DANCE
ON THE
WIND

BANTAM BOOKS

New York
Toronto
London
Sydney
Auckland

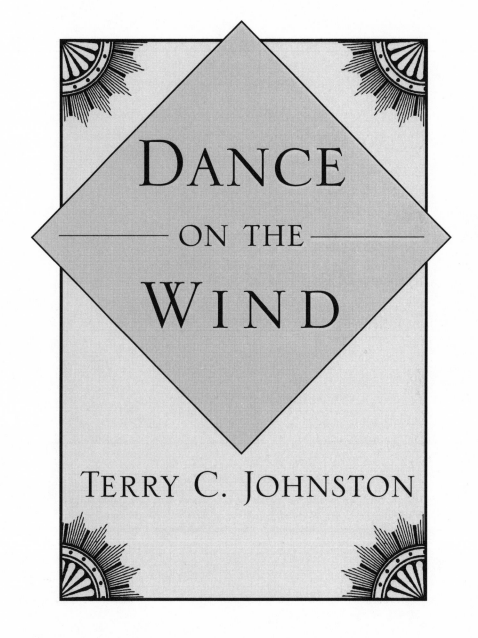

DANCE

— ON THE —

WIND

TERRY C. JOHNSTON

DANCE ON THE WIND

A Bantam Book / September 1995

ISBN 0-553-09071-2

Library of Congress Cataloging-in-Publication Data

Johnston, Terry C., 1947–
  Dance on the wind / Terry C. Johnston.
    p. cm.
  ISBN 0-553-09071-2
  1. Frontier and pioneer life—Ohio River Valley—Fiction.
  2. Young men—Ohio River Valley—Fiction.   I. Title.
  PS3560.O392D36   1995
  813'.54—dc20   *95-7558*
                                                      CIP

Published simultaneously in the United States and Canada

Bantam Books are published by Bantam Books, a division of Bantam Doubleday Dell
Publishing Group, Inc. Its trademark, consisting of the words "Bantam Books" and the
portrayal of a rooster, is Registered in U.S. Patent and Trademark Office and in other
countries. Marca Registrada. Bantam Books, 1540 Broadway, New York, New York 10036.

PRINTED IN THE UNITED STATES OF AMERICA

BVG   0 9 8 7 6 5 4 3 2 1

with my heartfelt appreciation,
I dedicate this triumphant return of
Titus Bass
to the
Bantam sales force
who first took
Ol' Scratch
into their hearts,
then shared him with the world,
nine years ago—
thanks to each and every one of you
for making this the ride
of a lifetime!

The first time I descended the Ohio and Mississippi rivers I left Cincinnati in December 1808 with five flat boats, all loaded with produce. At that time there were but few settlers on the Ohio River, below the present city of Louisville. The cabins on the river below Louisville were few and far between.

—Joseph Hough
An Early Miami (Ohio) Merchant

I have seen nothing in human form so profligate as [boatmen]. Accomplished in depravity, their habits seem to comprehend every vice. They make few pretensions to moral character; and their swearing is excessive and perfectly disgusting.

—James Flint
Letters from America

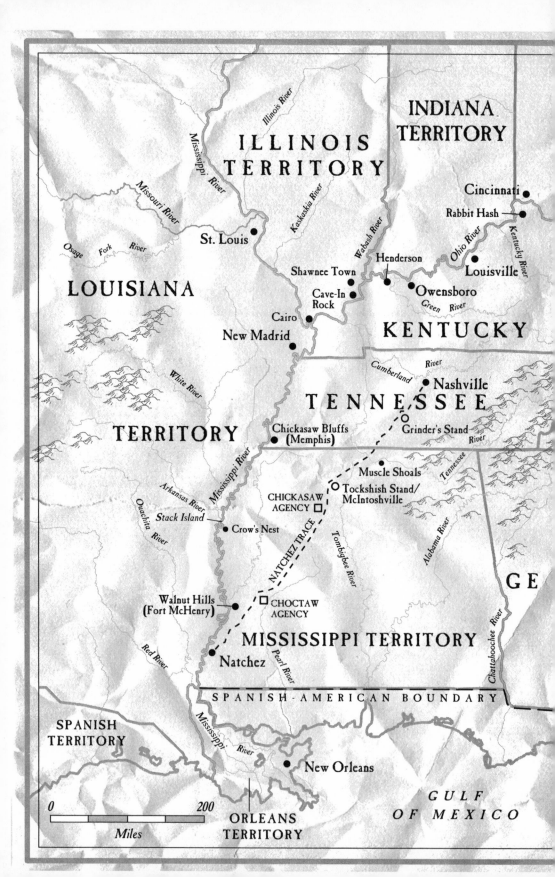

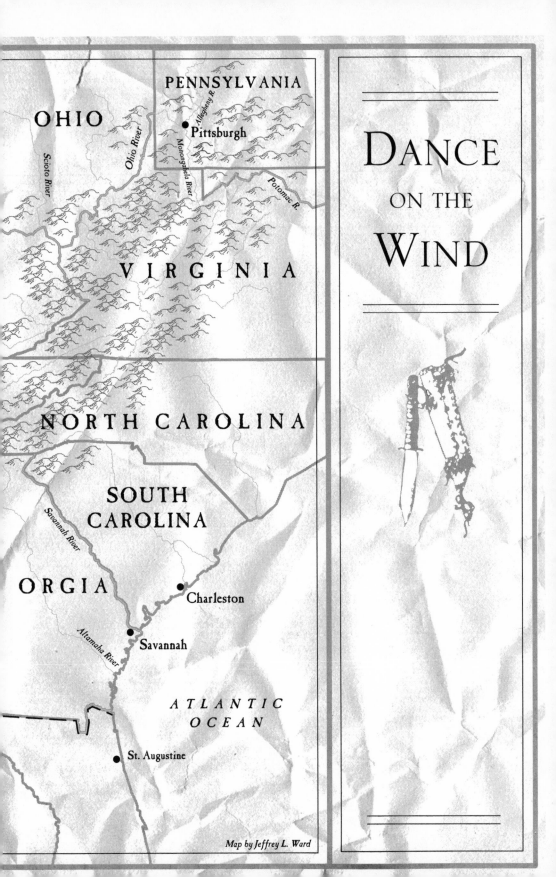

OHIO

PENNSYLVANIA

Pittsburgh

Allegheny R.

Ohio River

Monongahela River

Scioto River

Potomac R.

VIRGINIA

NORTH CAROLINA

SOUTH
CAROLINA

Savannah River

ORGIA

Charleston

Altamaha River

Savannah

*ATLANTIC
OCEAN*

St. Augustine

DANCE
ON THE
WIND

Map by Jeffrey L. Ward

ONE

Slick as quicksilver the boy stepped aside when the mule flung her rump in his direction.

Only problem was, he had forgotten about the root that arched out of the ground in a great bow nearly half as tall as he stood without his Sunday-meeting and schoolroom boots on. The end of it cruelly snagged his ankle, sure as one of his possum snares.

Spitting out the rich, black loam as fine as flour in this bottomland, Titus Bass pulled his face out of the fresh, warm earth he had been chewing up with a spade, blinking his gritty eyes. And glared over his shoulder at the mule.

Damn, if it didn't look as if she was smiling at him again. That muzzle of hers pulled back over those big front teeth the way she did at times just like this. Almost as if she was laughing at him when here he had just been thinking he was the one so damned smart.

"Why, you . . . ," the boy began as he dragged himself up to his knees, then to his bare feet in that moist earth chewed by the mule's hooves and his work with iron pike and spade.

On impulse he lunged for the fallen spade, swung it behind his shoulder in both hands.

"Put it down, Titus."

Trembling, the boy froze. Always had at the sound of that man's voice.

"Said: put it down."

The youth turned his head slightly, finding his father emerging from the trees at the far edge of the new meadow they were clearing. Titus weighed things, then bitterly flung the spade at that patch of ground between him and his father. The man stopped, stared down at it a moment, then bent to pick it up.

"You'd go and hit that mule with this," Thaddeus Bass said as he strode up, stopped, and jammed the spade's bit down into the turned soil, "I'd have call to larrup you good, son." He leaned back with both strong, muscular hands wrapped around the spade handle like knots on oiled ropes. "Thought I'd teached you better'n that."

"Better'n what?" the boy replied testily, but was sorry it came out with that much vinegar to it.

Thaddeus sighed. "Better'n to go be mean to your animals."

Titus stood there, caught without a thing to say, watching his father purse his lips and walk right on past to the old mule. Thaddeus Bass patted the big, powerful rump, stroked a hand down the spine, raising a small stir of lather near the harness, then scratched along the mare's neck as he cooed to the animal. She stood patiently in harness, hooked by leather and wood of singletree, the quiet murmur of her jangling chains—the whole of it lashed round a tree stump young Titus Bass had been wrenching out of a piece of ground that seemed too reluctant to leave go its purchase on the stubborn stump.

Titus flushed with indignation. "She was about to kick me, Pap."

Without looking back at his son, Bass said, "How you know that?"

"She was hitchin' her rump around to kick me," Titus retorted. "Know she was."

"How hard you working her?"

Dusting himself off, he replied in exasperation, "How hard I'm working her? You was the one sent me out here with her to finish the last of these goddamned stumps."

Thaddeus whirled on his son, yellow fire in his tired eyes. "Thought I told you I didn't wanna hear no such language come outta your mouth."

He watched his father turn back to the mule's harness, emboldened by the man's back, braver now that he did not have to look into those eyes so deeply ringed with the liver-colored flesh of fatigue. "Why? I ain't never figured that out, Pap. I hear it come from your mouth. Out'n Uncle Cy's mouth too. I ain't no kid no more. Lookit me. I be nearly tall as you—near filled out as you too. Why you tell me I can't spit out a few bad words like you?"

"You ain't a man, Titus."

He felt the burn of embarrassment at his neck. "But I ain't no boy neither!"

"No, you rightly ain't. But for the life of me, I don't know what you are, Titus." Bass laid his arms over the back of the tall mule and glared at his son. "You ain't a man yet, that's for sure. A man takes good care of the animals what take care of him. But you, Titus? I don't know what you are."

"I ain't a man yet?" Titus felt himself seething, fought to control his temper. "If'n I ain't a man yet—how come you send me out to do a man's job then!"

"Onliest way I know to make you into a man, son."

He watched his father turn and survey the stump partly pulled free from the ground, some of its dark roots already splayed into the late-afternoon air like long, dark arthritic fingers caked with mud and clods of rich, black earth.

Thaddeus straightened. "You wanna be a farmer, Titus—the one lesson you gotta learn is take care of the animals gonna take care of you."

The words spilled out before he wanted them to. "Like I told you before, Pap: it's your idea I'm gonna be a farmer."

The old man's eyes narrowed, the lids all but hiding the pupils as he glowered at the youth. "You not gonna be a farmer like your pap, like your grandpap and all the Basses gone before you . . . just what in blue hell you figure on doing with your life?"

"I . . . I—"

"You ain't got it figured out, do you?" Thaddeus interrupted. "And you won't for some time to come, Titus. What else you think you can do?"

Titus watched his father step back in among the leather, metal, and wood of the harness, tugging at it, straightening, adjusting the wrap of log chain his son had placed around the resistant stump.

"I like hunting, Pap."

Without raising his head from his work, Bass said, "Man can't make a living for his family by hunting."

"How you so damn sure?"

The eyes came up from the singletree and penetrated Titus like a pair of hot pokers that shamed him right where he stood.

"Sounds like you're getting a real bad mouth these days, son. Time was, I'd taken a strop of that harness leather to your backsides, teach you to watch your tongue better."

Titus felt his cheeks burn. No, he wouldn't let his father raise a strap to him ever again. In as low and deep a voice as he could muster, the boy replied, "You'll never lay leather on me again."

For the longest moment they stared at one another, studying, measuring the heft of the other. Then his father nodded, his shoulders sagging a bit wearily. "You're right, Titus. If you ain't learned right from wrong by now, it ain't gonna be me what's teaching it to you. Too late now for me to try to straighten out what needs to be straightened."

Titus swallowed, blinking back the tears of anger that had begun to sting his eyes as he stood his ground before his father. Suddenly confused that his father had agreed with him. It was the first time in . . . He couldn't remember if his father had ever agreed with a single damned thing he had ever said or done.

Thaddeus Bass patted the mule on the rump and stepped closer to his son. "But you heed me and heed me well: if I ever hear of you using such words around your mam, if I ever catch you saying such things under my roof—then we'll see who's man enough to provide for his own self. You understand me, son?"

With that dressing down Titus fumed under his damp collar. "I ain't never cursed under your roof, and I sure as hell ain't never gonna curse in my mam's hearing."

"Just make sure you don't, son," his father replied, stepping back of the mule and taking up the harness reins. "It'd break your mother's heart to hear you use such talk—what with the way that woman's tried to raise you."

Turning, Thaddeus Bass laid the leather straps in his son's hands. "Now, get back to work. Sun's going down."

Titus pointed over at the nearby tree where he had stood the old longrifle. "I been at this all day, and I ain't had a chance to go fetch me no squirrel yet."

"It's fine you go playing longhunter when you get your work done, Titus. That stump comes out'n that ground and gets dragged off yonder to the trees afore you come in to sup at sundown."

His stomach flopped. "If'n I can't get the stump up afore the sun goes down?"

His father looked at the falling orb, wagged his head, and said, "Then you best be making yourself a bed right here, Titus."

Anger was like a clump of sticky porcupine quills clogging his throat with bile. Time and again he tried to swallow as he watched his father's retreat across the field. Thaddeus Bass never turned as he headed purposefully for the far trees. Above the verdant green canopy beyond the diminishing figure rose a thin, fluffy column of smoke from the stone chimney of their cabin. He wondered what his two brothers and sister were doing right then.

Grinding the leather straps in his hands, Titus seethed at the injustice. He knew the rest of them would eat that night and sleep on their grass ticks beneath their coverlets. While he'd be right here in the timber, sleeping with the old mule and the other critters. Mayhaps that wasn't all so bad—but his belly was sure hollering for fodder.

Maybeso he could slip off with his old rifle and shoot some supper for himself, bring it back to roast over an open fire—then at least his stomach would be full for the night.

Titus took a step behind the mule, then stopped, staring down at the reins in his hands.

If he set off on his hunt to fill his grumbling belly, just what in blazes would he do with the mule?

"Hell, she ain't going nowhere," he reasoned, looking over the harness that bound her to the stump. "Can't get that stump out, she sure as the devil ain't running off from here."

Quickly he tied off the reins to the harness and leaped around the tangle of upturned roots. The rifle came into his hands like an old friend. More like an accomplice who had helped him in hunts without number in these very woods—ever since he was big enough to hoist his grandpap's longrifle to his narrow, bony shoulder and stride right out the cabin door to disappear within the forest's leafy green shadows.

Dusk was settling on the woods in just the way the mist gathered in the low places by the time he stopped at the edge of the narrow stream and listened. Titus jerked at the sudden, shrill call from a shrike as it dived overhead and disappeared in the coming gloom of twilight. The forest fell silent once more.

He figured he was too late to catch any of the whitetail coming here to water before slipping off to their beds for the night. Their tracks pocked the damp earth at the bank near the natural salt lick the deer sought out. No matter anyhow. Titus hadn't really figured when he'd started out from that stump that he would scare up any critter at these riffles in the stream. More than anything, he had come here just to get away from the mule, and the stump, and the work, and his pap.

On the far bank a warbler set up a song as the spring light disappeared from the sky. Another joined in, then they both fell quiet. Far off he heard the cry of a riverman's tin horn on the Ohio. A boat plying the waters—coming down from Cincinnati, which lay a twisting forty-some miles from where he knelt in the damp coolness of that dark forest glen. Perhaps a big flatboat speeding downriver to Louisville, on down, down to the faraway Mississippi with its rolling ride south all the way to New Orleans. Maybe even one of those keelboats that would eventually point its prow north on the old river to St. Lou. Seemed everyone in nearby Rabbit Hash, here on the Kentucky side of the Ohio, was talking about St. Lou these days.

"The place holds promise," claimed one of the drummers who came to town regular from Belleview, just five miles upriver.

Thaddeus Bass had snorted and wagged his head as if that was the most ridiculous assertion ever made. "Maybeso for shop-folk like yourself. Not for this family. We be farmers. Work the soil. Worked it since my grandpap come into Kain-tuck and staked himself out a piece of ground he and others had to defend from the Injuns. Naw, let others rush on to St. Lou. They been rushing on west, right on by my ground for three generations already."

"Opportunity enough for any man, I'd imagine," the drummer smiled benignly, pulling at his leather gallusses.

"To hell with opportunity," Bass retorted. "Opportunity's the retreat of a weak-spined sort. Hard work is what makes a man's life worthwhile. Ain't no better blessing for a man than to feed his family with the fruit of his sweat and toil."

Breathing lightly, Titus listened to the nightsounds, cradling the old flintlock, and wondered if he could ever forgive his father for keeping him chained to a mule, mired waist-deep in the muddy fields that surrounded their cabin and barn and outbuildings. Could he ever forgive his father for throwing cold water on his dreams?

"You'll get over it, son. Every boy does when he grows to be a man," Thaddeus had explained. "That's the difference between a whelp like you and a man like your pap here. Feller grows up to do what he has to do for them what counts on him, and he's a man for it. A boy just got him dreams he goes traipsing off after and he don't ever come to nothing 'cause dreams is something what cain't take him nowhere."

In the rising fog over the surface of the Ohio, the cry of the tin horn faded off. Titus closed his eyes, trying to imagine what sort of boat it was. Oh, he'd seen plenty of those flatboats and broadhorns, keels, and even those ungainly rafts of logs lashed together for the trip downriver, every small craft's wake lapping the surface of the Ohio against Titus's bare feet year after year. Summers without count had he wanted to hail a boat over and beg its crew to take him on.

But instead he sat there, listening until that horn was no more in the thickening fog that clogged the valley of the Ohio.

In the quiet that settled around him he heard the faintest rustle of brush. Held his breath. And a moment later his ears itched as something moved off into the night. Whatever critter it was had scented him.

Wind wasn't right, he decided, easing himself to his feet. Time to be moving off to home.

Times like these when he wasn't back to the cabin for supper, his father warned he'd get none. Still his mother always wrapped up a slice of cold ham and some corn dodgers, maybe even a sliver of dried apple pie, folding it all within a big square of cheesecloth before placing her treasure just back of the woodbox that sat to the left of the door on the front porch. Again tonight he knew he would be sitting in the dark, listening to the muffled voices of his family inside the firelit cabin as he chewed on his supper and washed it down with the cool, sweet water from the well his grandpap had dug generations before.

As much as he was certain he'd likely die early if he stayed on to become a farmer, Titus knew he'd feel like a rotted stump inside if he disappointed his father. So through the past few years he had walked this narrow line between what his pap expected of him and what he had to do just to keep from dying inside, a day at a time.

Warm, humid starshine streamed down through the leafy branches of the trees as he felt his way barefoot along the game trail that would take him back to the field and the stump and that old mule he realized had likely grown just as hungry as he himself had become. He stopped and listened a minute, leaning his empty hand against the bark of a smooth sumac tree. A frightened chirk overhead startled him. Black squirrel. Something amiss in that warning.

He did not stop again until he reached the edge of the meadow Thaddeus was having cleared for cultivation. Beneath the half-moon and the bright starlight he could make out the stump he had been uprooting across the open ground. But he could see no mule. Titus burst into a trot now. His throat seized with his thundering heart. Skidding to a halt on the turned and troubled ground around the stump, he found the singletree and chain harness still lashed around the wide trunk. But no mule.

Collapsing to his knees, he quickly inspected the leather for some sign that the old girl had snapped her way out of harness. Yet nothing there suggested she had freed herself. Around on his knees he crawled, inspecting the ground for hoofprints, bootprints, anything that might tell him how she got loose. Mayhaps some of grandpap's thieving Injuns. Or, worse yet, a white man come to steal the mule. But there was nothing untoward about that churned-up soil surrounding the stump.

"Take care of the animals gonna take care of you."

The voice seemed so real it near made him jump out of his skin. Titus turned this way, then that, just to be certain. Assuring himself he was alone, he settled on his rump, back against the stump, and cradled the rifle into his shoulder. As his head sagged, he struggled with what to do about the mule, about his running off into the woods and leaving her to get stole.

Finally he decided. If she was anywhere, she was chewing on some grass at that very moment. It made his stomach grumble in protest to think the mule was eating, and here he was worrying about her with an empty belly of his own.

In the starlit darkness it took something less than a half hour to reach the glen where the cabin stood, its chimney lifting a gray streamer to the night breeze. The wind was off from the wrong direction, but now and then he could pick up the faintest fragrance of supper. It made his belly growl in anticipation. Behind shutters and sashes drawn against the night outside, narrow ribbons of yellow lamplight squeezed free, a wee patch of light oozing out at the bottom of the door. Across the yard stood the separate kitchen, used from spring into the fall so the cabin wouldn't grow overly warm in those seasons of baking and cooking. Beside the kitchen stood the small smokehouse. Across the yard, the springhouse and corncrib. Beyond all of them still, the barn—taller even than the cabin with its sleeping loft.

Heading at an angle for the structure that blotted out a piece of that starry night sky, Titus kept to the shadows. Years before, so his father and grandpap had told him many times, the men of the family were required to keep an eye open at night for Injuns. Any shadow seen stealing across the yard was likely an enemy, and subject to be shot.

It had been years since the tribes had last made trouble. Back to the war with the Frenchies, later the revolt against the Englishers. It made his grandpap choke in anger to think that his father's own countrymen had made life so hard on their fellow English citizens that the colonists had gone and fought to throw King George right back into the sea. But as distasteful as it was to admit, grandpap's countrymen had turned out to be conniving, vicious lobsterbacks who had set the Injuns on the rebellious settlers. An army and all those Injun tribes come to make war against a few hundred farmers scattered over hundreds of miles of wilderness.

Titus slipped into the barn through the narrow door and held his breath.

His imagination soared as his eyes grew accustomed to the fragrant darkness. Recalling his grandpap's stories of how a few brave young men had carried word of an uprising or the English army's advance from settlement to settlement. How the farmers had reluctantly abandoned their fields and gathered families around them, hurrying to the nearby fort erected by a group of settlers for their mutual protection—each individual farmer's outlots in the fields surrounding that communal stockade. There had been one such stockade near Belleview where the Bass clan had gone in times of emergency. Where nearly everyone in Boone County fled when the British set their Shawnee and Mingoes loose on their own white-skinned countrymen.

Now Titus's eyes were big enough that he could make out the low walls of each stall, to discern the backs of some of the animals, the spines of a rake or a loop of harness draped over a nail. Enough light crept through tiny openings in the wall chinks that Titus could make his way down to the last stall, past the milk cows. One curious one came up and stuck her wet nose over the gate. He stroked it as he went past, feeling her long, coarse tongue lap over the back of his hand.

As he reached that last stall, he held his breath and hoped. It wouldn't be right to say he prayed, simply because he never had really prayed for anything. But at this moment he hoped harder than he had ever hoped for something before. And if such hoping was another man's prayer, so be it.

Daring to turn his head slowly, Titus looked into the stall.

Against the back wall stood the old mule. And on the nearby wall hung the harness.

Turning on his heel, his knees gone to mush, the youngster sank with his back against the stall door, where he leaned the rifle, catching his breath.

Leastwise the old mule was here. She wasn't took. He swallowed hard, knowing who had come to fetch her. Likely come to fetch him for supper. More likely, come to see how he was doing on that dad-blamed stump.

Titus wondered if his pap would count "dad-blamed" as cursing.

"I don't give a good goddamn if he does or not," Titus whispered to the lowing animals. "His damn ol' mule anyway—so he can take proper care of it hisself."

He listened as the mule moved closer, right up to the stall door. Looking up, he saw she had laid her bottom jaw atop the door and seemed to be peering down at him with one of those dark, iridescent eyes.

"I'm sorry, Lilly," he suddenly apologized. "Nothing against you. Shouldn't've left you be there all by yourself. Something might've happened to you. Sorry, girl."

Her head seemed to bob once before the mule retreated back into the stall once more.

Sometimes, he brooded, these animals were downright spooky. Like they understood what you spoke at 'em. Mayhaps—he feared—even able to outright read a person's mind.

Slowly clambering to his feet, he saw that she'd been fed. The bucket hung from a peg inside her stall where the mule could reach it, feeding herself from the grain provided her every night. His pap had done that too. Likely brushed her down good. Like Titus was supposed to each night after he worked over the stumps on the far edge of the ground they were clearing for next season's planting. Not time enough this year—what with the good ground already turned and the seed already covered, more than a dozen good, soaking rains already.

He put his hand in the canvas bucket and brought out a handful of the grain. Holding it beneath his nose, he drank in the faint sweetness of oats, the fragrance of molasses. Then he extended his hand to her. She came to the stall door, curled her lips back, and lapped at the offering as he patted the solid bone between her eyes.

When she finished, Titus swiped his damp palm across his worn britches and took up the rifle. It was time he had something to eat himself. Careful not to let the small door slam against the side of the barn as he eased it back into place, the youngster crept amongst the shadows toward the cabin. As he had done so many times before, he would eat his supper, then wait until all the lights were out before he would climb the roof and steal in through the window to find his bed in the dark.

After setting the longrifle against the side of the porch, Titus heaved himself up without using the steps. They were creaky with age and use, and more often than not apt to make more noise than one of the rooting pigs down in the pen behind the barn. Kneeling at the side of the woodbox, he reached around to the spot where his mother always left the cheesecloth bundle for him. He felt a little farther. Still nothing. Leaning all the way over the hinged flap atop the woodbox, he put both hands to work, stuffing both arms clear under the box. Nothing. No cheesecloth bundle. No supper.

At that moment his stomach growled so loud, he was sure they heard it inside the cabin.

Quickly hunching over and wrapping both arms over his belly, Titus limped away from the woodbox to the edge of the porch, where he sat dangling his bare feet while he stared up at the half-moon. It had climbed to near midsky, and the breeze was coming up. Damp, rich, rife with the smell of rain by morning despite the cloudless sky overhead.

In the starshine the edge of the hog pen stood out on the far side of the barn. Closer still, the small corral where his pap kept their wagon team. Titus had straddled the wide backs of those old, gentle horses ever since he could remember. As much excitement as it had been when he was a pup, these days he yearned to climb atop a real horse. Not one of those working draft animals. A lean, slim-haunched horse that would carry him across the fields and down the wooded trails with the speed of quicksilver. A real horse like those he saw from time to time in Belleview. And the once-a-year trip upriver to Cincinnati, only some twenty miles if a person took the overland route that dispensed with most of the meandering course of the Ohio.

Yes, sir. A real horse like fine folks rode. He deserved that, Titus decided. Here in his seventeenth summer, on the verge of manhood, a hunter like himself deserved a fine horse. After all, times were good. The Englishers were gone, thrown out for good, and when the men got together, they cheered one another with talk of times being good now for their young country as America slowly spread her arms to the west. Four summers back Lewis and Clark had returned from the far ocean, with unbelievable tales of tall mountains and icy streams teeming with fur-bearing animals. Stories and rumors and legends of fiercely painted Indians who attempted to block their journey every step of the way.

The only Indians Titus had seen were a few of the old ones he saw from time to time, come to Belleview or Rabbit Hash, civilized and docile Indians who no longer hunted scalps but tilled the land like white men. They came to the towns for supplies but for the most part kept to themselves when they did. Wouldn't even look the white folks in the eye.

"They're a beaten people," grandpap had told young Titus. "We whupped 'em good when we whupped the lobsterbacks."

At first Titus had been scared whenever he saw one of those farmer Indians. Then, he grew afraid he never would see a real, honest-to-God Injun for himself, ever.

About as much chance of that as him ever forking his legs over a strong, graceful horse.

He sat in the darkness until the last lamp went out. Everything was quiet down below, quiet up in the loft where his two brothers and sister slept. Waiting while the moon moved a few more degrees off to the west to be sure all were asleep, just as he always did, the youngster crept back to the door, took hold of the iron latch, and carefully raised it, easing forward on it to crack open the door just wide enough to—

Damn!

He tried again, thinking perhaps he hadn't raised the iron latch high enough to clear the hasp. Titus pushed gently against the door again—

Goddamn!

It couldn't be stuck. He tried harder, noisier, as iron scraped against iron.

The door was barred from the inside. He was locked out.

This had never happened before. Always the door was left unlocked for him when he went hunting of a night, or off to gig frogs, or maybe only to wander down the road to Amy's place, hoping she would sit and talk with him about mostly nothing at all. But that door was never locked.

And his mam always had supper waiting under the woodbox in that piece of cheesecloth.

He leaned his forehead against the door, suddenly wanting to cry. So hungry he couldn't think what to do next. So tired from fighting the mule and the stump and his pap that day that he wanted only to lie down upon his tick, pull the covers over his head, and go to sleep despite his noisy, snoring brothers.

With a sigh Titus turned from the locked door. Mayhaps he could pull himself up onto the porch roof and make his way across the cabin roof and lower himself onto the sill where a lone window opened into the sleeping loft. Maybe his old man wasn't as smart as he made on to be.

After hiding the rifle behind the woodbox, Titus shinnied up the pole and clawed his way onto the roof. As quietly as he could move across the creaking timbers and shakes, the youngster crept to the cabin roof itself and hoisted himself up. Keeping to the sides where the support beams had more strength and were therefore less likely to groan and protest his weight, Titus leaned over the edge and found the window. Lying on his belly, he scooted out as far as he dared and reached for the mullioned windowpanes. Nudging. Then pushing. Straining. Neither side would budge.

Frustrated, he tried again, and again. It acted as if it were nailed shut. It was always easy to open that window, he thought. Both sides flung open for summer breezes. Never before had it been so hard. He tried once more. Unable to budge it.

A nail or two could do that, he thought. Wouldn't take much to keep him from sneaking in that way.

As he dropped barefoot to the ground at the side of the porch, he boiled with indignation. Wrenching up the rifle from its hiding place behind the woodbox, Titus seethed to have it out with his pap. But as tired as he was, it could wait until morning.

Back across the damp shadows of the yard, he could already smell rain coming. Into the barn he crept once more and waited for his eyes to adjust to the darkness. To his right stood the faint hump of a hayrick. After leaning the rifle against a nearby post, Titus kicked at the soft hay with his bare feet until he had a pile long enough, and some four feet deep. On it he lay down and began pulling hay over him for warmth.

Curling an arm under his head, the youngster closed his eyes, his breathing slowing as the anger and disappointment and hunger drained from him. All he wanted now was some sleep. In the morning he would have words with his father about locking his son out of the cabin.

Even if he had gone off without tending to the stump and the old mule, nothing was so serious that he should be locked out of his own home.

Titus felt the warmth of the hay envelop him the way the cool of the swimming hole would wrap him on those hot summer days yet to come.

No matter how important any *thing* was to his pap, nothing should be more important than family.

Bringing the old girl home, feeding her, putting her up for the night in her stall. No two ways about it—that mule was getting better treatment from his pap than Thaddeus was giving his own son right now.

With the hay's heady fragrance filling his nostrils, the quiet lowing of the animals droning about him, and his dreams of riding one of those fast horses the woodsmen owned, Titus drifted off to sleep.

He shivered once and pulled more hay over him. Growing warm once again. Not to stir for what was left him of that short night.

• • •

"Get up, boy. You've got some righting of a wrong to be at."

He blinked into the gray light, then rubbed at his gritty eyes, staring up sidelong at his father, who stood over his bed of hay. Thaddeus had the collar to his wool coat turned up against the morning dew, a shallow-crowned, wide-brimmed hat of wool or castor felt pulled down on his hair.

It was cold in here, Titus thought. Damp too. Must have gone and rained.

"I said get up!" Thaddeus Bass repeated more urgently. And this time he added his own boot toe for emphasis.

Titus pulled back his bare foot. "I know I done wrong—"

"Get up! Afore I pull you up by your ears!"

The youngster stood, shedding hay as he clambered to his feet, shivering slightly, hunch-shouldered in dawn's dampness. His breath huffed before his face in wispy vapors. Outside a mockingbird called. "Jest lemme explain, Pap."

"Nothing to explain, Titus. You left off work to go traipsing the woods. Left off the mule too. No telling what'd become of her I didn't come back to see to your work at that stump."

The look in his father's eyes frightened him. He could remember seeing that fire in those eyes before, yet no more in all of Titus's sixteen years than the fingers on one of his hands. "It was getting on late in the day anyhows—"

With a sudden shove his father pushed him down the path between the two rows of stalls in that log barn. "Grab that harness."

"Yes, sir," he said with a pasty mouth, too scared not to be dutiful and obedient.

A rain crow cawed on the beam above him. He shuddered as his bare feet moved along the cold, pounded clay of the barn floor. But he wasn't all that sure he trembled from the morning chill. Not knowing what would come next from his father's hand was all it took to make the youth quake. Alone Titus had faced most everything nature could throw at this gangly youth—out there in the woods and wilderness. But he had never been as frightened of anything wild as he was of his father when Thaddeus Bass grew truly angry.

As Titus took the old mule's harness down, his father said, "G'won, hitch her up."

The boy pushed through the stall door and moved into the corona of warmth that surrounded the big animal. She raised her head from a small stack of hay to eye him, frost venting from her great nostrils, then went back to her meal as he came alongside her neck and slipped the bridle and harness over her.

"Bring her out to me."

"Here, Pap," he said, almost like whimpering. "I . . . I'm sorry. Never run off on the work again, I swear—"

"I don't figure you ever will run off again, Titus," his father snapped. "Not after I've learned you your lesson about work and responsibility." He pointed to a nearby post. "Get you that harness."

"What for? I got the mule set—"

"Jest you get it and follow me."

He trudged after his father, out the barn door and into the muddy yard, where a faint drift of woodsmoke and frying pork greeted him as warmly as the dawn air did in cold fashion. How it did make his stomach grumble.

"Can I quick go and fetch me something to eat while we're off to the field, Pap?"

In the gray light shed by that overcast sky the man whirled on his son. "No. You ain't earned your breakfast yet."

"But—I didn't have no supper last night."

"Didn't earn that neither. Off lollygagging the way you was."

He swallowed and walked on behind his father, bearing south toward the new field they were clearing. Suddenly appearing out of the low, gray sky, the bright crimson blood-flash of a cardinal flapped overhead and cried out. In the distance Titus heard the faint call of a flatboat's horn rise out of the Ohio's gorge. Was it one of those new keels with a dozen polemen? Or was it one of those broadhorns nailed together of white oak planks the boatmen would soon be selling by the board-foot on the levee at far-off New Orleans?

"Here, girl," Thaddeus said as he put the mule ahead of the harness-tree and himself at her head, beginning to coax her back a step at a time. "Titus, hitch her up."

Titus hoisted the oiled hardwood and locked both harness traces in place. Then he straightened, watching his father pat the mule between the eyes.

Gesturing toward the tangle of leather and chain his son had dropped onto the ground, Thaddeus said, "Now you hook up that harness to the tree."

Maybe he didn't want to know any more than he already could guess. Maybe he refused to believe his father would really make him do it. No matter—Titus didn't ask, didn't say a thing as he bent over his work. His cold hands trembling, he found it was a tight fit lining up all the metal clasps into the harnesstree's lone eye, but he got it done and stood again. Shivering in the cold air as a breeze rustled the green leaves of the nearby elms.

"We gonna pull the stump out and then we go to breakfast?"

His father slapped the mule one time on the rump as he moved back to take up the reins. "We gonna pull out the stump, that's right. We'll see for ourselves what comes next, Titus. Now, step in that harness and cinch yourself up."

"M-me?"

"You heard me, son."

"Y-yes, Pap."

For a moment longer he stood there, gazing at his father. Thaddeus had taken the long, wide leather reins into his weathered hands, shifted it all to his left, then took one long double length into his right and began to wave it over the mule's wide back.

"You seen what your pap has to do if'n an animule ain't obeying, ain't you, Titus?"

Quickly, he turned and stepped into the harness. "Yes, Pap."

"Buckle yourself in and take up the slack," the man ordered, then ever so gently laid the long strap of leather onto the mule's back. Obediently she leaned into her harness and raised the harnesstree off the damp ground, then stopped, awaiting the next command.

"Aside her, I'm just gonna be in the way—"

"Lean into it, boy!"

"You ain't really gonna make me pull this stump out—"

"I'm gonna make a farmer outta you, Titus—or I'll kill you trying. Now, lean into it, goddammit!"

"Pap!"

"There's work you left afore it was finished, son." Thaddeus's eyes glowed like all-night coals.

"Lemme pull the stump out by my own self with the mule. I'll get it done—"

"Damn right, you'll pull it out with the mule," his father growled, savagely bringing the leather strap down on the animal's back.

With a sudden snap she lowered her head, bobbing, her front quarters reaching forward for a purchase on the slick ground as her rear hooves dug in and both muscled haunches rippled while she locked herself against the stump.

Beside the snorting, heaving animal Titus pushed against the wide, soaped harness so hard, his feet lost their bite on the muddy ground. He spilled onto his hands and knees.

"Get up, boy!" the man bellowed. "Git, git, git!" He coaxed more effort out of the mule.

Leather stretched and the thick-linked log chain hummed as everything that could give was taken out of the links and latigo. Now it was nothing more than muscle and sinew and will against what grip this piece of ground still had on the stump.

Titus struggled back up, sickened, wobbly, nearly the whole of him covered in mud now. Looping his soppy hands inside the harness, he struggled to plant his bare feet again as the mule lurched forward a few inches. That sudden slack between him and the harnesstree they shared flung the youth into the mud once more.

"You ain't pulling, Titus! Giddup!"

"Dammit, Pap!" he spat, his mouth filled with the damp earth once more.

"What'd I tell you 'bout cursin'?" and he laid the leather strap down on the mule's back just enough to get her to strain forward again with those powerful rear haunches.

Titus's thin neck swelled, bulging as his hands cramped around the harness lashed tightly across his filthy work shirt. Pushing this hard, he was sure something inside him was bound to burst.

"That's it, son! Put your back into it and work with the animal! Work with her—not agin 'er!"

Out of the corner of his eye Titus glanced at the big mule; then he slowly turned to stare at her as he strained every muscle in the effort. Entranced, all but mesmerized by the two streams of vapor issuing from those great moist nostrils of hers. Then she seemed to roll her eyes his way as if to remind him that he was supposed to pull in tandem with her.

"Git, git, git!" Thaddeus clucked behind them.

Back against the harness he flung himself anew when he heard the leather crack across the mule's broad back. In the next instant he pitched forward again as she wrenched more of the stump from the ground.

"Good girl!" Thaddeus cried out jubilantly. "Git, git, git! Now, git!"

Time and again he laid the leather strop down on her back more insistently. Titus watched foam fleck at her nostrils as her front hooves pawed at the muddy ground, flinging clods back toward Thaddeus, spraying Titus with more dark, damp, fragrant earth each time she plunged a hoof down into the soil.

"Git, git!" he bellowed behind them both. "Git, Titus. Lean into it, boy!"

They lurched forward another two feet. The strop laid down on her back, again. Thaddeus coaxed her with his almost constant chatter. Then a yard more and they were out of the chewed-up ground. He and the mule now churned bare feet and monstrous hooves on grassy furrows—bull nettles and the Spanish needles that thrived in newly turned ground. He fought for a grip with his right foot as the mule shuddered with fatigue, then leaned back into the fight.

"You got it! By Jupiter—you done it!"

The words rang in his ears as the mule shot past him and Titus stumbled into the damp grass, the leather and chain and harnesstree jangling over him, pulling him along as Thaddeus leaned back against the reins, bellowing his orders to bring the mule to a halt.

Her massive sides heaving in throbbing quakes, she stood a few yards from the youth, frost rising in a ragged halo around her big head as she turned to wearily regard him. Then blinked her eyes once before she looked away from Titus.

Suddenly his father was on him, pulling him up by the back of his collar, pounding him on his shoulder, yammering as he shook Titus by the shoulders in exultation. Then Thaddeus Bass gripped his son's shoulders in those big, meaty hands of his and put his face right up to his boy's.

"Don't you damn well ever forget what you just done—you hear me? Don't you ever go and forget what a man and a animal can do together, when they work together, son."

Gulping down more of that moist earth on his tongue, Titus nodded, staring back at the fiery intensity burning in his father's eyes. Minutes ago he had been frightened to the core by those eyes. But that anger, that iron-nail-spitting rage in his old man's eyes had disappeared, and now Titus saw only mirth and joy and jubilant self-satisfaction.

Thaddeus tousled his son's hair, smeared some of the dirt from one of the boy's cheeks. "C'mon, Titus—let's go get you both some breakfast."

As he walked back beside that great, sweating animal, Titus wondered if he would ever be as satisfied with his lot in life as was his father.

TWO

How he loved the smell of her. A dusting of flour. The sweet mingling of creamy milk, maybe some rich yellow butter. Perhaps a dash of vanilla beans, or crumbling of cinnamon sticks, even the faintest hint of ginger. Most always the stirring tang of yeast whenever he dared get that close.

Never was there any smell of soap or laundry to her. Much less the earthy odor come of butchering farm animals that clung to other girls he knew. No, none of that—not even the stale, sourish fragrance of dust and sweeping and mopping out the floors rose from her skirts or hung about her hair when he chanced close enough to smell of it. Instead, Amy Whistler had the smell of baking about her, the promise of bread rising and pie crusts turning golden, of corn fritters and johnnycakes and nothing more grand than swollen butter-yellow corn kernels frying in a great iron skillet over the flames of the fireplace. Parched corn. How he had come to favor her parched corn.

"You set yourself on the porch there, Titus," she told him, grinding her hands into her apron, a tiny cloud of flour puffing about them. "I'll be out straightaway as soon as the dough is pounded and set to its second rise."

He watched her retreat back into the shadowy interior of the cabin lit by the glowing fire and those candles waxed atop iron pegs driven into the logs all about the big room, their fluttering giving the place the appearance of constant movement. Then he drank deep of the smell of cool milk and fragrant butter, fresh from the springhouse, and turned with a sigh.

Amy Whistler didn't grow food to eat in the ground like his father, by God. But from her hands she grew things nonetheless. Tasty and seductive concoctions, confections, and elixirs. Whereas a man who coaxed green vines and tender shoots out of the rich black soil might be called a wizard, Titus had long ago decided she was an angel.

It was more than merely the fact that she was two years older than he. Titus was in awe of the way her hands felt when she let him hold one of them. And only then when they were off and out of sight of her cabin, far from her younger brothers and sisters in that great Whistler brood. How they did flock around Titus every time he wandered down the lane or crossed the country as the crow flew to pay a call on their eldest sister. Out of sheer orneriness did they cling to his legs and arms when he came visiting, beseeching him to play their games with them, to swing on the rope from the great maple that stood squarely in the middle of the yard, or fashion something wondrous and new with his folding knife and a sliver of kindling from the woodbox by the door.

Most of them eventually wandered away this evening, as they always did, shooed from the porch by their mama and told to be off to play until sunset. Yet four stayed on, remaining every bit as silent as the bristles on the back of a sleeping hog, standing stock-still no more than a yard away from Titus, all of them staring like statues at him. Watching with such undistracted intensity as if he were going to change shape right before their eyes, sprout wings, and take flight—something that would eventually merit all their rapt, undivided attention. The youngest among them sucked on a thumb. Another repeatedly swiped at a runny nose. A third stood statuelike with his hands stuffed down inside his hand-me-down canvas drop-front britches with new patches repairing old patches. And the last brushed a thick rosy twist of her dusty-red hair in and out of her mouth, sucking on the strands as her green eyes studied Titus.

His eighteen-year-old angel had that same hair, those same eyes. For a moment that remembrance made him smile, to think how little he had noticed Amy Whistler in those days so far behind them now, when Amy had been this young. Hard to believe ten years had passed since he first remembered noticing the girl—not for the beauty of her hair and eyes, but for her lean, hard fists and quick feet. Far from being demure, Amy struck back whenever she felt aggrieved: swinging those tight little fists at an offender's nose, lashing out with her bare feet to wallop some bully's shins. No, Amy Whistler was not just a tomboy—she had quickly become one of the boys.

For years the two of them shared the same secret fishing spot, enjoyed the same rope that swung them out over the summer swimming hole, where they let go and dropped into the cool creek of a hot, muggy afternoon, or tracked the same fox and deer, raccoon and turkey, he with his grandpap's rifle, she with her father's in hand.

Then one day on the banks of their swimming hole a few years ago, when Amy found Titus gazing at her with unabashed amazement, she had little choice but to own up to the fact that she was no longer a child. While other girls her age had blossomed early, as they so often did on this Kentucky frontier, for the longest time Amy's figure remained boyish, thin and bony, almost as angular as Titus's . . . until she blossomed with a vengeance.

In the short weeks of that single summer years ago, it seemed Amy went from skinny and hard-boned to rounded, filled-out, and more than painfully shy about the sudden changes in her late-blooming body. By the time another year had passed, however, she had come to accept the inevitable march of time, wholly embracing her new station in life. With the arrival of each new summer it seemed Amy Whistler grew more beautiful, acquired new curves, learned more about the way she could hold a boy with her eyes, came to speak to the object of her attentions in that just-audible whisper, or could stand silhouetted by the falling sun to accent her ample figure just so.

It was in this last year Titus found his own body awakening. Oh, for certain he was still as skinny and angular and unsure of just what his muscles might or might not do to embarrass him from day to day—but the greatest changes occurred within. Those first stirrings of manhood. An awakening of the sweet juices of youth that fired his veins—in very nearly the same way as had the thrill of the hunt and the flush of conquest for all those years spent in the woods, along the game trails of this Kentucky hill country.

It wasn't just that Amy had changed into a woman right before his eyes . . . it was that now Titus looked at her differently. No longer as merely a best friend, a companion, a confidante who kept his secrets from all others. No, he could no longer confide in her his deepest secret now, unable to tell her the way she made him feel when she came near, when he touched her hand, smelled her hair, felt her soft lips press against his bony cheek each time they parted. These feelings were the first he kept from her, unable to find words for what confusion he sensed, something so deep inside that it shook him with a tangible lurch across his groin. It was a mystery he could not hope to have explained by a distant, critical father, let alone his mother. Perhaps what made things even worse was his position as the oldest in the family: there were no brothers to confide in.

So Titus struggled along through the days and weeks and months of his own coming of age among other boys who seemed to have mastered their arrival upon the threshold of manhood with no strain at all, much less break out into those sweats Titus suffered every few nights as he lay on his grass-filled tick up in that sleeping loft. Holding his own breath while listening for the reassuring deep-breathing of his brothers and sister, then carefully letting his hand wander down below the covers to touch and explore that part of him he no longer understood with any certainty, finding it hard and swollen, and so eagerly sensitive to his touch. Night after night he rolled over on that rigid flesh and tried to force out of his mind those images of a rounded, soft-skinned Amy Whistler—struggling to think instead on red fox and gray squirrel and turkey roosting in the low branches of the trees . . . anything but the smell and feel and roundness of Amy so that he could soften what had grown hard, so that he could go back to sleep before the coming sun nudged them all from their beds for morning chores.

On nearly every nocturnal visit of this mystery-made-flesh Titus had been able to will himself back to blissful sleep, yet less and less so these past few weeks as the air warmed and the snow disappeared from the timbered north-facing slopes while the ground budded and the wild things in the forest cavorted. For these weeks as summer approached he could not tear his mind off Amy, drawn again and again to the feel of her lips on his cheek—imagining how they must taste on his own just one time.

Most of all, it was how he looked at her anew this time of the year, this time of his life, not so much gazing at her face, but his eyes instead focusing on her body, how it moved, dwelling on how it might feel pressed against his, how its soft responsiveness would feel beneath his trembling hands.

My, how his heart raced and his throat constricted whenever he closed his eyes in the darkness of that sleeping loft and thought of how she would feel and smell and taste to his lips with her flesh laid against his flesh. Naked. The way they used to swim so many summers gone the way of their innocence.

If only one more time, he prayed. Just to swim together one more time as they had when they were children. So that he might look at her body for himself, see if she had hair beginning to appear beneath her arms and on her chest. Hair, even down there, right where it seemed thoughts of her stirred him the most.

Times were that he wondered if she awoke in the deep of night with such strange, frightening, and deliciously evil dreams stirring her as they stirred him.

"I'm done," she said as her skirts rustled up behind him. Amy settled beside Titus at the front of the porch. "Go on, now, you all," she ordered the four away. "Git!"

He watched the quartet of siblings turn and shamble off, each of them turning their head to look back over their shoulder at the intriguing pair when Amy slipped two hands around one of Titus's.

"You wanna walk?" he asked, hopeful.

She glanced back at the door. "I can't be gone long. Got things rising, other'ns baking. Mama needs help, and I can't leave my work for her to do."

"We got time," he pleaded.

Then she smiled at him in that crook-toothed way of hers and squeezed his hand. "Yes. We do got time, don't we?"

He rose, missing her touch already as he pulled his hand away from hers.

"Lemme just tell mama I'll be back straightaway."

He watched the swirl of that long dress drop again over her ankles, brushing the tops of her bare feet as Amy slipped inside. The murmur of voices came to him from somewhere within. Then Cleve Whistler came to the door with a length of peeled hickory in one hand, pulling the chewed stump of a cob pipe from his bushy face.

"Evenin', Titus," the man said, tossing the hickory strip atop a pile with others he would use to weave a strong chair bottom.

He nodded properly, as one did when one was courting a man's daughter. "Evenin', Mr. Whistler."

The farmer came to the edge of the porch and braced a shoulder against a post there beneath the overhang. "And a fine evenin' it is." He breathed deep. "I remember I was your age." And he pointed back at the doorway with the battered stem of his pipe. "I first come to spoon Amy's mama when I was your age."

"Yes, sir."

Whistler's brow furrowed. "You're serious about courting my daughter, ain't you, Titus?"

His head bobbed in time with his Adam's apple, just like a string toy he would carve for the younger children from time to time, the kind he could get to dance up and down a piece of hemp twine, clogging atop a white-oak shake.

"S'pose I am, Mr. Whistler."

He smiled at the youth. "That's good, Titus. Because Amy is the sort of girl could have any suitor she wanted. Lots of boys would love to come callin'. But she's set her eyes on you, so it seems."

"I . . . I see," he stammered, concerned what that might portend.

Leaning forward, Cleve Whistler confided in a lower voice, "I just want what's best for my eldest, you understand. I know your papa and his family—good people. So I figure you'll make Amy a fine husband, father to lots of her young'uns."

Titus swallowed again, blinked. Husband? *Young'uns?* Why, he'd just come to take him a walk with Amy, to touch her hand, to feel her kiss his cheeks, maybe even talk her into pressing her lips against his one time—to hold her body ever so close to his when they did touch in such a forbidden, bewildering way. Maybe tonight even to talk about his fears and this mystery of the fire in his belly if he felt safe enough with her . . . but here Mr. Whistler was talking about—

"—sure your papa will shave off a piece of that new ground he's clearing down by the creek and turn it over to you one of these days real soon."

"N-new ground," Titus repeated with an uncomfortable stammer.

Cleve Whistler pointed off into the coming dusk, wisps of fog gathering in the low place a hundred yards off on the path to the creek. "Such would make a good place for you and Amy to raise yourself a cabin, where you could start raising yourself a family."

A family?

How'd things get all so discombobulated so quick? How was Whistler talking about Titus taking a wife and having themselves children, with a cabin all to themselves, when he hadn't even kissed Amy for certain and for sure right on the mouth the way he had heard tell a man was to kiss a woman to announce he wanted her for his very own gal?

"You'll make a fine farmer, I'm sartin," Whistler observed. "Your papa is as fine a man as they come—so you come from good stock. Not that I didn't fret over you a time or two, Titus. Fret over giving Amy up to you. She bein' my firstborn and all. But her time's come."

"Her t-time," he echoed, his cheeks burning in embarrassment as Amy came out through the door.

She had taken off her apron and pulled a knitted shawl over her shoulders.

"Amy made that. Did you know, Titus?" Whistler asked, pointing at the shawl with the stem of his pipe as she stopped beside her father.

"It's . . . it's . . . yes. Real purty," he replied, looking into Amy's eyes, at the fullness of her lips.

"I think it's purty too," Whistler replied as he put an arm around his daughter's shoulders. "She's the kind of woman gonna make a fine man proud one day soon."

Titus watched Amy kiss her father on his cheek and wondered if she really did know any other way to kiss a man but on his cheek. Had she ever thought of his mouth, and how it must taste, how it must feel—the way Titus so many times had dreamed on the feel of her mouth, and how it might taste to his tongue?

"Now, don't you two be late, you hear?" Whistler said with a wave of his pipe, smiling at them.

Slipping her arm inside Titus's, Amy said, "We won't, Pa. Promised mama I'd be back to take the bread off the fire."

Cleve Whistler inhaled deeply as Amy turned her beau from the porch. "Fine evenin' for courtin'. A fine, fine evenin'."

Crossing the yard, Titus walked dumbly at her side while Amy shooed the younger Whistlers from their heels. As soon as they reached the edge of the woods, she finally spoke.

"Don't let my pa bother you none. He's just, well—I figure he's proud a young man like yourself is courtin' me."

"Y-young man like myself?"

With a squeeze of his arm Amy slipped her hand down into his. "Yes. A young man with what my mama calls good prospects."

"What's that mean?"

"It's what a girl's supposed to look for in a fella," she answered.

"How's that?"

"Someone take proper care of a girl he's married to. Provide for her and their family. The children they'll have."

"Whoa!" he gulped, stopping and wheeling on her. "You . . . an' me? Setting up a house and having children?"

"Yes, Titus," she replied, a small crease knitting her brow with worry.

"I . . . I was thinking we was friends, Amy."

"We always been friends, Titus." She squeezed his hand.

"Where'd all this talk of prospects come from?"

"I been thinking lately," she replied, turning him, tugging him into motion once more. "And talking to mama: she was your age when she married pa and my age when she had me."

"Y-you wanna get married to me?"

She stopped this time, dropping his hand and pulling the shawl about her shoulders. "You don't wanna get married to me?"

With a wag of his head he stared dumbfounded at the ground, at his bare feet a moment, then finally looked at her to say, "I can't say as I ever thought—"

"Never thought about it?" She turned away from him in a huff, pouting.

He brushed by her shoulder to face her once more. Amy only turned away again. "Have you thought about it, Amy?"

How his heart was pounding, looking at the way her eyes were lit with such fire here at dusk, stealing a look at the way her breasts heaved with each pouting breath there above the arms she had folded across her midriff.

"What's it all been for, Titus?" she finally asked without looking at him at first. Then her eyes squarely found his. "We knowed each other since we was children ourselves. You growed, and I growed. And . . . well, the way you been coming by to pay me court and all."

"I come by 'cause I like to be with you, Amy," he explained lamely. "I ain't got 'nother friend I can talk to the way I talk to you."

"You mean you ain't been paying me court?" she asked with a quiet squeak. "Wanting to hold my hand or my arm all the time. Telling me to kiss you so much. Looking at me the way you do with those eyes of yours. Don't go tell Amy Whistler you ain't been thinking about courtin' her!"

He waved his hands before him helplessly. "All right, Amy. S'pose I been courtin' you and just never knowed what I was doing, exactly."

She nodded once without a word. Not making it any easier on him. How small he felt standing before her at that moment. How much he wanted to put his arms around her and press his whole body against hers, to ask if she finally felt the same stirring deep across her groin that set fire to his.

"And," he started, "I s'pose I been wonderin' if'n you . . . you was really wanting me to pay court to you."

He didn't know where those words came from, but there they were, spilled from his tongue.

"Not wanting you to court me, Titus Bass?" Then she giggled behind her hand. "Oh, silly—how many girls has let you kiss them on the cheek, or gone and kissed you back on your cheek?"

With a wag of his head he answered, "None. None others, Amy."

"How many girls let you just come to call whenever it strikes your fancy to pay 'em a visit, Titus? How many girls you know hold your hand, hold your arm the way Amy Whistler does?"

"None. An' you know that too," he said, suddenly feeling on the spot, defensive. His heart's hackles rose like the guard hairs on one of the family's redbone hounds. "How was I to—"

"How was you to know I wanted you to pay me court, Titus?"

Amy leaned toward him, only their lips touching, mouth closed, but pressed hard and insistent against his mouth. He blinked all through that momentary kiss, looking at her, finding Amy's eyes closed.

Then she drew back, opened her eyes, and asked, "Now. Don't that tell you Amy Whistler wants Titus Bass to pay her court?"

For a moment while he struggled to breathe again, Titus touched his lips with two fingertips. Only now did he realize his flesh stirred with a lightninglike tingle clear down the inside of his thighs to weaken his knees.

"I s'pose it does at that," he admitted when he took his fingers from his lips. "You didn't give me no warning, though. Lemme try that again."

When he stepped toward her, Amy brought her hand up to her mouth and giggled behind it again. "Silly. I don't just give my kisses away."

Suddenly he was angry. "Who else you been kissing?"

"No one, Titus. No one."

"You better not," he declared gruffly.

"I won't—not if you tell me we're courtin' proper."

He nodded. Decided he could grant her that. "Yeah. We're courtin' for sure."

"Then I can tell folks."

"Yeah. You can tell your pap and mam."

"No, Titus," she replied. "Tell friends around these parts. Folks up to Rabbit Hash and over to Belleview."

"T-tell friends?" Now he burned with embarrassment again.

"C'mon," she urged, taking him by the arm and leading him on down the trail that would take them to the creek where they often sat on one of the limestone boulders above the swimming hole.

"Folks in these parts?" he repeated as his feet stumbled along the dusty path.

"School, too. You can finish up your schoolin' afore we're married," she instructed.

On the frontier, girls simply did not receive any education, informal or not. Such a privilege was left to the males. Instead, girls were to devote themselves to preparing for homemaking and motherhood. Like most young girls, Amy had been given a sitting of goose eggs as a start on her own dower: a goose-down tick and feather pillows. Once her birds were hatched and grown from goslings to geese, the down could be plucked once every seven weeks. Such was a skill handed down from mother to daughter, a task requiring the utmost patience as well as strength and not the least bit of courage in the face of a strong and struggling bird. A goose might well end up with torn skin, while the picker might come away with bites and bruises from the flapping wings.

For those nestled far away on the frontier, feathers were the most expensive item after gunpowder. Good goose feathers would cost a minimum of a dollar a pound. Or, in trade value, a pound of feathers was equal to a gallon of good whiskey. As the oldest in her family, Amy had long ago started on her dower. This very summer she had completed the feather-battened counterpane she intended to spread across her wedding bed—that, and two huge, fluffy goose-down pillows where she and her husband would lay their heads.

Amy continued. "Don't you see how I want you finish school first? Then you're ready to build us a proper place where we can set up housekeeping like my mama and papa done when I first came along."

"Amy—"

"And my pa told me your pa's gonna give you that new ground he's stumpin' this season . . . now that the other fields is all planted."

As they reached the boulder there above the placid waters where years before they had dammed up a portion of the narrow creek to create a swimming hole, he asked, "Don't you think they all rushing us a bit, Amy?"

"Who's they?" she asked as they climbed.

"Your folks. My folks." He shrugged and settled onto his haunches. "Anyone getting us to get married."

She quartered away from him atop the rock, drawing her shawl around her shoulders again huffily.

He could feel the chill from her. "Amy?"

"If you don't wanna get married to me, then why you paying me court, Titus?"

How the devil did he know the answer to any of these questions? he wondered right then and there. Ciphering and writing his letters were hard enough in school now, what with the way his mind wandered away to other things—like Amy or the cool shadows of the forest where he wanted to be walking with his rifle. But as difficult as they were, ciphering and writing his letters were nowhere near as tough as the questions she was flinging at him. He wondered if his pap had struggled this hard growing to be a man.

Was it all worth it?

"Well?" she asked him. "If you don't wanna get married, then why you wasting your time on me? And why the devil am I wasting my time on you?"

He watched her slide down off the far side of the rock. "Amy—c'mon back up here."

"No. I'm goin' home."

"Amy," he coaxed.

"Got bread due to come off the fire," she explained, standing still at the foot of the rock below him, yet with her back his way. "Mama be expecting me."

"They damned well know we gone off to court, Amy."

Lord, where did those words come from? Right out of his mouth that way, so smooth he sounded like he was sure of himself. Why, when he didn't feel smooth and sure of himself, no ways?

"Is that what we're doing, Titus?" she asked finally, turning partway back to face him, looking up at him still seated atop the rock. "Are you paying me court now?"

"I can't very well spoon you with you down there and me up here."

She gathered up her long skirt and planted her bare feet along the slope of the rock, clutching her shawl with one hand while she clambered her way back up to sit beside him. His heart was hammering like all get-out by the time she settled and swept up one of his hands. Amy held it between hers in her lap, the way she always did, gently stroking the back of his with her sure, hard fingers.

He smelled the yeast and the flour on her hair as the breeze came up. Smelled the milk and butter and a hint of vanilla. She baked bread like her people had for centuries. Folks what was Englishers from long back.

Titus's grandpap said they was from a long line of Scottishers, but they'd give up on fighting the English years before and come to the colonies when the lobsterbacks were trying to hang all the rebellious highlanders. Grandpap had many a tale of huge, double-bladed claymorgans wielded by wiry Scots. Legends of lowland battles against the mighty English ranks while small, brave youths swirled in among the lobsterbacks' herds, stealing the finest horseflesh to drive back north into the moors and sheltering hills amid the angry shouts and whistling gunshots.

He lifted a lock of her dusty-red hair and smelled it. And found his flesh stirring, hardening, heating up.

"You . . . ," he began tentatively, then swallowed and licked his lips. "Amy, you ever think back on them times we come here to swim of a summer afternoon or evenin'?"

"Yes. I do, Titus. Sometimes I wish we was children again. Do you?"

"No. No, never." He dropped that lock of her hair and stared at the water below them. "I can't wait till I'm on my own. Never wanna be a young'un again."

"When you're on your own, I'll be there with you," she confided softly.

He stared at her mouth as she formed the words, wanting his mouth to touch her lips the way the words just had.

She continued, "We won't be living with our folks no more. Just each other, with children of our own."

"I don't . . . I never done nothing . . . with a girl. . . ." And suddenly his cheeks grew hot with shame.

"Me neither," Amy admitted, turning away.

He felt better when she did turn. Maybe she was as shy about it as he was. Scared to talk of it, as afraid as he was to talk of his fears. "Don't know nothing about having children—how it happens 'tween a man and woman."

"Atween a husband and wife, Titus." She fixed him with her eyes. "Atween two folks what love each other and are making a life together. He works the fields, growing things. And she takes care of all else, growing their young'uns up."

Young'uns. Hell, most times he was so bewildered, Titus figured he was still just a child himself. Not that he'd let anyone know what he thought. Not Amy and not her folks. And sure as hell he wouldn't let his pap know. Certain it was that Titus knew he wasn't grown-up. All he had to do was look at Cleve Whistler, look at his own pap, to know that.

Being a man meant settling down with a woman on your own land, raising up a cabin and starting a family. Leaving your bed before light each morning and working the dark, moist soil into every crack and crevice of your hands all day until you stopped for a cold midday meal of what had been left over from last night's supper. Then you went back to turning the soil behind the oxen or an old mule, watching each fold of the earth peel away from the share blade as you were pulled along by the animals you coaxed and prodded, whipped and cajoled ahead of you up and down the fields you had cleared of rocks and stumps, fields that you walked over so many times that your bare feet must surely know them by rote.

Being a man meant you hunted only to make meat. You never took up your rifle and disappeared into the woods just to walk among the shadows, across the meadows, along the game trails. Never did a man just go to sit and listen to what the quiet told him. There to watch the deer come to drink, or gather at the salt licks, and not once raise his rifle against them. No, only a boy wasted such precious time like that. Never a man.

A man never played with the same zest and fervor that Titus felt when he stepped past the last furrow of a field at the edge of the trees and looked back, his rifle on his shoulder, then slipped on into the timber, the squirrels chirking their protests above him, the drone of flies and the startled flap of other winged things singing at his ears.

No, sir—only a boy could play as much as Titus wanted to play. A man had more important things to be about than walking in the woods with no purpose at all. Just as Amy had explained it: a man had to provide for others. When all Titus wanted to do was to be left alone to sort out why he wasn't yet ready to be a man.

How many times had he looked at his pap—really looked at him— studying the way Thaddeus went about things, dealt with situations, reached out to folks and was regarded by his neighbors . . . only to realize he himself was a long way from being the same sort of growed-up man his pap was? Titus wondered if he ever would be that growed-up. Wondered if such a state just came with time, this settling in to be a farmer, raising a family and crops, raising cows from calves and butcher hogs from shoats. Maybeso being a man just came with time, on its own and natural.

Problem was, everyone around him seemed to be saying now was his time. His own folks, and the Whistlers too. Even Amy her own self—all of 'em was saying it was Titus's time to grow up to be a man and put aside childish things. For certain he knew he was not a child no more. Not yet a man neither.

Leastwise, not a man in the way every other man he knew of was a man.

They all took responsibility on their shoulders like a yoke and stepped into harness like one of their oxen or that old mule his pap trusted to pull those stumps out of the fields. That was what made a man, he had figured.

They took on responsibility for others . . . when here Titus was having trouble being responsible for only his own self.

Her voice shook him. "I asked: don't you want that too, Titus?"

Startled, he looked at her face again. Wanting to tell her exactly what she wanted to hear. Some of those smooth, oily words that could come tumbling out of his mouth if he wasn't careful. Not knowing where they came from, except that maybe his own heat, his own tingling readiness was just the place from where they sprang.

Instead, he told her the truth. What he wanted right then and there.

"I wanna go swimming with you, Amy."

Her eyes widened. "What?"

"Yeah. I want us to go swimming. Just like when we was young'uns ourselves."

She shook her head, studying his face. "No. We can't. Not now. Not ever, I fear. Not like that again." With a sad look on her face Amy started to pull away. "I gotta get back home now. Don't want mama to have to pull the bread off the fire for me when it's my job, Titus."

He trapped her hands in his. "No. Listen. Just for a short bit. Let's go swimming."

"I can't," she repeated more emphatically, tugging to free her hands from his grip. "Not time now to do nothing but go back afore my baking's burned."

He pleaded, "Then promise me when."

"Promise you what?"

"We'll go swimming."

"I don't know—"

"Promise me."

She stopped wiggling, studying his eyes, cocking her head slightly to the side. "This something you really, really wanna do—like we done as children?"

His head bobbed up and down. "More'n anything I could think of doing with you, Amy."

Finally, after long moments of what seemed like tortured consideration, she answered. "All right. We'll go swim—"

"When?" he interrupted in a gush.

"Soon."

"Tell me when."

Her eyes darted about, as if searching the darkening woods for her answer. "Come Saturday. When your school be out for the rest of summer now that planting's done. I can get things done back to home so that we got us enough time to have alone, Titus."

"Saturday," he said, his mouth gone dry just to think of it, faced with the waiting.

She gazed into his eyes, as if trying to measure something there that even she could not sort out. "Yes. Saturday. You come fetch me up after supper. We head down here and be alone to go swimming like kids."

"But we ain't really young'uns no more," he wanted her to know as he let her hands go.

Amy placed them on either side of his smooth, hairless cheeks. "No. We ain't children no more." Then she pulled him to her and kissed him on the forehead. And turned to slide down the gentle slope of the swimming-hole boulder.

At the bottom she looked up at him. "You coming? Fella's always gotta walk his girl home when they're courting."

He glanced at the quiet surface of the pool they had made years before when they were young. Then he looked at Amy in the starlight.

"Yeah. I'll walk my girl home."

And realized he could never look back again.

Everything lay before him. Only memories of childhood rested behind him.

And as he walked out of the trees toward the Whistler cabin, Titus wondered if this was how a boy like himself became a man like his pap. Or like Cleve Whistler, who sat on the porch, idly stripping thin slivers of bark from a hickory limb with his folding knife.

"Evenin', Titus," he called out, his teeth clenched around the cob pipe. "Amy said you'd be dropping by."

"Yes, sir."

"You going for a walk?"

"Yes," he answered as steadily as he could, hoping his face would not give him away. Titus was afraid a man was sure to see a certain look on a boy's face when he was about to become a man. "Going for a . . . walk."

"Nice evening for it, son."

Whistler reached over and snatched up a small bundle of long hickory sticks, each more than four feet long. Every one he had peeled and carefully knotted with his knife. He untied the four long leather straps lashed around the narrow bundle, slipped in the limb he had just finished, then retied them all together as tightly as he could before knotting the straps.

In the near distance came the reassuring clang of an ox's bell, floating in from the fenced paddock.

"You 'scuse me a minute, Titus—I gotta go put these back to soaking an' bring that ol' beast in from his feed."

"Yes, sir. You go right ahead."

He swallowed as he watched the man's back disappear around the side of the cabin. Every man Titus knew of had a special trough somewhere close where a fella would keep peeled hickory shafts soaking and straightening, all bound one to the other in a tight bundle.

He sensed something behind him. When he turned, the four of them were there again. Each one of the children stared up at him from those expressionless faces that regarded Titus as if he were of no real particular interest, yet the only thing of any interest at all for that particular moment in their world nonetheless.

"I'm ready."

He whirled about, finding her on the porch above him. Behind Amy stood Mrs. Whistler framed by the open doorway, tucking a wisp of her hair behind an oversize ear. From the cabin came the strong lure of salat greens simmering in a pepper-pot soup over a fire. Daughter tossed mother her apron, then pulled at the loose end of a ribbon that had held her own hair back from her face.

"Here, Mama," she said, laying the ribbon in her mother's palm, then planted a kiss on her mother's cheek.

No different from the kisses she gives me, he thought.

But when Amy turned back to Titus, she wiggled her head, shaking out her hair, combing her fingers through the long, wavy tresses that caught the sunset with a hint of coppery shimmer. Oh, how he loved her for the way she tossed that mane from side to side. He was positive she had to know what a trembling pan of mush it made of his insides to watch her do something so seductive as flip that hair around, suddenly loosened from its ribbon.

"You young'uns have fun now," Mrs. Whistler cheered them, waving to them both as Amy leaped barefoot from the porch to his side.

Swallowing hard, Titus waved back and nodded lamely, not taking his eyes off Amy—for the moment he could dwell on nothing more than seeing her get loose of her clothing. He wondered how a woman looked skinned. Shet of her garments—almost like skinning an animal to get down past all the layers of concealment.

He thought he wouldn't be able to take another breath when she slid her hand into his and tugged him away, stumbling and ungainly as a new-born calf at her side.

"You been looking forward to tonight, Titus?" she finally asked when they had pierced the shadows beneath the timber at the far side of the yard.

He glanced back at the Whistler cabin, her brothers playing mumblety-peg in the yard and her sisters fluttering around that rope swing, not sure what to feel now that he found himself truly alone with her and on their way to the swimming hole. Anticipating to the point that he found it hard to speak.

"M-more'n anything . . . ever," he stumbled getting the words out.

Amy didn't say anything more on that walk through the woods until they reached the creek and turned south, using the game trail that ran close to the bank, a path likely every bit as familiar to their bare feet as it was to the four-legged creatures who shared this hardwood forest. An owl flapped low over their heads as they reached the pool, hooting once in the shrinking light that seemed to compress the world in around them. As far as he was concerned, there really was nothing beyond the ring of trees and tangle of brush that covered either bank, immediately surrounding them with a sense of privacy, intimacy. Despite the coming twilight, the yellow of tansy and whitish-blue of periwinkle were still evident among the fragrant wild clover.

For several minutes they stood at the side of the boulder, staring at the black water stretching to the far bank, not uttering a word. Then Amy finally turned and spoke.

"You still wanna swim with me way we done when we was children?"

"I ain't really thought of nothing else for days, Amy," he confessed. "Working that field for my pa, yanking stumps outta the ground—every-thing I done it made no matter: I ain't thought of nothing else."

Slipping her hand from his, she stepped away to the side of the boulder. "I'll shinny out of my clothes over here. You stay there and . . . I'll meet you in the water."

"Aw-awright," he answered, of a sudden dry-mouthed.

He felt that left hand she had been holding grow cool in a gentle nudge of breeze rattling the heavy green leaves on nearby beech and cedar trees. Cool enough to make him aware for the first time that the dampness had been there in his palm all along. He looked down at it, then swiped both palms down the front of his britches. When Titus glanced back up, she was gone behind the boulder.

For an instant he thought of following her, just closely enough to watch her disrobe—a little miffed that she robbed him of experiencing her shinny out of her clothes. Then he quickly realized he would see all of her soon enough. And that set him to tearing at the bone buttons on his square-shouldered, pullover shirt, ripping it from his shoulders and flinging it onto a bush close by. He fought with the wooden buttons at the wide flap of his drop-front britches, then tugged them down his legs and crow-hopped out of them a foot at a time.

The water was cold when he stepped off the grassy bank and into the shimmering pond, cracking the surface of the placid waters that flowed peacefully toward the Ohio River less than two miles off to the northwest. He gasped audibly as the water met his privates, but on he sank as his feet felt their way across the bottom. Within heartbeats his skin grew accustomed to the feel of the pool, and he sank to his chin, arms treading slowly as he moved away from the bank, then turned back to the boulder that stood overlooking the grassy bank.

He stopped, stunned into utter motionlessness.

Amy slipped through the starlight, more silhouette than shape. Just enough starshine and nibbled moon for him to see the milky whiteness of her skin as she emerged from the shadows of overhanging branches, and no sooner had he gasped again than she was swallowed by that shiny black surface of the water, which reflected the night sky the way a tortoise's shell shimmered like polished ebony. With his belt knife he had carved his mother a pair of hair combs from just such a shell for her last birthday.

Remembering that, he watched Amy sink slowly to her chin, her long hair trailing out behind her on the surface of the water as she slowly rippled her way toward him.

When she was a good six feet from Titus, Amy turned aside and stretched out her body, her legs bobbing to the surface, her feet kicking playfully at the water. Her white body merging with a distinct line against the black surface of the disturbed water, Amy rolled over and swam off toward the far side of the creek.

He watched her feet splash at the water, the curve at the back of her legs where the ankles ran up to meet her calves. There at the crook of the knees she moved up and down ever so slightly as she kicked in a great arc while turning back. And he stared transfixed at the tight mounds of her rump exposed above the water's plane like a rounded hillock draped with the first snow of the winter in this silvery light. Against that black, glimmering slide of the roiling surface she plied back toward him.

Her legs ceased kicking, her arms no longer crawled through the water as she came close. A little breathless, Amy spoke.

"I forgot how good this feels. Been some time since't I come down here. So busy helping mama with the chores, with all the rest of the babies."

He only nodded, and swallowed hard. Unable to speak as she drew up to arm's length.

She whispered. "I'm glad I come, Titus."

"Me too." His eyes sought to divine a vision through that black water. How he wanted to see bare what he had never seen before.

Inching closer, now well within his reach, Amy stopped and bobbed slightly as she settled her feet to the creek bottom. As her shoulders emerged, the tops of her young breasts broke the surface of the water. He felt himself stir, twitch, strengthen like nothing before in all those nights alone beneath his blankets.

"This . . . this is important to me," she whispered, as if it were a secret that could not be shared even with the creekbank. "Important to us."

"Us," he repeated. Then reached out a hand, hoping to touch.

She felt it brush the underside of one breast, then seized it in one of her own, inching his down along her ribs to rest at the soft curve of her pelvis. Amy shuddered.

"There," she said. "When you touched me . . . there."

"I want to."

For a moment she didn't say anything, only stared back into his eyes. Then admitted, "It made me . . . not like you was tickling me. Just a . . . a nice tingle."

"I want to, Amy."

"Yes," she replied. "I want you to."

As she said it, Amy moved Titus's hand up her ribs to place it on her breast. He gasped at the soft, slippery feel to it cupped in his hand. She closed her eyes halfway, and he sensed the shudder shoot through her.

Beneath the surface Amy sought out his left hand, pulled it to her, placed it on the other breast as she eased a step closer to him.

"That's—oh! You're making me shiver like I was cold," she confided. "But it ain't really like I'm cold. Shivering 'cause you're making me warm there to touch me."

Her palms brushed across the flat hardness of his skinny chest at the same time he felt a hardening of some of the skin at the middle of her breasts. She had to be made the way he was, Titus decided. Not all that different: with nipples just like him and the hogs and even the bitch hound that slept under the porch, out of the snow and out of the sun. But as he gently raised her breasts out of the water, he saw these were not at all the same nipples. Amy's were something deliciously different.

And in looking at them, he felt all the more stirring as he rose beneath the surface of that tranquil pond.

Or perhaps it was the way her eyes half closed once more when she tilted her chin back and slowly slid her hands down below the water, just barely brushing the skin of his chest until she reached his belly and held there as Titus rubbed his hands across her hardened nipples.

With a groan emanating from the back of her throat, Amy's hands inched on down—suddenly reaching his engorged flesh.

"Oh," she said, opening her eyes and bringing them down to look squarely at him.

How they glistened in the starlight there as the moon rose.

"What's this?" she asked.

When she ran a single, roughened finger down the length of it, his flesh quivered. "My. Did you feel what it did when I touched it?"

"F-feels good, Amy," he begged.

Hurried, with one hand he traced a path from a breast down to her belly, and stopped as he felt the mat of curly hair. Made different from him, constructed perhaps like half of those coupling critters he had watched in rapt amazement over the past few years. He sought to go lower, finding that the hair ended and her privates parted in two soft folds of skin. Just like the cows he had observed. Of a sudden he realized it was there he was to put himself, to slip within as the males of other species mounted their females.

Her breathing had become ragged, short and raspy. Inching his finger farther down, he gently moved the skin apart. Amy gasped deeply. And clamped her hand around him, hard.

He felt his flesh jerk as if it were about to leap free of him, even free of her lock on him, a sudden constriction seizing his lower belly.

Titus had to bury himself in her. Now.

Clumsily he dragged her hips toward him, working his groin upward as he pulled her thighs apart. With her arms Amy tread water, her widening eyes locked on his, their faces marked with strained intensity. Time and again he thrust himself at her, his hands grappling violently at the small of her back, yanking her down on him, seizing hold of her buttocks as he thrust against the water's buoyancy, which made her rise from him.

"N-not like this," she ordered as she kicked her legs off his hips. Pointing, she added, "The bank. Up there."

In despair he watched as she turned away, laying out on the surface of the water, kicking her legs and stroking with her arms, the long hair playing out behind her. Titus was within reach of her as they arrived at the grassy bank and stepped out of the pond, both of them trembling with the summer's breeze as it kissed their wet skin.

With a sudden sense of how he was to mesh his body with hers, Titus was on top of Amy even as she settled quickly to the grass and rolled over from her hip. Barely lying back before he was atop her thighs. Legs that spread beneath the press of his weight.

Looking down at her, his long hair dripping into her face, Titus suddenly closed his eyes, dipped his head, and laid his mouth fully on hers. She sucked at his lips hungrily, thrusting her hips upward at the same moment. He sensed that same tightening across his lower belly and drew back, confused at this all-compelling need to concentrate not on her mouth, but to get himself between her legs.

As he rose on his hands, he looked down at the soft, rounded mounds of her breasts, the skin pale against the darker pink of her nipples. Then attempted to thrust himself farther against her.

"Not, not like . . . ," she said huskily.

And in the next moment Amy had seized his hard flesh and was guiding it against a softer spot, lower between her smooth thighs. Making the end of him brush the folds of flesh as the sky seemed to light up all around him with shooting stars, the earth quaked beneath him, as if to swallow them up.

He felt that first explosion—no doubt of that—yet it was the second and all those that rocked him afterward that seized Titus with such force he knew he would likely never see again. Everything had turned black except for the shooting stars. Again and again his hips flung forward against her, his hot flesh still enclosed in her hand, trying desperately to bury his rigid penis in her without success as he spent himself in great waves against the inside of her thigh.

She sighed as he trembled to a halt, and laid his head in the curve where her neck met a shoulder.

"We'll have lots of babies," she whispered, clutching his head to her chin, the other hand still gripping his softening flesh. "I'll give you lots of children, Titus. I'll raise them, and you raise the crops. Man and woman supposed to be like that."

He shuddered again, this time from fear. Of a sudden afraid at what he had just done. This talk of babies and joining Amy on the land. Knowing he was not the sort who could sink the rest of his life into the ground with her.

Afraid he would never be man enough to stay.

THREE

Titus slapped at a big blue-black fly droning in the hot, sticky air right in front of his nose. Noisy enough with all the clatter and racket, all the people moving past, with beeves mooing, pigs grunting, and sheep baaing. Yet none of it bothered him—except for the incessant, bothersome drone of that fly.

Then he had it, snapping his hand around the pesky insect in a blur. When he opened his palm, there it lay, stunned, wings flitting lamely, buzzing inconstantly. Without remorse he slapped the palm against the side of his old britches, swiped off the hand on the pants, then closed his eyes again after tugging down the old floppy-brimmed wool-felt hat.

It wasn't cool here, even tucked back in the shade. But at least beneath this weeping willow he found it was a damned sight less hot than out there in the late-summer sun where the afternoon dragged on and on. He had a little time to rest before the next relay of shooters was due on the firing line at three. Right square in the hottest part of the day. The ten competitors who qualified from these last five relays would all compete come early evening after the sun began to sink and the air might cool to something bearable.

As for Titus, it had proved to be a long day already.

Last night he hadn't been able to sleep all that well—not that sleeping rolled up in his blankets on the ground had ever bothered him. No, it was more that his excitement, anticipation, eagerness to be about this contest kept him tossing until he finally drifted off sometime shortly before the sun made its appearance that Saturday in mid-August.

"These dog days," is what his mother muttered repeatedly, no matter was she at home or here at the fair.

Dog days came once a year, visited upon northern Kentucky with summer's last vengeful fare-thee-well. Here after the crops were all in the fields, growing to beat the band, and just before that slick-eyed schoolmaster would again ring his bell signaling that first day of school for the new year, eager to get in a few weeks of book learning before classes would be suspended while the young boys stayed to home, helping out in the fields during the harvest time. Only when the crops had been gathered and all was securely put up would the farmers think of sending their children back to school.

Dog days. Beside him lay the old redbone, his hunting partner of the last handful of years. Tongue lolling, eyes glazed in fatigued stupor, the hound lay on his back upon the patch of shady grass, his belly exposed. Gnats swarmed in clouds around his watery eyes. The dog snorted at them, dragged a paw down his long muzzle in frustration, then rolled onto his side to plop a leg over his nose.

Nearby the rhythmic booming continued nonstop from the long firing line staked out at the edge of the meadow. Interposed between each rumble of the muzzle loaders he heard the squeals of children at play, the giggles of the young girls eyeing the summer's crop of prospective beaux, and the laughter of adults passing this way and that among the meandering knots of marquees and wall tents, canvas awnings, and fire-smudged lean-tos stretched across a modest framework of poles. From every one a barker gave nearly the same call—something to entice passersby into viewing their wares: baked goods, fruits and vegetables, needlework, woolens, leather goods, harness and plowshares, woodwork, ironmongery, all of it for sale at this once-a-year carnival begun long ago.

The Boone County Longhunters Fair—a celebration of the county's own namesake and his blazing of a trail into this land of the canebrakes—was held on this same ground this time every year to insure the greatest turnout, and therefore sales, for each of the merchants who traveled here from as far away as Pittsburgh and as nearby as Cincinnati. Besides, a person had the opportunity to browse past the displays of fine mercantile goods spread out atop crates and display tables by the local merchants of Rabbit Hash, Belleview, and Petersburg, and even this sprawling village of Burlington as well, not to mention what many of the poorer families set out atop worn blankets spread upon the ground before their lean-tos, hoping to sell their modest, homemade crafts.

This carnival of baking, quilting, and other contests each summer brought a growing throng here to Burlington for the better part of three or four days. Families arrived on the fairgrounds to select a spot down by one of the two creeks, perhaps choosing something back against the woods, and there raised their tents and dug their fire pits. Friends greeted friends they had not seen for an entire year. Men hailed one another and spoke of their crops, their hogs and sheep. Women shared recipes and spoke of loved ones gone to their reward with the past winter. Children frolicked and dogs scampered with abandon through the meadow until fair officials came through, as they always did, ordering all animals tied up in camp.

That's why Tink had a short length of rope loosely knotted around his neck, the end of the loop stuffed into Titus's belt. Just so the old hound wouldn't get himself into trouble, maybe even shot by some man whose wife screamed out that a dog had just run off with their supper, plucked right from the fireside. Such a thing had happened at noon, and the squire of Burlington, along with his duly elected town constable, had to pull that dead dog's owner off the dog killer for the sake of not charting up more of a human toll than the town fathers counted on every year.

For certain, there was plenty of celebration flowing free enough. The wines and brandies and beers brewed every year for just this festival were most often consumed in moderate quantities. Just enough to enliven each festive night's music and dancing. Still, there were always a few of the young wags who could not hold their liquor and ended up taking offense at some snub, those who got nasty and often pulled up a chunk of firewood, if not a knife, to settle whatever wrong they believed done them. Most times others merely pulled the quarrelers off to opposite sides of the sprawling camping grounds, where they could cool down and eventually sleep off their revelry. Rarely was the constable called in to hustle someone off to his modest jail.

But this shooting of a man's hunting dog was considered by many serious enough an offense to warrant the owner shooting the dog killer. Both had been dragged away to jail minutes ago, there to languish for the rest of the fair, one offender in each of the constable's two cells, where they could glare at one another, curse a blue streak if they chose, and likely try their marksmanship spitting at one another between a set of crude iron bars.

After that pair of scrappers had been dragged off in irons, the fair quickly resumed its atmosphere of merriment and music, a celebration of rural frontier life at its best. Back on the shooting range, the judges returned to their task of determining who was to be known as the best shot in Boone County.

It was serious, this shooting contest held each summer. Merchants in nearby Burlington put up the finest in the way of a purse for the winner, with a few prizes donated for second, third, and fourth places—those who had been bested. Serious enough business that the contest had long had three divisions: one contest held between all those men who were clearly long in the tooth yet still possessed a clear eye and a steady hand; another match that allowed the county's youth to pit their skills one against the other; and the final competition—the annual fair's most-watched event—pitting young men from sixteen and up from all the farms and towns to compete for the right to be known as Boone County's best marksman.

For the last three summers Titus had carried home his prizes from the fair, taking first place against the county's other youth each August. For the last two years how he had looked forward to this seventeenth summer: eligible to match his skill against the finest marksmen he had watched shoot ever since he was a wee lad big enough to load his own rifle.

In the last few months Thaddeus Bass had been preaching to his son, "It makes little shake what those men do toeing that line and firing their muskets at a distant mark. No, Titus—in life what matters only is what a man does to provide for those who count on him."

More than just about anything, Titus wanted to change his father's tune—to have his pap pound him on the back gleefully once he won the shooting contest and say that, yes, there was something worthwhile in being the best, after all, something worthwhile in his son having a dream different from his own. He knew he could never be what his father wanted him to be, for he realized he was not stamped to walk the same path his pap had taken. So it was that this year Titus carried great hope in his heart that once he proved himself not only capable, but the best, his father would finally relent and remove the tight harness he had buckled around his eldest son.

"Titus?"

He pushed back the floppy brim and gazed up at the sound of her voice. The summer's light lit the copper strands in her dusty hair with tongues of flame. How he stirred to see her, gratified she had come to find him.

"Amy. I looked for you this morning down at the shooting line."

With a shrug she replied, "Helping mama with her baking. Lunch is done and the other'ns're all fed, so she said I could come look you up for a bit. Leastwise till it's time to go help her put supper together. The young'uns is going crazy—running here and there."

He shifted himself up against the tree and pulled the hat off his head, pushing back a thick shock of dark, damp hair out of his eyes. "I . . . I need to ask you something."

"What?"

"Something been . . . what I been meaning to ask for last couple weeks."

"Yes?" she prodded, settling near his knee, her legs folded to the side in that way of hers that hid her bare feet and ankles beneath her faded dress, one of her mother's best.

"You . . . ," he started, then cleared his throat as his eyes retreated from her face and he went to scratching at the old hound's ear. For some time now he'd been brooding on just how to get this said—choosing his words carefully from what he realized was a most limited vocabulary of a young man totally ignorant of such mysteries in life. "I figure a girl knows about such things. 'Specially you since't you was around when all your brothers and sisters was borned, and it seems only natural that a girl pays proper attention to such things."

Her eyes darted back and forth between his. "What you wanna ask me, Titus?"

Again he looked into those green eyes. "T-tell me how a woman knows she's gonna have a baby."

Her cheeks flushed with a tint of pale strawberry, and her eyes dropped a moment. Amy yanked up a tall blade of grass and brought it to her lips. Sucking on the green shoot, she finally said, "If a woman ain't with child, once a moon she gets a visit of a particular ailment, Titus."

"Ailment? Like'n you got the ague?"

"Not 'sactly. She don't feel so good. Her belly gives her fits, cramping up—like that."

He shook his head, still bewildered. "So?"

"So if she's gonna have a baby—like you said—those visits once a moon don't come to trouble her."

Still he was having trouble making the connection, unable to fathom what it all meant as he sat there in the shady, sticky heat of that August afternoon. Nonetheless, he leaned toward her, undeterred from his quest. "You saying if she don't have that visit for two or three months, that woman knows she carrying a child?"

"That, and my mama was always sick for the first few months she was about to have another young'un."

"Sick?"

"Like"—and she rubbed her belly—"the heaves and all that."

He nodded. "Oh."

"Why you wanna know about that, Titus?"

Looking away now that she had asked a question, his eyes crawled to the canopy of long weeping-willow branches swaying on the hot breeze. "You . . . Amy—have you got your visit . . . since we—since we . . . there at the swimming hole. Have you?"

"Is that what you're asking about?" she replied, wide-eyed and gaping in surprise. "Y' was thinking I'm carrying your baby?"

"Yeah," he admitted. "I need to know."

"I ain't had my visit since we was at the swimming hole, Titus. I'm telling you, jus' so you'll know."

He swallowed hard. There it was—as unexpected and bad a piece of news as any could have been. And he suddenly felt a little hotter, a little more suffocated by the damp heat.

"Then you might'n be carrying m-my baby?"

Placing a hand gently over her abdomen, she said, "If'n it's a baby, it's your baby, Titus."

He wagged his head, feeling dizzied by the announcement. "My baby."

Amy patted the back of his hand, then held it in hers. "Mama says a woman don't necessarily get herself with child every time she's with a man. Don't always happen."

"Just when you don't get your visit each moon."

"Right," she answered. "Things gotta be right, I guess, atween a man and a woman for a baby to grow in the woman's belly."

He was confused again. "Things gotta be right?"

With a shrug Amy replied, "I s'pose my mama meant that the man and woman loved the other, they was married. Maybeso like us, they gonna get married."

"G-gonna get married," he repeated with a mumble.

"If . . . if I was carrying your baby, I'd be right happy, Titus."

"Happy?"

"We could have a head start on our life together that way—getting our family going early on."

"Family."

Just the sound of it rang with such finality.

But he had climbed atop her for only a few seconds, for what seemed like the blink of an eye, one thump of his leaping heart—and for that fleeting moment he might now have a baby to feed and clothe and care for until it was growed up enough to go out on its own. Like he damn well was this very summer.

Beyond a row of chestnut trees a bell rang out, tolling six gongs.

He sat up straighter, listening and counting each toll of the nearby bell. "I'll have to go in a half hour."

"Why?"

"They was calling the fellas for the final relay."

"The championship?"

"Yes," he replied, taking the longrifle into his hands and laying it across his lap. The old hound stirred. Tink looked at Titus beneath a drooping eyelid, then rolled over and went back to sleep. "Time come soon for me to show 'em all what I'm made of."

"I already know what you're made of. Gonna be so proud of you, Titus," Amy declared with a smile. "You doing this for the both of us." Then she glanced down at her belly. "Maybe even the three of us."

"Three?" His throat seized, feeling more constricted at that moment than when he had tasted the corn mash a friend of his pap's had brewed up for this year's fair.

"Could be," she answered. "You know how it is when a man and a woman love each other and wanna be husband and wife. It's how we was at the swimming hole a couple weeks back."

"I . . . I—"

She prodded him coyly, "You remember, don't you?"

"Ain't never gonna forget."

He pulled a gay red bandanna from a front pocket of his britches and swiped it across his forehead, glad it was so hot that she wouldn't ever tell how it made him sweat just talking about this with her.

"In a way," Amy said, her voice softer now, those big doe eyes of hers darting left and right before she leaned forward confidentially, "I've been thinking on how good that made me feel—how I'd like to feel that good again sometime soon."

"S-soon?"

"Maybe real soon," Amy answered, leaning back and bringing her legs under her to rise. "Maybeso tonight: you come look me up over to my folks' tent after supper chores is done."

"Tonight. Yes."

He rose unsteadily beside her, his temples pounding, hoping it was just the heat that made his head swim on rising waves of pressure. Then she was pressed against him, rubbing a breast against his arm. He looked down at the contours of her straining beneath the thin fabric of her dress.

"You want to touch 'em again, don't you, Titus?"

"I, I surely would."

Planting a kiss lightly on the singed redness of his hairless cheek, Amy giggled and turned away. Over her shoulder she said, "Look me up, Titus—an' we'll sneak off so you can do all the touching you want."

Godamighty!

He watched her sway side to side, moving off through the grass and sunlight toward the bustle and din of the fair, her long skirt sweeping this way then that as she threw those rounded hips of hers about. It made his mouth go dry just remembering how those hips felt in his hands, how he hadn't just held them, more even than a frantic grope, but had clawed at them as he attempted to drive himself into her there in the cool black water of that stream.

Into . . . inside . . . he never had been inside her, if there was an inside to women. Maybe there wasn't and everything was all outside, like he was. And a man was just s'posed to get his pecker laid down atween their legs, getting hisself pointed just right afore he shot. And that was what made babies grow: was when a man shot center—the way he was determined to shoot center this evening—and his juices landed in just the right place on a woman's privates.

And then he felt some self-imposed embarrassment, just in thinking about it. There was no one he could ask. Nary a friend from the Rabbit Hash school he dared mention his fears to. Sure was he that they were as ignorant of such primal matters as he was. No father he could present himself to and ask for answers to such vital questions. Maybe only Amy herself held the key.

He'd have to learn the mysteries from her—if he dared.

Dared . . . because he was scared, frightened right down to the soles of his feet that he had put her with child already. Lying down atop a gal and pointing his pecker in the right direction, then shooting center to make a real mess on her, to make a mess of their lives.

It was one bit of marksmanship Titus wasn't all that sure he was so proud of right now as he leaned over and nuzzled the redbone hound.

"C'mon, you ol' ranger. Time for me to take you back to the folks afore I mosey off to the shooting range."

Tink whimpered a bit, mostly howled as he leaped against the length of rope tied around his neck when Titus left him behind, secured to a tree beside his folks' pair of poor lean-tos.

Thaddeus had pitched their camp right beside a Cincinnati pot merchant who was selling his kettles and ovens beneath an awning of bright-blue Russian sheeting. In cherrywood boxes he also displayed the medicinals he had to sell, English ague and fever drops, as well as butter tubs and cream jugs made of fired and painted clays. On the other side of them sat the red-trimmed marquee tent of a glassman from Pittsburgh. Here in the first decade of the nineteenth century glass was relatively plentiful, not yet overly priced for those settlers pushing against the western frontier. Forty of the twelve-by-twelve-inch panes sold for fourteen shillings, little more than a nickel apiece.

Titus had to force himself to turn his back on the disappointed dog and walk away hurriedly, as sorry as he felt leaving Tink behind at camp. But trouble it would be with the dog at the shooting line, the noise and the press of people. The match would be tough enough for him to concentrate on without Tink lolling there between his legs the way he'd done that morning during the qualifying relays.

"Titus!"

He turned.

"You didn't even gimme a kiss good-bye," Betsey Bass scolded her son as she stopped before him.

"Ain't good-bye, Mam."

She brushed her fingers along his cheek. "You're away to the big match, ain'tcha?"

Titus nodded. "Where's pap?"

She shrugged, saying, "Don't know. Went off with some others to go talk seeds, they was when I last saw 'em." And she leaned up on the toes of her worn, scuffed boots to kiss his cheek. "That's for luck, Titus. You go show 'em."

"I will, Mam. You gonna come, ain'tcha?"

"Course, son. I'll be there shortly."

"An' pap? He coming to watch me win?"

His mother's lips quivered in deliberation before she answered. "I'm sure he'll be looking in on the match, Titus. Now, you go show 'em your best."

He set off again toward the shooting range on the far side of the meadow, where they fired into the side of a tall, wooded hill. He hoped his father would show, knowing the odds were against it. Touching his cheek where his mother had planted her lips, it made him wonder—when a man got old enough to be having girls kissing on him, was he too old for his mam to kiss on him then?

He was sure it sounded right—that there came a time when mothers should damn well stop embarrassing their sons by kissing them like they were children—then thought on fathers and their children. He struggled to recall any embrace from his pap, trying desperately to remember if he had seen his father hug his other three children. A kiss from Thaddeus—why, that was purely out of the question! A man, leastways the men Titus knew of, they never would be caught kissing. Not a woman, and surely not one of their children.

The sun had settled so that the bottom of its orb rested on the tops of the far trees back of the range. It would be warm on his neck. Already a crowd had gathered, knots of spectators sprinkled here and there, most all of them settled on the grass in the shade of trees and brush, a few standing. Some of those were women who sported new bonnets of the brightest calicoes and ginghams. Perhaps an arm wrapped around a husband or a sweetheart who wore his finest drop-shoulder shirt. As Titus stepped into line at the judges' table, he looked down at his own faded hickory shirt, spun and woven from the Basses' own flax and wool by his mother, then dyed a light brown with the natural dye of walnut shells she saved for just such a purpose. Folks on this frontier rarely called such cloth linsey-woolsey. Instead, what they wove to clothe their family they called mixed cloth.

Maybeso with his prize money he would have enough to buy himself a new shirt for this coming year's schooling, his last. Mayhaps enough even to buy his mam something pretty. And a special gift for Amy.

"You're the Bass boy, ain't you?"

He nodded to the man seated in a straight-backed, cane-bottomed chair behind the table where sat several inkwells and packets of ink powder amid large sheets of lined foolscap where names and numbers had been inscribed. "Yes, sir."

"Titus?"

"Yes."

The man nodded to his assistant, who hoisted a burlap bag across the table with the clatter of wood and said, "Like I'm telling every one of you last ten fellers, we'll start off at twelve rods. Each shooter will have one chance't at his target. If he don't hit it—he's out, and the rest go on to the next targets set up two rods farther on. In this-a-way, we keep going till there's only one feller."

"And he's the champeen."

The man smiled. "That's right. Like you been last couple years to the junior side of the shooting."

"What's in the bag?"

"Your targets," the man replied. "You go and mark each of 'em in the same way. With your initials. Or your mark, if you prefer: a scratch, a line, or carve your hull name if'n you want. But we must all be able to tell just whose target it is in the case of a dispute."

"They're all like this," said the sharp-nosed farmer assisting the shooting judge. He held up a square of rough-hewn hardwood, less than a foot on each side and no more than two inches thick. At the center of the block a small circle had been blackened by smudging a candle's flame against the flat surface.

"The range judges check every target after all the shooters is finished at a certain distance. Them what qualifies, anyway. If there's a hole inside the black—you go on with the others. If we cain't find no hole in the wood, or you didn't get in the black—"

"I go home empty-handed," Titus finished. "What if I put one on the line?"

The sharp-nosed assistant answered, "It don't count."

And the judge added, "You got to make it a clean shot in the black smudge."

"Certain enough." Hoisting his bag off the table, Titus said, "I'm ready."

"In just a shake now we'll call out for to start," the judge replied as Bass started away, motioning the tall man forward who had been standing behind Titus in that short line of finalists.

For the better part of a half hour Titus kept his eyes moving across the crowd continuing to grow in the shade of that rim of trees swaying with the gentle, warm breezes. None of his family had shown, not any uncles nor cousins. Disappointed, he tried telling himself it made no difference about them—not one of them saw any value in the things Titus held to be important. Nonetheless, with every minute that crawled by that late-summer after-noon, he found his young heart sinking lower and lower.

"You gone and set yourself up prime for taking a fall, Titus," he murmured to himself.

All through the years he had competed in the youngsters' matches, Titus had hoped his family would attend the shooting, supporting him as one behind their own. But time and again his father and mother had made their excuses, saying there were other more pressing concerns they had need of attending to at the same hour the matches were held. Matters of seed and discussions of weather cycles. Something, anything more important than coming to see their son strive to do his best. If only once a year he tried so hard to be the best.

So it was he had promised himself that this year it would be different for his family, convincing himself they would all show up now that he was shooting with the finest marksmen in the county. No longer among the boys, now he would stand at the same line with the menfolk, ready to show one and all that he had the stuff of a winner. And surely his pap would finally see he was worthy of his love.

At long last his father would congratulate him for a job well-done, would put his arms around his son and tell him how proud he was of him. Mayhaps even tell his firstborn son just how much he loved him.

"It's all right, Pap," Titus whispered to himself aloud, still snared in his reverie as the judge called out for the contestants to move up to the shooting line. "I know how hard it is for a man to say such a thing to his young'un. Just you being here tells me enough—"

"You coming, boy?"

Titus suddenly snapped to with a shake of his head. Before him stood one of the shooters, a tall, lanky, bearded man with a graceful fullstock slung at the end of his arm.

"Me? I'm coming," he answered, striving to make his voice sound as low as possible—angry at his shame to be caught talking to himself, off in another world.

Eight shooters waited for him and the tall marksman to reach the line.

"You're 'llowed to grease your bar'l 'tween each shot—with a patch if you're of a mind to," one of the judges kicked off.

"Other'n that," the first judge said, "it's pretty much straight-up shoot-ing. Off-hand. No rest. You can take your time on each target. Ain't being judged on how fast you shoot or load. Just how pretty you make each shot."

"Let's get on with it," one of the older men said with an impatient growl.

Titus nodded and moved off to the right end of the line.

Out close to seventy yards across the grass, which barely undulated in the faint breeze, stood a crude framework. As the judges called out names of the ten contestants from left to right, two men were placing the corresponding wood targets atop the highest plank on that framework. The shooters spread out a little more along the firing line as the crowd fell to a hush. That pair of range marshals scampered off to the side in different directions.

"Finish loading your weapons—then fire at will," said the man who had registered Titus for the contest.

Bass stood at the end of the line, his target the last on the right. Titus pulled the stopper from the large powder horn he had made himself of a scraped bullhorn, and measured out his charge of black powder into a section of deer antler hollowed out to hold just the proper number of the coarse black grains he used shot after shot.

From this twelve rods—he ciphered as he stuffed the stopper back into the narrow end of the powder horn—it would take little to put a ball from his grandpap's .42-caliber fullstock into that black circle of candle smudge. With the round ball of soft lead barely started down the swaged muzzle of the barrel, Titus pulled the long hickory ramrod free of the thimbles along the bottom of the forestock. He gave a push, moving the ball partway down the barrel, the lead sphere surrounded by a linen patch cut just a bit larger than the outer circumference of the muzzle itself, that piece of cloth soaked in the oil rendered down from a black bear he had taken not far from Amy's swimming hole early last winter. One of the few he figured hadn't been killed or run out of that part of the Ohio River country.

His mother had taken the thick yellowish fleece Titus had sliced away from the connective tissue between the hide and muscle, melting it into an oil in one of her cast-iron kettles over low heat on a trivet she swung over the coals he tended in their fireplace. It was something she had not done very often for her husband, seeing how little he hunted for the family. Thaddeus had harumped several times during the rendering process, content to leave that as his only comment from the chair where he rocked on the uneven plank floor while repairing broken leather harness using a big glover's needle threaded with thick strips of waxed linen.

"Waste of time, that oil," Thaddeus had said. "A lot of work for little gain."

Titus remembered again that winter's evening and how he had realized his father's skimpy appreciation for the pleasure a person might reap from a task far from work, a task taken on for little more than its own sake. To accomplish nothing productive but for the joy of the task itself. With his father, and his mother most times as well, everything had to serve a purpose, every day's value weighed only by what had been accomplished before one laid one's weary body down that night.

As he threaded the ramrod back into its thimbles below the barrel of the fullstock, Titus knew he would never be a man such as his father—at least the sort who found little joy in each day's modest passing for its own sake.

Thumbing the dragon's-head hammer back to half cock, he snapped forward the frizzen a Belleview gunsmith had resoled two years before so that it would once again bestow a plentiful shower of sparks into the pan where Titus now sprinkled a dusting of the fine-grained priming powder from the smaller of the two horns hanging from his possibles pouch slung over his left shoulder.

By the time the youngster brought the frizzen back down over the pan and dragged the hammer back to full cock, two shooters had taken their crack at those first targets.

He raised the butt to the curve of his shoulder and nestled it in against the thin strap of muscle beneath the worn, much-washed hickory shirt his mother had made him years before.

Another of the finalists touched off his shot. The firing line began to drift with the gray gauze of powder smoke suspended on the heavy, muggy air.

Titus laid his cheek along the smooth half heart of the small cheekpiece carved into the buttstock, trying hard to shut out the sounds of the nearby crowd murmuring, laughing, cheering on their favorites, the clamor of children at play, the unsteady and surprising boom of other shooters firing their rifles behind him. If he wasn't careful, Titus reminded himself, some man's shot just might surprise him, and he would end up jerking on the trigger instead of concentrating on nothing more than his own squeezing caress of the trigger.

When his longrifle went off, he watched through the curl of gray muzzle smoke while his target went spinning to the ground. As he brought the weapon's buttstock down to rest upon his instep, Titus turned slightly, finding the other nine shooters watching him as if he were delaying them.

" 'Bout time, boy," harped one.

Another cried out, "You may look young as a pup an' wet behin't the ears—but you take much time to shoot as a ol't lady!"

Some of the nearby crowd roared in approval. While most of the other shooters finished reloading without a complaint, a few guffawed at Titus's expense before they went about their own business.

Again his eyes anxiously raked the crowd, searching for family. Not finding any, he dropped his gaze back to his shooting pouch, where he raised the tiny iron pick he used to probe and clean the vent hole bored in the breech, then put his pan brush to work. He had crafted it last winter from the hump bristles taken off that bear.

"It's awright," he confided to himself, lips barely moving as he screwed a jag onto the end of his wiping stick. "Likely they're running late still. That'un was just the first shot, anyways. They'll be coming along directly."

As he drove a greased patch down the length of the barrel, then pulled it free of the muzzle coated with a thick swirl of powder smudge, the youth glanced downrange at the men who were hefting the framework back another two rods—some eleven yards—to the next set of distance stakes driven into the meadow. For the first time he noticed those wooden shafts some four feet tall, standing at regular intervals, each one topped with a long strip of pale cloth barely nudged by the wispy breeze.

With the ten new targets lined up and his assistants dashing off the range, the judge hollered, "Fire when ready!"

Titus finished seating the ball and patch against the breech, then brought the hammer back to full cock before the first shooter touched off. Sporadic cheers erupted for a few of the contestants as they struck their mark across that fourteen rods.

Then sixteen. And finally eighteen rods—a hundred yards of meadow. And that's when their number began to dwindle.

At twenty rods one old shooter missed his black smudge.

Two more rods from that, another pair just grazed the rim of that black smudge with their shots—not near good enough to stay on with the other seven.

At twenty-four rods they lost a man who jerk-fired and missed his chunk of wood entirely.

As Titus stood reloading to fire at twenty-six rods, he looked over the crowd once more, expecting to find his family standing somewhere near, to be close at hand, there to cheer on one of their own. Still he could not find them as he ran the ramrod home through its thimbles, then stole another look at the crowd directly behind him to be certain.

When he turned back to gaze downrange, Titus felt about as alone as he had ever felt in his seventeen summers. What he did this afternoon was damned important—yet evidently not important enough for his father to give off talking of seed and sheep and hogs, or his mother to leave off chatting about babes and spinning, baking and midwifing. . . .

Then he saw her, squeezing right through the tight first row of spectators.

Amy raised her arm and waved.

Silently he mouthed the words across the distance. "Where's my pap?"

With a shrug of her shoulders the young woman held up her empty hands and shook her head.

"Damn them anyway," he grumbled, turning from her. "Just teach me to do for myself from now on, that's what it does."

Bringing his rifle down to reload for the relay at twenty-eight rods, his eyes glanced her way, finding Amy clapping, raising her arm to wave when she found him sneaking a look in her direction. He tried to smile, if only to speak his thanks in that simple way, then primed the pan as disappointment soured his stomach.

Already two more shooters had trudged away from the firing line, leaving only four to aim at those shrinking black circles burned into wood planks set atop the stands 150 yards away.

As he brought his rifle away from his shoulder after that next shot, he heard another man curse at the unfairness of some judge's call while he trudged off in noisy protest. Just when he was about to drop his eyes to set about reloading, Titus noticed something out of place downrange as the targets were being moved out to thirty rods, drawing ever closer to the far side of the long meadow. It was the way he had learned to hunt: spotting something not quite right, not quite in place. A color where it shouldn't be, some shape out of the ordinary. And if you paid close enough attention, you were bound to discover some game hiding among that patch of brush, lying to against those shadows.

While most others might find a tree stand or lie in wait for their quarry to come down a game trail to them—young Titus Bass had taught himself to track his prey, to stalk, eyes moving constantly, searching for something that just did not fit.

For all this time he hadn't even noticed it here at this end of the meadow where the firing line had been staked out with a long piece of hemp string. The breeze hardly stirred the frayed cuffs of his drop-front britches, hardly tousled the long hair that hung in brown curls spilling down the back of his neck. But off yonder, 160 yards away, those cloth strips knotted to the tops of the tall stakes told him more than just where the targets were to be placed every two rods across the meadow. The strips fluttered, raised, flapped out straight, snapping in an eddy of wind tormenting the far end of the range.

He glanced to his left as he snapped the frizzen down over the pan, wondering if any of the three others had recognized what he had, if any of them paid the slightest heed. Two of them were intent on brushing out a pan or reloading. Only one, the tall shooter, stared downrange with knowing intensity. As Titus watched him, the lanky frontiersman slowly tore his eyes off the distance to find the youth regarding him.

Within his dark beard the man grinned so slightly, Titus wasn't sure it was a grin at all. Maybe nothing more than a squint there in the late-afternoon light. Nothing more. But no—the youth decided—the eyes had smiled, if nothing else.

Titus thought he'd sight in on his target, get his range down, and fix on where to hold the front blade in that notch filed in his rear sight—holding just so and high enough.

He brought his rifle to his shoulder and settled it in, snugging his cheek down on the smooth curly-maple of that half heart. He blinked and found that tiny black smudge way off there, all but blotted out by the front blade. He let out half a breath. Beginning to squeeze on the trigger. Then quickly flicked his eyes over to see what the cloth strip was doing on that faraway stake closest to the targets. Eyes back on the front blade he used to cover the black circle.

Continuing to squeeze ever so slightly, he blinked again and watched the strip flutter out of the corner of his eye. Titus went back to concentrating on his sight picture, then once more glanced at the strip as it suddenly dropped like a cow's tail after shooing a bothersome fly.

Readjusting his sight picture, Bass squeezed a little more insistently. Afraid to hurry, but knowing if he didn't get his shot off at that moment, the breeze might again rise.

Another shot echoed his, fired almost simultaneously. Without realizing what he was doing he turned to look at the tall man, saw those eyes smile. Plain as sun, it was he who had fired just as Bass had touched off his shot.

"Shooter two—drop off!" came the judge's cry as he relayed the determination of those range marshals far downrange using small red flags as semaphore.

"And shooter seven—you drop off!"

"What?"

"Seven missed the circle," the judge repeated. "Last two shooters can reload."

Titus watched the judge turn away, then focused his attention on the far end of the meadow where the range officers were again moving the framework back. Just two targets now. Flicking a glance at the tall man, he found the smile gone out of those eyes. Nothing there but concentration.

"You can do it, Titus!"

He jerked up in surprise, finding Amy bouncing on her bare feet at the fringe of the crowd, her hands cupped around her mouth as she cheered him on. For a fleeting moment he remembered how he had cupped his hands around those breasts that heaved now with every leap she took.

He promised himself he would win this match and they would celebrate tonight, his skin against hers. That hunger suddenly reminded him that she might very well be carrying his child, and all anticipation of being with her, getting his hands back on those breasts, of laying his own hardness down between her legs and finding such exquisite release inside the fuzzy smoothness of her thighs—it all flew off with the great flapping of a monstrous pair of wings.

He turned his eyes from her, his ears echoing with the crowd's clapping, rolling over them in a continuous din now.

"Load up, son," the tall man instructed.

Titus jerked about, finding him standing a few yards off, both wrists looped over the upright muzzle of his rifle.

"W-waiting on me?"

" 'Pears it's just the two of us now."

"I see that," he snapped testily.

"Don't take offense, young'un," the tall man replied with a shrug. "Weren't hurrying you none. Take your time. I wanna whip you fair and square."

That rankled Titus good. He growled, "Pretty damned sure you're gonna whip me, are you?"

"Don't forget to prime that rifle," the man said smoothly, in a friendly sort of way. "A hang-fire sure gonna make you more nervous'n you are right now."

"I ain't nervous!" Bass snarled, jabbing the cleaning patch down the barrel. "Whyn't you just leave me be?"

"I can do that," he replied, turning away. "Meant no offense."

"Just leave off me, will you? I come here to shoot, not to jaw with the likes of you."

Taking his big, low-crowned felt hat off his head and dragging a shirtsleeve across his forehead, the tall man turned back to repeat, "I just wanna beat you fair and square. 'Cause I'm a better shot. Ain't good to beat you 'cause you done something wrong. A good, hard victory is better'n a easy win any day. So you take your time."

"I don't need no more time to beat you," Titus replied, jabbing the stopper back in his priming horn. He snapped the frizzen over the powder in the pan.

"That's odd, young'un," the tall man said with a sigh as he brought his rifle up. "From what I been seeing of your shootin'—looked to be you knew the difference atween firing quick . . . and firing smart."

"I'm just as smart as you, any day." And Bass turned his back on the tall man, dragging the hammer back to full cock and nestling the weapon into his shoulder.

His right eye watered. He blinked twice, trying to clear it. Thirty-two rods, 170 yards, was a tall order. And rattled the way he was, that made him think on the man he was trying to beat. It was down to the two of them now, their targets out there across the entirety of this grassy meadow on the outskirts of Burlington, Kentucky.

That far cloth strip was dancing, not near as much as were the others in that thirty-two rods. But he knew enough that the lead ball would have to cut itself through a lot of crosswind to reach that distant target. He inched the muzzle a wee bit farther to the left. Then feared he was holding too far off the target, was allowing too much for that breeze.

Licking his dry lips, Titus glanced at the long procession of stakes where the cloth strips fluttered between him and the far target. He let half his breath out and began to squeeze, flicking his eyes again to that distant flutter. Against his cheek the air moved. All around him the crowd fell to a muted hush. Dogs barked and yowled behind them, off somewhere in that great camp. He vowed to allow none of it to distract him.

Would no longer let his family's lack of caring matter. Only, absolutely only thing to dwell on was this shot—this shot to win. The first shooter ever to win at sixteen years old.

The distant cloth fluttered down like a red-elm leaf drifting slowly to the autumn grass. The tall man's gun roared.

Titus fired a heartbeat later.

Behind him arose a loud groan.

His heart rising to his throat, the youth strained to see through the gauzy strips of their gray gunsmoke. The murmurs grew louder. It looked as if his target had fallen, hit by his ball. But the spectators were grumbling, disappointed—for there in the distance atop that wooden frame sat the tall man's target.

"Y-you didn't hit yours!" Titus exclaimed, his mouth going dry with the realization he had won.

"Looks like you beat me, young'un." The tall man stepped over to Titus and held out his hand. "Fair and square."

Taking the man's hand, he began to shake, jubilance at his victory just beginning to sink in.

"Hold on!"

They both turned at the shrill cry from the judge. Across the meadow the range marshals waved their little red flags back and forth. The judge turned to both shooters as an ominous silence descended upon the crowd.

"You fellers stay put. We'll see what they need me for."

For those long moments Titus tried to remember to breathe. So close to winning . . . it all seemed so cruel to drag out his victory with this little drama down there near the targets. Certain that he had hit his, for it had spun off to land in the grass while the tall man's hadn't budged at all.

Now the judge was returning, the two range officers close behind him.

"It's over," the man hollered as he came up.

Behind the shooters some of the crowd roared their approval while the rest pressed in, hundreds of curious gawkers wanting in on the reason for the delay.

"We have us a for-certain winner," the judge added, coming to a halt, the pair of officers at his elbows.

Both nodded as if they had had themselves a hand in deciding its finality.

The judge held up one of the two targets, a bullet hole plainly visible just outside the black smudge. "This'un here's marked for shooter number ten—the young'un here."

"He didn't hit his mark, did he?" a voice asked behind them.

"No, he didn't," the judge replied. "But if the only other shooter left in the match didn't hit his target at all, then the contest would go to the man who at least hit closest to the mark."

"Hear! Hear!" a few shouted. "The boy won it!"

There was a surge of movement at the edge of that jostling crowd pressing in on the shooters and judges. Amy slipped through them and stopped at Titus's side, gripping his left arm in her two hands, eyes bright and moist, dancing with glee at his victory. She rose on her toes to plant a kiss on Titus's cheek.

"Only problem is," the judge continued, holding up both the targets and waving them to get the crowd to quiet down, "we can't for the life of us figure out why shooter eight's target didn't fall."

The tall man leaned forward, reaching for the wood plank. "Didn't hit it at all?"

"That's what we thought at first," the judge replied, handing the shooter his target. "The men here thort you'd missed your target clean. 'Cause it didn't fall off the stand. Meaning the boy here beat you."

"Yeah, but lookee there, will you?" the tall man declared, holding his target up high at the end of his arm so the crowd could see. He stuffed a little finger through the hole.

Titus's heart sank.

"Near square onto the middle," the judge said. "An' for some reason your target just got itself notched down in that stand so that it couldn't fall. No matter—as you can all see, this man's shot went through the black while the young'un's here didn't but nudge the black."

One of the range officers immediately leaped forward to hoist the tall man's arm, and the crowd instantly raised its boisterous agreement.

"We got us a new champeen!"

Amy was squeezing his arm as folks shoved past, anxious to press in on the winner.

"You done just fine, Titus," she tried to cheer him. "Second outta all them shooters your first year, and shooting all that way over yonder—why, my pa said he ain't seen such shooting since he can remember."

"How come I don't feel just fine, then, Amy?" he whimpered.

"Maybe you gotta learn how to win."

He jerked up to find the tall man, his hand held out before him.

"Just like a man's gotta learn how to lose. You damned near shot the pants off me, boy." He was smiling broadly now as he pushed that floppy felt hat way back on his head. "Ain't been that skairt of losing for a long, long time. Purty, it was: the way you know how to handle that ol' squirrel gun of yours."

"It were my grandpap's."

He pushed his hand closer to the youth. "What's the name you go by, young feller?"

Titus finally seized the man's hand again and shook hard, one sturdy pump of his arm. "Titus Bass, mister."

"Nice to meet you, Titus Bass. A good grip you got." He brushed the brim of his hat with a pair of fingers for Amy, then quickly looked back at Titus, eyes twinkling. "My friends call me Levi Gamble."

FOUR

Summer had a way of redeeming itself on an evening like this. These long, hot, and sticky Kentucky summer days grew tiresome in the Ohio country come late August.

Yet redemption arrived after sundown when the flies ceased droning and the mosquitoes no longer raised angry welts on what bare skin one had provided for their feast that afternoon. Cool breezes stirred the weeping willows and rustled the leaves of the red elm. The heavy air hung rich with the fragrance of sumac and trumpet-flower vines climbing the dogwood and pecan trees. Fires twinkled through that encampment like a sugar-coated crusting of flickering diamonds against the indigo seep of night.

It was as if Titus could breathe again. After the heat of that long afternoon. After the drama of the rifle match.

With Amy's supper in his belly they had set off hand in hand in no certain direction once the youngest of the Whistler brood had been put in their blankets, seeking a stroll through camp beneath a half-moon this last night before the revelers would pack up come morning and drift off in all directions for home, to talk across another full year of the Longhunters Fair just past and gossip on what next summer would bring.

As long as this year was in passing, he doubted 1811 would ever arrive.

Days like this one went far to prove how reluctant summer was to lose its grip on the land. Yet day eventually gave way to night—balanced in the sort of evening that could stir a young man's juices, cause him to think on little else but getting his girl off to himself—to touch all those forbidden places on her young body once more. As exciting and compelling as was his desire for Amy at this moment . . . his dread that he had already put her with child cooled his fevered ardor.

Once during their walk she had pulled him into the shadows of the overhanging umbrella of long weeping-willow branches and there put her mouth on his, stoking his fire with the sudden, fierce intensity of a black-smith's bellows. Amy took his hand and raised it to her breast, squeezing his fingers around and over that soft flesh covered by a thin layer of her summer dress. In that brief and stolen moment she groaned at the back of her throat, exciting him while aroused herself at the same time.

Her lips were moist, wet enough so that her mouth slid across his. It seemed she became hungrier as he grew breathless. Rolling her hips upward, Amy pressed herself into him, more insistent still as she sensed his flesh harden and grow. He had to have her.

Titus whispered, "Got to find us a place . . . some place—"

But as his mouth left hers, fear drenched him with cold once more.

A child. Marriage. Settling on the land. Rooted to one spot the way his father, and grandpap before him, had sunk their lives into a particular piece of ground. Great-grandpap before them had been a different tale: come here in the beginning when it was a new land, fresh and unwalked, when adventure waited among the wild critters and the Injuns too. Perhaps great-grandpap hadn't realized what he was doing when he'd brought his family here to raise up a cabin and a passel of young'uns too.

Such was a legacy Titus feared he could not live up to.

"What's wrong?" she whispered at his ear, her breath hot and moist. "Find us a place. Yes, yes! I promised you—touch me all over again like you done at the swimming hole."

"You . . . you're," and he wanted desperately to find a way to say it. "Gimme a chance to figure it all out."

Amy stiffened, drawing herself back to arm's length. "Figure out what?"

"This being a father."

"Already you learned that it don't take nothing much to be a father," she said, stepping back against him, her head below his chin. "I liked how quick you learned."

"Scares me."

"The babe scares you?" she asked, taking up his hand again, this time placing it against the flat of her belly. "This little child what brings us together as husband and wife?"

Extracting his hand from hers, Titus turned slightly, staring out at the flickering fires that pricked the meadow like dancing fireflies, campsites extending from tree line to tree line to tree line. In a gust of laughter carried to them on the breeze, he thought he recognized a voice drifting over from a nearby camp.

Turning to Amy, he said, "Ain't the child what scares me. What I'm afeared of is living the life my pap cut out for hisself."

"Don't you want the same things he has, Titus? A home and family, making a living for us outta the ground?"

He looked away from her face, not able to gaze into those frightened eyes. "I think you always knowed the answer to your own question, Amy. Down inside, you knowed the answer all along."

"There's still time to decide, Titus," she replied, pressing herself back against him. "Time for you to finish your schooling. Then you can figure out what we're gonna do about a family and where we can put down roots."

Gripping her shoulders, he stared intently into those doe eyes. "Sounds like you don't have no idea what I'm trying to tell you. This ain't about deciding where to put down roots, Amy. This got all to do with not putting down any roots at all."

She lunged for his arm as he turned away. "Where you going?"

"C'mon," he replied, taking one of her hands in his. "You come with me."

As they stabbed their way through the spindly branches of weeping willow, Titus was sure, all the more determined, especially when he heard another burst of laughter. It was his voice.

Drawn to the tall, freedom-loving hunter every bit as much as he was drawn to the soft flesh of Amy Whistler. The sound of his laughter and the merry talk drew Titus on, tugging on her hand to keep up.

"Yo, ho!" Levi Gamble called out, turning as he spotted them come into the light. "Look here who approaches camp!"

He watched Gamble stand from the stump where he and three others were calling out their bets in playing quadrille, a most popular game played between four persons with the forty cards left in a deck after the tens, nines, and eights had been discarded. At that moment, backlit in firelight, the woodsman seemed even taller than he had that afternoon.

Titus shuffled nervously, explained his interruption. "We was out taking ourselves a walk and I heard your voice."

"C'mon. C'mon—you're among friends here, Titus Bass. Sit yourselves and join us." He turned to the others at the fire as he swept up the greasy cards into his hands. "Titus is the lad nearly whupped me in the shooting match today. A likely hunter he'll make one day soon."

"Titus an' me getting married," Amy blurted to those gathered in that ring of firelight. "Settlin' in to start our family."

Each of them stared at the young couple for a heavy moment. And as quickly as the young woman had shattered the mood, Levi Gamble jumped in to work his magic.

"Then congratulations are in order!" he cheered. "You there—pass over that jug of cherry flip and we'll send her round the circle for this young couple."

They did, and Titus took him a taste of the sweet brandy after he and Amy settled atop a large tree trunk rolled close to the fire. At times his father cooked up some corn mash or made a strong potato beer, but nothing that had the sweet decadence of that brandy. He took a second taste upon his tongue as the first warmed his belly and handed it past Amy to Levi.

"The young lady here gave her husband-to-be a kiss when we all thought Titus was the winner of the shooting match," Levi explained to the circle of those at the fire. Then he brought his hand to his chest expressively to continue, "But she never give me a kiss when we discovered I beat the lad by a hair."

"Maybe next year, young Titus Bass," a moon-faced man across the flames called out. "Levi Gamble here tells us he won't be here to steal first prize from you."

"Why not next year?" Titus asked.

Gamble's eyes took on a glaze weighed both in time and distance. "I'll be far, far from the Ohio country come this time next year." Of a sudden he turned on Amy. "So—sweet lady. What say you to giving Levi Gamble a winner's kiss?"

Her eyes dropped. "I cannot."

"Why?" he asked quietly.

"I'm spoke for, and it would not be the thing to do when a girl's spoke for."

"Titus?" Gamble asked, raising his head to look at the youth. "What say you about my kiss? Will you let your sweet Amy put a kiss here, on the cheek of the winner who whupped you in our gallant match this day?"

"Sure," he replied after a moment's hesitation.

"Now, sweet Amy—come give me my prize." Gamble turned his face to the side and leaned toward her. "I'm ready when you are."

The girl glanced once at Titus, then turned to Levi and leaned his way with her lips puckered. Just as she drew close, Gamble suddenly turned and planted his mouth on hers with a resounding smack. Amy leaped back so far she collided with Titus, and they both spilled over the tree trunk.

Gamble rose to his feet and held out his hands to them. "I've never done that before, Amy. Honest. To kiss a beautiful young woman and knock her off her feet that way—and you was even sitting down when I did it!"

The group at the fire roared anew with laughter as Titus and Amy settled once more. Gamble bowed to them.

"If I have caused you trouble in any way with my silly prank, I beg your forgiveness. It's only my happiness to be off to the western waters, with money in my purse enough to see me on my way."

"You said you'd be far away from here come this time next year," Titus replied, seizing hold of Gamble's wrist with worry. Now he was confused—wanting to know more about this Boone County neighbor. "You're not staying on here?"

"No, I move on tomorrow."

"You leave family behind?"

One of the men at the fire explained, "Levi's from Pennsylvania."

"P-pennsylvania?" Titus asked. "What brings you here to our country?"

"Just the road, Titus," Gamble explained. "Going west to see the far mountains and the rivers so mighty they say a man can't dare cross 'em come spring when the snow on those high places is melting."

"W-where is it you come from?"

"I hail from western Pennsylvania. Family from a little town called Emsworth on the Ohio, just downriver from Pittsburgh. I was following the river west when I happed onto a shopkeeper in Cincinnati what knew of this fair taking place across the Ohio. Every fair I know of has a shooting match —a likely place for me to win some money to fatten my traveling purse."

"Money to go west," Titus repeated, his eyes going to stare at the fire as Amy took his hand in the two of hers.

"If I make good time, I should be well downriver come the first hard snow, and by then I can find me somewhere to winter up and wait out the spring if'n I have to. Work as I need to. Always work and wages along the river, I say. And if'n I ain't there afore spring, then I can go on down to the Mississippi, north from there."

"Where?" Titus asked. "Where is it you're bound for?"

"St. Louie."

A large man leaned forward, his elbows on knees as he asked, "What do you know of this St. Louie?"

"I've heard it's a lively place ever since Tom Jefferson's expedition come back from the western ocean with word of beaver and other fine furs to be got from those western lands."

"What of the Injuns?" a woman asked, speaking for the first time as she came into the firelight, wiping her hands on a long apron.

"Yes," a man replied. "There must be Injuns there the likes have never see'd a white man."

"And perhaps they're better for that," Gamble said, "what with the way the English stirred up these Injuns agin us during the war for our freedom, as I hear it."

"They did, that's for sure!" one of the men roared.

"But those Injuns out there," Levi continued, "I hear they come walk the streets of St. Louie—looking to talk with the redheaded chief who went west to find them."

"Who's that redheaded chief?" Titus asked.

"William Clark," Gamble replied. "Aye, they come to St. Louie dressed in all their feathers and shells, paint and hides. From what we heard last winter back to Pittsburgh, the Injuns up the Missouri River been quite peaceable 'bout traders coming among 'em."

"That what you're fixing to do out west, Levi?" Titus inquired. "Go into the trade with them Injuns?"

He wagged his head. "No. I'm fixing to join up with a man called Manuel Lisa. He's been working the Injun trade on the upriver for three years now."

"Sound of his name," a man commented, "he must be one of them Frenchies."

"Spanish, he told me," Levi answered.

In a flush of astonishment Titus asked, "You . . . you met him?"

Gamble nodded. "He come through Pittsburgh late winter. Town was all abuzz with it. He'd been up to Vincennes looking to supply a whole new

kind of outfit. Couldn't get what he needed up there, so he had to keep on
east. Come to Pittsburgh, and that's how I happed onto talking with him."

The moon-faced man asked, "You said a whole new kind of outfit.
What's new about it?"

"That's what got my attention, it did," Levi answered. "Manuel Lisa
was the first to go farther upriver than any of them Frenchies out of St.
Louis, but ever before he'd allays just traded the Injuns for the furs. Took
'em blankets and powder and coffee and bells, that such."

"What's he figure to do now that's so different?" the big farmer asked.

"Lisa told me that last year he was the first to take some white men
upriver—not to trade with the Injuns—but to trap for themselves and sell
their beaver back to him."

"Injuns take to that sort of thing?" one of them asked. "Taking the fur
out of their country like that?"

"Yeah," agreed another of the farmers. "That Spaniard better be careful, or he'll find his hair gone."

"Yup—we ought'n just leave that country for the Injuns. We got plenty
enough this side of the river for ourselves. Let 'em have whatever's left over
yonder."

Gamble said, "I aim to find out just how much country is left over
yonder."

Titus watched the tall man's eyes, his entire countenance—a bit relieved to consider that Levi Gamble just might have the same fear of taking
root in one place that Titus Bass himself suffered. Ever since their afternoon
match he had hoped Gamble was a Boone County man, someone Titus could
look up from time to time, someone he could confide in and take solace with,
kindred spirits they.

But now he had learned Levi wasn't from Kentucky at all. And worse
yet, the hunter was merely passing through, taking first place in Titus's
shooting match only to pay his way west, there to push on for a far country
filled with beaver and Injuns and all the adventure a man could want for
himself.

"And now," Gamble continued, patting the skin pouch that hung at his
belt with a dull clatter of coin, "I am flush enough to pay for food, lodging,
and what fare my journey might need of me."

"I still say it should have been Titus's money," Amy grumbled.

Gamble grinned. "Second place to Levi Gamble is nothing he can be
ashamed of."

"It's a lot of money he should have won," Amy added. "It would've give us a good start on our life raising young'uns and settling down."

Gamble studied Titus a moment before he said, "Aye, I will admit that was a goodly sum of money I won me for first prize. But money is not the object. Leastways not for me. Look here," and he tore the pouch from his belt, yanking at the drawstring to open it up. From the pouch he poured a few coins into his palm with a clink.

"You can go far with that, Levi Gamble," the moon-faced man commented.

Ignoring the farmer, Gamble leaned closer to Amy and Titus. "Look there. It's hard. It's solid." He bit on one of the coins. "Meaning it's only a thing. Nothing magic about it. Don't make this money I won more than it is, young people. You'll be doing yourselves a great shame if you ever make money more than it really is."

The big farmer asked, "What is it, then, if not a wondrous thing to have?"

"Ah, money can be a wondrous thing only when it lets you reach for what you want most. Money ain't nothing in and of itself, you see. Only importance comes from how it keeps you going after your dream."

"So money's important, after all," Titus concluded with a nod of his head.

"No," Levi said quickly. "The only thing important is your dream."

"So what's yours, Levi Gamble?" asked one of those at the fire.

He looked up at the canopy of stars. "Those faraway rivers where the beaver pelts are so big they say a man can sleep under one of a winter's night."

"A blanket beaver?"

Gamble nodded to the farmer. "Aye. To lay eyes for myself on that land Manuel Lisa spoke of in the quiet tones a man uses when he's speaking of something religious."

"This Lisa claim he found him God out there?" snorted one of the older men at the fire, who spoke up for the first time.

With a grin Levi replied, "Perhaps he has, the way he talked. The way he told me come west to St. Louie and he'd put me to work that next season when his boats pushed upriver."

Titus leaned forward anxiously. "You'll go?"

"Aye—I will at that."

"What's those places you're going?" Titus asked dreamily.

Gamble turned sideways on his stump to look at the youth. "Magic names, young Mr. Bass. Rivers called the Yallerstone. Another one Lisa built a post on called the Bighorn. Said there's wild sheep out there in the hills, and the males get horns so long, they wrap right back around on themselves in a curl."

"Pure poppycock!" someone spouted, and others guffawed.

Levi held up a hand. "Lisa and them as was with him swore by it when I told 'em I doubted all they told me, the size of animals and such. Claim everything's much, much bigger out there in that big, big country."

"Like what?" Titus asked.

"Take any critter. The deer, sure. But they got one Lisa called a elk. Big as a milk cow, with a rack o' horns on his head would cover a dining table at a country inn."

"The man's daft, and he pumped you up with his wild stories!"

"No," Levi told the doubters. "There's bear out there the likes of nothing we seen here in these eastern forests. Said there's some called silvertips. What some call grizzlies. Stand half again as tall as a man on their hindquarters. Claws a good six inches long tear the heart out of a elk or rip a man's arm off in one swipe!"

Amy leaped back as Gamble's arm suddenly swung in a great arc toward Titus, his fingers stiffened into the curve of imaginary claws.

Bass did not flinch at Levi's frightful pantomime. Steady and sure, he asked, "What other critters out there what's big?"

Gamble stared into the youth's eyes for a moment, then answered, "Lisa told me 'bout buffalo, bigger'n a cow an' a elk an' a grizzly too."

Titus whispered huskily, "My grandpap tol't me 'bout buffalo."

The tall woodsman held out his arms wide. "A great and shaggy animal." Then put his crooked fingers on either side of his head. "Big black horns they scrape and keep shiny for to do battle when it comes time for the rut each year. Thick fur from the top of their head back across a big hump on their shoulders. Seems they crowd together in herds a man likely couldn't walk through in a hull day."

"This Lisa and his boys ever try that?"

Gamble looked across the fire at the farmer. "No, they didn't say they ever did."

"Poppycock stories!"

"No, listen," Gamble said. "They saw 'em, great herds of 'em. Saw 'em with their own eyes as they was pushing north on the Missouri River."

One man wagged his head and commented dryly, "Just hard for me to believe there'd really be such a critter, and so damned many of 'em."

"We ain't none of us never see'd any back here," claimed another.

"I heard talk once, long back," an old man spoke up for the first time, "used to be a woods buffler in this country."

"Must've been long back," the man's grandson replied.

"Surely was," the old one continued. "But there was always talk that a critter even bigger lived on west. Talk was we killed off all them woods buffler in this country, but folks said we'd likely never kill off all them big critters out yonder."

"If Manuel Lisa and his men are right," Levi added, "folks'll never make a dent in their numbers."

"Buffalo."

Gamble turned back to young Bass. "That's right, Titus. Buffalo. Biggest thing on four legs God ever made for this country."

"A man walk all day and not get through a herd of 'em."

Levi nodded. "For six days running, Lisa told me, they was pushing upriver, poling and warping their keelboats past just one herd. Six hull days it took 'em."

"So that's where you're headed, Levi? To see them buffalo?"

He wagged his head. "I'm going for the beaver, Titus. To see for myself those mountains and them rivers a'foam with melting snow. Rivers so muddied up they're gobblin' away at their banks, chewing trees right outta the ground in one bite and drowning buffalo by the thousands every spring. It's them rivers I gotta see me afore I die. And trust me, fellas—Levi Gamble being tied down to one place is a fate wuss'n dying."

Titus asked, "What your father do in Emsworth?"

"He's a blacksmith. Like his papa before him, an' before him too."

"So you learned the family trade?" asked one of the older men.

With an affirmative nod Gamble said, "A good thing too: I don't recommend nary a man going west what can't do some simple blacksmithing work."

"True, true," was the assent of most.

"Not just to repair his traps, but to care for his guns as well."

The moon-faced farmer commented, "Out across the Missouri a man is going to be too durned far from the settlements, from the help of those he's used to counting on to help."

Turning then to Titus, Gamble said gravely, "From all what them upriver men told me when they come through Pittsburgh, it takes much more'n just good shooting to make your mark out yonder to the far west."

"I imagine so," the big farmer echoed the general sentiment. "Out there a man's bound to be all on his own."

"Most times he's got no other to call on but his own self," Levi replied.

"Not a lot of folks, neither—I wouldn't imagine," an old gray-head commented. "Not a lot of *white* folks out there for company."

The big farmer guffawed at that and slapped his hand down on his knee. "Farther west a man goes, I've heard—less an' less civilization there be to count on."

"For some of us," Gamble replied, "maybe we're just looking to get someplace where there's a little less of that civilization to close in around us."

"Hell, son," declared the oldest man there at the fire, "all a feller has to do is get a mile away from any of these here farms, back into the woods, up into the hills . . . and he's as far away from civilization as any man needs."

"When'd you come here, mister?" Gamble asked the gray-head.

"Come here myself back when I was a tad. Seventeen and fifty-three. We took this ground from the Injuns. Held on to it against the French, and agin them Englishmen too when we was through with the crown saying we had to do this, a king saying we had to do that."

Levi Gamble leaned forward, the fire's light leaping across his face in a moving dance. Bass leaned forward too as the tall woodsman began to speak in soft tones, something wistful, almost a whisper that emerged from someplace deep within him. "This land was good then, weren't it?"

The old gray-head only nodded, his lips pursed, eyes half-closed in reverie. "T'weren't no others but you and the land back then."

Bass quickly glanced at the old settler, seeing those old eyes glisten with pooling moisture in the dancing firelight.

"But the others come in," Gamble continued. "They always come. One or two other families at first, I'd imagine. Then a handful not long after them. And the word was spreading, weren't it? They was coming like bees to the honeycomb. Next thing there was towns where once lay only campsites. River ports and landings where you used to run up your canoe on the bank and not see another soul all evening. Roads where once there was only game trails or Injun footpaths going from one place off yonder t'other."

The old man dragged a gnarled, wrinkled finger beneath one eye and said, "Land's bound to change, man comes to it."

"Don't you see?" Gamble whispered, forcing the others to lean in to hear him over the crackle of the fire. "I want to go someplace where the land ain't changed yet. Where it's old, and new at the same time."

"Ain't much new land what ain't been walked across to this side of the river," one of the farmers said.

"There is out there," Gamble said, pointing.

"There's allys been two types of men, way I sees it," the old settler spoke up. "Them few that comes to a place first—to discover it. And then there's all the rest of us, by the hunnerts and hunnerts, and even more'n that: we come once the place's been found. We come and move in, settle down. And them few what come first—well, that's when they got to move on."

"My time to move on," Levi added.

The moon-faced farmer said, "There'll be our kind what will follow along after you in the years to come."

"We ain't moving no more," retorted the farmer's wife, patting her husband on his shoulder as she stepped up behind him. "I come here when we was young to set down roots and raise up a family. We done that—so here we'll stay."

He looked up at her, taking her hand in his. "I was speaking of others, Mary. Others of our kind what will follow the first to go into a new land."

"We've got young'uns," she explained. "A man with babes to care for and feed don't have no business uprooting his family to go traipsing off to the west."

When Amy squeezed his hand in agreement, Titus looked down at it held between the two of hers. His eyes rose to find her smiling at him. From the look in her eyes he knew she was thinking about the baby. Their baby. The baby he had made for her there by the swimming pond.

And when he looked up, Titus found Levi gazing at him.

Gamble slowly took his eyes from the youngster and looked at those other, older men gathered round that fire this last night of the summer's fair. "I ain't got no babes, no children. Ain't got no roots either, ma'am. I figure I don't go west now—I won't never have the chance. Man gets married, starts him a family . . . why, then—he never will move on."

"True, true," murmured the old settler.

"Time for us'ns be off to bed," the farmer's wife said, tugging lightly on her husband's arm.

Reluctantly, that middle-aged settler rose beside her, draped an arm over her shoulder. His right hand he held out to the tall woodsman. "Levi Gamble, I wish you God's speed on your journey."

They shook as others stood and moved up to offer their own fare-thee-wells and parting words of encouragement.

"Man's only young once't," the old settler advised, leaning on his cane. "Your sap only runs once in a young man's life."

"And a man should always go where his heart leads him," Gamble replied.

In a matter of moments the hands had ceased shaking his and slapping the woodsman on the back. Shadows moved out of the ring of firelight, back to their tents and canvas shelters. Across the meadow in all directions, a number of the fires were still blazing strong. But most were dying, their caretakers moving off to blankets and blissful dreams of another summer's Longhunters Fair come now to a close.

"Where's your camp?" Titus asked.

Gamble swept his arm across the ground where he stood. "Any place I choose to lay my blanket for the night. Here's as good a place as any. Fire's banked good. Don't need nothing else to make a place for Levi Gamble to sleep."

"We oughtta be getting back to my folks' camp," Amy admitted.

Turning to the young woman, Levi smiled and said, "I'll forever treasure your kiss, Amy. Even more'n the money I won for the shooting—your kiss for the winner is something I'll remember for a long, long time."

She blushed in the moonlight and turned toward Titus, her arms tightening around one of his.

"Ain't there some way you'd stay on, Levi?" the youth finally blurted out his fervent wish. "Leastways for a few more days, a week or two so we got time to talk."

Laying a hand on the young man's shoulder, Gamble said, "Much as I'd love to, I best be moving on. Autumn coming. Winter right behind. Hoping to make it to the Mississippi before then, up to St. Lou afore the first snow if'n I can."

Titus watched the tall woodsman bring up his right hand. He shook with Gamble, feeling tongue-tied with all that he wanted to ask, everything he wanted to say. Here was the sort of man he wanted to be: a man who had the will to leave everything behind in taking the risk of what might lie out there. The sort of man who wasn't tied to place and people. A free man. Not a slave to the land.

Someone who would see and do things far west of Boone County before Titus would ever get the chance to clear the last of those stumps from that damned field.

"Let's go, Titus," Amy reminded. "I don't wanna worry my folks."

"You're with me," he replied sharply. "They damn well ought not to worry, you being with me." Titus saw the wounded look in her eyes as he turned back to Gamble. "Maybe you write me when you get yonder, Levi."

He looked at his moccasins a moment, his eyes lowered. "I don't write at all, Titus. Not a lick."

"Can you have someone else write a letter for you? Tell me you made it downriver, or when you reach St. Louie?"

"You'd like to know, wouldn't you?" Gamble asked with a grin. "Yes. You damn right I'll send word back to you, young'un."

"I'll count on it."

"Count on it. Levi Gamble will send you word that I'm there and ready to jump off to the up-country. See them rivers, catch them beaver. Lay my eyes on places no white man ever laid eyes on. I'll write to say when I'm going."

"An' say when you might be coming back this way."

"If'n I ever come back this way," Gamble admitted. "Not likely, Titus. Once a man gone out to see the elephant—he can't really ever come home again."

"You won't ever be coming back? Not even to St. Louie?"

"Maybe there. Most like," Levi replied.

"Then I could look you up if'n I come to St. Louie."

Amy whirled on Titus, tightening her grip on his left arm. "Just when the devil would you be going off to St. Lou and for what purpose?"

He shrugged off her question, saying to Gamble, "You lemme know where you're gonna be. When you'll be coming back downriver—I'll see you again, Levi Gamble. Count on it: I'll see you again."

Gamble gave a gentle slap to Bass's shoulder, then turned from the young couple, settling down among the stumps where the others had been seated that evening. He snapped out his blankets and settled upon them with a sigh, his back to Titus.

It was another long moment more before he led Amy from that fire. From the tall man's back. Into the darkness.

And though she was on his arm, even though they walked through that great summer's crowded encampment, Titus Bass felt not only lonely, but unsettled, almost empty.

She was talking to him about their future once he finished his schooling that year, how she'd care for the babe and all those babes to come. Saying how he would take his place beside his father and all would then be right in their lives.

But Titus Bass heard very, very little of her words.

The night was simply too crowded with the crushing silence of his need to be gone before he became everything his father was.

He cursed his ignorance as much as he cursed this farming, even as much as he cursed the father who imprisoned him to the land.

But right now it was his ignorance of women and how nature made babies that made him feel as if he were locked inside a tiny wooden box, suffocated and cramped, hollering to get out.

"Mama told me I'd miss out on them visits of the terribles each month," Amy had explained in recent weeks most times she talked of the expected child. "Woman with a baby coming wouldn't have no bleeding each month neither."

"Bleeding?" he asked. She hadn't told him anything about that.

"Sure," she explained in that matter-of-fact voice she saved only for the times she wanted to flaunt her two-year head start on life over him. "That's how a woman knows for certain she ain't carrying her man's baby—she starts bleeding when her monthly visit time comes."

"W-what sort of bleeding?" His mind was instantly busy on his remembrance of her naked moonlit body stretched out on the grass beside the swimming hole. Where in the devil would she bleed? And the image in his mind became that of a game animal, sprawled out on the forest floor as he dressed out squirrels and rabbits, turkeys or deer, before setting off for home with the family's dinner.

Her eyes dropped as she laid a hand softly on her belly. "You know, don't you?" When he shook his head, Amy explained, "From down . . . there. Where a man puts his seed. Like you done, Titus."

"My seed?"

"That's what mama calls it. The seed what a man gives a woman so she can carry his baby inside her till it's time for it to be born."

He nodded, swallowing hard, remembering how he had exploded across the soft flesh on the inside of her thighs. Thick and sticky. Seeds that landed on a woman's fertile ground and were thereby made into a child by some mysterious force of nature. The way he and his father prepared the ground for planting, then walked slowly across that ground they had turned, fresh and fertile, warm and upturned, dropping their seed into the folds of the earth like the folds of a fertile woman. Sun and rain did the rest.

God must surely have made a woman like the land. And a man was always the farmer, sowing his seed.

Farmers!

Damn! he cursed himself in silence. Now more than ever he wanted to flee as far away from farming as he could go.

"I been counting, Titus," Amy went on, slowly rubbing her bare feet back and forth on the cool grass beneath that maple at the far end of the pen that held the Bass family's milk cow. "It'll still be winter when I have the baby. Likely you'll be finishing up school sometime after spring planting."

He sensed his last shreds of hope tumbling out of his life the way crumpled clumps of earth spilled between his father's fingers just after newly plowing a piece of ground. More so like long coils of purple gut spilling out of the belly of a deer he had dropped. . . .

"—know my folks let us have the wedding right there in the yard," Amy was explaining. "Let all our kin and friends know, even up to Burlington, over to Union and down to Beaver Lick. I'm sure there'll be some real celebrating for us—what with as long as our families been settled here in Boone County."

Squeezing his eyes, Titus could not help but imagine that sight: he and Amy standing before one of those circuit riders or civil justices speaking marriage words to them out of the Holy Book.

"—then all there is after that is deciding on where we're gonna live till you and your pa get to raising up our own place for us to live in."

"Where?"

Amy looked at him hard, her gaze showing she realized he had not been paying her the heed due her as the mother of his child. "Yes, Titus. Either here with your folks, or over to mine. We'll have to thrash that one out atween us all."

"I don't know about living here—"

"No matter. We'll make room for ourselves, wherever we are," she said with that air of confidence exuded only by one who is nearly shed of her teens. "Just you think about finishing your education, Titus Bass. Our children gonna be counting on their father. So you think about getting this last year of school learning under your belt so you can put your mind to helping your pa with the family farming." She extended her arm in a slow arc across the yard, cabin, barn, and outbuildings. "One day this all be yours . . . ours. But first you finish up your schooling."

He looked up to find his father coming across the yard toward them, walking as if with a real purpose. That soured his milk all the worse—

already Titus was in no mood to have someone yanking on his rope, Amy or his pap. Here a woman was wrapping him tighter and tighter, not to mention that his father kept him fenced in, no different than if he was that milk cow held prisoner in her tiny pen. It rankled him, the way Amy had taken to preaching at him. The same as his father did: about responsibility and family and the land, and responsibility all over again.

"How do, Amy," Thaddeus Bass called out as he came to a halt.

"Mr. Bass. Nice to see you, sir."

"Titus," he said, turning to his son, "I come to tell you not to be out too late tonight. I want you back in the fields tomorrow."

He looked at Amy quickly. "Tomorrow?"

"I want you to finish up that stump work afore you go back for any more of that school business."

For a heartbeat he felt elation that his father was giving his permission to stay off from school. But that elation burst just like a bubble in his mother's lye soap when he realized the substitute would be farmwork.

"That's a lotta work," Titus grumped.

"Not if you get after it the way I know you can. I need that field cleared so I can turn the ground afore winter. Lay it fallow to catch as much rain and snow as the sky will give us this winter. Planning on planting over there come spring—so I need to have that ground turned afore winter."

He sighed, his head sagging between his shoulders, feeling his father's eyes on him, waiting for an answer, judging.

"You can forget your hunting till the work's done, Titus," Thaddeus declared impatiently. "I put your grandpap's rifle in the corner by the fireplace, and there it's gonna stay till the stumps is all pulled."

He jerked up at the admonition, as if his father had pulled on a halter rope attached to a bit shoved inside his mouth. "That's *my* gun. Grandpap give it to *me*—"

"I know. But you're still my son, living under my roof—and there's chores to be done afore you go slipping off with any more of that hunting foolishness in mind. This is a farm. And this is a farming family, Titus. That comes first. You best remember that."

Wagging his head in disbelief, Titus groaned. "I come this close to winning myself some real money with that rifle. That ain't no foolishness."

"You come in second and you're right: that's nothing no man can be 'shamed of, son," Thaddeus replied sternly, his hands braced on his hips.

"Never gonna be 'shamed of nothin'," he said, his jaw jutting angrily.

"But even so that you beat all the rest but one fella—it's time you realized you was home now. Time you got back to what is really important: raising crops to feed this family."

"Didn't ever tell you I couldn't hunt and help out 'round here," Titus snapped.

"Well, it's about time you was forgetting you ever tried to do both," Thaddeus Bass snapped. "That rifle stays in the corner till your farming is done to my satisfaction."

Titus glanced over at Amy, seeing by the look on her face that she clearly agreed with the elder Bass. He turned back to glare at his father. "You wanna kill something in me, don't you?" he snarled, seeing his words bring his father up short.

Then Thaddeus Bass glowered, his lips working for a moment on just what to say, what to do with Amy right there. "Long as you're under my roof, Titus—you'll do as I say you're to do. Best you remember that, and remember I raised you better'n to back-talk your elders. 'Specially in front of company."

"I'm sure Titus didn't mean to back-talk you, Mr. Bass," Amy said quietly, tugging slightly on Titus's arm.

Both of them, ganging up on him and his dreams.

"I'm sure he didn't, Amy."

Titus growled, "I don't think neither one of you give a good goddamn what I really meant."

His father took a step toward him, taking one hand off a hip to poke a thick finger in his son's face. "Best you learn what really means something in life, Titus. That shooting, any of your hunting—none of that don't mean a hoot. Only thing important for a fella your age is just how good a farmer you're gonna be."

Titus watched his father nod his leave-taking to Amy, turn, and move off toward the cabin in the waning light of that late-summer afternoon.

"Your pa only wants what's best for you, Titus," she said gently in the softening light. "What we all want for you."

He turned on her. "How you know what's best for me, Amy? How's my pap know? You tell me that!"

"I know what's best for you because it's what's best for me too: to take care of our family. Neither of us can just go off an' do what we want anymore. Not with a child coming to us." Her cheeks flushed with an angry crimson. "You best realize that when you laid me down and made me with child, Titus Bass—that was good as marrying me in the eyes of God Hisself. We're married and I'm having your baby. And that means you start acting like a man and quit running off from your responsibilities like you been doing."

"I think it's time you went on home, Amy."

"Ain't you gonna walk me there, Titus?"

He looked at the cabin, the first lamp being lit behind one of the four isinglass windows. Then he gazed at Amy. His flesh stirred again, the way it always did when he looked at her in soft light. He knew he could just as well take her—grab her and throw her down into the shadows nestled back in the timber somewhere on the path to the Whistler place. He knew she would not resist. After all, hadn't she said they were married? His anger at his father, his anger at her for agreeing with his father—it had aroused such passion in him, and he knew he would explode if he didn't find a way to spit out all that was choking him.

There was simply no way now to swallow it down the way he had swallowed it down every time before.

"C'mon, let's start me home, and maybeso we can find us a quiet place 'long the way."

He let her take his hand in hers and start through the trees. For a moment he looked back over his shoulder, seeing his father sitting on the porch, that old hickory-bottomed chair of his tipped back against the cabin wall, silhouetted against the waning light. A dove cooed somewhere above them in the green canopy as they were absorbed by the shadows.

As scared as he was of what price he might have to pay, his fright was swept aside by his sudden, overpowering hunger. Stopping, whirling Amy about, he pulled her back to him, watching her eyes widen as he laid his mouth on hers fiercely. His hands came up and slipped one button after another from the holes down the front of her dress; then both hands slipped inside.

She gasped as he fondled the soft, firm mounds, her hips rocking forward against him.

"You're right about one thing, Amy," he said, his voice low and husky with lust as he cradled her to the ground. "Time I become a man."

FIVE

As his mother handed Titus a heaping platter of soda biscuits, she said, "Amy asked me have you come over after supper, Titus."

He stared at his beans and side meat, finding it hard to swallow that last bite. "She say what for?"

"Just said it was real important she talked to you, son."

Titus finally raised his eyes, of a sudden realizing how a great silence had settled over the table. Thaddeus, as well as his brothers and sister, gazed at him—waiting to see some reaction in him. He would not give them that pleasure, turning instead to glance out the open window, measuring what remained of that day.

"Maybe best I should go right off," he told no one in particular as he turned back to stare at his food. "Night coming down soon."

"Yes," his mother replied. "You should do that."

He slid the wooden trencher away and pushed himself back from the table, his short, backless bench scraping noisily across the puncheon floor. "I'll be home straightaway I get done."

"Take your time," she answered, clattering his trencher atop hers as she scooped up iron and pewter eating utensils from the plank table. "Amy's a fine girl, Titus. Has the making of a good wife for some man. I want you to take good care of that one."

"Already him and Amy planning on getting married off," his sister blurted.

Her words seized him at the doorway, his hand hovering on the wrought-iron latch. Slowly turning, Titus glared at the girl some two years younger than he and demanded, "Where you get such a idea?"

She glanced at her mother, then her father, both appearing surprised with the news, then cocked her chin slightly to answer, "They all talking about it at school."

"Who's they?" Thaddeus inquired.

Twisting round to face her father, the girl said, "All Amy's brothers and sisters, Pa. Said she told 'em about her getting married off to Titus come spring—less'n it's sooner, what I heard."

"Spring?" his mother asked in a gasp as she settled on the empty bench, stunned with the sudden announcement. "Why, I s'pose I had no idea, Titus, that you was thinking—"

"Ain't nothing to it," Titus growled, glaring at his sister.

Although he realized she wasn't to blame for starting the dad-blamed story, he knew just how much she enjoyed being the one to carry home this tale, being the first to lay out the shocking news for all to marvel at.

"Amy will make you a fine wife and a good mother to your children," his mother repeated as she got back to her feet, swept down her apron, and once more gathered up the trenchers and utensils.

With her matter-of-fact declaration his mouth went dry. Painfully conscious that they were all waiting for him to say something, anything, perhaps even agree with his mother, Titus looked in turn at each of them gathered there at the table. Mute, and motionless as stone bookends, his young brothers continued to stare at him impassively.

Finally his father broke the uneasy silence in that cabin.

"Maybe this is just what you're needing to get shet of all your foolish notions, son," Thaddeus declared, laying both of his roughened hands flat on the table in front of him. "Finish your schooling this winter and get yourself married to Amy. You'll be seventeen come spring. Ready to shoulder an equal load here on the farm, Titus. Not a boy no more. Time for you to leave behind all that tarnal foolheadedness about slipping off to hunt every chance you get. Time now for you to leave off all that talk about seeing what's downriver, or over the hills yonder to where the sun sets each night."

He stood there numb, as if rooted to the spot. His eyes locked on his father's seamed and tanned face, Titus asked, "What of it I turn seventeen and I still want to go off in the timber rather'n walking behind a mule like you?"

For a moment Thaddeus pursed his lips into a thin, bloodless line, as if weighing the heft to each of the words he would use to answer his son. "With a good woman for your wife, and hard work for your hands—why, in no time you'll forget such utter tomfoolery and become a man, Titus. In that I got no doubt."

He wagged his head angrily. "I ain't so sure my own self," he replied, jerking up the iron latch and yanking open the door. Titus dragged it closed behind him at the same moment he heard one of the benches clattering across the cabin floor, heard the last of his mother's warning for his father to stay put.

No one followed. He was relieved his pap did not tear open that door he had just shut. No other sound behind him but the sharp-edged words flung between his parents that quickly faded as he leaped off the low porch. Slapping the side of his leg, Titus whistled low. The old hound loped around the side of the long cabin, tongue lolling, watery eyes glistening with anticipation.

"C'mon, boy," he said quietly as the dog bounded at his knee. Titus scratched at its ears, patted the top of its short-haired head. "We gotta go see us what Amy wants—besides her getting me in a whole lot of hot water with them back there."

By the time he reached the game trail that wound through the woods toward the Whistler place, Titus grew even angrier. But this time he was mad at himself. Able at last to admit that this was not Amy's fault, he realized he had gotten himself into hot water all on his own. Oh, sure and certain she had smelled good and felt soft and appealing, and damn well was the prettiest girl he'd ever laid eyes on in Boone County—but a fella ought not be so weak he couldn't keep himself out of trouble with a girl.

Tink bolted away with a sudden burst of youthful energy, bounding through the matting of red-and-white trillium undergrowth as a fat gray rabbit exploded out of the brush.

What an exquisite mess he'd made of things. About to be a father, get himself married, and start farming for the rest of his life—when he knew well enough that he was nothing more than a boy who loved the woods and had a hankering to see what waited in that country on down the Ohio.

The hound bayed from deep in the timber, the faint echo a mournful, plaintive call with night coming down as it was.

Never to chance riding one of those big Pittsburgh keelboats, even a Kentucky flatboat, down the river. No more use of dreaming he would ever see St. Lou, that city Levi Gamble spoke of where a man could jump off into the unknown. Hell, anything beyond ten miles downriver was as good as unknown to him. And as bleak as things looked from where he stood, he was bound to stay ignorant of the whole rest of the world from now on, knowing nothing more than the village of Rabbit Hash here in Boone County, Kentucky.

She sat at the edge of the plank porch as twilight squeezed itself through the clouds in the autumn sky, watching her younger brothers and sisters at play in the yard. Smoke curled up from the stone chimney. Titus sighed in looking at her, sensing that this was how things would be for the two of them soon enough. Their own place, a passel of children too. His young life over before he ever really had a chance to live it.

As he strode into the yard, Titus gazed at the swirl of her long dress billowing up at her calves as Amy swung her legs back and forth, ankles wrapped one over the other. Upon seeing him she leaped to the ground, snugging her shawl about her shoulders.

"Titus!"

He sighed, drinking in the delicate fragrance of honeysuckle on the breeze. "Heard you was wanting to see me. I come right over."

Flicking her eyes toward the cabin, Amy stopped right in front of him. "I got . . . news. We're needing to talk."

"News?"

"Sort of bad news."

He swallowed hard, gazing into her eyes, hoping to read something there. Hell, how much worse could things get?

Titus asked, "Can you go down to the swimming hole with me?"

With a shake of her head Amy replied, "Better not. Mama asked me watch the other'ns for her till bedtime so she can get some work done inside. Maybeso we go over by the big elm there. You can help me watch 'em from there—and there ain't nobody hear us talking."

He watched her settle at the base of the great, old gnarled trunk, curling her legs up at her side and snugging the dress down over her bare feet. She adjusted the shawl on her shoulders and smiled up at him, patting the grass beside her. For the longest time after he got comfortable on the ground, Amy didn't say anything. They both sat in silence, looking after the Whistler brood scampering back and forth among a new litter of pups all ear and tail and tiny, exuberant yelps as the animals loped after the children zigging this way, zagging that.

"It happened yesterday—but I waited till today to come look you up. Since it was bad news."

Bad news, he thought, not yet looking at her, knowing she was looking at him. Just how bad did bad news have to get? What with her having his baby in her belly, their folks already laying plans to get them married off, and his father poised to have him settle in being a farmer for the rest of his natural life?

Something eventually tugged at him, and he turned to her, their eyes only inches apart. He slid an arm over her shoulder, wondering at the thinness of her at that moment. Both times he had skinned her out of her clothes, she had seemed so rounded and fleshy. But right now she felt frail, downright bony, beneath his grip.

As brave as he could make it sound, Titus said, "I'm here with you now. S'pose you tell me your news."

In one great gush it came spilling forth. "I got my visit yesterday. Didn't wanna come to tell you till this morning."

"Your visit."

"Remember I told you 'bout women, and them carrying their man's baby."

He nodded. "When she starts missing her visits—yeah. She's gonna have . . ." Then it struck him like a slap across his cheek. "B-but . . . you just said you got your visit?"

"Started bleeding yesterday."

Anxious, scared as all get-out, afraid to be relieved just yet—he sensed his hand tightening on her shoulder. "Means you ain't carrying my baby?"

She didn't answer for a long time. Instead she reached over and took hold of his free hand and pulled it into her lap, squeezing it between both of hers as she stared down at it. When she finally spoke, her voice croaked with emotion. "I'm so sorry, Titus. I know we was counting on getting our family started. After all the times we . . . the times we done what it takes to make a baby—I was hoping."

"You wasn't gonna have a child all along?" he asked, trying to make sense of it.

"I missed my bleeding twice't, I did. But it come yesterday, and mama says there's no mistake when I asked her. I ain't with child. So that's when I figured I oughtta come tell you—come to look you up at school."

He swallowed hard, sensing what was to come.

"You wasn't there, so I figured your pa had you stay home to give him a hand this morning. I headed over to your place from school—but your mama got worried: said you took off for school with the others after breakfast."

Turning to her anxiously, he asked, "You tell my mam you didn't find me at school?"

Wagging her head, Amy said, "Nothing of the kind, Titus." She stroked the back of his hand. "I know you'd get in a bunch of trouble if your pa finds out you been staying off from school—so I'd never say nothing about it."

Relieved, Titus leaned back against the tree, sorting through the jumble of it all. She wasn't carrying his child. After all these weeks of having others make their own plans for him, he suddenly felt like a man freed from the gallows.

She laid her head against his shoulder. "Why didn't you go to school today?"

He set his chin atop her head and said, "Truth is, I ain't been going last few days."

"If you weren't helping your pa, and you wasn't in school—what you been doing?"

"Nothing much," he admitted.

"We talked about this," she said, lifting her head to look at him disapprovingly. "You needing to finish your schooling so we get married come spring."

"We talked," he agreed. "Just seemed to me like it was everyone else making up their minds for me."

"Don't you wanna finish your school?"

"Don't see no need in it."

"Can't you see no need in reading and writing, in knowing your ciphers?"

"I know me a little. Cain't see how it's ever gonna help me, Amy."

She squeezed his hand. "We get married and you work the farm—all that schooling's gonna help a whole lot, Titus."

"I ain't figuring on working a farm."

With a hint of a smile that told Titus she did not quite believe him,

Amy said, "Just what you gonna do to support us, you don't finish school and work on your pa's farm?"

"Haven't thought that far ahead on it."

Wagging her head as she would at one of her errant siblings, Amy scolded, "You got to finish school. You don't—why, I can't marry you, Titus Bass."

For some time he gazed into her eyes, looked at the fullness of her lips, wanting to lie with her again the way they had times before. So much did he want that. Almost enough to change his mind and tell her everything that she wanted to hear. Maybe he was stupid, after all, just like his pap and some other grown-ups made him feel most nearly all the time.

"I thought some on this, Amy," he began. "I figure I can support a wife wherever I go."

"Wherever you go?" she asked with a shriek. "W-what's that mean?"

"Means I'm figuring I won't stay around Boone County for long."

Shaking her head emphatically, Amy replied, "No. I ain't going nowhere else, Titus Bass. This is where I was born, where I'm going to birth my own children and raise them up. Here's where I'm staying till I die. Ain't you gonna stay on this land with me?"

A great gray owl flapped over their heads as Mrs. Whistler stepped onto the porch and sang out for the younger children to come in for the night. Then she called, "Amy?"

"I'm over here, Mama."

"You two don't be long," the woman said, hustling little ones through the cabin door. "Night's getting cold, and Titus has his school in the morning."

Once her brothers and sisters were shuffled inside the cabin, Amy turned to him, beginning to push away so she could get to her feet. "You got school in the morning. I best be going in too."

He sensed a sudden chill around her, more than the autumn twilight lent a frost to the air. "If I take a mind to do something else, ain't going to school tomorrow."

"What else can be more important than your schooling?"

"Hunting. Watching the boats down on the river. Wondering where all them folks is going. What they'll be doing down the Ohio to Louisville and on yonder. There's places futher still. Lot futher."

She stomped a foot in the cold grass. "All that talk from Levi Gamble got your head filled with having yourself adventures, don't it?"

"Maybeso it does."

Pulling herself away from him, Amy whirled about, crossing her arms. "Then maybe you better figure out what it is you want more: me or some old adventure downriver."

Looking up at her, Titus asked, "Why you make me have to choose?"

"Can't have both," she answered coyly, smoothing the bodice of her dress beneath the firm mounds of her breasts. "You want me, you're gonna finish your schooling and get yourself a way to support a family. My pa and yours see to their families by working the land. Such as they do is good and honorable work, Titus. Work any man be proud of."

"If'n he was cut out to be a farmer."

"You was cut out to be a farmer," she snapped. "You was born to a farming family. It's what all your kin done since they come into this country years and years ago."

"Don't matter what they done afore me—"

"It's what you're expected to do," she interrupted.

As he stood beside her, Titus felt enough resolve to declare, "I ain't cut out to work the land."

Her words took on more frost. "You're making a great mistake: you don't want to marry and settle down with me."

"You're telling me I gotta pay too big a price, Amy. I can't be a farmer. Don't see no sense in schooling neither."

"You'll never amount to much, then, you go off on your own now," she said haughtily. "Never be as good a man as your pa—make the mark on life that he's making, Titus."

When he reached for her hand, Amy pulled away from him. Instead, he stuffed his hands into his pockets and said, "There's more for a man to learn than reading and writing letters, working numbers, Amy. What I want to learn is waiting for me out there."

"Oh, damn that Levi Gamble!" she grumbled. "Damn that devil for making you—"

"Don't blame Levi," he protested. "I knowed I wasn't no farmer long afore I run onto Levi at the Longhunters Fair."

"He went and filled your head with such poppycock—"

"I told you," he interrupted her with a snap. "I decided long ago I was one day gonna be leaving all this life behind."

"Leaving?"

"There's a bigger world out there than what is right here in Boone County. I aim to see me a share of it afore my dying day, Amy."

Her eyes narrowed as she asked, "And if that means losing me?"

"Sounds of things, you'll be better off without me."

She turned on her heel again, staying in that same spot. He could see her shoulder shudder in the mercuric light of the autumn moon rising out of the east. He even thought he heard a muffled sob from her. Titus reached out to touch her shoulder, but she shrugged him off.

"I aim to learn more out there than what I can learn in school, Amy."

"All you'll ever need to know is right here—living your life with me, Titus."

"I'll learn more out there than I could ever learn following the rump end of a god-blamed mule."

Her face tightened as she turned from him again. "Sounds like you made up your mind, all for certain."

For a few moments he looked at her back, that dark spill of her hair tumbling nearly to her waist. He wanted to touch her, knowing she had only to hear the words she needed to hear and they would lie flesh to flesh. As much as he wanted to reach across that few inches remaining between them at that moment—it might just as well have been a chasm. Something kept him from retreating, from giving in to what his body begged for.

"This ain't easy," he confessed. "Not just you I'm leaving behind. Thinking about my mam and pap too."

"You think hard on them. Think about me tonight—how we been together. Then you come tell me for sure you're going."

"I don't have nothing to decide, Amy. I'm going. Only thing left to figure out is when."

She twisted round on him, her red eyes brimming, fury written on her face tracked with its first tears. "I'll make some man a damn fine wife, Titus Bass. That's for certain. Just as certain is the fact you're never gonna make a husband for no woman."

"Likely I never will, Amy," he admitted, watching the look of surprise come to her face.

"That's right," he continued. "Seems what a woman wants is more'n I think I'll ever be likely to give. If being a husband to you means staying here to work behind a mule, being a farmer like your pa and mine—then, no: I'll never be husband to no woman. If it means I gotta feel yoked in like an ox to what my pap 'spects of me, no—I won't ever be settling down with a woman and making a family for myself."

He said the last few words to her back as she dashed across the dusty yard while night came down around him.

◆   ◆   ◆

"I want you to do some reading for me," Thaddeus Bass said to his firstborn son as he rose from the table.

"Reading?" Titus asked, confusion raising alarm within him. Why would his father want him to read. . . ? "Can't it wait?"

"Wait? Wait for what, son?"

Titus shrugged. "I was looking to sit outside till it got cold after sundown, then I'd come in."

He watched his father go to the stone mantel and take from it a piece of foolscap twice folded.

Shaking the paper out before him, Thaddeus said, "You ain't going much of anywhere for a long time, Titus."

His eyes kept flicking from the foolscap to his father's face, back and forth, eager to figure out the suddenness of his father's turn on him. Titus quickly glanced at his mother, his face filled with appeal. But she turned away, busying herself at the washbasin over the trenchers and utensils the family had just used at dinner. His eyes climbed toward the roof, finding above him in the shadows those three faces peering down from the edge of the sleeping loft, all of them watching the tense scene below. As soon as his father began speaking, Titus's gaze locked on Thaddeus's face.

"I been needing your help around here last few weeks since school-master started up again, Titus."

"Yes, sir." Uneasiness squirmed inside.

"School taking up all your time, has it?"

"Yes. I s'pose it has."

"Learning a lot, I'd wager," Thaddeus said, slowly crossing the cabin floor toward his son.

"Some."

"Then you won't mind sharing all you been learning with me and your mam. How 'bout reading to us?" Thaddeus held the paper out at the end of his arm.

He shuffle-footed on the spot, his nervousness growing. He tried begging his way out. "You and me both know you're a better reader'n me. Just make me out to be a fool in front of everyone—you go and make me read that."

"You was learning to read of a time, Titus. If'n you'd keep learning the way you was, why—I figured one day you'd be a better reader'n me."

"Maybe I can be, at that."

Thaddeus shook the paper. In the cabin's silence it rattled noisily, like a huge elm leaf, autumn dried to a parchment's stiffness. "Won't be, you don't keep learning."

He glanced at his mother, finding that she had turned and was watching them both now. "I'll just have to see that I do."

"Read it, Titus."

With reluctance he took the paper and unfolded it, surprised at first—for he had suspected it was something written in his father's own expansive hand. Instead, this was written in a very neat and crimped penmanship. He did not recognize it.

Clearing his throat, Titus began, faltering, halting at nearly every word as he sorted out the marks and the sounds of the tongue each one took.

"Mr. Bass. I . . . write you . . . this day over . . . something most . . . t-troubling . . . to me . . . c-concerning your . . . eldest child, Titus."

His eyes flew to his father's face, then shot back to the bottom of the page, trying to conjure what the name was.

"Go on, Titus. Read it to me."

He pleaded, "What is this?"

"You gonna read it to me, son?"

By now he could see the anger beginning to rise in his father's eyes, the pressure throbbing up and down the thick cords in his father's neck. Titus grew frightened.

"I . . . I don't think I can—"

Thaddeus ripped the paper out of his son's hand and snapped its folds taut. "Then I'll damn well read it to you!"

Glancing at his mother for a moment, Titus found her staring down at her feet, twisting the scrap of muslin rag in her hands.

"Mr. Bass. I write you this day over something most troubling to me concerning your eldest child, Titus. When the new season began, I was in hopes that you would allow your son to complete his last year of schooling without interruption. I'm sorry to see that you've seen fit to have him stay home to work with you in the fields for the last two weeks. If you can free him up to finish his schooling with me, it would be in the best interest of you both. I pray you will agree with me. Yours ever sincerely, Henry Standish."

For a moment Titus moved his mouth to speak, but no sound came out.

"You know me and that schoolmaster ain't never shared nothing much in common before, Titus. But now you've gone and got him thinking the worst of me. Keeping you home to work the fields, is it? Bah!"

He watched his father fold the page as he returned to the fireplace. But instead of throwing it into the flames, Thaddeus set it atop the mantel again.

"Were you to lay out of school—least you could have done was to give me help in the fields. Where'd Standish get such a notion you was here helping me? You tell me that."

In a frightened, pale voice he replied, "I t-told him."

"What? I didn't hear you!"

"I told him."

"You told him I wanted you to stay away from school to help me in the fields, is it?"

He nodded, sensing his palms grow moist. "Yes."

Laying an arm across the stone mantel, Thaddeus suddenly roared, "If you weren't at school, Titus . . . and you weren't here working in the fields —just where the devil were you?"

"Thaddeus!" his mother whimpered. "Please watch your tone."

He wheeled on her, shaking. "I'll mind you to keep out of this, woman. I've a good mind to get angry at you as well. Likely you're to blame for allowing his foolheadedness to go on as long as it has. And now look what you've done, look what we've got for it. He's lied to us and lied to his schoolmaster. If you'd've helped me cram some responsibility into him from the beginning—he wouldn't be in the fittle he is today."

"Tell him you're sorry, Titus," his mother begged.

"We're long past the point of his apologizing, Mother," Thaddeus growled, and whirled back on his son. "What have you been doing with yourself?"

"Hunting."

"Hunting, is it?" he thundered. "And with you doing so much hunting —just what have you been doing with all the meat you've shot?"

"Been eating it every day," Titus answered, staring at a knot in the floor.

"All of it?"

"Most I been drying. What I learned to do—"

"Not bringing any home to help feed your family?"

"With all we got here, I didn't figure—"

"You ain't helping in the fields," Thaddeus interrupted. "And you ain't been helping put food on this family's table. Maybe you ought just go off and live in the woods like you've been wanting so bad."

For a moment he thought his ears had deceived him. Perhaps it was a trick his father was playing with words. How wonderful the idea sounded—too wonderful to hope for!

"I can bring in some meat tomorrow, I promise."

"If you do, it won't be with my permission. And you won't do it with that gun yonder in the corner."

"You taking my gun?"

"That was your grandpap's."

"He give it to *me*!"

"It's going to stay right there. A damned poor example you been to your brothers, and your sister too. I counted on you—and you let me down bad: running off with your squirrel gun every day like you done."

He felt the anger surge in him like white windblown caps frothing on the gray surface of the Ohio. "You can't take my gun away from me—"

"I can and I have. It stays here. I won't have you wasting your life on tomfoolery."

"Wasting my life?" Titus roared so suddenly that it caught his father by surprise. "You telling me I'm wasting *my* life? I'd be wasting my life if I was to settle for being a farmer like you! I don't wanna waste my life the way you done!"

He watched his words visibly slap his father in the face, as surely as any man's blow would make him flinch in pain. The arm Thaddeus had braced against the stone mantel came down slowly, that big hand tensing into a fist. Those dark, brooding eyes, shielded behind hoods of sudden rage, fixed Titus with their fury.

"Thaddeus!"

He sensed his mother's alarm as she took a step, stopping immediately when his father pointed at her—instantly nailing her to the spot.

"Stand right there, woman! This is between the boy and me."

"I ain't no boy no longer!"

Thaddeus whirled back on his son, scorn dripping from his every word. "Not no boy? Sure as hell are! A man owns up to his responsibility. Owns up to his mistakes and goes on. You ain't no man, Titus!"

"I ain't a boy no longer."

"You're my boy, and you're gonna do as I tell you long as you're under this roof, eating my food!"

"Don't make you right!"

Slowly, he started moving across the cabin toward his son, his words ominously calm. "I'm your father—and that's enough for you to show your respect for me."

"Thaddeus—oh, dear God, don't!"

"Just gonna teach the boy a little respect for his father, woman."

"You can't teach me that," Titus argued, setting his feet for what he feared was coming his way. "You gotta earn it."

"Then—by God—I'll beat some respect out of you!" Thaddeus roared. "Telling your old man he's wasting his life working the land? Just who the hell you think you are?"

He shuffled his feet, readying himself. "Don't come any closer, Pap!"

"Tell me not to come—"

"I said don't come any closer!" Titus snapped, beginning to bring his arms up, hands clenched. "I ain't no boy no longer . . . and I ain't gonna take no more of your whuppin's!"

Thaddeus stopped short, drew back, then snorted, "Just what the hell you think you're gonna do if'n I take a mind to give you the whippin' you're deserving right about now?"

"You ain't gonna ever lay a hand on me again."

His father brought both his hands up, fingers spread in claws of rage. "What in hell's name—"

"Thaddeus!" she cried.

"Don't ever you raise your hands to me no more," Titus warned. "You go to lay a hand on me—I'll lay you right out."

That brought Thaddeus up short. "You'll do what?"

"Don't make me, Pap. Please don't make me. Not in front of my mam. Not in front of her."

"Oh, God—please don't, Thaddeus," his mother whimpered, twisting that piece of muslin in her hands.

"You'll lay me out, will you?" his father asked, his voice gone thoughtful, eyes gone to slits.

Titus watched his father's face, saw something register in those eyes as Thaddeus looked him down, then up again. It was only then that Titus realized he stood nearly as tall as his father, shy no more than an inch of his father's height. Though Thaddeus carried more muscle upon his frame, that which came of wrestling animals and harness and pitting himself against the land, although Titus might well be as thin as a split cedar-fence rail, he was nonetheless every bit as tough in his own sinewy way: as solid as second-growth hickory.

And in that moment of indecision he knew his father realized the same thing for the first time. That pause he had caused Thaddeus served to give Titus a glimmer of confidence that he would not have to grapple with the man, here below the wide, muling eyes of his brothers and that troublesome sister. Here before the fright-filled eyes of his mother.

"You heard me before, Titus," Thaddeus finally said, his shoulders sagging as he retreated to the fireplace. "Your rifle stays in the corner. In the morning you go to school or stay to work with me. There'll be no hunting till spring when planting time is done."

"Till s-spring?" he said, swallowing it like gall.

"And you can't see Amy for a month," the man continued, his back to his son, placing both hands out wide on the top of the stone mantel, his head sagging between his shoulders as he stared down at the fire at his feet. There was resignation, if not outright defeat, in the way he held himself. "Maybe it'll take a month. Maybe it'll take all winter and into the spring . . . but maybe by then you'll have some respect for your father and the work what's fed you, the work what's put the clothes on your back for sixteen summers."

"I can't hunt till spring?"

Without turning his father repeated his stricture. "Not till you learn to respect your father, Titus. Damn, but you hurt me when you said I been wasting my life being a farmer. Damn you for that."

He looked at his mother. She shook her head in warning, put a finger to her lips.

"Go on now, Titus," Thaddeus instructed. "I turn around, I don't wanna see you down here. Time you went to bed. Morning's coming soon, and you'll either go to school, or be up afore then to help me on that new ground I want to plant come spring."

For a moment he didn't move, despite his father's directive. It was so quiet, Titus could hear the stuffy-nosed breathing of one of the children in the loft, the crackle of the hardwood in the fireplace.

"You hear me, son? Get on up there to bed like I told you."

He wanted to bolt away, out the door and into the night with the tears of rage he refused to let fall. Instead he swallowed them down, turning again to look at his mother. She nodded her head and gestured toward the ladder. Titus started that way.

"You plan on staying away from school, that's all right with me, Titus," his father said, his back still to his son. "I can use the help around our farm. But if'n you ain't up in time to help me, I 'spect you to be off to school with your brothers and sister. Go on now and get to bed."

Titus shuddered as he crossed the few steps it took to reach the foot of the beechwood ladder that climbed to the sleeping loft. As he took hold of a rung, Titus was suddenly compelled to turn back and recross his steps, wanting to embrace his mother, to somehow reassure her that all would turn out right. She stood with that twisted scrap of muslin still snaked between her hands, her red-rimmed eyes watching him silently approach. He stood nearly a head over her as he came to a stop, gripping her shoulders. Then he bent to kiss her on the cheek and brushed his hand across the other side of her face, wrinkled with worry and work, childbearing and thirty-three winters enduring this land. Her eyes flooded, and she bit her lip as he turned from her.

Quickly he clambered up the ladder, scattering the three youngest as they scrambled back to their grass-filled ticks and their wool blankets like a covey of chicks.

It would be a frosty night, he told himself as he lay down in the darkness, watching the last of the fire's light flicker in reflection against the roof of the cabin above him. Colder still come first light.

His father was right: he did have a choice to make.

And he knew he'd have to make it before first light.

Some of them squeaked, so he reminded himself to count the rungs on the ladder as he settled his weight on each of them one by one. Fifth one down he skipped altogether, sliding past it, his hands and feet gripping the ladder's uprights as he descended into the cabin's darkness suffused only with a faint crimson glow from the coals banked in the fireplace.

Even at this murky, early hour just before pre-dawn gray drained from the sky above, the puncheon floor wasn't that cold beneath his bare feet, although from time to time he could see red wisps of his frosty breath before his face in what muted light the dying fire radiated. Especially when he turned in the direction of the stone fireplace, moving one slow step at a time, making his way toward the corner where his father had leaned the rifle.

From the moment his head had struck the pillow stuffed with wool batting, Titus had slipped in and out of sleep for the rest of the night. At first he listened to the sounds of his parents arguing, then talking. Eventually his father was the only one saying anything. His mother had gone about her business of making dough to rise before the hearth overnight, then made her way to bed. Thaddeus wasn't far behind her, delaying only to finish his pipe there in the glow of the fireplace as the candles were snuffed. There in the silence of his home.

Gazing down on him from the sleeping loft, Titus thought how at peace his father looked as he sat in his chair. Satisfied, secure, perhaps completely content with his lot, with the niche he had carved out for himself in life.

At long last Thaddeus stood and laid his pipe on the mantel, perhaps near that letter from the schoolmaster, and pushed past those three blankets hanging from nails to separate his bedchamber from the main room. Titus heard the rope bed creak in protest as his father settled next to his mother, then a shuffling of blankets, followed by a sigh of making one's own place— like that of old Tink when he spun round and round and finally made a nest for himself under the porch.

Still Titus waited, awake beneath his blankets and down coverlet, propping an arm under his cheek to doze as he let the next few hours pass. He would awaken with a start and immediately turn to look through the small mullioned panes at the sky—trying to assess the passage of time by the whirl of the stars in that small patch of speckled black suspended over the Ohio River country. His sister was a noisy sleeper, more so than either of his brothers, so when he rose to his hands and knees to push open the hinged window, he timed each minute application of pressure on the window with her resounding snores. With one side finally cracked open just far enough, Titus slipped out the long wool cylinder—heard it land with a muffle.

Along with three pair of moccasins, his hand-cobbled boots were tied in the blanket roll, in addition to his heavy wool coat, and that shooting pouch. In it and a small belt pouch he carried everything a young man might need to survive out there in the woods. Fire steels and a good supply of flints, not only to start fires for heat and cooking, but flints for the rifle too. Tinder he kept in a small tin stuffed at the bottom of his possibles pouch. Greased patches for the rifle were to be found in another small tin that lay at the bottom of the shooting pouch. Screws and worms for cleaning the weapon. A large vial with cork stopper filled with grease for his patches. The brass-trimmed knapping tool to shape an edge to his flints. Not to mention a crude pair of pliers and a driver to use on the screws that held the lock securely in the rifle's stock.

Somewhere deep among it all lay his bullet mold and half a dozen extra bars of pig lead. Enough to last him until he could find a job and thereby purchase some more of the necessaries. Folded in a piece of oilcloth was a coil of strong, thin hemp line and a few hooks of varying sizes for fishing. Besides his two belt knives, he was taking along the small patch knife in its scabbard sewn to the strap of the shooting pouch.

On thongs suspended from that pouch strap hung the thin, delicately curved Kentucky powder horn. Last night in the dark of this loft as he hunkered over his few treasures, Titus had quietly shaken the heft of the horn. Nearly full. He hoped it would be enough to last until he could buy more powder as well as lead. If anything, powder would be what he needed first off.

So with everything else dropped outside and the window snugged back into place beneath the low rumble of his sister's snores—Titus had only to get the rifle and himself out of the cabin without awakening anyone. Most of all his father.

Through those hours of dozing and fitful, anxious wakefulness, he had been lying there thinking mostly on that: getting his hands on his grandpap's rifle. Trying to get some measure of just what he should do—no, what he *would* do—if his father awakened while he was reaching for the rifle in the corner, when he was making for the door the way his grandpap told him Injuns made their sneak.

Last night his father had been coming for him—sure and certain of that. But he had been stopped in his tracks, just shy of an arm's length from Titus by the boy's mother, perhaps by Titus himself—a youngster standing there ready to fend off blows and land some of his own in anger and frustration. No more to take his punishment, the whipping with straps of mule harness, as he suffered when he was a child.

Somewhere through that night Titus had decided he wasn't about to be treated as a youngster no more. Decided that in the next few minutes he would defend himself and do everything he could to leave the cabin with that rifle . . . if it came down to it.

The rifle. It meant damned near everything to him right now. Oh, he realized he might likely make it downriver without the rifle and find himself some work. But having that rifle along made things just all that much easier, while it gave Titus that much more freedom. It meant he could eat when he wanted to eat, camp where he pleased, freed from depending upon villages and towns. And he could defend himself against others, such as those thieves and pirates the loose talk claimed were working the shadows up and down the Ohio along with honest riverfolk.

In the dim, cold light Titus took a step at a time, staying as close to the hearth as he could. At least where the stones lay, there was little chance of the floor puncheons creaking their warning. It was warm there beneath his bare feet too. With one hand gripping the top of the mantel, he leaned forward, slowly reaching out with the other arm. Just past the end of the fireplace his fingers touched it, confirmed what it was by touching the brass thimbles that held the wiping stick beneath the long forestock. Afraid to drag it across the floor, he raised it carefully, bringing the weapon slowly around the corner of the stone fireplace. Into both his hands with an anxious sigh. And a leap of his heart.

He had his rifle.

Now he could leave. Moving off the stone hearth, Titus shifted his weight carefully, one foot at a time—testing the boards that no one gave any notice to other times. But at this moment, when all was quiet and the rest were asleep . . .

Of a sudden he thought on old Tink outside, dozing the way hounds would on the porch, or beneath it. Likely he might set up a clamor—a howl or a yelp of happiness, some declaration that he too wanted to come along on what the old redbone would believe was to be a hunt, off for a romp through the woods.

Maybe if he found something to give Tink to eat, something to chew on as soon as he got out the door. Keep the old hound's mouth too busy to yowl or bay. Titus inched foot by foot toward his mother's table.

Not until he got right to it did he see that on the table lay the new shirt his mother had been working on for Thaddeus. She must have finished it last night after pap had sent him up to the loft, he thought. And beside the shirt sat a pewter bowl of the biscuits left over from last night's supper, piled within the folds of a clean square of muslin. Gathering up its four corners, smelling the yeasty dusting of flour that made him think not only of his mother but of Amy as well, Titus rolled the biscuits into the center of the shirt and knotted the sleeves. All the biscuits but one, that is—he clutched one in his hand, then stuffed the shirt beneath his arm.

Step by step he moved off from the table, then suddenly came to a halt when his sister's snoring stopped. Balancing on one foot, he waited those long, breathless moments, his thundering heart climbing out of his chest and into his throat until she began snoring once more.

At the doorway he halted again. From a peg where they hung their coats he took down a small pouch, fingering it a moment to be certain. Inside he felt the scrape and rattle of a handful of rich amber French flints. His father's prized flints for his own rifle. Titus dropped the pouch inside the neck of the shirt he wore. Patted them against his belly. His father wasn't much of a hunter, nohow. Thaddeus would never use all them flints anyway.

As he raised the iron latch within the door's slot ever so slowly, some of the metal growled faintly. He stopped, his ears pounding as the rope bed creaked a few feet away behind the blankets divider. Breathlessly he waited, the latch half-raised, watching the wall of blankets, his eyes straining, ears working so he might have first jump when his father emerged to catch him. He would yank up the latch all the way and be out on the porch before Thaddeus truly realized what was going on. Off the porch and into the shadows of dawn, off to the cover of woods. Once there—no one would ever catch him.

His father snorted, coughed, and the rope bed creaked again. Then came an audible sigh, and all fell quiet once again. His eyes rose to the edge of the loft above him, and he nodded one time in farewell. Turning back to the door, Titus released the latch, pulling the heavy oaken planks toward him an inch at a time so the door would not drag across the puncheon floor. Open . . . open just wide enough, he told himself. Only that much. There.

And he was out, into the shocking cold of that autumn dawn. Dragging the door carefully toward him, latch raised—quietly pulling it closed and lowering the iron back into place.

He turned at the sound of the padding feet to find Tink had pulled himself out from under the porch and stood there stretching in a great flexing of his back, followed by a shake of his head with those long ears that slapped his muzzle. The dog was at the steps, ready to leap up in greeting, his mouth just opening when Titus reached out and stuffed half the biscuit into Tink's jaws.

Sweeping past the hound as fast as he could, in hopes of getting the dog far enough away from the cabin before either of them made the sort of noise that would awaken his family, Titus held the other half of the biscuit out for Tink to see, for him to smell. The hound followed obediently, quietly. Jowls flapping like this was turning out to be some game to go on.

Titus did not stop to feed the dog nor to look back until he had slipped around the side of the cabin, snatched up his blanket roll, and finally stood at the far edge of the trees. The gray of dawn was oozing out of the sky. Beneath the autumn canopy he had come to a halt, turning to kneel as the dog loped up to his side. With the biscuit held out in one palm, Titus scratched the hound's ears for what he knew was to be the last time.

"You got to go back, Tink," he whispered, sensing the sour clutch of sentiment burn at the base of his throat.

A good, old friend. Many, many hours had they roamed the timber and hills together, looked down on the boats plying the Ohio from the same rocky prominence.

"I don't wanna tie you up, you gotta understand that." He cupped his hand beneath the moist lower jaw and raised Tink's head so he could look into the dog's sad, watery eyes. "But you can't go with me this time. This is something I gotta do on my own, and you're better off here. Don't know what's out there, so it's safer for you here."

Then he finally stood, gazing back at the cabin where a thin streamer of smoke from last night's fire lifted itself from the stone chimney.

"G'won, Tink. Get."

The hound looked up at the youth with a bewildered expression, cocking his head to the side.

"I said, get. We ain't hunting today." He pushed the dog toward the cabin. "Get."

More gray was seeping into dawn's coming. He felt anxious to be gone before his father arose and stoked the fire as he always did before moving out to the barn to begin his day.

He shoved the old dog again, and Tink finally loped off twenty feet, then stopped and looked back at Titus—as if hopeful this was just one of the games they had played when the boy was younger. Many, many years gone now.

"Get! I can't take you with me."

Then Titus realized his eyes stung, and that made him mad, mostly at himself. "You gotta stay and look after them others now. G'won—get! Shoo!"

His head hanging morosely, the hound turned away from Titus and plodded one slow step at a time toward the cabin, as if being punished. Halfway there Tink halted one more time and looked back over his shoulder at Titus.

He waved both hands at the hound, to keep him moving.

By the time Tink got close to the porch, Titus was crying. And that made him madder than anything.

Angrily he squatted, scooping up the new shirt and the biscuits, retying the arms around an end of the rolled-up blanket with the rest of his necessaries before he unknotted the thin strip of leather he had used to secure the boots to the bundle. These he pulled over his bare feet, then dragged a hand beneath his drippy nose.

Looking one last time at Tink as the old hound clambered up onto the porch, turned, and lay down with his muzzle between his front paws, Titus was almost certain he heard the dog whine. Mournful.

A dove called out from the canopy being brightened by day with more and more of autumn's fire.

Swiping a shirtsleeve under both eyes, Titus took one last, lingering look at the family's place, that cabin where the rest would live out most of their lives. The barn where his father's animals were kept, critters that helped Thaddeus in the farming. The hog pens. The summer kitchen and the smoke shed.

He didn't belong here, he knew. So why was he crying?

Swallowing down the sour taste of his empty belly, Titus turned from the glade, stepped into the timber, and was lost among the shadows and the game trails, all those sounds of the small things up and moving to water that dawn.

He didn't fit in here no more, he had decided. Knowing it was now up to him to find someplace where he did.

SIX

He kept moving that first day. Not once did he stop any longer than it took to lay the longrifle down atop his small bundle of possibles and stretch out from the bank of some small creek or stream, his upper body held over the trickling flow to immerse his face and slake his thirst. Renewed and refreshed, he moved on at a trot, reaffirmed in the rightness of his quest.

If his pap came looking after him, he wanted to be far, far ahead. Mindful to leave as faint a trail as he possibly could. Titus wasn't so sure how a man accomplished that. As he brooded on it throughout the morning and into the short afternoon, he decided a hunter was always able to find game by following the game trails, by looking for the spoor of his quarry: antler rubbings, tufts of fur torn loose against brambles, piles of droppings.

So it was he was mindful not to let his rifle's stock rub against the bark of trees, taking care not to allow the brambles to snag and catch at his pitiful few belongings wrapped in that roll of wool blanket. And the one time he was forced to stop for longer than stolen moments, Titus made sure he found a patch of old undergrowth where he could kick the vines and creepers aside, pull down his leather britches before squatting to do his business, then kick that undergrowth back over what he left behind. Unlike the deer or fox or even the bear, he was not about to leave as plain a sign of his passing.

"Damn well smarter'n that," he had told himself as he set off once again at a trot.

But more than anything else, Titus Bass made sure not to stay with the game trails as did the other animals. Heavy with the scent of the hunted as well as the hunter, such faint and narrow paths crisscrossing the forest plainly would be the way his father would come looking for him. Instead, the youngster kept to the heavy timber, crossing the trails but never using them as he hurried north to the river, then turned west.

For something longer than a moment that dawn, Titus stopped at the edge of the trees and looked down from the rocky bluff as the autumn sun paled the sky in the east. Back yonder—upriver it was—sat Cincinnati. A seductive place, that one. A town grown big enough to be called a city—and thereby luring to a man. Even if one weren't quite yet a man.

But that would be the first place they'd likely come to find him; at least to learn word of him.

No, his best bet lay downriver, where he wanted to go anyhow. East and upriver—why, that all represented the past. West and downriver—now, that carried with it the promise of the future.

He looked down the sixty or so feet of adamantine slate dotted with brush and trees sunlit with the fires of the season at sunrise, gazing down at the slow, rolling current of the river. And turned his face to the west. No matter that he knew not how far west his intentions might take him this winter. Or the next. Maybeso only to Louisville. He had heard of Louisville. Just someplace down the Ohio before another winter grew old. How little it mattered. Only that he was moving west step by step, following the river for as long as it would let him.

"*Oyo,*" he said quietly as he set off in earnest above the westbound beacon.

O-ee-o. Long ago some white man had garbled the Iroquoian name for the waters moving past his rocky bluff. *Oyo.* Ohio.

Which got him to wondering on the Indians west of him. Over there, after all, on the north bank of the river sat the place named for them— Indiana. This all was country to the Miami. Seneca. Shawnee. And Mingo. All the whole damned Iroquois confederation. They had been England's Indians during the war with France to determine just who would rule North America. Soon enough England had set those very same Indians down upon her colonists west of the Alleghenies when it came time for herdsmen, and farmers, and cottage craftsmen to tear themselves away from the crown.

Titus scratched and scratched at his memory throughout that day, wary of every new sound from the forest—afeared it be a black bear or a roach-topped Seneca—yet he could not come up with a recollection one of any recent troubles with the tribes.

"Moving on west, they are," folks had said with no small gratification.

As the upper Ohio Valley was slowly settled, cleared, surveyed, and mapped, the wild creatures were pushed on. Bear and elk, lion and Indian too.

"It's the way of civilizing folk," Thaddeus Bass had repeated many a time. "As the hand of man crosses the land, the godless heathen and the beasts are driven before him."

In the end maybe that was the reason Titus had sneaked out that morning, so he told himself while he cleared a small ring of leaves on the forest floor as night fell quick and cold about him. He scratched at the bottom of his pouch and pulled out his fire-steel and flint, struck it to catch a spark on the charred cloth. Blowing against it to keep the cloth glowing, Titus laid it in a small piece of old bird's nest about the size of his thumb, then blew gently some more. With the tinder caught, he set it upon the ground, where he began laying slender twigs on the single struggling flame.

As he watched the tiny dancing tongues of blue and yellow catch hold, Titus remembered the only stop he had allowed himself that day. After trotting less than five miles downriver from the young settlement of Rabbit Hash, he tarried long enough to see one last time what drew the common and uneducated rivermen to land and go ashore for more than fifteen years already. As time went on, word spread of the Big Bone Lick where the *Ohio and Mississippi Navigator,* a river pilot's indispensable guide, stated a visitor could view remarkably large bones that must have belonged to some monstrous animal now extinct.

Gazing down at those partially unearthed bones of some creature once as big as his folks' cabin had given Titus the shivers. He trembled again, thinking of the size of such a monster. Wondering if there were any animal at all in those western territories where Levi Gamble had gone that could rival such beasts.

As he shivered again now over his tiny fire, Titus told himself such stories were nothing but hokum. No creature could ever grow to be that big. Those bones had to be nothing more than rock.

Night came down quickly. It grew cold. And he lonely. Even more lonely than that night he'd spent in the barn, locked out of the cabin. Titus chewed on a biscuit and washed it down with the small tin cup filled with creek water. It tasted good, this long, cool draft of freedom. So each time he grew lonely, or anxious at some sound come to him from the dark, Titus took a drink. Savoring its taste upon his tongue. Telling himself he had done right.

For every man there came a time to leave home. A time to try out his wings before he beat himself to death with them struggling against the confines of his parents' nest.

The water had never tasted so good as it did that night.

He kept his little fire going through the night more for companionship than for warmth—although he was cold, chilled through that single blanket he found crusted with frost when first light seeped across the glade to touch his stand of gum trees. It had been the coldest he had ever been. Surely the coldest night he had ever spent. Then he realized he had never slept in the forest before.

As much as he hunted, as much as he had haunted the forest, he had never once set off and slept out on the night's own terms. All of his journeys, all of his hunts, had found him back to the cabin at night. So he congratulated himself as he arose within that crinkling, frost-laden blanket and carried the tin cup over to the creek, where a layer of mist hung across the bank like a wispy fragment of Amy's petticoat. He dipped the tin into the cold water, the creek rimed with a thin layer of ice—sensing the warmth her remembrance brought him. It was as easy as closing his eyes there on that streambank, in the overwhelming silence of that forest, to remember the feel of her beneath him.

That served only to make his mouth go dry, causing his heart to hammer all but uncontrollably. Titus opened his eyes and stood, feeling the cold once more, remembering he was alone. Cold and alone by his own choice.

Laying some more twigs on the embers of his fire, he dragged out another biscuit and sat eating it, feeding wood to his smoldering, sputtering companion. Besides being cold and frosty, the air was damp. The wood struggled to catch the flame, more often than not only smoking without real heat.

It was his own stupidity, he cursed himself.

From now on he'd simply have to learn better to protect some wood from the dews and damps if he intended on having himself a morning fire.

That's how it was for a man, Titus convinced himself. A man had to teach his own self. No one could do it for him.

After lashing everything together into a tight bundle he could loop over his shoulder, he retied his crude moccasins. He hadn't walked long yesterday morning in his hand-me-down boots before yanking them off and putting on the moccasins.

Like most folks who had settled on the borderlands, he preferred the softer, conforming footwear. Besides, most frontier settlers simply did not have what it took in the way of money to purchase shoes and boots for expanding families. No matter—they were stiff and cumbersome, simply could not take the soakings you could give moccasins. A lot simpler to patch up the sole of a moccasin, laying in a new piece of leather. He had two extra pair in his possibles, older ones, some he had almost outgrown. But Titus figured he could always put them on, get them duly soaked, and thereby stretch them out to wearable if need be.

That second morning of his journey, he felt no pressing need to worry on his feet. Surely there was plenty of time for him to shoot a deer to fill his belly—which would as well provide a hide he could soon learn to cure, just the way the tanner back in Rabbit Hash did with the pelts and skins brought him by the settlers in surrounding Boone County. The place had stunk, smelled to high heaven of death or worse still, what with the pelts stretched out and nailed to every wall of the tanner's sheds or lashed inside great rectangles formed from elm saplings. All manner of skins cluttered that tanner's place at the far edge of town, every hide to one stage or another scraped free of fat and loose tissue.

Titus set out at a walk this day, the sun rising at his back, intending to bring down some meat before that sun would set. Perhaps even that morning, as the critters moved out of their beds and went down to water, went in search of graze. This would be the time of day to keep his eyes open for sign, his ears alerted to any sound the cold breeze might bring him. If nothing presented itself this morning, then he'd just wait—evening would be the next-best time of the day to run across game.

His belly's angry, rumbling protest convinced Titus he shouldn't wait until the end of the day.

With cold, wet feet and a belly filled only by the last of his mother's baking-soda biscuits, shivering within the linsey-woolsey shirt he wore beneath the thick wrap of a leather jerkin, he strode on into dawn's mist tumbling over the great river. He promised himself he'd buy a needle and some thread once he reached Louisville. Already he felt one of his long stockings wearing thin across the toes. If he walked all the way to Louisville —why, surely, his stockings would be in sore need of repair after all those miles.

Morning passed without so much as a chance for a shot. Not that he didn't see a few deer. But they were too far off, or bounded away too quickly, or he simply knew no more of them than the sound of their flight through the forest that swallowed all trace of them. The forest denied him all morning long.

Near midday he came across an outcropping of slate that hung some two hundred feet or more above the wide river. As it tracked low in the southern sky, the autumn sun graced the rock with a sharp slant of light and, so he hoped, with warmth. Clambering up to the flat shelf, Titus shed his blanket and shooting pouch before leaning back against the gray rock. He turned his face toward the sun, soaking up the warmth from above, greedily drawing in what heat radiated off the slate beneath him. The river below lay twisted, a great tawny road that snaked its way almost due north toward Cincinnati in this, the great bend of the Ohio.

Off to his left the river flowed. Yonder to the unknown. Away to far places he could only dream of—for no man he knew could lay claim to setting down tracks out there.

Oh, like so many others in Boone County, Titus had heard tell of a band of his nation's explorers setting out for the far western sea, returning three years later, taking that long to cross everything in between. There had been lots of wondrous talk about that journey at the Longhunters Fair every summer the last few years. Fragments and shreds of speculation and legend, rumor and fable: the size of the animals, the sheer number of the beasts, those high mountains one had to cross, heights where the snow never melted . . . and the Indians. Yet what stuck more than anything else in his memory of such talk was the description of the land. The sheer immensity of it. The way some folks claimed a man must feel all but swallowed up by the land.

Too, some spoke of the way a man could see much, much farther than he could in this closed-in country, could look back behind him all the way to yesterday . . . look all the way ahead into day after tomorrow.

Titus closed his eyes. Trying desperately to imagine. Struggling to picture just such a land. Hoping to capture a glimpse of it somewhere in his mind, if not his heart. Perhaps one day. One day in the years to come, when he was finally ready to look back into all his yesterdays, ready at long last to look ahead into all his tomorrows—then he would find a way to take himself toward that unknown land.

But for now he sat at the edge of what was frontier enough for most any man. Behind him lay most of what passed for civilization. Ahead stretched a wilderness dotted irregularly with little sign of the white man save for outflung settlements huddled by the river, separated by many, many miles of thick forest still dominated by the beasts and the Indians.

He sighed behind those closed eyes, conjuring up an image of an Indian. Not the sort he had seen a few times back on his one trip to Cincinnati years before, or on those annual treks to Burlington's summer fair. A handful of Indians always showed up with squash and other crops to barter. But he imagined they could not be real Indians—not the way they had taken to wearing the white man's shirts and vests and tricornered hats. Seemed just about all the Indians Titus had ever laid eyes on took a real fancy to the white man's headware: poking feathers and birds' wings or some other totem into the tricorne's folds for decoration.

No, he decided as the sun's warmth cradled him: those Indians upriver simply couldn't be the real thing. Downriver—that's where he'd find some wild Injuns. But, then, he knew nothing about anything downriver. At the same time, he was certain his pap and the other men of Boone County knew something of what lay down the Ohio. Being farmers sending off their produce to sell downriver every harvest, they had to have dealings with the sort of man who plied the Ohio in the flatboats Titus and other youngsters watched floating south and west with the current in all seasons. Kentucky broadhorns bound for the unknown just around the far bend. Even if his pap had never once directly engaged a riverman to carry the family's produce west, then Titus was sure his father had many times talked with men who had.

With a twinge of remorse now, he regretted that he hadn't paid more attention each fall as their harvest of corn and wheat was carted into Rabbit Hash, there to be joined with the produce of other farmers, and flatboat pilots contracted to take the year's harvest down to Louisville, farther still. Perhaps down to the mouth of the Ohio at the great Mississippi. To places that had foreign-sounding names on his tongue when he repeated what others spoke of with such a mysterious air. Perhaps if he had paid more attention—at least one time—he might now know more of what lay downriver.

As it was, all he knew lay up the Ohio. Cincinnati. Pittsburgh.

The first to recognize the crucial military importance of the confluence of the Allegheny and Monongahela rivers, which joined to form the Ohio, were the French who built Fort Duquesne in 1754 near the site. Following their defeat of the French, the British changed the post's name to Fort Pitt, and by 1803 that surrounding community of nearly two thousand inhabitants was already known among area settlers as Pitts-burg, "The Key to the Western Territory." As early on the frontier as it was, the town nonetheless claimed a sprawling public market, a pair of glass factories, cabinet and coopers' shops, nail works and tobacco manufactory, along with more than forty retail shops, all thriving on the steady influx of settlers.

Yet it was flatboats and their bigger cousins, the keels, that made Pittsburgh truly famous in its early days. For more than half a century one out of every two citizens in the town was involved in boat building, boat selling, or boat buying.

Those waters of the upper Ohio were littered with boulders and stones —a serpentine river, treacherous to the unwary and unskilled. Yet the water upriver was clear and clean—much more so than the lower Ohio—perhaps because of the lower river's snaking route. River travelers had long commented on the overwhelming magnificence of the forested mountainsides that loomed right over the Ohio's winding path as it flowed past Virginia and on to eastern Kentucky. "The Endless Mountains" was the term westerners used when speaking of those foothills of the Allegheny range.

A lush growth of grapevine, blue larkspur, and purple phlox covered both sides of the river, along with a profusion of tall grasses and the dark hardwood timber: beech, hickory, walnut, poplar, red maple, and at least three varieties of oaks. There were places where the winding path of the Ohio so narrowed beneath the verdant overhang that a trip down the river appeared to be a journey through a green and meandering tunnel.

Downriver from Pittsburgh lay Wheeling, Marietta, Gallipolis, Limestone, and finally Cincinnati—each new settlement outgrowing its own modest beginnings in but a few years as more and more emigrants flooded over the mountains in search of land, peace, and freedom. Through the past decade the population of Kentucky itself had more than doubled: folks looking for better ground to farm, there to put down their roots.

Between each of these larger towns lay the smaller villages, farms, and orchards—places named Vienna, Belpre, Belleville, near the mouth of Ohio's Big Hockhocking River, and Point Pleasant at the mouth of the Great Kanawha River—many of which sprouted up around what had originally been forts or stockades erected for the common defense during Indian scares

of recent wars. From western Pennsylvania all the way to where the Great
Miami River met the North Bend of the Ohio at Cincinnati, census takers
estimated as many as one hundred thousand folks lived along the river,
bringing some small measure of civilization to what was nothing more than
a forbidding and all but impenetrable wilderness a generation or so in the
past.

Sitting across the Ohio from the mouth of Kentucky's Licking River,
Cincinnati was just then becoming known as the "Queen City of the West."
Land speculators had first laid out its streets in the 1790s, and folks came
flocking to the territorial capital growing in the shadow of the new nation's
army garrison at nearby Fort Washington. By 1810 a thousand residents lived
either "in the bottom," or "on the hill," all of them squeezed between thickly
timbered heights and the Ohio itself as the settlement became a beehive of
activity for boatmen moving downriver with produce, wood, iron, and hemp
supplies, as well as settlers. In the town's influential newspaper, *Sentinel of the
Northwest Territory,* they even boasted to folks along the Atlantic coast of
having two cemeteries: one for the Methodists and one, presumably, for
everyone else.

Beyond Cincinnati a man afloat on the Ohio plunged into a region
thinly settled with a few farms and even fewer infant villages the likes of
Rabbit Hash. By the time he journeyed farther still, halfway between the
great bend of the Ohio and Louisville, he left behind those tall slopes burred
with thick forests, the land slowly gentling, giving way to more hills, the
rolling landscape softening here and there where farmers settled to till the
fertile bottomlands dotted with swamps and ringed by deep woods.

Titus awoke with a start.

The air had grown cool, and with the sun's setting the slate shelf where
he had drifted off to sleep was quickly losing its warmth. Wearily, yet with a
sense of urgency, Titus clambered to his feet and swept up his shooting pouch
and horn, then his blanket-wrapped possibles. Turning back into the timber,
he once again vowed he would find game before nightfall. He had to: sleep
had been the only way to relieve the painful gnawing of his empty belly.

Shadows lengthened and the wind picked up, rattling the bright, fiery
colors of what leaves still clung to the branches like hailstones battering oiled
canvas. The minutes ground past, and with them step after step through the
cold timber, all without a single sign of game. No tracks, no droppings, not
even a faint or narrow trail.

He cursed his luck. Then with a growl he cursed his rumbling belly.
Sensing the sap running out of him, his strength failing after two days of

nothing but a handful of soda biscuits to eat, Titus slowly sank to the ground and leaned against an old elm. How he wanted to cry out loud. For a moment he became convinced he had done wrong in fleeing home. Mayhaps, he told his miserable self, it wasn't so bad a thing having his mother's warm food in his belly and a roof over his head. Mayhaps the plodding certainty of a farmer's life wasn't all that bad, after all.

But go back?

Titus hefted that option as a man would weigh two objects, one in each of his hands. Back and forth he considered. And in the end his pride won out. Not to have to face the look in his father's eyes if he limped back home with his tail between his legs. No, never, he decided. He simply couldn't bring himself to turn about and return home.

Yes . . . eating crow, one foul-tasting bite after another to swallow, washing it down with a healthy draft of his battered, wounded pride, would surely be far, far worse than going one more night without real food. Without meat.

With that renewed resolve came the stinging realization that hunting because he enjoyed it, hunting for fun, was one thing. Whereas hunting when you had to feed a hungry belly was something altogether different.

Cradling the rifle across his lap, Titus stuffed his hands into his armpits for warmth as the wind swirled noisily through the branches overhead. A squirrel chirked in the high branches, protesting the cold, complaining about the wind, perhaps even snapping at the young hunter sprawled beneath the tree.

It came over him the way his mam might nudge him gently awake of a school morning. He put his teeth together, opening his lips slightly, and chirked. Like most farm boys on the frontier, Titus had grown quite good at imitating the sounds of forest animals.

There it was, by God! Close by. Near the fork of that gray limb.

Titus slowly stood, drawing the hammer back to half cock. He looked down at the pan to be certain of priming powder, then brought the frizzen down over the pan once more. Easing the hammer back to full cock, he chirked again. The squirrel snapped back at him angrily, bounding down the limb, then leaping out of sight momentarily. Yet he found the tree, spotting the squirrel in a big knobby maple less than five yards off.

Near its base he circled slowly, a step at a time as the animal inched out of sight. Titus studied each of the high branches, for he knew a squirrel liked to lie along them as it peered down on the forest floor. Mostly he regarded each and every fork, as that was where the savviest of the creatures hung back in hiding. At first he could not be sure, but he realized he had to freeze where he stood, motionless, peering up at the gnarled fork of a thick branch. In the fading light of autumn's afternoon it was all but impossible to be absolutely certain. Then he saw the flicker of the squirrel's tail. Perhaps only tousled on the wind as the sun continued its descent into the west.

Taking a few heartbeats more to study his shot, eyeing the path his bullet would take, Titus took one step backward as he slowly brought the rifle up to his shoulder. From there the round ball would have far less chance of striking the tiniest of branches that could deflect it just enough to miss his target. He let out half his breath, held it, and brought the front blade down on the dark and narrow fork in the branch where he had seen the tail flick in the wind.

No, he told himself. If he shot the critter from this direction, there wouldn't be much meat left at all.

Gingerly stepping to the left as quietly as the dry leaves allowed him, Titus inched around the base of the trunk, keeping his eyes moving to the ground before he set each foot down, then to that fork in the branches. Finally he allowed himself to take another breath, and with it he came to a stop. There in the dimming light he thought he could make out the tail curving back on itself, saw where the tail root attached to the shadow of the body, and at the far end, some of the squirrel's head.

If he could make a head shot, none of the best meat would be ruined. Sighting in on that part of the shadow, Titus squeezed off his shot before any more light drained from the sky.

For an instant the bright flare of the pan flash-blinded him. As the roar of the flintlock was swallowed by the deep woods, he blinked, inching forward, intent on the ground blanketed with fallen leaves. His attention was drawn by a rustle.

The squirrel thrashed among the dried leaves as he came up and knelt over it. He had missed its head, but by striking the limb it sat on, had stunned the animal out of its hiding place. Taking his knife from his belt, he held it by the blade and brought the antler handle down on the squirrel's head with a crack.

As he picked up the plump squirrel, Titus glanced into the tree. Too dark to look for any bark knocked loose from the branch above him. It didn't matter really, he thought. For certain it wasn't good shooting that got him the squirrel this time. Perhaps the forest itself had given one of its own to feed him.

"Thankee," he said softly, looking around him.

As good a place as any, he determined. Might as well make himself comfortable right here.

After clearing a spot beneath the tree and striking a fire, Titus pulled out his tiny kettle and retraced his steps back through the trees until he found the narrow trickle of water he had passed after leaving the adamantine ledge. He drank long and slow after dipping the kettle into the oozing flow. Then he waited while the kettle filled a second time before returning to his fire.

There he began skinning his supper, his mouth already beginning to water, anticipating the taste of meat. Cutting off head, tail, and paws, he slit the squirrel up the belly, opening it up to gut it. That done, he selected a long tree limb, as big around as two of his fingers, to skewer his supper. Shoving one end of the limb into the ground so that the squirrel could sizzle over the low flames, Titus turned to preparing his bed as the night wind hooted through the skeletal trees, making him feel all the colder.

Kicking over piles of leaves from some of the surrounding trees, he made himself quite a mound near his fire. Turning the squirrel once, he returned to collecting. With enough of them spread out to make for a soft and deep pallet, he flung down his thin blanket. Then Titus settled cross-legged at the fire and sighed. Cold as it might be tonight, he vowed he would not allow the sounds of the forest, the wind, even the cold itself to keep him from sleeping as they had last night. If he were going to make it downriver, even as far as Louisville, he was simply going to have to master what it took for a frontiersman to be at home in the forest.

He turned the squirrel over the flames, then probed at the browning flesh with a finger and sighed, his thoughts suddenly on Levi Gamble. How he wanted one day soon to be as sure a backwoodsman as Levi was already. Why, he knew he was nearly as good a shot, likely might even be better than Gamble soon enough. Still, he remembered Levi's words that there was more to the life Titus Bass hankered to lead than being a good shot.

As darkness dripped down from the leafless branches overhead, the wind came up. And with it the smell of rain. Gazing up at the sky, he could see no more than a small patch of stars off to the southeast. Chances were there'd be wet weather by morning. Just one more thing he'd have to learn to deal with if he was going to make it downriver as far as Louisville, where he figured a man might give himself a new stake in life.

Folks talked about the place. Said it was where a young man could make a go of things. The whole area was opening up. That sense of boom and bustle appealed to him more than most anything right there and then.

Second only to the aroma wafting off that squirrel. Titus fed a limb into the fire now and then, and from time to time juices plopped into the flames, each drop sizzling, every sizzle causing his mouth to water all the more until he knew he couldn't wait any longer.

Scrambling onto his knees, he pulled out his knife and sliced free a thin sliver along the backstrap. Stuffing it into his mouth, Titus half closed his eyes, savoring this taste of red meat. Licking his lips, he freed another sliver of meat, then washed it down with the cold water.

Before he realized, he was squatting beside nothing more than glowing embers, gnawing the last tiny morsels from the squirrel's scrawny bones in the dim ruby light as his fire died. Sucking the final drops of grease from his fingers, he took one last drink and stood, moving off a few yards to find a place where he could sprinkle the forest floor in the cold and dark that were his only companions again this night.

Returning to his little camp, he fed the embers a few twigs until they caught, then laid on some thicker limbs for the first part of the night. That done, he scooted back onto his blanket and lay down, dragging his pouch and rifle in alongside him. After pulling half of the blanket over himself, Titus scooped leaves over his feet, then his legs, and finally covered his torso. Just as thick as he could burrow himself beneath.

For a long time Titus cradled the rifle in his arms, the lock protected between his legs, watching the flames and listening to the forest around him, reminded of the sputter and crackle of a limekiln fire back home. How something so simple as a sound aroused his reverie. He wondered what Amy was about at that moment. Did she even know he had taken off? Was she missing him, or had she already made designs on some other young fellow?

And then he thought on his mam, remembering how the pumpkins grew untended among the tall stalks of corn. Licking his lips, Titus tried to remember the taste of his mother's pumpkin butter and pumpkin molasses boiled down in the fall.

The first good cold snap like this every autumn brought on the hog killing, the menfolk butchering those animals fattened all year on cane roots and mast made of beechnuts, acorns, and chestnuts. Hogs were knocked in the head with a maul, their throats quickly slashed, and then hauled up on pulleys lashed to a strong tree limb for proper bleeding. Below the gently swinging creatures mam always caught as much of it as possible in cherrywood pails and churns to make the rich blood pudding she would stuff into a cleaned intestine and smoke over green hickory chips in the smokehouse. He was almost able to taste it—served under a thick white gravy with yellow hominy on the side. Memories laden with the remembrance of sausage strong with red pepper and sage, sousemeat or headcheese.

Yes, on the frontier October came to be known as killing weather.

But with the remembrance he began for the first time to worry about her, sensing some remorse for the worry he was likely causing her. But no remorse for his loss of Amy. No, his only regret in not turning back was his mam, and all the anxious concern he must likely be causing her.

A beat of wings passed over his head with a startling rush as he closed his eyes, so weary. The great-headed owl, prowling the forest.

Titus wondered if his mam had stood there at the front of her porch across those past two days—just the way she had when he was so much younger. Calling out his name.

Calling him home.

He came awake in the morning slowly, smelling the heady fragrance of damp, loamy earth strong in his nostrils.

A time or two before he opened his eyes for good, Titus heard the rain's patter softly through the trees. A gentle, cold, soaking rain, most likely. At least he thought so from its soft cadence against the stiff parchment of the maple and gum leaves he had pulled in over himself, burrowing down like a deer mouse in its snug little hole.

Warm it was in here. A damned sight better than the night before, he said to himself as he decided to open his eyes for good and not drift off to sleep. The irregular concert of misty drops had tapered off, and the forest fell quiet. He shifted his hip, making it more comfortable on a new spot among the thick pallet of leaves, and curled his legs up within the blanket.

No need in rushing on his way. Warm as he was. Comfortable too. Almost as soft as his grass tick back at home. Except . . . it wasn't home no more.

He opened his eyes, finding it still dark. It took a moment or two more for him to realize he had tucked his head back into the blanket like a turtle retreating into its shell. Slowly dragging a hand up from between his thighs where the rifle rested, he brushed it past his face and poked out with his fingers at the leaves. With a damp rustle he parted them slightly. The light was gray. His fire gone out—nothing more than a heap of blackened char and gray ash beaten down by the steady, gentle rain. Some of the squirrel bones lay at the far side of that ring of ash. A misty fog clung back among the trees all around him.

Not the sort of morning for a man to be rising bright and early.

Some time later he realized he had closed his eyes again, maybe even been sleeping—coming awake slowly, as he had earlier. This time the rain wasn't pattering on his leafy burrow. Without a lick of wind the forest lay stonily quiet about him. So quiet he could hear a low snuffling. If it didn't sound like a dog.

Parting the leaves again, his heart beginning to hammer anxiously, he peered out through a tiny opening in his burrow and spotted the reddish fur. Moving more leaves, he could make out the hind end of the animal, the thick, bushy tail nearly as long as the creature itself, then ringed with black and tipped in pale hair. As it rooted around his fire with its nose and front paws, the fox turned slightly, its jaws crunching down on the leavings of last night's supper.

So quiet was the forest that Titus could even hear the snap of the bones with every close of the fox's jaws. He watched as it finished off the squirrel and sniffed at the small kettle before putting its nose along the damp ground, rooting for something more to eat. Had it been dry, the fox likely would never have approached his little camp. But the damp weather kept down the smell of man, burying it beneath all the other odors of a dank, musty forest.

Through the leaves he watched the fox turn in his direction, slowly sniffing its way toward his side of the fire, going this way a step to smell something, then darting a couple steps to the other side. Inching closer all the time until it was all but eye to eye with Titus's burrow, about to stick its nose right into the youngster's face.

"Haw!" he roared as he flung back the leaves, every bit as scared those last few seconds as the fox was. It leaped back, bared its teeth, and lowered its head, snarling and yipping.

"Get!"

He waved his arms as he burst out of the leaves, scattering them all about him in a wild flutter of color and motion as he emerged. With a throaty whimper the fox whirled about and disappeared into a patch of fog.

For some time he sat there in his bed of leaves, buried nearly up to his armpits, the blanket tangled around his waist. Waiting. Peering into the fog that had swallowed the fox whole.

As good as that scrawny squirrel had tasted last night, he realized his belly was empty once more. Already he could recognize the beginning torment of its complaint. He would have to find more substantial fare today. No other choice but to hunt until he had some game. Even if it meant he wasn't able to move as far downriver as he had vowed he would each day. Food had become his highest priority.

But for now he had to take care of something else first.

Kicking back his blanket and the thick layer of leaves, Titus emerged from his burrow at the base of the tree and looked about until he found a likely spot at a downed tree nearby. Backing up to it, he pushed the wooden buttons through their holes on the front of his britches, tugged them down around his ankles, then settled the backs of his thighs upon the cold, wet bark. As he emptied himself out and gathered a handful of wet leaves he used to clean himself off, Titus watched the patterns of frost that puffed before him with every breath.

Snugging his britches back into place, he plodded back across the sodden ground and went to his knees by his blanket, drawing his kettle over. From it he took the last long drink of creek seep mixed with rainwater, then wrapped the kettle up with the rest and lashed it into the long roll he flung over his shoulder as he got to his feet.

Draping his shooting pouch over the other shoulder, his rifle at the end of his left arm, Titus moved off, into the cold fog and his third day.

Both times he stopped to rest that gray morning that bled itself into a grayer afternoon, he chewed on a peeled twig he had cut from a gum tree. Something to quiet his roiling stomach as he sat looking at the river beneath a sky brushed the same endless color. In Boone County as elsewhere on the frontier, it was often the older child who taught younger ones what they could eat when off to the woods gathering herbs for a mother's cook pots. Some children came to favor dogwood with its taste of quinine, spice-wood preferred by others, or the stomach-soothing taste of walink, commonly called walking leaf. But they learned never, never to chew poison vine, or buckeye, or a bright, shiny, tempting poison-oak berry.

Thinking back on how he had learned to feed himself from these woods as a child couldn't help but aggravate that empty hole gnawing away at the pit of him, making him madder at himself for his failure, chipping away at his resolve piece by piece. As he walked on and on, it wasn't a matter of thirst that made him drink as much as he could hold of the creeks and streams and every last trickle he crossed that long, wet day. He only knew that if he kept his belly filled with as much water as he could stand, it didn't complain quite as badly.

"Sun going down again," he muttered aloud, then realized he had spoken out loud, looking left—then right—embarrassed.

"Who the hell you talking to?" he said, wagging his head. "Ain't no one to listen anyways."

Damn. Here he was, someplace he didn't know of. Hadn't eaten an honest meal in days, and he hadn't scared up any real game to speak of.

"Good goddamned hunter you are," he grumbled, bringing his legs under him and rising to his feet, fixing to press on through the hard, leaden plop of that cold October rain.

He didn't know why—except that he was feeling the first twitches of fear. No longer merely disgusted with himself. No longer mad, the way he had been for most of that day. Instead, Titus was sensing the first self-doubts rattling within him like stones inside a dried gourd. And that made him afraid. Try as he might, he couldn't for the life of him figure out why he was failing. Never before had he failed to bring down game, no matter what season he hunted. Why now? When it counted? When it meant the differ-ence between surviving and starving? What had he done wrong?

Through those tiny cracks in his confidence seeped the growing fear that reared its ugly head, tangled up with no small measure of superstition. Long ago he had learned from hunters much older than he that if a man had himself a run of bad luck in hunting, chances were he had been enchanted. His heart hammered twice as fast, just to even think on it. Possessed of a spell or hex that he would have to break.

But there had to be a reason he had been hexed.

"Think," he chided himself, squeezing his brain down on it the way he stood there in the rainy forest squeezing a hand tightly around the leather straps that bound up his wool blanket.

Maybe it was a curse put on him because he'd wronged Amy Whistler, maybeso wronged even his pap. Then again, maybe it had only to do with him: what had been happening to him in the last three days was simply telling him he'd chosen wrong, taken the wrong path for his life. Maybe . . . he was being told he should turn back.

Titus stopped right there on the game trail, and for the first time in three days he looked back. Turned around and peered into the wet, soggy forest, back the way he had come. The tears were there before he could squeeze them off. A stifled sob was all that came out as he stared into the east. Upriver. Back to Boone County. As cold as his cheeks were, he could sense the track of every hot tear as it spilled from his eyes.

Looking down at himself—his pacs, those double-soled moccasins, and leather britches soaked clear to the knees, forcing the rain's chill straight to his core—only made him cry harder. He had never been so alone.

"This is what you wanted, dammit!"

And he swiped at the tears with a trembling hand, still looking down at his miserable self. Then, suddenly, he began to chuckle.

Wagging his head, he murmured, "You . . . you surely are the sight, Titus Bass."

That chuckle felt good. Like a warm, dry place right down in the center of him. So good did it feel that he started to laugh. He was unsure about really laughing at himself there at first, but then he picked up one moccasin and looked at it hanging soggy and floppy from where it was lashed about his ankle with a buckskin whang. He sat it down on the wet forest floor and picked up the other moccasin—in just as sad a shape. Now he was laughing for real. That good, great belly sort of laugh. What a damned poor sight he was! Some great woodsman!

Likely he'd be nothing but a rack of bones by the time he limped into Louisville. Looking like something ol' Tink'd drag into the yard out of the woods.

No chance I'll go and land myself some work on the wharf, looking so puny and poor the way I do. A hiring man take one gander at me and think: man as can't provide for hisself surely ain't worth hiring on to be doing no heavy work.

As his laughter withered, a faint and distant sound pierced the forest clearing where he stood. Not sure at first, he listened with all his being while human voices became distinct. A slight echo reverberated behind what was clearly an attempt at song. With that echo, and its direction, Titus realized the voices came not from the forest surrounding him on three sides. Instead, the off-key melody rose from the timbered canyon of the Ohio River somewhere below him.

Through the wet leaves and soggy grass he bolted away in the song's direction. Perhaps only to see another human. Perhaps to assure himself that his mind hadn't been teched after going without real food for so long, and three days without the sight of a human face, the sound of a human voice.

Standing on the edge of the tall granite escarpment less than a hundred feet above the river, he gazed up the Ohio anxiously, not seeing a boat upon the water. Downriver he turned expectantly. Nothing there. Turning to peer upriver once more as the echoing voices drew closer, he watched a single flatboat emerge at the far bend from the great, green, verdant tunnel of the Ohio. How many men stood on its deck, he could not tell at the distance, yet as the flatboat closed that next mile, their forms began to take shape.

Foremost was the helmsman, standing as he was at the rear of the boat, one arm drooped over a long rudder pole set down in the forks of support that reached as tall as the man's waist. Coming out of the turn, this steersman worked to inch his craft over toward the far bank, yard by yard, keeping his flatboat guided down the main channel of the river.

Bass waved, hoping he might catch the pilot's eye. But there was no sign of recognition from the boat.

Closer they came, until Titus could make out two more men, one on either side of the craft, each squatting down inside the low gunnels of the boat, gripping a short oar they worked at from time to time as the pilot bellowed his orders above their song. Then Bass spotted a fourth man, who until now had been hunkered down in the front of the boat, getting up from his knees among the barrels and kegs, chests and bundles of goods. Crawling over and around them, he made his way slowly back through the center of the craft and disappeared beneath an awning of cloth stretched taut from a ridgepole that ran along the midsection of the flatboat. He emerged from the back end of the low, sideless awning and went to stand near the helmsman.

Although Titus could not make out the words of their spoken voices, he could tell that those two were talking while the two oarsmen were singing their joyous air. For a brief moment it appeared they looked up his way among the trees at the edge of the escarpment. Bass waved again.

Still no one waved back.

"Halloo!" he cried out.

It echoed back from the far side of the forested canyon.

On the flatboat below, the singing immediately stopped. It seemed all four looked up to study both sides of the river, turning their heads this way and that, searching the forested banks.

"Up here!" he cried out, waving his hat, holding the rifle out at the end with his other hand.

Then one of the oarsmen spotted him and hollered out to the others, pointing with one arm. They all seemed to turn his way, so Titus waved his rifle again. Two of the boatmen took their hats off and gave a salute. They called out with a garbled, distant greeting he could not make out.

It mattered not, for that place within him burned warm to catch this sight of others, his ears to hear the sounds of voices speaking, even singing. As they bobbed on below Titus, the two continued their off-key song. He watched them, his eyes bouncing over all four men as the helmsman began to ease his craft to the south channel of the Ohio before slipping through another bend in that mighty river where the mist and fog clung like dirty linen.

Smaller they became, smaller still, until the flatboat disappeared around a piece of land, keeling to the north into the distant rain. Swallowed by the river and its canyon. In the silence of their wake, Titus could hear their voices fade for some time after they had gone from view. Then that too was gone, all traces of boat and crew.

So close to others, for only moments. And gone so quickly that he felt strange, as if something had been torn from him whole. The loneliness returned, this time with a vengeance—a solid, metallic ache to it as he continued to watch the very spot where the flatboat had disappeared.

Of a sudden he realized how quickly the sun was falling from the fading light. The river's canyon below grew darker still as he gaped into its depths.

He had to push on, keep moving until he ran across some game—or until it got too dark to hunt. Either one, and he'd finally give up and stop for the night.

Turning back into the timber was like peeling away a strip of flesh from his own body, forcing himself to press on—back into the wet, soggy forest, teeth chattering, his nose so cold it had begun to hurt. Trudging on, he followed step by step the game trail as it wound higher along the side of the canyon, through the forest—as he prayed he would run across something. Even another squirrel.

His stomach tumbled. Yes, even another damned squirrel. Far better than creek water and sucking on a gum twig.

What little light there had been all that gloomy day was eventually squeezed right out of the river's canyon, seeming to shimmer for a moment as the last rays peeked from beneath the western clouds. And with the sun's sinking the wind came up, as cold as it had ever been. Enough to drive a damp, chilling finger all the way to his marrow.

With no supper, and no prospect of bringing anything down—not even another squirrel—Titus ached all the more in every bone, knowing that when he would make another fire tonight, this time he faced climbing within his blanket-and-leaf burrow without even a few poor mouthfuls of some small, bony creature who haunted the ceiling of the forest above him.

As it grew steadily darker, Titus found himself squinting at the ground, forced to let his feet in those soggy moccasins make out the narrow game trail for him. Feeling his way up the last of that climb along the south side of the Ohio, he slowly started a gradual descent as the river bent itself around to the right, flowing north by west.

Once on that trip down he stopped and listened to the night, staring up

at the sky. Back to the east no moon could he see. Everywhere else the sky
thickened like blood pudding without a single star to mar its ominous
monotony. In a matter of minutes he would have to think of moving up the
slope to find himself a place to spend the night. A good chance of rain. The
dark and the cold settled into his spirit. To stop and rest, however, would
make for too much time to think. To brood on mistakes made, to conjure up
the faces of folks left behind.

As he hefted the rifle across his shoulder and stepped off the trail
toward the timber above him, Titus heard something—a sound out of place.

The way a man hunted the distance in a thick forest: looking for
something that did not belong.

But this was a sound the forest did not own.

Immediately he stopped. Listened. Downriver. So distant he wasn't
sure. He might tell better if he moved on a while farther. Perhaps make it
around the rest of that bend in the river. Then he would know for sure.

Both his eyes and his toes strained to make out the trail as he leaned
into a faster pace, spurred on by the prospect that those sounds promised.
One hundred yards, then two hundred and he stopped again. Listening for
several moments without hearing a thing.

Just when he had convinced himself that his mind had been charling
him—as cold and wet as he was, as hungry as he was for human company—
just when he was about to give up and give in and make a camp of it for the
night . . . he heard the voices.

Bounding off into the dark, he found his heart thundering in his ears.
Hurrying him ever faster.

The closer he got, the more his ears made sense of things. Not just
voices, but singing. A few thready notes of a wheezing squeeze-box. Behind
it the low thump of someone drumming and another of them clacking
tinware spoons in back rhythm.

The trees a few hundred yards ahead seemed to part, and he caught a
glimpse of light. Titus lunged to a stop, unable to see it now. Took a step,
then another back and spotted it again. Flickering. Dancing. Firelight.

Warmth. And they were sure to have food.

On he surged, renewed, invigorated. Assured of closing the distance in
no time now.

And even sooner than he could have imagined, Bass stood at the edge
of the trees, gazing down at the bank some thirty yards away. In those
moments he remained motionless at the last fringe of timber watching that
fire. The half-moon made its brief appearance below the clouds in the east.

Below him lay a wide strip of the river, a flatboat tied up at the bank, gently bobbing in the cold, silvery light tracing lacy patterns on the black water.

Laughter drew his gaze back to the fire.

What that sound could do for his young soul.

Laughter!

His heart rising in his throat, Titus moved out of the timber, watching two of the men rise from their stumps.

"Who goes?"

He stopped, called back, "Just me." And stayed rooted to that spot a moment more. "I was the one hollered out to you while back. Upriver, it was."

One of the forms moved in front of the fire now, coming his way. He stopped, backlit by the cheery, yellow, beckoning flames.

"You're alone?"

"Just me."

That one signaled Titus on. "You've got our welcome."

Bass inched into the light, licking his lips at the fragrance of something frying, smelling biscuits baking in a skillet to the side of the fire. He couldn't take his eyes off that steaming kettle, the simmering coffeepot as his mouth worked at a gallop, salivating like a hound's.

"Hell, he's just a boy," one of the others grumbled, placing his fists on his hips.

"Yeah," the closest one cheered as Titus came closer. He had on a worn flannel shirt and buff-colored nankeen britches. "C'mon over here, boy. You look a mite hongry."

"I . . . I am. Real hungry."

The one in greasy flannel stepped close. As hairy as any man Titus had ever seen. "We got us plenty. You're welcome to share."

"He don't get none of my share," a third, short and stocky man grumbled, then spat into the fire with a loud hiss. He wore a jacket and waistcoat of quilted Spanish silk.

"How long it been since you et last?" asked the first man with his Kentucky accent.

"Been a day . . . or two," Titus said, his eyes wandering nowhere from the frying pan and kettle at the fire's edge.

"God-glory-damned, Ebenezer," the last of the men exclaimed. "I do b'lieve this here boy's done runned away from home!"

SEVEN

He couldn't ever remember eating so much. It seemed his mouth and gullet and belly kept crying out for more, for every last bite he could lay his hands on.

"How long you say it been since you last et?" asked Hames Kingsbury, the head oarsman, who wore beneath his blanket coat a shirt of poor man's tow cloth, topped with a bright-red handkerchief for a cravat. Crowning it all was a dark-green hat in which a long red feather was prominently displayed—a strutting cock of a boatman's symbol of martial prowess.

Titus looked over the rim of his coffee tin at the blond, short-cropped man with a matted beard. "Two . . . two days."

Kingsbury glanced up at the one called Ebenezer Zane, the long-haired, heavily bearded pilot and patroon of that flatboat bobbing gently nearby in the black water of the Ohio. "This boy's got him a natural appetite, Ebenezer. If he gets hisself this hongry in two days—think what a pitiful sight he'll make if he happed to go a week 'thout a bite."

Zane squatted next to the youngster, grinning within that black beard and unkempt hair of his that surrounded his ruddy face like the mane of a lion. "Don't you give none of these river riffraff no mind, Titus Bass. G'won and eat your fill."

"I had a way," Titus garbled around a chunk of the boiled salt pork, "I'd do something pay you back for the victuals."

"Now, don't go and tell our patroon that!" grumbled Reuben Root, just about the sourest-faced man Titus thought he'd ever had the displeasure to run across. Besides his jacket and waistcoat of Spanish silk that had seen finer days, Root sported a shapeless, low-crowned hat, the like of which protected a man from rain. "Man always pays up for what he eats."

Stopping the corn dodger at his lips, Titus looked over at Root across the fire. "I . . . I ain't got no money to pay for this food."

In his fox-fur cap, with its legs dangling from either side of the pilot's head and the tail bobbing down his back, Ebenezer Zane clapped a hand on the back of Bass's shoulder and said, "Told you not to pay these'r hired fellers no mind. Eat your fill. An' if'n that ain't enough, we'll boil up some more."

"We go giving our food away, how we sure to last till Louisville and the Falls?" demanded Root grumpily.

"Shit, we'll make it awright," the fourth man cheered as he knelt close to the fire and picked up the bail to a large kettle where the boatmen had boiled their coffee. Like the other three, he too wore the thick moccasins preferred by rivermen, all well greased with tallow, as well as fustian britches, made of a coarse cloth woven from cotton and linen. The one called Heman Ovatt continued, "Cain't be more'n another night on the river afore we reach port at Louisville."

"Ovatt's got the sense his folks give him," Zane replied to the others.

"You're the pilot—you tell me," Root spat. "Pilot's the one what's supposed to know this river like every wrinkle in your own honey-dauber. Leastways, that's what you claimed to me when you hired me back up to Pennsylvania."

Zane leaned close to Bass as if intending to whisper a confidence, but his voice remained clear and loud as he said, "This sack of whorehouse catshit named Reuben Root really ain't so bad a heart as it may seem, son. Just that, well—he's a Pennsylvania boy. And not a Kentucky man."

"Ovatt ain't a Kentucky man neither!" Root protested. "An' 'sides—I ain't a sack of whorehouse catshit. That's 'bout the worse thing you could call a man what hates cats much as I does."

"Hell, Ebenezer knows that!" Kingsbury said. "Why you think he gone and called you that?"

The pilot nodded, smiling hugely. "Hames there"—and he pointed at the oarsman across the fire—"he a Ohio man. Same as Heman there. But I'll 'llow they're good Ohio men . . . seeing as they came from about as close to Kentucky as you can come."

"We're from Cincinnati," Ovatt explained. "This here's my third trip downriver."

As were many who took up the nomadic, rootless life of a riverman, the flatboat's patroon was himself a discharged soldier, a veteran of the Continental Army. Kingsbury, Root, and Ovatt had been the sort of vagabonds who naturally clustered in the river ports like Pittsburgh, Cincinnati, and St. Louis when Ebenezer Zane had come upon them—otherwise homeless men who had become a class by themselves in the late eighteenth century.

Zane turned to Bass. "I figure since't we saw you on the south side of the river—that's gotta make you a Kentucky boy."

"Yep, I am," Bass answered.

How his ears already hung on every word these four spoke. While they might all be from the same general part of the frontier Titus had once called home, these boatmen nonetheless spoke with an accent that was all their own. From time to time their unique speech was spiced with the jargon peculiar to their trade, with a few Spanish, French, Creole, and Indian words thrown in for good measure.

Zane asked, "You got a place you call home?"

He glanced at the pilot a moment, then at two of the others around the fire, all of them gazing at him in expectant silence.

"It's all right, Titus Bass," the patroon finally said. "You don't wanna say, makes us no difference. None of us gonna haul you back to home nohow."

"R-rabbit Hash," he said around a mouthful of meat.

"That ain't far down from Cincinnati," Ovatt remarked. "Heard of it."

"Ain't much to the place," Titus replied. "Few shops, a cooper and blacksmith is all."

"Don't matter how big a place is," Kingsbury said. "All that matters is what you feel 'bout it after you've gone and left it behind."

"You got you plans, Titus Bass?" Zane asked. "I mean—now that you've put Rabbit Hash at your back?"

He swallowed that bite almost whole, sensing it slide all the way down his gullet. Titus didn't think he could take another bite, his belly suddenly complaining that it was stretched to its limit.

"Wanna go down to Louisville. Heard lots 'bout it. I was figuring on looking up some work."

"Some work?" Root snarled acidly. "Why, who'd hire a skinny strap of chew leather like you to do anything?"

"I'll do anything. I handled mules and a ox in the fields, an' I can hunt—"

Root let out an explosive grunt. "Shit! Man can hunt wouldn't come in here near starving like you was."

His shoulders rounding with the man's crude laughter rolling over him, Titus hung his head. "I just never . . . didn't see no sign of any game."

"Don't pay him no mind," Kingsbury said. "Root's just the sort of critter what ain't happy less'n he can complain till every other man's feeling low as he is."

"That's right," Zane added. "His mama raised him on sour milk!"

"Least my mama knowed better than to take a full-growed skinny boy like this to wet-nurse."

Ebenezer Zane turned on the youngster. "Titus Bass, tell me true now: ain't you been weaned and whelped?"

His eyes muled, not knowing just how to respond to such a damned silly question. "Sure . . . certainly I am. I'm full growed."

Three of them roared with laughter, and Zane slapped his thigh while grumpy Root flung out the last of his coffee at the fire with a hiss.

"That settles it, Reuben," Kingsbury said matter-of-factly. "The boy's been weaned, so you don't have to worry 'bout none of us gotta wet-nurse him." Ovatt and Zane roared anew.

"That is, if Titus Bass figures on asking us for a ride down to Louisville," Zane said.

Ovatt stepped closer as his laughter sputtered to an end. "What you say, Titus Bass?" He pointed toward the nearby river. "You wanna float down to Louisville on that there Kentuckyboat?"

"Kentuckyboat?"

The pilot answered, "Just 'nother name for a flatboat, Titus Bass."

"Some calls 'em broadhorns too," Hames Kingsbury explained.

"So, tell me, now," Ebenezer Zane said, "you wanna walk downriver to Louisville—or you feel like floating with us?"

He studied the big flatboat tied up at the bank some twenty-five feet away and felt his mouth dry. "I ain't . . . never been on a boat afore."

"How long you been in Kentucky?" Kingsbury asked.

"All my life."

"You was born a Kentucky boy?" Ovatt inquired.

He nodded. "My grandpap come in long back."

"Before or after the French got throwed out?" Zane asked.

"Afore."

Zane leaned back, smiling in that dark hair that fully framed his big face. "By damn, fellas—this here boy's about as Kentucky as they come. Now, me, I was borned on the Kentucky side of the Big Sandy River—just 'cross from Virginia. Near a place called Savage Branch. But I was still young when my folks up and moved back to Point Pleasant in Virginia. My pa figured out he never was gonna be no good at farming."

"That's why I left to get down to Louisville," Titus admitted.

"Makes us both Kentucky boys," Zane replied. "You had your fill?"

"Yep, I have."

"And you decided to float with us?" Ovatt asked.

"You might as well float," Kingsbury said. "Damn sight easier'n walking."

"He gonna ride for free, Ebenezer?" Reuben Root growled. "While'st the rest of us work?"

"I figure I can use Titus come the rapids below Louisville."

Titus asked, "Below? You mean after we gone past Louisville?"

"We'll be tying up at the wharf in Louisville—see if there's any load we can float down to New Orleans. Then you help us get on through them chutes," the pilot explained. "That'll pay for your passage down. We'll put over to the shore and let you off a few miles down from Louisville. You can walk back up. That work for you?"

After running it over in his mind quickly, he nodded once. "I s'pose it'll do nicely."

"By the by, Titus Bass," Kingsbury said, "can you swim?"

"Yes, sir. I been swimming down to the crik ever since't I was a young'un."

"You ever swum in the Ohio?" Ovatt said gravely.

Bass only wagged his head.

"It's different'n swimming in a swimming hole, son," Zane declared. "Sinkholes and whirlpools, chutes and undertows—you a strong swimmer? Keep your head above water?"

"I can do that good as any man."

"All right, then, I won't feel need of tying a rope around you to keep you tied to me when we go through them Falls. You'll be on your own—like the rest of these'r hired men." Zane stood. "The bunch of you best bank that fire for the night and get to your blankets. I smell more rain afore morning, and that'll make for a soggy getup. I figure we'll cook coffee on the boat to make us a early start."

Wiping the back of his forearm across his mouth, Titus asked, " 'Sides the river giving you the fits—what about Injuns?"

They all stared at him a moment with strained faces. He felt his stomach flop, thinking he might just have hexed them for some strange reason.

"In . . . Injuns," he repeated. "I just figured—"

"We don't got no more worry 'bout Injuns," Zane interrupted. "Least-wise, not on the Ohio no longer."

With excitement tingling up from his toes, Titus leaned forward and prodded, "How 'bout down on the Messessap?" And he watched how they all went about their own affairs, their eyes busy at the fire, or what they were whittling, perhaps a new tattoo Heman Ovatt was scratching on his bare ankle.

"Injuns on the Messessap is just one of a whole shitbag full of dangers a boatman has to stare in the eye ever' trip down to Norleans."

Then Kingsbury chimed in, "Likely you won't even see a Injun what ain't got hisself drunk down to Natchez or Nawlins."

"Don't you even worry 'bout it, for the Ohio's got real quiet these days, and the Messessap is a big, wide river," Zane said, exuding confidence.

With Mad Anthony Wayne's stunning victory over the Wyandot at Fallen Timbers in 1794 and the resultant Treaty of Greenville, Indian problems for Ohio riverboatmen had been eliminated. But—that was on the Ohio. South on the Mississippi and its tributaries the bellicose tribes continued to ambush, attack, and kill unwary boatmen.

Kingsbury suddenly stood and rubbed his hands down the front of his thighs. "You got a blanket there, Titus?"

"I do."

" 'Nough to keep you warm?" Zane inquired.

"It's done me handsome so far."

"You get cold—tell me," Kingsbury said. "We got more blankets on the boat."

"And if it starts to rain," Ovatt added, "you can allays find a dry place with us up there under that roof."

Bass looked over at the flatboat, nodding when his eyes came to rest on the canvas awning stretched over the ridgepole that ran nearly half the length of the flatboat. "Keeping dry does sound good. I thankee for the company."

"And the victuals," Reuben Root snarled.

Titus replied sheepishly, "Yep—and thankee for the victuals too."

"Think nothing of it, Titus Bass," the pilot said as he turned away and strode off. "I'll give you your chance to work off those victuals and more—come the Falls of the Ohio."

"Get back from there, you idjit!" Heman Ovatt bellowed.

Suddenly Titus was snagged and whirled backward, stumbling over a coil of thick oiled hemp lying underfoot.

"The boy didn't know!" hollered Ebenezer Zane, piloting the flatboat at that fifty-five-foot-long stern rudder.

Ovatt grumbled, gesturing off along the gunnel, "Just go piss somewhere down the side."

His face burning in embarrassment, Bass stuffed himself back into his britches and scooted past the angry oarsman.

"Anywhere there will do, Titus Bass," Zane advised.

Feeling all four sets of eyes on his back, Titus turned toward the brown, frothy river and pulled his penis out again, hanging it over the Ohio flowing slowly beneath their flatboat.

"Ain't your fault," Hames Kingsbury explained from his thirty-five-foot-long starboard oar on the far side of the craft. "No one told you it's bad luck to piss off the bow of a boat."

"Only one thing worst'n pissin' off the bow of a man's boat," Reuben Root growled, then spit some tobacco into the water. "That's having a god-bleemed woman on a boat."

"I'll know now," Titus replied, dog-faced with shame. "Won't never do it again."

"Make sure you don't—you know what's good for you," Root snarled as he settled back in behind the larboard oar, one of that pair rivermen might also refer to as "sweeps," used more for helping the pilot navigate the flatboat than for propelling it.

"Don't pay him no mind," Zane reminded. "Just sit back and enjoy the ride, boy. Think on all the fun we're gonna have ourselves come we make Louisville."

For another moment Titus watched Ebenezer plunge the wide, flat end of his huge rudder back into the water, angling it from side to side as the pole rested in a waist-high, Y-shaped wooden fork at the stern of the boat. Turning from the pilot, Titus found Kingsbury motioning him over to the right, or starboard, side of the flatboat. He heaved himself up atop the wooden crates containing nails, from there crawled over some huge oak casks filled with flour, then finally sank onto a few open feet of the deck just in front of the oarsman.

"It's like anything, boy. First time for ever'thing. You'll learn."

"I never rode a riverboat afore."

More than seven thousand board feet of straight yellow poplar had been felled, milled, planed, and drafted in the construction of Ebenezer Zane's flatboat back up the Ohio in Pittsburgh. In that city, and downriver at Cincinnati and even Louisville during this golden era of river travel, hundreds of master carpenters and woodworking craftsmen were kept extremely busy right along the banks of the stately Ohio. Gunnels, cross ties and stringers—all were held together by hammering in more than three thousand wooden pins hand-carved from seasoned white oak. To this framework, built upside down at the water's edge, were then fastened the long sections of poplar planks. That done, all seams were tightly caulked with more than fifty pounds of oakum, untwisted hemp rope pulled apart and soaked in oil or tar, then hammered into every joint across the bottom and up the entire six feet the flatboat's sides rose above the waterline where the craft might take on some of the river in passing through whitewater rapids or the white-capped river swells during a storm.

To complete a flatboat having reached that stage of construction, the builder would pile rocks on one side of the craft until it tipped right side up. From there on the craftsmen would fashion one sort of raised cover or another, to provide protection for the crew and their sandbox fire pit as well as what cargo they would not chance leaving out in the rain and the river's worst elements—that roof made either out of wood with shake shingles of oak or cedar, or, in the case of what Ebenezer Zane had come to prefer, a simple oak framework over which he stretched the versatile, and much cheaper by far, oiled Russian sheeting.

Averaging sixty feet or better in length, at least fifteen feet or so in width, the flatboat was normally called upon to carry a minimum of forty or fifty tons of cargo downriver. Such craft came to be known by many names: Kentuckyboat, from the land of its crew's origin; New Orleans or Natchez, for that crew's destination; broadhorn, after its huge steering oars, fastened at both stern and bow; in addition to being affectionately called ark, after the boatman's biblical predecessor.

Ebenezer Zane outfitted every one of his craft with "check-posts"— what boatmen sometimes referred to as "snubbing posts"—those ends of a half dozen of the cross ties extending at least a foot or more above the gunnels every ten feet or so along both sides of the boat; with a muscle-powered capstan the crew could turn with capstan poles to slowly haul in the hawsers of oiled rope by which the rivermen would secure the boat to the shore or wharf at both bow and stern; in addition to a foot-powered leather boat pump, in the event the craft began to take on more water than the men could bail before they would tie up for the evening and replace any oakum guilty of leaking between the boat's seams. Here in the early part of the nineteenth century, flatboats were constructed for the nominal cost of $1.25 per linear foot, about $75.00, American money. By the time Zane had his craft fully outfitted, he had invested less than a hundred dollars before dickering over the purchase price of his cargo.

There were some businessmen who operated their floating stores, blacksmith shops, tinners, and cooperages, as well as river-going taverns— those "dramshops" and whorehouses—from their gaudily painted flatboats along limited stretches of the Ohio. These were commonly referred to by locals as "chicken thieves" because of their propensity for thievery from settler farms nearest the riverbank. Yet most flatboat owners used their craft to transport cargo from the upper Ohio to the lower Mississippi. To those who preferred the aesthetic lines of a canoe or even a crude bateau or pirogue paddled by buckskin-clad frontiersmen, the flatboat was nothing more than a large, plain, rectangular box allowed to bob in the river's current with some help from a pair of boatmen on their rudders as well as other crew who manned the oars along the sides. But while it would never win a beauty contest, the Kentucky-born flatboat got the job done: moving early-American commerce downriver.

"You any good with that rifle of your'n?" Kingsbury asked, giving his head a nod toward that part of the deck nearby that was covered by the awning. It was there that Ebenezer Zane had stowed the youngster's few belongings.

"Thought I was," Titus answered after a moment's reflection. "Always had good luck when I went out hunting. Don't have a idea one why I've been off the mark last few days."

"Said you ain't seen any sign?"

"Not a thing. And that's strange too."

"Only two things my pappy told me would run game out of the woods," Kingsbury replied. "A storm coming, or Injuns."

For a moment Titus studied the sky downriver to the southwest. "Must be a storm coming, like you said. Can't believe it'd be Injuns."

"Sure it could be," Heman Ovatt commented as he clambered over to the side of the boat and unbuttoned his britches. "Injuns still thick as ever south side of the river. Every now and then you'll hear what they do, jumping boatmen coming back home up the Trace."

"The Trace?"

"Natchez Trace," Kingsbury explained. "We float down with the goods to Natchez or Nawlins, sell the empty boat too—and then we hire us a wagon back north to Natchez on the Mississap. From there on a man has to buy himself a horse to ride, or he walks."

"Walks all the way back where?"

Ovatt answered, "Clear up here to the Ohio country where he can put hisself out to work another trip that same year."

"Man can make two trips a year if he hurries back north on the Trace," Kingsbury added.

"Why don't you just float on back north?"

Ovatt snorted, grinning as he fastened his buttons and turned around to look at Bass. "Look out there at that water you pissed in not long ago. Which way it taking us?"

"Downriver."

"That's right," Ovatt replied. "Ain't no getting a flatboat back upriver less'n it's more work than it's worth."

"Some crews used to pull their boats back upriver from Nawlins," Kingsbury said. "Most sells their boats along with the freight."

"Man like Ebenezer Zane there can make him a tidy profit from this trip," Ovatt said. "Tell the boy what you paid for this boat, Eb."

The pilot called out, "Less'n a hundred dollars, Pennsylvania value. Listen, boys: let's move 'er more to the center of the channel."

"Up to Pittsburgh," Kingsbury said as he put his shoulders into the oar and Ovatt crawled forward to resume control of the bow rudder, "a flatboat like this'un costed Ebenezer a dollar and a half for each foot. Some hunnerd dollars, since't this boat's just a little longer'n sixty-some feet."

"And she'll sell for ten times that much we get on down to Norleans," Zane boasted. "Fifteen dollar a foot or more for the lumber. They hongry for good hardwood down there." He slapped his hand on the gunnel beside his rudder. "Close-grained poplar. None better, Titus Bass."

"Damn, but she's fogging up, Ebenezer!" Reuben Root growled from the port side of the craft.

"Soup gets up much more," Zane flung his voice the length of the boat, "get huffing on that horn, Heman."

For several minutes Titus watched the fog coagulate on the brown surface of the Ohio, obscuring most of the banks on either side. Growing more and more worried, he finally turned to peer back at the bushy-headed pilot. Wisps of fog-mist clung to the wild sprigs of Zane's hair as if it were smoldering. Ebenezer suddenly threw all his weight against his long-tailed rudder, giving the flatboat an ungainly lurch.

Frightened, Titus turned back around, peering forward, his face gone as pale as the grain of newly hewn oak. "H-how's he know where to point this boat?"

Kingsbury started to grin, concentrating his squint on the bow piercing the wisps of fog, as he replied, "Don't you worry, boy. Ebenezer Zane knows this river, and he can push through soup better'n most men. Feels his way."

"Feels . . . feels his way?"

"Watches for signs on the bank when he can see 'em, but mostly he keeps his eye on the water. Water out in the middle of the channel runs different than the water close to either of them banks. 'Sides," Kingsbury explained, "if he gets into real bad trouble, he'll call me to take over up there on the gouger for Ovatt."

"Gouger?"

"That front rudder," Hames explained, his jaw working hard. He was so skinny, his sagging jowls appeared ready to topple him. "He knows I'm about the best gouger on the river. Working together, Zane and me, we could turn this here sixty-foot boat around on a ha'penny 'thout no trouble we get in a real fix. And if Ebenezer don't feel good about making it down a certain stretch, then he'll sing out and we'll all put 'er to one shore or t'other."

The rain came into his face, gentle at first, but cold. Then as it began to lance down harder, the fog began to dissipate, clinging only in long, thick patches strung along either shoreline, puffed back among the trees and brush that huddled just above the water.

"Heave back, Ovatt!" Zane bellowed.

Heman raised his gouger out of the water and secured a loop of rope over the end of the rudder to secure it just above the surface of the river. Turning back to the other three boatmen, he grinned as he began to sing loudly.

"Some rows up,
but we rows down.
All the way to Shawnee town.
Pull away! Pull away now!"

For the answering chorus Zane, Root, and Kingsbury joined in: "Pull away! Pull away now!"

"Tomorrow you'll be in Louisville," Kingsbury explained as the other three went on singing their chantey in the pelting cold rain. He snugged his shapeless hat down on his head as Titus scooted closer to a stack of crates to escape most of the driving rain. "We'll get you your first taste of likker, Titus Bass. You ever drank afore?"

"Never," he answered, pulling his oiled leather jerkin up around his cold ears, wishing he had brought himself a warm hat. Perhaps one of those ones his mother knitted for her entire brood. "My pap always had likker around, and he drank it come a wedding or a funeral or a reason for all the menfolk to say serious words about something."

"Never just for the fun of it?"

He looked at Kingsbury as if he were crazed. "Why, no—I never saw a man take a drink of likker just for the fun of it."

"Allays had to be a reason?"

"Yep. An' he said I'd get my first drink when I was finished with my schooling and joined him on the farm."

"I see," Kingsbury replied. "Didn't finish your school neither, did you?"

"Nope."

"An' you sure as hell ain't joined him to work the farm, have you, now?"

"Nope."

"Way I see it, you ain't done nothing your pappy told you to do—so it don't make no sense to me for you to go drink the way your pappy told you to."

Inside him there was a sudden leap of freedom, almost like a fluttering of wings. "We gonna get us a drink of likker when we get to this here Louisville?"

"Get us *a* drink?" Kingsbury roared. "What do you say to that, Reuben?"

Root cried out, "We'll damn well drink that river town dry if they ain't careful. And we'll get our honey-daubers wet too!"

"Just for good measure!" Ovatt joined in.

"You boys don't go spending everything I give you to last the whole trip, now," Zane cautioned. "There's still a hell of a lot of river left after Louisville."

"Natchez!" Ovatt sang out wistfully. "Sweet, sweet Natchez!"

"Norlins is the place! By damned, I'll wait to have my spree come Norlins!" Root cried out exuberantly.

Kingsbury leaned forward, lowering his head toward the youth, both of his arms wrapped along the shaft of his oar. "You ever had you a woman, Titus Bass?"

"S-sure I have. Had me a special girl."

"An' you run off, leaving her behind?"

He gazed down at the deck slick with rain. "She wanted to get married up to me right off."

"But you had you other things to do, right?"

"S'pose you might say."

"Damn right, Titus Bass," Ebenezer Zane roared. "Lots of gals out there in the world, many of 'em ready to climb the hump of a likely young lad such as yourself."

"You had you that special gal of yours?" Kingsbury pursued.

His head bobbed. How eager he was to be a man among these men. "More'n once."

"Whoooeee!" Kingsbury exclaimed. "Then you're ready for a real man-thumpin' woman, Titus Bass!"

"I . . . I don't—"

"Not that young gal of your'n back where you run off from," Kingsbury interrupted. "We're talking about getting you a real, live, honest-to-goodness, fleshed-out woman who'll just love to take you under her arm and teach you all she can teach you."

"T-teach me?"

" 'Bout getting your stinger wet, Titus Bass," Zane added.

Kingsbury leaned forward and slapped the youngster on the shoulder. "I'll even put up the price of getting you diddled!"

Ovatt asked, "Before or after you get him drunk, Hames?"

"Before, during, or after! Don't make me no difference—Titus Bass here's the young'un gonna get his pecker stretched as long as a riverman's gouger! I figure I'll just pour some likker in him, and the boy here will tell me when he's damn good and ready to climb aboard a gal."

"Mathilda's house?" Zane asked.

Wide-eyed, Bass quickly turned back to look at Kingsbury.

Hames nodded and replied, "Mathilda's house, it is. Not a finer lick in all of Louisville."

"Lick?" Titus asked.

"A whiskey house men flock to," Kingsbury explained. "Just like the critters you hunt flock to a salt lick."

Then Bass inquired, "Who's Mathilda?"

Again it was Hames Kingsbury who explained, "It's her inn what has the sort to make any man happy, by damn!"

"That's right," Root said, a rare smile creasing his face. "Louisville's the last place on the river till a boatman gets down to Natchez or up to St. Lou."

"St. Lou?" Bass asked, remembering. "You ever go up there?"

As he looked from man to man, they all shrugged their shoulders. Then Ebenezer finally said, "None of us ever been upriver to St. Lou afore, boy. Place might be coming of age soon, what I hear. But for right now it ain't much of anything but Frenchies."

"Just like down to Norlins," Root added.

"Ain't nothing for us up to St. Lou," Kingsbury said. "We make fine money floating goods from Pittsburgh and Cincinnati downriver to Nawlins. St. Lou just filled with Injuns and them fellas trade with the Injuns for the furs. More of them all the time."

"Got all the Frenchies I ever wanna rub shoulders with down to Norleans," Zane declared. "I don't need to go looking for more up to St. Lou."

"Less'n it's the sort of gals come out of Madame Lafarge's," Kingsbury said.

The pilot grinned widely in that bushy, unkempt beard and nodded. "Them kind of Frenchies I can stand to rub on all the time!"

Turning back to Titus, Hames Kingsbury winked. "We'll get your pecker dipped in the honey-pot tomorrow at Louisville. An' downriver at Natchez—that's Ovatt's favorite place. Then we'll see about getting you up on top of a fine French gal down at Madame Lafarge's come we reach Nawlins."

"Titus Bass," Zane hurled his voice, "a stroke of real luck you running onto *this'r* boat of rivermen, it was."

"With us—by damn—you're gonna swaller your first likker," Kingsbury agreed with a smile. "An' go dip into your first real woman too!"

By the time Ebenezer Zane began shouting his orders for them to put in at the little harbor at the mouth of Bear Grass Creek the next afternoon, the eastern sky behind their backs had turned as gray as the slate lining the canyon of the upper Ohio, and the west ahead of them roiled with dark thunderheads, whipped to a froth by a wind that shoved the taste of a cold rain straight into their faces.

"Steady on that gouger!" the pilot ordered, watching the river, his two oarsmen, and Heman Ovatt struggling at that bow rudder.

"Get ready to bring her over!"

"Ready when you are, Ebenezer!" Ovatt bellowed.

From where he crouched out of the cold wind and coming mist, Titus watched less and less of the four rivermen as he turned his attention to the increasing signs of civilization they had been passing in the last few miles. Infrequent squatter farms had eventually given way to larger spreads until there were more and more lamps lit in the windows of cabins and shops as Ebenezer Zane eased them over to the Kentucky side of the Ohio.

While there were three other towns in the immediate area—Shippingsport in Kentucky, along with Jeffersonville and Clarksville across the river in Indiana Territory—Louisville had not only been the first river port, but from the start had remained the most successful, primarily due to the small harbor that lay at the mouth of the Bear Grass, which made for an ideal patch of calm water where boatmen would tie up and lay to before braving the Great Falls of the Ohio—just downriver from the town.

"Aport! Ho! Bring her hard to port!"

With the pilot's command Ovatt lunged against the small gouger, clutching it beneath his armpits, pushing the rudder toward the starboard side of the craft. At the same time Zane was performing the opposite maneuver with his larger, longer, deeper-plunging stern rudder. While the bow of the flatboat began to swing out toward the main channel of the river, the stern was already inching in toward the south shore as they cleared the northern boundary of the bay, a grassy, timbered fingertip of rocky land.

"Goddammit! She's cluttered up, Ebenezer!" Root bellowed his warning as they all got their first view of the crowded port.

"I can damn well see that!" Zane spat. "Loosen up on that gouger, Heman!"

As soon as Ovatt brought the rudder out of the water, the flatboat's bow eased back into line with the stern as Zane worked his rudder back and forth in long, sure, deep strokes. More than half a hundred flatboats already bobbed in the bay, tied up bow to stern all along the shore, every last one of them awash in the saffron light of at least one oil lantern as the rainy twilight flooded out of the western sky. On shore the wharf bustled as men shouted and barked their orders, hefting loads on and off the boats, clomping up and down the sagging gangplanks, laughing and cursing.

Beyond, on up the southern bank, lay the flickering yellowed diamond dots of Louisville. Titus hadn't seen this many people in one place at one time since last summer's Longhunters Fair—likely not since his family's last trip to Cincinnati.

"Hames, you and Reuben give me some drag!"

At the steersman's order both Kingsbury and Root dipped their oars into the murky Ohio and braced their legs in the bottom of the boat as they sought to slow the flatboat's speed. The river tugged, shoved, popped its might at the oarsmen, both of them grunting, huffing, hunching over their work as their voices blended with the loud creak of wood and iron strained to the limit at both gunnels.

"Likely we can put to on the far side of the harbor," Kingsbury advised, his words no more than a growl as he fought to hold his oar deep in the moving water.

"Figure you're right," Zane replied. "Heman! Swing her about and take her across to yonder side!"

Once more Ovatt plunged his gouger into the water, bringing the bow out more in line with the main current of the Ohio as the pilot sweated in concert with him, together keeping the flatboat all but on a dead reckoning for the far side of the Bear Grass harbor.

"Dig in, boys!" Zane reminded his oarsmen. "More drag! More drag! Mind you, I've never landed over here, so we don't know what we got in store for us."

In the fading light Titus found himself growing more scared as the broadhorn rushed on across the mouth of the harbor toward the south side.

There the number of flatboats thinned out and dwindled down to nothing as the lights of Louisville lumbered past on their left, then winked out of sight behind them.

Bass inched around to ask of Kingsbury, barely above a whisper, "What happens we don't land here?"

"Ain't no *don't,* boy. We gotta land here. We don't—we'll face the Great Falls of the Ohio in the dark."

A shudder ran down his spine. "In the dark?"

"And a man might just as well put a pistol to his own head as head down them chutes at night, with this wet weather blowing into our teeth way it is. You know how to pray—you might wanna give Ebenezer a hand."

"He p-praying?" Bass asked, feeling himself go weak inside. He'd never been on rough water, much less any falls.

"Hell no, he ain't prayin'!" Kingsbury replied with a grimace as the oar just about dislodged him where he had his legs braced between some kegs of nails. "Ebenezer's too damn busy saving this boat—"

"Hard to port, Heman! Put everything you got into it!"

"She's fighting me, Ebenezer!"

"Stand on it!" Zane commanded. "Don't let 'er throw you off!" Then he flung his voice down at the youngster. "Titus Bass! Crawl up outta there and lay on that gouger with Heman!"

He started to rise slowly, cautiously, frightened.

"We need you up there right now, Titus," Kingsbury urged.

"That boy ain't gonna do us no good!" Root snarled.

"He will too," the pilot snapped, fighting his rudder. "Get up there now, Titus—and help us get this goddamned Kentuckyboat landed."

Clawing his way around barrels and over crates, Titus eventually slid down onto the slippery deck in what foot room there was standing opposite Heman Ovatt.

"Lay on it!" the gouger ordered.

Bass hurled himself onto the short shaft of the rudder, face-to-face with Ovatt.

"You don't weigh much, do you?" Ovatt grunted.

"My mam . . . she always trying to fatten me up. Said . . . I had me no tallow. Only b-bone and gristle."

"Push! Or pull, Titus Bass!"

Zane hollered above the cry of the wind and the hammer of the rain, "We're doing it, boys!"

Titus didn't allow himself a look right then, able only to feel the lurch and bob of the flatboat's bottom as it passed out of the river's main channel, heaving over toward the calmer water near the Ohio's south shore. By now the mist had become a steady rain, cold as springwater running down the back of his shirt and jerkin.

"Bring 'er over hard, Heman. Bring it over, Titus Bass!" Zane cried out. "Reuben, bring your oar out and get this'r stern line ready."

In less time than it takes to tell, Root had pulled his oar from the hammered surface of the brown water and slid back to the rear of the craft, where he laid a loop of thick oiled hemp over one shoulder.

"There's some likely stumps up ahead, Ebenezer," Reuben suggested. "They been clearing more and more land."

"I'll bring you over and you snag a likely one," the pilot advised with a grunt.

As Zane brought the slowing flatboat side-sliding to the shore, Root bent and lunged toward the bank in a smooth, practiced motion. He landed on the shiny grass, his moccasins slipping on the mud. He went to his knees but was up in a fluid motion, ripping the coil of rope from his shoulder to fling a great loop of it around the stump of a long-ago girdled tree.

"Tie 'er off stout, Reuben!" Zane advised as the flatboat began to ease on past the stump where Root stood knotting the length of hemp as thick as a man's four fingers.

At the first straining creak of the stretching rope, it proved certain the huge, oiled knot was going to hold, bringing the stern of the craft closer to the shore as it bobbed on down the bank.

"Bring it about, Heman! Show the boy what to do!"

"Push, goddammit!" Ovatt commanded. "Now's the time to push!"

Together they plunged the gouger deeper into the water speckled with icy, hammering rain. Beneath him Titus could feel the bow of the boat beginning to sweep around, held firm astern by the one line to their rear, the front of the craft being nudged over by the strong muscle of the river's current against the gouger and the two men who clung to her.

"Hames! Take the bowline ashore!"

Against the steady drumming of the rain atop flat oaken kegs and barrels, against the hardwood crates, he heard Kingsbury grunting up behind him with his burden, listened as the boatman dragged the rope across the top of their cargo, heard him land in the sodden mud onshore. Kingsbury flung a loop once around a second tree stump, and working in concert with the two men straining at the gouger, he steadily took up the slack in the rope, easing the bow into the shore.

"Tie 'er off," Zane commanded, stepping away from his rudder pole for the first time in those long, anxious minutes. He twisted from side to side, working a kink out of his back, then tugged down the brim of his shapeless hat before disappearing beneath the awning.

"You can let go now," Ovatt said.

Only then did Titus realize he still had a deathlike grip on the gouger pole. It took him a moment before he could get his cramped fingers to obey his wishes. When they finally came off, he flexed them.

"C'mon, fellas," Zane called out, reappearing from the awning. He scooted to the left side of the craft and heaved himself down into the mud.

Ovatt was next, while Bass was the last to land. His legs felt unsteady beneath him at first, what with struggling to keep his balance on the bobbing, weaving flatboat.

Ebenezer Zane was beside him, grabbing his shoulder, helping him straighten there on the shore. "C'mon, boy. I owe you a drink. This Titus Bass did fine, did he not, Heman?"

"He did better'n fine, Ebenezer. He did a man's work this afternoon."

Zane pounded him on the back. "Then a man's drink it is for Titus Bass."

"At the Kangaroo?" Kingsbury asked.

"Hell, yes," Zane replied. "There is no better place where we could celebrate this boy's passage to manhood in Louisville."

Twenty families accompanying George Rogers Clark on one of his many forays in the Old Northwest during the Revolutionary War had first settled in the area in 1778. Until Thomas Jefferson purchased the Louisiana Territory from Napoleon Bonaparte, Louisville officially served as the young country's western port of entry, with headquarters for a single U.S. customs agent. Now some thirty-two years later the town boasted a population of at least five hundred, and growing. Besides the grogshops, alehouses, and inns frequented by the rivermen, there were a score of more respectable hotels and restaurants, as well as two long blocks of shops and stores of all description. The town even boasted its own theater, recently built in 1808, establishing what the Louisville *Gazette* called a true home for "the golden era of Drama in the West," where theater patrons had "created a high standard of taste and judgment."

But try as Louisville's respectable citizens might, it was still the river that had created the town, and it was the river from which Louisville drew its sustenance. Here, close to two out of three men in one way or another owed their livelihood to the Ohio flatboat trade. All along the wharf surrounding the harbor pulsed the bustling commerce of boat building and repair, the riverbank crowded with wagon masters loading goods for their trek inland to the heart of Kentucky, from dawn till dark throbbing with the jostle and shove of draymen and hired lackeys.

Louisville was just about the most exciting place Titus had been in his life. All he had ever dreamed of already, and he hadn't yet moved a step from Ebenezer Zane's flatboat.

"The ever-loving Kangaroo!" Hames Kingsbury sang out prayerfully as they pushed on up the soggy bank. "God, but I hope to lay eyes on sweet Mathilda."

To which Zane exclaimed, "That ain't all you want to lay on her, I'll wager!"

All five of them belly-laughed as they strode through the mud into the splotches of hissing torchlight fronting the infamous low-roofed Kangaroo Tavern. Titus stumbled into something, leaping over it as he peered down at the ground.

"You'll have to watch where you're walking," Ovatt advised, "there's more of 'em." He pointed out the half-dozen or more bodies sprawled here and there among the mud puddles shimmering in the torchlight dancing on the breeze outside the tippling house.

A crude door blew open and out poured three men, two of whom had a secure hold on the third. A burst of noise, squeals of womankind, and sharp gusts of cruel laughter rolled out in their wake. Intent on their business, the two shoved their way right through the boatmen, stopped, and heaved the one between them into the night. Bass watched the man hurtle a good ten feet through the air until he landed facedown in the rutted muddy lane, where he struggled to rise on all fours at first, then gave up and sank back into the mire.

"Such'll teach you: don't never get yourself thrown out, Titus Bass," Zane warned with a wag of his finger.

The other three rivermen laughed as Titus's eyes followed that pair of monstrous, stoop-shouldered bouncers back into the Kangaroo.

"Maybe there's 'nother place—"

Heman Ovatt snatched him by the arm, Kingsbury securing the other as they set him in motion between them, all four laughing.

"There ain't 'nother place holds a candle to the likes of the Kangaroo!" Hames cried as they passed beneath two wavering, spitting torches and plunged into the tavern's raucous, smoky depths.

"Man overboard!"

Titus whirled at the frantic cry of alarm, finding a disheveled riverman perched high atop the huge stone mantel fronting the fireplace, weaving for a moment before he flung himself out into the crowd with abandon. A half-dozen others caught him, some grumbling their curses, many laughing, a few splashing ale on his head as they lowered him to the soppy floor below. There on his belly he thrashed with his legs and stroked with his arms disjointedly as if swimming, worming his way across the floor's mud and muck in good fashion as more and more of the drinkers continued to splatter ale on the swimmer.

Titus found the noise almost ear shattering, unable to make out a single voice in the mad, raucous cacophony—

"Man overboard!"

Another cried out, causing Bass to whirl and look as he was swept along with his crew. This caller as well flung himself out from the wall into the crowd, which broke his fall, then dropped him without ceremony onto the muddy puncheon floor. But like a great beached carp, this one flopped over on his back and began to mimic something of a crude backstroke. Keeping his mouth open for the most part, the swimmer gaped like a fish as he inched himself along in that worming backstroke, swallowing most every drop of that ale bystanders sloshed upon him from above. Titus watched until the swimmer, his front completely soaked, disappeared among the tangle of legs in the milling throng.

"Three Monongahela rye for these fine boatmen," Zane was ordering as Titus clattered to a halt within their fold, the pilot immediately drawing Bass to his side as he held up two fingers on the other hand, "and a spruce beer for me and my young friend here."

Three men worked the bar, tapping kegs of ale with great bung starters and mallets, pouring out mugs of the Ohio River's most famous rye. With a clatter and a slosh their five pewter mugs appeared before them. As the other four all grabbed for theirs, Ebenezer Zane took his in hand and picked up the last, unclaimed mug.

"Here, Titus Bass. I figure you ought'n go slow—this being your first night's carouse as a man. That pissant rye these boys love to swill takes some getting used to. Me? I prefer my ale, with a foamy head or no. Potato squeezings or spruce drippings—it's all the same to me. Drink up, lad!"

Titus watched the pilot throw back his chin and take a long and mighty draft, his hen-egg-sized Adam's apple bobbing up and down between those muscular cords in his neck that throbbed beneath his thick beard.

Taking the mug from his lips, Zane dragged a forearm across his hairy face and whirled on the barman. "Another of that fine ale, my good man!"

When he had his second and had turned back to his crew, the pilot leaned in to Titus, saying, "Now it's your turn. Drink the first one fast like I, boy. And the second you can savor the taste."

"Swaller? Swaller it all . . . like you done—"

"Just like I done."

"G'won, Titus Bass," Kingsbury prodded as the other three boatmen crowded close, faces gaping apishly.

He figured it would be nothing much to fit his belly around that mug of ale—just a matter of swallowing until he had drained it all. With the first sip he found it not unpleasant, a woodsy taste to it, some effervescent tickling his tongue. Then he was swallowing in good order, barely aware of the boatmen around him chanting their encouragement as he tipped the bottom of his mug up higher and higher. From the corner of his eye he watched them cheer him on, hoisting their own mugs in waving salute until there was no more for him to drink.

"What'd you think of that?" Heman Ovatt asked with a slap to the back of his shoulders.

"Yes, you li'l river rat—what'd you think of that?"

At the sudden, strange, and very female voice, he whipped around to find a skinny woman sliding herself into their group, picking up Kingsbury's arm to drape it over her shoulder.

"Ah, Mincemeat," Kingsbury cried out, his eyes come alive with an inner fire as he seized one of her ample and half-exposed breasts in a huge hand, then clamped her jaw in the other, holding her prisoner while pressing his mouth on hers.

"I'm next, I'm next!" Ovatt cried, standing right there to press himself against the woman when Kingsbury drew back to take a breath and another swallow of his rye.

"An' how 'bout you, Ebenezer Zane? You want your welcome kiss too?" she asked when Ovatt had finished kissing her.

Still aghast at the woman's sudden appearance, how she allowed the men to hungrily fondle and kiss her, Titus stood there dumbfounded, his eyes muling as he watched Ovatt reach up to fondle the flesh across the tops of her rounded breasts, exposed as they were all the way down to just above her nipples, pushed up to their full extent by the bodice she had laced beneath them. Skinny as she was, they were about as big a pair as any breasts Bass had seen.

At that moment it grew warm in the Kangaroo. He became discomforted inside, gazing as he was at her pale, mottled flesh there in the murky, smoky lamplight.

"Thankee anyway, my sweetness. Mathilda working tonight?" Kingsbury asked as he brought his head up from kissing the woman's cleavage.

"Ain't she working ever' night?" the woman asked in reply, her full eyes coming to rest on Titus. "After all, she owns this place where you pigs come to rut, don't she?"

"Any new girls?" Reuben finally spoke up before he drank at his rye.

"Nary a one," she replied. "Mathilda had a signed writ on three more new ones to come downriver from Pitts—but a feller down Natchez way made 'em a better offer."

"Bet that made Mathilda a wild one!" Zane declared.

"Wild? You bet. None of us could live with her for a week after that," she explained. "Then she up and sent a writ back to Cincinnati for what new girls she could get to come down on the next boat."

"When'll that be?" Root asked.

She turned to him slowly, her distaste for the man plain as paint on her face. "Be a long time."

"What?" Root complained. "There's boats like ours coming down all the time—"

She snorted as she took hold of Ovatt's mug, saying, "Not boats hauling people cargo."

As she tossed back some of his rye, Ovatt said, "Settlers going downriver—we see 'em all the time."

"Not the same as a bunch of women, now, is it, you mud rat?" she snarled at Heman, her eyes flicking back to the youngster. "Not many wanna take up valuable cargo space with whores, now, do they?"

"Think Mathilda be happy to see me?" Kingsbury asked as he snugged her tighter against his hip.

One side of her chemise slipped off a bony shoulder, exposing just a bit more of one breast. Yet she did not take her eyes off Titus. "She'll be happy to see you. Seeing that you're one of the few don't punch her so she's gotta throw you out. One of you pig rutters gonna tell me who's this skinny river rat you dragged in with you?"

"This'un?" Zane replied, slinging his weighty arm over Bass's skinny shoulder. "Why, this be our new hand. Joined up couple days back on the river. Kentucky side of the river, that is. Like me, the lad's a Kentucky man: southwest of Cincinnati—where you say them new girls be coming from."

"What's your name, boy?"

He licked his lips and looked away from her face. "B-bass."

"What's your christened name?"

For a moment that stumped him.

"His name is Titus," Ebenezer answered for him.

With a bob of his warm head he echoed, "Titus Bass." Immediately he turned to Zane to ask, "Can I get another?"

"Like that, eh?"

Bass agreed, glad to tear his eyes from the roundness and cleavage of the woman's flesh. "Tasted real good. Makes a fella thirsty for another." His head felt warm, the skin on his face burning too.

And he felt warm low in his belly when his eyes yanked back to look at her.

"S'pose you go find Mathilda for me?" Kingsbury asked. "You do that, Mincemeat?"

A loud voice suddenly called out, "You staying with them, Mincemeat?"

The five of them and the woman all turned to look at the table where a trio of men hard at their cups motioned her back over their way.

"I'm staying here, Briggs."

A second man grumbled sourly, "You was here with us first."

Zane slid in front of the woman protectively. "The lady said she was staying with us. There's plenty others here for the likes of you."

"The likes of me?" the third one of the trio cried out like a branded mule. "You're a fine one—"

Then the woman shoved back in front of Zane, holding her arms out between the two of them. "Briggs, you and the rest ain't never met this'un before, have you? If you had, I figger you'd know better. He's a real snapping turtle—"

"Don't look all that mean to me," Briggs snorted. "Kinda old, ain'cha?"

"Shuddup, Briggs," she snarled, slapping a hand against his chest, causing his two companions to guffaw. "Makes no matter, 'cause I'm sure you heard of him somewheres on the river anyway. Eb—this here's Nathaniel Briggs. Briggs, this here's Ebenezer Zane."

The stranger's eyes went wide as his mouth stammered, "Eb . . . Ebenezer Zane, is it?" The color drained from Briggs's face as he repeated the name.

"Then I wasn't wrong: you heard of this here half snapping turtle, half earth trembles, I take it?" Mincemeat asked. "Learn't what happened last time he tied up here in Louisville."

"Some talk of it," Briggs said, his voice quieter as a few others around them at the crude bar squeezed in closer. "Last summer, wasn't it?"

"I don't aim to have no trouble here." Zane clasped an arm around the woman's waiflike waist.

"Naw," Briggs replied with a quick wag of his head. "Just like Mincemeat said, there's other girls hereabouts."

Titus watched the riverman turn and urge the other two off into the crowd. Then Bass shouldered his way back into that group, anxiously asking, "What happened last summer to you what made them three back away?"

Zane bent over and whispered into the woman's ear. Titus saw the tired expression on her face change to something a bit more animated as she brought her eyes to rest on Bass.

The pilot straightened to say, "I'll tell you about it some other time, Titus Bass. But right now—we've got beer to drink, and Mincemeat here has agreed to be your friend for the night."

She patted the wide, colorful sash the pilot had knotted around his waist. "Just as long as it's money what's good for a girl to spend here in Louisville."

"Since when you become particular what you get in trade?" Ebenezer asked. "Guineas, pistoles, or shillings. Even hard American dollars—"

"What you're to pay me with this trip down, Ebenezer Zane?"

"Coin," Zane boasted. "American and English too. Hard money you can spend anywhere." He whipped back around to the bar, where he slammed down his pewter mug. "Barman! Another beer for my friend and me." Then, twisting to look at the woman, he asked, "What you drinking, Mincemeat?"

She eyed the youngster and said, "I'll have what it is Titus Bass is having himself."

"Another beer, good man!" Zane ordered.

At the same time the woman slid out from under the pilot's arm and pressed her hip against Titus's groin, threading an arm around his waist, rubbing her cheek right up against his so that he could smell her breath. Already she had likely drunk her fill of Monongahela rye. He found her face pocked with the ravages of some past pox, her cheeks flushed as she pulled back from his face and peered up into his wondering green eyes. With her skinny fingers Mincemeat stroked first one of his cheeks, then the other.

"Been a long, long time—it has," she said huskily to the rest of them, pressing her hip into his groin all the more insistently. "A goddamned long time since't I last had me a peach-cheeked boy like this'un!"

EIGHT

When she took his hardening flesh in her hands and began to stroke her fingers lightly up and down the length of him, Titus didn't know whether he was going to laugh out of sheer unabashed joy, or cry from the bliss he felt flooding over his entire body.

This was more than the feeling he had experienced with Amy, twice even. But instead of the nerve-jolting joy lasting but a few seconds at most while he exploded, this woman prolonged his eruption to the point Titus became certain he was enjoying more pleasure than any one man could endure.

"Why you called Mincemeat?" he had asked her when she'd first led him back to her tiny, cramped shanty across the muddy rear yard behind the Kangaroo, where she, like the rest of the bar help, was given a crude bed frame of saplings and rope, a musty tick filled with moldy grass, a chamber pot, and a small sheet-iron chimney beneath which she could build a cooking fire. It was the only thing that could chase the damp, bone-numbing chill from the room.

At least that's what Titus thought until the skinny woman

rose from striking sparks to kindling in that rock-lined fire pit and came back to the tall, gangly youth—intent on starting a fire in him.

"It just a name what don't mean nothing," she answered as she peeled off his oiled jerkin, then gazed up at his eyes smokily.

God, how thirsty he was, his tongue thick and pasty. He asked, "You got any more of that ale left you?"

"Little bit," she said, reaching across the narrow crib for the small table where sat her mug. "You can finish it off, sweet boy."

My, but it still tasted good, although some of the sparkle and bite on his tongue had diminished. The spruce beer Ebenezer had started him out on still had that earthy body to it as he let it wash back against his tonsils, just the way he saw so many of the others in the Kangaroo do throughout that evening and into the long night. After a while he had stopped counting how many mugs Ebenezer and the others bought for him, and now he couldn't even remember what the tally was when he had stopped caring. For so long there it had seemed like the thing for a man to do—to know how many he had put under his belt—what with this being his first drunk.

She had stayed beside him all that evening, even when they'd moved from the tavern, through the low-beamed entry into the dining hall, passing men who sat on crude benches at long tables where they clattered their mugs down to get the attention of at least one of the maids busy balancing steaming platters and trenchers and even more pitchers of ale from the kitchen fireplaces at the rear of the room where a half-dozen old women and men tended the fires and the food. The venison and pork, along with heaping helpings of potatoes and corn, took the edge off his lightheadedness, yet not so much that he wasn't anxious to head back into the tavern once all of them were bloated with solid food.

The rest of the night proved all the more raucous as he grew warmer, his forehead and the end of his nose more and more benumbed as time seemed to slither by without notice, and people with it. After the longest time now he suddenly remembered the boat crew and took the mug from his lips, turning slowly around so he wouldn't topple over as he slurred at her.

"Where they go?"

"Who?"

"Ebenezer and the rest."

"They got their own places to be tonight," she replied, back at the tiny fireplace, where she laid more of the kindling on the first licks of flame. It was finally beginning to drive the chill from the narrow room constructed of chinked logs, a low, sloping roof overhead of oiled canvas on which saplings had been laid, then brush, followed by a thin layer of sod to turn out the heavy rains and wet snows that battered the Ohio country three seasons out of the year.

He gazed down into the mug, saw there wasn't much left. He swilled it back, then leaned forward to plunk the mug back upon the table. That made his head swim and he felt mushy in the knees, as if he might go down. As heavy as his eyelids were, Titus struggled to prop them open as he tried to figure just what to do, weaving slightly on that spot where he was rooted for the moment.

Then he lunged forward with one step. From the corner of his eye he saw her turn slightly, saw her cheeks flushed with the warmth of the fire she was tending; then he kept on trudging flat-footed toward the bed near the fireplace. Banging into it with a shin, he grunted more in surprise than in pain and clumsily wheeled about, causing his mind to swim in a great, sweeping wave as if it were unhinged and adrift, rocking back and forth within his skull. Like a tow sack filled with rocks, he collapsed back onto the bed, let out a sigh, and sank backward across the rumpled quilts and wool blankets.

"Lift your foot up," she told him. "Best we take off these here moccasins afore your feet get froze."

After she flung them over to the pounded clay floor by the fire, the woman kicked one leg over him so she could straddle him. He stared up at her face, trying so hard to focus, just to keep his eyes open. He groaned from the effort it was taking, sleep calling him more fervently now.

"You ain't gonna get sick, is you?" she asked. "You get sick—you'll be cleaning your own mess up."

He tried smiling at her to let her know he wouldn't as his eyelids grew too heavy to fight them any longer. Not sick. Just sleepy.

She was tugging on the long tail of his shirt, yanking to get it out of his leather britches. He felt himself giggling softly. So damned warm, inside and out.

Titus did not know how long he had been asleep, but he was sure he had been. Time had passed. He knew this feeling, coming awake slowly, drifting down in the warm immersion of that land between sleep and wakefulness. He giggled again, not really sure if he made a sound with it, or just laughed within.

Then he groaned. And remembered groaning for the last few minutes, sensing the rise of pleasure. He felt his breathing grow shallow, increasingly rapid as the fixed, physical joy intensified, warmth radiating from his groin.

Slowly he opened his eyes, hoping to discover just what was overcoming him when he found her hands working over his rigid flesh.

The woman had it standing up straight as a poplar volunteer bursting from the ground, about as hard as one of those hickory wiping sticks Amy Whistler's pap kept curing in that trough all the time. And just as he worked a pumice stone up and down a new wiping rod he was making for his own rifle, the woman kneaded her hands up and down his hardened flesh, making it almost too hot to be comfortable.

Groaning again, he closed his eyes, not wanting to wake up and find out that this feeling was nothing more than one of those dreams he used to have back in that darkened sleeping loft outside the tiny hamlet of Rabbit Hash. Such pleasure simply could not last this long. This exquisite torture hadn't lasted anywhere near this long with Amy—none of the times at the swimming hole or in the woods when he had decided it didn't matter anymore and he no longer gave a damn, he was going to have her body whenever he wanted.

This time when he opened his eyes halfway, she looked up and found him watching her.

"It don't matter you gone and got yourself drunk."

"I'm drunk?"

"Had yourself a man-sized snootful this night, I'll tell you," she declared. "But Mincemeat's real glad you ain't had you so much she cain't get your pizzer hard for our fun."

"Our . . . our fun."

He looked up from the tops of her breasts in that bulging chemise to find her eyes burning into his.

"You wanna touch 'em?" she asked, her whole face alive with a knowing smile.

"Touch 'em?" he asked in reply, then brought a wobbly hand up.

But as he did, she reached up and yanked down the front of her chemise. Both breasts spilled out over the top of the chemise and the leather bodice she had laced around her midsection. He was startled at the size and shape of them, larger than any he had seen before. Hell, he had only seen Amy's, and only then in moonlight at best. Hers had been smaller, hard and firm. But these—as he brushed his fingers across the flesh of one—were soft, pliant, and seemed to have a strange and direct effect on just how he felt down there where she continued to rub him.

She inched back, withdrawing the breasts just beyond his reach, saying, "Tell me if'n you like this."

Once she laid his hot flesh within her cleavage, she used both her hands to press her breasts inward, encircling him as she began to rock back and forth on him, moving slightly up and down as she squeezed and released her breasts against him while keeping her eyes locked on his.

"Don't you worry 'bout nothing," she cooed. "I can tell just from looking at you when you're 'bout ready to toot. An' I won't let you toot till I'm good and ready for you to do just that."

His mouth had gone dry again, so dry. Rolling his drumming head to the side slowly, he spotted the mug on the table. Then remembered he had drained it. There had to be something else hereabouts for him . . . but in another heartbeat Titus's thoughts no longer dwelled on his thirst.

He felt her shift her weight atop him, taking her breasts from his flesh as she went to her feet beside the bed. There she yanked furiously at the oiled-leather whang that lashed the bodice beneath her breasts. After pulling it and the rumpled chemise over her head, she tugged at her belt and shimmied out of her long skirt, skipping out of the long, quilted pantaloons at the same time, while he stared hypnotically, captivated by the sway and bobble of her heavy breasts.

By the time she had placed one knee back on the low bed, he had rolled to the side and reached out for her, locking her shoulders in his hands, flinging her down to roll atop her.

"Think you know what you're doing, do you, young river rat?" she murmured.

He was rocking back slightly to plant himself when she took him in her hand and drove him against her.

"Right there," she groaned. "Gimme all what you got for Mincemeat— right there, now, li'l river rat."

He wanted to stop and tell her he wasn't a river rat. He wasn't a man who worked the Ohio like the others. He was just a runaway farm boy wanting something different. Something more. But Titus didn't stop, and he couldn't make the words come out of his mouth, what with all the whimpering he heard himself making as he worked himself in and out of her growing wetness that clung to him all the more with every thrust.

It had never lasted so long—not this high-pitched ringing in his ears as he clawed up toward the pinnacle, expecting to explode any moment as he fought his way upward. With Amy it had been so earth-shattering the first time, so violently short the next times—none had lasted like this.

He thought he could feel her raking her chipped and battered nails along his back, digging furrows along the straps of muscle as he hammered harder still. Sensing the woman's ankles lock behind his buttocks as she throbbed back into him with every one of his strokes. For just a moment he gazed down at her face, finding her eyes become catlike slits, the tip of her pink tongue just peeking between her browned teeth. Lower still he noticed that the firelight glistened on her neck, some strands of hair plastered against her damp skin. Dewdrops of sweat stood out like clusters of diamonds on her soft breasts, the shape of those mounds changed somewhat—perhaps flatter now—as she lay on her back, moving against him.

In that next moment those flickering droplets he watched seemed to explode into a million fragments of whirling, shattered particles of light. Shooting stars was all he thought of as the first explosion rocked him to the core. His hips drove forward to plant himself ever deeper within her center. As he slowed over her with the succeeding thrusts, Titus could feel her shudder beneath him at last, her chin arched back as her hips continued to grind upward against him.

With one last quiver he was finished, and he looked down at her, feeling an immense weight suddenly piercing his head from temple to temple. His body relaxed from the center outward, an inch at a time as he sagged upon her. Sensing the sharp angularity of her hips against his, the boniness to her rib cage beneath those breasts where her breathing eventually slowed like his, he slowly let go.

So tired was he that he thought he could rest his head in the crook of her shoulder for just a little while. Feeling his nakedness all the way down to the soles of his feet. Later he could drag his clothes back on and wander back to the tavern to look up the rest of the boat crew. Have some more of that beer.

And—mayhaps if he was lucky enough—Titus would talk this woman into bringing him back here to her bed one more time before he had to join Ebenezer Zane and the rest in pitting themselves against the Great Falls of the Ohio.

It all sounded good enough to be a dream.

His tongue felt like he had dragged it all the way up the trunk of a black walnut tree, tasted like he'd used it to clean out the stall muck caked within all four of the plow mule's iron shoes.

Thirsty, Titus thought of getting his hands on more of that spruce beer . . . but that only made his head throb all the more. Slowly becoming aware of the pressure on his shoulder, he opened his eyes and looked down —finding her sleeping against him. The fire in the corner pit had all but died out.

Been asleep at least that long, he thought. And the tiny Betty lamp on the small table flickered low, its wick floating in oil the only light in that tiny room.

The arm she laid her head upon had gone to sleep, filled with painful pinpricks: he knew he had to move it. Inch by inch Titus dragged himself from beneath her, then slipped out from beneath the rumpled blankets she had pulled over them both—spilling onto the clay floor. Landing on his knees and one hand beside the bed, his head thumping like wind-driven waves slapping against the hull of Zane's flatboat, Titus tried to remember some shred of what had happened since swallowing that first spruce beer. There was a piece of the night here, and there.

When he cocked his head around to see for sure, finding the length of her bare thigh and a portion of one naked breast peeking from beneath the greasy blanket—he was sure he had humped her. No . . . maybe she had humped him.

That would've been a first, he started to snort, yet it made not just his head, but his whole body, hurt. Then he recalled a pale vision of sitting with the four carousing boatmen in that stinking, noisy tippling house, their table wet from spilled ale and rye. Two more women were there, one bouncing animatedly atop Ovatt's lap, and the other laughing as she stood directly behind Kingsbury, her partially exposed breasts secured on either side of his head like a wool muffler while he fondled her flesh and she rubbed his belly. She was a big one, that woman, and older than the others who plied their trade in the Kangaroo.

A voice or two came clear as he dragged his knees up and slowly squatted beside the bed. Titus remembered how the others had poked their fun at him while the skinny woman ran her hands over him, exploring more and more boldly as the night got older and older, kissing on his neck, pushing his curly brown hair back from his ear to breathe huskily in it— tickling, teasing, taunting him until he figured he just couldn't take it no more and stumbled back here with her.

Now she was snoring lightly. And when he looked at her face, he recalled how Kingsbury, Ovatt, and especially Zane had all winked at him again and again throughout the evening, as if they were privy to something he had yet to learn.

Maybe he would eventually find out why she was called Mincemeat.

From the disheveled end of the bed he carefully yanked one of the striped wool blankets so he wouldn't disturb her, then draped it over his bare shoulders with a shudder. Scooting along on his knees, his head sagging heavy as a chunk of rain-soaked granite between his shoulders, Titus inched over to the table and peered down into the small tin where floated a feeble stump of wick in what his nose told him was bacon grease. It saturated the tiny room with the rank odor of cooking pork. What with supper last night, and all those meals the crew ate on the river—so much pig meat he sensed his stomach revolting, about to heave at the stench.

He dragged himself away, gasping for breath to keep from losing his stomach on the floor, sliding on his bare legs over to the fire pit beneath that sheet-iron chimney, and blew on the coals. Finding plenty of life in them, Titus began to lay bark chips and slivers of kindling on the glowing embers until he had a warming fire stoked once again. It did not take long for it to knock the chill from the log-and-chink lean-to constructed at the back of Mathilda's alehouse and road inn.

In the corner sat a short three-legged stool supporting a copper kettle. What caught his eye was the handle of an iron ladle poking over the lip of the kettle. Ladling out some of the liquid in the kettle, he took a cautious sniff. Water. He drank his fill, dipper after dipper, nearly emptying the kettle before he got himself sated. His mouth was no longer so dry, but his eyes still hurt with a hot, gritty pain. Maybeso he could sleep some more now that he had taken care of his thirst.

But then he was reminded of the immense pressure in his groin. In searching under the low bed he found a copper chamber pot and dragged it over to a far corner. With his back to the bed and the fire, he pulled the blanket apart, rose upon his knees, and relieved himself. From a wooden bucket with a rope handle he took a handful of red cedar shavings and tossed them into the chamber pot so the small, closed room would not reek so badly with the stench of his urine.

That business seen to, Titus kneed his way across the pounded clay floor, reaching the side of the bed, where he crawled back under a second wool blanket. He had no more got himself settled and let out a contented sigh than he jerked in surprise, feeling her hand tickle across the flat of his belly, her fingers descending to encircle his limp flesh. Startled, he lay there, partly frightened, partly hypnotized with sensing his flesh grow and harden as quickly as it did.

"You be a good boy now and give me another one of your rides, river rat."

"M-my name's Titus," he said cautiously. "Told you last night I wasn't no riverman like the rest of them. Don't you go and call me a river rat."

"Awright, Titus," she purred, sliding her body up against his once more. "You're just a boy long, long way from home, ain't you?"

"Ain't no boy."

"Awright," she agreed. "So tell me where you're headed."

"Always aimed to make it here to Louisville."

She kept on kneading him, saying, "Ain't all that much work round here. Might find work for the army down there to Fort Knox."

"Don't know what I'll do," he replied, one of his hands moving as if on its own accord to find her thigh, climbing to stroke the curve of her buttock. It felt good beneath his touch. Almost immediately he grew curious about her breasts. Dragging the blanket back from her shoulder, Titus looked down at them.

"Go 'head. Kiss 'em," she said in a husky whisper. "They want you to kiss 'em, Titus."

Not at all sure how it should be done, he planted a chaste peck on each one.

"No," she instructed, reaching up with her free hand to force his head down onto a breast. "Open your mouth. Lick 'em. Suck on 'em too. That's the way you can make 'em feel good."

Obediently, he did as she asked. Finding that not only did she respond with a growing murmur in the back of her throat, but he found himself becoming inflamed with hunger the more he fondled, kissed, sucked, and licked on her. And through it all she pressed his face down into that pliant fleshiness of her.

"Don't be selfish, now, Titus," she finally said. "The other'n wants some attention too."

He let her shove his face over to the other breast, where he continued his enjoyment of her damp skin. While he was, there came a couple of times when he thought he just might explode, so fiery was the stimulation she was giving him between his legs. Then he put his head between her breasts, licking down, down, down to her belly.

As she arched her back, he continued to kiss back and forth across her flat, smooth belly, from one sharp hipbone, licking the groin to the other hip.

"Do this," she said huskily, taking one of his hands now and pushing it down upon the soft hairiness of her thigh. Moving it up and down twice in a heated flurry, the woman finally positioned his fingers on the inside of her leg.

"C'mon up with your hand to where you'll find me getting wet."

"W-wet?" he asked, more than a little concerned. Perhaps there was something wrong—maybe even her getting her monthly visit like Amy finally did. Scared that maybeso what he was doing was making the woman bleed.

"It's awright, Titus. Just what happens to a woman. Feel it—how warm I got for you aweady. How wet I am for you to climb up on me now."

"Now?"

She shook her head. "We can wait a bit. Just touch me all over down there and see just how wet you're making me. This be the best way for a young'un like you to learn all 'bout a woman."

As he began to explore with his fingers, climbing higher and higher until he reached her warmth and wetness, hearing her groan low and feral, the woman dragged his head back down against her flesh: tangling her fingers within his hair as she pulled his face back to her breasts once more, rubbing him there with an urgent need. His fingers continued to explore her, studying the rise and fall of the contours of her body, afraid at first with its newness when he discovered her skin grew all the more moist the more he probed along that parting of her flesh between her thighs.

"There," she whispered. "Right there. Put your fingers in." Then without ceremony she reached down and roughly guided his hand against her flesh, positioning him, easing his fingers within her with a groan. Gripping his wrist with a trembling lock, the woman moved his fingers back and forth within her as her hips began to rock upward, just as she had rocked against him earlier that night.

When he felt her shudder convulsively, tossing her head from side to side, Titus again grew scared—fearful he had hurt her, but as soon as he tried to yank his hand from her, the woman seized it, dragged it back against the same moist warmth. Afraid to move, ignorant of what had just happened with her, he lay there still as a cat about to pounce on a mouse.

"You done good," she said eventually when her breathing became more regular. The woman stroked his hair with the hand that held his face against her breast.

Wanting to sort out the mystery so badly, but not sure how to ask, Titus finally said, "Tell me what I done good for you."

"Ever'thing. Bet you done good in school—quick as you are at learning. The kissing and licking, and how you learn't to touch me where it drives me near crazed. That all come to you pretty fast, Titus Bass."

"You done most of it yourself."

He could feel her wag her head.

"I just showed you—an' you done the rest like you was born to make a woman's body happy."

"Is that what I done?" he asked, lifting his head and looking down into her face.

"Damn right. Just you remember me whenever you want a woman to hump. I'll allays save time for you, Titus-from-upriver."

"What about all them others what come back here with you—"

"Shit," she grumbled sourly, shifting position slightly. "All the rest of them just interested in their own good time. Not that I don't make a living at it, mind you, now—but they don't think about me a'tall."

" 'Fraid I don't rightly understand."

"See, I'd rather take me a young'un like you and teach him what a man ought'n do to make a woman happy, 'cause all them older ones only worried about themselves. An' speaking of that: it's about time Titus climbed on me with that hammer of his and knocked a few pegs loose hisself. C'mon, lover."

She kept her fingers locked around his flesh as he rolled over her, positioned himself, and rocked forward. He was beginning to think there wasn't much of anything better than that feeling of getting inside a woman. For a fleeting moment he thought how he had lain atop Amy beside their old swimming hole last summer and never really gotten his pecker buried in her. Only between her thighs. It wasn't until the second time that together Amy and he had gotten him inside her, both of them moving frantically, urgently before he repeated his first performance and exploded all too quickly.

But now this, the way the woman showed him to make it last precious minutes longer. If something felt so damned good, it just made sense for him to find all the ways he could to prolong his pleasure.

Locking his elbows so he could rock above her, hurling his hips into her with a growing insistence, Titus sensed the fire rising, the flames climbing across his lower belly for no more than a matter of heartbeats before the stars exploded back of his eyelids.

Once his breathing had slowed, he lay with a hand cupped on one of her soft breasts, fingertips sensing the bony ribs beneath it. "How you come to be called Mincemeat?"

She didn't answer for some time, then replied, "You see'd my face in the light. That oughtta tell you. I been called that name since't I was no more'n a wee child. Back to Virginia where I was raised, whole valley had us a time with the pox. Some got it real bad and died, burning up with the fever. Some didn't get it at all. But most young'uns was like me. Got real sick, closing in on death's door—but we come back to the land of the living. Only our faces to show that we'd been marked by the pox."

"Why call you Mincemeat?"

"The pox on our cheeks looked red and angry, crusted and weepy for the longest time. My older brothers got to calling me Mincemeat 'cause my face looked like the meat mama chopped up and mixed in her mincemeat pies."

"What's your real name?"

"Awright to call me Mincemeat. Ever'body does," she answered, turning her head away.

"No," he insisted. "I really wanna know your real name."

"Ain't been called by my real name in longer'n I can remember."

"You know mine. So tell me yours."

When she finally answered, her voice sounded distant, sad. "Abigail," she replied softly.

"That's pretty, your folks naming you Abigail."

"Abigail Thresher."

"And you're from Virginia?"

"Family's all back there."

"Some of my kin come from Virginia."

"You born there too?" she asked.

"No. Like Ebenezer said, I'm a Kentucky man. But my grandpap come from Virgin'a. By the time he got over the mountains with the others to settle, I s'pose it weren't Virgin'a no more. They was already calling the place Caintuckee. That's where I'm from—downriver from Cincinnati an' Fort Washington."

"Your folks farming?"

"Long way back, we been farmers. What they wanted me to be too."

"But you're gonna be a riverman like Ebenezer Zane and them others now, ain'cha?"

"I'd be lying if I told you I didn't think hard on it some last two days— but I first set my sights on coming here to Louisville. Still think I like the forest better'n the river."

She cleared her throat and replied, "Probably better for you, Titus. I seen enough these last few years to know river life can be mean on a man. On the women what work 'longside the rivers too. Ain't all men gone bad—

some of 'em like Ebenezer. He's half horse, half alligator like the best of 'em, but he's still got him good feelings inside. You're damned lucky you bumped into him coming downriver. Been some of them others, they'd had you stripped of all you owned and killed you just for the fun of it. Dumped your body off the side of the boat."

"I can take care of myself," he bristled.

"You're still just a boy—"

"I ain't a boy!" Titus snapped, rolling away from her angrily, shuddering with the cold as he pulled out from beneath the blanket.

She eased against his back. "Sorry if I hurt your feelings. What I meant to say was you 'pear to be growing into a fine young man. It's easy to tell you ain't got no business on the river . . . less'n you learn the riverman's life from someone like Ebenezer Zane."

"You said Ebenezer ain't mean—like most of 'em are," Titus began. "S'pose you tell me 'bout what happened that made them three ugly fellers want nothing to do with tangling with Ebenezer last night."

For some time she lay quiet, nestled into his back. He could hear her breathing, feel the rise and fall of it against him as he watched the dip and dance of the fire's light on the far wall.

"It was to last summer," Abigail eventually began, in too quiet a voice. "The run Ebenezer made afore this'un. Most crews can make two trips downriver a year if they try—"

He was instantly edgy at the way she took her own sweet time to roll out the story, interrupting to say, "Just tell me what happened when he come through Louisville last time."

"There was two of 'em he picked a fight with."

"Ebenezer Zane?" he asked in disbelief. "Picking a fight?"

"This is the God's truth, it is," she explained as she laid a scratchy wool blanket over his body once more. "You push any man far enough—"

"All right, so I believe you. He picked a fight with two of 'em."

"Ebenezer had his reasons. Trust to that."

"They was?"

"Them two he picked a fight with were hard users."

Bass wagged his head slightly. "I don't know what that is—a hard user."

"The kind's rough on women," she explained. "This time it was Mathilda."

"Same one's your boss?"

She nodded. "Mathilda owns the Kangaroo and keeps us girls working.

She don't have nothing to do with the men no more—bedding down with 'em—unless they hap to be favorites of hers, like Kingsbury is. Mostly she just keeps out there in the tavern, making sure all folks are happy and them that aren't get throwed out."

"So what does she got to do with Ebenezer and them two he picked a fight with?"

"It all went back to the day before when Ebenezer's boat landed and his boys come in for some supper and a good time," Abigail continued her story. "Ebenezer stayed down to the boat—said his belly wasn't feeling all that good. But Kingsbury come up here, and him and Mathilda was having themselves a drink together when a bunch of Pennsylvania riffraff come in. Their steersman set his eyes on Mathilda, right off—and when she told him she wasn't bedding down with the customers no more, that big fella sour-mouthed her but he went off so's to keep on drinking, like it wasn't gonna matter."

"You gonna tell me how Ebenezer picked a fight with 'em?"

"You're jumping way ahead in the story," she snapped, sitting up and letting the blanket fall from her upper body. He watched her breasts and bony shoulders as she rolled away from him on her hip. Then he stared at the mottled skin stretched over her bony back like a plucked bird's folded wings as the woman swept up another dirty blanket from the end of the bed and wrapped it around herself. "You ever smoke afore?"

As she rose, Titus swallowed hard. "No, I ain't."

"Ever care to? Like now?"

Abigail went to a small walnut lap chest beneath the lamp table and from it drew out a drawstring pouch and a small clay pipe. She continued her story while she settled back on the edge of the bed beside him.

"Later on that night it seemed that bunch from Pennsylvania watched that Kingsbury and Mathilda was gone from the tavern for a long time together. And when the two of 'em come back, I was there to see the big steersman come over to grab hold of Mathilda—telling her he wanted some of her too. When she got angry and tried to explain she didn't do that no more, he slapped her and dragged her up by her arm from the place where she was sitting."

As he watched Abigail taking finger-pinches of fragrant tobacco from the pouch and dropping them in the tiny clay pipe bowl, Titus could clearly picture the scene in his mind: the hazy, lamplit tavern, so noisy and raucous no one would know what was happening right at first.

"That's when Kingsbury got up and jumped for the steersman. About as far as he got, 'cause some others got him and started whopping on him while the pilot knocked Mathilda around good."

"But when I come in last night, I watched a couple of fellas throwing a man out," Titus said. "What about them she hires to protect her place?"

"She has help now. Since last summer, anyways," Abigail explained, rising from the bed, clutching the blanket around her upper arms, her shoulders naked as she stepped to the fire. There he watched her squat, bare feet and ankles exposed as the blanket slurred out across the floor around her. He smiled to see that flesh while she took a straw from a bucket and for a moment held it in the fire. "But back when Kingsbury and her got whopped on, there was nobody in the place who could help. They all just backed away and let them strangers beat up that woman, and a good man too. Four of 'em throwed Kingsbury outside in the yard, good as dead. While'st the pilot dragged Mathilda outside too—carried her off down to their boat, where the bunch of 'em held her down and started using her bad."

"Using her bad?"

Taking the burning straw from the fire, Abigail held it over the pipe bowl and inhaled, sucking noisily to light the tobacco. Then she pulled the stem from her lips and blew a great gush of smoke toward the low beam-and-mud roof, finally saying, "Like you and me just done, 'cept it's one man right after 'nother—and none of 'em gentle about it," she commented sourly, her pocked face gone hard again. "The more they hit her, the more she cried and bled. And the more she cried, the more they hit her."

"How'd Ebenezer get in all of this?"

"Said he heard a woman moaning. The more he listened from where he was sick on his boat, with his belly hurting him—the more he figured out what was happening: a woman crying and men laughing. Said he could even hear them smacking her, they was whopping on her so hard."

"That's when he jumped on 'em?"

She nodded once as she rose to return to the edge of the bed. "He got him his cutlass—you ever see his cutlass?"

With a wag of his wide-eyed head, Titus looked down at the pipe she held out to him and said, "No, I ain't."

"Ask Ebenezer to see his cutlass sometime," she advised knowingly. "Right then he come on that boat and got right in the middle of 'em afore he even saw it was Mathilda they was beating bad. When he started swinging that cutlass around, two of them sonsabitches run right off, wanting nothing of Ebenezer Zane and that big knife of his'n. Here—take this."

He took the pipe, but when his palm met the heat of the clay bowl, Titus let it fall to the earthen floor.

"Silly man," she said, bending over to pick it up by the stem, the blanket parting to expose most of those fleshy mounds, enough for him to see how her breastbone stood out beneath her pale skin like a freshly pressed sheet draped over a drying line. "Here, hold it like this." She presented it to him again. "You try it again."

"What of the other two?" he asked as he took the pipe, gripping it back on the stem, fingertips away from the hot bowl. He brought it to his lips, and his eyes met hers as he began to suck in.

"Them two what gave Ebenezer the worst of it? Well, now—one snatched out a pistol and brung it up to shoot, but Ebenezer was quicker with that cutlass, cleaving off a couple of fingers of that bastard's pistol hand. But right about then Ebenezer went to his knees, a knife in his back. Say, you don't gotta hold that smoke in so long, Titus. Let it out now if'n you want."

With a gush it exploded from his mouth.

"Did you swaller it down into your chest?" she asked.

Titus swallowed, sensing the strong taste of it. "I dunno."

"Then try it again. Just like breathing in. You'll feel it down there in your chest, then you'll know."

"One of 'em, you said he stabbed Ebenezer?" and he put the stem to his lips.

Abigail waited to answer, watching his face as he drew long and slow on the pipe stem, pulling it into his lungs with all that was in him. The potent heat hit him hard: he found this smoking stuff like trying to force down a coarse old horseshoe file. As soon as it began to hurt more than he could stand, Titus coughed it right back up, gagging and retching, his face hot with embarrassment.

"That's awright, Titus. Best to take it gentle and slow—not so much all at the first. Go 'head on and give 'nother try."

He closed his eyes as he brought the pipe to his mouth a third time. Had to admit he'd always liked the smell of it, what with menfolk smoking around him all those years back in Boone County—something mighty flavorful. But getting it past his mouth into his chest appeared to be another matter. Still game for it, this time he did as she had suggested, drawing the smoke in slow and easy, a tiny bit at a time. He held it for a moment without coughing, opening his eyes wide in self-astonished celebration at his own triumph, then exhaled every bit as slowly as he had just pulled the smoke into his lungs. It was nothing less than a wonder to watch it all come back out in a steady stream.

Abigail smiled at him. "That's it, Titus. Now you try some more."

"G'won and tell me about Ebenezer getting stabbed." Only then did he bring the pipe stem back to his lips.

"The pilot done it. With a big ol' guttin' knife—but lucky for Ebenezer Zane that the tip of the blade hit a rib and only sliced up some skin. Hurt him enough I s'pose that he went to his knees. That's when Mathilda watched that bastard yank the knife back, ready to plant it in Ebenezer's back again—'bout the time Zane grabbed hol't of that pistol one of them others dropped out'n his chopped-up hand. Ebenezer turned and fired."

"Who'd he hit?"

She wagged her head, insistent on telling the story her own way. "First thing Zane done was pick Mathilda up and wrap a blanket round her—what with the way them four had tored every stitch off her. She asked him if the pilot was dead, and when Ebenezer said he didn't know, Mathilda said they should make sure he was. She told Ebenezer go pour some powder and coal oil all over the cargo."

He blew out a gush of smoke, so damned proud of himself that he hadn't coughed anymore nor made himself sick like his pap had warned him he would. Titus asked, "But he still didn't know for sure if that river pilot was dead?"

"Didn't matter," she said matter-of-factly. "Mathilda wanted the bastard dead her own self. She was the one used that pistol's flintlock to drop a spark down on the powder, setting it off and putting the coal oil to flame just as Ebenezer was loosing the mooring ropes. He pulled her onto the wharf afore he jumped back onto that flatboat and steered her long enough to get it out of the harbor into the main channel of the river."

"Then what'd he do?"

She took the pipe from him, sucked on it twice without results, and said, " 'Pears you're out'n tobacco. I'll get us some more."

He sat up at the side of the bed and pulled a blanket around himself, anxious to hear the rest of the story as she went back to the skin pouch in the walnut chest, then squatted by the fire. "Tell me what Ebenezer done out on that burning boat headed into the river."

Holding the stump of the straw in the flames, Abigail explained, "Why, he gone and jumped in the river—an' don't you know he was cut up and bleeding pretty bad—but he swum right back to where Mathilda was waiting for him at the wharf. By the time he got hisself swum there, a goodly crowd was watching, and they dragged him out of the water. I was there by that time too. We all stood, with the rest—watching that boat drifting off across the Ohio, burning to beat the band. Ever' now and then there'd be a poof, and come a big shower of sparks like a cannon firing. And soon enough —there weren't no more fire, and no more Pennsylvania flatboat."

This time he readily took the pipe from her and put it to his lips.

"I gotta pee," Abigail declared, as if she made such a confession to men all the time.

His eyes widening, he snatched for the blanket with one hand, pushing himself off the bed. "I'll go stand . . . go outside—"

"You silly," she chided, her smile one that involved her whole face. Abigail inched over to the chamber pot. "Just turn away and look at the fire."

From the corner of his eye he watched her for a moment as she turned her back to him, then flipped out the bottom of the blanket to squat over the chamber pot. As she rose, he quickly looked back at the fire and sucked on the pipe. Once more he glanced from beneath the shock of brown hair that spilled across his brow, finding her scoop a handful of red cedar shavings from the copper kettle, which she tossed into the pot. He heard her slide open the crude door and carry the pot out.

While she was gone, the door hung open—the small fire's warmth scurried from the room in one long draft. Then she was back, closing the door behind her, seeming to bring with her an aura of cold and dampness that clung about her threadbare blanket.

"I feel like I ain't et in a week," he said as she took the pipe from him. "How about us going out for some breakfast?"

"Ain't time for breakfast yet," she said, setting the pipe on the table and turning back to the bed.

Glancing at the door, he asked, "Ain't morning yet?"

"Still dark out there. Hardly a soul moving."

He watched her lie back on the bed, slowly sliding the blanket back from her body in that firelight and frail, wispy lamplight. Not able to help himself, he swallowed hard, staring at her bony hips, that dark delta between her legs, then up across her flat belly to those fleshy breasts. He licked his lips, mouth gone dry as he found her staring at him, her eyes intent.

Patting the narrow bed beside her, Abigail said, "C'mon in here with me, Titus. I'm certain we can find us something to do till it's time for victuals."

NINE

Ebenezer Zane chose to set off downriver in the worst possible weather yet to batter the valley that autumn.

The sky overhead hung just out of reach, every bit as cold and the color of a great slab of the rain-soaked granite that protruded from the barren, skeletal forest that formed both sides of the channel the Ohio carved out of this western land. Yellows, oranges, and reds had been long ago stripped from the trees, nipped by frosts, turned by the crawl of time toward winter, hurried on their way before every gust of the season's winds. Everything smelled of dank decay and humus, coated with ice and frost.

And then the sky unleashed itself, beginning to fling down a sharp, needling sleet borne on the back of a twisting, thrashing gale.

Titus gulped the last of the coffee in the bottom of his tin cup and turned on the rough bench to pull on a second pair of moccasins, dragging them over the first he had tied over his thickest pair of woolen stockings. Not without their holes and worn fabric, they nonetheless still climbed to his knees. And they

would simply have to do. Like the rest of what little he had plopped beside
the table where he hunkered with the rest of the crew finishing their hearty
breakfast of hominy and great slabs of bacon, as well as baskets filled with
biscuits and plenty of steaming coffee. Here in the Kangaroo other rivermen
tied up at the wharf were beginning to show up for a hearty meal. But they
would have to do without this choicest of tables near the fireplace, where
Ebenezer Zane stuffed the other four who would that morning dare the
Great Falls of the Ohio with him.

"Looks to be you're still dead set on killing yourself, Ebenezer," one of
the other pilots growled as he came up to the table, wagging his head.

"Plan on getting my boat all the way down to New Orleans before the
devil even knows I've cleared out of Louisville," Zane replied. "Have some
coffee, John."

The boatman took the offered cup, cradling it in both hands just under
his nose, soaking in the steamy warmth and aroma. After that first sip he
said, "Looks like snow out there."

"I'd just as soon it did," Hames Kingsbury commented.

Zane nodded. "Better that than the ice I fear most."

"It's froze to everything," Heman Ovatt said. "Hard for a man to lock
on to the gouger. Even an oar. Everything coated thick with ice, Ebenezer."

"Nothing what can't be chipped away." Zane glanced at a wide-eyed
Titus for a flicker of a moment, then said, "Snow's fine by me."

The boatman looked up from his coffee and replied, "You nary was
one to be afeared of that river, Ebenezer. Afeared of what it could do to your
boat."

"No sense in being afeared now."

"Times we wondered if you was born with any sense at all," the older
pilot commented with a snort. When he looked around over the rim of his
cup and found no smiles among the others, he quickly sank back into his tin.

Other rivermen continued to crowd in as the minutes passed, some
hobbling over from the tavern side, where they might well have slept off
their liquor sprawled on a table or crumpled under a bench, perhaps lumbering in from one of the barmaids' beds, most hurrying up from the wharf,
where they had sought shelter aboard their flatboats bobbing in the crowded
harbor while the white, icy arrow points had begun to lance out of the gray
sky. At least half of those who entered the Kangaroo came over to make
some greeting to Ebenezer Zane, more still to give their farewell—having
heard the news that the pilot was pushing off downriver this nasty, forbidding day.

Three nights had Zane's crew tarried there in Louisville while their steersman bartered himself more cargo, itself a bit of a problem to begin with, seeing how little of the deck a man could walk upon, crammed to the gunnels as it was with crates, kegs, and oaken barrels bound for the mouth of the Mississippi. It ultimately turned out they had taken on a load of oiled hemp destined for use on great oceangoing vessels—huge coils of coarse twenty-four-strand rope, each one a hundred feet long and looped into a bundle it took three stevedores to burden on board. There the coils were lashed down atop the rest of the cargo.

"That rope's just about the only thing Ebenezer could've figured out for us to haul pitched up there on top of everything else," Ovatt had declared yesterday as they'd secured the last coil.

Reuben Root spat into the water alongside as twilight sank around them. "Could've done 'thout it at all, to my way of thinking. Jest lookee the way we're a'setting in the water now."

"We'll ride just fine," Kingsbury said. "Got plenty of room left to draw water up the sides."

"Which is just what we're gonna do we hit them Falls," Root replied with a sneer.

Kingsbury waved his arm for them all to follow him off the boat, saying, "Just pack that squeeze-box of your'n in some waxed paper and lock it up high—you won't have a lick of trouble, Reuben."

"Don't none of you realize that extra cargo I just bought me after three days of haggling will make this trip all the sweeter for every one of us?" Zane asked them as they joined him on the wharf nearer the Kangaroo where they had moved the boat earlier in the day to begin their on-loading. There the broadhorn would remain moored until dawn.

All four carried belt weapons that night as they put solid land under their feet. Zane had assigned each of them a four-hour watch, keeping a fire burning in the sandbox there close by the stern rudder, something to warm their hands and coffee over too.

Bass glanced over the others as they put away their pistols, then said, "You didn't gimme a watch, Mr. Zane."

With something of a smile Ebenezer turned to Titus in the swelling darkness of that autumn evening. "These here men're my crew, Titus Bass. They hired on for work such as this."

"Back at the start you said you needed me through the Falls."

"I did say that, and your help is much appreciated."

"Then you count me like one of the rest—if I'm to work through to the other side of the Falls."

Kingsbury nodded. "Boy's got him a point, Ebenezer."

"You're up to taking a watch, are you?" Zane asked.

But before Bass could answer, Ovatt declared, "It's lonely work. Out here by yourself. Just you and the river and any others what wanna raise some devilment with our load."

"That's right," Root added. "The whole town knows we're setting off come morning. Lonely and cold out here—'specially since't Mincemeat gonna be inside 'thout you tonight."

Bass turned back to Zane, steadfast. "I'll take the watch you gimme. First, last, or middle. I figure to pull my share of the work for 'llowing me come downriver with you. All you done for me since we got here."

Zane said, "I'll see 'bout sending Mincemeat out to visit you."

Wagging his head, Bass replied, "Treat me just like the rest of 'em here. I got work to do—don't want a woman around."

"Jumpin' Jehoshaphat!" Kingsbury exclaimed. "Did you hear that? Titus sure got serious about work, going and turning down a woman coming out to keep him warm—"

"Maybeso the rest of you learn something from Titus Bass here," the pilot declared. "When you're working, you keep your mind on work."

Bass said, "Yessir. That's what I was saying."

"All right, son. With you added on, that shorts the watches to three hours apiece. Titus takes this first watch." Ebenezer drew his two big-bored belt weapons out of his greasy red waist sash and handed them over, butt first, to the youth. "Here. Keep these handy. Rest of us be right up the slope at the inn. Any trouble, just call out or shoot. We'll huff down here straightaway."

His eyes got big as coffee saucers when the pistols came into his skinny hands, in awe at their sheer weight. All Titus did was bob his head as the four turned to go.

"You want supper brung out?" Ovatt asked.

"I'll wait."

"When he finishes, he can have his ale and stew," Zane declared as the four slogged up the slope toward the Kangaroo in the cold. "And Mincemeat too."

Bass thought he had struggled with loneliness before—those first nights in the forest. Believed he had battled cold too. But nothing like this:

the dampness penetrated him to the bone despite the coffee and the fire he hunkered over, flames flutting in that tin sandbox he fed with more and more kindling. But, then, cold and lonely always seemed to go hand in hand, he brooded. Never had he been lonely on a summer night.

How easily he thought back to Amy then. Her memory still a bright thing he could feel inside his breast despite the miles and all the days. How sweet her mouth had tasted last summer, so unlike Abigail's—her mouth strong with the whiskey and the tobacco. But it was not to be, he decided again, surprised that he still was making peace with that.

Had his father come searching for him? Had they finally given up? Would his folks ask of him all the way upriver to Cincinnati? Perhaps even this far downriver to Louisville, he convinced himself. Maybe not. Maybe his pap already figured it was for the best, ridding himself of a son not wanting to become a farmer. So much the better—and now they would go on with their lives.

But what of his mother? Strong as she was, he nonetheless worried most for her. She had always been the one to quietly set herself against her husband when it mattered: she who hid supper for Titus; she who had seen to it the new shirt and biscuits were set out where Titus could get his hands on them that dark morning of farewell. Such was the real remorse he felt, about his only regret, leaving the way he had without explaining to her. Sure even now that she would have understood.

There wasn't a star he could make out in the sky overhead. Clouds thickened like coal-blackened cotton bolls, reminding him how his hands hurt, rubbed raw and cut, whenever they had to pick what little cotton they had taken to growing on a small patch of ground by the smokehouse. Better was the flax the family planted, woven with wool to make a strong cloth that would turn the weather without being as heavy as pure wool. Between that mixed cloth his mother had woven and the animal skins she'd tanned for coats, britches, and moccasins—a body could count on staying reasonably warm, no matter what the weather.

In such deep thought his watch passed, and it was with reluctance that Titus turned over the two horse pistols to Ebenezer, who came to relieve him three hours later.

"Likely there's some stew left, but if not, they'll get you a pullet or two and a loaf of that black bread. There's plenty of beans to fill you up. But stay away from the spruce beer this night, Titus," Zane had warned as he settled onto a crate to start his watch. "I need your head clear come morning."

So until that dawn he had filled himself with nothing more than

Abigail Thresher, as hungry as he was for her, having done his best to pay no heed to the taunts of the other three boatmen when they warned him the whore would have nothing more to do with him once Ebenezer Zane had gone, taking his fat river pilot's purse with him.

"She said she likes me," Titus had protested.

"Playing with your diddle ain't the only thing Mincemeat gets paid for," Root explained, always the one out to pop another man's bubble. "She gets paid for saying what she's told to say."

"Ebenezer told her to tell me that?"

Kingsbury only shrugged. "Who knows?"

"She's just a whore," Ovatt said. "There'll be others on the ride down. Why, if'n you was floating along with us, you could count on tasting some fine girls we reach Natchez-Under-the-Hill."

"And all them sweet Creole girls down to Nawlins," Kingsbury added with a smack of his lips.

"I ain't got me any need to go south," Titus argued with a doleful wag of his head. "West is where away I'm bound."

"St. Lou?" Heman Ovatt asked.

"One of these days soon," Bass answered.

Kingsbury said, "A man goes west—you'll need money to give yourself a stake. That's fur country out'n St. Louie. Ain't white man country west of there. You'll need fixin's."

"I'll get me some work."

"What the hell can a farm boy like you do to make a man hire you for pay?" Root inquired.

"I can find work," Titus snapped quickly, wincing at the pain he'd felt with their talk about Abigail.

"Yes, you can," Kingsbury replied quietly, holding a flat hand against Root's chest to quickly silence the other boatman. "No doubt you'll find work here in Louisville real soon."

Titus had drowned himself in her flesh that last night, at least every time he awoke enough in rolling over against her, placing the woman's hands on his flesh to harden it to stone once again. If in the end it was true that Mincemeat was feeling nothing more than any working girl who got paid to do what she was told, then—Titus decided—he'd sure as hell make sure Ebenezer Zane got his money's worth out of that last night in Louisville.

As good as it felt with her at the moment, as excited as she could get him with her body, it was afterward that got him to thinking. Like he was doing now in this damp, fragrant tavern as they finished their coffee near the fireplace as if soaking up all this warmth for what ordeal was yet to come, waiting for Ebenezer to tell them it was time to push away.

And he wondered what it was that made a man want to stay on with a woman after they were through coupling. It had to be something more than just a man's knowing he could climb atop that woman again whenever he wanted. There must surely be something else he had yet to learn of this mysterious tangle of things between a man and a woman—more than he had learned at the threshold from the pretty Amy Whistler, and now from that full-growed woman what could please a man no end and was called Mincemeat.

What made some men stay on and on with a woman, while at the same time urging him to move on from both of those he had known so far?

"It h'ain't getting any better out there, Ebenezer," Root grumbled from the open doorway where the cold air gusted. Beyond Reuben was a gray streaked with white slashes.

"Best us be going," Zane said with resignation.

"We could stay over, sit it out," Ovatt declared.

Ebenezer turned to them slowly, hitching up his belt, and smiled inside that hairy face. "We got everything tied down and we're ready to put off. Nothing's holding us no more. I want out of Louisville and put the Falls behind us."

Kingsbury started, "Maybe Ovatt's right, Ebene—"

"Any of you's free to stay what wants to," Zane interrupted, though his voice remained quiet and calm. He turned to the youngest among them. "Even you, Titus. No reason for you to get on that boat now. We'll do just fine 'thout you."

"Said you needed me."

Zane shook his head. "Weather like this, it don't matter much anymore. Best you stay."

"I made a promise," Titus said, sensing the curiosity of the other men nettling him. "You an' me made us a bargain. I aim to keep up my end of it."

Zane regarded him briefly, then took a step forward, slapping a hand down on Bass's shoulder. "Good man." Looking at the rest of them, he explained, "Any of the rest of you decide to stay, Titus here can take your place."

For a moment they looked at one another, almost furtively, perhaps waiting for one of their number to stave in. Then before any of them could, Zane suddenly emboldened them with his words.

"Good for you, men. Like I always been proud of you—taking on this river, no matter what face it showed us. And now Heman's got him a new man to help with the gouger when the water gets rough."

Ovatt nodded at Bass. Titus swallowed, for the first time in his life feeling as if he was a part of something bigger than himself. One of these reckless men who would once again pit themselves against the icy river.

That was when Ebenezer held up a clenched fist at waist level, speaking not a word in explanation. Kingsbury immediately set his clenched fist atop Zane's, then Ovatt's atop his. When Root had added his to the top of the stack, they turned their eyes to Bass. Eagerly Titus slipped between the muscle-knotted shoulders of Zane and Kingsbury to join that small circle and made his short-fingered hand into a fist that looked so outsized by all the others.

With that fifth hand atop the rest, Zane declared, "This is the shaft that water and wind may bend but will never be broken as long as we stay together as one."

"Let's go to the Mississippi!" Kingsbury roared.

As the four men yelped and cheered, turning aside to sweep up their blankets and oiled coats, Titus stood for but a moment in that spot, somehow still sensing the power of those clenched, veined fists his had joined, no matter how briefly, feeling as if the others had just vowed to prop him up, support him, watch over him like one of their own. A short, strong staff carved of man's will and camaraderie. In that moment all doubts took to the wing, freeing with them all remorse in leaving the Kangaroo and the woman behind.

Once more his life appeared black-and-white, without shades of indecisive gray. Just as it had when he'd determined to leave home behind, Titus sensed the certainty of what lay downriver. The sureness that he was being pulled on by what lay out there.

"You'll stay with Heman," Ebenezer ordered as the four of them pounded up the cleated gangplank, clambered over the gunnel, and began to scramble off in different directions as the sleet spat at them in gusty sheets out of a leaden sky.

Bass turned to find Root still onshore and leaning into his work, lunging against the thick rope that held the flatboat's bow fast to the wharf. With the knot eventually loosened, he heaved the rope toward Ovatt, who began to coil it up near his feet as Root trudged back through the icy mud toward the last rope securing the stern. With that second knot freed, he flung the loose end of the rope to Zane while making sure the loop was still secured around one of the wharf's stanchions. When Root had crawled on board and was dragging the cleated gangplank atop some of the crates, Zane dropped the free end of the rope and released them from the wharf. The thick hemp flopped to the surface of the ice-flecked water like a huge oiled snake suddenly dropping from a great height. Kingsbury began to haul in the rope as the pilot whirled about to seize up the long arm of his rudder.

"Push us free," Zane ordered.

Root and Kingsbury took up fourteen-foot hardwood shafts, each of them going to the gunnels, where they planted the ends of their poles against the wharf and heaved with the thrust in their legs. Foot by foot, grunt by grunt, the two lunged against the poles, easing the laden flatboat out from the tangle of other craft moored at the wharf. Slow it was, the gray water slogging beneath them little by little. Back and forth Zane worked his rudder, shouting an order from time to time to Ovatt on the gouger as they edged on out into the middle of the harbor. Then, just beyond the last finger of land surrounding that cove on three sides, Titus felt the perceptible nudge of the Ohio against the hull beneath him. Now the water seemed to pick up speed, and the boat with it as they rounded that last glimpse of Louisville and Zane piloted them into the current.

"Sing out—you see anything a'floating!" Ebenezer called to the others. "We done this many a time, so ever' one of you knows what we're needing to draw for water!"

"What's he talking about?" Bass inquired as he leaned on the short gouger pole across from Ovatt.

"This ain't a high-water time to be floating down the Ohio," Heman explained. "Come autumn and winter, water gets low so we might just see us a lot of planters and sawyers from here on out downriver. 'Specially when we get yonder to the Falls, where the water gets all boiled up."

"What's he mean by drawing water?"

"We're heavy," the boatman explained. "Sitting down in the water some, instead of riding on top. So we're gonna need deeper water to run the chute."

"Chute?"

"There's three of 'em at the Falls. One of 'em's better'n the others sometime during the year. Depending on how deep the river is, how fast she's moving. It's up to me to sing out to Ebenezer soon as I can tell which chute is the one he ought'n take us through the Falls."

As the boat picked up speed, with the wind whipping the icy sleet into them out of the west, Titus felt his insides drawing up like someone had dashed them with pickling spice. Water was one thing. Swimming in it— hell, even floating on it was one thing. But this bobbing within an onrushing current, totally at the mercy of the Ohio as it suddenly narrowed itself southwest of Louisville, rushing them onward to the Great Falls, was quite another.

He quickly looked about at the other three boatmen. Root had one hand gripping the gunnel as the icy water began to slap against that side of the flatboat. Time and again he swiped his face clear of spray and sleet as he squinted downriver.

Then Titus heard the sound that made his blood go cold.

Turning with a jerk, he peered into the sleeting mist ahead of them. Not only was it that low rumble which seemed to pull them perceptibly closer still, but also his inability to make out the source of the nearing thunder which caused his belly to churn and flop. In all that gray he could find nothing ahead of them that gave him the slightest clue—nothing but the gradual narrowing of the river's channel between its timbered, rocky banks.

"You hear it, don't you?"

Without tearing his eyes from the far bend in the river, he nodded to Ovatt.

"That's the Falls," Heman went on. "You allays hear 'em afore you see 'em."

"Jumpin' Jehoshaphat!"

With a start Titus turned from downstream to look at Kingsbury, finding the boatman intent on watching the river channel as he clung to a rope with one hand, the other clamped on an oar he held just above the frothing water. Beyond Hames Kingsbury he watched Ebenezer at the stern, yanking downward on the soggy brim of his wool-felt hat, pulling up the woven muffler over the lower part of his face before he leaned against the rudder to urge the flatboat a little closer to the northern shore.

"Keep 'er coming some more, Ebenezer!" Ovatt bellowed into the growing noise of their plunge.

Zane asked, "It look to be the Indian chute?"

Ovatt nodded, shouting, "Not as bad as one time we rode through here!"

"Keep your eye peeled on that rock at the bend like I teached you!" Zane instructed. "You tell me when we reach that."

"See the rock yonder coming at us," Ovatt explained now, his voice quieter against the swelling of sound around them. "By the time we reach that rock on the north bank—Ebenezer's gotta have to choose which't chute he's gonna put us through the Falls."

"If he don't do it then?"

"There ain't much time left if he ain't ready," Heman replied. "See how he's doing now? Lookee, see how he's moved us into the middle channel of the river. That way he can go to the Kentucky chute. Or he can stay here in the river chute. Or the likeliest way at low-water time like it is now gonna be for him to jump us over into the Indian chute. Off the starboard side here," he said, pointing off to the right shore.

"How come they call it Indian chute?"

"Hell, Titus. 'Cause that's Indiana Territory there you're floating by. That's how come."

Despite the rising growl of the water, the Great Falls of the Ohio weren't actually falls at all. More precisely, they were a long series of terrible rapids that churned up the river to a froth between the banks, narrowing as the river passed Louisville. Anyone on the Ohio could plainly hear the water pounding on the rocks for as much as a mile upriver. A trip through the chutes was much, much easier at high-water time, anywhere from late spring to late summer, but as Heman Ovatt had explained, the rapids became all the more troublesome during the autumn and winter due to low water and many more exposed rocks. While a pilot always had his choice of which one of the three chutes he would select to negotiate the Falls—such a decision became critical to the lives of his crew and the safety of their cargo during low-water time. In earlier days of canoe travel on the Ohio, many of the more faint of heart even chose to put over to the Indiana side, unload, and portage their cargo past the rapids.

"Some cap'ns hire on a pilot back there at Louisville what knows the Falls," Ovatt explained. "For two dollars there's a few guides what make a good living just getting flatboats through the Falls."

"But Ebenezer knows what he's doing?" Titus asked, wanting an answer to dispel his uncertainty.

"He's the sort would never let another man pilot his boat anyways. Sure enough—the Ohio might toss us around some this time o' year—but Ebenezer gonna get us through."

The growling belly of that thunder of water colliding with rocks grew until it seemed to drown out all other sound but the nerve-grating creak of the flatboat timbers. Looking at the icy, wet boards beneath his moccasins, Titus watched them shift and twist. He gulped, as if to swallow down the panic he felt for fear the boat would break apart as the river flung it toward the point where Ebenezer Zane would have to make his decision.

The closer they raced down the middle channel of the Ohio, the lower the clouds and sleeting mist sank down both slopes on either side of the river, clinging among the sycamores and birch, ash and poplar, then spilled onto the surface of the river itself. Swallowing the rock Zane used as his landmark.

Ovatt called out, "You see, Ebenezer?"

"Hell, no, I cain't see it!"

"Can't see the rock up there—what you want me to do?"

"We'll just count to twenty. Should be there by then. Count 'long with me."

Heman Ovatt tore his eyes away from Zane and stared off downriver just as the craft took a noticeable lunge to starboard, nearly loosening Titus's grip on the gouger. Ovatt had begun to count, loudly, over the increasing noise of the water pounding on the sides of the flatboat, against the rocks around the far bend, and the increasing hammer of icy sleet beating against canvas and wood and flesh.

Every now and then during those next few seconds Bass caught snatches of Ebenezer's voice counting along with Ovatt. The gouger's voice rose in anticipation with each successive number as the entire crew struggled to catch a glimpse of something telltale along the starboard bank while the mist continued to swallow upon them.

"How's he gonna see where to go?" Bass asked anxiously.

"He ain't."

"Heman!" Zane called out. "Less'n you got a better idee—I'm gonna set her in the Indian chute!"

"Fine by me!" the gouger called back, his voice sodden, flooded out in some spray as Ebenezer suddenly heaved his bulk against the rudder and set the flatboat creaking as it hurtled across the racing current.

Titus clung to the short gouger beside Ovatt and worked up nerve enough to ask, "We gonna put over and wait till we can see what's ahead?"

Ovatt tongued his tobacco quid to the other side of his cheek, bent his head over the gunnel, and spit, the brown streamer smacking into the bow of the boat directly beneath him. "Ain't nowhere in the Falls a boat can put over. We gotta ride it through."

"R-ride it through," he repeated without conviction.

"Ain't nothing we can do now but ride, Titus. Just hold on and ride through the Falls—no matter if there's hell on the other side."

By the time Ovatt finished his words, they were all but swallowed up by the roar of irresistible liquid fury pitted against immovable granite. As the shifting winds nudged the sleeting mist this way and that, Titus captured a glimpse here and there of the shore on one side of the river or the other beneath the roiling fog. Closer and closer Zane moved them to the northern bank, the boat's timbers complaining audibly, protesting the strain as the Ohio flung the five men and their flimsy craft ever toward the upstream opening of the Indian chute.

"We in it now!" Ovatt sang out at the top of his lungs.

Barely able to hear the man right beside him, Titus turned to glance at the other three boatmen. Able to accomplish nothing with their oars in the rapids, Root and Kingsbury had laid their oars aside and crawled to the stern of the boat, clinging to the gunnel close by Zane in the event the pilot needed their muscle on the main rudder.

"This the start of the Falls?" Titus asked.

Ovatt nodded, then pressed his lips against Bass's ear, to yell, "It be just a matter of Ebenezer and the river now! Him alone agin it!"

Zane laid his weight against the rudder again and again. Moving the boat this way and that, feeling his way through the rocks and water and great gray slabs of icy granite, throwing his flatboat and its cargo toward one shore, then the other, as the other four men clung to the slippery gunnels, unable to assist, knowing only that the next few moments of their lives were most precious, for above them hovered the specter of an icy death.

For Titus this staring into death's face had a cold, metallic taste to it. Almost like sucking on an iron fork.

Time and again the pilot steadied himself, bracing his great, powerful legs within that square yard of icy deck, holding his own against the cargo lashed on three sides about him, holding his own against the frothing river that sought to snatch the rudder from his grip. Over and over the boat seemed to exercise a mind of its own, the great force of the Ohio flinging the flatboat out of the current only to plop down with a crash, its unyielding sides of strong yellow poplar groaning against the unmitigated forces of nature at her rawest.

Bass wasn't sure if he was shaking because of the cold—how wet he was, standing like the rest, soaked to the marrow with sleet, wind, and river spray. Or if he was trembling down to the very core of him out of undeniable fear. Either way, his teeth chattered like bone dice in a horn cup. Loud enough he was sure the others could hear them.

Then it struck him. He started to smile, looking at Ovatt. The gouger smiled back, both of them realizing that no more did the flatboat creak and groan. No longer did the river thunder about their ears. No more were they caught in the merciless grip of a watery hell.

There was only heaven. A quiet that slowly grew just the way the noise of the Falls had swelled and pounded at him. But now that pounding terror was behind them, and the persistent hammer of the sleeting rain was about all Titus could make out above the occasional dull slap of river against the flatboat's sides as Ebenezer Zane worked the rudder into the current, moving them closer and closer to the Kentucky shore once again.

"Yonder's Indiana," Ovatt said, his voice strangely muted now in the absence of that thunder. "Place called Clarksville over there right about so. It sits at the bottom of the Falls—just about the last village of any size 'tween Louisville and St. Louie. Wish you could see it, but for the clouds."

Titus could see very little of the Indiana shore, upstream or down. "Clarksville."

"Named for George Rogers Clark. You hear of him?"

Wagging his head, Titus said, "No, I ain't."

"Hero of Vincennes. He kept the Northwest out of enemy hands many a year ago," Ovatt explained in a reverent voice. "I see'd him once. Sure of it."

"You seen Clark?"

"He was a old man then. Thin as a broom handle, all wored down with age. But every day he come to the river, folks said. An' he'd wave to us what was going down. Clark's the one opened this country—held back the enemy, and pushed back the Injuns across the Wabash."

"What's that?"

"Wabash? A river comes into the Ohio from the north. We'll reach it soon enough. But for now, looks to be Ebenezer is about to put over to the Kentucky side and let you off."

With a start Titus whirled about, finding the pilot indeed easing the flatboat ever closer to the south bank. His heart pounding, his mouth gone dry, and his throat feeling like he had daubed with tannic acid, Titus started to scramble over the crates and kegs and great coils of oiled hemp smelling fragrant in the moist, icy air. Root and Kingsbury were at the port gunnel, both with loops of rope over their shoulders by the time Titus clambered his way to midship. As Zane eased the stern of his cumbersome craft crosswise to the current, slipping them toward a muddy section of land, Reuben and Hames freed the ropes securing the small two-man skiff at the side of the flatboat and let it drop into the icy river with a splash. Leaping on board with their heavy coils of hawser rope, the pair quickly paddled toward shore. Beaching the skiff among the leafless brush, they slogged about in the frozen mud up to their ankles to knot their mooring ropes around a couple of trees with roots exposed by the relentless Ohio.

"Gimme a hand here!" Ovatt cried out at the capstan, where he began to turn the wheel with one of the short, stout, removable poles, walking round and round in that cramped area left free of deck cargo clutter. Already the flatboat was beginning to jolt and shudder as the ropes snapped, went taut with a creak, and the timbers groaned, Ebenezer's Kentuckyboat bouncing against the current as she was drawn toward the bank.

"You heard the man, Titus!" Zane shouted. "Get up there and put your back into it so we can set you off on that shore."

"Eb—Ebenezer?"

For a moment Zane watched Heman Ovatt and the others over the youth's shoulder, then peered into the lad's face. "What is it, Titus Bass? You of a sudden got something agin hard work?"

"No . . . no, sir! You won't think ill of me if'n I go an' break our bargain, will you?"

"Goddammit, boy!" Ovatt growled menacingly as he struggled against the capstan. "Get over here help me out!"

"Keep your back into it, Heman! Titus got something to say to me!" Ebenezer hollered. Then, squinting sternly at Bass with one eye, the pilot replied, "So you ain't a man of your word, that it?"

"Nothing of the kind. I—"

Ebenezer interrupted, "Just how you figure on breaking our bargain? I brung you downriver like I said I would, and you rode with us through the Falls. Sounds to me we're square."

"But I didn't do nothing to help us—"

"Nothing nobody could do. Allays just river an' me"—then Zane's eyes flickered to the sleeting heavens—"an' God too what brung us through. It don't matter none that I didn't work you for your passage. But that ain't breaking your bargain. You get on up there and help Heman haul us in to shore."

His tongue felt pasty inside his mouth, his heart hammering and breath coming short and hard.

With sweaty palms Titus said, "I wanna stay."

"Stay?"

Root and Kingsbury slogged down the muddy bank clutching the ends of their ropes, both of them intent on trying to overhear the talk. Ovatt continued to grunt, pushing round and round a step at a time there at the capstan among the ice-coated cargo lashed near the bow.

"Wanna stay on down the river with you fellas."

"You know where we're heading?"

"Natchez you said. On to Norleans."

Zane wagged his head thoughtfully. "I dunno. Got me half a year's earnings here."

Bass said quickly, "I wanna go with you. See what's there."

"Thought you was wanting to go to St. Lou."

He tried out a smile on Zane. "I figure it'll still be there come next year. Plenty of time for me."

"I was young as you once," the wrinkled river pilot replied. "Seemed there was all the time in the world back then."

For a moment Titus looked around him at the other three boatmen, then said, "You consider taking me?"

"Figure to hire on, are you?"

"A man don't ride for free," Root grumbled.

Bass nodded. "Reuben's right. I don't 'spect to ride for free."

A grin grew within that great black tangle of hair Zane called his head. "I'll work you, Titus Bass. I'll work you hard."

Bass gulped, asking, "That the hardest piece of river we go through to get to Norleans?"

Zane tilted his head back and roared with laughter, so deep and hearty was it that he showed his tonsils. "Just about, son."

"Then I figure to ride the river with you fellas."

Leaning forward, he held out his hand to the youth. "Good to have you with us, Titus Bass." He straightened and hollered at the two on shore, "Loose that hemp, boys!"

"Jumpin' Jehoshaphat!" Kingsbury yelled in exasperation from the bank. "What in the goddamned hell?"

Zane waved his free arm, gesturing his crew in. "We're bound for the Mississip with a new man!"

Grumbling, Root and Kingsbury freed the double-fist-sized knots from their moorings, then pushed off, paddling furiously, heading out into the channel to catch the flatboat while Ovatt hurriedly coiled in the hundred or so feet of loose hawsers across the wind-whipped surface of the Ohio.

Coming alongside, Reuben and Hames tied off the skiff to a pair of check-poles along the flatboat's gunnel and clambered aboard.

Root asked of Zane, "This here green man you're fixing to hire on— ain't we gonna get him started right, Ebenezer?"

"How you mean—*started right?*" the pilot asked.

"Have the boy here scour and grease the anchor?"

Ebenezer chuckled. "You can sure be one mean son of a bitch, Reuben. No, sir. I never did cotton to pulling such pranks on a feller what sets foot on my flatboat for his first trip downriver."

"Not even a li'l fun?" Root whined, disappointment now where glee had been.

"What you figure to have Titus Bass do to make fun for you, Reuben?" Kingsbury asked.

He turned to Hames, saying, "I was figuring on him cooning the steering oar."

With a lusty guffaw Zane shook his bushy head like a lion's mane. "No, Reuben—less'n you're willing to coon it yourself."

"Shit! I ain't no green hand like him—"

"Hap that you remember I never made you do nothing of the kind when you was a green hand?" Zane snapped. "You hap to think back on that?"

Sullen, Root nodded.

Having watched and listened in confusion, Titus finally asked, "What's cooning the steering oar?"

All four of the boatmen roared in great peals of laughter.

Nearly out of breath, Kingsbury finally explained, "On many a boat the old hands will play some mean trick on a new hand—something like Reuben wanted you to do."

"Cooning the steering oar," Zane continued, "means we'd have you climb out to the end of this here rudder of mine."

Bass's eyes grew big as coffee tins as he stared at the water flowing around the back of the boat where the pole sank beneath the river's surface. He gulped. "You'd had me climb out there, hanging on to just the rudder pole?"

Root was still hooting, slapping his knee in merriment. "Make sure you touch the rudder out there now, Titus . . . or we don't let you climb back onter the boat!"

"It's easy enough," Ovatt confided. "Just hang on with your arms and legs. I done it years afore."

"Yeah!" Root roared. "Best you hang on real tight!"

"Or you get a cold bath in the river," Kingsbury concluded with a shudder. "Like I done."

"B-but, none of you gonna make me do that, are you?" Bass inquired.

"You're part of the crew anyways," the bushy-headed pilot replied. "I see no need for them silly games just to make these fellers laugh on your account."

"I thankee for that, Mr. Zane," Titus replied, wanting to sense some real gratitude, but not really sure how he should feel at that moment. Perhaps such a ritual of initiation was really necessary for him to become part of the crew. Maybe they never would accept him as one of their own if he didn't suffer some of their lighthearted pranks.

"No need to thank me, Titus," Ebenezer said, his eyes softening in that kind, hairy face.

Titus started to turn away, ready to head to the bow, where he intended to lend his muscle to Heman's efforts at the gouger, when Zane caught him by the shoulder, saying, "Why'n't you stay back here with me for now, Titus Bass? That's easy rope work for Ovatt now—and I could use the company, I could at that."

As Hames and Reuben reached the stern of the flatboat to tie the skiff off to a snubbing post before clambering up the side and over the gunnel, Titus settled in near Zane, his heart still hammering, desperately wanting this to be the right thing for him to do.

"I don't figure I done enough yet to thank you, Ebenezer," he began. "I was fixing on helping the rest of you get through the Falls. But I didn't do nothing. 'Stead of troubling yourself with me—why didn't you just leave me back at Louisville when I told you I was all for staying on there?"

Grinning into the slanting hammer of the wind-driven sleet, Zane replied, "I figured there was no other way to find out if you was a riverman or not—but to take you with us through the Falls."

"So what'd you find out?"

The pilot tousled Titus's hair, then peered on down the gray Ohio once more. "You'll do to ride the river with, Titus Bass. By damned, you'll do."

Autumn was all but done for by the time Ebenezer Zane's broadhorn reached the mouth of the Ohio. What ducks and geese and other species of winged creatures hadn't already flapped their way overhead were destined to struggle out the winter here in the north: all manner of doves, redheaded woodpeckers, and nighthawks too. The sort that stayed behind.

One day on the trip they spotted some gray and black squirrels, hundreds upon hundreds of them, all sweeping down from the north bank, plunging into the river to bob and swim with all their might against the current, like a mighty exodus that crossed to the south. Hundreds of heads dotted the murky brown water all about the boat, hundreds more pressing behind. And every day the men watched the shorelines for bigger species. Titus was amazed at the growing numbers of bear and deer, turkey and fox, he spotted as they rode the river farther west, heading for the Mississippi.

And always they sang—ballads of death and love and hard-hearted maidens.

> *"Rise you up, my dear, and present me*
> *your hand,*
> *And we'll take a social walk to a far and*
> *distant land;*
> *Where the Hawk shot the Buzzard and*
> *the Buzzard shot the Crow.*
> *We'll rally in the canebrake and shoot*
> *the Buffalo!*
> *Shoot the Buffalo! Shoot the Buffalo!*
> *Rally in the canebrake and shoot*
> *the Buffalo!"*

For the longest time he pondered that the old song said just what his grandpap had told him: there had been buffalo in the canebrakes. Which set Titus to brooding on how those who had gone before him had shot the buffalo until there were no more.

Then Hames Kingsbury would always lift Bass's spirits by singing what had long been Ebenezer Zane's favorite, sung to the tune of "Yankee Doodle."

> *"We are a hardy, freeborn race,*
> *Each man to fear a stranger;*
> *Whate'er the game, we join the chase,*
> *Despising toil and danger;*
> *And if a daring foe annoys,*
> *No matter what his force is,*

We'll show him that Kentucky boys
Are alligator-horses!"

Then Heman Ovatt started in on one of his own.

"Way down the Ohio my little boat
I steered,
In hopes that some pretty girl on the
banks will appear.
I'll hug her and kiss her till my mind is
at ease,
And I'll turn my back on her and court
who I please."

When Root bellowed forth with "Bird in a Cage":

"Bird in a cage, love,
Bird in a cage;
Waiting for Willie
To come back to me.

"Roses are red, love,
Violets are blue.
God in heaven
Knows I love you.

"Write me a letter,
Write it today.
Stamp it tomorrow,
Send it away.

"Write me a letter,
Send it by mail.
Send and direct it
To the Burlington jail."

"Burlington?" Titus asked Ovatt. "Is he singing 'bout the Kentucky
Burlington?"

"I don't know no other Burlington."

"Sing me 'nother of those I like," Ebenezer commanded from the
stern.

Kingsbury began to sing another to the tune of a 1766 hymn by Isaac
Watts.

> *"I'm far from home, far from the wife,*
> *Which in my bosom lay,*
> *Far from my children, dead, which used*
> *Around me for to play.*
>
> *"This doleful circumstance cannot*
> *My happiness prevent*
> *While peace of conscience I enjoy*
> *Great comfort and content."*

Titus took his eyes off Zane to ask of Ovatt, "Ebenezer married?"

"He was," Heman replied.

"And had he children?"

"Them too." But Heman warned, "Wouldn't do for you to ask after
them. It makes the man powerful sorry."

"What happened to his family?"

"They was kill't."

"Injuns?"

"Long ago, when the children was but babes," Ovatt explained. "All
boys, they was. Their heads smashed in by Shawnee."

Titus turned to gaze at the pilot, regarding the man studiously, wondering how it was to have one's family taken by a sudden act of savagery,
rather than merely an act of leaving.

Zane winked at Titus as he called out to Kingsbury, "Sing 'The Boatmen's Dance.' "

> *"High row, the boatmen row,*
> *Floating down the river of Ohio.*
> *The boatmen dance, the boatmen sing,*
> *The boatmen up to everything.*
> *And when the boatman gets on shore,*
> *He spends his cash and works for more.*
>
> *"Then dance, the boatmen dance.*
> *Oh, dance—the boatmen dance.*
> *Oh, dance all night till broad daylight,*

*And go home with the gals in
the morning!"*

Float time between sunup and sundown shrank a little each day, and there were mornings when they awakened to find a rime of ice slicking their cedar water buckets. As much as they could through the long, cold evenings of enforced idleness they stayed close by the sandbox fire before they would crab off to their blankets beneath the oiled awning cloth.

With their singing and their storytelling filling the long days and into the nights, how Titus often sat in pure wonder of these men who had welcomed him into their life, sweeping him along in their adventure, showing him how to make it his own. Rivermen, some called them. Others called them boatmen. Every last one of these restless souls folks on down the Mississippi had lumped together and called Kentuckians—these were the rough, rowdy, ne'er-do-wells Titus had come to regard as uncles, men who had taken him under their wings, to watch over, to teach, to open up the widening world to a young runaway from Rabbit Hash, in Boone County.

And if Root, Ovatt, and Kingsbury were his uncles . . . then Ebenezer Zane must surely be like the father he wished he had been born to. An unfettered spirit, instead of a man like Thaddeus Bass, who lived out his days tied down to one place—his dreams, his very vision, content to take in no more than what he could see of the forested hills around him. Less than a mile, no more than two miles at most—that was all a man could see in that cramped country his father had chosen to live out his days.

How was it that a man could satisfy himself so easily? Titus asked. How could a man content himself with so small a world, when the rest of it lay right out there for the taking? Had his father never had a dream like his own? Or was it simply that the older a man became, the more tarnished and smaller, the less important and more unrealized his dream became?

It was during the days as they floated toward the Mississippi that he thought on such things, with every new sunset and all the miles they put behind them, sensing all the more just what he had chosen to leave back there—pulled by all that which lured him onward.

Few people lived southwest of Louisville that early in the new century. No longer so hilly and broken, the countryside slowly flattened into a rich and fertile region.

"Good for the farmers what's coming," Hames Kingsbury stated. "Only a matter of time before they fill it up too."

Surveyed only nine years before, Henderson, Kentucky, was beginning to flourish as a crossroads for the state's Green River region. Floating on past Diamond Island, the boatmen then swept past the mouth of the Wabash, the western boundary of Indiana and one of the largest navigable rivers in the Northwest Territory.

Early one afternoon Kingsbury took to singing a jaunty tune.

> *"Some row up,*
> *Some row down.*
> *All the way—*
> *To Shawnee town.*
> *Pull away—pull away now!"*

"Ain't far to Shawnee town now," Ovatt declared, pointing downriver.

A few miles down from the Wabash they put to at Shawnee town, a wild and raucous river port then beginning to flourish on the north side of the Ohio, its new citizens finding easy profit in satisfying all a boatman's hungers. A little farther on Ebenezer Zane brought them to Cave-In Rock on the "Indian side" of the Ohio.

"Times was, there was talk river pirates hid out in this place," Hames Kingsbury explained to Titus as the crew put over to the north shore and climbed up to take in the legendary landmark.

"Pirates?" Bass inquired.

"Ain't no pirates working the river like they done of a time not so long ago," Ebenezer added. "Things pretty quiet nowdays."

Inside the cave the boatmen showed Titus where they had first inscribed their names on the walls, beneath them the dates of their first trips down the Ohio. The walls were covered from floor to a full arm's length above them with the names of hundreds of other river travelers.

"Here," Reuben Root said, holding out his belt knife to Titus by the blade. "Scratch your name in there."

As the youth finished the second *S* on his last name, Ovatt said, "You'll have to ask Ebenezer what day it is. He's the only one among us what pays heed to such things."

"It's your good fortune I do pay heed to such as that," Zane replied. "It's November the twenty-eighth, Titus."

"So that means the year still is eighteen and ten."

"Oh, you'll know when we get to the new year, all right," Kingsbury exclaimed. "That's good cause for celebration with this bunch."

"It's my birthday," Titus told them as he finished gouging out the last number.

"New Year's Day?" Ovatt asked.

Nodding, he turned and handed the knife back to Root.

"Way I hope things to go, Titus," Zane said, "we'll be on the Trace come 1811."

Titus asked, "The Trace? What's that?"

"It's the road we're walking home from the Mississap, through Tennessee and on to Kentucky," Kingsbury answered.

"A wilderness road that points us north," Zane added, turning toward the wide mouth of the cave. "Time we was setting off again."

Farther down the Ohio they passed the Cumberland River, commonly called the Shawanoe by the locals in the new nearby settlement of Smithtown, slowly spreading into the bottomland forest. In less than an hour they passed the Tennessee, both rivers flowing in from the south within a few miles of one another.

"That Smithtown is one place a man's life goes damned cheap," Root grumped as they passed by the wharf where a couple of dozen men came out of log cabins to hail the flatboat passing on by.

"Lots of knockabouts: fellas like you there, Titus," Kingsbury declared.

"Like me?" he asked, watching the men on the wharf wave, holler, attempting to attract attention and flag the boat over.

"Homeless runaways, I'll say. Young men with nothing but time on their hands. Even some boatmen what don't have jobs. They all waiting there to hire on as hands to any of the boats what hap to put in at Smithtown."

"A scurvy lot those wharf rats are," Ebenezer spat with a doleful wag of his head.

By this point the Ohio was becoming more and more crowded with river traffic originating all the way from the Allegheny and Monongahela, the Muskingum, Scioto, and Kentucky. Within some two hundred miles, four major rivers—the Green (what some locals still referred to as the Buffalo), the Wabash, the Cumberland, and the Tennessee, also known by the earliest settlers as the Cheraqui—all flowed into the Ohio. No more was she *la belle rivière* of the French traders. Yet she had become something quite grand, widening with mounting strength as each new river fed her its waters.

Past the Tennessee they floated by Fort Massac, first erected in the

Illinois country back in 1757 . . . then Wilkinsonville, a crude frontier station named after the young country's treasonous brigadier general James Wilkinson who continued to dabble in boating, soldiering, and conspiring to carve out his own empire in the West. Little more than clusters of cabins and riverside wharves, these were among a handful of tiny outposts cropping up here and there to signal the inevitable spread of a thriving frontier civilization. Over each village, smoke smudged the air as open fires, rock chimneys, and hundreds of smoldering tree stumps all raised their oily black columns into the late-autumn sky. Each of these riverside ports was simply a pocket of land stripped of its timber and brush to make room for a cluster of cabins, a common stockade, and a few cleared fields just beyond.

Why they hadn't left the forest the way it was . . . why men like his pap, and his grandpap before that, figured they could improve on what was there to begin with—Titus figured he never would know. Whoever, whatever, put the trees and critters there at the start likely had the best idea of all, he decided.

"It's up to man to bring peace to the hills and valleys," his father often repeated his litany of subduing the earth. "Up to man to pacify the land and make it fruitful—just as God commands us do."

If his pap's God wasn't the same what made all the hills and valleys and critters, then Titus would simply find himself another God to believe in. A God who could make such a luxurious garden of forest and timber and critters could never be a God that set silently with seeing his creation destroyed by man.

The farther west they floated, the more startling the contrasts became to him. With fewer and fewer settlements and outposts, with more and more long stretches of untouched wilderness—the differences between Titus and his father became all the more clear. While most came to a new land to conquer it, desiring to subdue all within sight, to make of it something in their own image . . . with every day Titus all the more sought the wilderness on its own terms.

As they approached the mouth of the Ohio, Titus realized he had flatboated from the gentle mountains and forests of the upper river, southwesterly to a region of flooded lowlands and great stretches of treeless, brushy wilderness as far as the eye could see. The Ohio was the feeder, bringing the races and cultures tumbling together: Scotch-Irish, Kentuckians, English and French, pioneers all, rubbing shoulders with Creoles, Negro slaves, mulattoes, and freedmen, as well as an array of tribesmen—Shawnee, Miami, Delaware, Peoria, Sauk, and Piankashaw.

"These Injuns ain't a problem to rivermen no more," Zane explained as they closed on the mouth of the river, where the often-roiling blue Ohio mingled with and lost itself to the coffee-colored, more sedate Mississippi. "Most of them redskins moving on into the Illinois country. Maybeso across the Mississippi to the west. White man's land over here. Let them red bastards have all that's left 'em over yonder."

His eyes widened as he stood, mesmerized and amazed in watching the great sweep of water come in off the starboard. Pointing, Titus asked, "What's that river coming in?"

"It ain't coming in, Titus," the pilot explained with a smile. "This'r Ohio coming into it."

In wonder at the sheer size of it he exclaimed, "That's the Mississip?"

Working his rudder beneath one arm to position them into the colliding currents, Ebenezer Zane replied, "Ain't none the other. You come to the mighty Mississip, Titus Bass." Nodding to the south, he said, "Over here is all the land any man could want to farm and raise up his towns."

Yet Titus stared off across the widening expanse of water at the far, far shore. He pointed to the west. "And over there?"

"Over there," Zane answered with a sigh, "is the beginning of a wilderness fit only for Injuns, critters, and wild men."

TEN

As Titus stood atop some of the hogsheads of flour to get himself the best view of that spectacular, unpeopled country, Ebenezer Zane heaved against his rudder to slip the flatboat out from the mouth of the Ohio and into the great, wide Mississippi already beginning to spread itself a mile and more wide in its slow roll to the south.

"Yonder's Cairo," the pilot called out, pointing off toward the collection of shacks and log cabins built around a tiny wharf at the end of that peninsula formed by the joining of the two waters.

Kingsbury brought his oar out of the water and leaned back with a sigh. "Farther on up there, Titus—a man comes to St. Louie."

"Like I said: time enough to get there, young as I am," Titus said, his eyes widening as he took in the vast sweep of all that stretched before him on that far western horizon.

"Young as you is," Root scoffed at his oar below Bass, "you can have you two or three big adventures afore you gotta figure out what it is you're gonna do for the rest of your life."

"Don't pay him no heed, Titus," Zane advised. "Reuben still ain't sorted out what he's gonna do when he gets growed up!"

While rolling hills and timbered bluffs dominated the Mississippi's shoreline above the mouth of the Ohio, from there south one could watch the landscape begin to flatten. Eagles dotted the cold, clear sky overhead, sweeping across the great expanse of the river in search of a meal they could pluck from the muddied waters in huge claws. Wild turkeys squatted in autumn's leafless trees along the riverbanks like stumpy, black-robed, wattle-necked old men, curiously watching the boatmen float past.

"Lookee there!" Heman Ovatt cried out, pointing to the eastern shore where loped a small pack of wolves, no more than a half dozen, slinking easily along the skirt of timber that frilled the riverbank.

"Hunting must be good in these parts," Titus exclaimed, already sensing an undeniable itch to have the ground beneath his moccasins and the woods at his elbow once more.

Zane scratched at his hairy cheek and inquired, "You figure you could find us some game yonder?"

With an eager grin Bass turned to the steersman, saying, "If you spot wolves along the bank, I figure there's a good chance I'd run onto something for us to eat over there too."

"Damn right," Kingsbury added. "Them wolves didn't look like they'd missed a meal a'tall!"

"I'll bet these fellas would appreciate you giving them a change in supper fare tonight, Titus," Zane continued, then looked off to the west to measure the fall of the sun in that cold sky. "Not far down here, I know a place where we can put over and let you off with your rifle. We'll ease on down a few miles and tie up for the night. Get us a fire going and wait for you to bring us in some victuals for supper. How's that strike you?"

"It sounds fine to me!" Bass replied, starting to scramble down from atop the great oak kegs, eager to have a chance to hunt for the crew once again, just as he already had done on several occasions while they'd descended the lower Ohio.

"Here's one man gets damned tired of eating pig all the time," Kingsbury grumbled.

"Speak for yourself," Root snapped. "A thick slab of salt pork allays better'n some gamy ol' slice of buckskin."

"Y'all got my hungers up already," Ovatt cheered from the bow, where he had been working at expanding one of his most elaborate tattoos, scratching at his forearm with a needle, then marking the artistic wound with India ink. More than any of the others, Heman was nearly covered in the gaudy blue drawings of sea serpents and devil's heads, water maidens and feathered Indians. He looked up from his work, saying, "Don't you give Reuben no never mind, Titus. This belly of mine could do wrapping around something new tonight, Titus!"

"G'won now and get yourself ready," Zane instructed. "It ain't far till we come to that stretch of shore where we'll drop you off to do some hunting. That is, if the river ain't et the bank away too bad since't last summer."

Even as slow as it moved, the relentless Mississippi had a way of doing that: gobbling up great bites of the riverbank from season to season. Come late spring, early summer, the river would lift twenty-five feet or more above its banks, cutting itself a new channel in the process, going here and there to alter last year's course. As it did so, the Mississippi would destroy old islands and create new ones, uproot trees from both the banks and the far end of those new islands, depositing that timber on the upstream end of the next island met downriver. At high-water times of the year, tying up for the night could be a ticklish proposition: a good river captain understood that to secure his boat beneath a high bank or large timber just might mean the Mississippi would cause that bank to cave in on his broadhorn, or chew away enough of the shore, toppling one of the huge trees to come crashing down upon his sleeping crew.

Flowing anywhere from three to five miles per hour, the Mississippi ran thirty feet deep in most places, fifty feet in some spots as it seesawed back and forth, making itself remarkably crooked. Despite the river's width, it still proved itself a real test not only of a river pilot's abilities at the rudder, but of the watchfulness of the rest of his crew as they kept eyes sweeping the roiling waters for all manner of dangers: sawyers and planters and submerged sandbars.

"You warm enough now?" Zane asked as he eased the flatboat out of the running current and headed for the eastern shore.

"I'll be fine," Bass replied, kneeling at the gunnel as Root lowered the skiff into the muddy water.

After Titus climbed into the tiny boat and he began paddling with Reuben, Ovatt played out a length of hawser lashed to the back of the skiff.

"Get on off afore we gotta push back into the running current," Root advised.

The youngster heaved himself onto the bank just as Root waved across those yards of icy water, signaling Heman Ovatt to pull the skiff back to the flatboat.

"Cold as it is, Titus," Reuben hollered over his shoulder as Heman began to drag him away from the shoreline, "lot better to be hunting now. Come the summer in these here parts, skeeters come pick you up and carry you off, you go hunting way you are in them woods!"

Such winged torment wasn't the only disadvantage to hunting the riverbanks come the summer season. The heat and humidity both conspired against a man laboring through the thick, semitropical brush, weakening many with heat-fevers.

Root waved his final farewell, saying, "Skeeters down in this here country twice't as big as the ones we grow up to Kentucky! Big as a god-damned sparrow!"

Waving in kind, Titus watched the skiff and flatboat move away, slipping back into the current, sensing a rush of emotions tumbling through him. Excitement and sheer anticipation had to be most prominent, as well as a good deal of pride, what with the trust the others placed in him to bring supper eventually to their evening fire.

Titus clawed his way up the bank, into the brush and trees, then stopped with that shadow-drenched cover and looked again at the flatboat one last time from hiding. Perhaps he should be a bit scared, he told himself. Left here on his own in country that was as foreign to him as a desert. Maybe he ought to be frightened, Titus thought as his eyes slowly moved in a long sweep from left to right, listening with all his might to those sounds the woods brought to him.

But in a matter of moments he was scolding himself for ever thinking about fear, telling himself that the apprehension he felt was a natural part of the anticipation of the hunt.

What with the way those wolves were moving downriver along the bank, he decided he would have to work his way inland a bit. A pack like them surely had to be scattering game away from the riverbank itself. Chances would likely be far better if he did not hunt in the wake of those gaunt, four-legged predators flushing most everything before them.

Angling south by east, he struck out, plunging into the brushy timber, taking in this terrain and plant life so new to him. In less than a mile, and after something on the order of a half hour, he ran across a groove worn in the woodland floor. A game trail that arced off to his right toward the river, tracked and clawed with the prints of many animals. Titus rose and eagerly turned left, following the trail deeper into the timber. Within a few yards he came across a pile of deer droppings. As chilly as it was, with skiffs of sleety snow coating nearly every plant and gathered at the base of every tree, he didn't expect to feel any warmth from the spoor as he took a handful into his palm. Nonetheless, the cold discovery quickened both his heartbeat and his step as he pushed deeper into the timber. It was good sign. Showed that the critters did use this trail.

The farther he went, the brush thickened around him. Titus slowed his pace, his eyes searching ahead of him so that he would not scare up the white-tailed deer he hoped to sight before it bolted off. Buck or doe—it did not matter, although he preferred the flesh of the doe for its tenderness and flavor, especially this time of the year after the males had gone and worked themselves into a hormone-driven frenzy during the rut.

It was a thought that made him chuckle quietly as he moved along through the cold shadows. Now that he had experienced the rut himself, it was damned easy to understand how those bucks got themselves into such a ferocious state over the thought of climbing atop a female!

Something snagged his attention. A faint rustle of brush that hadn't been there before. At least some sound that had failed to pierce his consciousness until now. Yes . . . there it was again . . . moving toward him. He backed up a few yards, out of that small clearing the trail crossed, then crouched within some brush and pulled the hammer on his grandpap's rifle back from half cock. Waiting as his heart pounded and the sound of leaves rustling drew ever closer.

He swore he even heard the deer breathing before he saw the frost streaming from its glossy black nostrils, the chest heaving in fear, perhaps exhaustion too, as the doe bounded into the clearing and stopped, stiff-legged. In fright it twisted its head one way, then another, studying the open ground before it—then jerked its head over its shoulder to gaze along its backtrail with wide, frightened eyes Titus now watched above the front blade he nestled down in the narrow crescent of the backsight.

Just as it wrenched its head forward and twitched its tail—always a sure sign that the deer was about to set off once more—Titus squeezed back on the trigger.

In that next heartbeat it appeared he had missed, for the deer bounded off on all four legs. His greatest fear right then was that the doe had started away before he had touched off the shot. He peered through the brush and gray smoke, hearing his rifle shot swallowed by the timber and the cold, damp air.

But instead of the clatter of the deer's hooves galloping off into the trees, the only sound that followed the fading gunshot was the silence that echoed back upon him. That, and the thrash of the deer's legs as the animal struggled on the ground at the far side of the small clearing.

Immediately bolting from cover, Titus raced across the open ground, laid the rifle against some nearby brush, and knelt near the deer as the legs slowed their wild fight. A big brown eye stared up at him. He looked down at the ragged, bloody hole torn in the heaving, lower chest, then back to that eye. Already it was beginning to glaze. And then the legs moved no more.

Quickly he pulled out his big belt knife and slit the throat in order to drain off most of the blood from the carcass before he dragged the blade down the length of the body, from windpipe to rectum. Since this was a doe, which ran smaller than most bucks, he thought he might try carrying the carcass over his shoulder down to where he would find the boat crew having made camp for the night. By cutting off the head and gutting the animal, along with getting rid of the weight of the green hide, he could easily drape the rest of the kill over his shoulders and hurry it downriver.

He had never been the strongest youngster in Boone County, hardly the strongest right around the village of Rabbit Hash either. Truth was, Titus was mostly bone and sinew, with a few strap-leather-lean muscles knotted to his wiry frame. Because he was stronger in his legs than elsewhere on his body, Titus early on had learned he simply could not heft the weight other fellas his age could lift and carry, much less do what a full-grown man could. Standing just shy of six feet in his moccasins, but weighing less than 140 pounds by the wharfmaster's scale at Louisville scant weeks before, Bass truly gave off the appearance of a much smaller man when he stood with his shoulders slightly rounded as he shrank back into himself, shy as he was. Because of his spare size and rail-thin frame, the youngster had learned to make do for the lack of muscle. No matter how much he ate in the last few years, no matter how much he demanded of his body, he never seemed to fill out and put on the pounds the way so many other Boone County boys had.

Didn't matter anyhow, he reminded himself as he carried on with removing the internal organs and flinging them into a nearby gut-pile. Time would come, Titus knew, and he'd put on some weight, finally getting those muscles every man eventually earned.

Shadows lengthened across the cold ground while he worked, his breath beginning to frost before his face in his exertion. Yet his hands remained warm, working in the blood and the carcass as they did. He cut the last of the windpipe and lung free, then flung them onto the gut-pile . . . when he froze.

Motionless. A new sound. Something that did not fit in with what he had been hearing from the surrounding forest as he labored over the doe.

Perhaps it was another deer, he convinced himself. Much the same sound too—moving through the brush and coming from the same direction as the doe had. Closer and closer. He might be lucky and get two of them, he convinced himself. Then he'd have to cut down a few saplings and make a crude sled he could use to drag both carcasses downriver to the boatmen's camp.

Quickly he wiped most of the blood and gore from his hands in the frosty, icy leaves, then swept up his rifle before ducking back toward the brush where he had been hiding when the doe had made her appearance along the game trail.

What meat Zane's men didn't gorge themselves on that night, they could spend the evening slicing and drying by the fire. Maybe carry along the bigger hams with them on board, as long as they were out of the sun, tucked away under that oiled awning on the boat. Along with the dried strips of venison, those roasts would give them several meals across the coming days before Zane might have him again hunt for them.

Crouching there in the brush, he dragged the rifle up and pushed back the frizzen. Snugging his shooting pouch against his thigh, Titus pulled the stopper from the priming horn and sprinkled a dusting of powder into the pan—for the first time realizing he hadn't reloaded after dropping the doe.

Damn!

Yet he had no more time to curse himself for his stupidity as the faint rustle came ever closer.

He grew angry with himself: if he didn't get his rifle reloaded, he was going to miss his chance to drop a second deer. No matter that it might be a buck this time.

Quickly pouring powder into his palm, he found himself quaking slightly as he spilled the coarse black grains down the muzzle—then became still as a stone. His own eyes widened, his breath choked off in his chest as the creature stepped to the far edge of the clearing.

Instead of a four-legged buck moving beneath a set of antlers, what made young Titus's heart freeze in his chest was a two-legged Indian in smoked buckskin who slowly emerged from the brush in a crouch, then sank to his knee.

Now his heart began hammering so loudly, he was certain the Indian could hear it. Starting to sweat in the cold of those shadows, Titus found himself every bit as scared as he was mad that his gunshot had drawn the redskin to the clearing.

This way, then that, the Indian's own dark, black-bead eyes searched the timber enclosing the clearing, before he inched forward a bit more, easing toward the deer. Kneeling over the gutted animal, the Indian put a bare hand down into the gut cavity.

He's feeling how warm it is. How long ago I kill't it.

All the while the Indian's eyes kept moving across the glade, watchful and attentive. From the looks of the warrior, Titus figured the man could be anywhere between his age and his father's. Hell, he thought—he never had been very good at guessing such things as a person's age.

Swallowing hard, he suddenly realized this was the first real Indian he had laid eyes on. Not that he hadn't seen some come wandering into the settlements back in Boone County. The sort what had taken to white man's clothes and even wore hats. But never had he seen a redskin like this: complete in fringed buckskins, with a deerskin vest tied with thongs, the lower part of his leggings lashed tightly around his ankles and calves with long whangs.

Titus glanced down at his own smooth britches, figuring fringe would only snag in the thick underbrush. Nodding to himself, he decided that tying them up that way made for easier, quieter hunting too, as the Indian moved through the thick timber.

Quietly settling on the far side of the doe, the Indian laid his bow across his thighs, then dragged a big knife from the scabbard at his waist. Beginning at the long opening Titus had made from neck to anus, the Indian started working to free the green hide from the carcass on either side of the rib cage.

Why, this son of a bitch was fixing to take his meat! That damned hide didn't matter—but it was the meat the others were expecting him to show up with at camp shortly!

A goddamned red thief! All that grandpap told me 'bout Injuns is true —thievin' sonsabitches!

Now his temples pounded more from anger than from fear. That was his meat.

Mine—what's 'bout to get stole from me!

Clenching his teeth was the only thing that kept him from hollering out right then and there—to tell that Indian the doe was his. Instead, Titus struggled to fight down that impulse, his mind racing to sort out what to do with a problem he had never before confronted. A man could figure out an answer to everything, he reminded himself. If he just had enough time, and thought on it hard enough. It wasn't like he was the smartest fella in school back there in Rabbit Hash. Not the quickest, but he could learn, once he put his mind to it. And this couldn't be any different, he told himself.

Just maybe he could show himself and somehow work it so the Injun and he could split up the doe. At least he'd have half the meat that way . . . and a damned good story to tell the others when he finally showed up downriver a ways.

Yet just about the time he was convincing himself of the wisdom he would show by negotiating half the doe with the Indian and was finally ready to show himself, Bass snapped to a sudden stillness.

A chirping whistle floated from the nearby woods.

That's a Injun. Damn, if there ain't another'un out there.

As he crouched lower in his stand of brush, frozen and wide-eyed, Titus watched the would-be thief stop and listen, then eventually put a hand to his mouth, answering in the same chirping birdcall. Another whistle came from the forest, this time from a different direction than the first. This second call, too, was answered by the meat thief.

It was with the keenest curiosity that Titus stared at the four warriors who emerged from the woods to join the first. One of them carried what appeared to be an old smoothbore musket. For a few moments all five appeared to share some words, yet their talk was so quiet, he could hear nothing of it. From the far timber came another chirp, which one of the newcomers answered. They all turned to gaze toward the north.

Like them, Titus watched that fringe of the timber, when his wonder turned to nothing but cold, dry fear in his belly. Swallowing hard around the lump swelling in his throat, he counted six more of them emerging from the shadows—four carrying short bows, and another two with guns, what appeared to be a pair of old French fusils. Half of them already dragged some haunches of meat and green hides they had rolled up, all of it placed on improvised sleds they had constructed from saplings cut down and lashed together with ivy and grapevine. It would be easy enough to pull those sleds over the brush and what little icy snow slicked the ground.

They all came to the doe, talking a little louder now that there were so many to discuss what had been found by one of their number. Still, he could not make out much of the words at all, only fragments of sounds that meant nothing to him in the least. Except to realize that these were red men. Hunters and warriors. The sort his grandpap had fought back in the Shawnee War and two years later in the Cherokee War. These were the sort of Indian the white settlers were driving right up against the Mississippi, he figured. Not the sort of Indian to take kindly to a solitary white hunter caught alone and far from his own.

The breeze tousled their hair, some of which was left long. For others the hairstyle of choice was a roach greased so that it stood straight up from the forehead to taunt any would-be enemy into taking that war trophy. Yet none of them wore any paint. From his grandpap and the old men, Titus had heard so much about the hideous paint—looking now to study each of the faces of the eleven who continued to argue something with growing urgency.

One of them pointed—south. An older man wagged his head emphatically, pointing off in another direction. Back to the north.

A third stepped forward, gestured to the doe, then gestured to the south with his bow. Several of the group grunted their agreement with whatever he had declared, for they nodded as they inched up to stand behind him.

Honest-to-goodness Injun warriors! It sent a new shiver down his spine.

A heartbeat later it began to sink in. They were discussing him! Talking over who must have killed the doe. They had to realize the hunter was somewhere close—simply because the carcass was still warm when found. They had to figure the hunter couldn't have got very far before the deer was discovered.

He wasn't sure he breathed at all, afraid even to do that right then in his hiding place. With growing certainty Titus feared these warriors were sure to hear his heart hammering against his ribs if it continued to get any louder—what with the way the blood rushed up his neck cords and roared in his ears, thundering in his temples.

Some of them crouched to study the ground around the gut-pile and the carcass, then peered off into the forest, talking to one another, gesturing. There wasn't any one thing he could put his finger on to tell him that they knew of him—maybe just the way they turned their heads to regard the woods around them, the way their voices got quiet, the way the eight of them strung their bows and the other three slowly brought up their long-barreled guns, those huge muzzles swinging out toward the timber surrounding the small glade like wide black eyes.

He could not remember ever finding himself on this end of a gun before—staring down the barrel of a weapon that might well be used against him.

With that moment came clarity of thought, the sharp-honed realization they were bound to discover him once they spread out and crossed those few rods between them and where he crouched in hiding, his legs beginning to cramp in pain. He had to act.

Simple, untarred fear was what compelled him to move at last. Nothing as complicated as the consideration of his options. To his uncluttered mind in this, his first confrontation with real Indians, Titus decided he had no options. It was run or die.

As he exploded from the brushy undergrowth, heading back toward the river at a sharp angle to the southwest, Titus heard them shout to one another behind him. Surprised, confused for the moment—perhaps even afraid there might be more than one. How he hoped their fear might delay them, if only for a moment or so to contemplate what they should do, how many they might be facing down, if there might be more enemies lying in wait for them to make a mistake. Oh, how he wanted them to be seized with some of the uncertainty, nay—the outright fear—that drove his cramped legs into frantic motion.

Leaping, dodging, sprinting, making for the far-off riverbank still at least a mile away. How far down the others had gone before they put to and tied up to await his delivery of their evening meal . . . he had no idea. Only a hope. Nothing he could call a real prayer—the way his folks prayed, or the prayers of that circuit man who came around to hold his Bible meetings, then went home with one family or the other, gone to dinner and a dry place to sleep before moving on to another village the following day.

No, what Titus did as he sprinted through the icy forest, trying his best to stay where the thin layer of wet snow did not blanket the ground near as deeply, was to try to will those four boatmen to sense the danger he was in. To call out to them with nothing more than his thumping heart, since he could not cry out with his throat grown raw from every gasp of the cold air he dragged into his lungs. So far away, they wouldn't hear him anyway, he told himself.

But Titus could hear the hunting party coming: whooping, hollering, crying out in shrill voices. Those yelps, more than the crashing brush he heard whipping his pursuers, drove him onward. Wishing he had loaded the rifle as soon as he had shot the doe. At least he would then have one shot. One last shot before they came within reach of him. To drop one of his killers—a way to even things up, he thought.

But that didn't matter either. He cursed his luck. Cursed his stupidity. None of it mattered because he hadn't loaded his rifle. Never had to think about it before. Forests where he grew up, hunted, came of age as a woods-man—those wooded hills were no longer haunted by red men. His grandpap's kind, and a few expeditionary army forces—they had pushed the Injuns farther west. Bass had simply never had to worry about bumping into redskins before.

He stumbled, spilling to one knee, the rifle skidding from his grasp in a skiff of snow iced across a patch of leafy brush. Lumbering to his feet, Titus told himself to forget the pain crying out from his knee. Scooping up the rifle and a handful of dead leaves, he pushed on through the woods, trying to forget the bare limbs and thorny branches that whipped at his face.

They thundered behind him, breaking through the underbrush, some exhorting the others with chants and war cries—he swore he could even hear the hard breathing of a few of the closest ones, grunting as they chased him.

Plunging into a thicket of bramble, he felt the thorns claw at his jerkin, catch at the cuff on his britches, slash the back of his hands to ribbons as he swept ahead—struggling to hack his way through to the far side of the briars. Now he had a good-sized gash on one eyelid, and it was beginning to ooze enough that it hindered his vision from that eye. As slow as he was in breaking through to the other side—Titus was certain with his every step that he would feel a bullet catch him, maybe an arrow driving deep into those thin, sinewy muscles of his back. By their growing shrieks he knew they were closing on him faster than he would have ever imagined possible.

But then he remembered this was their forest. Not his. And he became all the more frightened—figuring they knew where he was going much better than he. Something cold clutching his belly in a knot made him fear some of the fastest ones might even get somewhere ahead of him and be waiting for him.

The breathing, the grunts, the yelps he heard at his heels, all made him fear that his first run-in with real Indians was going to be his last. Something he simply would not live to tell his grandchildren of, the way his grandpap had sat the young'uns around his knee and told them the chilling, hair-raising stories of just what a dark and bloody ground that Ohio River canebrake country had been of a time not all that long ago.

An angry whine sailed past his ear, followed a heartbeat later by the roar of a musket behind him. He'd never been shot at. Now he felt as if he had become the fleeing game, the bounding, hard-pressed buck or doe, pursued by the hunters, chased through the thickets, driven across the snow as his heart pounded in his chest until he was sure it was going to burst with its next beat.

What a fool he had been to go so far inland to hunt!

His stupidity, along with the fear, the exhaustion, and the utter hope-lessness of ever reaching the boatmen alive . . . it all came slipping in on him like separate fingers to claw the courage right out of him. At least a mile inland, and they must surely have gone much more than a mile downriver. That meant that no matter how he cut back to the river at an angle, he still had more than two miles—maybe even twice that—before he would reach the boatmen's camp.

How he wished Ebenezer had been with him when the first Indian showed up. For sure he wouldn't have frozen in fear, Titus thought. Not the way Abigail had told him of how Zane had waded right into the rivermen fixing to abuse a friend of his, Mathilda. The river pilot would do no less for Titus, would he, now? Any of them, maybe even Reuben, the sourest of the lot, would have helped him take care of that first Indian . . . and they could have slipped away before the others had happed onto the clearing.

His breathing came a little easier. Titus figured he was getting his second wind. Chest didn't hurt so much now. And the soles of his feet inside that double pair of moccasins didn't pain him near as much as they had there at first. Maybe they were simply numb. He couldn't tell, really—not able to feel anything from the ankles down. Like something cold clinging from the end of his legs.

What a fool he was for going so far inland to hunt. A fool for seeking the aloneness with the woods and what game he might find . . . for now the boatmen could not hear his yells, even if he could have forced his dry mouth, his aching throat, to break free a yelp of warning. There were two things he realized had a crystal certainty at that moment: the Indians were still behind him, crashing through the brush in his wake; and the boatmen were still somewhere ahead of him, floating somewhere downriver before tying up for the night to await him and the game he was to bring in.

That almost made him laugh, and almost laughing made him want to cry. Instead of carrying in some haunches of fresh venison, he was bringing in some Indians right behind him. As the limbs and thorns whipped across his face, slashed at his eyes, Titus tried to focus on each of their faces, one at a time, to imagine how the four rivermen might look as he came down upon the camp they had made.

Sitting there circling their fire.

Fire!

He could almost smell it. Wanting so bad to stop long enough to get himself a good, long whiff of that fragrance on the cold wind. But he dared not stop for anything . . . hearing the Indians renew their yelps and cries close behind him. Perhaps they smelled that fire too. Maybe it wasn't his imagination, after all.

Then he realized warriors would figure on redoubling their efforts to get to him before he got any closer to any sort of help.

It was his sensitive nose that led him across that last half mile of chest-heaving sprint. As an animal might catch the scent of danger on the wind, this time Titus followed the scent of man's woodsmoke toward the east bank of the Mississippi.

Then in the murky light of that late afternoon as the air seemed to grow all the colder, he thought he spotted a distant twinkle of light. Almost like a faraway star flung against the dark shimmer of twilight coming down upon that river valley, a flicker of something against the dark, rolling band of the Mississippi itself. The light danced and rose, quivering from side to side. Their fire!

He tried to yell, but nothing came out—finding his tongue pasted to the floor of his mouth, unable to budge it free.

Then he saw movement cross in front of the light of that fire, remembering how he had happened upon the four of them early last autumn, back on the upper Ohio. Their black shadows momentarily cut off the light as they moved about the fire. He tried again to yell, his tongue freed a bit, and sensed his warning come out as a squeak escaping his parched throat.

One of the shadows ahead of him stopped, backlit by the fire. Then it seemed that they turned. He could hear the sound of voices suddenly raised in alarm ahead of him, no longer just those cries and yelps behind him. Then the four were all on their feet, looking at him.

Didn't they know! Couldn't they see!

Clumsily he tried to twist his upper body as he ran, pointing behind him with the empty hand. In doing so he nearly stumbled on the last clumps of some low brush just as he reached the muddy, sandy bank. The final thing he saw before he began to pitch forward was Ebenezer waving his arms and the other three breaking in different directions.

He felt the grit of the icy sand and snow bite the bloodied skin on his face, sensed it scoop into his mouth, rub raw against the cuts on the back of his hands as he got to all fours, crawling, scrambling to get back onto his feet at the same time he swiped a forearm across his eyes to clear them of sand and blood and stinging sweat.

And before he realized it, he was sprinting again.

Heman Ovatt was already on the flatboat, lunging from the awning to the gunnel, something in his hands. There he threw the long object to Kingsbury, a second to Root. While Ovatt turned back to that awning of oiled Russian sheeting, Titus knew those had to be longrifles, muskets, smoothbores, fusils—firearms! As Ovatt reappeared at the gunnel with two more, Titus watched Kingsbury and Root scurry in his direction, where they dropped to their knees and brought their weapons to their shoulders.

Zane swung about with a rifle in his own hands, bringing it to his shoulder as Ovatt leaped over the side of the boat. The steersman hollered something. Titus wasn't sure what he said. The words sounded garbled at first.

"Hold your fire, boys!"

Then he understood, as Kingsbury rose from his knee, his rifle still at his cheek.

"C'mon, Titus Bass! C'mon—you can make it!"

Hames strode toward Bass confidently, the muzzle of his weapon pointing at whatever might be pressing down on Titus from behind.

"Get on in here, Titus!"

He lunged past Kingsbury as Root got up from his knee and began to move backward, a step at a time. Ovatt and Zane were there to catch Bass as he stumbled against them.

"Get him on board!" the pilot ordered Heman.

Ovatt turned, clutching Bass as they careened down the riverbank past the big, warming fire they had built. How he wanted to stop, to rest, to feel the fire's warmth. He found himself stumbling.

"Get up!" Ovatt hollered.

Zane became frantic, shouting, "Get yourself in the boat!"

He did as he was told, scrambling over the gunnel as the first shot rang out.

Yet it wasn't fired by any of the four boatmen. The shot had come from the brush, where he glanced to see a whiff of smoke, saw glimpses of the Indians converging, then moving apart at the edge of the timber.

"Ease back to the waterline, boys," Zane ordered his crew. "Hold 'em so they don't break on us."

The three of them continued to back slowly, slowly toward the flatboat, training their rifles on the timber, holding the Indians at bay. Bass stuffed a hand down into his shooting pouch, dragging out at least a dozen round lead balls he then popped into his mouth.

"Heman—you got them hawsers?"

Ovatt turned from the last of two lines securing the flatboat for the night. "Done, Ebenezer. I'm getting on up so I can pole us off soon as the rest of you're here." Heman leaped against the side of the flatboat and kicked a leg over the gunnel, rolling himself aboard.

Pulling the plug from his powder horn, Titus spilled more of the coarse black grains onto the deck than he got into his palm. Trembling more now with the exquisite excitement of their predicament than with anything resembling fear, he turned that quaking hand over the muzzle and poured the powder down the long barrel. One of the lead balls he popped from his lips and dropped down the muzzle without a patch.

Without taking his eyes off the enemy still clinging to the shadows, Zane said, "You get on up first, Reuben!"

They were less than five yards from the boat now—just about the time the Indians were making a clear, stand-up show of themselves at the edge of the timber. Yelling, screeching, pounding their chests and taunting the boatmen, a few even pulled aside their breechclouts and exposed their manhood at the whites from the river.

As Root turned his back on the Indians and raised his arms to clamber over the gunnel, Bass and Ovatt both reached down to help him get on board.

Titus asked, "What's that mean, them showing us their . . . their privates that way?"

"Just their way of telling you they think you ain't much of a man like them," Root grumbled as he turned and crouched atop a pair of large oak casks, pointing his rifle at the edge of the timber.

"You next, Hames!" Ebenezer ordered, only his eyes moving back and forth as the two of them backed right to the water's edge. He eased back a few more steps, the water lapping at his knees before he came to a stop.

"We can both climb on at once't, Ebenezer!" Kingsbury protested.

"No!" he growled. "That'd take two guns off them red devils at once't. Get!"

His lips pursed in resignation, Kingsbury turned and splashed out to the flatboat as it drifted lazily away from its moorings. He slogged through water midway up his thighs before he could toss his rifle up to Ovatt, then held up his arms for help.

Bass did his best to sprinkle a dusting of priming powder down into the pan while he kept his eyes darting across the crescent of Indians pointing muskets and arrows at the boat and its white men.

Kingsbury shrieked, "C'mon, Ebenezer!"

"You all got your guns ready?" Zane asked, cocking his head slightly so he could snatch a quick glance at the flatboat.

"Gotta come now, Ebenezer!" Kingsbury shouted. "We're loose and drifting off!"

Bass's heart leaped into his throat as he felt the river jostle the boat to the side as they inched out into the channel where the Mississippi's pull became increasingly stronger. They were easing away from the pilot.

"Zane!" Root cried.

Ebenezer waited no longer. Suddenly wheeling, the steersman lunged around into the water, struggling as the river bottom sank deeper, desperate to reach the side of the flatboat before it drifted out of reach.

"I'll get the rudder an' work us back to shore!" Kingsbury shouted, starting for the stern.

"No, goddammit!" Zane bellowed, the water up to his waist as he fought his way into deeper and deeper water. "Keep your gun on them!"

The first bullet smacked into the gunnel, just past the pilot's head. Titus snapped up, wrenched from watching Zane's struggle to find the Indians emerging onto the open beach where the white men had tied up for the night. The arrows began to arc silently into the twilight. Making no noise until they struck the thick yellow timbers, snapping at times like dried cane stalks underfoot in the ripe, moist bottomland every winter. A few sailed down through the oiled awning with a brief hiss as they ripped through the heavy fabric.

"Listen to 'em, will you?" Kingsbury called out. "That's a Chickasaw war whoop if'n I ever heard one!"

"Shuddup and shoot, goddammit!" Ebenezer called out.

As Titus pulled the hammer back to full cock, he watched Root reach down and snatch the rifle from Zane, who now stood up to his armpits in the river. Bass whirled away as the boat twisted slightly, starting to come broadside against the current, throwing the blade down into that back buckhorn sight—not knowing where the hell to hold on those tall figures. Sure as anything, he knew game: where to hold his sights on a turkey or squirrel, deer or even a black bear. But . . . those were men! Red bastards to be sure, just what Zane had called them. And they would've likely killed him and raised his hair if he hadn't run so fast, what with being so damned scared. Shooting a man?

He held squarely on the middle of one of the bodies—an Indian who stood reloading his rifle. And Titus squeezed, clenching both eyes shut.

When he dared open them in the echo of the gun's blast, he watched the Indian spin like a string top, his rifle cartwheeling out of his grip. Ducking down on one knee to reload, he saw from the corner of his eye Zane kick one leg onto the top of the gunnel. Then heard the pilot grunt.

More and more arrows slapped the surface of the water, thwacked into the side of the boat with a hollow, leaden sound.

"Jesus God, Ebenezer!" Ovatt cried.

"He done caught one!" Root said, desperation in his voice.

"Get us the hell out of here!" Zane snapped as they dragged him over the gunnel and onto some crates. "Hear me, Kingsbury! Get to that rudder!"

All at once the men seemed to explode in different directions, every one of them hollering as the Indians came on down the sandy bank to the water's edge, shooting their old muskets and loosing their arrows, screeching and crying out in frustrated disappointment.

"Goddamned Chickasaws," Zane growled as he rolled onto his belly.

That's when Titus glanced away to the beach—then immediately looked back at the pilot, his mind suddenly realizing what his eye had seen: the long shaft of an arrow, its fletching a'quiver with the muscle spasms in Ebenezer's leg as the pilot struggled to make himself small among the crates.

"Titus—go help him!" Ovatt ordered from the bow where he had seized the gouger and was working it frantically back and forth to help Kingsbury speed the flatboat farther out into the current.

Stuffing the rifle between two of the kegs filled with iron nails, Bass scrambled toward Zane.

"Goddamned Chickasaws . . . goddamn, goddamn, goddamn," the pilot muttered repeatedly.

"That what they are? Chicka . . . Chicka—"

"Saws. Goddamned Chickasaws," Ebenezer grumbled as he twisted onto his side. "Take a look at the son of a bitch for me. See how bad she's bleeding back there."

"Damn right, they was Chickasaws," Kingsbury bellowed from the stern rudder. "No other cry like a Chickasaw war whoop in the world—them runts hollering for blood the way they do."

"Ain't bleeding too bad," Titus declared, wide-eyed, staring down at the back of the pilot's leg.

"Cut it open," Zane ordered.

"Y-your leg?"

He wagged his head, biting down on his lower lip, then said, "No. Cut open my britches, goddammit—so you can see for sure if I'm bleeding bad."

Pulling his knife from his belt with one hand, the other gripping the thick canvas fabric of the pants, Titus pricked a long slice away from the arrow's shaft.

"How it be?" Zane inquired, dolefully looking over his shoulder in the coming darkness. "Best get me in there."

Titus watched the pilot nod to the open area beneath the awning, then lifted Ebenezer's arm over his shoulder, dragging him off the crates, hopping one-legged under the edge of the cloth.

"Light a few of them wind lanterns. We're bound to need some light," Zane ordered. As Bass set about pulling some tow from a kindling box, the pilot turned to fling his voice at Kingsbury. "Hames—best you get us on downriver afore putting over."

Kingsbury shook his head in protest. "I wanna look at that leg of yours first off, Eb—"

"The boy's taking care of it for now," Zane interrupted. "You just get us a few miles on downriver afore putting over to the west bank." Rolling on his hip slightly, he turned to holler at Ovatt. "You hear that, Heman? Up to you on that bow to find us a place to put in for the rest of the night."

Titus asked, "How many mile you figure we ought to put atween us and them?"

"Don't matter how many, son. We're gonna be on the other side of this big, wide ol' river. They ain't gonna cross the Messessap to get at us."

Root poked his head under the awning. "You want me to help, Ebenezer?"

"Yeah. Get me a little of your tobacco. Gonna chew up a poultice."

"Straightaway," Root replied, crawling on under the awning to search for his own belongings.

"Hand me some of that tow, Titus Bass. Yeah, that you got there with the fire-making plunder."

Bass's hands were trembling as he gave it to the river pilot. "I should've known better than to—"

"Known better'n what?" Zane demanded.

"Going so far in from the river," he tried to explain, unable to look at the steersman's face, even in the coming of night as they slid on beneath a cold, starry, moonless sky.

"You're the hunter, ain't you?"

With a shrug Titus replied, "I s'pose I allays thought I was a hunter."

"That's what I brung you along for, Titus. You was to be our hunter.

So you tell me: when you run onto those Injuns—was you doing anything different from what you do when you're hunting?"

He struggled, thought, then shook his head. "Nothing different. Just following a game trail."

"Then, goddammit—don't go blaming yourself. Damn, but this hurts."

"B-but I got you shot!"

"Ain't nothing tore but a little meat," he said just above a whisper, his face nonetheless etched with pain. "You boys'll fix me up right proper—and I'll be feeling fine in no time. Get back on my feet and take over that rudder—"

"No such a thing," Kingsbury snapped. "I'm near good a steersman as you, Ebenezer. And, besides—this ain't a tough river like the Ohio."

"Still the damned winter's low water!" Zane spat. "And the Messessap ain't no lark of a ride in winter, Hames!"

"Shuddup and let them two fix on you," the relief pilot ordered. "I'm kingfish of this here boat while you're down—an' you'll learn to take orders just like any of the rest of the crew."

Zane rolled back over onto his side, still gripping the arrow shaft as his leg trembled in pain. He looked up at Bass, grumbling, "You boys gonna get us some light to work with or not?"

"I'm fixing to get some char started on this tow—"

"Then get the goddamned candles lit so I can dig this son of a bitch outta my leg."

"Here's that tobacco you wanted, Eb," Root said, handing the pilot enough of the pressed leaf to fill his palm.

Taking a big bite out of the carrot-sized twist, Zane stuffed the rest into a pocket of his britches and growled, "Punch through the bunghole of that keg of rye and tap it, Reuben. An' be quick about it! I'm beginning to feel real puny, and this leg is starting to talk to me."

After lighting the wick on the second candle lantern, Bass turned to the pilot, holding the burning tow and asking, "W-what more you w-want me to do, Ebenezer?"

"Your knife a sharp'un?"

He nodded, his Adam's apple jumping like a great green grasshopper up the front of his neck. "Sharp 'nough to skin anything."

"Good," Zane snarled around the lump of tobacco puffing up the side of his cheek like a case of the mumps. "You get it out and slick it on that strop hanging yonder. I figure you'll be the one what can do the cutting on me."

"M-me?" His heart seemed to stop. Titus felt himself begin to quake, starting up right from the soles of his feet.

"Yeah, you, goddammit." He spit to the side, the brown tobacco gob landing in the sand of the firebox, where it raised a small cloud of old ash. "Now get a fire started down there an' heat us some water."

"You want me to c-cut on you?"

"Damn right I do!" Zane said, then raised his eyes to the frightened youngster's, his voice becoming softer. "Listen, boy—I figure you got the steadiest hand here in this here bunch of scurvy entrails."

"I don't think I could cut on 'nother man."

"You damn well just killed a man!"

For a moment he stared at the pilot, perhaps not wanting to believe. Then he answered quietly, "I . . . I killed a man?"

Kingsbury said, "Damn sure did!"

Feeling the certainty of that course through him, Titus replied, "I done what I had to do—save you, Ebenezer."

"That's why you're gonna cut on me now."

Bass wagged his head. "I . . . don't think I—"

"You hunt, don't you?"

"Yeah, you know I do—"

"An' ever since you was a sprout, you butchered out what you hunt?"

Titus only got to nod before Zane went on, pain written over his paste-colored face as he gritted on some of the words.

"Then you're the one I want cutting on me. Likely you done more work on hide and meat than all the rest of these here bastards," the pilot said, his eyes closing halfway, beads of perspiration standing out like diamonds on his forehead. "Besides, Titus Bass—there's 'nother goddamned good reason you're the one better do the cutting on me."

He tried to swallow, gulping at the hot lump clogging the back of his throat before he answered, afraid his words would come out as a squeak. "W-what's that, Ebenezer?"

"You're gonna cut this arrow outta the back of my goddamned leg 'cause you're the one I reckon got it put there in the first place."

ELEVEN

It was damned cold there in the dark—moonless the way it was. Their only light shook loose and rained down from those brilliant stars hoisted way up high in that tarry sky. Not near enough for him to tell much about where the crates and casks ended and the gunnel began.

Black, and bloody well cold enough that a man wanted nothing more than to stay wrapped in that blanket Titus had draped about him as he sat atop some hundredweight barrels of flour lashed near the front of the awning. The rest slept, soundly, from what he could hear of them.

Titus let his heavy eyelids fall. What little sleep he had grabbed during the first two watches wasn't near enough to let him fight off the mighty pull of slumber. What with the night quiet as cotton on the wind. Nothing more than the constant murmur of the river lapping against the yellow poplar sides of the flatboat, along with an occasional call of a owl on the hunt, maybeso the howl of a distant wolf on the prowl somewhere on that western side of the Mississippi.

Those nightsounds, and that muffled scrape at the stern of the boat. Likely a snag, he considered, letting his eyes close securely.

That was but one kind of terror that might "stove in" the bottom of a boat if a watchful crewman stationed at the bow did not push off that sort of hazard. A *snag* was nothing more than a branch, a piece of a tree trunk, "trashwood" freely floating downriver.

More dangerous still were planters and sawyers—both of them trees freed from the river's eroding banks. The *planter* had one of its ends firmly planted in the river bottom but otherwise plainly visible so that the flatboat crew could steer themselves away from the hazard. The *sawyer* was, like a planter, a fallen tree with its end firmly gripped by the river bottom, but the other end bobbing above and below the waterline—making it the greatest hazard of all.

Either one—planter or sawyer—could put a quick end to a flatboat's journey to New Orleans. Already Zane's crew had passed the wrecks of half a dozen flatboats since leaving behind the mouth of the Ohio. A tree branch of no mean size could nonetheless still gouge a hole in the hull of a broadhorn with no more force behind it than the river's current.

And when either hazard did crunch into a flatboat, the rivermen immediately had to begin bailing and using their leather pump while attempting to reach shore before they sank—there to effect repairs, if possible, before their expensive cargo disappeared at the muddy bottom of the Mississippi.

Come spring, the boatmen told Titus, the river was dang near choked full of planters and sawyers, sometimes so many that it might appear they were floating through a submerged grove of trees. Winter travel wasn't near so bad. Still, they had seen some on this trip down, sure enough—more here on the Mississippi than on the less rambunctious Ohio.

From the sounds of it, likely a small snag had just bumped against the upriver end of the boat, scraped, and floated on by.

He opened his eyes and looked back at the stern. Nothing. No more sound now. And try as he might in the pitiful starshine, Titus couldn't much make out anything on the surface of the river as the black water flowed on past.

Gone on by, he convinced himself. Then looked longingly at what few red embers remained in that sandbox where they had heated water he'd used in cutting on Zane's leg. About the time the brass kettle had begun to boil, Kingsbury and Ovatt had heaved the flatboat over to the far western bank and tied up in some brush. They hadn't needed to go ashore to secure the hawsers—simply lashing them to the roots of some sycamore trees exposed in the side of the bank like bared rib bones in some half-consumed carrion.

He turned and leaned against a crate, dragging the thick wool blanket back over his shoulder, smelling its musty river stench, then shifting the rifle across his lap Titus let his eyelids sink once more.

By the time they had secured the boat to those roots, Titus had pulled the kettle from the fire and sat there quivering as he honed his knife across the strop's greased surface. Having no idea where to begin cutting on a man's leg, digging out the shaft of an arrow from that man's flesh, Bass figured he'd just wait for someone to tell him what to do—even if it had to be Ebenezer Zane himself.

The pilot drank long and hard at the rye they sloshed out of one of the gallon kegs the crew kept for their own use.

"Messessap water tastes like weak mud," Ebenezer had explained in a slur.

"He's right," Kingsbury agreed as the rest gathered round, holding the lanterns close. "Ain't no use in washing with it—a fella ends up just as dirty, smeared up too. Maybeso in coffee it'll do."

That seemed reasonable enough an explanation why liquor was always the drink of choice for a Mississippi boatman. The river rendered such a disagreeable drink that most men took to letting a pail of it set overnight, hoping to settle most of the dirt. Even then, many of those working flats down the Mississippi drank it right out of the river for its "medicinal qualities," others claiming the Mississippi was a cure-all and "powerful cathartic," even "a purifier of a hardy man's blood."

"Do like he told you," Kingsbury said. "Cut that hole in his britches bigger so you can see to work on him."

Without a word of reply Titus brought his trembling hands back to the base of the arrow shaft that Kingsbury attempted to hold steady. A squat and powerful man, Reuben Root had positioned himself between Zane's legs, where he locked an arm around each ankle. Heman Ovatt squatted near the pilot's head, helping Zane drink his liquor and staying ready to bear down on Ebenezer's arms when the need arose. Across the steersman's body Kingsbury laid his weight, there to assist the best he could as young Bass finished tearing the thick nankeen cloth nearly the whole length of the wounded man's thigh from buttock to knee.

"You don't need the whole goddamned arrow no more," Zane slurred, the rye clearly beginning to work. "Figure you might just as well break off a big chunk of it and lemme have it."

Titus asked, "What you want it for?"

Ebenezer twisted his head slightly, still not able to touch Bass with his eyes. "Gonna bite down on it, you stupid young'un. When you finally get around to cutting that son of a bitch outta my leg. Now, do as I said and break it off!"

Bass's hands were shaking so when he took hold of the shaft that Zane yelped in pain, his leg twisting up, his body contorting in pain. Titus let go as if he had touched a hot fire poker.

"Here, lemme," Kingsbury suggested softly. "See if I can do it."

Steadying one hand against the back of Zane's thigh and around the shaft, the boatman wrapped the other hand just above it, looked up at Titus, and closed his eyes, gritting his teeth as he gave the shaft a snap. It broke smartly, making the sharpest sound in that quiet night tied against the west bank of the Mississippi.

Zane huffed, slowly quieting his breathing. "Gimme that, Hames, goddammit."

Titus watched the pilot take the arrow shaft and jam it between his big teeth. Then he laid his cheek upon the blanket they had folded beneath him once more. He grumbled something Bass could not understand.

"W-what'd you say—"

"Get it done!" he ordered, having yanked the shaft from his mouth so his words weren't so garbled.

Looking up at Kingsbury, Titus asked, "You figure we should see just how hard it's buried in there?"

Kingsbury only nodded.

Taking hold of the last six inches of shaft, Bass pulled slightly. Zane groaned, but made no great cry of pain. Titus gave another, harder yank—and this time Zane nearly came off the deck of the boat with a stifled shriek. When Bass let go, Ebenezer lay there panting as the pain passed over him in waves.

"Gonna have to cut it out," Root advised. "Just like he tol't you at the start."

"Y-you knowed I was gonna have to cut it out, didn't you, Ebenezer?" Bass said.

Zane raised his head wearily and nodded once, his eyes glazing.

"Then I reckon you been stuck by an arrow afore," Titus replied.

"Neber," he said quietly around the shaft.

"Seems that makes two of us, Ebenezer."

Zane asked, "How's dat?"

"I ain't never cut a arrow outta a man afore neither."

Suddenly a little scared when he saw Zane turn slowly to peer back over his shoulder at him, Titus tried to look away but could not tear his eyes off the pilot's clay-white face as Ebenezer took the shaft from his mouth.

"That's good, Titus Bass," Zane said, his glassy eyes smiling more than his lips. "A man what can make me laugh just when he's fixing to go cutting on my leg—that's all right, Titus Bass. Like I said afore: you'll do to ride the river with."

He watched Zane return the shaft between his teeth, then turned back to Kingsbury. "I figure this cutting is gonna hurt him something fierce."

"We'll hold him," Ovatt said, locking Zane's arms under his.

"Just get on with it," Root said from the pilot's legs.

"You cut slow enough, maybe he won't feel it so bad," Kingsbury suggested almost in a whisper. "Not near as soon anyways."

It took all his strength to put the tip of his knife against that flesh, piercing the ragged hole cupped around the shaft, oozing blood shiny in the light spilled by the candles hung from the beam just above their heads. As he began to drag the blade through the soft, giving skin and down into the muscle, stroke by stroke by stroke below the shaft, Zane whimpered, groaned, growled around his piece of wood, but he lay amazingly still. Only the punctured leg quivered uncontrollably in something resembling a muscle spasm each time Bass's blade sank deeper.

"Try it now," Kingsbury said, then nodded to Ovatt and Root as if to tell them to lock down on Zane.

With his left hand Titus put some strain on the shaft. The pilot squealed in pain. While he heard Ebenezer gasping, Bass pressed on with his work and pried open the incision he had made with the bloody blade, pulling up with a steady pressure at the same time.

The shaft yanked free.

With a loud grunt Zane went limp.

"Ebenezer?" Ovatt called out. Then repeated it again more loudly. He touched the pilot's face. "He's gone, boys."

"G-gone?" Titus groaned. "I kill't him?"

"Jesus God, no!" Ovatt replied with a chuckle. "Zane's done passed out."

"Good thing, too," Kingsbury said. "He took that longer'n nary any man I know of would taken it. G'won now, Titus."

"G-g'won?"

"You've more to dig outta his leg."

"More?"

Snatching the shaft from Titus's hand, Kingsbury held it inches before the youth's eyes. "Can't you see, goddammit! Here's the arrow! But there ain't no point on the son of a bitch." He wheeled on Root. "Get over there to larboard and pull one of them arrows out'n the side of the boat, Reuben. I wanna have us a lookee at it."

When Root returned, he handed two arrows over to Kingsbury. "Side of the boat looks like a porkypine, stuck the way it is."

"I s'pose Ebenezer's lucky he only catched the one," Kingsbury replied. "Look there, Titus," and the boatman held both arrows to the lamplight. "These got 'em some iron points. Damn it all. See how they're tied round the shaft with that wrap."

"I see."

"It all come loose inside his leg. The wrap and the point too. Got wet in his blood."

"An' slipped off the shaft," Ovatt finished for them.

Root inquired, "Gotta dig it out, Hames?"

"Gotta try." Then he peered up at Bass. "Don't we, Titus?"

"I'll . . . try."

He went back to work, pressing down on one side of the incision with his bloody fingers, slicing down a little at a time with the point of his blade until he saw something fibrous. He snagged it between his trembling fingers and pulled slowly. Out it came in a long, thick thread.

"Just like I tol't you," Kingsbury declared. "Now, go back in there and get the head of it afore Ebenezer wakes up."

"I don't think he's coming to till morning, Hames," Ovatt reported.

"Good thing too," Kingsbury responded. "Finish it, Titus."

Back down into the meat of the river pilot's muscle he probed, until it felt as if the tip of the blade scraped against something harder than the soft, giving tissue. Hoping it wasn't bone, he slowly pressed two fingers deep into the incision, both of them feeling down the knife's blade until a fingertip struck it. Taking it between his fingers, he pulled. Slick with dark, warm blood—his fingers slipped off.

Again he grabbed hold of it, pulled, and slipped off.

"I c-can't get a hold on it."

"Stuck in the bone, most like," Ovatt grumbled.

"Yeah," Kingsbury agreed. "Don't you got something in your shooting pouch you can grab it with, Titus?"

"I don't know what you mean."

"What's a fella use when he's got a ball stuck down his barrel and you're wanting to pull it out?"

"I got a screw I put on the end of my wiping stick."

"Yeah, I know—but when you got the screw into the ball, what you use to yank hard on the wiping stick get that stuck ball out?"

It came to him all at once. "That just might work. Get me my pouch."

Heman Ovatt flung the shooting pouch his way. Scrounging at the bottom of the front section of the pouch, Bass pulled out the forged-iron tongs he had never used all that much.

"Them looks like they'll work," Kingsbury declared.

"Hames, help pull that meat outta my way," Titus told the boatman. As Kingsbury tugged the muscle in one direction, Bass eased it down in the other. Working his fingers back into the incision, he touched the rounded end of the arrow point once more. Slipping the small, narrow tongs into the incision, he guided them into position, clamped them around the point, and began to pull. "Damn, but that's stuck in there."

"Work on it—it'll come," Ovatt said.

Rocking it back and forth slightly, Titus felt it begin to give way, eventually freeing itself from its lock in that biggest bone in the human body. Carefully he slid it from the deep incision, captured between the tongs. Holding the point up to the light for a moment, Titus turned it around slowly so all could see.

"We best save that for him," Kingsbury said.

"That's for sure," Root agreed. "He'll be one mad kingfish gone alligator-horse if'n we throw that away!"

"He might even wear it on a cord round his neck," Hames predicted.

They washed the wound out with hot water, then pried open Zane's lips so they could extract a little of the tobacco quid he had pulverized inside his cheek before passing out. Kingsbury pressed the dark, soupy leaf and spittle down into the laceration. They finished by cutting a strip of cloth from the bottom of Ebenezer's spare shirt and knotting it around his leg. With a pair of blankets pulled over their leader, the three boatmen decided they would draw lots to take watch until dawn, when they would once more set off downriver.

Root happily sat up the first pull, and Kingsbury took the second watch. An hour or more back now, Hames had awakened Titus with an insistent nudge.

"Cold," Bass had muttered as he sat up, slowly coming awake.

"Real cold," Kingsbury said as he slid past the youngster. "And cold does a good job keeping you awake."

But it hadn't.

He awoke himself with a start, hearing himself snore. He sputtered, then fell silent, still half-asleep, listening to the other men snoring. He wondered if Ebenezer's was that loudest rumble, as much of that rye as he had swallowed down. As he let his eyelids slip back down and his chin go back to resting against his chest, Bass heard the muffled scrape of another sawyer against the side of the boat. It bumped so quietly, he wasn't sure. Then decided it was the tumble of the sawyer's roots, hitting again, here, then a third place along the side.

He glanced up at the starry sky to the east across the river where the sun would emerge—if it ever chose to—watching his frosty breath as he pulled the blanket up against his ears.

And froze in place.

Staring into the blackness of that moonless night. Holding his breath, Titus watched the shadow take form at the gunnel, pouring over the top of the poplar plank like a big bubble in a kettle of stew ready to boil over the fire, emerging slowly from the surface of the stew, just as this shadow emerged from the top of the gunnel back there near the stern. As if it were punching an inky black hole out of that cold sky dusted with a sugary coating of stars.

He swallowed, feeling his throat constrict in fear.

The shadow congealed in the black of that night, becoming a head, then one arm, and another—eventually pulling itself atop the gunnel. Beyond it another shadow. Then three more appeared at the stern. Heads turning this way, then that. Finally slipping themselves soundlessly atop the side of the boat. He wasn't sure, but he thought he saw bows at the ends of the arms. Saw them already strung with arrows. And then a shaft, perhaps a lance. No. Not that long. Those had to be the muskets.

Letting the blanket fall from his shoulders, he brought the hammer back to full cock in one motion as he lowered the muzzle onto the closest of the shadows and pulled in one motion. In his rush he forgot to close his eyes for the muzzle flash. That much sudden light hurt them as everything went black. The last he saw was the shadow pitching backward, spilling over the gunnel, where it disappeared among all that blackness beyond.

Around him erupted cries and yelps as the boatmen came awake and the Chickasaw screeched their war cries. At least a half dozen were on board before the other three boatmen fought their way out of the blankets and began a heroic defense of their boat.

Arrows thwacked into wood all around him, a gun roared, then another. He had no idea whose weapon it was: boatman or Indian. Men grunted as bodies slammed together in a match of strength pitted against surprise. Beneath the dull starshine he watched a tomahawk go into the air at the end of a warrior's arm—a gunshot—the tomahawk stopped its arc, then fell backward . . . the arm and the warrior spilled over the side of the boat.

Titus found his knife in his hand as he watched an Indian hurtling onto Kingsbury's back—something huge held out at the end of his arm.

On instinct Titus lunged forward, felt the blade that had sliced an arrowhead out of a man's leg with so much struggle now dig between another man's ribs almost effortlessly. He didn't know if he pulled the Indian off Kingsbury or if the boatman flung the Indian back to free himself like a dog shaking off water, but Titus fell over backward, his arm locked around the Indian's neck. Rolling to the side, he felt the warrior quiver, tense, then go limp.

Bass was on his feet, wheeling to leap beneath the awning, his eyes searching the red-tinged darkness for sign of Ebenezer Zane. In a tangle of arms and bodies the lump on the far side of the awning struggled beneath its blankets, crying out in pain, grunting under two attackers who pinned the pilot down, one of them raising his arm to strike a second time, then a third with something that cracked dully against Zane's head. Bass swept forward, tripping on the planks and falling against one attacker while the second whirled and fled. Bass's knife sank into the Indian's back but seemed to take no immediate effect. Titus spun on that first, fleeing warrior.

Drawing the knife back, Titus reached out and snagged a handful of hair as the Indian cleared the awning. Yanking the head toward him, Bass slashed at the Indian's neck once, then a second time. He was preparing for a third journey with that skinning blade when he sensed the warm gush spill across the back of his hand and wrist in the cold night. The body went limp beneath him.

Spinning to find another attacker, Titus cried, "Ebenezer!"

He had time only to yell out the man's name once before he felt the searing pain against his shoulder, delivered with enough stunning force that he was flung against the pilot's body. Spinning, Titus watched his attacker draw back a long, stone-studded war club for a second swing. Without thinking, Bass tried to raise his left arm to ward off the blow. But the arm would not respond to his command without a frantic, burning tongue of fire coursing through his shoulder. Suddenly crouching, Titus hurled himself at the Indian, slashing back and forth with the knife at the end of his one good arm while the attacker stumbled backward beneath the savage ferocity of the white man's attack, swinging his long club side to side in a vain attempt at fending off the white man's knife. At the end of one wide arc with that club, Titus dived, his arm extended.

The blade struck, slid to the side a little, then sank into the Indian's chest. He drew it out. Ran it home a second time. Drew it out as the Indian stumbled backward. Again he plunged it into the chest. Pulled it back, then jammed it into the enemy with all his might. Bass watched the Indian finally sink to his knees, the front of his buckskins glistening in the pewter light of that cold starshine. The warrior keeled to the side, his eyes opened wide, and he lay completely still.

At that moment it seemed the boat grew quiet around him. So quiet he could hear the lap of water against the poplar planks. Some man's raspy breathing nearby. The groan of another. Then a scrape against the side of the boat. The very noise he'd heard just before the Indians had come aboard. His mind swimming with a charge of hot adrenaline, his heart squeezed with terror in his chest, Titus knew the warriors were in canoes.

And now more of them were about to come over the gunnels!

Leaping from the awning, he reached the stern, ready to hack at the next warriors to climb out of their canoes. When the voice startled him.

"That you, T-titus?"

"Heman?"

He growled, "Pull me up, goddammit!"

Ovatt stood precariously, his legs shaky, in one of the canoes, holding one of his arms up the side of the flatboat. As Bass pulled, Heman clambered over the side and into the broadhorn with a grunt. Gasping, he asked, "Where the others?"

Only then did Titus turn, drenched with the chill of that darkness, fully realizing the significance of the great, cold, inky black silence around them.

"Kingsbury?" he called.

"Hames?" Ovatt cried in desperation.

"Here," came the reply. A shadow appeared halfway down the far side of the boat, hand to its head. "I . . . I need some help, boys."

Bass watched the shadow pitch to its knees, struggle up again, before he reached Kingsbury. "Only got one good arm right now," Titus apologized for his struggle in getting the other man to his feet.

"Me too," Kingsbury replied. Into the dim starshine he turned, showing his right arm, dark stains tracing its length from shoulder to wrist. "Cain't move it too good."

"Then don't," Ovatt ordered.

"Reuben?"

They heard a splash from the bow.

"I'm here," came the growl. "Just throwing one of the dead bastards overboard."

Root turned about, darkening a patch of the starry sky as he strode back toward the stern atop kegs and casks and crates.

"You hurt?" Kingsbury asked as he tore his own bloody sleeve asunder.

"I been better," Root growled. "A few scratches. Nothing I ain't ever had afore in a good brawl. You boys?"

"Looks to be Hames got the worse of it," Ovatt explained as he finished tearing the sleeve from Kingsbury's shirt, looping it quickly around the upper arm. "Gonna have to stop this bleeding for you. Me—I just headbutted a few of them red bastards and followed 'em over the side into the shallow water, where we tussled."

"You finish a few of 'em off?" Kingsbury asked.

"They ain't none of 'em left I can see of," Ovatt replied gruffly.

Root turned to the youngster. "Your arm—you stuck, Titus?"

"Just hit my arm, maybe my shoulder. A club. It'll be all right come morning."

"Ain't long till morning," Kingsbury said, settling clumsily to the deck. His head weaved wearily. "Well, now, Titus—that were your first Injun fight—"

"How 'bout Ebenezer?" Ovatt interrupted suddenly as he rose from Kingsbury's side, turning on his heel. "Eb—"

"I pulled one of 'em off him," Titus began to explain. "One what was smashing Zane with a club."

"Here that'un is," Ovatt declared, dragging the body out of his way to step over it getting to the tick mattress where they had worked on the river pilot beneath candlelight.

"Ebenezer?" Root called out, rushing to Ovatt's side.

"Maybeso he's still drunk," Kingsbury declared as he pushed up to join them.

"Likely so," Ovatt said as he rolled the man over, pulling the blankets down gently. He held his ear over Zane's face, listened. Then jerked back, his hands feeling around the pilot's head in the dark. "Shit."

"What?" Titus asked, inching forward a step.

Ovatt wiped his hands on the front of his coat. "Ebenezer's done for."

"Dead?" Root demanded.

"Just as dead as that son of a bitch there," Ovatt growled as he whirled and kicked the dead Indian with all he could muster.

Whimpering like a wounded animal, Heman fell atop the Chickasaw's body, pummeling it with his fists. Then seized the Indian's ears and drove the head down onto the deck repeatedly as Root and Titus struggled to pull him off the body.

When Ovatt finally let the mighty Root yank him away, he sank into Reuben's arms. Then he spat on the body, spat again. "Killed the best man on the river! That's what you done!"

Completely numbed, Bass stood rooted to the spot, unable to move, not believing what the others were saying. It simply couldn't be. Not Ebenezer Zane! Not the man who had taken him under his wing, promised to teach him the rivers, the flatboat trade, to introduce him to the right whores in Natchez and on down to New Orleans. The man who these last few weeks had become like a real father to him. Not Ebenezer!

"I'll throw this bastard over with the rest," Root said as Ovatt crumpled next to Zane's body.

"We gotta get downriver," Kingsbury commanded as he crawled back in under the awning. "Can't stay here now."

"Burn them canoes afore we go," Root said.

"Just scuttle 'em," Ovatt growled with a shake of his head, anger making the man tremble. "They'll sink sure enough."

"Ebenezer?" Titus asked in the midst of all their talk, taking another step forward.

"There might be more coming," Kingsbury declared.

"Ebenezer . . . dead?" Bass repeated with another step, staring at the body in the dim, starry light.

"Nawww," Root disagreed with Kingsbury. "Ain't no more coming. This is the same goddamned bunch the boy here run onto out hunting. They come downriver follering us. Ain't no more coming."

"Still the same," Kingsbury said, his voice edged with pain. "We gotta get on down past the Chickasaw Bluffs.* Safer water."

---

* Future site of Memphis, Tennessee.

"Hames might be right," Root said. "Them jumping us like this might just mean them red devils are out to put the steal on some of the river traffic."

"Awright—we'll go," Ovatt finally said as Titus reached his side. He looked up as the youth knelt beside Zane's body. "Decent thing to do . . . we gotta take Ebenezer on down. Figure out what we oughtta do then."

"What we gotta do from here on out," Kingsbury corrected with a wince of pain as he rubbed the shirt bandage around his arm. "With the boat. And this load."

Barely hearing any of the others' talk, Titus sank to his knees, reaching out his hand, pulling the blanket back from the pilot's face. "Didn't have a chance."

"What would Ebenezer Zane want us to do?" Ovatt asked.

Bass peered into the crushed and battered face of Ebenezer Zane, feeling the tears of frustration, of loss, come over him, ease slowly from his eyes.

"He'd want us to finish the trip," Root replied. "You always finish what you start—Ebenezer Zane always said."

A hand came out to rest on Bass's shoulder. Then a second. He looked up to find Ovatt standing over him now, Root as well. Kingsbury slid up nearby, clutching his upper arm tightly.

"He liked you, Titus," Hames said. "I never knowed Ebenezer Zane to take to young'uns afore."

"But he liked you, for certain on that," Ovatt said, patting Titus on the shoulder.

"Said you'd do to ride this goddamned river with," Reuben added quietly. He patted the youth on the back of the head as Titus hunched over, beginning to cry.

Heman added, "Ain't nothing better Ebenezer could say 'bout a man."

Hames Kingsbury dragged a bloody hand beneath his nose angrily, then snorted, "And by damn, fellas—that's something Ebenezer Zane was right about from the start. You'll do to ride this goddamned river with, Titus Bass."

More than a day before Titus's hunt had set a terrible wheel in motion, Ebenezer Zane had piloted them out of the mouth of the Ohio—for the last time.

They floated on downriver another day after the Chickasaw attack, deciding to take their chances that night by anchoring at the downstream end of a tree-lined sandbar where they figured no redskin on the river would find it easy to discover them tied up among the clutter of living brush and dead sawyers.

After scuttling the three canoes that cold night of the attack, they had wrapped the body within a section of oiled Russian sheeting Ebenezer kept stowed away for repairs to the awning, binding the dead pilot tightly within his shroud using a wrap of one-inch hemp before carrying Zane out to lay atop some casks containing cured Kentucky smoking leaf.

After that short autumn day of denying what needed doing, the four of them gathered beneath the oiled awning at their sandbox fire and boiled coffee, finally speaking of the unspeakable.

"Never thought he'd go this way," Kingsbury admitted softly.

"Still can't believe it," Root added, as if it soured his stomach.

Ovatt looked into the other faces, asking, "What you figure we ought'n do with him?"

The three only shrugged, stared back into the fire, each man deeply possessed of his own thoughts.

Eventually Titus asked, "What you think Ebenezer would want you to do for him?"

One by one in turn the three looked up from their reverie and stared at the youth.

"I just figured—you all knowed him much better'n me," Bass explained. "Thinking one of you should have an idea what Ebenezer'd want done. Maybe we ought'n talk about getting him back to his family for burying."

"He ain't got no family," Root explained. "Heman told you 'bout his woman . . . what happed to his boys."

"But he's gotta have a mam or pap," Titus declared. "Surely he's got some kin back to home." He watched the heads shake. "Aunt or uncles? Brother or a sister?" Still the boatmen wagged their heads.

"Got no kin he ever spoke of," Kingsbury said.

Kingsbury nodded as he stared at the tiny flames, rubbing one of his jowls thoughtfully. "He started floating the Ohio and Mississap years ago when he was just a young feller. Always said he didn't leave behind no family to speak of."

Ovatt stated, "I reckon that's why he took such a real liking to you, Titus."

"How old you figure Ebenezer was?" Bass inquired.

With a wag of his head Root said, "I don't have no likely idea. Man looked older'n he really was—or maybe he was older'n he looked. No telling with all that hair, and life being so hard on the river."

"He had no family, but he had to have a home," Titus protested. "Place where he come from."

"Don't think so," Kingsbury answered. "He done two floats south to Nawlins each year. Finish off selling his goods, then sell off the boat timbers, and we'd walk north on the Trace. Get back up to the Ohio, Ebenezer'd go straight on to Pittsburgh for to get one of the boat outfits started on a new broadhorn for his next trip downriver."

"No family?" Titus repeated as the sad and utter rootlessness of it sank in. "An' no home neither."

"River was his home," Ovatt stated.

Rubbing his palms along the tops of his thighs thoughtfully, Bass said, "Then you men was his family."

They looked at one another for a few moments.

Finally Kingsbury spoke. "Maybeso you're right. We was as much his family as any man's got family."

"Then to my way of thinking," Ovatt agreed, "it's up to us to decide what's best to do for Ebenezer."

"Gotta bury him," Titus said.

"Where?" Root asked.

Bass gestured with a thumb over his shoulder. "Where he lived. Out there. On the river."

"Bury him in the river?" Kingsbury echoed.

"Certain of it," Ovatt replied with a slap to his leg, then pushed back a shock of that red hair from his eyes. "Damn right—we oughtta bury him in the Messessap."

"Why not the Ohio?" Root asked, hard-eyed. "He was more a Ohio boy than a Messessap boy."

"Can't haul his goddamned body all the way up the Natchez Trace with us," Kingsbury grumbled.

"Why cain't we?" Root demanded.

"Jumpin' Jehoshaphat! He's gonna . . . he'll be . . . ah, goddammit!" growled Kingsbury. "Ebenezer gonna start going bad, and the man deserves to be planted afore he starts stinking enough to turn the noses of heaven!"

"Hames is right, Reuben," Ovatt stated firmly. "Nothing we can do about what's landed in our laps. We can't go a'hauling him all the way back up to the Ohio—so we oughtta just figure out what's best to do by Ebenezer down here on the Mississap."

"He allays liked Natchez," Kingsbury mused out loud, then looked up to gaze at the others around that low fire that reflected a crimson glow from each of their faces in the cold darkness surrounding their boat.

"Thought we decided we was burying him in the river!" Root snapped.

"We can," Kingsbury replied. "We'll just do it when we get to Natchez."

"He liked some of those places Under-the-Hill," Ovatt agreed. " 'Bout as much as he took to Mathilda's Kangaroo."

"Then we'll wait to bury him till we get to Natchez," Kingsbury said with great finality. "And put him to his eternal rest in the river opposite the harbor."

The next morning before full light they had secured the body of Ebenezer Zane atop their cargo, released the hawsers, and slipped away with the cold brown current of the Mississippi. Only four of them now: three boatmen, and a youngster who kept staring at that shroud, unable to shake off the feeling that it had all been of his own making.

"You're carrying more'n any one man ought'n carry," Kingsbury said that night as he relieved Titus at watch after they had tied up in a small, brushy cove against the river's west shore.

"Can't help it, the way things turned out."

"No man ever can say how things gonna turn out, Titus."

Bass wagged his head. "He's dead because of something I done, or didn't do. Dammit!" he grumbled under his breath. "I don't know rightly which it is."

"Listen and let me tell you the way Ebenezer lived his life, son," Kingsbury said as he settled beside the youth. "Life is only what happens to you after you get borned of your mama. You can't help it, so you go on living if you're lucky enough, if you ain't one of them babes what dies in the birthin'. You do what you must to stay alive for a few years, and then dying is something that happens at the other end of your life, he always believed. Just make sure it's a quick'un, Ebenezer said. Better'n going slow, painful."

Stifling a sob, Titus said, "I damn sure hope he went quick."

Hames continued, "I figure Ebenezer Zane got his wish, Titus. He went the way he wanted to go—and by damn, that's a lot more'n most of us'll ever get when our name's called on the roll up yonder."

"I don't know much of what to think about heaven."

"Ain't much to think about, really. We'll find out all about it when we get there."

Bass looked up at the boatman, then asked in that icy stillness, "You figure Ebenezer Zane is gone on to heaven already?"

Ovatt chuckled softly, patted Titus on the back reassuringly. "Hell, he's there already."

Kingsbury nodded. "I'd wager he's got a bunch of them angels already learning to tie hawsers and work a gouger, how to dip their oars an' turn their heavenly flatboats right around in midriver."

Even the sour-faced Root grinned when he said, "No doubt Ebenezer's even got 'em singing some of his bad songs too."

"Bad songs?"

Hames smiled, staring up at the dark canopy. "Songs what God wouldn't want none of his angels learning—them's the kind Ebenezer Zane will go and teach 'em. Probably got some chewing tobacco too."

The hurt overwhelmed Titus when he sobbed, "I miss him."

Kingsbury looked at the youngster's sad, hangdown face. "We all miss him. But God's got him now, so we're bound away to get Ebenezer Zane's last flatboat down to Nawlins—just the way he'd planned."

"Then we're heading back north?"

"Buy us another boat and hire us on another load—float on down again come spring," Kingsbury replied.

And Ovatt added, "Like Ebenezer allays done."

"Just like he'd want us to keep doing—even 'thout him here," Hames said.

It had been another cold day of floating, watching the land flatten even more while the river itself began to meander before they sailed past the settlement of New Madrid squatting on the far west bank of the Mississippi. Founded in 1790 by Colonel George Morgan, a New Jersey land speculator, who was in turn sponsored by the crown of Spain as a means of establishing a foreign outpost reaching far up the river, by 1810 the village was inhabited mostly by Americans who had been struggling against the fickle river for twenty years. Less than two dozen ragged houses sheltered a rough, indolent population that included a handful of Spaniards, some French Creoles down from the Illinois, and a few hardy German immigrants. A pair of poorly stocked stores charged outrageous prices for what little they had to offer, especially if a traveler did not carry the right nation's currency then in vogue and was thereby forced to pay a rate of exchange bordering on river piracy.

South from there the terrain flattened even more, the extensive floodplain preventing any real settlement through what appeared to be a boggy, impenetrable wilderness. In more than a week of travel the boatmen alternated periods of extreme boredom with snatches of terror while they negotiated treacherous stretches of the Mississippi popularly known as the Devil's Raceground—where to Titus it felt as if some unnatural force picked up the crew's flatboat and hurled it downriver a few miles at a dizzying pace . . . and later at the Devil's Elbow—where they had to fight constantly to steer the boat around a maze of innumerable sandbars while twisting this way and that through corkscrew turns as the river bent back on itself. Here Kingsbury had to battle the stern rudder, with Heman Ovatt on the gouger, both of them struggling to keep their broadhorn close to the east bank lest the strong current pull their boat right into what the rivermen called "the woods," that broad floodplain west of the Mississippi, a tangled, confusing maze of bogs where a crew would have little hope of ever returning to the river's main channel.

"See that high point yonder?" asked Ovatt of an early morning two days later.

Titus looked into the distance where Heman pointed south. "What is it up there?"

"That's the fourth Chickasaw Bluff."

"Chica . . . like the Injuns killed Ebenezer?"

Ovatt nodded. "Chickasaw. Up top there sits the army's post. Called Fort Pickering."

"S'pose them soldiers can see a long way up there," Bass replied as his eyes came back to watching the river for sawyers and planters. He sat at the bow, clutching one of the long, sturdy poles, ready to push off any dangerous object that posed a threat to their boat by bobbing too close in the muddy, sometimes swirling current.

"Keep your eyes open," Ovatt reminded as he got up to clamber away over the casks and kegs. "I'm getting me a little drink now that the river settles down for a while."

Bass returned his attention to the water, sweeping his gaze back and forth as he had been doing for days on end as they rolled on down the great, wide river. Most of the sawyers were easily spotted. Some were not, the others had warned him: hiding their danger just below the surface of the river. Some might poke only a solitary root or limb barely above waterline. A man had to be watchful and not become mesmerized by the monotonous roll of the murky water beneath a gray, overcast sky.

Spotting one, Titus rose to his knees, leaned back, and grabbed the long pole, ready to brace himself against some hundredweight kegs to push off the sawyer he saw coming up, still downriver more than a quarter of a mile. With a single limb raised, it bobbed in the current. For a moment the hazard appeared to roll, for the limb disappeared, then another arose to take its place out of the brown water. Funny thing, he thought, rubbing his eyes, then squinting into the distance again. For a moment there—that damned thing looked like it took a ghastly, human shape.

"Heman!" he shouted, heart leaping out of his chest.

Ovatt stuck his head out from beneath the awning as Root stirred fitfully from his nap atop some tobacco crates. "Just knock the goddamned thing off to the side, Titus."

"It's a person!"

Kingsbury craned his neck from the stern rudder, asking, "In the river?"

"Lookee there!" Titus said, pointing as Ovatt emerged from the shade of the awning and clambered over the cargo to the bow.

"I can see! By damn, it is a human person, Hames!"

Root had rolled up on his elbow, rubbing his eyes and grumbling to himself as Kingsbury began shouting his orders.

"Heman, get some of that rope tied around the boy's waist. We'll put him over the side and he can swim out: pluck that fella outta the river—"

"I! I can't swim!" Titus squealed.

"You can too swim!" Ovatt cried.

Wagging his head emphatically, he admitted, "Not good 'nough to pull nobody else outta no river!"

"Dammit!" Kingsbury snarled. "Ovatt, you tie yourself off. And, Titus, you work that gouger with me so we can slow this here Kentuckyboat down. Heman can grab that fella, and we'll let Reuben pull the two of 'em in."

With Kingsbury barking orders to young Bass while Ovatt knotted a one-inch line around his middle and Reuben Root secured the other end around his own waist, Hames and Titus began to work the flatboat over into the middle of the current, cutting a course directly for the man waving all the more frantically as the rivercraft bore down on him.

"Looks like he's hanging on to something—maybeso a snag or piece of timber," Ovatt announced as he squatted at the gunnel near the bow, ready to leap into the cold water. "Right when I go in, Titus, you cut that gouger hard to the left so the bow goes right—away from me. Understand?"

Bass nodded, more than a little nervous at having so important a part in this rescue.

Then it was time for the red-haired boatman to take his bath. Into the river Ovatt dived just as they were about to approach the man in the river. Immediately leaning hard against the bow rudder, Titus helped Kingsbury wheel the flatboat about, almost crosscurrent, suddenly slowing the craft with a sharp lurch as Ovatt splashed up behind the man and snagged him.

"P-pull!"

Root was already heeding Ovatt's command, dragging in the narrow rope hand over hand as the man from the river flopped and struggled to secure a grip on the one who had come to rescue him. The pair of them went under again, and then again, bobbing up, both men sputtering and spitting, Ovatt bellowing at his charge to settle down—but still the man fought against his rescuer, flinging arms this way and that, attempting to lock on to Ovatt. There at the side of the flatboat he finally did so as Kingsbury shoved the rudder hard to the starboard, kicking the bow back into the head of the current.

"Bring me up! Up, goddammit!" Ovatt gurgled, spitting water.

"Gonna help this fella first, you no-good half-drowned mudrat!" Root snarled in reply as he leaned over the gunnel and seized hold of the man they had just plucked from what appeared to be a wide plank of white oak. A hewn flatboat timber.

Gasping, the sodden, soaked creature collapsed from Root's grip right atop some casks, his chest heaving, spewing up river water, heaving volcanically.

"You done up there—get me up now, Reuben!"

Root leaned over the gunnel, grinning. "You ain't asked me purty, now, have you?"

With the flat of one hand, Ovatt smacked the side of the flatboat, growling, "Get me up there or I'll pin your ears back so far you'll be wiping them when you wipe your ass!"

Root and Kingsbury both roared as Reuben pulled Ovatt over the gunnel, where he landed in a heap, sputtering and gasping, gazing with the other three at the soppy-haired creature they had just pulled out of the muddy waters.

"How you come to be in the river, mister?" Root demanded as he pounded heartily on the survivor's back. Then, "Oh, my God!" he exclaimed, backing up a step clumsily, then a second and nearly falling as the creature raised its head and gazed up at them.

"He's a . . . she's a woman!"

True enough.

"What the hell have you just plucked from the river, Heman?" Kingsbury asked, his neck craning as he roared with a great laugh.

"D-don't none of you go blaming me for bringing no goddamned woman on this boat!" Ovatt cried.

Shivering with cold, trembling with fear, she looked at each one in turn as the three men stared back at her, stunned into silence. None of them moved. Titus was gaping openmouthed at the stringy-haired soot-smudged woman with the rest of them until Kingsbury jogged them all awake.

"Get her a blanket, goddammit! Woman gonna freeze in this wind less'n you cover her up."

As Root turned and bent to slip under the awning, Ovatt asked her, "You—ma'am . . . gonna be all right?"

Unable to utter a word, the woman only nodded, swiping muck off her face from brow to chin with the back of her torn sleeve as she continued to drip as much of the river on the deck as did Heman Ovatt. When Root laid an old wool blanket around her shoulders, she gazed up at the man with the sort of gratitude in her eyes that Titus always saw in the eyes of the family's hounds whenever he threw them the bones butchered from what game he brought in from the hills. It damned near pulled at his heart now, the way she looked round at all of them red-eyed and frightened.

Wiping her hand one more time across her face, where her hair continued to drip, the woman said quietly, "I know what you're all thinking: it's bad luck to have you a woman on your boat." She yanked the blanket tightly around her shoulders, her eyes falling to the deck. " 'Cause my husband . . . me an' him had a boat like this'un."

Root leaned forward to ask, "Where at's your husband, ma'am?"

With a wag of her head she replied, "River claimed him."

"You mean he's dead?" Kingsbury inquired.

Titus watched her choke off a sob with a quiver of her chin, then brave herself up enough to answer. "River claimed him . . . after the Injuns jumped us two day ago."

TWELVE

"The sooner we get her off our boat, the better things is gonna be for all of us," Heman Ovatt growled in a loud whisper that rumbled off the nearby water.

"We can't just set her off!" Titus protested, his eyes imploring the other two boatmen, who huddled with him near the bow, arguing out the fate of the woman they had plucked from the river.

At that moment the dark-haired woman sat alone beneath the awning, where she huddled out of the cold drizzle that leaked from a pewter sky, drier now, and warmer too, by the sandbox fire they tended for her. Nonetheless, she trembled, staring upriver into the distance as if she truly could not overhear their heated discussion.

When Bass glanced at the woman again, something tugged in his chest—the way she gazed upstream, transfixed, as if she were going to spot her husband's boat, as if she hoped to materialize her husband right out of the cold air. There had been occasions he saw his mother wear that same look on her face: worried for his pap not yet home from clearing a far field. At such times he already had come to know that both she and his pap were children of families who farmed and hunted their ground at great risk to their lives. In those early years on that bloody ground of the canebrakes south of the Ohio River, a man might be late for any number of things. So his mother bravely watched from the front door, and always lit a candle at the window as dusk settled like a fine talc among the hills surrounding their cabin. She, continuing to watch into the distance for her man the same way this woman gazed upriver for some sign of her own.

"The young'un's right," Hames Kingsbury stated flatly.

"He ain't got no say in this," Reuben Root grumbled, his face grown hard, chertlike eyes barely visible between the slits he made of them. "Only us three got a vote on her staying, or us putting her off right now."

Bass was about to open his mouth in hopes of cajoling, in some way to convince them into allowing him his voice in this, if not his outright vote, when the skinny Kingsbury wheeled on the explosive and powerful Reuben Root.

"Time you listen to me: I been first in charge of this boat for Ebenezer ever since't him and me started down the Ohio years ago," Hames said evenly, setting full measure by every one of the words he chose. "He picked him the best crew could be had on the river—so I damned well know any of us could be the one Ebenezer picked to watch over things if ever he wasn't around or was just sleeping off part of a day's float. Any one of us—"

"That's right!" Root interrupted.

"But he picked me, Reuben."

"Still, that don't give you no extra vote over us," Heman said, his own pocked and pitted face gone cold, suspicious, perhaps even downright superstitious in clinging to that riverboatman's oldest and worst taboo with such fervent and steadfast belief.

"I ain't taking a extra vote for me," Kingsbury replied. "I'm just telling you as pilot on this here boat now—that I'm doing just what I figure Ebenezer'd do hisself if'n he was here. He'd give Titus a vote."

"Like I said," Root disagreed with a snarl, "the boy here never was hired on like the rest of us."

"It ain't right, Titus having as much say as us what been working Ebenezer's boats for years now," Ovatt added.

"You don't wanna give the boy a vote, well—let's just set that aside for a minute and talk over something else," Kingsbury said with the sure ease of a man used to steering a boat out of troubled waters.

And something in the boatman's face told Titus that Hames was going to try something smooth.

Hames continued, "S'pose you boys sit there and ponder what Ebenezer Zane would do 'bout that woman we pulled from the river back there. Reuben? How you think Ebenezer would vote?"

Ovatt's eyes flared, knowing he'd been bested. "Ah, shit," he said sourly. "We all three of us know Ebenezer'd vote to keep her on his goddamned boat—and he'd throw any of us off if'n we grumped about it too."

"But Ebenezer ain't here to throw us off," Root declared, slowly crossing his beefy arms across his stout powder keg of a chest.

"Yes, he is," Kingsbury said with great conviction, and pointed at the corpse lying in its canvas shroud. "I figure we're carrying him on to Natchez . . . so we sure as hell can do the same for a living, breathing woman."

"Ah, sweet Jupiter!" Root cried out, flinging his arms about in frustration. "No telling what kind of bad luck we're going to have now!"

"Things in life ain't that simple," Kingsbury attempted to explain.

Ovatt laughed without humor, then said, "Listen to you, Hames! That woman sure as hell wasn't no good luck on her husband's boat. All the crew and him gone too—like she told it. The boat sunk in the river, scuttled by Injuns."

"That man and woman been working the river together for more'n twenty years, Heman," Kingsbury reminded. "Sure took that thing you call a woman's curse a helluva long time to catch up to 'em, didn't it?"

Bass watched the two of them grumble for a moment, then Ovatt turned to Kingsbury.

"She stays right there," Heman demanded with noticeable reluctance. "She don't come out to curse the rest of the boat."

"What's done is done," Root groaned. "We're already cursed, Heman. It don't matter where she stays on this goddamned boat. The whole lot of us is already cursed."

"But—she can stay, right?" Bass asked.

"Yes," Kingsbury answered with finality. "The woman's gonna ride with us till we get to Natchez—where we can let her off and put Ebenezer to his final rest."

Later that afternoon Titus was surprised to hear the first notes from Reuben's squeeze-box in a long time. Sliding mournfully up and down the scales with his wheezing concertina, the oarsman sat at the gunnel to begin playing snatches of melancholy ballads and slow airs in the cold drizzle that seeped from the brims of their hats, hammered the taut oil sheeting of their awning where the woman kept a fire going and coffee brewing throughout the day when she wasn't fishing.

"Funny," Bass said to Kingsbury quietly enough so that no one else would hear, then sniffed the aroma coming from the awning. "Never did I think of fish being something I'd get my hungers up for. That does smell good."

"Ain't ever had but one bite of catfish," Hames replied. "Never had me another. But from what I seen that woman doing all afternoon, if she hauls in a catfish on her line, she just throws it back. Only keeping the fish what don't taste like mud."

"S'pose she'd mind me asking for some to eat?"

"I reckon you can go ask her," he said with a smile.

Ducking out of the rain beneath the awning, Titus stood there, dripping, then thought to remove his hat. He found himself back in the company of women, where a man had to remember his good manners.

"Ma'am?"

She turned to regard him with her crow-footed face scored by wrinkles across her brow and reaching from her nose down to her chin in deep clefts. Pushing a long, unruly strand of hair from her eye, she did not speak to Bass, just stared as if expecting him to get on with his question.

As he watched her, he found himself liking the way working over the fire's heat brought a flush to the woman's leathery, tanned cheeks, after they had been so damned pasty and white the time they'd pulled her from the cold river.

"What's that you're cooking there?"

She glanced down at the big cast-iron skillet spitting and spewing the fish she'd halved and dipped into a cornmeal batter. And the woman smiled, her eyes softening.

"Fish."

"Not catfish?"

She chuckled a little as she leaned over the skillet with a long fork and speared the fish around in the grease. "Don't like catfish, me either. This here's perch. Good eating." Then she looked up at him, blowing the hair back from her nose and eyes. "You want you some?"

"I'd be awfully pleasured to have some, yes, ma'am."

"Gonna need more of that grease," she replied, turning back to her spewing skillet from which rose such enticing aromas. "Get me some more, and I'll dish you up a trencher of this hot perch."

In a long canvas-lined white-oak chest where the crew kept their mess utensils sat several clay pots into which the men always scraped the bacon grease left over after their endless, monotonous meals of pork. One of these he brought her, pulling off the metal latch that held the flat top on the pot. Stuffing her big iron fork into the congealed grease, the woman took a speckled, translucent gob over to the skillet and plopped it in with a spitting hiss. With the fork she pulled the largest piece of fish from the heat and laid it in one of the scooped-out oaken trenchers the crew used as plate and bowl in one. How Titus's mouth watered just to look at the deep, rich, golden brown of that cornmeal breading, just to breathe in that fragrance of something other than salt pork, bacon, and boiled hocks. The anticipation of this meal was enough to bring tears to his eyes.

"How long since you et?" she asked.

"Yesterday night," Bass replied, settling and pulling his knife from his belt.

"Acting starved to me."

"He's just a growing boy, ma'am," Kingsbury defended from the stern rudder nearby. "The sort what needs a lot of victuals."

Suddenly, with a second bite in his mouth, Titus was seized with another, even bigger, fear over his incomplete manners. "You ate, didn't you, ma'am?"

"I fed myself first, son," she answered. "Don't you worry. If I didn't eat first, I'd not had the strength to keep on fishing and frying. By the by—you might just as well be calling me by my name. I'm Beulah."

"Beulah. Yes, ma'am. So how long'd you go without food?" Kingsbury asked from the stern rudder.

"Better'n three days: from the morning we was set upon by them Chickasaws, till yestiddy afternoon you come downriver and finded me floating on that piece of the boat."

The pilot said, "Can't imagine them Injuns letting you off alive like they done."

"They didn't," she replied. "Figured us all being dead."

"You slipped off 'thout them knowing?" asked Reuben Root.

With a wag of her head she plopped another slab of perch into a trencher dusted with cornmeal, then laid it in the greased skillet. "Me and Jameson—that's my . . . that was my husband: Jameson Hartshorn," she said, seeming to choke for a moment, her eyes blinking in the smoke rising from the fire and the pork grease. "We was both in the water after the Injuns got the four other fellas on the boat. Busting up the cargo, those red devils was, tossing it all over the side, making a awful mess of everything. Yelling and screaming and kicking fire out of the sandbox, catching our boat to burn."

"They burned it right down to the water, I'll bet," Ovatt said acidly from the starboard oar.

"They might have," she answered. "I wasn't there to see it. Jameson and me—we was hanging on to some oak-cask staves, trying to slip off 'thout any of them killers spying us. We was just lucky to slip over the side them not seeing us, way I figure it. We was paddling and kicking out from the boat—I looked around once and saw 'em dancing and screaming, couple of them Injuns throwing one of our men into the fire they had burning the boat. That's when one of 'em spotted Jameson and me. They come to the gunnel shouting and pointing, shooting arrows, and finally one of 'em got his gun and shot Jameson in the back of the head."

A few uneasy moments passed while she pushed at the portions of fish in the spitting skillet. Then Kingsbury asked quietly, "That when you lost him?"

"No. He started to slip off the stave, but I held him up for some time while his eyes was still open. Jameson . . . he said a couple things to me afore he went under. Last thing he told me was it was all right to let him go. Said he was done for and I ought'n save myself."

"You waited to let him go till he died," Root said, some new, begrudging respect showing on his broad face. "You're a . . . a strong woman, ma'am."

"I let the river take him," she continued, pulling some of the fried fish out and heaping it into a big wooden trencher. "I'll fetch up some of this for each of you and bring it over, you just wait a minute more."

"It's a wonder they didn't shoot you too!" Titus exclaimed.

"They tried," she said matter-of-factly. "After the third shot I quit paddling. Just hung myself over that chunk of wood I was floating on, barely kept my nose and mouth outta the water."

"Playing possum, was you?" Ovatt asked.

"Playing dead is what I done," the woman replied. "Drifted off into some brush by the far bank and they never come to look after me then on out. Next morning I pushed away of that brush to try to make it to the east shore, but the tow caught me, and I ended up getting pulled on out into the river. Hung there for more'n another day afore you come along—the first boat I seen come down after them Injuns jumped us all."

"You was near froze by the time we come along," Kingsbury said.

"I'm mighty grateful to you fellas," she said, straightening, looking at each of them in turn when she continued. "I know how most folks look at a woman on a Kentuckyboat—but you still took me on for the trip down to Natchez. I promise you I won't be in your way none, you just get me to where I can start my walk back up the Trace to home. I'll help out all you want me to till then."

"I think you're doing us just fine, ma'am," Kingsbury said.

"Hames is right," Ovatt agreed reluctantly as he took the oak trencher from her. "This fish and all."

"I can make us up a mess of beans—you got any beans for supper tonight? I best get to soaking 'em."

"Titus, you're in there. Fetch off the top of that barrel got our beans in it for her."

After she had scooped out what she wanted into a brass kettle, the woman ladled some of their drinking water over it and set the beans aside to soak.

"Ma'am, you got any family, any friends, in Natchez?" Titus asked as she went back to breading more of the perch she'd dragged from the river that morning.

With a doleful wag of her head she answered, "We neither one had any family there."

Kingsbury asked, "You fixing on setting off up the Natchez Trace all by yourself?"

She began to wag her head, saying, "No, I don't." Then she shrugged and stared at the fire. "I reckon there'll be some wagons to ride in eventual. Maybe they'll let me ride along like you done, what with me working for my keep by cooking and cleaning all the way north."

"Ought to be a way for it to work out for you," Ovatt commented.

"Hope it's so: just ain't right for a woman to have to face all them miles alone by herself," Kingsbury said.

She looked up from her cooking, pushing some hair back from her sad eyes again, cheeks rosy with warmth, and said with courageous melancholy, "Looks like I'm bound to be lonely for a long, long time now. What with Jameson gone at the bottom of this here goddamned river."

"We lost us a good friend to the Injuns too," Root said.

"That him?" And she pointed to the shroud lashed near the bow.

"The pilot and owner of this boat," Kingsbury answered. "We all been riding the rivers with him for some time now."

She touched each one of them with her doleful eyes, baggy with fatigue and woe. Finally her gaze landed on the youngster. "How 'bout you?" she asked. "You don't look to be a riverman."

"I ain't. Truth is—"

"He wasn't till our pilot made a riverman out of him," Kingsbury interrupted.

"He don't got the look of a boatman," she replied, hunching back over her work at the sandbox fire. "I know boatmen and you ain't one, young'un."

"This here's his first trip down," Ovatt explained. "An' he's taking to it real slick."

Still she wagged her head. "That'un"—and she gestured up toward Bass with that long iron fork, not even raising her eyes to him—"he looks more like some lost mother's child what ain't got no business out here where he's throwed in with a rascal bunch like you at best, mayhaps he's gonna be killed at the worst of it."

Titus instantly bristled with shame, roiling with boyish pride. "I'm old enough to take care of myself!"

"I had seven young'uns of my own," she explained with a knowing smirk that made any man feel like a boy. "Lost two of 'em to the river. And now my husband—gone. Lemme tell you I know there's a mother some-where worrying herself sick about you. I never been able to own up to knowing all that much about a lot of things—but a mother knows something like that for certain."

Prickling with anger, Bass felt the eyes of the others clawing at him as he stared down at the woman while she aimlessly poked at the burning limbs beneath her spitting skillet. What could he say in his own defense, he wondered, that wouldn't let his words betray him when they come out?

"No matter that you might think different," Kingsbury said offhand-edly as he watched Bass turn without a complaint and silently shuffle away. "He's a man now, and one of our crew . . . here on what's to be Ebenezer Zane's last trip to Natchez."

"I heard how you put up for me back there when them others was wanting to set me off their boat," Beulah said to him in the gray light more than a week later. "I wasn't intending on being a burden—didn't even ask any of you go looking for my husband."

"He's . . . likely gone, ma'am," Titus replied.

She blinked, as if that worked something mechanical inside her to own up to the reality of it. "I might've asked—but I didn't have the shirt he was wearing."

"His shirt? How'd that help you?"

"Folks believe it—howsomever I ain't never had occasion to prove it wrong," Beulah explained. "You take a loaf of bread and wrap it in the missing person's shirt. Put it on the water and it will sink over the spot where we can find his body."

He thought on that, hard.

Finally she asked, "You don't think that's crazy, do you, young'un?"

With a shrug he replied, "Maybe not near as crazy as what some folks do. Hell—no matter that you didn't have your husband's shirt. We ain't even got any bread to do it with anyways. But if we had, I'd talked 'em into giving it a try for you."

She smiled warmly. "Want you to know I'm in your debt and didn't mean you to take no offense when I was calling you a young'un, talking about your ma."

"Wish you'd just left my mam out'n this," Titus said as he watched the river ahead for obstacles, scratching at the incessant itch under his arms, at his waistband.

"There's difference 'tween leaving home when it's time . . . and running off," she said as the cold wisps of river fog glided slowly past them.

"It was my time."

"Just looking at you, I can tell that ain't near enough the truth."

Bristling like a short-haired hog at butcher time, Titus replied, "Ain't none of your concern nohow."

"How long you been itching the way you are?"

"I dunno," he said, suddenly conscious of the fact that he had been scratching himself almost raw in places.

"Likely you got the Scotch-Irish itch."

"The what?"

"You got lice, young'un," she explained. "Never had 'em afore?"

He shook his head.

"Bet you got 'em now—just looking at this boat's crew," she chided, wagging her head.

"What can I do for 'em . . . stop this scratching?"

"Burn your clothes, pour coal tar on your hair," she replied.

"You're pulling my leg, ain'cha?"

"No—onliest way I know to get rid of them little seam-rats. Nits and graybacks—damn 'em all," the woman answered.

He swallowed, regarding her carefully, deciding she was serious. "Maybeso I can get something for 'em up to Natchez."

"Coal tar's good."

He flared with anger briefly as he gazed out at the river, watching. "I ain't gonna put no coal tar on my hair."

With a warm smile Beulah said, "G'won and get you some of that tar in Natchez. We kin daub some of it on them bites—keep 'em from itching you so bad."

"Thank . . . thanks, Beulah," he stammered, sensing something profound come from her at that moment.

For the longest time she had been staring off downriver as they'd slipped through the gauzy tendrils of gray fog, some of it clinging in her hair as if her head were smoldering. From time to time he caught sight of the river's edge and the sycamore trees, roots exposed by the eroding bank, high-water mud plastered halfway up the tall trunks. Long gray moss, what some of the rivermen called "Spanish beard," drooped in great, wavering clumps from the giant branches, dancing gently on the cold breeze.

"We'll be making Natchez soon," Beulah finally said. "Get close to Natchez, them others gonna bury the pilot in this river."

"We been planning on it ever since't he was killed."

"He was a good man to you, wasn't he?" Beulah asked. But without waiting for an answer, she continued. "So was my Jameson. How he stuck up for our three boys what run off from home—stuck up for 'em the same time he was doing all he could to ease my sorrow at their going."

"They run off, like I done?"

"Ain't ever see'd 'em since," Beulah admitted with a sigh. "Once a young'un you've tried so hard to keep in the nest gets ready to try his wings —if you don't step back and let 'em try flying on their own, they can damn sure beat you to death with those same goddamned wings."

"You watched all of your'n fly off," he said quietly.

The woman nodded. "And they ain't come back after all this time, likely won't ever show their faces again." Then, turning to him directly, the woman added, "You best send your mama word that you're all right—"

Shaking his head emphatically, Bass replied, "Don't want no one to know where I'm gone."

"You don't write her word, then you better go see your mother."

"Can't do that neither."

"Your pa?"

He went on staring at the brown water gliding past them beneath the cold gray of the wispy fog.

She said, "Men and their boys—every family has problems."

"Weren't just my family," Titus owned up quietly. "It were everybody wanting me to be something I wasn't."

"This what you was meant to be? A riverman?"

"No," he said. "Not that neither. Something akin to my gran'pap." He went on to tell her how his family had come into the Kentucky country to settle long ago—how his grandfather never really did settle down like he was supposed to, restless and yearning to move farther west to his dying day.

"There's men made what're never meant to settle long in one place," the woman said. "I saw that in my Jameson, right off. We both just made peace with it—and found us something to do what would keep him moving. Ain't no wonder to me anymore that a young'un does all he can to escape the labors of the field for a life on the river."

Heman Ovatt was clambering up over the cargo. "Titus, you best go back and get you some coffee. I'll spell you at the gouger."

"Hap that you fellas are ready for breakfast?" Beulah asked.

"We always ready to eat," the riverman answered enthusiastically as he came up to take the gouger from Bass.

Titus stopped a moment, sensing an immense sadness clinging to the woman here, days after her tragic loss. "You got sons back to Ohio?"

Beulah wagged her head. "Two of 'em the river took," she replied, staring off. "Them three I spoke of took off, and I don't have idea one where they've gone. But two of my boys, yes—they always been up to Ohio when Jameson and me come home from every one of our journeys."

"Then you got a place to stay when you get back there."

"Yes," she replied. "But you ain't got a home no more, do you, son?"

He watched her back as the woman moved off toward the awning. Perhaps no more acutely since he'd fled Rabbit Hash had he felt without a home than since Ebenezer Zane was killed. Almost as if he were adrift on the river now himself, but without a rudder or gouger, without a single paddle to use when life tossed him this way and that, very much the way this mighty river shoved and pulled their broadhorn downstream.

Over their heads that melancholy morning hung a pearl button of a sun glimpsed through the thinning fog. The other three boatmen grew more somber as the hours passed and familiar landmarks presented themselves along the eastern shore.

"We'll be tied up at Natchez before dark," Kingsbury declared early that afternoon.

Titus said, "Means we're gonna bury Ebenezer afore that."

"There's a place a few miles upriver he liked especial'," Reuben said. "I figure that's where he'd want us to let him over the side."

Ovatt nodded, his face twisting somewhat in an attempt to hide the emotions threatening to overwhelm him.

At the rudder Kingsbury said only, "We get there, I'll put us over to the east bank and we can all help put Ebenezer to his rest."

Since passing the Chickasaw Bluffs where they'd first brought the woman aboard, they had made reasonable time coming on down that great river road. Several days after Beulah was rescued, they had pushed past the wide mouth of a river joining the Mississippi from the west.

"There's some what says that water comes in from the far mountains," Kingsbury stated.

"That river?"

"Call't the Arkansas, Titus. Some thirty mile on up, there stands a old French village. Leastwise, there used to be when Ebenezer and me went there once of a time," Kingsbury said as he leaned against the long rudder pole. "Nearby, the Spaniards got 'em a fort. Some folks call the place Ozark Village, other'ns call it Arkansas Post."

"Spaniards still there?"

With a wag of his head Hames replied, "Naw. Nothing but backwoodsmen now—few hunnerd of 'em. Speak American—though most of 'em got French blood and French names, so it seems."

Titus gazed off to the west, squinting, attempting to conjure up the lure of that settlement. "What them Frenchies do living off over there?"

"Near as we ever made out, they hunt when they want, trade when need be. And ain't a one of 'em acts no better'n the Injuns in that country."

For the longest time Bass watched the wide mouth of that river disappear behind them, trying his best to replace the endless cane and cattail swamp with images of mountains as he knew them from the Ohio River country, those distant high places supplying waters that rushed all the way down to feed the Mississippi.

Just south of the Arkansas they glided past the treacherous Stack Island, and the next day Kingsbury pointed out the "Crow's Nest"—both at one time havens for Mississippi River pirates. That night they camped north a ways from the mouth of the Yazoo River at a well-known landing spot at Gum Springs in Choctaw country. The following morning they passed below the American Fort McHenry, standing high upon the Walnut Hills that rose along the eastern shore.* Now surrounded by some well-cultivated fields and a sparse dotting of cabins and girdled trees, these heights in an earlier time had been held by the dominant Spanish with a post they called Fort Nogales. That bold, rising ground proved to be a welcome sight after the last seven hundred miles and many days of monotonous bayou and swampy cypress and sycamore forest.

Still, the river was far from finished cutting a wide swath for itself in that meandering journey to the Gulf of Mexico. South from the Yazoo the Mississippi once again spread its waters through a wide and inhospitable wilderness stretching all the way from Grand Gulf, down through Bayou Pierre and on to the endless swamp at Petit Gulf. Through it all Zane's rivermen plied those brown waters, passing the sinister places named Devil's Playground, down to the Devil's Bake Oven, then on to the Devil's Punch Bowl, where whirlpools snarled across the surface of the river, forcing even the finest of river pilots to put all their skills and muscle to a test.

But by that last day's float above Natchez, the river once more moved along with a placid pace, if not became downright mournful, as they drew closer and closer to Ebenezer Zane's resting place beneath the Mississippi.

"That spot way yonder 'neath the far bluff—ain't that the one, Reuben?" Kingsbury hollered.

Root nodded, pointing. "That's just the place I was thinking."

"Yeah," Kingsbury replied. "It'll do just fine. Ebenezer allays thought this was a real purty place every time we come past."

It could well have been one of the most beautiful spots along the river at the height of summer when the wisteria bloomed in all its purple glory and the dogwood set the hills afire. Even now, after so many freezes had shriveled every leaf and turned the trees from monuments of glory into winter's contorted, skeletal refugees overlooking this wide bend in the Mississippi, Titus could nonetheless see for himself what beauty Ebenezer Zane might have always found in this place as Hames Kingsbury and Heman Ovatt eased their long Kentuckyboat toward that eastern shore.

Root jumped over the side and hauled the first of the thick hawsers into the shallows, where he stood shivering in waist-deep water to tie them

---

* *Future site of Vicksburg, Mississippi.*

off before clambering back over the gunnel. Beulah awaited him, holding out an old blanket as Reuben got to his feet.

As if struck dumb, Root stood there a moment, dripping and trembling, then took the offering, nodding shyly as he wrapped it around his middle and quietly said, "Thankee, ma'am."

Clearly the woman saved him any more embarrassment when she turned aside, ducking beneath the awning as Kingsbury moved up among the casks and crates.

"Heman, why don't you and Titus bring Ebenezer over here?" Hames said. "I figure we ought to put him into the water off the starboard."

Root nodded in agreement as the two brought the canvas shroud to midship, hefting it atop four large kegs. Reuben said, "Ebenezer never was much of a man for port, was he, now? Allays liked to be on the river, never quite as happy when we was making for to tie up."

"Thems is fine words to say over a friend, Reuben," Kingsbury replied, drawing himself up as if about to confront something difficult. "Any of the rest of you have something to say to Ebenezer before we see this through?"

Laying his hand on the canvas shroud bound with rope, Heman Ovatt said, "I just want Ebenezer Zane to know—wherever he is right now—I never met a man I respected more. A man what took me in when no one else on the river would give me a job."

"Amen to that," Kingsbury said as Heman stepped back. "You was the sort what was trouble: Ohio born, whiskey soaked, and quick to anger. But Ebenezer didn't never look at you that way. He said you'd make a good hand. And you allays have."

"It's 'cause of him I'm a different man today," Ovatt replied, then looked over at Root shyly.

With a shrug Root just snatched the floppy-brimmed felt hat from his head and stared down at the shroud. "All I know is I'm a better man for knowing Ebenezer Zane. 'Cept—I do know one more thing for certain— I'm gonna miss him something terrible from here on out."

There was a short period of silence until Kingsbury said, "We're all gonna miss him, if'n we ain't already. Come our walk back home to the Ohio. Come next summer's float south again."

"I dunno if I'm coming downriver again, Hames," Ovatt said.

"You'll come with us," Kingsbury replied. "Ebenezer wouldn't want you to go quitting on us, would he?"

"S'pose he wouldn't."

Then Titus felt Kingsbury's eyes touch him.

The flatboat's new pilot asked, "You got anything you wanna say afore we put Ebenezer over the side, Titus Bass?"

All of them looked at him, expectantly, even the woman. He stammered a moment, then finally said, "I still figure his dying was somehow my fault."

"It ain't," Kingsbury replied immediately, "and Ebenezer told you that, right after they run us off the beach—told you none of it was your doin'. So you just go and make peace with that. If not for your sake, then you damn well do it for Ebenezer's memory."

"That's right, Titus," Root stated. "Ebenezer weren't the kind to hold no grudges agin no man. So he wouldn't want you holding no grudge agin yourself."

Bass eventually nodded and said quietly, "I just wish things'd turned out different for us."

"Life never tells us what it's gonna do," the woman said suddenly, surprising them all as she bent to come from the awning to stand among them near the shroud. "We ain't got no call on life but to go on—no matter what's dealt us."

"Them's true, true words, ma'am," Kingsbury echoed with no small admiration as he gazed at her. "Thank you."

"I never had me a chance to say nothing over my husband's body," she went on, staring at the shroud. "Not like most women, they get to stand over the grave where the man they loved is gonna lie for all eternity. Never had me the chance for them words."

"You feel like saying something now—maybe over Ebenezer—what you'd like to gone and said over your own man's grave?" Kingsbury asked.

With a nod she glanced quickly at Titus. "Jameson and me, we buried one stillbirth, another two that didn't make their first year, then we finally raised up seven boys—only to see the rivers claim two of 'em. Maybe another three. I seen my share of troubles and woe, I have. My life been far from a pretty thing. But a man what sticks by his friends and cheats no other is a real treasure in this life. Seems to me that my Jameson and your Ebenezer Zane was two of that kind."

"He was at that. Amen," Kingsbury said, swiping a hand across a damp, jowly cheek.

Beneath her eyes Beulah dragged the rough wool of that blanket she clutched around her shoulders. "I suppose all we can really say about good men like this'un—what God don't already know His own self—is that there's gonna be a big hole to fill in our lives now that this man's gone. But God, and good men like this'un, expect us just to go right on."

As her voice dropped off and it got quiet, Titus looked up, finding her gazing at him with those intense, sad, red-rimmed eyes.

"Men like Ebenezer Zane expect you to go right on with what you were bound to do in this life," Beulah continued.

As her voice died away, the wind gusted, cold and toothy, whipping their coats and flapping the edges of their blankets at them like flags. In the sudden leaving of that wind, the soft slap of water against hard, yellow poplar filled the silent void around them.

"If you fellas are ready to send this man to his rest," she said, "I'll say a few words what I remember is always said over folks getting buried."

Without a sound Ovatt and Root hoisted the upper part of Ebenezer Zane's body while Kingsbury took hold of the legs. When Titus began to move forward to help, Beulah put out her arm, held him in place beside her, then curled an arm in his as she began to repeat the litany as she remembered it.

"Dust to dust, ashes to ashes," she said as the three boatmen hoisted the shroud toward the gunnel. "The Good Lord in heaven awaits thee, noble soul. Fly, fly now—and be quick to sit at God's feet. Know that your toil is done, and your troubles are behind you now. We who are left behind will remember. We *vow* to remember."

Bass watched them roll the shroud off the six-inch-wide plank that formed the top of the gunnel, heard the body splash into the river. By the time Titus got to the side of the flatboat, the gray shroud had darkened, taking on water as it slowly sank with the weights Root and Ovatt had tied to it.

We vow to remember, he echoed the words in his head, peering down with the rest of them as Ebenezer Zane sank slowly beneath the murky brown surface of the river, became a dark, oblong shape, then disappeared completely.

Once more the wind came up, and he had to swipe the hair from his eyes as he pushed back from the gunnel, stood, and moved away to the awning. In a moment more, the rest of them joined him there, all kneeling to warm their hands over the sandbox fire, eyes red-rimmed and the skin over their noses and cheeks flushed with the cold's cruel bite.

"We'll be putting up at Natchez in less'n a hour," Kingsbury said to the woman. "But you're welcome to stay over the night with us—seeing how you ain't got no family there to put yourself up with."

"Didn't I hear talk of you fellas planning on making a hoot of it this evening Under-the-Hill?" she asked, without raising her eyes to any of them.

"We allays do," Ovatt answered as he began to hold his right thumbnail over the flame of a candle in one of the lanterns.

"What the devil're you doing?" she asked him.

"Hardenin' my fingernails 's all."

"Whatever for?"

This time Kingsbury explained with a grin, "Why, the better to feel for a feller's eye strings, woman. Heman goes to gouging with them nails—he can make any bad son of a bitch tell the news! Natchez can be a damn hard town for a man what can't take care of hisself in a scrap. But just 'cause we go off and have ourselves a hoot don't mean you won't have you a place to sleep tonight."

With a visible shudder she turned away from watching Ovatt harden his thumbnails. "I'm 'bliged," she replied. "My boys, an' them others what hired on to work our boat—they never said much 'bout what they done when we reached Natchez, nary what they done at the Swamp when we got on down to Orlins too. Early on I come to figure it all just had to do with a man whoring and drinking, having himself a spree when his boat comes to port."

Titus peered at those three roughened men, surprised to find them suddenly shy and sheepish in the presence of this woman looking every bit as worn enough to be their maiden aunt, a woman who had just spoken moving words as she watched them bury their pilot—then minutes afterward forced them to own up to just what it was rivermen tied up at Natchez to do.

Poking at the embers with a twig she stirred some more life into the fire, then shrugged a shoulder as she pulled the big coffee kettle from the heat. "I suppose it's what men are about, and there's never gonna be no changing it. So don't pay me no mind. I'm much obliged for your giving me a place to lay my head on your boat tonight." She picked up a tinned mug and asked, "Any of you care for more of my coffee?"

As for anything remotely resembling civilization in this river wilderness, there were but three sizable outposts of settlement that joined those tiny villages, far-flung trading posts, and the occasional military fort: at the far northern end of the lower Mississippi Valley sat the old French colony, St.

Louis; all the way south at the other end of the river sprawled the even larger New Orleans; and between them squatted Natchez—a town more of dubious reputation than of any real note.

Not only could a boatman look forward to some ribald female companionship along with some head-thumping whiskey in the brothels and watering holes that sat at the river's edge—but there was still even more cause to celebrate. Reaching Natchez meant the most treacherous sections of the Mississippi were now behind them. Sitting where it did on the eastern shore, the town had quickly proved itself an ideal way station where the flatboat crews put in to resupply, rest, and recreate before making the last short run on down to New Orleans.

Long before, the place had been nothing more than a semipermanent encampment of the Natchez Indians. With the coming of the white man the first settlement high upon the bluff overlooking the river was eventually wrangled over by three European countries. First to arrive were the Spanish, followed by the French, and eventually the British brought their influence to bear on this Mississippi port. Ultimately the infant United States came to reign supreme in recent years. Each of those conflicting cultures had added the same full-bodied, international flavor any traveler would find in St. Louis and New Orleans. All told, the entire Natchez district numbered some seventy-five hundred souls, due in large part to the cultivation of the unusually rich soil found on numerous farms and expansive plantations. Yet the town served as the center of more than mere trade—early-day Natchez boasted an extremely varied and exciting social life of theater, balls, and what traveling acts happened by.

The winter sun had set and twilight was slipping down around them as the four boatmen climbed over the gunnel to stand on the wharf, peering past the rickety clapboard and canvas-topped shanties to the lights of the town itself on the heights above.

Kingsbury turned and asked the woman, "You're gonna be all right here?"

"Got me all I need," she replied, then gestured them to be off. "Now, get—and have yourselves a hoot. I'll be right here when you mosey on back."

"Likely be back afore morning," the boat's skinny pilot replied as he turned away with the others.

They pressed into the last throb of that busy wharf, pushing past all manner of those who made the river and this wilderness their home. Here beneath the Natchez hill Bass not only rubbed elbows with many other homespun boatmen and leather-clad frontiersmen, but with Brits and

Frenchmen, African slaves and freedmen, along with Indians, Spaniards, Acadians, and Creoles as well.

"What be that up there?" Titus asked, stopping to point up the bluff to the town built on the high ground at a distance of a mile from the river.

Kingsbury stopped with the rest of them right behind Bass, saying, "Natchez."

"Ain't we going up there?" Titus asked.

Heman Ovatt explained, "We ain't allowed."

"That's right," Kingsbury continued. "Rivermen like us get arrested if'n they go up there to the town where the proper folks live."

Bass looked up the bluff again, then quickly at the collection of vulgar shacks and hovels raised along the wharf in one long, jagged strip. "If'n that's Natchez up there, then what's this place down here where they 'llow us to go?"

"This here's called Natchez-Under-the-Hill," Kingsbury answered.

That name was not only picturesque, but apt and clearly fitting. Tucked here under the fine houses and rich shops catering only to the most cultured of Natchez residents sat the squalid, low-roofed sheds where the rivermen flocked to celebrate a bawdy and profane life. Above them stood the big houses, all finished off with ornate balconies and ivy-covered piazzas, the town's streets crowded by handsome carriages, while here beside the river huddled only those monuments to man's timeless attraction to the varied sins of the flesh.

Kingsbury set the group off again, draping an arm over the youngster's shoulder to say, "I'm wanting Titus here to have him a look at Annie Christmas's gunboat down the way."

"Gunboat?" Titus asked. "What the devil that be?"

"Just what they call a flatboat been left behind by a crew long ago and some working girls took it over," Ovatt declared.

Bass asked him, "Working girls? Like them at the Kangaroo in Louisville?"

"That's the idea!" Kingsbury replied. "It's their floating whorehouse."

"But why is it called a gunboat?"

"Don't you go there to shoot off your gun?" Root inquired.

"I didn't bring me my rifle—"

"Naw!" Kingsbury interrupted with a chuckle. "Didn't Mincemeat go an' teach you all about how to use your gun?"

"Yeah," added Root. "You was locked up with her for all that time—I figured you'd learn't you couldn't have you near the fun with your rifle you can have with your gun!"

It came over him slowly as he looked from face to grinning, gaping face in that deepening twilight. "All right," Bass said. "Let's go see this here gunboat."

Ovatt asked, "Maybe you'll shoot your gun off tonight, eh?"

"Count on it," Bass replied enthusiastically as they started off down the wharf once more, passing noisy whorehouses, grogshops, card rooms, and gambling dens where laughter and music, shouts and screams, as well as drunken men all came tumbling out onto the cold plank thoroughfare. Here and there a short street ran perpendicular to the single long avenue that corded itself beside the river—streets named: Choctaw, Silver, Cherokee, Arkansas, and Chickasaw, all of them littered with filth, trash, and human excrement. Hundreds of men poured from one dimly lit place to the other, hooting and hollering at the pinnacle of bawdy revelry, while half-feral dogs and other wild creatures slunk back in the dark places and fought wrinkle-necked vultures among the shadows over the rotting garbage heaved right out of each establishment's front door.

"Here you go, Titus," Kingsbury said when they finally reached the southern end of the wharf to stand near a long flatboat badly in need of repair.

"What's this?" Bass inquired as the pilot held his palm open and there laid three coins.

"A picayune."

"What's it for?"

"Man needs money to buy hisself a place to shoot off his gun!" Root exclaimed as Kingsbury handed the other two boatmen their picayune—the equivalent of six cents.

"What'm I gonna do with only this?" Titus protested.

Kingsbury snorted a loud guffaw, then said, "Here at Annie Christmas's gunboat, that there picayune gonna get you drunk, get you a woman near all night long, and a bed till morning."

"But you don't wanna let yourself fall asleep, Titus," Ovatt warned.

"Listen to him," Root echoed. "Don't you dare fall asleep with one of Annie's whores."

"Why can't I just sleep it off if'n I take a mind to—like I done with—"

"Ain't like Mincemeat," Kingsbury started to explain. "Most of these here gals got 'em steady men they flock with. The women work on their backs and those fellas go gamble off what the women make getting poked by boatmen."

"So? What's that mean to me?"

"It means a lot of them gals don't give a good goddamn about you after they let you poke 'em," Ovatt said. "You fall asleep, and you're likely as not to never wake up—at the bottom of the river."

He glanced down at the three coins in his palm, then clenched them tightly as he asked, "N-never wake up? How?"

Kingsbury slapped a hand on Bass's shoulder in the way of a big brother explaining sharp realities, "You go to sleeping, that gal you're with might let in her feller to do the blood work."

"B-blood work?" He was suspicious they were yanking on his leg.

Root dragged an index finger from one ear, across his throat to the other ear, making a distasteful sound as he did so.

"Or that gal might just be the sort of whore cut your throat her own self!" Ovatt said.

"Like a hog hung up at the slaughter!" Kingsbury added.

Wide-eyed, Titus regarded them all in turn, then blinked and asked, "Why . . . why all you fellas—and Ebenezer too—let me go off by my own self with that one named Mincemeat?"

"Shit!" Kingsbury replied, rubbing a hand across the top of Bass's head. "None of us, 'specially Ebenezer, gonna let you go off with some whore what'd open you up a new breathing hole in your neck! Ebenezer Zane was taking good care of you, sending you off with Mincemeat."

"She's a good whore!" Root exclaimed.

"Not like none of these here bitches in Natchez," Ovatt said. "G'won and dip your stinger in their honey-pot, then get on outta there to do some more drinking. Or get your bones back to the boat."

"That's the only way, Titus," Kingsbury warned. "Don't trust none of them spread-legged bitches here in Natchez. They all likely murdered a man or two their own selves."

Ovatt agreed, saying, "You just figure that's why they're working here, and not up to St. Louie, or on down to Norlins."

"Likely got runned out of those towns," Kingsbury said, "or escaped afore they was strung up for murderin' customers."

"Ain't much law hereabouts," Root said, gesturing this way and that. "Best thing for a man to do is to hang together with his crew when he ain't humping 'tween the legs of one of them bang-tailed bitches."

THIRTEEN

A hard, cold rain hammered the heavy oiled-canvas sheeting stretched over Bass's head like the rattle of hailstones against the white-oak top of an empty shipping cask.

At first he was too frightened to allow himself to be pleasured by one of Annie Christmas's homely castaways.

Instead Titus sought relief at the bottom of a clay mug filled with a fiery concoction of corn spirits, for the longest time unable to take his eyes off the gunboat madam. He'd never seen anyone, much less a woman, near so tall—over six and a half feet of her. She laughed and drank, roared and cussed with the other three boatmen, and then he watched her disappear in the back with Kingsbury. Bass found another big one to stare at. This one—just about as wide as Annie was tall.

From that point on it didn't take him long to start sensing the whiskey's effects as the tip of his nose steadily grew more numb and felt for all the world like it was swelling as large as a hog's snout right there on the front of his face.

Mysterious thing about what he had been swilling down—

the more he drank, the more beautiful that plump and fleshy half-dressed consort became.

It took a while as he sat there drinking, but that gunboat whore finally realized the youngest customer there that night at Annie Christmas's was giving her all his attention from across the small windowless parlor that fronted a half-dozen tiny cribs. In all, the parlor and those six cribs took up the entire length of a flatboat salvaged after its owner had been murdered in one of the many uninvestigated, unsolved, unquestioned killings that seemed to be an everyday staple of life "Under-the-Hill." It was seventy feet by eighteen feet of floating pleasure palace. No music save for the incessant humming and singing performed by the tall, bald-headed slave Annie kept behind the short, stinking bar. Patrons and the working girls had few tables to set their drinks upon, and only two chairs dressed the whole parlor. Everyone else had to satisfy themselves squatting on some soiled, grass-filled tick pillows covered in muslin or nankeen sheeting. There didn't appear to be a single one that hadn't recently seen a drunken customer pitch the contents of his stomach onto it, and a few even bore significant splotches of blood Annie's girls had failed to bleach before the stains set.

At long last she returned to the parlor to find Titus still willing to stare at her. Taking up a clay mug for herself, she came to stand over him. "How old are you, honey?"

He looked up into her big, round, expressive eyes staring into his as if she were about to hang on his every word because what he had to say was sure to be the most important news of that day. When she smiled he saw where the whore was missing three of those teeth squarely behind the middle of her lower lip. And for a moment he sat there transfixed, dumb-founded, wondering how it was going to be kissing that mouth, what with that big gap in her teeth that made her look much older than he supposed her to be.

There at the corner of the parlor, his head was beginning to swim crazily. He watched her kneel, coming so close, he had to pull his head back, blink and strain to keep her in focus, the way she became two whores when he wasn't concentrating.

"You hear me, sonny? Ain'cha gonna tell me how old are you?"

"Eight . . . eighteen."

When he started to giggle at how funny that seemed right then, she turned and motioned to the bartender, who wore a black Barcelona hat atop his smooth skull. "Hezekiah, get me and my young friend here another drink. Double up on mine 'cause it appears he's a long way ahead of me."

"Him paying, Miz Nina?"

Twisting about to shoot the muscular barman her most evil glare, she said, "You ain't the idjit you make out to be, Hezekiah—so you best just get me my rum!"

"Eighteen's what I said," Titus repeated, and struggled to keep from laughing at his untruth this time.

"You ain't eighteen, honey," she cooed, running one beefy finger down the front of his shirt, "no more'n I'm the lily-white virgin you been waiting for on your wedding night," then laid her hand on the inside of his thigh.

It grew warm where her palm pressed, those fat fingers kneading his leg ever so gently. He looked up when the canvas portal parted, two men coming in from the rainy deck, each one of them ducking out of the way of one of the many candle lanterns suspended from the canvas roof's cross beam. Stopping at the bar, they hunched over, whispering low to Hezekiah. As the Negro bartender clanged down a pair of tin cups and began to pour a potent libation from a large wicker-wrapped clay jug, Titus turned his foggy attention back to the whore . . . for now she had her hand firmly in position to get all of his attention.

Don't you dare fall asleep with one of them whores!

Recalling that warning was enough to scare himself: Titus seized her plump wrist, gripped it firmly.

"What you doing, honey?" she demanded in a coarse voice. "I was just getting ready to start pleasuring you."

"No . . . no, you can't—"

"We only gotta get you up and head on back to my crib—take off all your shucks so you can hump on top of me like I feel your young poker getting ready to," she declared without preliminaries.

He didn't move, staring instead at the deep crevice between her heavy breasts about to pour right out of that soiled chintz dressing gown she wore, its gay flowers dull and faded with too much use and too little soap. Everything about her was big, fleshy, overflowing. He looked more closely, noticing the scratches and teeth marks, moles and freckles, that marred the white skin rounded across the top half of those breasts.

"I'll bet you're the kind just needs to put his face right into 'em," she said, suddenly reaching behind his head and pulling him into her cleavage.

Soft as it was, as foul smelling as was her unwashed flesh, Bass drank in the pleasure of his predicament as if her earthy stench were sweet perfume. Feeling himself stir all the more beneath the hand she kept moving between his legs.

"Don't wanna sleep," he grumbled, reminding himself—becoming groggy with the growing numbness of the whiskey.

"Shit, honey—I ain't gonna let you sleep." She lapped at his ear, then slowly got to her feet, pulling him up beside her. "You're gonna be thumping Miss Nina: the biggest, roundest whore in all of Natchez. Like Annie says: there's more of me to pleasure a man than all the rest of 'em put together."

When she bent over to retrieve her cup, one of Nina's breasts spilled out of the dressing gown. Instead of taking care to cover herself immediately, she drained the rum from her cup, then stuffed her breast back beneath the loose folds of chintz.

Bass looked down into his own cup, saw his own dim reflection in what little of the tobacco-colored whiskey remained at the bottom. Then he turned it up and swallowed the last of the burning potion.

"You seventeen, boy?" she asked, nudging him away through the smoke, noise, raucous laughter, and the tangle of legs of those sprawled across the floor pillows. "For sure you ain't eighteen."

"Almost seventeen," he admitted, glad to have her big arm to hold on to.

Nina stopped and whirled on him. "*Almost* seventeen! You sixteen years old, you li'l river tramp?"

He held a finger to his lips and hushed, "Shhhh! Don't tell nobody how old I be."

"Shit, no," Nina replied with sarcasm. "We don't want no one thinking bad of you for lying 'bout your age, now—what with all your other bad habits. So tell me, child—you got money for a poke with Nina?"

"I got me a piggy-yune," he replied, slurring the word.

The whore held out her hand. "If you gimme your picayune, I'll make sure this'll be a night you don't ever forget."

"Just can't sleep it off with you," he repeated, stuffing a hand inside his oiled jerkin to produce the three coins.

In the blink of his bleary eye she snatched them away, stuffed them into that deep cleavage straining against the folds of her dressing gown.

"Say, Nina!"

She turned, with Bass clinging to her arm so he wouldn't fall. He came tottering to a stop, his head wobbling, trying to focus on the two newcomers at the bar.

One of the pair asked, "When you gonna be done with tender britches there?"

"Soon enough. You jest be patient, Will. Won't have to wait long."

"Make quick work of him so you and me can have us a poke."

Nina didn't say another word as she wheeled Bass about, leading him down a narrow hallway formed by sheets of canvas hanging from the oak cross beams overhead. Off to the right sat three cribs. Off to the left, the other trio of cribs. He thought he could hear an impassioned grunt from behind one of the canvas walls rising in crescendo as the two of them shuffled toward the end of the flatboat. By the time they pushed past the canvas door flap into her crib, the hard rain was slacking off. Using one candle she kept lit, Nina lit two more. In the dim light Bass could see his breath, squinting cross-eyed at it while the vapors danced before his face. Concentrating on it as hard as he was, Titus bent, and bent some more, and almost keeled over to the side. From the next crib he heard a familiar voice growl.

"I ain't giving you no money yet, you whore! First I lay, then I pay!"

Wobbly, feeling his stomach suddenly lurch, Bass put out his hand to keep himself from falling and stumbled against the canvas wall separating Nina's from that adjoining crib.

"Hey! Watch it there!"

Titus was sure now that he recognized the voice. He stuck his face right up to the wall and hollered in reply, "That you, Ovatt?"

"No—dammit! It's Root! Leave that wall be!"

Laughing easily with the sudden flush of companionship, he identified himself. "It's me, Titus!"

"Good for you, Titus," Root bellowed. "Now, just get on with what you're about and leave me to my honey-daubin'."

"Just don't you go falling asleep with that whore, Reuben!" Titus replied every bit as sternly as he had been told, then giggled as Nina came over to him to begin pulling off his jerkin.

She guided him over to her pallet on the floor all of the three steps it took to get Titus there, then nudged him backward. On his back, head dizzied, he sensed her pulling at his wet moccasins, then the bottoms of his canvas britches. His head felt lighter and lighter, as if it might just screw itself off his shoulders and go floating right up through the low roof he fixed with a stare as he fought down the rising intimidation of his troubled stomach.

Just about the time he felt her cold, fleshy hands wrap around his penis, Bass tried rolling onto an elbow, growling, "I'm gonna be sick."

She flew off him so fast he was amazed, struck at the way she moved for being so large. Nina reached over, snatching up the chamber pot that sat nearby, and stuffed its fragrant opening right under his face. It was there she held his head as he screwed up his face at the horrendous stench that filled his face and mouth. Titus emptied his stomach in one explosive lurch.

"That's a good boy," she cooed to him, running her fat, oily fingers over his forehead. "You just go 'head and fill that up if'n you need to."

His belly knotted up another half-dozen tries at wrenching itself free from its moorings in his gut, and then he was done. As he rocked uncertainly atop that single elbow, Nina took the chamber pot to set it in the corner, turned, and got back down on her knees over him, her hands wrapping around his softening flesh once more.

He looked up at her and smiled, gradually collapsing backward while the world slowly went warm and black.

Unable to part the blackness that enveloped him like a suffocating hood, Titus instead let his head hang as he shuffled blindly beside the one who was dragging him along, lunging forward beside him a step at a time. As much as he wanted to wake up, he couldn't. For all he knew, the big whore was dragging him off—maybe it was even one of those who had hollered at her from the bar a while back. They'd get him to the other side of the flatboat, away from the wharf, stab him—then throw his body into the harbor.

He wouldn't be able to swim—wasn't all that good at it anyway. Hell, he wasn't even walking for himself right now, getting pulled along as he was. And if they pushed him into the Mississippi, he was bound to die. Sober, he might well fight his way through most any water if he had to. But not like this. Titus knew he'd sink like a boundary stone, struggling only a little before he sank all the way to the bottom of the river—unable to stroke and paddle. Hell, he couldn't even open his eyes!

It was still black. As black as it would be on the bottom of the river where these killers hid the bodies of the men they robbed. They stumbled over something. A man grunted. Then Bass was wheeled suddenly, his shirt ripping.

If he was lucky, Titus thought, they'd slit his throat first, maybe shoot him in the head. No, they wouldn't do that. Too much noise. Just slit his throat, and then he'd never reach St. Louis to see if Levi Gamble had made it there last summer.

"What the hell business is it of yours?"

He felt the rumble of angry speech in the chest of the man who held him against his side.

"That's my friend you got there."

Titus wondered about that. Who was this friend of the one who slung him around again and took a few steps back toward the far voice? Sounded just like Root's.

"I seen you afore, ain't I?" the one holding him growled.

"Maybeso," the far voice said. "S'pose you put that boy down and come on over here in the light. Then you can take a good look at me."

The one carrying him lurched forward another step, then stopped. "Say, now—lookee there. Just what you got in mind to do with that big sticker, you ugly son of a bitch?"

"Told you, put that boy down."

"He a friend of yours? Whyn't you say so in the first place?"

His senses all firmly dulled, Bass nonetheless felt his body flung toward the far voice, tumbling, colliding with a man who tried to step out of his way as Titus hurtled past, limp arms and legs akimbo. When he struck the hard-planked floor, it was with enough force that his eyes blinked open in shock at the sudden blow.

Above him for a long moment he watched a candle lantern sway precariously, its dirty-yellow corona swishing this way and that above the two shadows grappling between the two dark walls at his feet. Then he remembered: this was the narrow canvas hallway strung between the half-dozen cribs. The grunting pair rolled through the foot of one of the walls, gouging at eyes and pulling at hair for all they were worth.

Within that invaded crib a woman's falsetto shriek rose above a man's low, angry curse as the combatants tumbled back from the canvas wall, rolling toward Bass.

He blinked, wanting to see, make sense of it all, slowly clawing his hands up the canvas wall, pulling himself to his bare feet.

One of them was yelling names, sprawling atop the downed man, holding his opponent with one strong hand gripping the throat and the other raised above his head in a cruel fist. But the other arched his back violently, unseating his enemy to immediately begin hollering out for help of his own. Names that, though muffled in his foggy mind, snagged a familiar chord within Bass:

"Ovatt! Kingsbury!"

Titus knew them. Ungainly, he lunged forward a step, stood there wobbling, ready to take another when the voice ordered him:

"Back off or I'll gut you like I done a hunnert afore you!"

Bass pitched to his hands and knees again.

"Christ a'mighty, they're gonna kill the boy!"

Someone was behind him as suddenly as he tried to pull himself up once more. Whoever it was grabbed hold of Titus, tearing his old shirt nearly off his shoulders as they dragged him aside and lunged past him into the fray. Now he wasn't sure how many there were as another kicked him aside and hurtled into that heap of grunting, cursing bodies . . . when the whole mass of them reversed direction in a blur, wheeling over him in cries of pain and gasps of exertion, that great roiling beast of many arms and legs careening this time toward the parlor, where women shouted and screamed in hysterics.

In that distance wrought of fog and the spiderweb of time distortion made sticky by his drunken stupor, Bass heard clay shattering—its aftermath echoed by the high-pitched, feral screech of a man's voice—sounds of some frightened, cornered animal. More and more hard body blows delivered against muscles and bone, each like a maul cracking against the tough, tight grain of newly felled hickory. At each blow came an accompanying grunt of pain.

Then the sudden, blinding flare of a muzzle flash, brightening the whole of that end of the parlor where the first pair of cribs began. Someone screamed, and a body crashed through the canvas siding with a great ripping of coarse cloth. The man scrambled and attempted to rise—but sank slowly back, crumpling to the floor.

Root's voice thundered down upon him, "Watchit! That bitch's got a gun!"

Lurching to his knees, Bass felt his head complain, blood throbbing against one temple, then the other, side to side like Mississippi trashwood adrift inside his skull—battering this temple with shrill pain before tumbling for the other. He grew thirsty immediately: his mouth tasted as if he'd been sucking on the bitter contents of a hog's gallbladder as he tried to speak, desperate for the attention of the shadows lumbering back and forth before him.

"I'll slit your throat, whore—you don't drop that gun of your'n!" Kingsbury threatened with a snarl.

Gazing up, with all his strength struggling to focus on the lunging shapes of lamplit shadows, he found them: Annie Christmas—all six feet eight inches of her—swinging a big horse pistol about, clutched in both hands, that skinny Hames Kingsbury clinging to her back like a tick on an ox, his wiry arms locked around hers as she careened past Titus, headed wildly toward the mahogany bar, and toppled against the wall behind it. As she came closer, all Titus could think to do was to lash out with his feet. He tripped Annie, the pistol flying into the dark as she pitched forward against the bar, toppling it against the wall behind with a crash and clatter of glass and clay and tin.

Kingsbury stuck to her like a cocklebur as they landed in a tangle. With a grunt she lay still beneath the boatman, groaning.

As those two had landed, Titus's wide, fleshy whore burst from the shadows to straddle Kingsbury, starting to pummel the sides of his head with her big, soft fists. Back and forth Nina rocked the river pilot as Bass painfully dragged his legs under him, put his hands out to steady himself, and laid one atop something round. Bringing it up before his eyes for all of a heartbeat, not consciously recognizing what it was. Yet in some dim, primal way realizing he held in his hands Kingsbury's fate.

Unsteadily Bass rocked backward, his head feeling like a burlap bag loosely filled with a load of stream-washed rocks. Righting himself, he rose to one leg. Closing one eye seemed to help him keep the fat whore in focus as he shakily got to his feet and careened forward, his hand swinging that leg busted from one of the broken chairs back and forth before him. Over his head he raised it, then brought the leg down across the woman's shoulders. Time and again he struck her on the back, with no effect but that she turned and cursed him, trying unsuccessfully to grab him with her left hand.

"You li'l pissant!" she screamed, fending off the chair leg with one fleshy arm while she choked Kingsbury beneath the other. "I'll cut your no-good pizzer off when I'm done here!"

In that instant he hated the mocking cruelty in her eyes, the angry curl to the folds of skin around her mouth. And struck out at them blindly, sneaking in beneath her arm to lay the hardwood leg against the whore's cheekbone with a smart crack. Her face immediately opened up in a long, dark line that spurted a glistening spray over the yellowish lamp-lit paleness of her skin. He dragged the lathe-turned hardwood leg back behind his head for another blow.

Spitting blood from the corner of her mouth, her eyes became even more menacing as she turned on him, rising from Kingsbury's body. "Now I'm gonna chop your balls off and feed 'em to you while I cut your heart out!"

As she was lumbering to her feet, he swung, connecting with the top of her skull just above the ear. Nina's head snapped to the side, she rocked unsteadily, stunned as Bass brought the chair leg to his left and swung it back at her head with even more force. She growled at him, both her arms held out in his direction, hands opening and closing like claws before her eyes began to glaze. A third blow—this time driving it under her chin. Blood darkened her lips as her eyes half closed. Nina weaved atop Kingsbury, both arms still outstretched to grab at the youngster, fingers clutching, releasing, clutching again, with nothing caught between them but the smoky air.

Bringing the chair leg over his head, Titus brought it down on Nina's skull as her eyes rolled all the way back, their sockets showing nothing but whites. With a loud snap her neck popped backward, and she toppled her great bulk into a heap beside the river pilot, like a forest slug spilling off the stem of some ground ivy.

Trudging forward one step, then another, Bass wobbled over to her, holding the chair leg high all the time, suspended there as he stared blearily at the whore sprawled on the floor . . . when the room erupted again with women's screams.

One of them screeched right in his ear, "You killed Nina!" just as she landed on his back and they both went down in a heap against the overturned bar.

At their feet Kingsbury clambered slowly to all fours, gasping for breath, dragging it in noisily, labored and wheezing, as would a drowning boatman who was just pulled from certain death beneath a turbulent river. Hames pulled his knife as he came up, clutching one arm against his side with a pasty grimace.

"Get off him!" Kingsbury ordered.

Immediately the whore riding Titus's back stopped pummeling Bass with her fists, whirled, and lunged for Kingsbury, baring her teeth like a fighting dog's. As she flung herself at the river pilot, the whore fell against the long blade of his belt knife—stumbled suddenly with eyes wide, her mouth moving without a sound—then stared down at his hands gripping that knife pressed into her belly, up to the hilt.

With a grunt of great exertion, Kingsbury dragged the blade to the side, splattering the youth beneath him with the whore's warm blood, then quickly snapped his head forward, cracking it against the woman's forehead smartly. She lurched back, only then pulling herself off the knife blade as the front of her dirty dressing gown darkened like the underbelly of a thunderstorm.

"Let's get!" Root hollered.

As the dying whore crumpled beside him, Bass turned slowly, numbed, to find Reuben holding down the Negro bartender, a knife at his throat. The slave's white eyes muled angrily as he glared up at the boatman, his great coffee-colored hands spread in surrender, but his face bearing nothing but undisguised scorn for the victor. Backing slowly away before he inched the blade from the glistening black skin of that muscular neck, Root finally straightened as Heman Ovatt limped over, having held a pistol on two of the women through the last minutes of their whorehouse fight. Kingsbury hobbled up beside Reuben, half-bent at the waist, his left arm wrapped around his middle as he wheezed in pain with each shallow breath.

"Get up," the pilot ordered Bass, his voice strangely hollow. It reminded Titus of how a person might sound if cast down a well. Hames turned to Ovatt and Root as they all three surveyed the scene. "Any of you know who them two was?"

With a nod Heman answered, "Think I seen 'em afore, yeah."

"I thought so—first they came in here tonight," Kingsbury replied, pointing at the white man's body sprawled half in the parlor, half in the narrow hallway. "They was on the crew what took Mathilda to their boat last summer."

"I cain't be sure as you, Hames," Reuben said as they stood huddled together, their eyes moving over the scene of blood and death, tattered furniture and broken clayware. "You two was what seen 'em in the Kangaroo afore Ebenezer took off on his own to break Mathilda loose."

"I'm sure of it," Kingsbury answered quietly, stonily. "They come in here tonight, looking us over—I got more sure of it. Can only be the two Ebenezer said jumped the boat afore he kill't them other two."

"All that over a whore," Root moaned, wagging his head as he kept the knife held on the big slave. "And now this—with some more goddamned whores."

"There'll be others comin' soon," Ovatt warned.

"You best take me to the boat," Kingsbury said as Root dragged Titus to his feet.

Ovatt asked, "You hurt bad?"

"Dunno," and Hames swallowed down some pain that grayed his face even more. "Just get me there now!"

"What we gonna do with these whores?" Root asked.

"Take 'em up back there in them cribs. Have 'em tie each other up and gag 'em," Kingsbury snapped, his eyes clenched fiercely. "Just do it quick—dunno how long I can stay on my feet like this."

Bass and Ovatt did just that. While the pilot and Reuben held a pair of

Annie Christmas's big horse pistols on the whimpering prostitutes and that big, bald-headed bartender, Titus and Heman tore dressing gowns and petticoats into strips they forced the whores into tying around ankles and wrists, as well as knotting a tight gag around each mouth.

"Get outta here 'fore I shoot you!" Kingsbury snarled.

Bass poked his head out of a crib to find two men standing at the door flap. Their eyes flew around the parlor's clutter, then back to that pair of wide muzzles Kingsbury and Root held pointed at them—before the pair turned and fled like frightened quail, bellowing like gored hogs.

"The fat's in the fire now," Root grumbled as the other two emerged from the cribs.

"Don't worry 'bout gagging her now," Kingsbury said, pointing his pistol at Annie Christmas, who, for the last few minutes, had been un-leashing her wrath on her slave-bartender. "Just get that son of a bitch tied—every last damned body Under-the-Hill gonna be crawling over here in a shake of a bear's tail. We gotta get when he's tied down."

"Where?"

Kingsbury glared at Ovatt. "You idjit! Back to our goddamned boat!"

"With them sonsabitches atween us and the boat—all of 'em coming this way to see what the ruckus is?" Root asked in a high pitch.

Titus didn't know how the idea ignited in his mind of a sudden, but it was there—with a certainty that startled him. Something so sure and sur-prising, it damn near frightened him.

"We can make it back through the woods," Titus suggested in a whisper so none of the whores would hear. When Annie Christmas stopped cursing the barman, Bass was frightened. Root held up one of the pistols, and the gunboat madam backed off while Titus looked at the Negro bartender, finding fear in the man's yellow eyes. He immediately turned his black face away, then stared down at his hands bound in whorehouse rags.

"Bass got him a fine idea," Kingsbury whispered, wheeling about to shove Ovatt ahead of him with a jab of his elbow. "Go! Go!"

Shivering in the shreds of his torn shirt, Titus stood there a moment in the wake of the others as they ducked out to the deck. Root stopped at the canvas flaps, whirled about, and leaned back in to snag Titus by the arm—hauling him right out to what there was of deck between the brothel's canvas wall and the gunnel's grayed wood.

"You're leading us, god-blessit!" Root growled, back to his normal ill-tempered self.

As Titus vaulted off the gunboat and landed on the wharf beside the others, Kingsbury pressed his face in close, staring intently at Bass's eyes, flicking his gaze back and forth. "Know where you're headed?"

Titus pointed.

Nodding, the pilot asked, "Your head clear enough to get us through that timber and away from any crowds?"

"Like them what's coming now?" Ovatt announced in a shrill voice.

They turned, gazing north along the crude wharf where the low rows of clapboard card houses and grogshops lay clustered. Two hundred yards off danced the flare of at least a dozen torches held high above a considerable knot of boisterous men. From the crowd came loud voices, noise without the words. Little matter: only a deaf and blind man would fail to understand the intent of that murderous crowd moving their way.

"Take us to the timber, Titus Bass!" Kingsbury hissed in agony, shoving the youngster ahead of him into that narrow patch of shadow between a pair of weathered buildings, each of those shanties about to lean its shoulder against the other as they slowly sank into disrepair with each new year.

Bass drew up at the back of the shacks, peered into the dark. Immediately behind the short streets that branched off the main thoroughfare stretched along the wharf, thick timber rose against the pale bluff. Without signaling the men behind him, Titus darted from the shadows of that alley, making for the shadows of the trees. Once he was beneath their cover, he waited for them all to catch up. Kingsbury was the last, hobbling up, gasping, clutching his side, his pasty face beaded in sweat.

"You gonna make it, Hames?" Root asked, wrapping an arm around the pilot's shoulder.

Kingsbury looked up, his eyes narrowing. "We allays have us some scrap or another coming downriver, don't we, Reuben?"

"I s'pose we do."

"Good you remember that," Hames replied. "I don't want neither of you go blaming Titus Bass for the trouble been dogging us this trip."

Ovatt and Root glanced at the youth a moment. Then both of them shook their heads.

"Only thing I wanna do is get you back to the boat," Heman declared.

"And get us the hell out of Natchez," Root added.

"Maybe things cool down by the time we get back here again come next summer," Kingsbury told them. Then with a thin-lipped nod he instructed Titus to lead on.

Bass swore his heart was going to leap out of his chest or pop right out of his mouth, the way it made his head pound, when they hadn't gone all that far and he had to shush them. They all knelt back in the timbered shadows when the frantic jig of torchlight drew close—splashes of light dancing just on the far side of the low-roofed shanties. More frightening still was the sound of that mob: snarling, snapping, its quest for blood like a living thing that snaked along the wharf, headed for Annie Christmas's gunboat. It reminded Titus of how he'd once watched a cottonmouth eat a field gopher, the dying prey slowly drawn along the length of the snake's scaly body.

As the mob thundered into the distance, they moved on into the welcome darkness. For now the four of them had a little time. Not much. But it might just be enough.

As he reached the side of the flatboat, Bass watched the woman sit up like a shadow suddenly taking shape out of the night. Her dark form stood, pulling that ratty old blanket about her shoulders. She stepped to the side when he stopped at the gunnel, able to make out the red glow of embers and low flames she had shielded behind her.

"You fellas home earlier'n I figured you—"

"Help us get Hames aboard, ma'am," Reuben demanded.

Immediately crawling over the crates, she held down both her hands, the blanket falling from her shoulders. Rearing back, she pulled with all her might as Ovatt and Root hoisted the wounded pilot from the wharf, his body dragged against the side of the flatboat and onto the gunnel, where Kingsbury lay gasping, groaning.

"You shot?" she asked.

He clamped down on his lower lip and shook his head, eyes moistening.

"They cut you?"

"No," he huffed, perhaps the pain easing.

"Your side?"

When he nodded, she carefully lifted his left arm braced against his belly. "I do believe they broke your ribs," the woman declared. "How many, we'll just have to find out."

"Ain't got time for none of that now," Ovatt snarled at her as he pushed past. "I'll take the rudder, fellas. Reuben, get them hawsers freed so we can push off."

She watched the two move off in different directions, then turned to look at Kingsbury once more before she snagged hold of Titus's jerkin.

"What happened out there tonight?"

"I don't know," he answered sheepishly, hungover already. As if his very own mother had caught him at something wicked and now he was about to pay the high price for having his fun. "I was drunk. I dunno—"

"We're leaving for Nawlins," Kingsbury announced, sprawled beneath them. "You ain't got folks to stay with here, ma'am—"

"No, I don't."

"Then you got one choice or another," and the pilot visibly sagged with the effort the talk took out of him.

So she spoke up while he gathered his breath. "I can jump off this here boat and take my chances till I can get a way north on the Trace," Beulah declared. "Or—I can throw in with you fellas all the way to Orlins."

The pilot swiped the back of a hand across his bloodied mouth and replied, "That's only choices you got."

"We're free!" Root cried, flinging the last hawser across the gunnel, then slinging himself aboard.

"Push us off, you two!" Ovatt bellowed. "Give him a goddamned hand, Titus!"

"I ain't rightly got but one choice," the woman said quietly as Titus started to move off, snatching up one of the long snag poles.

Bass stopped, turned to hear what she said so very quietly as Beulah knelt beside their wounded pilot.

"You fellas picked me out of the river. You give me a ride on your boat when every last one of you 'cept that young'un believed in all your hearts what bad luck it was to have a woman on your boat—"

"I ain't . . . none of us blaming you for this," Kingsbury interrupted, then coughed soddenly.

"Damn," she said with a sad wag of her head. "Sounds of it: bet you gone and poked one of them ribs right through your lights."

Kingsbury turned his head to glance at the wharf Root was pushing his pole against with a loud growl. As he heaved against his long hardwood pole, Bass noticed the flare of the torches bobbing in the distance, this time headed back upriver. In their direction.

The pilot rolled toward Beulah slightly, warning, "This be your last chance to jump off, woman."

With a shake of her head she nearly whispered, "And if I do jump off —just who the hell gonna take care of you men?"

•   •   •

"He ain't getting any better, is he?" Titus asked.

The woman looked up from the feverish, unconscious Kingsbury, then wagged her head. "Nothing more I can do. It ain't in my hands no more."

If it wasn't in her skilled, sure hands, Titus wondered—then in whose hands did the life of Hames Kingsbury lie? It troubled him that the woman expected him to understand her . . . when he had no earthly idea who might hold the power to save the man.

First off, he lost Ebenezer Zane. Now another man clung tenuously to life. No matter that he had people around him at this moment, Titus had rarely felt so alone.

He raised his eyes from the pilot's pale, clammy face, looking at Root manning the gouger, turning to gaze again at Ovatt stationed at the stern rudder.

"It's good water from here on down," Heman had told him earlier that morning as the sun came up milk-pale in a cold sky. "I could get this broadhorn down to Nawlins, steering it on my lonesome, if'n I had to. Easy enough, though there's cypress swamp what can fool a man if he don't keep his nose locked in the main channel. But don't you fret none, Titus. I'll holler when I need you on one oar or t'other."

Many, many night fires this crew of four had told him how they'd worked the rivers together for more than a decade, without much bloodletting at all: a few fights, a few knife cuts sewn up with the same thread they used to repair their clothing, mostly a lot of good-natured head thumping in the midst of one hell of a lot of work. As much as there had been Indian scares in years past, they had never caused much more than an anxious moment or two for Ebenezer Zane's boatmen—nothing more than threats from a far bank now and again.

But what with that old pilot resting among the mud and catfish and sawyers at the bottom of the Mississippi, Heman Ovatt was beginning to think things had changed for the worse. And what was usually nothing more than some bruises and perhaps a broken bone now and then whenever they tied up for a frolic at Louisville's red-candle district, Natchez-Under-the-Hill, or even the Swamp in New Orleans—now their raucous brawling had turned deadly. For no reason they could figure out.

Except that it just might have to do with settling an old score with Ebenezer Zane.

Kingsbury coughed in his sleep. Bass sensed the pilot slipping away from him too.

Hames had passed out about the time they were pushing free of the wharf, with that mob drawing ever closer below those bouncing torches, their discordant voices looming louder out of the dark. One of that drunken lot had spotted them making for the main channel of the river, shrieked his warning to the others, and a great cry of frustration and disappointment had gone up. More than a handful of that rabble had yanked pistols from their belts and fired at the southbound flatboat. Only one bullet had smacked against their craft, crashing noisily into a cask holding ironmongery. The clatter had made Bass jump there at the gunnel while the woman bent over Kingsbury protectively and the other two men hurried them away from Natchez.

For some time Ovatt and Root were convinced others would put up a chase, board some canoes or a pirogue and come slipping up after them. Overhead the stars in the Big Bear slowly slipped away from the middle of the sky and fell into the west as Titus fought a great weariness. He drank cup after cup of the woman's coffee sweetened with thumb-sized clumps of homemade cake sugar there beside the sandbox fire and watched Root stoically wince with pain each time he had to lean against the long rudder handle to keep them in the running channel.

By now Heman had a dirty bandage wrapped round his head. One eye was nearly puffed shut, yet he gladly took his place at the gouger when he and Reuben spelled one another, rotating pilot's chores at the stern rudder through that long night. Once more Natchez-Under-the-Hill had lived up to its rough-and-tumble, life-is-by-damn-cheap reputation.

Long after sundown the night following the fight at Annie Christmas's gunboat brothel, Reuben Root admitted they had to put over and tie up just past Fort Adams, which stood on Loftus's Heights at the thirty-first parallel, the southernmost military post erected on American soil in those days prior to Jefferson's purchase of Louisiana Territory.

"The river shrinks down here some," Reuben explained after he and Ovatt secured to the exposed roots of some cypress trees. "Don't run no wider'n two hunnert fifty . . . maybe three hunnert yards at the most. On downriver tomorrow we'll pass Wilkinsonville—named after the army general what wanted to be king his own self over all that out there." Heman swept an arm across the darkening western horizon.

Not so bad a dream, Bass figured as he slipped off the jerkin and removed what tatters were left of his old shirt. Bending over the tiny bundle of his belongings, he unwrapped the shirt his mam had finished for Thaddeus the night before Titus had slipped away. Ever since he had refused to wear it—feeling it to be ill-gotten, as if he had stolen that yoked shirt with its

square arm holes, but now as he slipped it over his head—Bass sensed his
mam just might have left it lying out on the table as she had because she
knew her eldest son was taking his leave. Them biscuits and this new warm
shirt: it was the best way she knew how to tell him good-bye without
embarrassing him with a mother's tears. Slowly he brushed his hand down
the front of it after he got the shirt tucked into his britches.

And felt the sudden stirring of homesickness that did not leave him for
the better part of a day.

By the time they approached Pointe Coupee the following morning,
Root could hardly move his left shoulder. Close inspection by Beulah discovered the boatman's shirt crusted to his back, right over the shoulder blade.
Once she coaxed and coddled Reuben into sitting near the fire and sent Titus
up to man the gouger, the woman clucked her disapproval as she slowly
dripped warm water on the coagulate to free the shirt from a nasty knife
wound.

"You're a brave man, Reuben Root," she told him loud enough for all
to hear. "Plenty brave . . . and mighty stupid."

When he started to rise in anger, she snagged hold of the back of his
shirt and held tight—making him wince in pain as he settled back atop a low
crate in a huff.

"Ain't nothin'," he grumbled. "Had worse."

"Have you, now?" she replied in that tone guaranteed to make any
man feel like a scolded child. "Ever you need someone to sew on you?"

Wheeling on her, his face blanched. "No. Allays kept my cuts bound
up with—"

"You're gonna need me sew on this'un. That much's for sure, Reuben."

"W-we don't got us needle an' thread," Root said, smiling lamely.
"S'pose you can't do no sewin'—"

"Ebenezer allays keeps him some stout linen thread and some glover's
needles down in a chest there," Ovatt reported from the rudder with a much
wider, and more genuine, smile. "Never know when you'll get your canvas
tore."

Wagging his head in utter disgust while glaring at Heman, Reuben
spat, "You mean-assed, mule-headed son of a bitch! Why, one day I'll make
sure—"

"Beulah says you need some sewin'," Ovatt interrupted calmly, "so
we'll see you get sewed up. Time for you be having your *fillee*."

"Fillee, hell!" he roared impudently. "This woman gonna sew on me,
I'll damn well drink my fill!"

Reuben promptly set about drinking much more than his boatman's ration of Monongahela rye—a *fillee*—and then some. Putting the backwoods liquor down on a stomach gone more than a day without food, and sedating a constitution having gone close to forty-eight hours without sleep—it wasn't long before Root slid in and out of consciousness enough for Beulah to announce that she might as well get to sewing.

Just south of Pointe Coupee, Heman put over, and Titus struggled before he got them tied off to the roots of a single great cypress. As the boat rubbed and chafed, timber against timber, Bass and Ovatt ducked beneath the awning where the sandbox fire always kept the air at least ten degrees warmer, there to join the woman, who took the knife from Root's belt and cut herself a length of fine linen cord. One end of this she placed between her teeth, soaking it with the moisture in her mouth before she began to peel back the tiny strands that formed the twisted cord. When she had one strand the thickness she desired for the job at hand, she peeled it from the rest of the cord and threaded her sharp three-sided glover's needle.

Raising her eyes momentarily to Bass, she ordered, "Pour some more of that Monongahela into his cup."

Sitting at Root's head, Ovatt said, "Don't figure you need to, Beulah—looks to be Reuben ain't gonna be awake to want no more. He's snoring through the rough water already."

"I didn't mean I wanted any for him to drink," she replied curtly. "I want you to pour some on that there nasty cut afore I start."

Holding the threaded needle in her mouth, she once more took the boatman's knife in hand, raised her long skirt, and this time sliced through the long hem of a dirty petticoat. "Tug his shirt out'n his britches for me, fellas. Pull it way up on his shoulders."

Heman and Titus did as they were instructed, both of them silent as sandbars and wide-eyed as deaf mules in a high wind, watching her every move as she dribbled a little of the rye along the crusty open wound. Taking an end to the strip of petticoat, she kneaded away a little of the coagulate. Time and again she dipped the cloth into the liquor and scrubbed at the neglected wound until the entire length of the angry gash lay raw and shiny with fresh ooze.

"Wish to God I had my medeecins," she grumbled to herself as she knotted the linen thread, then looked at Titus. "A body can't rightly do without some medeecins when folks need tending."

Wincing involuntarily, Bass watched her poke the needle through the right side of the laceration, continuing over to the left side before she pulled the thread through the flaps of flesh. Reuben grunted and his eyes fluttered a few times, but he never stirred.

"Take hol't of his arms there," she said to Ovatt. Then turned her head to tell Titus, "An' you, son—sit on his legs. There, like that. Just in case he decides to wake up and get in a fittle over this sewing I've got to do on him."

Tugging against the knot as if to assure herself that it would hold, the woman clucked once and drove the needle through the skin a second time. Wrap by wrap she worked herself down the eight long inches of severely torn muscle. Each time Beulah pulled her thread tight, she would dab more of the fiery alcohol on the laceration as it continued to ooze and seep bright-red blood.

"That's good," she told them as she neared the last of her labors. "Better that it bleed. Gets all the evil out, seeing how we ain't got no roots to put in it. My medeecins"—and Beulah bit her lip to stifle a sob—"all that I had in this world went down with that goddamned flatboat."

Her curse struck Titus as something foreign, never having heard a woman of her age hint at profanity, much less take God's name in vain. After all that she had said about Kingsbury's life resting in the Almighty's hand—he thought it strange indeed that she would pray to God one day and soundly curse Him the very next.

"Don't look at me so odd, boy," she commanded. "Close your mouth, or you're likely to have something crawl right in it with more legs'n a Chickasaw war party."

Knotting the linen thread, she cut off the excess and returned the bloody-handled knife to Root's belt scabbard. Then she slowly poured the last of the rye from the cup up and down the wound, washing away some of the dark ooze one last time.

Handing the empty cup to Titus, she said, "Now, wipe that cup out and get me some more likker."

When Bass turned to the side to use Root's shirttail to wipe at the crimson coated inside of the cup, Ovatt asked, "You gonna put more of that Monongahela on your sewing job?"

"Hell, no," she said. "I aim to drink my share, now that he's done and Kingsbury over there seems like'n he's turned the last bad bend in the river."

As she took the cup from him, a frightened Titus asked, "You mean he ain't . . . not likely to make it much longer?"

Swallowing long and slow with her eyes closed, the woman finally took the cup away and licked her lips, then swiped a sleeve across her mouth.

"Didn't mean nothing of the kind. Damn, but it's been a long time since I felt that particular burn down in my gut."

"Just what the hell you mean, then?" Ovatt demanded.

She looked offended, then peered down at her cup a moment more before answering. "Near as I can tell, fellas—looks like your pilot there is gonna be up and around soon."

"He's . . . he's gonna pull through?" Bass demanded, feeling the tingle of hope coursing through all the bleakness of what had been his despair these last few days.

"His color's lot better, the last little while, and he ain't breathing near like he was. No more choking and gurgling a'tall. I do believe Hames Kingsbury's gonna make it."

"Whooeee!" Ovatt cried out, reaching out both arms to embrace the older woman, who sat there stunned by the boatman's sudden affection.

When Heman took his arms from her, Titus leaned forward and clumsily hugged her, whispering in her ear, "Thankee, ma'am. For all you done . . . for the both of 'em." And just before he released her, Bass kissed her lightly on the cheek.

As he pulled away from her, an astonished Beulah brushed her fingertips across her cheek, gazing at the youth wistfully. "T'weren't nothing I wouldn't done for nary boatman."

"We had you with us, likely Ebenezer Zane be alive today," Titus said.

Taking his hand in hers, she patted it maternally and wagged her head. "Ain't nothing in this world gonna save a man what got his head caved in with a Chickasaw rock war club."

"She's right, Titus," Ovatt agreed as he pulled his collar up and rose from the bench to move past Root toward the bow. "I see it's time we got on down to Nawlins. Get on up there and get them hawsers heaved to on that capstan. We got us a boatload of cargo and these two ailing boatmen to get on downriver."

The thick hemp ropes nearly filled his hands in their own right as he struggled with his knots against the nudge of the current, but they were soon moving south once more, through the last of that myriad of false channels and swamps just below Pointe Coupee, where Lower Louisiana began. Here long ago the French had begun construction of a great levee, that work later taken up by the Spanish in their own attempt to prevent seasonal flooding of the rich agricultural lands of the lower Mississippi Valley.

"You see that," Ovatt called out, pointing at the levees on the eastern shore, "a riverman knows it ain't far now till he's with more and more folks. All this here stretch is called the German Coast."

In his own crude way Heman had just expressed the riverboatman's term for the civilization that began to dot the banks once he'd passed the northern end of the levee: behind its protection sat plantations, many small and quaint villages inhabited by the friendliest of French-speaking Louisianans. Here in the flooded fields they grew sugarcane and rice, along with cotton and one huge orange grove after another, many trees still heavy with fruit. A wondrous sight for young Titus to behold. Many of the inhabitants along the German Coast came to the riverbank to wave at the passing flatboat. Ovatt, Root, and Bass waved back in salute to the friendly riverfolk working their fields and orchards. And at the sight of every likely young maiden, the three all stood tall, boasting of their manhood while lustily crying out their claims of true love to her.

In three more days Kingsbury was able to sit up and take more sustenance than grease soup. They floated past Baton Rouge, the site of an abandoned Spanish fort and a small village still peopled by Acadians. From there south they were never out of sight of one small settlement, cluster of fishing boats, trading post, or fine, palatial plantation after another.

"I'm gonna get myself a drink of some real liquor," Beulah said one afternoon as she came up and settled on a cask near Titus at the gouger. Root and Ovatt both sat near the stern rudder, singing one of their riverman songs to the tune of "Yankee Doodle."

> *"Get up good sirs, get up I say,*
> *And rouse ye, all ye sleepers.*
> *See! Down upon us comes a thing,*
> *To make us use our peepers!*
>
> *"Yet what it is, I cannot tell,*
> *But 'tis as big as thunder.*
> *Ah! If it hits our loving ark*
> *We'll soon be split asunder!"*

Titus asked, "What's real liquor taste like?"

She regarded him a moment in that afternoon light as a warming breeze crossed the bow. Then, peering off again to the south, the woman answered, "I allays get me a bottle of long-cork claret. Have every trip down. Figure it's only fitting I should drink a final toast to Jameson. Only right."

"Drink a toast? Of course—to your dead husband," Bass replied.

"He damn well better appreciate it," she said with a ghost of a smile, reaching out to slap Titus on the knee. "First time I made it to Norleans without him!"

FOURTEEN

As much as Root, Ovatt, and even Kingsbury grumbled about the fact that Beulah hung their laundry up on that rope stretched from the awning to the snubbing post at the bow, those freshly scrubbed clothes snapping smartly in the stiff breeze for everyone else on the lower Mississippi to see, the boatmen didn't really mind at all the idea of having a clean shirt to pull on before they climbed ashore to celebrate their arrival in New Orleans in fine style.

Once she learned they had no extra clothing, the woman had ordered them all to pull off their dirty shirts, right then and there. When the pilot hesitated, then turned in retreat, the woman balled her fists on her hips and glared at him with motherly sternness.

"Hames! You—more'n the rest—need some soap put to that shirt of your'n."

With a sheepish look he glanced at the others. "I think it's fine just the way—"

"Give it here."

He could see the grins and smirks on the rest of that bawdy crew and likely realized he was never going to win against the woman. Ever so slowly did he drag the shirt's long tail out of his britches and waist belt, then yanked it over his head. As Kingsbury held it out at arm's length to Beulah, Titus looked at how skinny the man was, all ribs and backbone and shoulder blades, the skin stretched over them like a piece of fine white linen draped over the sharp newels at the top of a ladder-back chair.

She snatched the shirt from him with a look of smug self-satisfaction. "Now that greasy cravat of your'n."

With a look of fright crossing his face, Hames touched the red handkerchief. "Not my neck wrap!"

"Give it to me."

"Ah, shit, woman," he grumped, his bare skin beginning to show goose bumps.

"Won't take me long," Beulah explained. "Sooner you let me start on it, sooner I can get it done and dry."

Reluctantly he untied the square knot and handed the cravat to her by one corner. Beulah took it in her hands, spread it out at arm's length, and inspected it.

"Just as I thought," she grumbled. "C'mere, Hames."

Circling behind the pilot, Beulah raised up the hair that brushed Kingsbury's shoulders. "You see, boys? I'll bet you're all the same as this'un here."

Titus leaned in close enough to see how the skin at the pilot's neck was nothing more than oozy scab and raw, angry flesh. "What's all that from? He sick with something?"

Beulah clucked disapprovingly. "Only thing he's sick of is taking care of hisself. He's been givin' home and hearth to some verminous critters. These'uns here."

Holding up the red bandanna Kingsbury had long used as a neck wrap, the woman pointed to the long row of big white lice neatly arranged within one of the folds, each one every bit as big as the hog lice he had seen on the family stock back at Rabbit Hash. Looking like a strand of long white beads, the vermin had arranged themselves in a row with their heads all turned toward the raw skin of the pilot's neck, feasting away.

"When I get done with your clothes, fellas—won't be a one of these I ain't drowned. Then we gonna pick over all your blankets too."

"What 'bout his neck?" Titus asked, pointing to the raw flesh. "Maybeso we ought'n put something on it."

Beulah wagged her head, saying, "I don't have nothin' no more, none of my medeecins—"

"Most like, Ebenezer has him some liniment or oil you can put on it for me," Kingsbury said, scooting to lean forward over a long chest, where he began to rummage among Zane's belongings.

After smearing a thick daubing of some less-than-fragrant ointment Ebenezer kept in a cork-topped clay jar, Beulah proceeded to work up a lather from some river water and half a cake of lye-ash soap she found buried in the bottom of Ebenezer's kitchen box. The day not really warm enough for any of them to stand around sans shirts, all four pulled on coats made of canvas or wool blanketing. Without a tin scrub board, she instead scrubbed their grimy shirts against the white-oak staves that formed the side of a large water bucket. Titus watched her work, reminded of his own mother, recalling for a moment how Amy washed the clothes of all those brothers and sisters.

By the time Beulah got to Titus's homespun shirt of mixed cloth, the woman held the garment between two fingers at the end of her outstretched arm, her other hand pinching her nose in mock disgust. After she rubbed and scrubbed the best she could, she would pull his shirt from the soapy water and inspect it—both sides, neck, and cuffs—before plunging it back into the pail for more watery abuse. Again she pulled it out for inspection, then returned it to the gray, sudsy water. Over and over she dunked his sole shirt, then raised it from the pail for a look until it eventually passed her scrutiny. Only then did she drape it over a long line of half-inch rope they had tied for her to the awning support, stringing it all the way forward to the bow checking post.

Of varied tow cloth, calicoes, and linsey-woolseys, the four shirts dripped, drop by drop, before they began to dry, flapping in the cold air above Titus's head. Nearby Heman Ovatt clacked out a rhythm on a pair of pewter spoons he whacked against his palm and elbow, knee and thigh. Back at the rudder, Reuben Root whistled one of his squeeze-box songs as he steered them through the last few miles of shoals, while the closer they drew to New Orleans, the flatboat traffic grew thick as the strop hair on the back of a hog. Even Hames Kingsbury clanged an iron ladle against the back of a cast-iron skillet while trying his best not to let that big grin of his split his face half-open.

"Damn, but it's good to get back down here," the pilot exclaimed with a gush of excitement. "Put all that river behind me."

"Till May comes round again," Ovatt reminded them all. "We go and load up a brand-new flatboat with another season's cargo."

"We still got us that damn walk back to Kentucky afore we do," Root said, his dour expression quite a contrast to the healing Kingsbury's.

"Just a thousand miles—every one of 'em making you hunger for seeing the Ohio again," Ovatt said.

Hames called out, "Titus—you figure on walking north with us, don't you?"

Nodding emphatically, Bass replied, "I ain't staying down here in this country. Nosirree."

"Good to hear: we can likely use your rifle on the Natchez Road," Kingsbury declared. "Feed this bunch on our way home."

Ovatt turned to the youth and asked, "You changed your mind and decided on heading back to your family's place, Titus?"

He watched the passing of those lacy whitecaps stirred up by the wind like the bobbing of so many white-headed doves before he answered. "Nothing much left for me back there."

"Maybeso you'd like to join on with us," the pilot said. "With Ebenezer gone . . . well, we're a man short—and besides: you've already made yourself one of the crew. Come downriver, twice't a year with us! It's a damned fine life for a young'un like yourself."

As a matter of fact, Titus had already been working that over in his mind these last few days, ever since the night they escaped that mob on the Natchez wharf.

"There's girls, Titus," Ovatt said. "You seen 'em too. They come down to the bank to watch you pass. Wave to you. And you can call back to them, vow them of your love!"

"Figure I know what you got on your mind, Heman Ovatt," the woman declared sourly.

"Just what any youngster like Titus here got on his mind too!" Heman replied.

"We'd like to have you join us," Kingsbury repeated, getting serious once more. "Ain't that right, Reuben?"

"It be a life just made for you, Titus Bass," Root added.

With a slow, undecided wag of his head he finally raised his eyes to look at the crewmen seated here and there about the boat. Then he gazed at the woman one last time. "No. I been figuring on it some—and . . . this don't rightly seem the life for me. Not that it ain't a good life and all. But last few weeks . . . ever since Ebenezer, them Injuns and all—"

Kingsbury said, "I know just how you might feel, son. After Eb was kill't . . . we got you tangled up in that business back at Annie Christmas's gunboat. But cain't you see? That was for Ebenezer too, settling a score for the man."

"We done it for Mathilda too," Ovatt said.

The pilot seemed to study Bass's face for a few moments, then shrugged with resignation as he added, "Maybeso there's too damned much of the wrong kind of excitement on the river for our young friend here."

"Maybe too damn much . . . ," Titus began, then sighed and finished, "I ain't never killed a man."

"Them red bastards gonna kill you if'n you didn't kill them!" Ovatt argued.

"Worse'n that," Titus continued, "I never afore see'd a man die like Ebenezer Zane done."

"You pay me heed: that's one thing there's plenty of in a boatman's life," Kingsbury explained. "Lot of dying."

Ovatt nodded. "But I allays s'posed all that dying went right along with all the living."

"So what you figure to do, Titus?" Root asked.

With a shrug Bass answered, "Figured to get back to the Ohio, make my way yonder to Louisville, where I was bound away for when I run onto you and Ebenezer."

"Still got your sights set on finding work there?" Ovatt inquired.

"If I can't find none, maybeso I'll get on up to St. Louie eventually. Finally see what that place got to offer a man."

"The hull damned world, that's what," the woman said, stunning them all. "That St. Lou there's one of the four doors what opens onto the rest of the world, Titus. Don't you see?"

"Four doors?" Root asked at the rudder.

"Up yonder's Orlins," Beulah explained. "That's the southern door out to the world. A man can mosey on all the way up the Mississippi to find the northern door to them English lands, the lakes and rivers and all that country beyond where it grows mighty cold. Then, from Pittsburgh and Cincinnati country, you head east over the mountains where a body can go to the edge of the ocean, sailing off to just about anywhere."

Bass listened to her words with not just his ears, but even more so with his heart, pounding as it was. Finally he asked, "St. Louie's the w-western door?"

"That's what I hear tell."

Kingsbury leaned toward her to ask, "You ever heard of what's out there?"

For a moment she cocked her head to the side, as if trying to pull something from her memory. "Only what I heard when Jefferson's bunch—them explorers—come back years ago. You see, them other three doors—north, south, and east—they all open onto water. Water's the way you get to the rest of the world."

"But not from St. Louie?" Ovatt asked.

"Shit," Root growled. "Everybody knows St. Louie's on the river. Sure as hell a man can get west on the water."

"I s'pose that's true," the woman agreed matter-of-factly. "But I heard there's tall mountains atween St. Louie and the far ocean. Ain't no river through them mountains what takes you to t'other side."

Mumbling his unintelligible complaints while he scratched at the side of his hairy face, Root finally responded, "I don't figure a man got any business going to no place where there ain't a river to take him. I'm a waterman. Borned beside the river, raised up on it—figure I'll live and die riding the rivers."

"If there ain't a river going there, Reuben don't figure it's worth the journey," Kingsbury explained to Titus.

"Got to admit, Reuben's got him something there," Ovatt stated. "I allays found me everything I needed on the river, or right beside it."

Turning from the boatmen, Titus peered intently at the woman. "You ever hear anything more about that country out there?"

"Only what I hear'd listening to menfolk talk up and down the river after Jefferson's men come back from that far ocean."

Bass leaned forward, excitement coursing through him. "They say anything about them mountains?"

"Only that they was so tall they touched the sky," the woman replied, a look crossing her face that told him she understood. "Mountains higher'n anything we can't even imagine out there."

"And goddamned red-bellied Injuns too!" Kingsbury snarled.

" 'Thout no big, fine rivers out there," Root began, "sounds to me like that be country fit only for Injuns, and not at all fit for the likes of civil folk."

"There gotta allays be a place for Injuns and wild critters," Ovatt said.

"Place where we can put 'em so just plain white folks like us can go on about our business of living."

"Listen to you!" the woman cried. "Like you fellas was the cocks of the walk, wherever you choose to set down your boots!"

"Damn right—we are that!" Kingsbury shouted exuberantly. "Ever' last one of us is half horse, half alligator—"

"Don't even let me ever hear you go on and on about how you can whup up, outride, outdrink and all that better'n any other man alive."

"We're rivermen!" Root exclaimed. "By damn, we're ring-tailed roarers—"

"By bloody damn, you just get us to Orlins," Beulah interrupted the boatman's verbal strut. "Then we'll see if you can get us back north to Kentucky all to one piece."

Kingsbury leaned forward from his perch to slap her on her ample rear. Whirling quickly on him, she squinted a flinty glare at first, but no sooner did it quickly soften into a grin.

"Why, Mr. Pilot," she said, cocking her head coyly, "you do appear to be mending quite nicely."

"I am at that," Hames replied.

But now the woman doubled up a sizable fist and held it below the pilot's nose. "But if I ever catch you taking a swat at my behind parts again, I'll do even worse to you than you got visiting that whore's gunboat."

With a wide grin of his own Kingsbury ducked behind his arms as if about to be pummeled. "I hear you, ma'am. Won't never have me grabbing for a feel of your behind parts no more."

"Maybe since't you ain't making yourself useful steering this here broadhorn—you can grab one of them poles and do us some fishing for lunch."

"I can do that," Kingsbury said, starting to rise.

She laid a firm hand on his shoulder and shoved him back down on that rough bench beneath the awning. "And while you're fishing, mister riverman—suppose you think about how you just might treat a lady proper, and not like one of your whores."

Hames gazed up into her face, immediately contrite. "I'm sorry if'n I offended you, ma'am. Didn't mean to treat you bad—"

"Not like them women you pay to hike up their skirts for you!" she said.

Titus listened and watched, amazed—never having heard a woman talk in such a bold-faced manner to a man. At least one who was not a foul-mouthed, hard-case whore.

"Just get to your fishing there, Pilot," the woman ordered. "And prove to me you're of some use besides rutting with poxed-up pay-women, making yourself turrible drunk at every river stop, and shoving your way into a fight at the drop of a boot."

Hames glared, saying, "It's fish you want, then fish you'll get, woman."

By midday Kingsbury had pulled all sorts of creatures from the waters of the lower Mississippi: besides perch and trout, he had hooked some buffalo fish, carp, and sturgeon, along with pike and even a soft-shelled turtle. Over the coals of her sandbox fire Beulah cooked the pilot's catch, feeding them all until they were ready to burst.

"Maybe you'll do," she admitted to Kingsbury as he started from the warmth of the fire, intending to relieve Heman Ovatt at the stern rudder. "Maybe you are the sort of man what can provide for a woman proper."

The pilot stopped, turned back to look closely at her face, then said, "If ever a man was intending to get himself tied up to one woman, I figure one like you ought to do a man nicely too."

Bass watched her kneel back over the sandbox fire, her cheeks flushing with the compliment—Kingsbury grinning proudly as he took the long rudder pole from Ovatt.

As Heman resettled himself at the starboard oar, he winked to Titus. "Jesus God—look lively there, young'un. We'll be tying up in Nawlins afore nightfall!"

New Orleans.

How he stretched and craned his neck to see something of it far down that broad stretch of endless bayou cluttered with cypress where Spanish moss hung eight, sometimes ten feet long, like great gray beards tossing in the wind.

To come here at last.

So he could finally get on with starting back for that Kentucky country . . . just as soon as they sold off the cargo, along with all the timber in Ebenezer Zane's flatboat.

He was a thousand times farther away from home than he had ever been and right now was sensing a dull ache with that longing for familiar faces and well-known places and the reassuring smells that told him he was home . . . but that was purely impossible. There was no longer a home.

He was adrift and free, dancing on the wind.

But before he did return to that faraway Ohio River country, there still lay all those miles of wilderness they had yet to cross. On a road that would take them right through the red savage heart of the Choctaw and Chickasaw nations.

Any way he looked at it, that spelled Injun country to Titus Bass.

If he had believed Louisville, and later Natchez, to be bustling, sprawling river ports—Titus was in no way prepared for what greeted him when they neared the levee at New Orleans.

Their Kentucky broadhorn was but one of more than three hundred tied up along the length of a serpentine wharf, boats lashed together three and four abreast. The great clusters of unloaded flats cluttered against the New Orleans wharf reminded Titus of sprawling and forlorn stacks of empty chicken coops. In addition, there were more than a hundred of the bigger keelboats with their low-roofed cabins squatting midship atop their decks.

But beyond them in the deep harbor lay anchored the astonishing wonder that made his young eyes widen and his mouth gape: those tall-masted schooners and other oceangoing vessels ribbed in their dull-white canvas now tucked away high above their decks and crews, massive sailing creatures that rose out of the water at least as tall as three of his pap's cabins would be if stacked one on top of the other.

Kingsbury's crew tied up at the far north end of the levee for a seven-dollar fee paid to that dog-faced wharfmaster who plied the waters of the New Orleans harbor in a rowboat propelled by six oarsmen, each one with skin blacker than any Negro Titus had ever seen and all wearing the same smart waist-length jacket with gold braid and brass buttons that glimmered brightly in the Mississippi sun. The six sat quietly, nonetheless watchful, as the man ordered them to tie him alongside the flatboat just come from upriver. Kingsbury and the rest listened from the gunnel as the wharfmaster accounted for the docking fee and held out the possibility of severe penalty for nonpayment.

"We'll pay," Kingsbury growled, stuffing his hand into Ebenezer Zane's satchel of coins. "Ebenezer Zane allays paid what toll was due you."

"I thought I recognized you," the wharfmaster replied, his eyes searching the boat quickly, craning his neck this way and that as Kingsbury counted the coins into the man's beefy palm. "Where's Ebenezer Zane himself?"

The question was barely out of his mouth when the woman appeared from the awning, his jaw dropping agog in surprise.

"Dead," Kingsbury declared. "Buried him upriver. T'other side of Natchez."

Tugging down on the points at the front of his waistcoat, the man stated solemnly, "I'm sorry . . . sorry to hear that. He was a good man— the best. Well, hmmm. You understand you'll have to have Zane's bills of lading for all this cargo if you intend to sell it here to New Orleans."

"We got 'em," Kingsbury replied confidently, and stuffed his hand down into a flat rawhide pouch, pulling out a handful of papers.

Without another word the man clambered over the side into his boat and made a small, almost insignificant gesture with one hand. The six ebony oarsmen dipped their wood to water and stroked away along the levee as the wharfmaster settled midship, on about his business.

"Pleasure doing business with you too," Beulah said as she came to the gunnel and peered after them.

"Seven dollars a day, just to tie up. That's near robbery." Kingsbury wagged his head.

"We just be sure to get this cargo sold and off the boat in a couple of days," Ovatt reminded them optimistically.

"Stop all your fretting now," the woman snapped at them. "That fee ain't nothing, nothing at all—not compared to the small fortune you boys are bound to make when you go sell all this: hemp, flour, tobacco, ironworkings, and all."

A smile slowly crossed Kingsbury's face. "I suppose you're right. A small fortune. Yes. Well, maybeso."

"You're all gonna be rich men," the woman buoyed them. "Drink the finest wine. Smoke the finest cigars—not have to chew that poor stuff you boys been sucking on since you pulled me out'n the river. Times gonna change for you now."

"R-rich men?" Root asked, looking at the faces of the other three crew.

"Even Titus Bass," the pilot said. "You got your pay coming—"

"Pay?" Beulah demanded. "You three figure on giving Titus nothing more'n regular pay?" She whirled on Bass. "That's only some fifty dollars for a crewman to come all the way downriver with a Kentuckyboat."

"It don't rightly seem fair he gets a full goddamned share," Root snorted. "Not since't he wasn't with us when we put this here boat into the Ohio way up—"

"I don't 'spect it to be a full share, now," Titus interrupted with an apologetic wag of his head.

"Wait a minute," Beulah demanded. "What'd Ebenezer Zane pay you fellas ever' trip down? He pay only boatmen's wages? Like every other patroon on the river?"

Kingsbury's face went more sheepish than the others' as they dropped their eyes. "Naw," the pilot answered. "After he sold everything, Eb took his half off the top and split the other half atween all four of us, him included."

She nodded in wide-eyed admiration, saying, "That's a damn fine proposition for a boatman, I'll say. No wonder you boys stayed on with him so many years. Likely you all was making five, maybe six times or more what you'd make working any other man's boat down the river."

"We all had us a little piece of the cargo that way, Ebenezer always said," Hames explained.

"And all of this is yours to sell off now," Beulah replied. "So to my way of thinking, I say you boys do like Ebenezer done for you: give Titus here what would be one man's fair split of the boat's profits, and with all that's left you can split up atween yourselves. How's that strike you?"

Root and Ovatt looked at one another quizzically, then both turned in unison to Kingsbury for help. After cogitating on it a few moments, working it over in his mind a handful at a time, he nodded and replied, "Sounds fair; fair to everyone. Fair to Titus 'cause he'll get better'n a boatman's wages for the trip . . . and better for all the rest of us 'cause we ain't not a one ever had so much to split atween us before! It sound good to you, Titus?"

"I ain't never . . . didn't even count on no money coming—"

"Don't matter. You earned your money," Kingsbury interrupted, slapping Bass on the shoulder. "That settles it. What's fair is fair—right, boys?"

When they went ashore that afternoon for the first time, Titus sensed his excitement swell with every step they took down the meandering levee, moving closer and closer to the city's central business district. Never before in all those weeks and all the miles Bass had put behind him in coming downriver had he seen such a mix of colors and tongues, dialects and costumes, as there were here on the streets of New Orleans. Besides gaily dressed Indians from the region's various tribes, Bass jostled against pale-skinned foreigners from faraway European principalities, coffee-colored visitors from a host of Caribbean islands, as well as stopping dead in his tracks to watch long lines of half-dressed Africans—some dull-eyed with privation, others wide-eyed with fear at certain death—each one as dark and shiny as charred hardwood glistening after a rain, all of them chained together with massive iron shackles, their feet bound two by two, led along with the accompanying beat of a drummer, perhaps even a fife or two adding a lively air above the sad procession of human cargo making for the middle of the marketplace, where the Africans would be offered up—man, woman, and child alike—to the well-heeled bidders who journeyed here to this slave market from throughout the gulf coast.

Even now near the end of a busy day, slave traders cried out in voices shrill and falsetto, bass or soprano, announcing what they were buying. Each barker screeched or sang louder and louder to outdo his competition as the hawkers moved along through the throbbing mass of upriver boatmen, local stevedores, and sailors come from ports across great oceans.

Here in the market below the trees where the grass moss hung like tatters of dirty linen, the autumn air did not move near so well within such a crushing mass of bodies. It was then that Titus began to smell people. As he thought on it, he could not remember the last time he had been confined in a crowd, forced to smell the sweat and stink of other folks—but, surely, it must have been only last summer. Back in Boone County. Perhaps at the Longhunters Fair, where so many gathered. Yet nothing at all like this.

Back upriver at the ports on the Ohio, the commerce of a few prosperous communities, perhaps a few states at best, was all that was conducted. Yet here lay the crossroads of many cultures, many countries, all bringing their wares to this southwesternmost port of an infant nation.

The smells of these people from different lands mingled now with the fragrances of exotic spices, the hearty tang of generous quarters of beef, veal, and pork, along with headless poultry and monstrous, glassy-eyed oceangoing fish, all hung in the public market that crowded most of the levee's length, every morsel baking beneath the autumn sun, crusted with clusters of flying insects. In addition, from the backs of their carts some vendors hawked wild ducks and game from upriver in the Indian lands, while others sold what they held captive in their nearby cages: live turkeys, ducks, and geese, as well as varieties of barnyard fowl. As well, those men from upriver could purchase such exotic wares as packed vermilion from the Orient, French girdles of fine silk, embroidered shirts of Spanish linen, tiny round looking glasses, and dainty slippers for the tiniest of women's feet. Here at New Orleans the world came knocking at America's door.

On the docks lay a dizzying maze of goods just off-loaded from the downriver flats. Most Kentucky boatmen ran what they termed a "straight" load—consisting of one product easier to load, maintain, and unload en route. Things like pork, flour, coal, hay, and even cordwood. Fewer preferred a "mixed" load, hauling what they could buy cheap and sell for a considerable profit upon reaching New Orleans. Here on the wharf sat crates and kegs and casks of potatoes, dried apples, rolled cigars, lime, and tallow, very important to a lardless community. As well, the boatmen dodged around stacks of millstones and sprawling bundles of pig iron and corn brooms. Tobacco was a favorite of the Kentucky shippers: cured leaf purchased in Cincinnati or Louisville for $2.00 American for a hundredweight would increase in value to $9.50 by the time it reached the end of the line.

Everywhere was a splash of color and texture, with all the fruits and vegetables displayed at the top of open sacking or in huge wagon-borne boxes: all manner of melons, cucumbers, and Irish potatoes, both red and brown, along with the yams and sweet cherries, plums, and strawberries. Initially nervous at stealing—no matter how trifling—Titus nonetheless followed the example of the other boatmen as they threaded their way through the maze of vendors and displays, snatching up a treat here and there when they passed a veranda where no one was watching. Quickly stuffing their stolen treasure between their lips, sucking noisily, and commenting on the relative merits of the various purloined wares—finishing some while tossing the rest beyond the levee, where the refuse landed among that garbage floating on the chocolate-colored surface of the grand old Mississippi.

Originally founded by the French in 1718, New Orleans likely boasted a population of some ten thousand souls late in 1810. While the great fire of 1788 had destroyed nearly all of the original buildings, those tile-roofed wood and brick houses that arose from the ashes couldn't help but impress even the most cosmopolitan or international of travelers. A constantly expanding dike protected this low-lying city, that dike ever in need of repair. Within the confines of the old colonial port, New Orleans had long ago divided itself into three sections: Spanish, American, and the dominant French community. In a city French by birth and French at its marrow, the French inhabitants rarely dealt with other residents save for matters of business. At the center of town stood the grand cathedral, the town hall nearby, as well as a convent, hospital, and public market house, in addition to a large complement of army barracks and a notorious prison, which was used by the local constables for the many, many troublemakers who haunted the city's disreputable and world-infamous "Swamp."

Here all manner of music screamed for attention from every open door as the four boatmen muscled their way along the crowded, rutted, garbage-strewn streets to reach that most dangerous yet ultimately alluring section of

New Orleans where few streetlamps glimmered. As the sun sank from the sky, life in the Swamp grew more animated. Bustling billiard rooms and brothels, overflowing gaming houses and watering holes, the doorway of every public place teeming with those moving in and those coming out, along with those who shouted, barking to entice passersby with the prospect of whiskey, or women of all hues and colors, proposing that sailors come within for the sheer fun of unbridled debauchery now that they had reached this famous port.

"You never wanna go in there," Heman Ovatt warned.

Titus stared, mule-eyed, at the oversize barker waving, dancing, shimmying all his rolls of fat while chattering to all at once in the doorway to a card room. On each side of the door was painted a brightly colored hand of cards.

Bass asked, "Why not?"

"Swindlers," Ovatt said as if it hurt his tongue to have the word cross it. "Steal a man's money and throw him in the street with their cheating games. And the girls in some of these places ain't there to pleasure a man, neither."

"Then what for?"

"They just help get a man drunk. Help him drink up his likker so others can see to it he loses his money at their swindling tables. And that poor turtle won't even have a chance to get his pants down and climb a'tween their legs a'tall. Not in that sort of place. Stay close to us, young'un. And don't dare let yourself get hauled into one of them dark dens."

Dogs snarled at one another, fighting over the mounds of filth tossed from the many kitchens that lined these muddy, wheel-rutted, hoof-pocked streets. Men dead drunk lay propped here and there against the buildings, sleeping off their excesses, most with their pockets already turned inside out by casual thieves who leisurely worked over their unconscious victims. Not one of those drunks still boasted a pair of boots on his feet, most already stripped of hat and coat, perhaps a fancy shirt or sash—anything that might bring a thief a few pennies, ha'pence, shilling, or doubloon in exchange. The unwary and stupid proved themselves fair game.

In front of one busy saloon a large ring of people danced and cavorted in the lamplight, flowing this way and that in a great circle in time to the music of a fiddle and a concertina, along with a third man clanging out a steady rhythm on the bottom of a brass kettle.

Across that narrow lane from the revelers half-dressed women leaned on their elbows from open windows on both floors of a two-story brothel, many drinking and smoking expensive meerschaum pipes as they conversed with those below in the street. Flesh advertised because flesh was for sale. Necks and shoulders bared, breasts all but spilling forth from skimpy, wispy turns of cambric and calico, some of it trimmed with lace. Titus stood agog as one woman caught his eye, beckoned him over as she leaned out, her exposed and pendulous breasts hanging like fat udders craving a man's fondling.

He looked over, staring, unbelieving at their size.

"Get along here, Titus," Reuben snarled, snagging Bass's arm and yanking him away from the whore's outstretched arm. "We ain't here to-night looking to find a knocking shop for you. Think back to the last time you had diddling on your mind—we nearly got us all kill't."

Then Bass remembered Annie Christmas's gunboat. Natchez, and that mob intent on something unspoken, but murderous all the same. Recalled that bloodied scene: those dead men and the whore Kingsbury had gutted. Thinking on the look in those yellowed eyes, the dangerous, feral fear chiseled across the shiny black face of that big, smooth-headed slave who had worked the bar for Annie Christmas.

"Hey, you there: Kentucky boy!" the bare-breasted whore called out in singsong, lisping slightly what with missing some of her front teeth. She waved, tilting her head and lifting one of her breasts, beckoning him to her window. "C'mon over here and show me what it is all you Kentucky boys know about a woman!"

"That's Madame Laforge's place," Reuben declared, tugging Bass away from the window. "You go in there—a feller like you won't ever come back out!"

"W-why . . . they likely to kill me in that place too?"

The boatman snorted. "Hell, no! Not in there! Madame Laforge's girls just hump a young'un like you till there's nothing left but your moccasins!"

With a shudder he let Root turn him away, hurrying past the gay dancers to duck within the saloon behind Kingsbury and Ovatt. This mingling of dialects and tongues, a cacophony of odors and aromas that assaulted his nostrils as they pierced the lamplit gloom of that teeming grogshop, were enough to make Titus believe he had entered a whole new world. This could not be part of the United States.

"Lookee there," Heman Ovatt cried out, indicating the bar where stood a long line of customers, most of whom were copper-skinned Indians and indigo-eyed freedmen, "drinking just like they was white men."

"You of a sudden got something against a Negra having hisself a drink?" Kingsbury asked, slamming an open palm into Heman's chest.

Ovatt shook his head. "Naw, I s'pose not—just as long as they don't drink my share."

"You ever see a Injun drinking?" Root asked Titus.

"Nary a slave neither," Bass replied.

"Them ain't slaves," Kingsbury explained. "Them's the Negras bought themselves their freedom, or had it bought for 'em by their owner."

"Still ain't never gonna be like a goddamned white man," Ovatt grumbled.

"Negra works his job, same as you and me," Reuben began. "How you figure that's so bad?"

Shrugging, Ovatt declared, "Don't know what to think about it. I guess I just figured there'd allays be slaves, and there'd allays be those what owned slaves. It were the way of things when I was growing up—simple as that."

Sliding his arm over Titus's shoulder, Kingsbury said, "Down here things aren't near as simple as they likely was for you back home. Now, fellas —we ain't having ourselves but a couple of drinks tonight before we get on back to the boat and the woman. We all need our heads clear tomorrow while'st we sell our cargo."

"Just two drinks," Reuben repeated, looking at Titus. "Then we'll go."

Then Ovatt turned to Bass. "So I s'pose that means Reuben and me gotta keep a eye on Titus here, just so he don't go getting in any trouble with no fat whores this time!"

"Ah, leave the young'un be," Kingsbury protested as they reached the long, crude counter and waited for one of the bar lackeys to amble over. "Ain't his fault them two yellow-striped back-stabbers walked right onto Annie Christmas's gunboat when they did. Young'un was just there to get hisself diddled."

Ovatt turned to the pilot, asking, "Ain't we gonna visit none of them knocking shops cross the way this time down, Hames?"

"Back to Natchez, taking care of your pizzers near got us all killed," Kingsbury said as a barman approached. "So we get our work done, you just be sure this time you have your fun with some gals what won't try to lift your purse or slit your throat."

Came the bored question, "What'll it be?"

Kingsbury replied, "A goodly portion of your finest phlegm-cutter for my crew, good man!"

"Lemme first see the color of your money," advised the wary barman.

Onto the bar the pilot promptly hammered down his hard money.

"Don't want none of your usual stuff," Ovatt demanded. "Only your best antifogmatic will do for us'n!"

"Twenty shillings a bottle," the barman said, sweeping up what he needed from the scattering of coins. All manner of specie was welcomed in trade anywhere along the river, but no more so than in New Orleans itself, where a brief roll with a woman would cost no more than a mere fivepence.

"Just have you a look at these, Hames," Reuben complained a few minutes later as the mugs and bottle were slammed down before them and the raucous noise swelled around them. "These are all coarse frolickers and braggarts what ain't got no bottom! Hell—give us a chance and we could drink the balls off any of 'em!"

Instead, the four did as they were ordered and drank slowly at their green bottle of smooth corn whiskey, something of a pleasant change from their *fillee* of Monongahela rye that had been their mainstay on the trip down —that daily ration usually no more than a gill, or quarter pint. Why, to pick up and leave these riverside grogshops and beer-sties before he had himself a head of alcohol-powered steam under his belt went completely against character for most any Kentucky boatman. More often than not for those who reached New Orleans after a long, ofttimes monotonous, sometimes invigoratingly dangerous journey, it seemed the greatest desire was to determine who among them could swallow the most liquor, whoop up with the most abandon and brawling, and carouse with one whore after another until the peep o' day. After all, a riverman must always drink his full share, or he might well catch what their breed chose to call the "dry rot."

Come now to this most southern port of call, the watermen did their best to live up to that compelling reputation they had acquired: the "alligator-horse"—a hard-drinking, lawless, straight-shooting, crude, and ferocious fighter—the ultimate drifter.

But with that evening still young, they devotedly followed Hames Kingsbury from the rambunctious Mad Dutchman, threading the noisy, bustling alleyways, past lamplit corners, making for their flatboat secured at the far end of the levee.

In the midst of the marketplace, where vendors were closing their shacks and shanties in the murky twilight, Reuben dropped back a bit to walk beside Titus, where he whispered, "I truly do believe Kingsbury's gone soft for that woman we drugged outta the river."

"She seems a nice enough woman," Bass replied.

"Was a time it didn't matter to Hames how long we all stayed out the night afore Ebenezer was to sell off his cargo," Reuben explained. "Truth is, Hames was one alligator-horse what'd howl all night. A real damned snapping turtle! So tell me now: ain't it strange how a woman can change a man?"

"I . . . s'pose it is," Bass replied as Kingsbury hurried them all along.

Indeed, it was likely very strange for the three veteran rivermen from the Ohio country to be plying their way back to the boat so early on their first night come to New Orleans. After all those downriver miles, most new arrivals had a spree to get out of their systems, every bit like men who had wandered too long in a wilderness, making stops only at Louisville, Natchez, and eventually here to slake their thirst for strong drink and their appetite for soft-skinned women. Most of the commerce in the Swamp, that dangerous section of New Orleans catering to the rivermen, relied primarily on satisfying every last one of those intense hungers magnified by the long downriver journey for those half-feral American frontiersmen. Truly, the watering holes, whorehouses, and gambling dens here on the lower Mississippi helped the river live up to its reputation as "the spillway of sin."

Without hesitation the fun-loving, hospitable Creoles and Acadians of New Orleans opened their arms to all their visitors, gladly providing for the rivermen what those visitors wanted most. So warm was that welcome for the lusty boatmen that many Americans decided to stay on after cargo and boat were sold. A good number took up residence, never to return to the states from which they originally hailed.

Despite the hospitality of the longtime residents, Creole mothers in these parts nonetheless commonly scolded their children with the oath, *"Toi, tu n'es qu'un mauvais Kaintock!"*

"You, you're nothing but a filthy little Kentuckian!"

The wharf and levee this night were alive around them with crowds and music, laughter and torchlight. They found the woman sitting atop a cask near the awning, where she could watch the bustle of New Orleans after dark.

"Beulah?" Hames called out.

"That you, fellas?"

The four of them scrambled over the gunnel one at a time.

"Thought you'd make it a late night," the woman explained as she eased herself over by Kingsbury. "Our crew always did."

"We got us a shitload of hard work come early in the morning," the pilot explained. "After that these fellas can have their fun."

She watched the skinny boatman move past her, then asked of his back,

"And what about you, Hames? What you gonna do for fun now you come to Orlins?"

He stopped, but without turning around, Kingsbury shrugged, saying, "I been to Nawlins many times. Ain't nothing new I gotta see. Ain't nothing new I gotta do. Maybeso a man comes to a point where he's had him enough of the bad whiskey and humping on them bang-tails."

She replied softly, "Maybe a man comes to where he figures he wants a little more outta life'n what he's already had so far."

"I say we split the money up afore we set off for the Ohio," Heman Ovatt suggested.

Titus could see in the boatman's eyes some hint of what he himself felt inside at that moment. The four of them and the woman stood in a cluster at the far end of the levee, watching three strangers release the hawsers, wheeling them in on that crude capstan as they set off on that very flatboat which had carried Ebenezer Zane's crew down the Ohio, on down the Mississippi to New Orleans.

"Maybe that ain't such a bad idea you got," Kingsbury replied. "That way I don't have to watch over it all by myself."

Reuben nodded enthusiastically, licking his lower lip with a pink flick of his tongue. "I figure each of us watch out for his own share."

"Too much for one man to carry, anyway, ain't it?" Beulah asked.

The pilot held up the skin sack filled with heavy coins, then patted, with a muted rattle, the five other sacks he had weighing down the pockets of his greasy hide coat.

"I do believe it is. I ain't no packmule," Hames replied. "And sure as hell don't wanna carry all this up the Natchez Road by myself."

"Let's divide it!" Ovatt cried.

"Not here," Beulah said. "I gotta tell you that's more money'n I ever seen—and I been on the river longer'n any of you fellas."

"Ebenezer made sure he loaded his boat this time down with cargo what'd bring top dollar here in Nawlins for the season. Shame he ain't here to see just how much it brung him."

"He allays carried the money north hisself—in belts he wore under his shirt," Ovatt stated. "Don't know how he stood up under it all, though."

Titus turned aside a moment, watching their flatboat slip away down the wharf, under the control of its new owners—men who bought flatboats reaching New Orleans, taking the vessels to their woodyard on the levee, where in the shallow water the boats were knocked and sawed apart, the hard-grained yellow poplar from those northern forests sold plank by plank, foot by expensive foot to those who could afford to build their homes and shops of the very best money would by. Selling off that long flatboat Ebenezer Zane had built for him at the mouth of the Ohio in Pittsburgh was the last thing holding them there. The long trek north could now begin.

Over the last week their cargo had gone for more than any of the veteran rivermen could have imagined. The massive coils of thick, oil-soaked hemp rope taken on in Louisville went first. Then the northern flour, first sifted and checked for weevil larvae and other pests before stevedores rolled off those casks for the buyers. After that the crates of Kentucky tobacco leaf were inspected and sold among four competing middlemen, each of whom had an overseas buyer in the markets in Europe. And finally came the middlemen interested in looking over the kegs and casks of Kentucky and Pennsylvania ironmongery: candleholders and chest hinges, door latches, hasps and all manner of window hardware, every last fire-hardened piece of it hammered out somewhere along the northern frontier of the Ohio River country.

Seven days it took them to arrange for the sale of everything. This strange, new, convoluted process began by their searching out Ebenezer's longtime buyers for certain goods, scouring the levee for still others, bringing those savvy negotiators to the boat one by one to let them pore over the goods brought down from the Ohio country, and offer their best price for what they wanted most. There followed considerable discussion and ciphering among the three boatmen, arguing over how they might wrestle the best deal for every cask, keg, and crate of Ebenezer's cargo.

After the second buyer made his offer on the entire lot of their flour that first day of dickering, the boatmen even turned to Titus for help sorting through the maze of numbers for them.

"Why me?" he asked anxiously.

Kingsbury's brow furrowed. "We ain't none of us been to school in many a year—I just figured you'd know more about such things and wouldn't mind working out things on paper for us."

"I . . ."—and he swallowed hard with no little fear, forcing out the admission—"I don't remember much about how numbers work and such."

It was the truth, plain and simple: he could recall practically nothing of the mystical world of ciphering.

In bewildered frustration Kingsbury turned to the woman.

"If you're sure you'll trust me," Beulah replied without hesitation.

With a glance at Titus the pilot said, "You know how to work your numbers?"

"See there?" she snapped at him. "Just goes to show you don't trust me."

But Kingsbury was as quick to answer, "We'll trust you—just figure it out for us. Cipher what the offers mean for all them ropes. An' what that fella said he'd give us for that whole lot of flour."

From then on Beulah stood foursquare in the thick of the bargaining, selling, and in counting the hard money the buyers brought in pouches, all manner of specie: Spanish doubloons, French guineas, and sometimes even American silver. Money that had a real heft to it, cool to the touch, substantial. More of it than Titus thought he'd ever see in his whole life.

And now he watched the woman count out his share into his palm. More into his other palm, until he was sure he could hold no more in his hands. Into a skin pouch he poured his treasure, then dropped it inside his shirt, patted it. Maybe this was what it took to feel like a man. Not just the liquor and women—but to feel as if he was a real man like his father, earning a living. This long trip downriver had earned him a small fortune.

"I'm gonna show you boys what you ought'n do with your money," Beulah said that night as they settled into a small second-story room above a noisy gambling house at the edge of the Swamp. Against the walls lay pallets made with coarse hemp, old comforters for padding, and a wool blanket.

They joined her to sit squat-legged around a flickering grease lamp and some wax candles at the center of the room while the woman passed out four needles.

"You get all of these out of Ebenezer's plunder?"

Nodding her head, Beulah answered, "They was in his box on the boat what I saved. Them and this thread here."

She gave them each a long strand of linen thread to start them out, showed them how to lick it before slipping it through the eye of their needle despite their coarse, callused, clumsy fingers. Then she turned to their youngest member.

"Titus, I want you go over in the corner and take your britches off."

All four of them looked at her as if she had just whacked them all up alongside their heads with a snag pole.

"G'won, now. Put that blanket round you, if you're scairt to lemme see you in your woolens."

No one said a word as Titus crawled over to his pallet, laid the wool blanket over his legs, and loosened the buttons on his britches. When he had kicked them off his feet, Bass slid his rump back to the circle and handed the pants to her.

"Now watch what I'm gonna show you on the young'un's britches so you can get started doing the very same thing on yours."

Having peeled both legs inside out, the woman carefully sliced open the waistband. She pushed in a few of the youngster's coins before knotting her thread and beginning her repair.

"Here, son," she said, handing him the britches in one hand, the needle in the other, "now you keep on with it and get all them coins of your'n sewed away outta sight."

"Ouch!" Reuben cried moments later as he began. He sucked on a bloody finger. "Goddamn! I ain't s'posed to be doin' such woman's work as this." He flung down his britches in disgust. "Rest of you can play like you're a tailor—"

"So you want everyone you meet 'long the road home to know you're carrying all that money, is that right?" Beulah asked.

"That's my concern. T'ain't none of yours!" Root snapped.

"Damn well is my concern," Kingsbury said. "You go letting folks know you're carrying all that money—they're gonna rightly figure we're carrying all of ours too."

"Most folks coming north from Orlins gonna be poor—but 'nough of 'em gonna be rich," Beulah explained as she leaned over to hand Reuben the britches he had flung down. "Folks know if you're on the Trace, you either gonna be rich from selling cargo downriver . . . or you're poor as a church mouse, with nothing but the clothes on your back and a hankering to get back home fast as you can."

"So that's just how we gotta look to folks, ain't it?" Ovatt asked.

"Like we're poorest of the lot, and ain't worth the time of no robbers to shake us down for the lice in the seams of our old, wored clothes," Kingsbury added.

"You fellas all got your pistols, don't you?" she asked, her eyes touching each one of the four.

"Only thing you let us spend our money on today," Root grumbled.

"G'won and throw your money away like you fixed on doing at Natchez: whores and whiskey—just to get your throats cut."

"Aw, shit," Root said sourly. "This damned woman's right again."

"I wanna make the Ohio country with my fortune," Kingsbury declared. "To do that, we gotta be smart and use our money only for food, some new blankets, and these pistol guns we bought us for our journey. We go off buying too much fancy things—folks can tell we got money just by looking at us on the way home."

Ever since that morning when they had moved from gun shop to gun shop looking to buy enough weapons so that each of them would have a pair of pistols, including the woman, Titus had kept his tucked in the old sash tied at his waist. As he stuffed coins into the waistband he was sewing, he touched those pistols where they lay beside him. It reassured him now, to have such power—the long-barreled, big-caliber pistols, in addition to his grandpap's rifle. He let his chest swell again as it had many times this day, just to think how he would turn away any would-be highwaymen by simply pulling out his weapons. And once more Titus practiced that determined look he was certain would turn any thief's knees to water when they laid their eyes on him.

He was still dreaming on how he would convert robbers to cowards on the Natchez Trace when Heman Ovatt nudged him awake the next morning in that cold room they all shared.

"Them wagons ain't gonna wait for us," Root said as Titus came up onto an elbow slowly.

"Time to go," Kingsbury said as he stood, slinging over his shoulder that pair of blankets he had rolled into a tube, tied at either end with a leather cord.

Titus's stomach complained with a fading whine as he yanked on the second of his moccasins. "We got time for breakfast afore we catch up them wagons?"

Beulah shook her head, patting the big pouch that hung at her hip, suspended over her shoulder. "No, but I got us some biscuits and hard-meat from last night's supper. It will do once we get rolling north."

Leaving their tiny room, the five hurried into the cold mist and down the outside steps that were braced into the back wall of the gambling house. A few yards behind the brothel next door they stopped among the trees where three outbuildings were stationed. Titus was the last to have the chance to duck out of the cold dawn mist and settle himself on the plank with that hole sawed out for him to nest upon. While it was dry in there, he had to admit the air damned near choked a man. In enough of a hurry to breathe some better air, he shuffled outside, pulling his britches up. In the chilling mist he got them buttoned, shifting the new and unaccustomed weight of the waistband while he retied the belt sash.

Through the litter-clogged streets of New Orleans they hurried as the mist became a chilling rain. Among the heaps and mounds of garbage, children fought for any edible morsel, every one of them dressed in their tattered frocks, muddy and barefoot, noses running and eyes red and matted in disease. Ragged-eared dogs, soaked and shivering, slunk back in the shadows of the alleyways. Along those dark passages the boatmen and Beulah hurried, watching and listening for windows that would open above them, chamberpots emptied by the oblivious tenants on any unsuspecting pedestrians below.

Titus smelled the wagon yard a full two blocks before they reached the freight district—mules and oxen steaming in the downpour, the smell of fresh dung and old hay. Arriving at the proper yard just as a sheet of oiled canvas was being lashed over the walls of the last wagon, they found the head teamster, who looked them over, then held out his open palm.

"When you wasn't here right away, I thort you'd had you a change of mind," said the moon-faced, red-nosed man.

"We're here, and we're going," Kingsbury replied, glancing down at that open hand suspiciously. "We done paid you already."

"That was for my boss," he said, an ingratiating smile seeming to cut that bare-shaven round face right in half. "This morning you pay *me*."

"We had us a deal—"

"You had a deal with my boss." The wagon master smiled, snapping his fingers, then opening his palm once more. "He just owns the wagons. I'm the man what sees they get to Natchez and back with the goods."

"I wanna talk to your boss—where's he?"

That smile fading quickly from the moon face, the wagon master turned and began to step off. "Get yourself another ride north."

"Wait!" Beulah cried, lunging forward to grab the man by the elbow. "What do we owe you?"

For a long moment he looked down on the small woman; then the smile returned as he peered back at the four men who stood in the rain, small puddles growing at their feet. "Ten dollar each ought'n be about right."

She let go of his elbow, looked back at Kingsbury quickly, then shook her head. "We ain't got that kind of money."

"Don't tell me that crock of horsepuck," he growled, and laughed. "You're going north, back to home. Got you all kinds of money—"

"Five dollars each of us," she wheeled and interrupted with a snap. "That's twenty-five dollars for you. And I'll wager you ain't seen that much money for your own self at one time in many a month."

For a second the heavyset man was startled by her words; then his smile broadened and he licked his bottom lip. "I ain't in the business of arguing over money, ma'am. Ain't nothing for us to settle here. All you gotta do is get out your ten dollars for the each of you—"

"Five dollars," she snapped at him again, putting one finger against his chest. "We don't go, you don't make no extra this trip north. That'd be a real shame."

Cocking his head, he licked his lips again and let the rain drip off the floppy brim of his cheap wool-felt hat a minute longer, then said, "Eight dollar."

"Six."

"Seven."

"Six," she repeated adamantly.

"Awright," he grumbled, holding out his hand again, this time toward the woman. "Six and a half."

"She ain't got the money," Kingsbury declared as he shuffled forward in the mud. "I do."

Eyes dancing, the wagon master watched the coins clink into his hand one at a time, smiling with more largesse than ever. "Just figured she'd be the one to have the money, I did," he clucked, "the way this female panther 'pears to have just about all the brains and balls in your outfit."

FIFTEEN

"We stick to the Catholic streets of Natchez," Kingsbury whispered in the wavering shadows cast by the Spanish moss clinging to the tall cypress at the southern edge of town, "an' I don't mean the Irish Catholic streets, neither—we'll be awright. Wait till dark to start through, and get on out of town afore light."

The other two boatmen nodded, then looked at Bass. Grim-lipped, Titus nodded, sensing his Adam's apple bob high in his throat as he did.

"We need us food, Hames," the woman reminded.

Glancing now at her haggard features, Titus thought Beulah looked older than she probably was.

"Don't you worry—we'll get us food," Kingsbury replied. "Do that, first whack."

It was their nineteenth day since leaving New Orleans, well into December now, with the weather growing colder the farther north they bounced and jostled atop the tarped wagons hauling staples up a well-beaten road to Natchez, Mississippi.

Recognizing that they were nearing the outskirts of that settlement, Kingsbury bellowed out to the wagon master.

"You go 'head an' get off on your own now—anywhere you want," the teamster boss cried over his shoulder as he brought the leather straps down onto the backs of his plodding oxen. "From here on out only place I stop is in town."

When they realized the wheels would keep on rolling, the wayfarers crawled to the sidewalls and leaped to the hoof-pounded trail where mud puddles lay crusted in ugly ice lace.

Fearing that someone might well recognize them from the killings aboard Annie Christmas's gunboat, the five hid among the thick undergrowth at the edge of town. Not far away stood the first of the immense canebrakes, each shaft standing nearly thirty feet tall, measuring a good two inches in diameter. Nearby squatted a jumble of run-down shacks where a woman might well take in wash during the day and work at keeping her legs spread at night, all to provide for a growing brood of children. Even in this chill as a metallic sun sank in the west, children scampered and played near enough that Titus could not just hear them, but watched them through the timber and underbrush.

How these dirty, poorly dressed urchins reminded him of his own brothers and sister in earlier days, reminded him of Amy Whistler's own siblings.

"I could use a drink," Ovatt grumped. "Ain't had much of any since't we was at Annie's place."

"What'd that drinking get us?" Root demanded dourly.

Turning to Kingsbury in disgust, Ovatt asked, "Can't we just move around these here shanties and get on through town?"

The pilot shook his head. "You two just hush. We'll wait."

"Maybeso I can find something for you fellas to warm up on," Beulah declared as she started to rise.

"What you got in mind?" Kingsbury demanded, seizing her wrist.

"A little liquor for the bunch of you," she replied, glancing down at the hand he held around her arm. "A little ain't gonna hurt, will it, now?"

He let her go. "No, no hurt it be. A damn fine idea, you have."

As Beulah stood and straightened out her skirts beneath that secondhand coat purchased in New Orleans, then moved off toward the town as nonchalant as could be, Titus leaned back against the trunk of a chinaberry. Above him in its branches hung gray moss suspended like winter's own tatters, tormented by the chill wind. Only yards away the streets of Natchez this sunset were beginning to bustle with barkers and pimps and highly rouged women emerging into the coming night, along with an assortment of tame pigs and wild dogs, as well as more of those dirty, unclaimed children.

Beyond the last of the poor shanties, Bass watched Beulah reach the first of the low, broken, half-sunken plank sidewalks. She stopped, as if she wanted to wave back at them, then turned without a gesture and kept on until she disappeared into the gloom of those dark streets. Into the bowels of the wildest hellhole on the Mississippi River.

Whereas the French were the first to build there around 1716, establishing their colony some three hundred miles—or ninety leagues—north of New Orleans, it was the Spanish who first sent their military expedition to that part of the new world. Late in the summer of 1540, de Soto, governor of the Island of Cuba, traversed the plains out of the southwest before he crossed the Mississippi near the future Natchez, packing along his own Negro slaves. There the knight commander of the Order of St. James of Compostela made contact with the peaceful Choctaw Indians, who for generations had performed their own bloody sacrifices at their White Apple Village. De Soto marched on with his army to reach the Choctaw, the Chickasaw, then the Cherokee in turn. By and large a peaceful people, these natives did not at first resist the intruders, even when de Soto's priests began attempting to convert them from their heathen ways. For such Christians come to save unclean souls, their mission became a simple matter of converting the savages or killing them.

Yet it wasn't until de Soto asked too much of his hosts by demanding Choctaw women to warm the beds of his soldiers that the tribe finally revolted. They drove the Spanish back to the banks of the great river. As the terrified soldiers and priests fled from the forests that seemed alive with an enemy behind every tree, the Spanish left behind their holy vestments, their eucharistic ornaments, even their sacramental wine. Suspicious, the Choctaw broke the clay jars used in the white man's ceremonies, letting the fragrant crimson fluid soak into the ground. Every bit like that wine the priests had blessed, de Soto's blood was soon to seep into the mud, and there beside the Mississippi the governor of Cuba lay down to die, his anonymous bones to rot for all of eternity.

It took nearly two hundred years more until a European culture would again dare to settle in the Mississippi Valley. By 1716 the French had come up from the West Indies to establish an outpost close by the White Apple Village of the Choctaw. Like the Spanish, the French were Catholic, bringing with them their own black-robed priests in charge of the vestments, sacraments, and wine. With only a brief interval when the British assumed temporary rule over the great river valley, the Spanish next took over under Governor Galvez just prior to the coming of the Americans in 1795. That same year the first steam-powered cotton gin arrived on the lower Mississippi. Already the Natchez District had proved itself as good a region as any other in the south for the growing of tobacco, sugarcane, and corn. Now it prepared to stand head and shoulders above the others in cotton.

To the north, east, and south of Natchez sprang up the great plantations scoured from the canebrake and cypress swamps. Great houses were raised, fields were cleared from the bayous, and roads blazed. All of it accomplished on the backs of the African slaves brought to New Orleans on tall-masted ships, auctioned on that great, bloody block of misery in the market square, then hauled north into the wilderness, not quite able to understand they were now the property of one of those wealthy landowners.

More than an hour later Beulah returned, the four corners of a scrap of blanket suspended over her shoulder to form a pouch. Coming awake in the dark and the cold, Titus moved with the other three boatmen into a tight circle as the woman set her bundle at her feet, then sank beside it.

Beulah pulled apart the corners, exposing two clay jugs, and said, "I got you fellas some tafia."

Titus watched Ovatt pull the cork from one of the jugs and sniff it before turning the jug up to drink. He asked, "What's tafia?"

"Rum."

"But it's better'n that Monongahela we drunk all the way downriver," Root said, smacking his lips as he handed the second jug to Kingsbury.

"Try some," Ovatt suggested, giving the first jug to Bass.

It truly tasted sweeter than the American backwoods rum, and well it should—as it was made of the finest sugarcane in the French West Indies.

"What else you get us?" Kingsbury inquired, fingering a slab of something dark. He brought it to his nose for a sniff.

Beulah said, "You'll like that."

"I bet I will," the pilot replied, and took a bite.

"Salt meat fried in bear's oil," she told them. "Enough for you all to have a goodly portion for supper."

For the most part they drank their tafia in silence, using it to wash down the seasoned meat and what biscuits she could find to purchase. At the same time, Kingsbury made it clear none of them were to drink enough to hobble them when it came time to push on through town. Overhead more clouds rolled in, shutting out the stars completely as some of them dozed on their full bellies.

It was near the middle of the night when Kingsbury tapped on the sole of Bass's moccasin. The others were awake, dusting and shifting their clothing, shivering in the cold. Beulah stood at the edge of the brush, waiting expectantly.

"Like I told you, Hames—I figure you can keep to the edge of the woods until you get to the north side of town, where we'll pick up the Trace."

"There by Kings Tavern?"

With a nod she continued, "Place ain't as dangerous as it might be. 'Pears there's a train of slavers pushing through. They gone and chose to make a night of it at Kings Tavern."

"Slavers?" Ovatt asked. "Jesus God!"

"Wagons and cages and such?" Kingsbury asked intently, ignoring Heman's grumbling.

"Yeah," Beulah replied. "The place is packed with wagons. Men was all over the yard, in and out. Though most of 'em gone inside to the fires when it got cold."

"We'll keep to the woods," Kingsbury said, turning to the other three men. Then he led them out.

Snatches of wild, bawdy music joined discordant singing, the shrieks of drunken women, and the bellows of drunken men, along with the crashing of clayware and the cracking of furniture—all a river of sound pouring from the low shanties and shacks that bordered the river itself here in Natchez-Under-the-Hill. Where they could, the five pilgrims kept to the shadows and the sodden, quieter ground along the timber.

In reaching Kings Tavern they found the low-roofed saloon and brothel nearly hidden behind the many wagons parked haphazardly in the wide, muddy yard, every tongue down and teams staked out to graze nearby.

Kingsbury halted them as they all came abreast at the edge of the timber and studied the scene. "The first step home is just on the far side of that tavern, fellas."

"I say let's be putting this hellhole behind us right now," Beulah whispered.

"Me too," Ovatt agreed. "I'd like to reach Concordia Lake afore the sun comes up."

Looking at Root, the pilot said, "We'll push right ahead."

Then Kingsbury moved out of the solid wall of shadows into the cleared yard, hurrying toward the first wagon. As they did, a half-dozen dark human forms took shape from the floor of that wagon, rising one by one cautiously to peer out at the travelers with wide eyes yellowed bright as a new moon in their black faces. As the other boatmen and Beulah joined him, Hames slid down the sidewall, stepped over the long tongue, and darted to the next wagon, coming to a rest closer still to the side of the tavern. When the other four reached him there by a wagon near the back corner of the saloon, the pilot said, "Keep against the back wall. There's a kitchen door there—but I'll lay good money they got it closed tonight."

"Cold enough," Root grumbled.

Kingsbury inched toward the front of the wagon, peering around it as a solitary, silent figure sat up inside the last of three cages that filled the wagon's bed. Hearing the movement, seeing the huge shadow blot out some of the hissing torchlight that filled most of the wagonyard, Titus looked up, finding the slave's hands gripping the bars of his cage, pressing his swollen, bloodied face against them.

Bass looked away, then immediately looked again at the slave. A big man from what he could see in this light. Bald-headed too. Titus's breath caught in his throat as he stood, hearing the others shuffle off beneath the patter of the incessant, icy rain.

The slave had on only the tattered remnants of a shirt, clearly cut to ribbons across his shoulders and back by a recent whipping. Unsure at first, the big man slowly reached out one arm toward the white youngster, opening his palm. For a long moment Titus stared down at that lighter skin, then peered back at the man's face.

"Help me, boat-man."

Titus stumbled back. That voice: it was the goddamned Negra from Annie Christmas's gunboat!

"Don't you see me, boat-man?"

"I . . . I see you."

"Help me. Get me away from these bad men."

Just a quick look over the rest of the wagons in the yard filled with their cages of human chattel told Bass enough. "Y-you're going to work the fields."

"I dunno," the man replied, pulling his arm back into the cage and letting his head sink between his shoulders. "Know nothing 'bout that."

A voice rose softly from the cage next to his, and the big man whispered something in reply.

"What's that?" Bass inquired, his suspicion aroused. "Who's there?"

"Them others—they tell me we off to work the cotton for our new owner."

"But you was . . . you belonged to Annie Christmas."

He nodded, pressing his face close to the bars once more, one eye all but puffed shut. "White woman sold me two week ago. After big fight with you boat-men."

"She tell you why?"

"First she say she kill me—but she say a big man like me get her lots of money. So she sell me to work for the man who put me in this cage. Take me north to his home."

"She got rid of you after the killing at her boat?"

He nodded, his face a dark shadow within the dancing, torchlit shadows of that rainy night. "Say I no good to her no more—no good can keep her from trouble. Annie's whores get kill't. She get hurt. Her man friends get killed. She say her Negra man no good no more. Wanna kill me—but she sell me. Gonna get too much money for me."

"Titus!"

Bass turned, finding Kingsbury and the rest crouching at the corner of the tavern. The pilot hissed his name, waving him on. Titus turned back to glance over his shoulder at the man in the cage, starting to go, but got no more than a step when he turned to say something more to the slave.

At that moment an angry, frightened Kingsbury jutted out his jaw and issued his stern order, "C'mon, young'un! Ain't no time to dawdle!"

"Wait here," Bass whispered at the cage.

His ebony brow creased in bewilderment; then he smiled broadly and shrugged. "I h'ain't goin' nowhere."

As Bass slipped in among them back in the shadows of the tavern, Root demanded, "What the hell you doin'?"

"That there's the Negra from the gunboat," he tried to explain with a gush, his mind whirling madly.

"Annie Christmas's place?" Kingsbury asked.

"Yep. Said she up and sold him—"

"Leave his black ass be!" Root grumbled. "Bastard's where he belongs."

"Reuben's right," Ovatt agreed. "That skinhead savage nearly could've killed us."

Bass wheeled on Heman, saying, "That's just why he's in that cage, don't you see? Annie Christmas sold him 'cause he didn't kill us like he could've when he had the chance. Kill't us all, like she wanted him to."

Kingsbury scratched a louse from his beard, brought it out, and cracked it between his fingernails. "What the hell that mean to us?"

"Let's break him loose." Bass suggested it, suddenly as astonished as the rest that he had even considered it, much less uttered the words.

"B-b-break that Negra loose?" Ovatt sputtered in amused disbelief. "C'mon, boy! No more of this nonsense. We gotta be walking home."

"None of you don't help me," Titus argued, "I'll do it myself—"

"You can't do that!" Kingsbury said. "That Negra's some man's property."

Titus felt himself growing angry as he asked, "Just like he belonged to Annie Christmas, right?"

"Yeah."

"But if you'd had the chance that night, you'd gone and killed that property on the gunboat, wouldn't you?"

"Damn right we would," Reuben growled.

Titus grinned a little. "Ain't a bit of difference to my thinking 'tween you kill a man's property, or you let it go. Either way it ain't his no more."

"What you're talking about's stealing!" Ovatt cried, and was immediately shushed by the others. Quieter, he said, "You just don't steal another man's Negra, like you don't steal his horse, or his cow!"

"We ain't stealing," Bass protested, wagging his head, desperate for some way to make them understand. He pointed at the cage. "We're just letting him out to go off on his own. That don't make us thieves."

Inching up before Bass, Beulah asked, "It true what you said about that big black Negra not killing none of you in that gunboat when he had him the chance't?"

"Ask Kingsbury, any of 'em here," Bass replied. "It's the certain truth."

She turned on the pilot. "Hames, less'n you wanna tell me that the boy here's lying 'bout that gunboat fight—you best get ready to stop me too."

"Stop you?" Kingsbury asked, the pitch of his voice rising. "Stop you from what?"

"From helping Titus here set that there Negra loose."

"Jesus God!" Ovatt screeched, throwing his head back in disgust. "We can't do this! We gotta get outta Natchez afore any folks see us and make for trouble—"

"Shuddup!" Kingsbury interrupted, slapping a hand across Ovatt's chest as he leaned toward the woman. "Listen, Beulah. I ain't setting no darky free what belongs to another man."

"Don't need you," Beulah said. "C'mon, Titus. You got your knife?"

"Yes'm."

"G'won ahead of me," she directed, shooting Kingsbury a scorching look. "I'll be on your backside all the way over yonder to that wagon."

Bass took off, hearing her moccasins scratching the gravel and dry grass as they darted for the wagon. He ground to a halt on that fine-grained, yellowish-brown loam and glanced up at the prisoner, holding a single finger against his lips for silence.

The slave nodded, his eyes growing wide, a sliver of white evident above his chin as his lips pulled back over crooked teeth. Bass yanked his knife free from its scabbard and climbed up the hind, off-side wheel, holding on to the wagon's sidewall to steady himself as he stuffed the knife blade into the old padlock's keyhole. Twisting this way and that so hard he was afraid he would snap off the tip of the blade, he finally turned in frustration.

"Ain't working!" he whispered to the woman.

At that exact moment they heard voices, low and rumbling, around the far side of the tavern. Footsteps on the loose gravel. He dropped from the wheel as the woman slid beneath the wagon bed. Crouching down beside the wagon, Titus glanced up at the slave, frantically motioning him to get down. Instead the black man stared off in the direction of the voices as they hailed one another. One set of steps moved away. And a pair of boots scuffed right toward the wagonyard.

Bass was backing slowly, slowly, still bent at the waist when the voice caught him.

"What the hell are you doing by that goddamned wagon?"

Bass stood, whirled about, realizing the knife was still in his hand. He watched the man's eyes drop to the knife blade gleaming with a dull sheen in the flickering torchlight that continued to hiss in the falling mist. Those eyes began to smile as they climbed back to Titus's face.

"What you figure to do with that knife, son?" He took a step closer. "Hear me talking to you? Asked you what you doing here round my boss's wagons! Up to no damn good, I'll bet." Then his tone of voice changed as he tugged back at his cuffs. "Looks like I'll just have to box your ears, boy—teach you some goddamned propers about staying away from 'nother man's—"

He hadn't seen Beulah roll out on the far side of the wagon, nor had he seen her creep over the tongue and around the far corner of the wagon box. But there she stood now as the white man sank slowly to the icy ground, his eyes rolling back to their whites. Titus winced, sensing how the man's head would be ringing something fierce when he woke up, what with the wallop Beulah gave his head with that piece of firewood.

"Forget that lock," she ordered as she stood breathing heavy over the man who had crumpled near the hind wheel. "Get on up there and break that Negra free." Then she shot the other three boatmen a glance. "All four of you owe this here black-assed son of a savage your lives. Every last one of you."

It was as if they had felt the shaming sting in her harsh whisper like an indictment of their equivocation, maybe even their cowardice. Ovatt, Root, and Kingsbury joined Bass in clambering up beside the cage.

"Get me two big rocks," Kingsbury ordered.

"You gonna smash it?" Reuben asked as he climbed down to gather up the stones from the wagonyard.

"Break it clean off," the pilot answered. When the other two had a large rock held beneath the lock, Kingsbury raised his stone and brought it down with a loud, metallic crash.

"Jesus God! We're gonna get caught for stealin'!" Ovatt cried.

"They'll stretch our necks, Kingsbury!" Root gasped.

"Just hold that goddamned rock right there!" he demanded, bringing his stone up once more and down even more savagely.

The padlock fell free of the hasp with a clatter of metal on wood. Titus lunged between them, dragging the bolt from the hasp and yanking back the narrow cage door. Back in the corner, the slave hesitated.

"C'mon!" Titus yelled, reaching in to pull the black man's arm.

Quickly the big man ducked, sweeping up his black Barcelona hat before turning his shoulders to slip sideways out the cage door. As he squeezed past, Titus saw the long bands of welt and bloody crust striping the slave's back, visible only through the tatters and tears of what had once been a shirt. Those swollen wounds stood out in bold relief against the darker satin finish of the skin.

And numbers. A whole shitload row of numbers tattooed right on the goddamned back of that Negra's shoulder.

Kingsbury was pulling on Beulah's arm, urging her away from the wagon. Ovatt and Root were already halfway back to the corner as Titus heard a groan from the ground. The black man leaped from the wagon and sprinted past Bass. Titus turned, watching the white man groggily pick his face out of the gravel, swipe the tiny stones and mud from his cheek, then shake his head.

Bass brought the stone down on the back of the man's head with a crack loud enough that it seemed to echo from the wall of the tavern. Like an anvil the slaver dropped onto the gravel and icy mud with a grunt, arms sprawled, and lay still, his chest slowly rising and falling.

Bass stared a moment at the man, then looked at the others frantically signaling him on. Dropping the stone beside the slaver as if it had suddenly grown too hot to hold, Bass darted at a crouch for the shadows. When he reached the group, he felt his right hand yanked up, gripped as if between two fine-grained slabs of second-growth hickory, and squeezed in a vise as it was pumped. The others stepped back as the slave brought Bass's arm up and down, up and down.

"Just like white men do, this shake," he said, beaming. "Me thank. Me thank, so shake with you. You make me not go to Miss'ippi."

Kingsbury came between them, gently prying Bass's hand from the slave's. "That's fine now. Shoo, boy. Just be on your way."

"I go your way," he said, turning back to gaze at Bass.

"Oh-h-h-h, no, you ain't!" Root snarled.

"Just tell him you gotta be on your way, Titus," Ovatt implored.

"We . . . I gotta be going," Bass said.

The bald-headed slave remained steadfast, reaching out for Bass again. "Me go with you."

Kingsbury clamped his hands around the black man's wrists, saying, "We ain't going to Nawlins."

"Good." And he jutted his chin. "Never like Nawlins no good."

"And where we're heading, we sure as hell can't take you!" Ovatt added.

"G'won, now," the pilot demanded. "You're free, and you better be long gone afore that white man comes to with a lump on his head and finds you gone."

Kingsbury grabbed Titus by one arm, the woman taking the other as Ovatt and Root led the way, all of them looking back over their shoulder at the big black shadow standing there at the corner of Kings Tavern as they hurried into the brush and timber for the trailhead of the Natchez Trace.

Bass watched the man's eyes as he hustled off, how red-rimmed they were despite the blackness of the flesh. Then he realized that the Negra had to have his own feelings. Likely he had cried in anger and frustration at first, what with being sold off and put away in that cage like he was. Then those tears eventually changed to slow, sad ones as he felt his world closing in, and him shut off from the rest of it, torn away from friends and family, separated from everything he had come to know and understand over his short time in this white man's world.

And as he watched that black face disappear in the shadows behind him, along with the cold curl of the slave's breathsmoke and the spitting-hiss of those torches outside Kings Tavern at the far edge of Natchez-Under-the-Hill, Bass figured he knew just how that felt.

By damn, he knew how it felt to have his own world ripped inside out.

From the Mississippi River the Natchez Trace pointed roughly in a northeasterly direction toward Tennessee for close to six hundred miles through Choctaw and Chickasaw country, ending up on the Cumberland River at a place called French Lick, in the last few years come to be known as Nashville.

Some early-day historians were already claiming this was the oldest road in the world, originally used by the beasts to cross ridges and rivers and high-flowing streams; later followed by the Indians who came tracking those flesh-bearing animals, long, long before the Romans ever dreamed of their famous Appian Way. Here in Mississippi country it was often known as the Chickasaw Trace. The Choctaw Path was the name given to the southern end, while the new American government, which had in mind to use the road in moving its mails, gave the Trace a grand and imperially democratic title: the Columbian Highway.

For Titus Bass and the rest who fled north into the wilderness that cold and misty night in December of 1810, there was nothing remotely grand nor glorious about the prospect of making their way on foot through the swamps and bayous, fording streams and ice-clogged rivers, ascending countless ridges and stumbling down countless more valleys, hoping they did not freeze at night, nor fall prey to any of the beasts, savages, nor white predators who murdered and robbed all along that narrow footpath pointing the way north—home.

Indeed, more so in the latter part of the eighteenth century than now, it had acquired the reputation of a robber's road, a thoroughfare of the hunter and the hunted, prey and predator. Thrilling stories and splendid myths had already built up concerning the gruesome exploits of famous highwaymen along the Natchez Trace. The sort of brigands who painted their faces with berry juice and bark stain to appear like rogue Indians, for just often enough had the Chickasaw and Creek in fact swept down to make their raids on the long men and lean women who plied that lonely road.

All too often only a circling buzzard called attention to the fate of other, less fortunate travelers. Because they dared not leave evidence of their bloody crimes, some of the more barbaric of thieves ripped open the bodies of their victims, tore out the entrails, and filled the cavities with rocks to sink all evidence of their black deeds beneath the placid waters of the swamps and bayous. What with an alarming number of murders and short list of cele-brated outlaws, by the 1790s the road was commonly known as the "Devil's Backbone."

Most everyone on the frontier was a sojourner in those days, pilgrims all: traders and tinkers, medicine peddlers and missionaries, contract mail carriers and even an occasional settler on the tramp south to find richer soil. And always, always there were the Kentucky flatboatmen. Few if any were ever compelled to cordelle and warp their boats back up the Mississippi and Ohio, against the mighty current. Instead, with their cargo auctioned and their transportation sold by the board, the Kentuckians found themselves again afoot, staring at the prospect of a long walk home before they would begin to make plans for another float downriver.

Even young Tom Lincoln from Kentucky had made his trip to New Orleans back in 1806, then plied his way back home on foot, vowing never to return to such a wicked wilderness. He kept his promise, found himself a wife, and began to raise a family—the father of Abraham, the hickory-thin rail-splitter.

By the end of that first decade of the nineteenth century, the road pirates were all but a part of the past—no longer anything more than scary stories used to frighten young children in their beds on a dark and stormy night. Most boatmen returning home from their long trek downriver did so without giving a thought to any real danger from banditti. While a few took north a fat purse, most came back to the Ohio River country homesick and footsore. The hapless handful might well take north the bitter fruit of their bawdy frolics with the many-hued whores: blindness and idiocy for their offspring.

That first day on the trail after leaving the fertile, loess bluffs at Natchez, Titus proved his worth to the rest by bagging a fat turkey cock then out in search of his own meal. They took turns plucking the bird then and there that afternoon beside the worn footpath, building a fire to warm their cold, wet selves as night came down and the sounds of the wilderness began to swell around them.

"We're in Choctaw land now," Kingsbury explained. "Been past some of their villages a time or two walking north. I knowed 'em to strap small bags of sand onto the heads of their babes to make 'em flat."

Beulah placed her hand on her forehead. "They think that makes their skulls pretty?"

Indeed, the Natchez Trace penetrated the heart of what had once been a great wilderness ruled only by tribes warring over disputed territory. For centuries the route had been no more than a buffalo trail when the Choctaw, Chickasaw, and Cherokee came to blaze their own short woodland paths that took a man from the shellfish shore of the Mississippi to salt licks of steamy woodlands, past river and stream and hunting ground until the tribes eventually joined each small section to form the great road.

It wasn't until their third night out of Natchez at their camp on the Bayou Pierre River that the slave finally worked up enough courage to slip up on their camp and show himself at the far edge of the firelight.

"Figured you was out there," Kingsbury stated in a matter-of-fact tone as the black man emerged from the shadows.

When they all wheeled about, Titus nearly jumped out of his skin at the sudden sight of the slave. Staring up at him now, just as he had gazed up at him in that cage on the wagon, Titus thought the Negro seemed all the taller. Almost like a huge, ebony monolith.

"What the hell you doing, Negra?" Root growled, finding his voice after the fright the slave's surprise appearance had given him.

The man eyed the butchered carcass of a white-tailed deer, his hand across his belly. "Hungry."

"Ain't got nothing for you!" Heman Ovatt snapped. "Just get on with yourself and be gone!"

"Here," Titus said, standing on shaking legs. "I'll share what I got with you."

The others fell silent as Bass stepped toward the slave, holding out his tin cup. In it steamed hunks of venison and broth.

Snapping that two-cornered Barcelona hat from his head, he performed a quick bow, then snatched the cup from Bass and brought it to his face, where he sucked its contents down ravenously.

"There's more here," Beulah said, passing over what she had left of her portion.

As he ate, the boatmen argued over the slave's fate as if the man weren't even there, or at the very least completely deaf.

"Mebbeso we can sell him up to home," Root suggested eagerly. "Big Negra like him—sure to fetch us a lot a money."

"What the hell you need with more money, Reuben Root?" the woman demanded.

"Leastwise, it'd pay for what he'll eat on the journey!" Kingsbury replied.

"You all sound like addleheaded fools," Beulah scolded. She laid a hand on Titus's shoulder. "It's the young'un here feeding the lot of you. Ain't costing you a damn thing."

"Then I say we leave him," Ovatt grumbled. "Can't sell him—he ain't gonna be worth nothing to us."

"Don't you remember? We already tried leaving him," Kingsbury said. "You see what that got us."

"Maybeso we can tie him up till someone else comes along and finds him."

"No!" Titus said a little too loudly. The other three and the slave all turned in his direction, freezing in place. "No. You won't want that done to you. A man tied up, he can't protect hisself from the wild critters in these here woods."

"Boy's right," Beulah agreed, rising to a crouch to ladle more of the venison soup from the brass kettle into the slave's cup. "You'll just have to figure out something else. You fellas are so damned smart, ought'n be real easy."

With the way the disgruntled Root and Ovatt glared at Kingsbury as if to tell him to do something—and quick—about that sassy woman, the pilot could only shrug in helplessness.

Bass watched the slave suck at the stew, chewing up the big morsels of meat with his huge teeth. At each gust of cruel wind which sliced through that shirt torn to ribbons, the black man shivered, doing his best to cradle the tin cup in both hands to keep it from sloshing. Not knowing what prompted him to, Titus dragged up one of his blankets and draped it around the slave's shoulders. Those huge white eyes in that shiny black face looked up at him in the middle of chewing a bite. A look of stunned gratitude crossed the man's face as Bass turned back to his place by the fire.

"Then there ain't nothing else we can do but we send him back," Ovatt said.

"That ain't no better'n trying to leave him," Kingsbury argued.

"If we ain't gonna send him back, or leave him—I got me an idea," Reuben declared. "I say we take him north—"

"We ain't taking him north!" Ovatt repeated.

"I'm telling you we ought'n take him north and *sell* him!" Root declared.

The woman settled beside the youth. "How you feel about that, Titus?"

"Why you asking him?" Kingsbury demanded.

"I figure the Negra belongs to Titus—"

"That buck Negra belongs to him?" Ovatt whined.

Reuben snorted. "Craziest thing I ever heard of!"

Beulah paid them no heed and continued, "Belongs to Titus because Titus is the one busted the Negra free." Turning back to the youth, she repeated, "How's that set with you? Taking him north to Kentucky where you can sell him."

For some time he stared at the fire, then looked at the slave, then back to the flames again, rolling it over and over in his mind. At that moment he regretted not paying more attention to his schooling, figuring it might well have given him the capacity to resolve his dilemma. Finally, Bass said, "I ain't got no place to take him I get back there."

"You got a home," Root disagreed.

"Not no more," Titus said, fearful of the responsibility. "I'm going to Louisville."

"Take him with you," Kingsbury said.

Wagging his head, unable to sort it all out, Bass admitted, "Don't wanna take no Negra slave 'long with me."

"Then you just sell him when we get back to the Ohio country and be done with it," Ovatt suggested.

"I . . . I don't rightly know how I feel about that."

Root asked, "Ain't your people got any slaves?"

"No. My family ain't never had any. Work the land all ourselves . . . all by themselves."

"Maybe they can use a slave now," Kingsbury tried to add cheerfully.

"Said I ain't going back home," Titus told them firmly. "I don't want no slave. Can't use him."

"Sell him!"

"No!" Titus snapped at Root, his fist clenching in frustration.

"He's just a god-bleemed Negra—"

"He's a person!" Titus interrupted.

All three boatmen erupted in roars of laughter.

Kingsbury said, "This Negra? A person? Listen, son—that's money sitting right there. Like a good milch cow. Or a breeding stud. Just look at him! He'll bring you top dollar. Every planter from here to Kentucky'll wanna get his hands on him to breed with their Negra bitches. Have 'em strong li'l suckers to do the fieldwork in the years to come."

"Said I ain't gonna sell him."

"Then we'll sell him for you," Root said.

"He ain't yours," Titus snapped. "He belongs to me."

"So what the hell are you gonna do with him?" Beulah asked.

"I s'pose I'll turn him loose."

"He'll just follow us . . . till some law catches him."

Titus was worried again. "Then what?"

"If they don't kill him while'st running him down, they'll sell him off," Kingsbury said. "No two ways about it, the man's going for money, even if you turn him loose."

" 'Cept if you make him a freedman," Beulah suggested.

All four men turned to her, stunned. Then Titus looked at the slave. "A freedman?"

"That means you let him go legal, so he ain't no man's slave no more," she explained. "Means he's on his own from there on out."

Turning now to the stranger in their midst, Titus asked in a quiet voice, "You wanna be free to go your own way?"

He smiled. "Go with you."

Wagging his head, Titus explained, "No man's slave. Go where you wanna go, on your own."

The yellowed eyes slowly widened, as if he were struggling to make sense of it in his mind, translating, forming words like sturdy nets to capture the concepts.

"Me come across the big water . . . way down river," he started. "Big boat. Big boat many die. Me so sick come to river. Down in Orlins Town they sell me to Annie. She learn me fix whiskey, rum, brandy too. Help Annie's women. I not help Annie's women, she sell me. You take me now. Me go with you."

"Not no more," Titus replied adamantly. "Free man."

"Go home?" he asked the youth.

"That's across the ocean," Beulah answered. "Too far. You can go anywhere, make a new life for yourself."

"Go work anybody else now?"

"No," Titus said, sensing the warmth of something spreading inside his chest. What it was, he could not put a name to. "Work for you . . . what, do you have a name?"

"Hezekiah, she name me."

Beulah asked, "Your mama?"

"No. My mama far away," Hezekiah said sadly, his eyes misting as he stared off into the night. "She die when men come to village and take all people to big boat. Chains."

Titus asked, "Who give you the name Hezekiah?"

"Annie give me."

"Then that's what your name's gonna be," Titus declared. "Hezekiah Christmas."

A broad smile brightened the slave's face like a crack in burnt, blackened wood. "Like Annie name. Christmas."

"You like it?" Bass inquired.

"Like it, yes. Hezekiah Christmas."

His mind burned with possibilities as he said, "Now, soon as we get someplace where I can have folks write us up a paper says I'm freeing you, from then on you'll be a free man."

"Goddamned shame," Root grumbled. "Negra buck like him'd brung us his weight in coins, I'd wager."

"Just hope he ain't gonna be trouble to us," Kingsbury grumped.

"He ain't," Titus vowed, hoping it was a promise he could keep.

"That's a long goddamned walk," Ovatt said.

"He'll help out," Bass explained, then looked at the slave. "Pay for his keep."

Hezekiah nodded, handing his empty cup to Beulah.

"You done?" she asked.

"More?"

Beulah smiled and took his cup to lean over the kettle. "My, but you are a hungry one."

"Just look at the size of him," Ovatt said almost under his breath. "Bet he eats as much as a goddamned plowhorse."

North by east they pushed on the following morning, making for the Choctaw Agency on the Pearl River,* the heart of the Choctaw nation.

Only nine years before, General James Wilkinson had concluded a

---

* Present-day site of Jackson, Mississippi.

treaty between the tribes and the federal government that would allow passage through their lands. Four years later in 1805 the tribes agreed to establish and maintain a handful of settlements along the trail. While the first leg of the journey north from New Orleans to Natchez was one of relative ease due in large part to the frequent and comfortable way stations, once on the Natchez Trace, however, the "stands," as those half-dozen wilderness way stations were known across the next six hundred miles, were something altogether different: really nothing more than a few ramshackle cabins and tumbledown huts offering the crudest accommodations. Not a single town in all that distance. Only three Indian villages, a ferry at the Tennessee River, and two squaw men's cabins provided the only measure of civilization and company in that wilderness.

While the Trace did indeed serve as a mail route and was of some small military purpose for the infant nation, it remained of limited commercial importance. From the time of the Revolution until the coming of the steamboat—which one day soon would easily push its way upstream against the might of the Mississippi and the Ohio—the Natchez Trace was primarily a route for returning flatboatmen. Coming downriver, theirs had been a journey by shoal and suck and thunderous rapids. Walking north would present a man far different perils.

"Ain't near so bad making for home in wintertime like it is," Heman Ovatt said at their night fire several days later. "Summer's trip be the one what can kill a man with bad water, the fever and malaria, and all sorts of other bloody fluxes."

"Mosquitoes and gnats," Reuben Root joined in. "In that sticky heat they'll suck your blood and make you so sick you wish you was dead."

"Them's the only things you don't have to worry about come winter like this," Beulah snorted. "But going north, you're still bound to run into poisonous snakes—the likes of cottonmouths and copperheads."

"Only on the warm days," Kingsbury advised.

"I know 'nough 'bout 'em," Titus replied. "Sunny days you just gotta be watchful for the places them snakes is out to lay around and warm themselves."

Root trembled as if cold water had been poured on him. "What I don't like is them panthers crying in the night out there. Sounds just like a woman, wailing for help."

Night after night it had been the same for Titus. Awakened from a fitful sleep by the cries from all manner of shapeless creatures out there in the dark. He'd lie wide-eyed for the longest time, his back slid up to Hezekiah's, hoping to share their warmth and Bass's two blankets, as he listened to the night-things come into voice out there in the swamp.

Day after day it was to be the same for them as well. Up before first light to chew on the cold remains of last night's supper as they rolled their blankets, tied their few belongings over their shoulders, then trudged on across the frosty bayous and skirted the great, stagnant pools encircling the base of each cypress tree, intent on covering as much ground as they could, what with the few hours of daylight the winter granted them.

Every morning the others let Titus lead off, followed closely by the runaway slave. Kingsbury would follow with the others after a few minutes, wanting to assure that they would not frighten off any of the game Bass might run across throughout the day. Most evenings Titus provided fresh game for Beulah to cook over their supper fire. But every now and then they failed to hear a gunshot as twilight came down and the temperature dropped. It was then they would have to content themselves with what they had saved of last's night meal and hope that something would cross the youngster's path come the morrow.

Far beyond the Natchez District they emerged from the interminable bayou, at the edge of which stood the Chickasaw Agency,* where the foot-path grew worse. Below their feet the soil had become gravelly, eating away at their boots, chewing up Titus's moccasins, requiring nightly repairs and patching.

"They call this part of the road 'the Barrens,' " Ovatt declared that first night the landscape changed so drastically. "From here on out to Tennessee, the trail gets a mite rough."

Bass poked at a blister on his heel with the point of his knife and asked, "Can't imagine how it's gonna get any worse."

The following day they reached what most travelers considered the halfway point of the Natchez Trace: McIntoshville, named for an early Scottish trader who had come to the Chickasaw to trade but stayed on to father his own dynasty. More commonly known as Tockshish Stand† to the tribe and travelers alike, the village lay some 310 miles from Natchez—the first such village a wayfarer passed in all that distance from the Mississippi. Not another sign of civilization, not one mail carrier, merchant, or party of traders.

From Tockshish the path did grow worse, threading in and out from

---

* Present-day site of Houston, Mississippi.

† Present-day site of Tupelo, Mississippi.

open woods to sparse sections of inhospitable prairie as the ground rose, becoming more bushy and broken as they ascended the divide that would take them to the Tennessee River, still eighty miles beyond. Up, then down, the Trace led Titus through that unforgiving wilderness, as he listened through each short day only to the sound of his moccasins on the pounded earth, perhaps the haunting crackle of the dried cane as it shook, troubled by the winter wind.

There were times Titus stopped—not so much to rest his feet or to catch his breath—but for no other reason than to turn around and listen, hoping to catch the sound of Hezekiah coming up the trail behind him, or to turn around atop a hill and look back, hoping to spot the boatmen and Beulah, plodding along beneath the cold, gray, monotonous sky that each day offered them.

Already December was growing old. Just how old, he had no way of knowing for certain. The way things looked now, he might well be seeing in the new year still caught in this wilderness. A new year, and with it his seventeenth birthday. That afternoon he knocked a turkey cock out of its roost in the bare branches of a beechnut tree. While it wasn't the finest feast he had provided them, the meal filled their bellies as the gloom of winter's night closed its fist around them.

"We should be drawing close to the Tennessee," Ovatt declared as he picked his teeth and wriggled his feet close by the fire's warmth that night.

"Keep your eye peel't tomorry," Kingsbury said, turning to Bass. "The trail takes you down to the river crossing."

Titus asked, "We gonna have to ford it?"

"Time was, a riverman had to ford it," Kingsbury replied. "Not no longer. Years back a Scotch feller named Colbert come to trade among the Chickasaws and saw him the chance to make a nice living."

"King of the roost, that one is now," Root added.

Kingsbury nodded. "Married into the tribe, built him his ferry, and set himself up right nice."

Ovatt rubbed his hands together, teeth gleaming in the firelight. "Got him a mess of handsome daughters too!"

"Half-breeds they are," Root explained with a wink.

"Still as handsome a woman as you're likely to meet along the trail," Ovatt declared, then suddenly turned to Beulah. "Pardon me, ma'am. Not meaning that you ain't a handsome woman . . . just, that—well, considering you and Kingsbury, see?"

She grinned and dropped her eyes. "I took me no offense, Heman."

Then turned to Bass. "You just watch yourself there at Colbert's Ferry, Titus. Them half-breed girls got Injun blood in 'em, and there's no telling what they'll do when they see a likely young man such as you come round."

"M-me?"

"Yes, you," Beulah said. "Don't you go and run off into the woods with none of 'em."

"They'll just as soon slit your throat as wet your honey-dauber," Root grumbled. Then apologized: "I'm sorry, ma'am. It's me and my awful manners again."

"What Reuben says is right," the woman explained. "They're the sort won't think twice 'bout lifting a man's purse or knocking him over the head for his money. They ain't looking for your hand in marriage."

"D-daughters," Titus repeated, sensing that sudden animal urge cross his loins with a delicious electricity.

"Least seven or eight," Kingsbury declared. "Less'n Papa Colbert's married any of 'em off since't last summer when we was through here."

"Why would he go an' do a fool thing like that?" Root demanded. "Them girls is the best he's got to offer—'sides that river ferry."

"Reuben's right," Ovatt agreed. "Men on the Trace allays look forrad to talking with them girls, dancing some with 'em, after hunnerds of miles of no womankind to speak of."

"Wenches is what they are," the woman said. "The devil's own hand-maidens."

"Did you say dancing?" Titus asked, staring off into the distance.

Why, he had never been allowed to dance before. As much as music made his feet move, his folks had for all those years enforced a strong proscription against dancing during every visit to the Longhunters Fair, where he had always contented himself watching others jig and clog, reel and waltz to the merry music.

"Ah, hell," Beulah groaned as she glanced over to find that faraway look in the youngster's eyes. "Looks like we already lost this'un to that devil Colbert's half-breed daughters!"

SIXTEEN

The more Titus looked over those young half-breed Colbert women, the more he realized these dusky-skinned maidens of the wilderness appealed to him.

Something about the high, pronounced cheekbones not only seemed a deeper rose in contrast to the rest of their facial color, but also accented those big almond-shaped eyes. Dark as rain-polished chert, large and expressive, doelike in the way they took his measure. And every last one of those five daughters knew how to use those eyes on their male visitors to their advantage, every one of them—from the oldest at nineteen down to the youngest just turned twelve. None had taken after their mother, a squat, rotund woman; it seemed all had their father's blood when it came to the matter of height: even the youngest already taller than her pear-shaped mama.

When Titus and the rest reached that point on the trail where the Natchez Trace emerged from the timber on the side of the hill overlooking the river crossing, they could see family patriarch George Colbert working with two of the girls beside their big cabin below.

"That's Colbert's Stand," Heman Ovatt announced as the entire party came to a halt and looked down at the clearing, which extended to the river's edge, that large cabin joined by a small barn and four huts all clustered around an open yard.

"Seems he's got two of 'em chopping wood for him," Reuben Root declared, his flat hand shading his eyes. The afternoon sun was just then slipping out of the belly of the low clouds—its first appearance in more than three days.

"The man's got the kind of help I could use," Kingsbury said, then quickly glanced over to find Beulah glaring at him. "I mean to say—"

"I know damned well what you meant," she growled in a huff.

"Let's go get us some victuals," Reuben suggested, going around Titus and Hezekiah on the worn trail, starting off down the last fifty yards of slope that would take them to the cleared, open ground where stood Colbert's Ferry.

By the time the boatmen reached the packed earth of that great yard, George Colbert stood waiting to greet them—flanked by his wife and all their daughters, in addition to three young men, all in their early twenties.

Down there Titus finally saw the large main cabin was in fact two smaller cabins that stood some fifteen feet apart. Each had its own door facing the yard, as well as a door that fed into a covered hallway or dog run, which joined the two. Both roofs sprouted an unusually large chimney, although a trail of gray smoke billowed from only one at this hour. It was plain to see that in places the logs fit tightly together; in others there was as much as four inches in gap where they had been chinked with wood chips held in place with dried clay. Like most cabins on the frontier, Colbert's had planed oak doors—hung without a single piece of hardware in evidence. Instead, they were held together with pegged cross braces and swung on wooden hinges.

Even as cold as it was, three of the girls stood in the damp breeze that afternoon without benefit of jerkin or coat. One by one Titus quickly appraised each one from the corner of his eye as Kingsbury and Colbert discussed the terms of their lodging for the night—finding that it excited him to see how those cold, hardened nipples pressed against their blouses. Three of the five wore long skirts gathered at the waist beneath wide, colorful sashes. But the two who most captured Titus's admiring attention preferred men's britches. Never before had he seen a woman wear a man's clothing.

"What ye want done with your Negra for the night?" asked Scottish-born George Colbert, his brogue heavy with the mist of the moors.

Kingsbury turned and regarded Hezekiah for a moment, seeming to cogitate on it until Bass grabbed the bald man's arm and declared, "He stays with us."

"That right?" Colbert turned from the youngster to gaze at Kingsbury. "The Negra staying with ye?"

"I s'pose—"

Colbert suggested, "I can have my boys see to him: lock him in one of the cabins, or we can tie him up outside."

"L-like he was no more'n a dog?" Titus demanded.

Appearing taken aback by the brassy youngster, Colbert rocked on his heels, saying, "Why, lad—he's barely more'n a animal himself. An' ye don't want him running off while the bunch of you're sleeping, now—do ye?"

"He'll stay with me," Titus protested, glaring at the Scotsman.

Kingsbury nodded with a shrug. "The Negra stays with us."

"Suit yourself," Colbert replied with a raise of one disapproving eyebrow. He turned to point at the two huts directly across the yard from the cabins. "Them two. C'mon—I'll show ye where the woman can stay. And the men can stay in the cabin aside her."

"I'll sleep in with them," Beulah said, glancing at Hames.

"Now, that's up to the bunch of ye. I only be offering the woman a private place of her own."

"We'll take the two cabins," Kingsbury said firmly, glancing quickly at Beulah. "The rest can bunk in together, and I can allays bunk in with the woman here—making sure she feels safe, having someone around at night."

"Like I said before: suit yourself. Them two the best cabins we got. Bear robes and grass pallets to lay your wee bodies down tonight. Won't find nothing softer, all the way down to Natchez." Colbert turned to wave away his eight offspring, saying to them, "Ye children know what needs doing—now, be off and do it. Look yonder," and he pointed. "Seems we got folks coming down to the landing on t'other side."

With the rest Titus peered across the Tennessee River to the north shore where a half-dozen mounted men appeared from the timber and came to a halt by the water's edge where Colbert had cleared away the brush and graded the bank to form a landing for his ferry.

"I'll be off to see these fellows across," he explained. "Ye make yourselves at home in those first two cabins."

"They're brazen women," Beulah murmured a moment later when Colbert had turned away to march down to join his sons poling the ferry across the river toward the waiting horsemen. Ovatt, Root, and Titus ducked inside the first of the two small huts, while Hezekiah stood outside and waited dutifully. Kingsbury and Beulah went to inspect the other. Each structure stood some ten feet square, and like the main cabins were constructed of chinked logs.

"Least there's a fire pit in the corner, and a hole up over it in them shakes on the roof," Kingsbury commented minutes later as he emerged into the fading sunlight to find Titus waiting beside Hezekiah, with that two-cornered cap of black silk twill perched upon the slave's bald head. The pilot turned to the woman, asking, "What you mean they're brazen women?"

"Them Colbert girls: they get more daring with their eyes every time I come through here," Beulah clucked. "Did you see the way they held themselves for all you men to gander?"

"One thing I'm sure of—Titus here saw all he wanted to," Kingsbury said with a grin and a wink in Bass's direction.

They peered down the low bank to the ferry, which was just then reaching the far side. One of the young men on board leaped onto the bank as the flatboat came close enough, carrying a long hawser over his shoulder, which he looped round and round a tree stump, tying up to take on passengers.

Kingsbury laid an arm over Beulah's shoulder without a complaint from her.

Heman Ovatt said, "What daughters Colbert ain't married off likely make him a good living—sold out by the night to keep travelers warm."

"Just like a livery owner," the woman said under her breath.

"He do that?" Titus asked innocently.

"Shit," Kingsbury grumbled. "There you two go, giving this youngster the wrong ideas. No, Titus—I don't think his girls are whores."

"They're just as brazen as them poxy trollops what work that gunboat you boys raided at Natchez," Beulah replied.

The pilot scoffed at that. "Now, you all been by here enough to know Colbert makes a good 'nough living on that ferry of his 'thout putting his own daughters out like common lay-down women."

"Damned pretty, ain't they, Titus?" Root strode up from the other dirt-floored hut.

"Glass windows and a glass pane in every door," Beulah clucked, turning to regard the cabins again. "I should say this family's making a fine living off travelers like us."

"I'd rather pay my fifty cents and ride over on his goddamned ferry," Kingsbury retorted, "than ever again have to ford the Tennessee on foot in the winter."

"Or summer," Heman agreed.

"For the devil!" Root exclaimed. "With the money I'm carrying, sure as hell I'd sink like a rock."

"The man's due what he's got, Beulah," Kingsbury tried soothing her. "He come out here to the wilderness many a year ago to trade with the Chickasaws in these parts—an' he's worked hard for everything he's got him today."

"Looks like the man married smart, though," the woman said sourly.

"Who put the goddamned bee under your bonnet?" Hames said, wagging his head. "The tribes got 'em a treaty says if full-bloods don't run the stands, then only half-breeds and squaw men like Colbert can make their living on Injun land." Kingsbury turned away to regard the last of the six riders urging his skittish horse onto the ferry. Hames quickly patted the waistband of his canvas britches, saying, "Can't ever blame a man for wanting to get enough money ahead to make life easier for hisself, now—can you, Beulah?"

"See there," Root said. "He's just made himself six dollars, bringing over them riders and their horses."

Beulah squinted at the landing in the fading light. "Who you s'pose pushing south on the Trace this time of year?"

They all turned their attention to the ferry heaving away from the north bank beneath the thick rope strung from shore to shore, each end attached to a great tree on either bank, while the ferry itself was hooked to that rope with another that slid along it, which prevented the flat, unwieldy craft from being swept downriver by the force of the Tennessee's current.

"Maybe just some folks looking to find some warmer weather," Kingsbury commented with a shudder as a biting wind came up. "C'mon, fellas. Let's get us some of that wood took inside afore they call us all to supper."

While most stands along the Natchez Trace offered both bed and board for the night, which included a supper of such questionable taste that it was guaranteed to deaden even the hungriest man's appetite, Colbert's Stand was a different matter altogether. Over time the old man's squaw had learned something about the proper feeding of a white man from her Scottish husband, combining that knowledge with her native Chickasaw recipes. Although the family patriarch had gone so far as to nail down a rough-hewn puncheon floor in the family's sleeping cabin, the floor in the combination kitchen-dining room was in no way fancier than the floors of those sleeping huts provided their guests: bare earth pounded as smooth and solid as any clay tile beneath thousands of feet across the years.

"I'll pay you good money for that Negra of yours," one of the horsemen offered over a dinner of white beans and corn cakes, some slabs of salted pork simmered in the beans for a hearty flavor.

"Not selling," Kingsbury replied around a mouthful of the savory beans.

"Ain't you 'fraid that Negra's gonna run off on you?" asked another of the horsemen as he swabbed his corn cake across the bottom of the wooden trencher to soak up the last of his bean juice.

"He ain't the kind tends to run off," Titus answered testily this time, then dragged the back of his hand across his mouth. He pushed his trencher back, finished with supper, although he did hunger for another cup of that coffee, especially if it would be poured by any one of those smiling, doe-eyed half-breed Colbert girls. He wasn't the only one giving his eager attention to the old Scotsman's daughters—what with those six horsemen hungrily sizing them up. He raised his cup, signaling the pair nearest the huge kitchen fireplace.

"All Negras gonna run off," the first man said with a slit-eyed smile on his lips. There was an angry fire in those eyes.

"James here oughtta know," a third horseman spoke up for the first time, indicating that first speaker with a thumb. "He's 'bout the best man-hunter there is in this country."

"Man-hunter?" Ovatt asked.

The second horseman nodded, saying, "We all of us hunt down runaways. Make a pretty fair living by it, we do."

Now James spoke again. "Always plenty of work for us, you see. Lots of folks pay a good reward for bringing back a runaway Negra."

Kingsbury finished a swallow of coffee and asked, "Why'll folks pay you such good money just to get one Negra back?"

James held up his cup, signaling the daughter filling Titus's. "It ain't just the one Negra that may happen to run away from a man's plantation that causes worry for that owner. It's all the others still back at his place, you must understand." He set his full cup down and adjusted the pair of huge horse pistols he carried in the wide woven sash tied around his waist.

"All the others," the second man repeated for emphasis.

"We're talking about a lot of money," James continued. "Because if that plantation owner doesn't get back that one runaway Negra—chances are damned bloody good some of the rest are going to try running off too."

"And no rich plantation owner wants that to happen," added the third talkative horseman.

"That's why rich land barons will pay such good money to get back just one poor Negra what dreams his foolish dreams of freedom," James said with a wry grin. "So my men here and me afford to drink the finest whiskey, we smoke the best cigars, and lay with the best whores . . . pardon me, ladies, for my thoughtless tongue. We work hard for our money, and the money is very, very good."

"Bet you're tracking some Negra now, ain'cha?" Ovatt asked.

"You're a smart fellow, boatman," James said after he drank some of his coffee. "I'm being paid well right now as we speak. A man by the name of Lewis Robards—biggest slave trader in Mercer County, Kentucky." Then he smiled immensely, saying, "Tell me, was your journey south a successful one?"

Kingsbury's eyes touched his crew, then he answered, "Same as any year. But prices for near everything are down. Hard to make much of a fair living anymore. Not nowhere near the money you fellas make in your line of work."

"I'm sure you're not going north empty-handed," James commented with a disarming smile. "Enough perhaps to build you another Kentucky boat, to load it with goods for another trip south. That's always the way of things for rivermen, isn't it, now?"

"The way it's s'pose to work ain't allays the way it does work," Kingsbury replied.

"We run onto some trouble in Natchez." Beulah suddenly entered the conversation. "This crew can be foolish a'times—not ones to walk away from a real hoot of a celebration. They tore up a gunboat and dramshop."

James leaned his elbows on the table, slit eyes narrowing even more. "What's that got to do with—"

"To get these boys out of that miserable jail," the woman explained, "they had to pay a judge practically all we made for the trip—just for the damages their spree cost 'em."

"And vow we wouldn't show our faces back in Natchez for a year," Kingsbury added, taking up Beulah's fanciful story.

"A full goddamned year," Root echoed dolefully.

"Not much a man can do, is there?" James asked. "When he gets thrown out of a town—a real shame. You fellas must be hellions."

"Regular ring-tailed swamp panthers," Kingsbury boasted. "Every last one of this crew is half horse, half alligator."

"Even the young'un here?" asked the second horseman, pointing at Titus with the knife onto which he was scooping the last of his beans.

"Him? Oh, he just got his first trip down under the belt," Kingsbury answered. "He might have the makings for a riverman."

"As for the Negra?" James inquired. "What you plan on doing with him?"

"Told you," Titus snapped, banging his coffee cup down on the plank table. "He ain't for selling."

His face hardening, James turned to Kingsbury. "I'm sure as leader of this group, you are the sort who recognizes a good offer when you see one."

"What you talking about?" the pilot asked.

"I'm certain I can sell that Negra for a good dollar," James instructed. "In fact, I know plantation owners who would snatch him right up for top dollar tomorrow—and all I'd have to do is show up with that big buck in tow."

"Tell him he's wasting his breath," Titus growled at Kingsbury.

Grim-lipped, the river pilot replied, "The Negra belongs to the young'un here. So if'n he says he ain't for sale, he ain't for sale."

The cool smile returned to James's face as he leaned closer to the table, rocking on both elbows, clunking the big curved butts of those flintlock pistols against the tabletop. "I'm sorry to hear that, my good man. Since your trading venture downriver in New Orleans didn't turn out very well and you spent nearly everything you had just to get out of Natchez—why, I was certain you might be interested in turning a quick and tidy profit on that Negra out there."

"We ain't talking about this no more, Kingsbury," Titus snarled angrily as he stood, pushed back his end of the bench, and stepped over it. He moved to the open doorway, which allowed fresh air into the heated kitchen, then stopped before he would move into the splash of torchlight just beyond the dining room.

"You heard him," Hames repeated. He turned to Beulah, saying, "I s'pose we ought'n be off to bed now. Morning will come awful early."

James leaned back, pulling from inside his shirt a buckskin pouch he had hanging around his neck. From it he pulled a thick cigar. "Traveling in a hurry, are you?"

"Winter's coming strong," Kingsbury said. "Want to cover ground. January be here afore too long."

"Tomorrow, in fact."

Titus turned in the doorway. "Tomorrow? It's January?"

"A new year, lad. The first of 1811," James said. "Which makes this a night for us all to celebrate and fittingly frolic—to see in the new year in proper fashion."

"My birthday," Bass said quietly.

"Your birthday, is it?" Beulah exclaimed. "Why, yes! We ought to all celebrate that, even if we don't celebrate the coming of the new year!"

Turning to the proprietor seated in his cane-backed chair beside the fireplace, James declared, "Mr. Colbert, be good enough to bring us your finest libations—whiskey, rye, what have you."

The Scottish Colbert bowed graciously, saying, "My wife brewed us a good batch of potato beer not long ago. Perhaps you'd like to give that a try."

"Yes, yes," James replied, stroking one side of his mustache. "Along with any sweets you might have about. And see to it that your daughters stay close until the new year has arrived in all its glory . . . for I'm sure these boatmen love to dance even more than do my men."

Those first hours of the new year brought with them the black belly of midnight as clouds bubbled across the heavens on the heels of distant thunder.

Lying there in that tiny hut with the two boatmen, sharing his blanket with that slave who had skin the color of rich, fertile humus, Titus listened wide-eyed to each celestial peal as it rumbled toward Colbert's Ferry on the Tennessee River. In the throaty dying of every bark of that thunder he heard the raucous laughter of the horsemen as they reveled ever closer to dawn.

Eager to see in his birthday among real grown folk for the first time—especially since Bass fancied himself just as grown-up as the next man—he held out and wearily stayed up well past the ebbing of his own candle. Always before it had been parents and siblings, in later years some visiting friends come from across the county to celebrate that momentous day. They would bunk in and stay over, making for quite a time of it . . . but never anything as bawdy and uproarious as had been the merrymaking that began right after supper when all of them pushed back the long tables and benches, clearing the center of that packed-earth floor while Reuben Root scurried off to fetch his wheezing concertina.

"No matter what them others ask you to do when it comes the new year," Kingsbury warned in a hush against Bass's ear as everyone else hurried here and there, "don't go showing 'em your guns."

"M-my guns? What're you talking—"

"Keep 'em hid, Titus. Better that way."

"Why's it better?"

The others had drawn too close for more talk then. "Just better we don't ever have to find out."

It wasn't long before Heman Ovatt purloined a pair of pewter spoons, which he clacked against thigh, knee, and elbow, while one of the horsemen produced a jaw harp, and George Colbert pulled out his Tennessee mouthbow, both of which added the right rhythmic twang to accompany the sweating, heaving dancers as they jigged and clogged, pranced and stomped, the ten male wayfarers keeping the Colbert daughters whirling nonstop, while the old man's three sons took turns spinning across the tiny dance floor with Beulah and their beaming, dark-skinned mother. Hezekiah squatted in a corner near the warmth of the fireplace, clapping, bobbing his head, and near grinning his face loose.

As midnight approached, the one called James announced the advent of the new year by his watch and ordered everyone out into the yard beneath the darkening skies as the first clouds rolled in to obliterate all traces of the moon and the far-flung stars. At the proper moment the horsemen and Colbert's sons all pulled free their heavy armament and let roar at the deepening black of the heavens. In response to that gunfire, and what hooting and shouting accompanied the momentous hour, those oxen in the nearby corral bellowed while the nervous horses set loose their own shrill protest.

Not long after they all crowded back into the Colberts' dining hall, Bass had grown bone weary and begged off, paying his respects to the ladies. He had made it to the open doorway when his hand was caught up and he was spun around, flung back into the arms of one of those tawny-skinned daughters. She led him spinning around the dance floor, bumping into some, bouncing off others as the unattached horsemen glared their jealousy while clapping in time with the wheezing music's frenetic pace.

Before they circled the floor a fourth dizzying time, Titus realized he was smitten. Hard-bodied and rawboned, this tall half-breed girl smiled eye to eye at him, her cheeks flushed with excitement and energy and all that she put into her dance as they swung round and round. Almost more than anything, he liked the way the sweat glistened on her tawny skin, drops captured in that shallow cleft at the bottom of her neck, the way the rivulets of it streamed down to converge within the salty heave of her cleavage. Already the dancing lather plastered her blouse against those breasts, sticking to the flat of her belly. While she might not have been the best-looking of Colbert's five, the one who seized hold of him at that moment did have one definite advantage over her sisters: she made no bones about just who it was she wanted to pair herself with.

As much as she threw herself into the dance, it did not surprise Titus that a short time later she asked him to take her outside for a breath of the cool night air. Once immersed in those shadows playing against the wall of the cabin near the dog run, she pressed her mouth right against his. Stunned, he stumbled back, wide-eyed as one of her arms trapped his waist, slamming his hips against hers until she bumped him back into the wall. He was pinned as her free hand roamed up his belly to the neck of his shirt, then wandered across that bare skin drawn taut over his shoulder.

Of a sudden she had her tongue pressing against his lips. This was new, an unsettling sensation. As his lips relaxed, she pressed hard with her tongue, separating his teeth, searching out his tongue, exploring his mouth voraciously. Every bit as hungrily he swallowed the taste of her, the flavor of her father's potato beer on her tongue, still so fresh on his own. Each time he closed his eyes, his head swam, sensing again a great tingling that swept over him like the lick of a burning flame.

Then his eyes flew open when he felt her hand tugging at the waistband of his britches—more than eager: the girl was downright hungry.

"Ho— . . . hold on," he sputtered, seizing her hands in fear she would discover the coins sewn there where she fumbled in her hurry to get at his engorged flesh. "L-lemme."

"Now," she whispered. "Jest do it now."

The girl pulled away from him, moved back beneath the covered dog run where the shadows lurked even deeper. As he fought those buttons out of their holes, Bass lurched close behind, nearly falling over her clumsily as she dropped to her knees, rolled over on her back, and hiked up her long cloth skirt. Placing himself between her outflung legs, he fumbled to get his flesh freed from his longhandles and the nankeen britches, feeling those two big pistols spill from the back of his waistband as his pants fell open. At that moment he cared little for what became of them.

Quickly he went to feel along her bare legs, surprised to find they were covered with what he felt were buckskin britches much like his. When she seized hold of his hot, rigid flesh in one hand, the girl grasped one of his hands and guided it between her legs. It was then he discovered the britches were instead leggings. His appetite rising, Titus danced his fingers over the bare flesh of her loins, seeking that moist patch of hair where she wriggled as soon as he brushed his hand against her heat.

Roughly she dragged his engorged flesh forward as if it weren't attached to him at all, forcing him to rock over her as she planted him within her moistness. Certain was he that he would spend himself right then and there—exactly as he had that first night at the swimming hole with Amy Whistler. But just as he began to tense and shudder, she suddenly stopped moving, reaching down to grab his scrotum, pulling on it gently, but insistently, until he sensed that overwhelming need to explode slowly dissipate.

He welcomed that wash of relief by immediately throwing himself back into his energetic thrusts. Likewise she imprisoned him with her legs, locking his head in a death-grip with both arms, flinging her hips up against him in a clumsy dance by this half-dressed two-headed beast.

When she began to groan—low at first—he quickly stopped and reared back in wide-eyed surprise: mystified, more afraid than anything. Great God, if he went and hurt her, what the devil would her brute of a father and half-breed brothers do to him?

"No! D-don't stop!" she ordered, squeezing her legs about his hips even tighter, dragging his head back down as her hips gyrated insistently.

Obedient was he, willing captive that Titus was. A prisoner of his own sudden appetite, aroused to a fever pitch by those patches of smooth flesh he stroked beneath the crumple of her dress pulled high above her waist, compelled by the moistness he had penetrated, made dizzy by the strong smell of fragrant wood chips, sweat, and potato beer clinging to her like hickory smoke clung to his pap's hams suspended above the smoldering fires in the smoking shed.

It wasn't long before her groan became an insistent whimper. As the sound grew in volume at his ear, the primal grunt of it began to hammer at him every time they collided. Then she nearly scared him out of his skin when she suddenly grabbed one of his hands and clamped it over her own mouth as she thrashed back and forth. He ripped the hand away.

"Keep . . . keep it there!" she huffed in a high-pitched whine.

Seizing his hand again, the girl slapped it back over the bottom of her face as she went back to lunging up at him. He'd never had a woman throw herself into this mating with such fight, at the same time wanting him to keep her quiet.

Then he knew why she had clamped his hand where she had.

The instant she began that muffled scream, he stopped his thrusts and started to pull the hand away. Terrified at the wild shriek from the beast below him, he clamped the hand back down over her mouth as she threw herself into a hissing, snarling tantrum there in the shadows of the dogtrot. Titus jerked his head this way, then that, afraid to his core that at any moment the elder Colbert would appear at the corner of the cabin and find him not just rutting with his daughter—but bodily harming the frightened young girl to boot.

Why, it sounded as if someone were killing her!

Then, as her hips slowed their lunging gyrations, she reached up and took a bunch of his hair in each hand, dragging his face down so she could lather it with her wet mouth.

"Ain'cha ready?" she huffed breathlessly at his ear.

"I . . . got so scared—"

"Do it. Just do it now," and she let go of his hair, locking her hands on his buttocks poking above the wide waistband of his britches like two bare hillocks rising above a line of timber below.

She clawed and scratched them, kneading his skin while thrusting herself up to him. No longer did she have her eyes closed. Now they were intense, snakelike slits. Her lips pressed together in a line of determination.

Again she asked, "You're ready, ain'cha?"

For the moment he could not answer. Suddenly everything above and below his groin seemed shut off from all sensation, incapable of any function aside from assisting what eruption was about to occur. And with his first explosion she moaned and whimpered beneath him again—small, feral yelps of pleasure.

As he ground to a halt, fully spent within her, the girl slowly, softly stroked those bare mounds she had been pulling tight against her.

The next thing he grew conscious of was her voice in his ear.

"We cain't sleep here all night."

"No . . . no, we can't." His mouth tasted pasty, as if he'd been sucking on a trencher filled with lye ash.

Groggily Titus raised his head. The air was cold, damp too of a sudden, on the bare flesh of his buttocks. He was surprised to find that she and he lay just as they had finished—fallen asleep locked in that final embrace of afterglow.

But then she was pushing him to the side, rolling the other way herself.

The cold shocked him all the more as his limp flesh flopped against his belly, shrinking quickly.

Scrambling to her feet, the girl tugged down her skirt, shuffled that loose blouse back into place, and smoothed it over those young breasts he had wanted to taste so badly while they had been dancing. He realized he wanted her again. When he reached up for her, the girl pushed his hands down.

"Get your britches pulled up," she ordered in a harsh whisper.

"C'mere. I wanna—"

"No," she answered harshly. "Maybe 'nother time. My father come out looking for me if I'm gone too long."

"Just go let him see you, then come back."

"Maybe you go on to your bed. Your cabin yonder," she countered coyly. "Maybe I'll come find you later. You was good, boy. Better'n a lotta the men I had me."

That raised his ire. "I'm every bit a man like them."

Behind her hand she giggled, turning away. "Like I said, better'n most every one I had."

The shadows absorbed her so quickly, he never got another plea out. It took a few moments more before the cold breeze brushing his bare flesh seeped back into his consciousness. Hobbling to his knees, Titus heaved himself from there to his feet, hopping about while yanking up the britches.

With them buttoned he slipped around the side of the cabin, stole a long last look in the open door. There he found everyone still in full revel. Kingsbury turned, saw him, and motioned Bass back in.

Titus shook his head, pointing to the hut. After the pilot nodded, Bass moved out of the splash of flickering torchlight as the wind picked up. The night air smelled rank with rain as he reached the second of the two huts where the boatmen had stowed what blankets and belongings they were packing north to the Ohio. Inside the shanty, out of the wind, his nose pricked with the smell of another. Eyes were slow growing accustomed to the dark as he searched the walls, while dancing torchlight from across the yard spilled in through the hut's single, small window.

"Hezekiah?"

"Yes. Me."

"You're awake."

"Not sleep. The noise. Guns."

"Yeah," he said, searching the floor with his hands. "You got both our blankets?"

"Right here."

Titus settled in beside the big slave as Hezekiah held up both blankets. "Cold night."

"Sure is," the slave agreed. "Warm now."

He let out a sigh and closed his eyes, sensing the body heat from the big man's back beginning to warm him.

"Ask you question, Titus?"

"What's that?"

"You with woman tonight?"

"How you mean?"

For the longest time there was no reply. Then Hezekiah said, "With woman: like you was with Nina back to Miss Annie's boat."

"Yepper," he answered, remembering Ebenezer Zane always answering in the affirmative just that way.

"Thought me so. Goo'night, Titus."

For a moment he wanted to ask the slave how he knew, then decided he wouldn't. Eventually Bass said, "Good night, Hezekiah."

Sometime later he had awakened, hearing that first roll of thunder come their way from across the ridge to the west, the same heights they had struggled up, over, then down to reach this ford on the Tennessee River. For the longest time he lay there in the dark, feeling the Negro snore with a rumble like dull thunder itself, listening to the other two boatmen snore.

He was just slipping back into sleep when he heard footsteps outside. Sensing immediate alarm, he laid a hand on one of his pistols as the small oak door creaked open on its own swollen wood hinges, grating across the pounded clay floor beneath it.

"Reuben!" Kingsbury's voice whispered harshly like the rending of new canvas. "Heman! Ho, Titus! Pull yourselves up."

Then a sudden flare of lightning backlit the river pilot, stoop-shouldered in the half-opened doorway. At the crack of thunder he vaulted into the hut, stumbling over a pair of feet before catching himself against the far wall.

"That you down there, Titus?"

"My feet, yes."

"Get you and that Negra up," Kingsbury ordered as he straightened. "We gotta be off now. Up, up—be quick about it now."

"By the devil—it ain't even light yet, Hames," Root hissed as he sat up, rubbing grit from his eyes.

"Gonna be soon enough," he replied with an urgent bite. "I wanna be long gone from that bunch afore dawn. Now, up with all of you and get down to the ferry. I'm off to fetch Colbert and his boys now to haul us away to the far shore afore this storm breaks."

The first drops fell as they were nearing the north bank of the Tennessee, hauled across by the power of the Colbert muscle. The half-dozen wayfarers hurried off the rough planks of the unwieldy craft as rain slicked the wood and bare ground where they turned momentarily to watch the old man bark orders at his three boys. The sky chose that moment to open up as the ferry disappeared behind shifting sheets of rain. When they struggled up the slick bank to huddle beneath the first of that canopy of trees sheltering the well-worn groove of the Natchez Trace, another flare of that terrifying electrical storm lit up the whole of Colbert's Landing.

In that daylike brightness it was plain to make out the main cabins, the wayfarer huts. The corral.

"Shit," Kingsbury growled.

"Them horses ain't there," Titus said.

"Jesus God," Ovatt added his own oath.

All six of them stood there, soaked and chilled, staring across the river as another flash of lightning starred the far settlement of crude buildings. The post corral was empty—not one of the eight horses the six slave hunters had brought with them still there.

"Where you figure they gone?" Root asked, something pinching his voice into a taut string.

As Bass hunched over, squinting in the sudden flares of the storm, searching the muddy ground for some clue, Kingsbury shouted against the roar of approaching thunder.

"Wherever they gone—it's for no good."

"W-why you say that?" Beulah asked.

The pilot turned on her, gripped her shoulders firmly. "They ain't gone to bed—pulled out afore us. None of that's no good."

"What we do now?" Ovatt asked.

They looked at one another for a moment, then Beulah said, "There ain't no ferry coming to fetch us, fellas. We just sit here, or get on down the way home like we 'tended."

"Woman's right," Kingsbury said. "Maybeso the dark help us more'n them sonsabitches."

Root grabbed hold of Kingsbury's soppy coat. "How you so sure they ain't just gone looking for runaways?"

"They're coming after us, Reuben," the pilot answered with a wag of his head. "Didn't you see it plain as paint? They want this here Negra."

Root whirled on Hezekiah. "I say we get rid of the son of a bitch right here and now. Let 'em have him."

"No!" Titus bellowed against a clap of thunder.

Root turned to Bass, snagging up a big handful of his oiled jerkin in both hands, shaking the youth. "That bunch hunts down men for money. Likely they kill't their share."

"So have we," Ovatt replied.

"But they're the paid killers," Kingsbury argued. "And we mean nothing to 'em but money."

Root flung Bass back from him. "Get rid of the Negra right now!"

"Maybe Reuben's right." Ovatt aligned himself with Root. "We give 'em the Negra—they'll leave us be."

The wind came up, strong in Titus's face as if it were siding against him too. "You can't—"

"It won't help a damned thing," the woman suddenly interrupted Bass. "Hames, you know damned good and well they ain't after just the Negra here."

Nodding with some reluctance, his skinny face glistening with rain as the next bolt of lightning lit up the countryside, Kingsbury said, "She's right. It ain't only the Negra. They're coming after the money."

Ovatt scoffed, "They don't know we got no money."

"They goddamn well do know!" the pilot replied. He seemed to square his narrow shoulders as he turned to Bass. "Best keep our guns under our coats—right, Titus?"

He swallowed hard, seeing the rest of those wet faces staring intently at his. "Yeah. Keeps your pan powder dry, out of the rain."

"Not just that," Kingsbury added morosely, gazing up the dark corridor of the Natchez Trace, "that bunch never did see for sure that we was armed, the hull lot of us. Maybeso they show up, that ignernce'll count for something."

"I pray it does count for something, Hames," Beulah agreed. "When it comes down to the killin'."

The horsemen had gone sometime in the night. It had to be after that gal had finished with Titus and he looked in to find everyone still celebrating —going off to bed himself. Had to be after Kingsbury, Ovatt, and Root had limped across the yard to their blankets. When the one called James had ordered his men into the saddle only then.

Bass wished he knew more about horses, to know how far and how fast an able man could travel on one. Then he would have some idea how far the boatmen had to go before counting on bumping into those slave trackers.

But then—he thought, with his teeth chattering like a box of ivory dominoes in an ox-horn cup—the how far didn't really matter, did it? Because once a man was out ahead of you, he no longer had to travel any great distance. He could pick his place. A spot most favorable to acting on his plans. Just hunker down and wait for you to come along at your own pace.

They could be waiting up there no more than a hundred paces. Or as much as a hundred leagues. That was the thing about not knowing that scared him down to his roots. This wasn't like any of the dangers he had faced before. Oh, he had been scared in having to face the Falls of the Ohio, just as scared of the prospect of running the Devil's Raceground or the Devil's Elbow on the Mississippi. Deep water had always frightened him.

Still, he had confronted his fear time and again—staring it in the eye, and not giving an inch. But this . . . Titus had never had to stew in his own juices over the very real possibility of staring down danger in the form of another man driven by deadly intent.

Not even when that Chickasaw hunting party had caught him alone in that timber. Not when that war party had slipped down the river to surprise Ebenezer Zane's flatboat crew. Not when Titus had been so crazy drunk he couldn't even get his pecker excited and that eye-gouging fight had broken out on Annie Christmas's gunboat.

On every occasion Bass had suddenly found himself thrust into the vortex of events. With no time to fret, or worry, much less get himself scared until all of it was damned well over and done with. And—by God—there really was a tangible advantage to not having to put one soggy moccasin in front of the other, minute by minute, yard by yard, worrying all the while when and where in the rain-soaked darkness of this wilderness they were going to strike.

"I don't like this," Root grumbled after they had moved something more than a mile up the trail.

"Reuben's right," Ovatt said when Kingsbury halted and turned around. He glanced back at Titus and Hezekiah before continuing, "I say we make fine targets, all of us bunched up the way we is."

For a brief moment the bony pilot appeared to heft that around as he stared at the wet leaves and dead grass beneath his feet. "Awright. Maybeso you're right. Beulah, you wanna stay on with me?"

"Told you I was," she replied with a sharp edge, her tone a bit haughty in her confusion.

"Then you and me'll go on down the road first," he said, then turned to Root and Ovatt. "Give us a short bit—just when you see us get to the far shadows, then you two move out. Titus, you wait and do the same after these fellas go, then bring that Negra with you."

Bass glanced quickly at Hezekiah, fear pricking the small of his back. "We're breaking up?"

"Maybe they won't do no good in catching us all if'n we ain't all together," Root explained.

No longer was it fear. Now his anger rose in him like a case of hives: sudden, and hot. "I know what this is," Bass snapped. "You're just getting rid of me an' him 'cause I won't let you get rid of him."

Kingsbury took a step forward, offering his hand in the misty rain. "We ain't leaving you behin't."

Swinging an arm, he pushed the pilot's hand aside. "G'won, then—if it's gonna be this way. Git. All of you."

Beulah moved up beside Bass. The lightning filled the sky overhead with a yellowish phosphorescence. "You'll be right behind us."

A clap of thunder raised the hair on the back of Titus's neck. He felt the small hairs on his arms rise as the odor of riven ozone burst through the canopy of trees while the rumble died off in the distance.

"We can't run off from you," Ovatt declared.

"I know you can't," Titus snarled. "You might try, but I can still catch up—"

"No," Ovatt interrupted. "We can't run off from you, 'cause you're one of us, Titus."

Kingsbury came closer to the angry youth. "You proved you was one of us ever since you said you'd ride through the chutes with us back to Louisville. You didn't have to, young'un—but you did. Right then and there Ebenezer figured you was part of his crew. And now . . . well—you been a part of us through it all. You say so, we'll all stay close together. Just to prove we ain't running out on you."

In the teeth of that raging storm he looked from one face to another, all three of those boatmen. Of a moment he felt ashamed. With no call to judge these men who had watched over him like uncles, protected him like older brothers, and scolded him like fathers. But even more, he again experienced that deep regret he had swallowed down ever since losing Ebenezer Zane, that shame that told him he was to blame for the riverman's death.

Skin prickling, Bass waited for the next peal of thunder to rock the ground where they stood, causing all of them to shudder with its nearness, knowing he owed these Kentucky men more than he could ever repay—simply because it was his fault Ebenezer was taken from them.

"The rest of you, g'won now," Titus said quietly. "Me an' Hezekiah, we'll bring up the rear."

Bass watched Kingsbury and Beulah, then Root and Ovatt slip from view up the footpath, really nothing more than a game trail beneath the skeletal overhang of beechnut and pin oak, black ash and chinkapin. When the next muzzle flash of lightning came, Titus could no longer see them. He nudged the slave into motion. It seemed colder now. The rain falling somehow harder, more insistently. Perhaps it only seemed that way because he felt all the more lonely. Down to just him and a big, black Negra who Annie Christmas paid for down at the slave pens in New Orleans and brought north, teaching him to speak a little of the white folks' tongue so he could serve liquor and throw any unruly customers off her gunboat.

But at that moment Titus put one moccasin in front of the other, listening to the rain hammer the forest around them, the thunder voice coming in a mighty roar before it slipped off in a whimper, only then able to hear the slog of the Negra's old, worn boots on last autumn's dead leaves lying in a black mat of decay on that ancient buffalo trail.

But the buffalo were no more. How well he had learned that from his grandpap. Big critters like the buffalo were all but gone when the first settlers had moved over the mountains from Virginia into the canebrakes of the land they would one day call Kentucky. Farmers—driving the Indian, like the buffalo, before them.

Anymore, most all that was left for a man to hunt in Kentucky were a few deer, and the smaller game: turkey, squirrels, rabbits, coon, and the like. Not like the olden times his grandpap used to talk on and on about. Time was when a man had nothing more to feed his family but wild game.

In that rainy forest, where it seemed the sun refused to rise of a dark and deadly purpose, Titus remembered how his grandpap seemed caught between what had been and what was. The old man used to say that now it was a good thing the settlers could provide for their families with all that they could grow, along with raising those domesticated farm animals a man could slaughter when times grew lean and desperate—simply because the big animals had all moved on.

This hunger to see what lay beyond the Mississippi was like a nettle poked into the seam of his moccasin—working its tiny barb into his flesh so that he was always shy of being comfortable when he set that foot down. Too, it was a remembrance that again released a great remorse in him, just like an oozy boil festering around that nettle worked down into his flesh. How dearly he missed that old man who had seemed to understand his grandson far, far better than did Thaddeus.

Titus did not have long to dwell on his loss.

Hezekiah clamped Bass's arm in one of his great hands, pressing a finger to his lips. The rain poured mercilessly from the black man's smooth head as he blinked. Then he motioned Titus to follow. They left the foot-path, twisting through the broom pine and dogwood trees as the lightning flared, igniting the whole of the sky above them like midday every few moments. Then the slave stopped him and pointed.

Out there in the sodden darkness left behind by a retreating peal of thunder, a familiar voice growled, "Where's that boy?"

He could not remember ever feeling cold like that: the sudden chill splash down his backbone like January snow-melt spilling off the cabin roof.

"He didn't come with us," Kingsbury answered, staring up into that ring of slavers.

One of the horses moved, sidestepping with fright, jostling another at a new clap of thunder. Nearly all of the animals fought their bits. Titus could see them wide-eyed in the excruciating flare of each tongue of lightning as the maw of the storm settled over them.

The slave hunters had his four friends surrounded. Clearly outgunned and caught dead-footed. Like the pilot and Beulah, Ovatt and Root had their hands raised as they stood at the center of that wide circle of horsemen.

"You're telling me he's back at Colbert's Stand?"

"We left him sleeping," Kingsbury lied. "He . . . he didn't wanna sell that goddamned useless Negra to you, so the rest of us up and figured to leave him behind for good. Son of a bitch has been too much trouble to us already."

The leader named James rocked back in his saddle as if he was consid-ering something. Then he looked down the backtrail. "He still have that slave with him?"

"They was cuddled up back to back, like bedbugs," Ovatt declared.

"Yep," Root added, his voice edgy. "Didn't wanna get up and move out when we did—so we left 'em."

"Goddammit," James growled. He waved one of his pistols down the trail. "You—Harrison—take McCarthy with you. Get back there and hold those two. I don't want them going nowhere."

"You coming on later?" Harrison asked.

"Yeah. Soon as I figure out what to do with the rest of these."

The two horsemen peeled away from the rest, parting a pair of led-horses as they set off back to the ford. At first the eight hooves clopped away on the soggy ground and fallen leaves, but that leaving was quickly swallowed by another loud rumble of thunder that followed the next lightning hurled from the low clouds suspended like black coal right over their heads. He watched the pair of horsemen disappear in the dark, then turned back to study the four who remained.

"The Trace has it quite a reputation," James was saying. "Murderers and thieves. All sorts of vermin been known to haunt this road. And they all share one thing in common: every last one of them leaves their victims speechless."

"That's what we'll do with 'em, right?" one of the others asked.

"Yes," James said, an edge of resignation in his voice. "I suppose we have no other choice."

"Leave the woman go," Kingsbury pleaded, taking a small step to move in front of Beulah protectively.

The slaver must have enjoyed that, for James laughed, throwing his head back lustily. Then he said, "Shit, now. I never knew a man who could hold a candle to a woman when it come to dangerous talk. No—a woman wags her tongue sooner, and a lot faster'n any man I ever knowed. The bitch'll die with the rest of you."

"Let's just get it over with," another of the horsemen growled.

"Not just yet," James snapped, his horse sidling nervously, fighting the bit. "Not before I see if these three rivermen are carrying what I think they're carrying."

The trio of boatmen backed closer together, Beulah between them.

"What about her?"

"Yes," James answered one of his men. "She might just be carrying some of the money too." He looked hard at the woman, saying, "You've got it under your clothes, don't you?"

"Haven't got nothing of no value," Kingsbury said bravely, his teeth chattering with cold.

Bass's heart whimpered with a twinge of sympathy for that brave man as he tapped on Hezekiah's shoulder, nudging him toward the horsemen. Leaning over to speak into the slave's ear, Titus whispered, "Grab you something big and long. Get you a branch off the ground."

While he kept his eyes on the horsemen, Hezekiah hunched over, creeping off in search of a limb among the dark, decaying leaves.

"You first," James said, wagging his pistol at Kingsbury. "Open your shirt."

He did as he was told. And the horseman James had ordered out of the saddle to search the river pilot found nothing.

Wagging his pistol again, the slaver thundered, "Off with your britches!"

"You heard him!" the man beside Kingsbury growled, pounding him on the back. "Take 'em off."

Kingsbury pulled free his wide leather belt from its buckle, allowing it to drop to the sodden ground. He yanked at the fly buttons, shinnying them down to hop out of his soggy pants.

The slave hunter snatched them up from the ground, shook them, then tossed the britches up to the leader. "They feel heavy, James."

"Aye, they do at that," the leader replied. "The rest of you, off with yours. Now!"

"And you, woman." The thief on the ground whirled on Beulah, reaching out and stuffing his hand inside the neck of her blanket coat, flinging open the flaps. "You I'll search my own self."

The moment he grabbed hold of the top of her blouse and rent it in half, Kingsbury lunged for him. The thief brought up his pistol in a back-swing, catching Hames across the temple. The river pilot stumbled backward. Root caught him as the thief hurled the woman down into the mud. Standing over her, his pistol in one hand, he fought his belt and britches with the other. Kingsbury came to and tried to fight off Root and Ovatt, struggling to reach Beulah, who refused to let out a cry.

"Stay where you are, boatman!" James ordered, urging his horse forward a yard, wagging his pistol at the three rivermen. "This ought to be a pretty sight to watch."

"I swear—I'll kill you," Kingsbury growled. "I'll hunt you down. I'll see you hang—"

James's pistol barked in that hammer of rain, spinning Kingsbury around. He crumpled from the grasp of his two companions, spilling back into the leaves and dead grass beneath the bare branches of a hickory tree.

Beulah scrambled to the side, attempting to crawl to her feet and reach him, crying out only when the thief struck her across the jaw with a flat hand. She sprawled back, and once more he stepped over to straddle her, exposing himself as the two other horsemen dismounted and slogged over.

"I get some'a that next."

"Hell with you! I was on the ground afore you."

The first shoved the second. The second reached out to grab for the first, squabbling.

"Stop it!" James bellowed in the dying growl of thunder. "Just take her and be done with it! And you," he said to one of the two on the ground, "get back in the saddle and keep your gun on the rest of these here."

"I'll damn well be next," the man grumbled in disappointment as he stuffed a boot into the stirrup and rose to the saddle.

Wincing, Kingsbury slowly rose to his elbow as Ovatt and Root knelt beside him.

"You hit?" Reuben asked.

Touching the top of his shoulder, the river pilot nodded. "I'll live," he huffed, clearly in pain, glaring up at James, who was pulling a second pistol from the sash at his waist. "Long enough to find you."

The man climbing back onto his horse guffawed nastily. "You ain't gonna live nowhere near that long, you dumb son of—"

In that next flare of lightning the man began swinging a foot over the rump of his horse—when he suddenly pitched sideways from his saddle, his horse bounding away from the falling body, colliding with another riderless horse.

That's when a piece of that black night tore out of the bowels of the forest and flung itself like a crazed, demonic shadow right into the midst of those two dismounted horsemen.

SEVENTEEN

As Titus stuffed the fired pistol into his waistband, pulling the loaded one into his right hand and drawing back its hammer, Hezekiah burst past him, through the tangle of trees and shadow toward the ring of frightened horses and slave hunters thrown into instant confusion.

There the big slave lunged through the frightened animals, landing among the two thieves standing over Beulah. Hezekiah swung a huge limb at the end of his powerful arms. Every time it cracked against one of the slavers' bones, it rang with the smack of a maul splitting hard oak.

At the same time, James's mount reared wildly, but he struggled it back down, wagging a second horse pistol this way, then that, trying to hold it on the black terror pummeling two of his men senseless as the woman crawled off on her belly through the leaves.

Suddenly Kingsbury leaped, snagging the famous slave hunter's wrist, yanking, snapping his head forward to lock his teeth in that pliant web of flesh between thumb and forefinger of the hand holding the pistol, gritting his teeth together as James flung his arm up and down, fighting to free himself from the wild beast pulling him from the saddle . . . when the pistol went off, the muzzle flash a bright, painful flare in the darkness of that thunderstruck forest.

As Kingsbury hurtled back, arms akimbo, the leader cruelly drove his spurs into the horse's flanks. With something close to the sound of human pain, the animal cried out as James savagely wrenched his mount's head to the side with the reins, hammering the beast into furious motion.

Clearing the last fringe of trees surrounding that deadly clearing, Bass brought his pistol up, marking a spot on the slaver's broad back. With the instincts of a hunter he quickly considered, then decided. Stuffing the pistol back into his waistband, he brought the longrifle up to his shoulder as he snapped the goosenecked hammer back, flicking off the greased leather sock that kept the powder dry in its pan.

He blinked. Then once more, trying desperately to clear his eyes of the swirling rain that drove down on them in dancing sheets. Unsure in that darkness, he touched off the trigger.

Thirty yards away, the slave hunter twisted to the side, arms flung up, screwing partway out of the saddle as his hands flapped down, fighting to secure a purchase on the horn, seeking to regain the reins that flopped out of reach. Boots freed from the stirrups, James hurtled from the back of that terrified animal in a low arc. He collided against the great trunk of a chestnut tree, spilling to the damp ground with a great rush of air from his lungs.

Just beyond the slaver, the horse came to a stop, gazed suspiciously from side to side, then calmly dipped its head to forage among the moldering leaves for something worth nuzzling in the way of graze.

Root was the first to reach the slave hunter, standing over him as Titus came up—trembling. Bass tried to stand just so, mindful that if he didn't, the others would surely tell his knees were rattling like all get-out. He'd never shot a man in anger. Standing there at that moment, he finally realized his veins burned with a fire never before this hot, adrenaline pumping through them still. His mouth gone dry, he could only stare, slack-jawed, at the body sprawled on the ground.

James gurgled, something bright and dark oozing from the side of his mouth as he gazed up at the moment Ovatt came to a stop beside Bass. The slaver's eyes rolled back to their whites for a moment, fluttering, his face contorting as if he were struggling to hold on. Then those cruel eyes appeared to brush across Root before coming to rest on Titus. They seemed to smile, laugh even—perhaps laugh at himself as he choked out something unintelligible.

Then he hacked up a great dark gob of gelling blood puffing from his mouth in a shiny bubble before he locked his eyes on Bass once more. "I didn't think you sonsabitches'd leave the boy behind. Maybe the Negra, leave that black bastard behind for me—just to keep me off your trail . . . but . . . I should've known . . . you'd n-never . . . leave the boy."

"The one you call a *boy* just killed you, you worthless hide hunter," Root growled. "You realize that?"

Bass watched James take his eyes from him, to gaze down at his chest and the shiny stain oozing around that exit hole. "I do believe," he started, gasping for air, staring cruelly back at Bass before the eyes began to roll slowly back. "Do . . . do believe he . . . he did . . ."

For the longest time Titus stared down at the slave hunter—numbed, unable to move, watching for any sign. Perhaps the face to twitch, his eyes to roll back and fix him with their steely gaze, maybe even see the slaver move a bit this way or that—he lay so like a disjointed rag-sock doll, the sort his mother had made for his sister years before. But nothing moved. Not a sound but the crunch of the horse nearby as it tore at the old grass, snorting and blowing aside the dying leaves with their stench of decay.

"Yep, you sure kill't that bastard. Kill't him dead," Root finally said.

At first Titus wasn't sure he'd heard Reuben speaking. The blood thundered at his ears so.

After he had worked his throat, worked his tongue around a few times before uttering a sound, Bass finally said, "I . . . couldn't stand by and let 'im kill Kingsbury like he done."

"That bastard didn't kill me," came the pilot's voice.

Whirling on his heel with surprise, Titus found Kingsbury approaching, leaning on Beulah's shoulder.

Sputtering, Bass shook his head, saying, "I saw . . . h-he shot you close—"

"His pistol went off right aside my face, sure enough," Kingsbury replied, pulling a hand away from his shoulder to expose a black oval of drying blood that spidered toward the armpit. "But he didn't hit nothing that second time—just blinded me."

"Lookee here what the young'un here done to *him,*" Ovatt said, his red hair sopping into the collar of his fustian coat. "Jesus God, Titus! I been one to cut my share of white men in my time—but I never out an' out killed a white man. Jesus God!"

"Killing that there son of a sow pig ain't really like killing a white man," Root declared, coming forward to kneel over the body. "This'un's no more'n a animal the boy here just put out of its misery."

Bass watched the boatman lay a hand on the slave hunter's chest, wait long moments, then lean forward to place an ear directly on that dark blossom of blood.

"Jesus God, Titus," Ovatt repeated with a wag of his head. "You gone and kill't a white man!"

"Shuddup, Heman! What the boy done ain't murder," Kingsbury snarled. "They was all fixing to kill us, then stuff our belly-holes full with rocks so we wouldn't float to the top of this here bayou."

"Hames is right," Beulah agreed, gripping the river pilot's arm. "Titus here done what needed doing when this son of a bitch took to running."

They all turned upon hearing Hezekiah's sodden steps. He had his waistband filled with pistols and carried a rifle in each hand. Shocked at the sight of an armed Negro, the three white men and one white woman stared speechless as Hezekiah came to a halt. He gazed back at each of those frightened faces, then handed the first rifle to Reuben Root.

"You need this'r more'n me," the slave said quietly. Then Hezekiah turned to Ovatt, handing the Ohioan the other full-stocked rifle.

Titus sensed a sudden relief wash over all four of the white people standing with him.

"You take all them guns from them others?" Root inquired, gesturing toward the bodies.

Hezekiah nodded with a simple shrug. "They ain't gonna need 'em. We might'n, somewhere down this'r road."

"What you aim to do with them belt pistols?" Ovatt asked.

Turning to Bass, the slave answered, "He tell me what to do with them."

"I don't own you, goddammit!" Titus snapped, his mind burning, turning away to look down at the dead slave hunter. He'd just killed a man —how was he expected to know the answer to every goddamned question in the world right now?

"For the devil, Titus! You just can't let a goddamned Negra have a gun," Root squealed. "Just look at him, will you! The son of a bitch took six of them pistols off them slave hunters!"

"Give him the guns you got," Ovatt ordered the Negro. "Titus, you take 'em from him now."

"Why?" Titus demanded.

"I don't want him at my back with a gun," Root said, his eyes narrowing.

"Don't matter to me if'n he's got a gun at my back or not," Bass remarked quietly, his throat burning with the first taste of gall as he looked back down and stared at that slaver's face going ashen in the rain. Pale as limestone chalk.

Right then Bass was afraid of what he knew was about to overwhelm him. It had happened with the first animal he had ever killed, out hunting with his pap and an uncle. They had run across a rabbit—caught far from the safety of its burrow. The flop-eared critter had stopped dead in its tracks as the hunters had closed in on the clearing.

"Shoot 'im," his uncle had ordered harshly, slamming his rifle into Titus's hands.

Instead, the frightened and confused young boy had stared down at the cocked hammer, then gazed at the rabbit before locking his eyes on the gun once more.

"Like your uncle said, shoot 'im, Titus!" Thaddeus Bass had whispered harshly.

Still the rabbit had sat there, staring at the three humans.

Shaking like a cedar sapling beneath the onslaught of an autumn wind, Titus had dragged the big rifle to his bony shoulder, aimed as he had been taught, and gazed down that long barrel at those dark beads of eyes just beyond the front sight—then squeezed his own eyes shut and pulled the trigger.

The body was still so very warm when his dad and uncle had come back with it, slinging the rabbit against Titus's chest. "Now skin it," the uncle had demanded.

Feeling the animal's heat, looking down at those eyes that had stared back at him, Bass had choked on the first flood of gall. Much as he tasted the rise of gall now, staring down at those white eyes rolled back in the slave hunter's head.

Stumbling in his hurry to flee, he pitched over the dead man's legs, caught himself with the rifle as crutch, and made it behind the tree as his stomach began to empty in great, volcanic waves. He was finishing the last heaves as he sensed a hand on his back.

"You feel better now?" Beulah asked.

Straightening, Titus nodded as he wiped his lower face, stinging with shame as he peered over at the others. His mouth boiled with the burn of acid as he said, "I . . . don't know what come over me—"

"Don't matter to us, none," Kingsbury replied. "Likely it's what happens as a natural thing, Titus. Nary a man here ever went and kill't a white man afore. Surely we'd do the same."

With his eyes smarting Titus tried to explain. "Thought you was . . . thought he'd gone and killed you."

"You done what any man do for his friend," the pilot replied. "You're a good man, Titus Bass."

"I'm glad you was here," Ovatt declared supportively. "None of us shoot near good as that, drop that son of a bitch off a running horse."

Beulah glanced down the backtrail, saying, "Maybe we ought'n figure on them other two coming back from Colbert's soon."

"She's right," Kingsbury said, suddenly stiffening as he peered down the road in the direction of the ford. "Likely they heard the shots."

"Shit. I ain't worried about the noise of them guns," Root argued. "Likely they'll just figure this here son of a bitch is busy killing the rest of us."

"But soon enough them two gone back 'cross't the river gonna find Titus and the Negra ain't there no more. They'll be on their way back here," Kingsbury said.

"That's why I say we ought'n be leaving here fast," Beulah suggested more forcefully, pulling Kingsbury's collar aside to inspect his bullet wound.

"What 'bout them?" Ovatt asked, holding a thumb over his shoulder. "This'un too."

"You boys're rivermen," Beulah chided them. "Drag the lot of 'em off into the brush yonder. Away from the trail."

"And them horses?" Root asked.

"I say we ride back to Kentucky, folks," Ovatt suggested.

"Damn fine idea," Kingsbury agreed. "Titus, you think you and Hezekiah catch up them horses afore they get too far away?"

He glanced at the slave, then nodded. "Don't see why we can't. I never had much to do with horses—"

"None the rest of us never did neither," Kingsbury explained. "Figure you two can catch 'em up so we can get out of here."

Self-consciously he licked his lips, still stinging with the sour taste of bile as the rain began to slacken. Nodding to the slave, Titus led out, heading first for that horse ridden by the dead leader of the slave hunters.

"You . . . you really kill them two other'ns?" Bass whispered after he had the reins in hand and they had started back toward the scene of the ambush.

Hezekiah nodded.

"Just like that?"

The slave shrugged. "I kill men afore. Annie Christmas tell me—I kill. Allays kill for her. Never before I kill for friends. These peoples here— makes no matter now. You, for first time to kill, it feel bad in here." He tapped a long black finger against his chest. "Maybe it get better sometime for you, like it done for me. No hurt no more in here."

"Yeah," Bass replied as he handed the slave the reins to the horse and moved away to inch up slowly on one of the other animals.

In minutes the slave took the second set of reins to stand there gripping both horses. "Don't think on it too hard, Titus. It could hurt."

Titus stopped, recalling that vivid memory of his first rabbit, considering its import this day in light of all the game he had tracked, hunted, killed.

"I s'pose you're right. Maybeso killing does get easier with time."

Titus never did run across the sixth horse, which meant he and Hezekiah ended up riding double. Natural enough—seeing how Bass was not only the youngest among them all, but the lightest as well.

On out of that far northwestern corner of Alabama they hurried. Putting the Muscle Shoals of the Tennessee at their backs, they set off atop those horses at a punishing pace, hurrying north for the Duck River. At the end of that first long day after leaving Colbert's Landing and the slavers far behind, Titus found half of the horses weary with exhaustion. Inside his head he heard the scolding voice of his father—prompting him to remember Thaddeus's admonishments that a man must always pay proper heed to the care of his animals.

That night at the fire he instructed the others that from then on out they should take care not to drive the horses so hard.

"You . . . you're serious! You want us just to walk 'em?" Root demanded in a scornful tone.

Titus nodded. "Don't think we should push 'em much faster'n we'd cover ground our own selves," he said, "walking on our own two legs, that is."

Root wagged his head as if confused by the logic. "What good is them horses, if'n we cain't get upland faster'n we can walk without 'em?"

Ovatt reminded, "Best we all paid heed: we got two of them sons of bitches still behin't us."

"Them two don't matter now," Kingsbury said, gazing at the two worried boatmen. "Way I see it, the two behind us, they'll keep on coming, no matter how slow or fast we get north for Nashville." Turning to the youth, Hames said, " 'Bout them horses—we all thank you for teaching us such a lesson, Titus Bass."

How his heart felt all the bigger, touched with the warmth in the pilot's words, when he had felt his heart slowly growing so icy throughout that long winter's day. Cold and dying inside was just what he had feared he had become after killing another man. Maybeso the others had been right after all in how they'd talked it over in those frantic, hurried minutes while they'd gathered up what little they had been carrying north, climbing unsteadily aboard the slave hunters' mounts. Maybe their wisdom was true: to kill a Injun or a Negra wasn't of much consequence at all, like Ovatt said. But to kill a white man . . . now, that was something. Bass even saw it in their eyes, the subtle change in how they looked at him after that terrible instant of decision when he had squeezed the trigger and took another's life.

As the hours had crawled past, he had slowly come to realize that Hezekiah knew the difference, perhaps even could feel the same confusion Bass suffered—maybe because of the physical contact between them throughout the day, the slave sitting directly behind him on that horse's back the way he was.

So he was damned grateful for Kingsbury's kindness that night at their fire holding winter's cold at bay. Titus thought back on the way he had suffered the terrifying fear that Hames Kingsbury would slip away from him, what with how Beulah had said that rib was poking a hole through his lights . . . and that come right on the heels of mourning the loss of Ebenezer Zane.

As they sat at their fire and wrapped themselves in the steaming, soggy wool blankets, Titus reflected back on his sixteen winters, thought on friends who had crossed his trail. Try as he might, the only person he could recall ever truly wanting to spend time with him had been Amy. Even with all the confusion and disappointment she had caused in him, with all the shattered expectations between them, here now in these cold woods he nonetheless sensed some strong regret that things hadn't worked out differently between them. Looking back, he realized she must surely have been his first true friend.

So terribly painful was it that in the end even Amy had turned out not to be what she professed to be.

Maybe—he brooded as he stared at the mesmerizing flames while the others talked in hushed tones and picked venison from their teeth with slivers peeled from a beechnut tree—just maybe these crude, unlettered Kentucky boatmen were the first *real* friends he had ever had.

And of their number Ebenezer Zane had been the first to step up and offer his hand to Titus. After the river pilot's death Hames Kingsbury had been the one to take up the slack in Titus's rope. But not just him, the woman too: Beulah. Eventually even Ovatt and Root, both of whom came to stand by him as only friends would, no matter their rough and less than polished ways of expressing their affection and loyalty.

Still all in all, it wasn't only the four of them. Titus looked now across the dancing flames at Hezekiah, suddenly reminded in this fire's bright flare that the man was nearly as black as charred oak.

True enough, back home in Kentucky, Bass had known a few simple farming folk who owned a slave, maybe even a pair of them—purchased off a slave block somewhere farther to the south, then carted over the hundreds of miles to their new owners' small farms, there to work out the long days of their miserable lives beneath a terrible yoke. This night such a tragedy was brought home to him with a metallic ache as he stared at the weary, worldly, yellowed eyes of the one an angry Annie Christmas had sold away as retribution. As he looked at that black face, Bass filled with a flush of sadness for Hezekiah, the many, many more like him: for all Negras he imagined would never know what it was to revel in the freedom one felt in simply walking into another valley for the first time, that unfettered luxury of setting off to go where one wanted to go.

All and still—Titus admitted to himself—it seemed there damned well weren't that many white men who ever really hungered to experience that feeling of true freedom. How very few in number were those who set out, not knowing where their journey would take them, not knowing what they would learn along the way, what they would find if and when they got to the end of their quest.

Men who lived as if it did not really matter, reaching the end of the trail. Their lives measured only in the journey. Spirits cast upon the winds, like a feather dancing, dancing.

Better that his spirit were chanced to dance on the wind, than to be mired in a plot of upturned ground back in Boone County.

Here at that fire in the deep of those woods blanketing southern Tennessee, Titus was once again rock-certain the spirits of those few old wanderers still followed the ancient trails of a bygone time, trails once pounded by the hooves of the long-gone buffalo. Every bit as sure was he that the spirit of his very own grandpap had picked up and moved away from the ground that the man had come and settled upon in his youth, the land where Titus himself had been born and raised, the ground it seemed Thaddeus Bass would farm until the day he was buried beneath its thick, cold, loamy blanket. There at last his father's soul would be at rest beneath the ground where he had labored his whole life through.

So unlike his grandpap's own restless spirit cast out to dance on the wind: forever wandering in the wake of the west-seeking buffalo. That spirit never to find its rest until it had journeyed far enough to discover that mystical place where the sun laid its head at night, out there beyond the farthest reach of man's most westward settlement. That old man's spirit never to find peace until at long, long last it one day reached the land where the buffalo ruled.

Generations ago new settlers come to the canebrakes and the Cumberland had scared off and driven away what buffalo the Indians hadn't yet killed. Yet with an unnamed certainty buried there in the core of him, Titus somehow knew the buffalo existed—out there, somewhere still. Undoubtedly it was a realm far enough away from the white settlers and town builders, well beyond all the school benches and church spires and small-town mercantiles, a land far gone, where those great mythical animals could at last wander free, every bit as free as the spirits of those who hunted for that faraway land where the buffalo reigned.

One day, perhaps. One day.

Four more frosty nights and four more grueling days later, as the sky wept a drizzle from low clouds, Bass stood silently staring down at the smooth gray river rock the Grinder family had heaped over an otherwise unmarked grave dug back in the woods no more than a few steps away from their roadside inn. All any of the three boatmen knew was the dead man's name. Only that—along with how he and another had taken a Corps of Discovery west to the far ocean, crossing the high mountains and fighting raging rivers in the process, returning home in triumph and adulation in 1806. Story was that about a year ago in the fall of 1809 Meriwether Lewis had begun his journey east along the Natchez Trace.

"He come in here on that awful October night," the elder Grinder loved to regale travelers with the hoary tale, pounding a fist into an open palm, "none of us knowing he 'tended to kill hisself right here and then."

Here beneath this pile of cold, rain-washed river rock lay the final resting place of that daring young wanderer who had pointed the way west for Thomas Jefferson's brave young country.

"Ol' Grinder says the man shot hisself in the head—but didn't do all that good a job," Ovatt repeated the story now as they all stood beside the cairn, paying their respects. "So he called out, begging others to finish him 'cause he knew just how hard he was to kill."

"How'd a man like him ever come to wanna take his own life?" Root asked. "Ever' time I come up this here road and spend the night at Grinder's Stand since it happened, it fair gives me the willies. Like I feel the man's ghost hanging on round here."

"A troubled soul perhaps," Beulah replied.

"Maybeso he'd already been across't them far mountains and out to the great ocean beyond it all," Kingsbury attempted to explain, "so likely he figured there was nothing left for him to see. Gone and seen it all. I s'pose a man like that figures it's just as well to snuff out his own candle."

"Gotta hand him that," Ovatt replied. "When there ain't no more to see, maybe you're right, Hames—no sense in going on, taking up room."

With the clang of the iron gong suspended from the Grinders' porch calling them to supper, Titus watched the others turn away from the grave, Kingsbury leading the rest back down the gentle slope to the gathering of squat cabins where they could take refuge from the drizzle and suffer the Grinder woman's distasteful cooking. In moving off, Hezekiah looked back over his shoulder, stopped, then returned to stand quietly beside Bass at the cairn.

"You g'won now and get yourself something to eat," he quietly told the slave.

"Folks ain't gonna feed me with them others," the slave said, wagging his head. "I'll stay till you come down. We eat together."

With a sigh Bass turned slowly. "I'm finished here, done trying to sort out why he done it."

"Maybeso he was kill't."

His face rose as did the realization. Bass stared into Hezekiah's yellowed eyes.

The slave continued. "Folks like them . . ."

"The Grinders?"

With a nod Hezekiah went on, "They just might'n figure a feller like this'un be carry him lots of money. 'Portant man like him allays got lots of money."

While it seemed so far-fetched, Hezekiah's explanation seemed probable at the same time. Bass replied sullenly, "So they kill't him for it."

"Then their kind go an' bury the man 'fore anyone come round asking questions," Hezekiah replied.

Wagging his head, Titus slowly shuffled away from that low pile of rock. "I ain't hungry no more."

Feeling as if his belly trapped a cold stone, Bass grappled with the greed and avarice of those he had encountered—whether it was pirates on the river or highwaymen haunting the Trace, or even the insatiable greed of stand owners like the Grinders.

Just what was it that made such men hunger after money more than love, more than adventure, more than happiness? Why did most men look for security in a full purse, while but a few searched for contentment beyond themselves in a land yet unseen? He laid his hand across the waistband of his britches as he watched the others take their pewter trenchers from one of the Grinder sons and stand at the stove while the old woman ladled out their supper. Perhaps the meaning of life came down to choosing gold, or the journey.

If need be, he decided, his would be the journey. Like his grandpap before him, he could live without the gold. His spirit must dance on the wind.

The next day they forded the Duck River at Gordon's Ferry, now come eighty miles from Colbert's Ford and the ambush by the Tennessee River. Another two nights in the wilderness of the Barrens brought them to the Big Harpeth River, where they slept in crude sheds erected near the house of the last American full-blood white man known to have lived between there and Natchez itself.

"We're less'n thirty miles from Nashville," Kingsbury explained as darkness came down like a cold, sodden blanket. "Place folks once called French Lick."

It was there at Nashville they left the Natchez Trace and pushed on to the northeast, following a trail that left behind the Cumberland River, their feet plying a path long ago blazed by boatmen returning to the Ohio River country. From there they pushed into the highlands of Kentucky, fording the Great Barren River, then the Green. At each crossing they stripped off what they could, tying it up into tight bundles they carried over their heads, thereby allowing themselves something warm to pull on once they reached the far shore, where they built a fire and drove off the chill the winter sky was whipping overhead.

Then on to Nolins Creek and Elizabethtown. Beyond there few miles remained before they crossed the icy Salt River, drawing close to Louisville and the mighty Ohio itself. Come nearly a thousand miles through the wilderness by wagon, foot, and horseback.

"More land getting cleared every trip," Heman Ovatt grumbled as they passed a growing number of settlers' cabins the closer they drew to the bustling riverfront town.

"Folks cutting down the forest for corn and wheat," Kingsbury replied.

"There's more'n enough forest to go around," Reuben Root argued. He swung his arm in an arc. "Lookit all this! You really figure they'll ever cut down all of these?"

"Settlers gone and drove off most of the critters," Bass said acidly. "I figure the trees just might be next to go."

"Sounds to be you're still nursing on sour milk over them buffalo," Kingsbury said.

Root agreed. "Yeah—an' you ain't never see'd a buffalo neither."

"Don't need to," Titus said, "to know they been drove off—gone out yonder someplace."

"That where you're fixing to take him?" Kingsbury asked, thumbing a gesture at Hezekiah.

"Ain't taking him nowhere with me," Bass replied. "He ain't mine no more."

"Then you must figure on setting him free?" Root inquired.

"Like I said I was."

"Ain'cha got no use for a Negra?" Ovatt asked.

For a moment he looked into the slave's yellowed eyes. Then Bass wagged his head. "I don't wanna be tied down by him."

"He'll bring you a fine profit," Kingsbury reminded.

"I ain't sellin' him," Titus snapped. "Gonna have someone up to Louisville write me a paper to sign and give to Hezekiah, sayin' to all what read it that the man been give his freedom."

"Him were mine, I'd sell him," Ovatt declared. "Good slave like him, bring top dollar this far north—"

"But he ain't yours," Bass interrupted. "An' he ain't mine no more. We get to Louisville tomorrow, I'll give him his freedom papers like I said I would."

"You're a man good on your word," Kingsbury added.

"Man ain't good on his word," Titus said, remembering a virtue taught him by his father, "man ain't good on nothing."

The following day when they reached the girdled trees that marked the outlying areas of a growing Louisville slowly extending into the forest, Titus Bass, true to his vow, searched out a local justice of the peace.

"You're certain this is what you want to do?" asked the red-faced shop owner with neck jowls pouring over the top of his buttoned collar as he measured the tall Negro. He reminded Titus of an old turkey cock with so much neck-wattle recently scraped red with a shaving razor.

"Yes, sir. I do intend to do this."

"Don't know as I can do it, son," the justice clucked.

"Why not?" he demanded.

"Like you said, you ain't got you no paper giving you rightful ownership of this here Negra. Gives a man pause, it does—maybeso this Negra belongs to your daddy."

"My pap never owned a slave in his life!"

His eyes narrowing in contemplation, the justice said, "Now, I don't suppose we could talk with your daddy about this matter, could we?"

Feeling the first itch of anger growing in his breast, Titus answered, "My pap lives back in Boone County. But I don't live there no more."

"Maybe you run off to Louisville with your family's Negra?"

"No!"

With a condescending smile the fat-necked justice wagged his head, saying, "But you got no way to prove the slave is yours to free."

Burning with sudden anger, Bass whirled on Hezekiah and asked in a voice cracking with emotion, "Are you my slave?"

Hezekiah nodded glumly. "I'm your slave."

"Makes you my property, right?"

"Yes, you my master."

Whirling back on the justice, Bass said, "There it is. What more you need from us? This man knows who his master is—and his master gonna free him for all time. You don't do it, I'll find someone else who will."

His scraped and scalded face turning crimson at the youngster's rebuke, the justice rose from behind his cherrywood desk and slammed a hand down with a resounding thud that echoed in the small office to the side of his store. "That's just what you're gonna have to do then, sonny. I ain't gonna have it on my conscience that I let a young boy like you go off an' do something foolish: turning your Negra into a freedman! I'll declare! Where you ever took a notion like that?"

Bass watched the fat-jowled man walk off, removing his sleeveless robe, returning to his shop next door. He stopped once, turned back on the two of them, and waved them out of his clapboard office. Bass turned to go, finding the boatmen pressing their noses against the murky panes of window glass, watching it all.

"So you get it done proper?" Root inquired when Titus and Hezekiah stepped out the door onto the board walk.

A gust of wind closed the door behind them. On the street again. In the cold. Bass looked up at the faces expectant of his answer. "Any of you got a idea where I can get me a paper says Hezekiah here is a freedman?"

Kingsbury rocked back on his heels, saying, "This be the only man what can do it right for you."

"No matter now. I stay with you, Titus Bass," Hezekiah replied. "Till we find right man to do it."

Beulah wagged her head. "That old frog. Shame on him."

"Ain't no other but him," Kingsbury argued.

"Sometimes, I declare, Hames—you're so addleminded," Beulah said, then turned to Titus to say quietly, "We just have to find us someone what can write."

Turning to stare at the woman, Titus found himself dumbfounded by the simplicity of what she was suggesting. "You saying we get someone to write up a paper for us?"

Beulah's eyes glanced at the boatmen before coming back to rest on Titus's. "And we have 'em sign that old frog's name to it."

"That's gotta be about as close to stepping outside the law as anything I ever heard!" Kingsbury complained.

"You get found out," Ovatt squealed, "there'll be stripes to pay on your back, Titus! Not just this here Negra's."

Beulah poked a finger into Kingsbury's chest, saying, "And you're telling me you ain't ever done all sorts of foul things at the edge of the law?"

"I ain't never used a goddamned man's name to do anything wrong!"

"It ain't wrong," Beulah protested. "I figure it's about as right as right can be."

In that moment Titus felt as proud as he could be for her, the way she gave the three boatmen pause, struck them dumb, unable to convince her.

Kingsbury's eyes blinked, as if he were working on something hard and fast behind them. "Right, or wrong—we get caught, this here is more serious'n causing a ruckus on a gunboat—"

"More serious'n killing a man—or a whore, Hames?"

"They was . . . she was fixing to kill us."

"So it was the right thing to do," Beulah said. "Just like this is the right thing for Titus here." With the three boatmen silenced, each of them standing there gape-mouthed, she turned to the youngster. "Now, you remember what that justice man's name was?"

Twisting his neck this way and that to search for some writing on the door or the window, Titus squinted, making sense of the letters and their placement. "Lu . . . ther L. P-pond."

Seemingly of a changed mind, Kingsbury slapped an arm around Bass's shoulder, his eyes darting up the street, then down. "Just get your paper writ up so we can get us over to Mathilda's place."

"Mathilda's place?" Titus repeated.

"Don't tell me you forgot awready," Ovatt said.

Root snorted, "Hell, I'd a'figured Mincemeat made Titus here a real comeback customer of hers."

"Hold on there, Hames Kingsbury! You ain't taking me to no such a place!" Beulah scolded. "Never been in one before, an' I don't intend to start now."

His palms coming up apologetically, Kingsbury started to explain, "Just a place where we can get us a square meal and a stout drink—"

"An' half-dressed women all hanging off you too!" Beulah snapped. "Wanting to dip their hands in your purse."

"But we got us old friends there," Kingsbury protested.

"Not no more, you don't." And she crossed her arms, turning from him huffily.

The pilot stepped around to face her, but again she whirled from him. "Beulah?"

"You fixing on marrying me like you said, your whoring days is done, Hames Kingsbury."

"M-marrying?" Root stammered. "That right—"

Kingsbury gestured for silence from them all as he took hold of Beulah's shoulders. "Course I'm gonna marry you—"

"You won't never again need no whore, Mr. Kingsbury," the woman told him. "I'm going downriver with you every trip."

With a mixture of excitement mingled with awe at the sudden announcement, Titus watched and listened as Beulah and the pilot finally declared what the two of them had been discussing for much of the long journey up from New Orleans.

Ovatt whirled on Root and asked, "An' you're telling me you didn't know?"

"I . . . I knowed they was thick," Reuben sputtered sheepishly.

"Yeah, real thick. 'Bout as thick as your skull," Ovatt said, then held his hand out to Kingsbury.

"Maybe you three ought'n go on over to Mathilda's by yourselves," the pilot said as they shook in turn, nodding at Beulah. "Me and the woman find us another place to bed in for the night."

"Mean you'll meet us down by the wharf come morning?" Root asked.

"Count on finding me there, waiting for all you late sleepers," Kingsbury replied, glancing down with no small satisfaction as Beulah finally stepped to his side and threaded her arm through his. "This crew still got us a few miles left afore we get all the way back up the Ohio to Cincinnati, where I can buy us 'nother flatboat. Ain't nothing changed my mind 'bout you an' Heman still working the river with me."

Root flicked a glance at Ovatt, then asked, "So you still figuring you need us?"

"Need you? Why, the hull lot of us been making a home on the river for years," Kingsbury snorted.

Then Beulah leaned forward to say, "You think just because me and Hames gonna be a pair now that we don't need you fellas? That it? Damned nonsense! If that's what you're thinking, you're both crazy as a mad coon. Me being your pilot's wife don't change a thing."

"But, well . . . there's some fellers what'd be afeared of having a woman on their boat—not saying it'd be me, you unnerstant," Root explained.

"Are you such a man?" Beulah asked.

Root smiled gamely and tried to shrug it off. "Maybeso you ain't no more bad luck than anything else, Beulah."

She leaned over to him and planted a kiss on Reuben's cheek. "That mean you figure it's awright for me to be part of your crew?"

While Root blushed, wide-eyed, Ovatt was the first to nod his head. Reluctantly, Reuben finally spoke up. "You're part of the crew—just as long as you keep us fed and the coffee on."

"I can do that," Beulah replied as she slipped back beside Kingsbury. "And since Titus here ain't gonna be part of the crew no longer, you'll likely need me to spell you fellas on an oar or the gouger from time to time."

A look of surprise crossed Ovatt's face. "You do that man's work too?"

"I been a boat pilot's woman since I can remember," she answered with a confident tilt to her chin. "So don't you think I can put my hands to every chore on a flatboat, including taking my turn at the rudder?"

"See, boys?" Kingsbury said confidently. "Just like I found out for myself—this here's one woman what can take care of her own self when it comes to a Kentucky broadhorn on the river."

With a happy wag of his head Root cheered, "Looks like we're back to being a foursome, it does at that!"

Ovatt nodded in agreement, saying, "When Ebenezer was kill't, I figured Titus here was the one bound to fill out our crew. S'why I got real worried when he said he wasn't gonna make a life on the river with us."

"No matter that he's going off on his own to do what he wants—now there's four of us," Kingsbury summed it up, then suddenly turned to the skinny youth. "Still, I wish I could find the words to make you wanna stay with us, Titus Bass."

Titus struggled to explain how he wanted to press on, reaching for his dream. "Far back as I can remember, I been thinking on making for Louisville."

Ovatt asked, "Come here to stretch your wings a bit?"

"Likely I will do that—if'n there's any stretching left to do after that float down to Norleans with the lot of you."

"Out yonder lays a great big world, Titus—just waiting for you. And there's allays the women and the whiskey while a young feller's tasting it all," Kingsbury said, stepping right up to Bass. "I'm gonna miss you."

"Only till you get back down the Ohio come spring," Bass reassured them, sensing a sour ball of sentiment begin to clog his throat.

"That's right, Hames," Root added. "Titus says he's gonna be right here in Louisville where we can look him up every trip down."

"Less'n Mincemeat kills him first!" Kingsbury joked, then clumsily threw his arms about the youngster. Into Titus's ear he whispered, "You'll take care of yourself now, hear?"

With the salty smart of his own tears and the sudden self-conscious silence surrounding them all, Bass could only nod, locked within the pilot's crude embrace. He was unaccustomed to such a sharing of emotion between men. Finding this thing of hugging a strange custom, yet discovering that embrace made him feel truly accepted. There and then he thought back with some regret, wishing his father had been the sort to show just this sort of affection. Still after all, none of his family had ever stood on that physical side of things. Not even his mother, not with all that she said and did. None of his kin had ever been much taken with outwardly showing warmth and affection.

So much did that river pilot's embrace mean to him that as soon as Kingsbury released him and took a step back, a sudden and chilling sense of loss swept over him. So much so that Bass was about to say he just might reconsider staying on with them—when Kingsbury reached up, tousled his hair, and gazed into Titus's face.

With glistening eyes the pilot said, "Just look at you, son. Come a long way from being that poorly critter what walked outta the woods on our night fire way back last fall. Cain't no man dare say you ain't come a long way, Titus Bass."

Try as he might to fight it, he could feel a tear escape from one eye, his lips quivering slightly as he fought to find the words—damning himself for such a childish display, angry at showing that sort of weakness here in the company of these strong men. But when he looked up, Bass saw Kingsbury's tears spill into his short-cropped, matted blond beard.

The pilot swiped at them carelessly as Beulah gripped his arm tight, her own eyes red-rimmed and brimming. With a voice suddenly sounding like a door dragged over its sill, Kingsbury said, "We'll see you here by the Ohio come late spring."

In the next heartbeat he had Beulah turned and moving away into the fading light of that winter afternoon.

"C'mon, Titus," Ovatt said, stoically refusing to let sentiment get the best of him as he grabbed hold of Bass's arm. "We gotta get over to Mathilda's and see if Mincemeat still remembers you."

Locked there between the two boatmen sweeping off to have themselves a spree, Titus was pulled away a few steps before he realized he had forgotten someone.

He jerked to a stop, turning around there in the last reddish splash of winter's afternoon sunlight, gazing back at the Negro. "You comin', Hezekiah?"

With only a shrug of his big, broad shoulders, the slave answered, his head hung, chin to chest. Confused, Titus hurried back to him, saw the tracks of moisture tracing shiny indigo furrows down the tattooed ebony cheeks.

Softly, Titus asked, "You're comin', ain't you?"

The big man answered, "You be going away from me soon, yes?"

"Hezekiah—I'm gonna see that you're set free. Ain't that what you want?"

"Free, yes. Free and go with Titus Bass."

"Maybeso you ought'n not be free with me no longer," Titus replied, trying to explain. "Maybeso you ought'n move on, go and try out your own wings now, Hezekiah."

The big chert-black eyes sought his out with their moistness. "Then we say good-bye soon."

"Not soon. Not tonight, anyways. Don't have to be tonight. C'mon, you go with us over to Mathilda's place. A fine place, with good food and lots of noisy folks."

"T-titus," Root began tentatively in a harsh whisper. "They don't 'llow Negras in Mathilda's place."

"The hell they don't!" Bass snapped indignantly. "I seen some back to the kitchen."

"They the help. So that's right where he can stay when we go in the place," Ovatt suggested. "Back with Mathilda's help."

Titus turned on the slave. "That be awright with you? Get your meal and maybe a place to curl up for the night back in the kitchen?"

"Be good to eat," he answered. "Good to find a warm place to sleep too."

Titus patted the tall slave on the arm. "Then in the morning we find us someone what can write, to make out my paper says you're a freedman now."

"Damn!" Root exclaimed, slapping himself alongside the head. "Why didn't I think of it sooner?"

Titus asked, "Think of what?"

"Mathilda her own self," Root said, grinning. "She knows how to make her letters and cipher her numbers with the best of 'em. There ain't many in Louisville gonna be any better'n her at it."

A sudden relief washed over Bass, despite all the raw tearing away and loss. The whorehouse madam would be the one to inscribe for Hezekiah that handwritten gift of freedom, thereby lifting a yoke from Titus's own neck with the same stroke of her quill. Now more than ever Bass realized no man should ever belong to another.

"There, Hezekiah!" he cheered. "Tomorry you'll be a freedman. You can go where you want. When you want. Ain't gonna belong to no man but your own self from then on."

"But," the big slave said, his eyes still brimming, "I allays belong to you."

Bass shook his head. "No, don't you understand? I'm freeing you. Don't belong to no one no more. Never did belong to me."

Hezekiah wagged his head emphatically. "No, Titus Bass. You not understand," he replied sternly. "You go make me a freedman, sure enough. But in here"—and he again tapped a single finger against his chest—"no matter what: I allays belong to you."

EIGHTEEN

Mincemeat wasn't there when Titus showed up at Mathilda's that bittersweet night of parting mingled with homecoming.

"She's up and left me to work downriver," the madam said a little huffily.

"Downriver?" Titus asked anxiously. "How far?"

"Place called Owensboro. Gone off on her own—and the trollop took two of my girls with her!" the madam explained. "Said the three of 'em going into business for themselves."

Turning to Root, Bass hurriedly asked, "Where's Owensboro?"

"If'n it's the place I'm thinking it be, wasn't much there—"

"Where?" Titus interrupted.

"Only a few poor cabins 'long the wharf—"

"Where?" And he grabbed the boatman's coat flap.

"Downriver a ways," Reuben explained. "They was just clearing a spot for it on the south bank when we come past few months back."

"On the Ohio?"

Root nodded. "I'd make it 'bout halfways to the Messessap from here."

"I took her in, give her a chance to make something of herself," Mathilda grumbled as she turned away, waving toward one of her Negro lackeys. "I'll see that the help brings you boys your supper while I go off to fetch my writing things . . . if you're still of a mind to free up that skin-headed Negra of yours."

Titus bobbed his head. "Yes'm. I am."

Mathilda smiled as she started away, smoothing the chintz cloth that covered only half of her ample bosom. "Anyone who's got manners enough to call me ma'am gets my attention, fellas."

When she returned, the madam eloquently worded two copies of the same declaration freeing Hezekiah. One, of course, would go with the freedman, and the second Titus chose to keep for himself, protected inside a small waxed fold of foolscap. Then she had one of her lackeys escort Bass back to her own room, where a steaming kettle of soapy water was soon delivered. With a scrap of cambric cloth he scrubbed himself from the washbasin in the corner of the lamplit room, then found the plush softness of her feather mattress an inviting contrast from the crude grass ticks he had so far encountered.

When at last he was awakened there in Mathilda's bed, all but one of the oil lamps had been snuffed. Soft, pudgy fingers were at his flesh, arousing him gently. A hot whisper clung to his ear as the madam declared she would give him all the sweet delights she could that night, in fact, whenever he wanted to visit her, seeing how he was going to stay on in Louisville.

As good as it felt, what with her fingers raking up and down the hard, hot length of him, the way she smelled good and sweet from cinnamon and tamarind she had rubbed on her neck and down her heaving cleavage—how he found her fleshy plumpness so startling after Mincemeat's angular hardness—right then Titus didn't have the will to tell Mathilda that he had determined to move on.

That hadn't even come up at all when he'd slipped out to gulp down some coffee and swallow the hot breakfast the Kangaroo's kitchen served. There among the great boiling kettles and the sweaty, shiny faces of Mathilda's black-skinned help, Titus retrieved one of the declarations from inside his shirt. As Hezekiah held one corner of the wrinkled paper, Bass held the other, preparing to read it aloud for all in that stunned kitchen where thick aromas swirled up from three fireplaces.

"I cain't rightly read all these proper words Mathilda put down on this here paper," he explained to the freedman with some frustration. "But I do recall what I told her to put down, and she read it over to me when she was done. This says I was your owner. Says I fair and square are setting you free, a slave man no more. This paper tells that you're free to go where you want from here on out. Then I put my mark down right here. She signed her name to it, and here's where two other gals she got to come in put their names last evening after watching the both of us put our marks to it. G'won now, as a freedman. That paper you carry is your'n to show any man what don't believe you be your own man from here on out."

That dawn the kitchen cradled them in such warmth, downright steamy and fragrant was it. Just like the embrace he suddenly gave to that tall black man.

"You're free, Hezekiah."

"I never forget you, Titus Bass."

"You damn well better not," he replied, then pulled his blanket roll off his shoulders and handed it to the freedman. "Here, now. Want you to have this."

"But it's your'n," he exclaimed in a harsh half sob of a whisper, his yellowed eyes brimming.

"Your'n now. This morning I seen to it I put some fire-makings in there, my old tin cup and that knife I first brung me from home . . . 'long with a li'l pouch of coins just in case you need buy yourself some food or a place to stay till you get where you're wanting to go."

His big hands trembled as he clutched the thick roll of blankets enclosing the precious gifts to his breast. Hezekiah said, "Going to do like you said —see what's west, Titus. Maybe even a place for me out there."

"If'n I stood in your place, Hezekiah—I'd likely be looking for to find me a place where a man can be just a man. Where there ain't no slave owner. No man made to be a slave. Out yonder there's bound to be a place for you. Just like there's bound to be a place for ary man . . . we look hard enough, long enough."

"You stay here when I go?" the freedman asked.

"No. Last night I figured I'd just push on," Titus replied. "Want to see someone I know—now they gone west to a new place downriver. Maybeso we can walk that road west together. Least as far as Owensboro afore we say farewell."

They took their breakfast together there in the kitchen, squatting in the corner with steaming mugs of coffee, before Titus went out as the town's shopkeepers were beginning to put out their wares for the day. Slipping more coins from the waistband of his britches, he bought himself a new pair of blankets, a small tin in which to carry his new fire steels and flints, along with a new belt knife in an oiled leather sheath that he proudly hung at his hip. At the side of the river he and Hezekiah bade the rest a farewell as the boatmen and Beulah moved off toward the light of a climbing sun, while the youth and the tall freedman pointed their noses west.

For more than eight short winter days and something on the order of 130 miles, the pair followed the twisting course of the Ohio's south bank until they reached the timbered hillside overlooking the land being cleared for Owensboro. Girdled trees strained for the sky as others were felled, then quickly dragged off by grunting teams of oxen while knots of men poured oil atop the fresh stumps and set them afire until the sky was corduroyed with black streamers. Still more laborers laid log upon log, raising the walls of cabins that would hold at bay the last of winter's chill from these hardy pioneering folk pushing west with the migrating frontier. Below Titus the air hung ripe with fresh sweat and steaming dung, burning hardwood and lye soap coming to a boil, those open fires attended by women who slowly worked great paddles round and round in the pungent brew, fingering sprigs of hair back from their rosy faces as the trail-weary pair pushed through their midst toward the cluster of shacks and lean-tos and cabins gathered close by the river's edge.

There in the cold shadows of that late afternoon he found her in the makeshift watering hole not any bigger than his folks' cabin back in Boone County. Mincemeat had one stockinged leg kicked up on a crude bench hacked from half a length of a tree trunk supported by four wobbly pegs, her arm draped over the shoulder of an old man whose five-day stubble showed more gray than it did the same mousy brown of what little hair still remained atop his sunburnt head.

"Mathilda told me I'd find you downriver," he began in a happy gush.

At first she only turned her head, squinted at him through the musty haze of that poorly drafted fireplace and the smoke of more than a dozen pipes, candles flutting the air with their dancing fingers of light. The room fell to a hush; all the customers turned to study not only Bass, but the big Negro behind him.

"Mathilda?" Then the woman dropped her skinny leg in its worn stocking to the pounded clay floor and turned on him wearily. "Do I know you?"

"Sure you know me, Mincemeat," he replied with sudden alarm. "We knowed each other up to the Kangaroo."

"I just come from Louisville," she said sourly, her bleary, bloodshot eyes peering over his shoulder at the tall, bald man behind him. "It's a good place to be from. He'll have to go—his kind ain't 'llowed in here."

"He's with me."

"Looks to be you'll both have to leave too," she replied a bit acidly, almost too wearily. "C'mon back when you're by your own self and ready to have some fun with Mincemeat."

His heart was sinking. Titus felt himself beginning to tremble. "You . . . you don't know me?"

"I supposed to?"

"I come all this way to find you."

"Find me?" And she laughed a bit too forced and shrill. "Must be you're wanting a roll." Mincemeat put out her hand. "As you can see, I'm still a working woman, mister. That means a roll will cost you a shilling—an' that's good till you're satisfied. Half-shilling for each time you're satisfied after that till the night's done." She began to turn back to the small group of hardened, dirty men she had been regaling at the moment Titus walked in. "You come back when you ain't got him along and you fix to spend some money on Mincemeat."

Smarting in anger, Bass quickly glanced at the other two bawdy women looking on with amused attention, their arms draped over their customers. Shreds of memory placed them as Mathilda's girls too.

"Abigail—" Then he watched as she smarted with the name. Flinching as if struck with a flat hand, slowly turning back to gaze at him with a studious squint.

"I'm Titus," he continued softly as the noise in that grogshop started to swell once more, like a deer's bladder he would fill with tiny pebbles from river gravel, to stretch it out while it dried to make himself a pouch. "Titus Bass. Don't you remember me?"

Shoving a long strand of unruly hair back from her cheek, she whirled away from the others, stepping his way with one red-rimmed eye clenched. "By damn, you don't say! It for certain is the boy what come to the Kangaroo not long back—all ready to become a man, this'un was."

At the table behind her some of the others snorted. Bass sensed the first burn of embarrassment. But as suddenly her face became open and lit up with undisguised glee. Mincemeat lunged against him, her bony arms wrapped around his waist.

"Course I remember you," she exclaimed, then whirled to explain to the room, "I'm sure you older fellas understand if I spend some time here with the young'un." She sniggered, saying, "You all ought'n remember what it was like when you had you a peeder what stayed hard all night long. Lemme tell you when this girl gets a chance to slip one of them atween her legs—she does it!"

The rest of the men laughed and hooted, as crude and foul a bunch of flatboaters and wood-raftsmen as he had ever seen clear down to New Orleans. He could still hear some of those poor, sick, womanless drunkards plain as anything when she took him out the low front door of that cabin and pointed to some tarps stretched between some nearby trees.

"Tell your Negra he can bed down there. You an' me going over yonder way."

When Hezekiah moved off to spread his blankets beneath the sections of oiled canvas lashed above a fire pit where sat a three-legged stool and cooking pot suspended on a chain from a tall tripod, the woman yanked Titus away, leading him through the folds of a canvas door into her small log lean-to. No sooner had he tried to stand inside than he banged his head on the rough-barked logs of the low ceiling. Bass dragged off his crumpled hat and rubbed his scalp.

"Get down here with me," she instructed as she pulled back the pile of blankets from a thin pallet of bear and deer hides before she began yanking off her own grimy, smoke-stained garments. "C'mere an' gimme what you gimme before at the Kangaroo. Dangerous up there, ain't it, Titus?" She quickly pulled her long dress up and over her head. "Banging your head on that roof 'stead of being down here banging on me."

When he collapsed beside her on the pallet, Bass found she smelled of stale whiskey, old meals, a day's suffocation of tobacco smoke, and the rancid stench of other men—but, God! how he found himself ignited by the mere sight of her naked flesh, the feel of the generous curves to her as he hurried out of his shucks and slid beneath those icy blankets atop her. It didn't stay cold in there for long.

That first time the woman didn't fall back on ceremony or any of the preliminaries; instead she stroked him so savagely that he had no choice but to rise to the occasion before she placed him home and thrust her bony hips upward against him. Within moments Titus spent himself in great waves of relief, then slept against her, awakening in the darkness of that winter's night to find himself hungry once more.

"You can take me all you want, when you want," she vowed with a whisper in the dark. "Long as you promise you'll never call me Mincemeat again."

"I . . . I promise . . . Ab-abigail."

Back again with her body now, the way she flung herself at him with such fiery abandon in the dark and the cold of that shanty, he came to realize how he had yearned for her.

Only with the coming of predawn's dim, gray light did he remember Hezekiah. As cold as it was in that log and canvas shanty, Titus grew ashamed—rock-certain it must surely be much, much colder for the freedman who had joined him on this journey downriver to Owensboro. Tugging on his clothes as he ground at the sleep crusting both eyes, the youth hobbled through the low doorway, past the canvas flaps, surprised to find Hezekiah squatting on a nearby stump, waiting for him.

"Dis morning I gotta go," the tall man explained softly, gesturing downriver with a slight bob of his head.

Bass glanced over his shoulder to the shanty at his back. "I . . . I didn't mean to—"

"Don't make no big matter of it. I got me a good night's sleep in them blankets you give me. Et me on some meat left over in that fire pot. Time now to do my business getting on 'way from here."

Titus stuffed in his shirt, shivering with the cold, sunless chill, and pulled his belt tight in the buckle. "You wasn't going 'thout saying nothing, was you?"

"You see'd I was waiting for you, Titus Bass. Tell you my fare-thees right to your face. Tell you my thanks for making me a free man."

He stood looking at the big man, that bald head covered with a bright red bandanna Titus had bought him in Louisville. "You need find you a hat." Then he impetuously pulled his own shapeless felt from his head and set it atop Hezekiah's. "There, now. How's that fit you?"

A big smile illuminated his face like a Christmas bonfire, his eyes rolling upward to regard the floppy brim. "Like it was made for me."

"It's your'n now."

"I'll pay you back someday, Titus Bass."

"No need. It ain't much."

"Said I'd pay you back."

Titus nodded. "All right. I know I can count on you to do just that."

"Saying my fare-thees is a hard thing."

"Harder thing for me was to leave you standing there in that cage—

bound away for some man's fields," Titus answered. Then he shook his head, remembering Boone County, and said, "Working the ground is hard enough for a man what wants such a life . . . I just can't imagine what possesses a man to buy another to do his work for him."

For a long moment they both stood all but toe to toe, perhaps both in wonder at what to say next as wisps of thick ground fog swirled at their feet and the cold breeze nudged at Titus's hair across his shoulders.

"That woman in there," Hezekiah began, "she good poon?"

"Poon?"

"Poon-tang," he explained in a dumbfounded sort of way, and shrugged. "What men come to Annie Christmas's place told me was what they wanted from a hoah."

"Poon-tang," Titus repeated, and glanced back at the shanty. "Yes," he answered. "Maybe good enough for me to stay on here for a while."

The freedman shuffled his feet for a bit, then finally blurted out, "We come 'cross't each t'other one day?"

That stunned him for a moment. Then Bass brought his eyes back up to look at those yellowed ones of Hezekiah's. "I hope so, my friend. Cain't say as it's likely, even possible to count on. I hear there's so much country west of here—man can get lost out there if he's a mind to."

Titus watched some of the brightness drain from the freedman's features.

"I was hoping . . ."

"Why don't you count on it, then, Hezekiah?"

Some of the smile came back as the big man's eyes pooled. He swept the youth's hand up in his, shaking it tightly between both of his. "I count on that, Titus Bass. I pay you back for all you done one day. Pay you back in spades."

"I know you will," he answered, choking on the words when he saw Hezekiah's eyes begin to spill.

"Gotta go," the freedman said clumsily, half turning away with great reluctance.

"Man's gotta leave when a man's gotta leave," Titus replied, holding his hand out again.

"No, like this," Hezekiah said softly, pushing the hand aside and pulling the youth against him. "Is the best way to say my fare-thees."

"A damn good way," Bass whimpered against the Negro's chest.

Eventually Hezekiah released him, whirled on his heel, and sprinted off all before Titus realized. He raised his hand to wave at the freedman's back, not saying a word, and stood still as stone, feeling the loss of that last, fierce embrace, sensing that great emptiness come with the going of that friend after the farewells of so many friends. Now Bass was alone again. Except for the woman.

The slithering gray fingers of ground fog and the sharp, black, skeletal fingers of winter-bare trees swallowed Hezekiah as the man pushed west, away from the coming sun.

Titus felt the cold of a sudden. He stood there, barely seventeen. No home to speak of but a tarp and log shanty that belonged to a whore. No friends left in this settlement but Abigail. He had killed some Indians, a white man, and saved the lives of others. Bass wasn't sure if growing up to be a man was all that great a thing or not anymore.

Turning slightly, he gazed at the shanty. Figured he could likely find work in a new place like Owensboro—an infant settlement sorely in need of strong backs and iron constitutions. As far as it was downriver from Louisville, chances were a man would make a go of it down at the landing, unloading goods from far upriver one day, loading timber and other staples for downriver the next. He felt certain he would find work and just might venture out to do so that very afternoon.

Just about the time the sun was sucked into the dark gut of the clouds overhead, the first icy snowflake struck his cheek, sharp as a patch knife and cold as the belly of the earth itself in these last weeks before spring. A time of year when it seemed spring would never come. When it seemed he had said good-bye to just about everything he had ever known, everyone he had ever come to care about.

Quit miserating, he scolded himself. At least here he would find work. At least here he had her. No matter that he would have to share her with others day and night. Titus figured there just might be enough warmth left over for him when Mincemeat quit for the night and dragged herself back to that pallet of bear hides and dirty wool blankets where he had banged his head before he had banged her.

Turning east, he looked upriver. Not sure where Kingsbury and the others might have put in for the night. Suddenly wondering how his mother had passed his seventeenth birthday. For the first time caring that his brothers should be giving their father a hand in the fields.

Then he looked to the west as it began to snow with a surprising ferocity. Hezekiah was gone into the teeth of that storm, alone. Truly alone now.

Already Titus had struggled against just about everything else and come out all right. Yet there remained one final struggle to pit himself against.

One day soon, when he was finally ready, he would move on as Hezekiah had done: by himself. Knowing he could not until the day when he could finally hack up this great pain of loneliness like a man hacked up something choking him, damn near suffocating him.

Hack himself free of it. And move on.

When that first great quiver of the earth's crust rocked the lower Ohio River valley, Titus was on the cleated plank leading him across the icy water from a flatboat's gunnel to the Owensboro wharf, where another two dozen broadhorns were tied up.

All that December morning long he and others had been hiring themselves out to merchants from distant points overland, and to upriver boat captains, taking cargo off the flats to begin its cross-country journey by horseback or wagon, perhaps hoisting bales and kegs and barrels onto what rivercraft were bound for Natchez and New Orleans. The icy air clung about a man, hoarfrost wreathed about his face, a sharp chill in every one of those wispy strands of fog that danced like greasy gauze clear across the river to the north bank of the Ohio. A pewter-pale, buttermilk-colored sun sulled in the sky overhead, every bit as cold and devoid of warmth as were the cast-iron hoppers squatting here and there along the dock where the stevedores kept fires going, over which they warmed their hands, rubbed their frozen fingers, even turned and kneaded their numbed asses over the feeble warmth that itself seemed to shrink beneath the mighty onslaught of this most recent cold snap gripping the lower Ohio.

Ice coated everything: tree branches and trunks, thick sheets of it whirling out of the northwest over the past three days to plaster the sides of cabins and shops, to slick the wharf itself. If the sun had ever chosen to put in a grand and bright appearance, it would have made for a dazzling show. But, instead, the sun hid behind the thick layer of icy frost blanketing the earth.

At dawn that morning Titus and some of the others had dragged in handcarts filled with mounds of sandy earth scraped from the bank east of town. This they scattered with their shovels over the crude, wide planks of the wharf, even spreading the sand up the length of those cleated planks that stretched from dock to flatboat like bands of thick and mortified connective tissue.

So it was that one moment he was plodding toward the wharf, planting each thick-soled, fur-lined pac moccasin deliberately along the sanded plank, glancing inquisitively at the ice riming the river below him around every trunklike stanchion supporting the dock . . . when the next heartbeat found him freed of the ninety-pound keg of ironmongery bound south for the settlement at Bowling Green. Like a dog flinging water from its hide— the keg flew one way, Bass the other. Just before he hit the water, the oak cask crashed against the side of the wharf with a great metallic clatter, splintering and splashing . . . but by then he was beneath the surface of the Ohio, numbed immediately, shocked by the cold immersion, his mind slow to react—until he realized he damn well might drown.

Not that he really hated water. It was something he might admit to drinking every now and then. And water enjoyed a fair enough reputation on those rare occasions when a man wanted himself a bath. But, by and large, if Titus was about to confront water, he wanted it on his own terms: shallow enough for him to stand in, no deeper. Those months floating down the Ohio and the Mississippi on a flatboat manned by a good and savvy crew had been one thing, but to confront water all on his lonesome—that took an entirely different sort of courage. The very courage he found himself still in want of at that moment.

Sluggishly clawing his way through the black, icy water, Titus burst to the surface, gasping at the freezing air, teeth chattering uncontrollably, his heavy woolen clothing like great stones capturing his limbs, dragging him down. Struggling through the water for the side of the wharf, he found his arms heavy and unresponsive, his legs sodden, reluctant to help him. The frosty air above the choppy water was alive with screams and wails, the cries of bellowing animals lashed to wagons they jerked and reared against, frightened screeches of the people who careened off in all directions, crashing into one another as the wharf suddenly heaved itself up right before Bass's eyes.

As if the riverbed below him had sunk in that instant, the mighty Ohio surged back from the bank with the strength of some unseen, mighty hand —and in that momentary lull he struggled to reach a wharf piling. Clutching it with all his might with both arms and legs, he turned, trembling, to gaze at the main channel of the Ohio and beheld a terrifying sight. What water had been mysteriously sucked away toward the northern bank was at that very

moment cresting against itself in a frothy gray tidal wave rearing some
fifteen feet high, one long and billowy wall of dingy-brown water beginning
to hurtle back his way—aiming right for the dock at Owensboro.

"Gimme your hand!"

Titus jerked around, looked up, stared at the bony hand extended
down to him—recognizing those wide eyes in that half-pretty face of hers—
then lunged to grab hold.

Straining, Mincemeat rocked back with all she had in her frame—
succeeding more from a long shudder the wharf itself underwent with the
next severe, rolling tremble of the earth's shell . . . and dragged him just
far enough that Bass could fling an arm over the end of the rough planks,
hoist a leg up. She freed his hand and grabbed that leg, yanking desperately
on his soggy pants turning to ice in the frigid air, heaving back with all her
might. And when she wasn't grunting with her Herculean efforts, she
bawled with the most hair-raising scream Titus had ever heard.

Sprawled on his belly across the roiling, sand-coated dock, Bass gasped
for air, sputtering as his belly spewed up river water. From the corner of his
eye he watched that monstrous wave thundering down upon him; he scrambled to his feet, pulling her up with him. Beneath them the wharf creaked,
groaned, then screamed as it tore itself apart, hurtling them both into the air,
thrown a dozen feet toward the bank as the dock wrenched itself free of the
southern shore. Down into the last of the sand scattered atop those planks
slanting toward the water like jackstraws they both tumbled as that great
wooden structure screeched in protest against what long iron spikes still held
it together, moaning in protest of the last few moorings imprisoning the
wharf against the riverbank that itself was peeling away in great crumbling
gobs of what, until moments before, had been solid ground. Sheet after sheet
of that dark loam was shredding itself away with each jolting shudder of the
earth's crust. The Ohio was all but back upon them.

That rampart of foam crashed against the two dozen or so flats and
keels, raising them like children's toys on its icy, boiling surface, flinging
some high into the top of the leafless trees sheltering the riverbank being
shed piece by piece into the Ohio, other craft flung into what remained of the
dock with a deafening thunder as wood splintered against wood. Great
planks of oak cartwheeled through the air as if they were no more than mere
whittling splinters. The force of the river's collision with the wharf shattered
more of the trunk-sized pilings into kindling.

With a great, long groan of agony, the wharf beneath them keened to the side, collapsing at long last toward the fevered river as if the Ohio were a giant, gaping maw swallowing, devouring everything within reach of its monstrous appetite.

"Titus!"

At her shriek he whirled, the fingers of one hand all that held him from sliding toward the black, roiling waters. Just feet above him Mincemeat slipped, slid his way on her belly, her own hands clawing uselessly at the icy planks as she spilled ever downward. Lunging toward her with his free arm, he felt the ground shudder beneath him. Then as suddenly the wharf heaved once again, flinging them both into the air. Spinning, wheeling, he landed in a heap beside her, the air driven from his lungs. Now she had a grip on his leg, and he had a purchase on the end of a plank that teetered precariously sideways as the rest of the wharf's superstructure slowly creaked to the side, giving way toward the river.

"Keep hol't on me!" he shouted to her above the screams and bawling of those terrified people on shore: the frightened ones who huddled on higher ground, watching the ground split like overripe pecans below them, those excruciating wails of the wounded and maimed, beaten and broken and crushed by the riverbed's cruel tremble.

Then he began to claw with his free hand, trying for a grip on another plank before he dared free the first hand, swinging a few feet closer toward the bank and solid ground. One wide plank at a time he slid his bloody hands pierced by splinters as the river heaved and frothed at their feet, like a yapping, monstrous, living thing devouring thick planks of once-great flat-boats now nothing more than creaking, groaning timbers hurtled together and flung against the sinking wharf like so much flotsam.

Titus clung to a piling with one arm while he twisted to reach down with the other, and snagged Mincemeat's wrist, pulling her free of his leg. Whimpering like a small, frightened animal caught with nowhere to run, she clawed her way up his legs to cling at his waist and refused to let go as two men slogged up to their knees in the mud to yank and drag them onto the last fixed portion of the wharf. Together the four clambered to their feet.

When the next shudder of the earth came, Bass lunged forward, one watery leg moving, then the next, the woman clinging to him like a deer tick sucking its fill until they were above the river street, standing in the midst of those who were to survive this great and mysterious quake of the earth.

There on the icy, trampled ground he collapsed onto his hands and knees, his every breath feeling like a handful of painful shards of glass splintering inside his chest. Mincemeat rolled onto her back, gasping as well, her eyes clenched as tight as her mouth was open, tongue lolling like a hound out of breath. Across her forehead and down into one eye ran a nasty, oozy gash. Her hands were dirty, bloodied. His a mass of bleeding wounds. Bass looked down at himself. His pants were torn, both legs cut and plastered with mud. Only then did he feel his whole face begin to throb. Touching his cheek below one eye made the rest of his head ache with a sudden fire. He had broken something in his face on one of those flights he'd taken across the wharf, he decided. But at least they were alive.

Slowly Titus turned, squatting in a heap beside her, there among the many who had been fortunate enough to clamber to higher ground when the first roll had struck Owensboro.

"How . . . how'd you know?" he asked her in a gasp.

"Know what?" she replied without opening her eyes.

"To come get me."

"I was already coming down there," she explained softly, only then opening her eyes. "Bringing you something to have your noon dinner with me."

"You damn well may've saved my hash," he admitted, staring down at the woman who had warmed his bed through what had been left of last spring, followed by a long and humid summer, then finally into these first cold, sleety weeks of another winter.

It had been something on the order of a year now since Ebenezer Zane had first led him into Mathilda's Kangaroo tavern. Just shy of a year since he had first experienced her back in that tiny crib. In all that time he could not remember sensing anything beyond an animal need for her. Yet here and now, as the thunder of the earth's great crumbling shudder died in the distance, great flocks of shrieking birds blackening the sky overhead, Titus realized he truly did care for this bony whore. Not that he believed she might ever love him the way he imagined a woman could love a man and be loved in return.

Yet here he sat, in the flush of that moment of terror—having been saved by Mincemeat—only now beginning to realize what he must mean to her. Perhaps even more important, sensing for the first time that she meant much more to him than a warm place to sleep, more than a moist receptacle for his peeder when it grew hungry for relief, more than a companion at his side to help drive away the long and lonely hours of these seasons while he sorted out what next to do with those years yet to come.

"Hell, I'd done the same for anyone," she said gruffly, rocking up to one elbow and swiping gently at the eye where the blood oozed.

He seized her by the shoulders. "No, you wouldn't."

She glared at him harshly a moment; then her face seemed to crack, softening, her eyes deepening in hue. "You bastard," she whispered, those eyes pleading. "Don't you ever, ever take advantage of me . . . now that you know what I . . . how I—"

"I swear. Never will I."

"Can I trust you, Titus?"

He gulped, blinking the tears back as folks flooded past them, heading for what was left of the south riverbank where once had stood a street bustling with frontier commerce, a wharf where riverboats had tied up, and the town's population helped inch settlement farther and farther west.

"You can trust me with your life, Abigail."

Her lips moved as if she were trying to say something, then she collapsed against him instead. Wrapping her skinny arms about him tightly, she buried her face in his chest, sobbing. "Don't care what you say, I know I cain't ever trust you now. Ain't never been able to trust no man. Your kind is here today. Gonna be gone off tomorrow. You'll just go away, tearing yourself off a little piece of my heart when you disappear."

"Didn't ever have no intention of leaving you . . . least like that I won't."

"You bastard," she groaned with a shudder, as if in saying it to Titus Bass, she could lump all men together in him. "You're no better'n a lying sack of pig's entrails—all of you!"

And the harder she sobbed, the tighter she clung to his icy coat. All around them stunned people trudged this way and that in shock, as if struck half-dead at what had just befallen them. But there on that tiny piece of icy, sodden ground, their sodden clothes freezing in the frightfully cold air, the two of them sat. Bass rocked her in his arms.

"I won't never leave you like that," he whispered into the wet sprigs of her wild hair that still smelled of too much tobacco smoke and the musty stench of their bedding gone too long without airing, those blankets and hides they retreated under every night she trundled back to him, for a few hours all done with lying on her back in those stinking cribs behind the saloon that once stood at the river's edge.

"You damn right you won't leave me, Titus Bass," she promised harshly. "I'll leave you first. Afore you leave me hurting. I'll say my fare-thee-well to you, you bastard. Just like I been wanting to say it to every man I ever come to care for just a little . . . when he up and leaves me."

Suddenly she jerked back, snagging the lapels of his dripping coat. "Some of those sons of bitches even had the balls to steal what little money I had at the time. Can you beat that? They'd hit me, made me bleed, then stole't what little I had hid away for myself—"

"You're hurt. Bleeding," he interrupted, suddenly drawn from the tremble of her blue lips to the darkening gash at her brow. "Let's go see to it."

As Titus dragged her to her feet, he said, "How's a fella s'posed to thank you for saving 'im?"

She stood quivering beside him. "Onliest way I know is just don't ever run off from me like them others done. That's how. You'll thank me by waiting until I take off on you."

Looking down into her frightened eyes, he knew he had no way of ever understanding her terror that she might fall in love with him. "I ain't gonna hurt you. Ain't gonna ever hurt no one like that—"

"You just let me go, Titus. Let me leave you behin't when the time comes."

Without saying anything more Bass turned Abigail toward the path of girdled trees that would take them west toward the edge of town, where the settlement of Owensboro had stretched itself more and more every week this past summer. There he had raised them a new place, a dugout a little bigger than her shanty had been, with a bit better roof of all one pitch, just like a lean-to. A single door and window in that front facing the river. They hadn't needed anything more, because he worked by day and she worked by night, and they gave themselves to one another in the moments of passing. For the time being it was enough to share what little they had with one another.

For the time.

The center of that great earthquake struck in Missouri, some seventy miles below the mouth of the Ohio, at a settlement called New Madrid, once a Spanish military post on the west bank of the Mississippi. For more than a hundred miles in every direction the earth convulsed.

Although Owensboro lay 130 miles away as the crow would fly, even that part of the lower Ohio River valley wasn't spared much of the devastation that eleventh day of December, 1811. Not only the Ohio, but even more so the Mississippi, both rolled back in their beds, flowing north for a short time while the earth heaved beneath them. Hundreds upon countless hundreds of keelboats, Kentucky broadhorns, log rafts of all description were torn apart, dashed against sandbars and riverbanks, the surface of the great rivers strewn for weeks and weeks with the debris of craft and cargo alike.

Five nights later near ten o'clock the crust of the earth trembled once more. Waterfowl clacked and squawked overhead, afraid to put down and roost as they were scattered to the four winds in their fear.

Then again the next day, December 17. Once more the banks caved in, carved away by forces stronger than the rivers that reversed direction in their beds. Great chasms splintered open across forest and field—raw, gaping lacerations in the earth that drew the curious and the frightened and the truly awed in the weeks and months to come—brought there to stare and consider. And when folks returned to the river, they always found it foaming, littered with a tangle of drift timber and uprooted trees. The thick forests were now a maze of sundered stands of maple, elm, oak, and beech. Those caught in more open country had witnessed the earth undulate in regular waves advancing at close to the pace of a trotting horse. In those first few days following the initial quake, there were times when the day became all but dark as the night, times when the sun failed to show its face, hidden behind a yellow pall, a haze wrought of dust and fires and hell on earth.

By Christmas many folks had begun migrating away from that tormented land. Where they were bound for sure, they did not know. But word already had it that the worst of things had devastated the region south and west from the mouth of the Ohio. Best to head back east and north, they figured. If a wagon could be had, settlers loaded it with all they could carry out of that dangerous country some said was condemned by the hand of God Almighty. If nothing else was available, they strapped what they could to the backs of their horses, mules, oxen, and milch cows, setting off to get as far as possible from that land of the devil, often forced in their travels to bridge the great chasms of earth rent in those mighty upheavals.

Even the wildlife migrated for a time, panthers and turkeys, deer and bear, wolves and waterfowl, all huddling in among the frightened fleeing from the maw of hell, taking what comfort they could from humankind in the wake of so great a catastrophe. Just to get out of that damned country.

And *damned* that country was, they believed. Nothing but the wrath of God could have caused so great a calamity as to make the earth shake as it continued to do from time to time, right on into February of 1812 with no fewer than twenty-seven full-scale quakes. All too many of those pushing east believed this terrible retribution was being visited upon the unclean, the impure, the unholy and unrepentant who had flocked to the lower Mississippi Valley to feast themselves on flesh and whiskey, wine, women, and debauchery, in the devil's playgrounds of Natchez and New Orleans.

Those who fled often looked back over their shoulders as they left the downriver settlements like Owensboro. Some merely clucked and shook their heads. Others ranted out the last of their sanctimonious warnings. Look to the heavens! Why, a burning star had foretold of catastrophe! That very same comet that had streaked across the heavens back in August and on into September and even October, with each fiery trip warning of God's hand soon to be unleashed on the land of the sinners. Even the righteous who would not listen, so the warnings went, would be swallowed up with the unclean.

"Go! Go now!" shouted one of the prophets of doom standing there at the edge of what was left of the Owensboro wharf Titus and the others labored to rebuild that cold, icy January.

With a singing of hymns the doomsayer led a curious flock in song and fervent prayer before he unleashed that brimstone tirade castigating those who sinned against the Judgment Day. It took him no time to gather a sizable crowd of those still clinging to Owensboro, women who now huddled beneath shawls or shreds of Russian canvas, a few men who shuddered beneath wool blankets to listen to that dire warning from one who, by the conviction of his powerful words, appeared to have a much greater knowledge about such things both physical and metaphysical than the mere common man.

"The end is coming!" he bellowed, holding up his scuffed and worn text at the end of his arm, a long staff in the other, exhorting his gathering. "In this—His own word—God Himself has ordained the end to arrive in just such a way. Take heed of my pronouncement, for the mouth of that comet unleashed by His great hand has brought nigh the end of man."

"The comet!" some in the crowd shouted in eager response.

"Yes—the comet!" the anointed one shrieked. "The earth has quaked because of the comet that made its appearance across God's firmament months ago. A comet with two great horns, like the devil has horns himself!"

"Work of the devil!" one in the crowd roared.

"Two great horns!" the prophet shouted. "And this frail, temporal scrap of earth where man has made his home now quakes because we have rolled over one of those horns on that comet, and now lie lodged betwixt that pair of horns that adorn the devil's own brow!"

So it was they flooded east in small groups and by droves, all those who feared lying in the lap of the devil when the hand of God returned to smite them again . . . leaving behind those who did not believe in such superstition, those who relished the depravity of living there in the lap of the devil himself, and even one lone man who had vowed he would not be the first to leave.

After all, enough folks remained behind, or migrated downriver, that Titus still had his job, could go on working through each day, spending each night waiting for her and wondering if the following morning would be the dawn when she failed to return.

Here in Owensboro there were many who celebrated their deliverance from destruction by merrymaking. When the aftershocks rocked their houses and saloons in the following weeks, they clung to one another or the walls until the trembling subsided, and they dared dance once more. It was this indomitable spirit that had brought such hardy souls to this land. Only those who truly belonged at the edge of that new frontier elected to stay on.

They always had.

The French and their Indians hadn't run them off their holdings sixty years before. A generation later the English and their Indians had failed to scare off their kind. Those of pioneer stock were not about to be deterred by something so insignificant as the trembling of huge plates of rock beneath the surface of the earth. They had the matter of living to be about. And whether it was enemy armies, or skulking Chickamauga and Shawnee, or whether it was capricious skies and stillborn babes, those steadfast pioneers hung on. Some had no choice: they had come to make a stand and dared not return to what lay behind, what they had fled, back over the mountains. If anything, they would move from this ground torn and rent asunder—move on to new land they could clear and make fruitful.

Time and again in those days and weeks and eventually months of tumult within the unsettled earth, Titus thought again of his grandpap. Once more he realized there was no threat big enough to frighten away those who were truly westering, truly moving toward the setting sun, seeking that most fertile of valleys. After all, that breed of folk believed, a man could be buried anywhere. A man had himself a choice: back there where they had come from, where most folks claimed it was one hell of a lot safer to keep his woman and raise his family. Or he could always lay his bones down here in the western extent of the Illinois country, here along the lower Ohio, or those new settlements of Missouri. Just as well a man be buried after making his life count for something, no matter how short.

Better to live their lives full, than long, some of the hardy ones declared. Better to be buried in sod where few men would ever walk than lie a'moldering beneath ground trampled by the boots of thousands.

In late winter word drifted downriver to Owensboro of something folks were calling a steamboat. Talk was that Nicholas Roosevelt's *New Orleans* had made it down to Louisville about the time of the first earthquake in early December—all one hundred tons of her, pushed along by a paddle wheel churning at her stern, primitive wood-burning fires heating steam that powered an engine mighty enough to push itself against the strongest of river currents.

The bearer of the news shared his report with his wide-eyed, yet skeptical audience there in Owensboro late that March of 1812: "It reached Louisville in the middle of the night, rousting folks from their beds to come scurrying down to the dock to watch it tie up. Didn't dare take on the Falls —water too low. So the captain turned it about at the harbor and marched that boat right back upriver to Cincinnati."

"Against the Ohio?" asked an astonished citizen.

"Yep."

"They had to have 'em a big crew paddling," Titus scoffed.

Others in the crowd agreed, doubting this outlandish monk's tale.

"Not a one," the reporter went on undeterred. "Not an oar in sight. Only that wheel paddling agin the current."

Less than a week later the *New Orleans* showed up at Owensboro, having finally braved the Falls of the Ohio, the water rising enough to resume that voyage to its namesake city.

Nothing short of a pure wonderment, that was, Titus thought, standing at the new wharf in awe. Why, to push upriver and down at will, that crude, hissing engine throbbing noisily, black smoke chugging against the winter sky. By some mysterious force able to sail upriver against the Ohio that long ago had borne the downriver fleets of the great prehistoric mound builders, then the birch-bark canoes of French and English explorers, next the dugout pirogues of Indian traders and Kentucky longhunters, followed by the bateaux of George Rogers Clark in his daring conquest of the Old Northwest, not to mention the first flatboats of those westering pioneers come to that new land little seen by white eyes.

What would become of these great, untamed rivers now—Bass wondered with a twinge of painful regret—if man could construct a craft such as this? Why, all the wildness would go out of the rivers, and eventually the land itself. The Ohio would soon be tamed, and the mighty Mississippi no longer feared by rivermen.

Only the Missouri remained.

The same faraway river that had beckoned Levi Gamble to join Manuel Lisa's fur brigades yearning toward the distant, as yet unseen, spaces. Farther on, those mountains few could speak of having seen, fewer still could claim to have crossed.

The world was changing around him, too damned fast for his comfort. Something on the order of a year and a half had passed since he'd fled those fields tilled by Thaddeus Bass. This second winter on his own, having watched the frightened and weak of heart turn about and take their families back, despite the relentless press of others surging ever westward.

Nothing would stop the killing. The wildness of the land was dying still.

Who was he to expect that it would be any different out here? Generations gone had crossed the mountains and flooded into the canebrakes, streaming down the Cumberland, killing the last of the buffalo not already run off. Now their kind was killing off the great rivers that for so long had been the final barriers holding back those of lesser fiber.

Now with a wet squeal of a whistle, the steamboat announced its coming. True enough, he had seen only one. But Titus knew there would be others, one day soon. Such noisy, belching monsters would put an end not only to the great mysteries of the western rivers, but to the rivermen as well. No more would the Kentucky boatman float and pole, cordelle and warp his way up and down the waterways that had moved America west. No more would there be any room for that breed that had spawned the likes of Ebenezer Zane and Hames Kingsbury.

And when the wild rivers no longer served as a final, immutable barrier, and every last person in the east could come west, then it would be time for him to move on again. If there was no more wildness in that move west—there was no heart in the journey. No spark in the spirit. No dance on the wind.

But move on he must.

For he had come to sense instinctively there in the first months of his eighteenth year that his feet itched perhaps every bit as much as his grandpap's had. So he prayed there would always be country to see, rivers to ride, those mountains to climb.

And winds to dance upon.

NINETEEN

The air was pregnant with the fragrance of early summer while his nostrils drank in the heady aroma of fresh-cut grass even before he opened his eyes to the sun creeping over the horizon. Without looking he knew it was morning's call: clearly making out the gentle lowing of a half-dozen cows below him all chewing their breakfast in their stalls.

Titus stretched, yawned, rolled over, and pulled the blankets over his head, grinding out a new place for both his shoulder and hip down in the soft crunch of the fragrant stalks that cradled him in the barn's loft. Moments of blissful reverie swallowed Bass until that voice jarred him.

"You coming down to help out today?"

Damn.

Titus shoved his blankets back from his face and replied, "I'll be down straightaway, Mr. Guthrie."

Instead he lay there for a few moments more—listening, hearing the settler murmur to his cows, settle atop a stool and begin milking. The first stream of milk struck the red cedar piggin loud enough for Titus to hear it. He had slept in again, later than he'd intended. Right now he didn't know whether he should be angry with himself, or the girl.

But then he smiled. How could he possibly be angry with her for keeping him up late into the evening after a long day, talking as they did on the porch to her parents' cabin? A few days ago he had decided there were no two ways about it. He simply would have to work hard not to fall in love.

For certain, this wasn't anything like what it had been with Amy Whistler. That was nothing more than some mutual exploration and discovery, wherein she was seeking a dutiful husband and Titus was craving some relief from all those greatest mysteries of youth.

Nor was this at all like what he had experienced with Mincemeat back in Owensboro for close to three years. That had only been a matter of his hungers and his loneliness. Nothing more to it, he had kept himself convinced. All Abigail Thresher had done was guide him into manhood; then in return she was free to take all that she wanted from him through their season upon season together as that Kentucky frontier settlement grew like a gangly child.

When he awoke one cold morning this past spring to find that she hadn't come home to the tiny shake-and-pole cabin he had built for them, Titus went off asking to round her up—fearful at first she had been hurt by one of the violent men who were a river-port prostitute's only clientele. That's when he was told Mincemeat had run off for New Orleans. As much as she had talked about it over the years, he had never once truly believed she really aimed to go there.

That morning he was unable to understand why anyone would want to go to New Orleans. Bewildered and shaking his head, Titus trudged back to their shanty—to find that Abigail had not only run off with what little weekly pay he had just earned from his work at the wharf, but over the past few days, with him gone to work, she had evidently been rooting around until she found his secret cache of what coins were left him from his trip downriver on Ebenezer Zane's Kentucky broadhorn bound for New Orleans.

As spitting mad as he was at first, it didn't take long at all before he found himself laughing until he cried, there and then in that shanty leaking with a cold early-spring drizzle, thinking how his New Orleans pay was on its way back down the Ohio and Mississippi right about then, traveling full circle without him.

That very day Titus determined to up and set out downriver himself. Just shy of the mouth of the Ohio he decided he'd make camp and wait to fetch himself a ride to the far shore of the chocolate-hued Mississippi. After three days of signaling to every passing keelboat and broadhorn and even the ungainly log rafts, a flatboat finally pulled over to tie up at the bank nearby late one afternoon. In return for bringing in a couple of deer for the hungry crew's supper, Titus was awarded a trip to the west shore of the old muddy river at dawn the next day.

Waving in farewell, he watched that boat's crew urge their broadhorn into the main channel. On south lay the mouth of the Arkansas and the White and all the rest of those rivers he had floated past when he was younger. Now he stood there on the far side of the Mississippi at twenty, turning expectantly to face the north that spring of 1814. Upriver. New country he had never laid eyes on. Nothing else really concerned him now but moving north. His eager feet set themselves in motion.

St. Louis lay somewhere beyond the horizon. How far, he had no idea. At the time it really had mattered little when he would reach that mythical place. For the time being, he exalted in the journey itself. He was young, feeling the fiery surge of every heartbeat as the wide breadth of his life seemed to stretch out before him. For now, time as measured in days, months, or years was of little concern for him.

He was on his way to see for himself the city that had lured Levi Gamble out of the eastern forests . . . when one evening Titus heard nearby the lowing of cows, about the time he was ready to roll himself up in his blankets that twilight. How his mind whirled with memories of home and barns, turned earth and the heady aromas of a cabin kitchen. No, sir— those surely weren't wild critters he heard. Why, one of them even wore a bell by the gentle clang of it.

Titus had followed the lowing to its source, and near dark he'd found the shed attached to a corral and paddock. Beyond stood a cabin where a telltale thread of smoke rose from the stone chimney. In the lengthening shadows Bass decided he didn't feel all that much like company. Quite the contrary, the possibility of warmth in that cattle shed beckoned him even stronger. After a solid night's rest, he figured to be up and on his way early enough, scaring up something for breakfast somewhere down the trail.

Besides, this settler might even have him a chicken or two roosting in that shed. And chickens just might mean eggs. Even pullets, those young chickens less than a year old, would mean eggs for a settler. Titus sorely missed his eggs. In these years since fleeing Rabbit Hash, he hadn't eaten anywhere near as many as he used to eat back in Boone County. Yes, indeed. It had all sounded like a fine, fine idea to lay out his blankets in that shed for the night, then purloin himself some eggs come dawn and cook them in his cup over a breakfast fire once he had put a few miles between himself and the settler's place later that morning.

Trouble was, Titus was about to learn that Able Guthrie was an early riser.

Which meant that he awoke not to the gentle cluck of a chicken or two as they went about laying his breakfast. No, Bass awoke instead to someone tapping the bottom of his bare foot, just barely opening his eyes enough to squint up at the muzzle of that big fowler the settler had pointed down at his privates.

"You wanna keep all your parts in working order, I'll pray you tell me what you're doing here in my shed."

While there had been guns pointed at his head and his heart, never had Titus Bass had one aimed at that most tender piece of his anatomy. A downright pleasurable piece it had proved itself to be too.

"Ju-ju-ju—"

"Spit it out, son."

"J-just sleeping."

The settler poked the muzzle of that gun firmly against Titus's crotch. "Where you from?"

"Nowhere . . . n-now."

"Don't fun me!"

"Ain't gonna try funnin' you a bit."

"Best you tell me where you hail from."

"Owens . . . Owensboro."

"On the Ohio?"

"Yes, sir."

"What you doing here in this country?"

"Set on seeing St. Louie."

"So you sleep good?" the settler asked him, something easing around his eyes.

"I'm beginning to figure I slept too damned good," Titus grumbled, looking cross-eyed down at that rifle stuffed into his crotch.

"Don't pay to be sneaking into a man's cow shed and sleeping the night away less'n you can get up afore that man stumbles onto you, does it?"

"No, sir," he replied as polite as he could, watching something slowly crossing the man's face that convinced Titus he might soon be breathing a bit easier.

"Way I figure it," the settler said as he leaned back, dragging that big muzzle away from Bass's most responsive part, pointing at the floor as he continued, "you owe me a little of your time and muscle."

"T-time . . . and muscle?"

The farmer quickly gazed around him at the small shed and sighed. "This ain't gonna do me much longer, son. Already I've gone an' laid the corner posts for a new barn. Staked and stringed everything else. I figure you can help me today afore you push on tomorrow."

"Tomorrow?"

"You're likely to be real tired after I work you hard as I'm gonna today. You'll wanna sleep another night right there in that hay."

Bass had to grin with relief. And that had made the settler smile, finally raising his fowler away from its delicate target.

"My name's Able Guthrie."

He held his hand up to the man. "Titus Bass."

"You come down from Owensboro of recent, yes—I remember," Guthrie replied. "Well, c'mon, young Mr. Titus Bass. The woman's waiting breakfast for us."

"B-breakfast?"

"Damn right, er—pardon me," Guthrie apologized sheepishly. "I don't but rarely curse. The woman don't like it—not a hoot—and I promised the Good Lord I wouldn't do no cursing around my girl."

Bass threw back the blankets and stood, dusting hay from his clothes. "Girl? Your family?"

"Only the one. Marissa. After her my woman couldn't have no others. Had hoped for at least one boy to have my name. Carry on the family, like any man would hope for." He flashed a courageous smile, his eyes crinkling with such brave, good humor in that way Titus would come to appreciate in those months still ahead of them. "But I got me a fine, fine girl. A strong woman she'll be real soon. Gonna raise her mama and me some handsome grandbabies. You come now and have your breakfast afore we start the day."

"Don't believe it," and he wagged his head. "You're gonna feed me."

"Sure as hell am. . . . Dear Lord, there I go again!" He whispered this last, his eyes flicking at the cabin, where the door opened and a full-framed woman waved him in from the cow shed. "Sure I'm gonna feed you. I can't expect a man to work his all for me without first putting some fodder down into his belly."

They had crossed the muddy yard, dodging greasy rain puddles and fresh cow dab close by the paddock to reach the cabin, where they climbed onto the low porch and pushed through the open doorway that faced south like most settlers' places erected foursquare with the world. It made perfect sense for the main entrance to look out on the southern side, which stayed sunny in the winter, cool in the summer, where the hard-driving rains and sleet and snows that mostly came out of the north and west of those hard months of the year could not beat in upon those taking shelter there.

Guthrie led him into the main room, thick with the heady perfume he had long ago forgotten. Like a warm flood the seasoned memories washed over him. Titus drank in the aromas of sizzling sausage, fragrant biscuits just scraped free from the Dutch oven, pungent smoked bacon piled high on a big platter at the center of the table where Guthrie went to settle. The seductive allure of boiled coffee made his mouth water almost as much as the sight of that pitcher of creamy milk and an apple-tree knot that served as a bowl for freshly churned butter just waiting to be lathered on those biscuits.

Looking around the room in amazement, Bass took in the hutch table covered with wooden bowls and pewter trenchers and utensils, several three-legged stools and a handful of half-log benches, on the shelves near the fireplace a hominy block, deerskins laid out for rugs across the uneven floor, brass tinder boxes with their dull sheen near the hearth, lug poles for the tea kettles and cast-iron cookware handy by the mantel, pepper grinders squatting on the table before him, a well-used cherry seeder atop a small table stuffed back in the corner, joined there by a coffee mill and a butter paddle, yellowed by use and age, lying among it all.

"This here's the woman, my missus," the settler said, steering Titus's attention away from the table to the woman rising from the fireplace with the bail of her Dutch oven at the end of her arm, still scraping loose the pull-apart biscuits that had baked themselves together in a mounded loaf beneath a golden-brown hue. "Lottie, the young fella's name is Titus Bass."

"Ma'am," Titus replied, glancing once at the woman's flushed face as she dragged the entire biscuit loaf onto a platter with her wooden spatula. In wet-mouthed wonder he went back to gaping at that table. He hadn't eaten like this in . . . in longer than he could remember. A real sit-down family meal, complete with all the fixings he could ever hope to have for breakfast.

"How would you like your eggs?"

He turned dumbly at the new voice, startled to discover the other female at the fireplace had turned to him, a great iron spatula in one hand, a coarse linen towel in the other, hand and towel both wrapped around the handle of a large cast-iron skillet. She squatted beside it so she could swing the trivet it sat upon over the flames in the fireplace made of stones daubed with a proper plaster of lime and gypsum, the chimney of fine-grained sandstone.

"Eggs?" Titus answered her with his voice rising, stunned by the surprising beauty of the girl, finding her cheeks flushed by the heat at the fire, sensing a thrill at the way her chestnut hair spilled down each side of her neck in curls she kept pushing out of her way . . . then suddenly he felt guilty as a pig snatcher, remembering last night how he had planned on gathering up a few of those very same eggs for himself, then stealing off into the dawn before anyone in the cabin was the wiser.

"Maybe you don't like eggs?" she asked him.

Able Guthrie nudged into the discussion, saying, "Mayhaps he don't, Marissa."

"Eggs?" Bass repeated, and swallowed hard again, locked into looking at her deep, round eyes. So much like a doe's. Heavy-lidded, long-lashed, and damned near as big around as that skillet she sat beside. "I l-like eggs a whole lot. Yes, ma'am. I mean miss. Sorry. Yes. Eggs. I'll take me some."

"How many?"

"A couple maybe."

Atop his crude cane chair Guthrie snorted, turning to his daughter and waving a hand in her direction as he said, "Just g'won and fix him a half dozen for starters, daughter. I'm planning on having you women stuff this here young fella so I won't feel the least bit guilty 'bout working the bedevil out'n him till dinnertime."

Titus grew wide-eyed, asking, "Dinner too?"

"I figure by midday I'll work your breakfast off you," Able explained, planting his elbows on the rough table. "So these two here gonna fill you back up come dinnertime. Then later on—by supper—it'll be getting dark, so it's only fair I feed you again at the end of the day. So tell me: that sound like fair pay for using your muscle and 'llowing you a place to sleep out to my cow shed?"

"I'm making syllabub for dessert this evenin'," the girl at the fireplace said.

He looked from Able Guthrie to the girl. "S-sylla . . ."

"Syllabub," Lottie instructed, coming to his shoulder. "It's a fine and heady drink we make by mixing fresh cream with our own apple cider and whipping it up to a fine froth."

It made his mouth water just thinking about how sweet it might rest upon his tongue. The girl at the fireplace smiled softly as she turned back to her chore of cracking eggs over the skillet. For the moment he wasn't sure if it was the flush of the fire's heat, or the crimson of her own embarrassment that had brought such a lovely blush to Marissa Guthrie's face.

"Yes, sir," Titus eventually said, turning on his stool to look at the settler. "That'll do . . . I mean them meals—they'll do just fine for my pay, Mr. Guthrie."

"Then sit yourself and dig in," the woman said, moving past the table in a swirl, a tangy cloud of sourdough clinging to her. "I'm Lottie—seeing how Able forgot to introduce us proper. You eat, and make yourself to home, son. We don't get much folk out here. Not much folk at all."

"What folks there is seem to be on the hurry north to St. Lou," Guthrie explained as he speared some fat sausages onto his pewter fork and freed them into his shallow wooden bowl. "While other folks is scampering south —getting as far away from that place as a person can get."

Lottie Guthrie turned to Titus, asking, "You want to see St. Louis yourself?"

"Yes'm. Figured I would see it for some time now."

"Don't be in such a rush, young Mr. Bass," Able Guthrie warned. "There's far more to life than the push and shove of folks when they get all crowded together, more to living than the hurly-burly of wine and song and the great trouble all that can bring a man."

"Able Guthrie! Leave this young'un alone," Lottie snapped as Marissa came to the table with the skillet still sizzling with more than a dozen eggs popping in hot grease. She settled on a bench opposite Bass.

"Just giving Titus his due, as I would warn and watch over my own son, missus."

"Just like you keep me from ever knowing anything about St. Lou," Marissa suddenly spoke up.

"Many are the times I think I done the wrong thing to come across the river to set down new roots here—just after the earth shook more'n two year back," the settler grumped. "The farther away from that sin hole, the better, you ask me."

She leaned toward Titus as if exchanging a confidence. "My pa claims the devil makes his home right up there in St. Louis."

"He truly does!" Guthrie bawled, dragging some eggs out of the skillet, piercing the fat yellow yolks in the process. "And that's a fact."

Just looking at those fried eggs made Titus's mouth water with an unaccustomed tang.

"Hush and let the boy eat his breakfast," Lottie scolded. "You gonna go off and work him so hard, then I say, hush: let him have a minute's peace to put away all this food and 'llow it settle in his stomach."

"Maybe you're right, woman," Able said, grinning at Titus. "We treat this young man good, I might just get more'n just a day's work out of him. Might talk him into staying on so's I got a extra hand to see that barn gets built before he skedaddles off north to see all the devil's temptations what wait up in St. Lou."

"You hush yourself and eat, Able," she scolded.

The settler grumped under his breath, but spoke not another word as Marissa slid Titus's tin cup toward her, pouring him some foamy, cream-rich milk from a dented pewter pitcher. That hand of hers she had wrapped round the cup lingered a moment too long in passing it to the visitor, just long enough that his roughened, callused fingers brushed hers as he took it from her. She'd pulled back as if she was scalded, then shyly looked up from her hand to peer across the table at him from beneath some of those chestnut curls spilling across her great, round calf eyes.

He had sensed the sudden flight of tiny wings across his belly. Bass swallowed hard, all but choking on the bacon he had just bitten off. "I . . . I think I might just do that, Mr. Guthrie," he forced the words out, almost embarrassed as he turned to look at the settler. "Might like to hang on a while and help out with raising your barn."

How he liked the way those calf eyes sparkled when he said that to her father, how one side of her pale, pink lips curved up in just the faintest hint of satisfaction. It was as if she were admitting to what he had just then owned up to. And that would mean moving St. Louie to the back of the fire for now—off the hottest of the coals. Way he was feeling right about then, Titus figured this girl mayhaps would make the delay worth any cost in days, or weeks, or even months. . . .

"I asked if you was coming down to breakfast or not, Titus," Able's voice cracked through his reverie, dissipating his remembrance of that first morning he happened on the Guthrie place.

Yanked back to the present, Bass kicked his way out of the covers and reached for his britches, pulling them over his bare legs.

"Coming, Mr. Guthrie."

"That mean today?"

"Now, sir," he said, crow-hopping his britches up his legs.

He so enjoyed lying naked with her, his legs pressed against hers, locked around hers, the two of them knotted within a tangle of heat and perspiration as they struggled together nearly every one of these short, hot summer nights. A strong tingle twitched through his groin now, stirred just by thinking about Marissa and the pleasure her body gave his.

He pulled his working shirt from the peg driven into the beam right over his makeshift bed and dragged it over his head. A yoked, drop-shoulder shirt with three bone buttons in front. She had made it for him, sewn it with her own hands, having dyed the tow cloth a pale buckskin color from crushed walnut shells. It smelled strongly of him from that first day, all sweat and dust and fresh-sawed lumber, even some hint of the animals in the paddock below. The honest, earthy smells of a settler.

Heading for the ladder, Titus listened to the wood thrush singing of late summer and decided what smell he liked best was hers. The heated eagerness of her these brief, sultry nights as summer reached its peak. The taste of her sweat trapped in that small cleft at the bottom of her throat. The hot earthiness of her mouth once he had taught her how to kiss back with her tongue and her teeth, her lips scampering all over his body like a ravenous beast he had unleashed within this lonely settler's girl.

She was waiting on the porch for him that morning. And Lottie stood in the doorway, just as she did every morning.

From the look Mrs. Guthrie had been giving him these past few days, it was certain the woman had already figured out how her daughter felt about this young stranger who had wandered into their lives last spring. Lottie's warm smile this morning said it all, said how she approved of Marissa's choice.

"They been fighting north of us for some time now," Guthrie declared that late-summer evening when they gathered in the cool of twilight.

"You getting worried for us, Able?" Lottie asked from her chore of setting a new hackle on the spinning wheel.

"No," the settler admitted. "Not with St. Louis north of us. Chances are slim that place will ever fall in British hands even if them redcoats and their Injuns come down the Mississip."

"My grandpap fought the British," Titus explained. "Back to Kentucky. They sent the Injuns down on the settlers then too."

"Oh, dear," Lottie exclaimed a bit breathlessly.

Guthrie shot Titus a severe, disapproving look before he turned to his wife. "It's a different time, dear. And a different place now. My own pa fought against the soldiers of the British crown just afore he come back home to marry my ma. No, them redcoats and their cutthroat Injuns can run all over hell up there on the lakes—"

"Able!"

"Sorry, Lottie," he apologized. "They can run all over that north country they want to, it ain't gonna do 'em a bit of good."

"Your pa and me heard yesterday the talk from that neighbor of your'n," Titus said to Marissa. "There's word of the Britishers landing at the mouth of the Messessap."

"New Orleans?" Marissa asked of that evening, the air filled with the joyous calls of whippoorwills and scritch of the katydids, noisy of a summer night, along with the soft but reassuring clang of the old cow's bell down in the paddock. She turned to tell her mother, "Titus told me all about New Orleans."

Lottie's eyes widened in disapproving exasperation as she glanced at her husband.

"Yes," Able replied. "Word was that folks fear the redcoats gonna attack New Orleans."

Exuberantly, Titus added, "Which means them Britishers likely to try squeezing us atween 'em."

"From the north up there at the big lakes with all their wild and bloody Injuns," Guthrie said. "And now from the south."

"Where they just might get them Chickasaws and the rest to join their fight agin the Americans," Titus added as he set the peg he had just whittled into the Cumberland basket with all the rest he had finished that night.

Instead of what frontier folks called an "Indian basket"—one made of cane splints or even grass stalks—the Cumberland was woven of white-oak splits, the very same material the pioneer used to weave chair bottoms, that oak peeled in the spring at the same season he peeled his hickory bark.

Sitting atop split-log benches on the narrow porch, Titus and Able worked beneath the light of two candle lanterns, each of them carving out a different size of peg. Like expensive, hand-forged nails, these oak pegs were used for all sorts of construction and repair on the frontier farms.

Nearly every evening the males all along the border country spent their last few hours after supper and before retiring to bed repairing wood and leather farm equipment, if not whittling the pegs they would use in making those repairs to buckets and kegs, yokes and plows. Whittling at pegs as well as buttons for the barn door, grain-mill gears from good, strong hardwood, beech or oak carved into a dasher for the red cedar butter churn—although every good farmer knew that beech always seemed to decay far before its time—maybe even a wooden door hasp, complete with turning key. Seemed that a man never stopped whittling—even as he sat up with a sick relation taken to bed with a fever, waiting for the ague to loosen its grip on a loved one. All time was precious in and of itself on the frontier, and so best used in keeping one's hands busy.

While panes of glass could be had inexpensively, iron wasn't cheap in this country. What there was of it found its way down the Ohio, thence up to St. Louis, where the price of the long iron bars just the right thickness for making tenpenny nails easily quadrupled with the cost of its transportation. Like most settlers, Able Guthrie was a fair enough hand at the hot and sooty work over a forge and bellows, although most men on the frontier generally used the cabin fireplace for their forge and a block of wood topped with a thick plate of iron for their anvil. There they could repair a broken grubbing hoe or fashion a badly needed log chain—for pulling up stubborn stumps—from strips of iron cut with a cold chisel, even reshape and sharpen a worn plowshare, and always, always repair their most vital tool on the frontier: firearms.

True enough that, for most things, repairs with wood and rawhide proved to be far cheaper than repairs with expensive and hard-to-come-by strap iron. Not to mention that most settlers preferred to weld all their wood construction together with pegs hammered into hand-drilled holes lathered with a generous dollop of oakum, which would swell each peg and seat it with no possibility of give, instead of investing in the cost and time to forge-cut and hammer out all the iron nails the same job would require.

"Over in the Illinois I've heard tell a time or two of them Chickasaws," Able said. "That bunch you told us jumped you, then killed your flatboat pilot. They sound just like the sort the redcoats could talk into making war down on the lower Mississip."

"Just as long as we got warning," Lottie said as she settled back onto her stool beside the spinning wheel, shifting her skirts up to lay a moccasin on the treadle. "We can get ourselves out of here afore they come tearing through."

Indeed. Such worry had always been a fact of life on the borderlands.

For more than a year now there had been growing unrest along the western frontier, an uneasiness wrought of rumor and speculation, to be sure, but more so born of a genuine fear that a real threat of Indian invasion once again existed. Like Able Guthrie and Titus Bass, frontier folk were people with family who had fought in the French and Indian War, and a short generation later battled against the British—this time in bloody rebellion against the crown.

Word carried up and down the river in the last year or so that every Indian nation between the Great Lakes and the Rocky Mountains had come under British influence, summoned to revolt against the Americans by none other than Tecumseh, whose very name struck fear into the hearts of many white settlers strung out along the borderlands. Robert Dickson, the sinister British Indian agent upriver at Prairie du Chien, had himself been fomenting all the unrest and insurrection he could—sparking serious fears that thousands of wild-eyed, painted warriors were about to descend the Mississippi and Missouri rivers in a grand assault to wipe the frontier clear of Americans.

Despite the fact that they had launched an invasion of the Illinois in 1813, and a year later Clark himself had led a campaign against the British at Prairie du Chien, they had been less than successful in choking off the possibility that Tecumseh's federation might just thunder across the sparsely settled frontier. Rumors continued to ignite American passions as those hardy souls waited in the darkness of their lonely cabins, watching and listening, keeping their guns primed and always within reach, whether by the door, or in the fields as harvest neared. These were not a people easily frightened, nor given to hobgoblins of their own making. Folks who had cleared land and settled in that fertile band of country extending from the lower Missouri to the mouth of the Arkansas all had very legitimate fears when reports came north of redcoats down the Mississippi.

Now with all this talk of the British bringing in their huge men-of-war to New Orleans, there to off-load lobster-backed regulars in preparation of launching a pincers invasion on the entire Mississippi valley . . . why, it only gave the faint of heart another reason to dwell long and hard on heading back east somewhere, anywhere the British weren't coming ashore and the Indians weren't skulking.

"I'll tell you this for a fact," Able declared, dusting shavings off his lap onto the porch and standing to stretch backward, working the kinks out of his spine. "The Injuns don't need no British to help 'em make trouble in this country. Forests thick as they are hereabouts, the Injuns got millions and millions of friends."

"Friends?" Titus asked, nicking a finger with his knife.

"The trees," Guthrie answered, jabbing his knife into the dark. "Trees what can hide them savages as they come sneaking up on a settler's place. Hide 'em again after they've done their devil's work and are skulking away into the forest, getting off with scalps and prisoners and everything else the durn blooders can carry away."

"There simply ain't no way of figuring what goes on in an Injun's mind," Lottie added as her foot rocked the treadle, the hackle spinning in rhythm with the giant wheel as the wool fibers wrapped themselves around one another in a long, continuous strand she was carefully taking up on another spindle.

Marissa sat nearby atop a three-legged stool as the air cooled and the twilight deepened, carding more of last spring's wool sheared from the family's sheep. He looked at her a long moment, watching her hands at work, remembering his mother at work on her own linsey-woolsey, the cane splints clacking as she moved them back and forth in the weaving sleigh, making her coarse cloth for those loved ones needing new shirts and britches, dresses and stockings.

"The missus is right, Titus," Able agreed. "No way of knowing when Injuns will break loose. That's why my folks kept the doors barred tight, and come summer they plugged the chimneys too."

Bass looked up at Able. "Injuns come in down the chimneys?"

"They sure as . . . they sure do," Guthrie said, barely catching himself. "They'll come to get you anyways they can. Mingoes, Wyandots, them Shawnee what your grandpa fought in his day. Any and all of 'em. They're the devil's seed, that's the gospel. Their kind's the red offspring of ol' Be-Hell-Zee-Bub himself!"

"Didn't you and Titus tell me word has it Kentucky, Tennessee, and Ohio are all clamoring for war the loudest?" Lottie asked.

"It's the God's truth there," Able replied. "Folks what settled in country the farthest from the fight with the redcoats appear the most eager to stir things up now."

Bothersome gnats had gone with the fall of the sun, as had the buzz of the hummingbirds, but still Titus could hear the reassuring chirp of the cicadas clinging to the trees, thinking about how Able had said every one of those big trees was a friend to the Indians coming to wipe the valley clear of Americans. A threat so real that it took on shape and body as he remembered his footrace from the Chickasaw hunting party, the smell of them strong in his nostrils as they boarded the flatboat, grappled hand to hand with the crew, leaving Ebenezer Zane dead.

"While'st it's the rest of us out here—we're the ones who'll fight their war when it comes," Guthrie eventually added.

"If'n them Injuns was coming," Titus said in that tone of his when he wanted most to prove he knew whereof he spoke, "they'd long come by now, Mr. Guthrie."

The settler's knife stopped in the middle of a long peg, a tiny curl still wrapped over the blade and Guthrie's finger. After a moment's contemplation he said, "Maybeso you're right, Titus."

"They was coming, they'd come in the first full moon of spring," Bass explained. "Even first full moon of early summer."

Guthrie's brow crinkled. "How you figure it by the seasons like that?"

"I don't," Titus replied. "Just recollect what my grandpap allays said. The Injuns, they come right after winter breaks up. Now, well—it's getting too late in the raiding season."

With a great harump the settler turned to look at his wife. "See there, Lottie. This young man's got him some good sense 'bout such things, don't he, now?" He looked back at Titus. "Let's just pray your grandpap was right."

" 'Nother thing too," Bass said as he selected another oak limb to whittle on from the pile at his feet. "Injuns fight for what they figure to be their land."

"Your grandpappy teach you that too?"

"Yes, sir. Them Injuns folks say are far up the Missouri—'bout them coming down here to raid? No, sir: they won't get all that fired up 'bout coming down here to fight when this ain't the land where the bones of their grandfathers are buried."

Slapping his knee, the farmer exclaimed, "I'll be damned!"

"Able Guthrie!" Lottie scolded.

"Oh, hush now, woman. I been minding my mouth long enough that I'm due a damn now and again!" He twisted on his half-log bench to gaze at Titus wonderingly. "So you know something of Injuns, do you?"

"Not near enough," Bass replied with a disarming smile. Then he remembered. "What I didn't know almost got me kill't in Chickasaw country four years back."

Guthrie rocked against the cabin's wall, gesturing with his knife at the youth. "Just my point, son. Just my point. Don't you ever forget it. No matter how right or wrong you are in them Injuns invading us here in this country . . . you just remember that as soon as a fella thinks he's got an Injun figured out, that fella's made him a big mistake."

That made immediate sense, sinking in the way it did all at once. He grinned back at Guthrie. "I do believe them are words a man can live by, sir. An Injun is a real uncertain critter. Yes, sir. An Injun is a most uncertain critter."

"You ever said anything to your ma about us?"

He sensed Marissa's hair glide across the bare skin of his chest, that flesh feeling a little tighter now as the sweat dried.

"No, I ain't said a word."

"She knows."

"I know she knows," Marissa replied, then fell quiet for a time, and finally added, "I guess a mother always does know when her only daughter falls in love."

He wondered how it felt to be so completely swallowed up in love like she was, like he was afraid to be. He lay there listening to the cicadas and the peeping of the tree frogs, and her breathing against his chest. The sweet, heady fragrance of forsythia and redbuds exuded a delicate perfume on the air. A few yards away the thick, verdant woods abounded with violets and wild plum having just come to bloom.

"You think she knows you're slipping out to come see me most ever' night now?"

"She can't help but know, Titus," Marissa answered. "There's just something atween a woman and her daughter what I can't put into words. But one woman always knows when another woman's in love."

"How 'bout your pa?"

"Him? He's a sleeper. A hard sleeper. Works hard every day, so he needs his sleep every night. Not like ma. She don't get much rest anymore. Last few months. Something's changed with her—but she won't own up to it for me. But I know she gets real weary and that sometimes she ain't sleeping when I come slipping out to see you here. Times I know she's already awake when I go sneaking back in afore first light."

"How you feel about that?" he asked, already knowing how he felt: more scared of hurting those good people who had taken him in than he was scared in facing any punishment meted out for dallying with their daughter's heart.

"If she knows about us and ain't said anything to me—I figure she don't have a problem with it. Any way you look at it, my ma's give us her blessing."

"Blessing," he echoed in a low whisper, knowing what Marissa meant.

"I ain't never asked you if you love me," she finally whispered against his chest, "even though I been telling you my feelings for some time now."

"I told you I'd say the words when I knowed I could say 'em."

"And I always told you that's fine by me."

She brushed her fingers across his belly, nails scratching across the bony prominence of one hipbone where the skin was stretched taut. He twitched. It was almost a tickle, but not quite. Something more urgent, deeper and less easily stilled than a tickle that she aroused in him with her wandering touch. As little as she had known about her body and the way of men when they had first grappled in the hay one hot night back in June, Marissa sure had made up for lost time with how she threw herself into their coupling. Some folks was just natural-born riders, or swimmers, maybe even runners. But to Titus, Marissa Guthrie was a natural-born humper. Unashamedly she hungered for him every bit as much as he hungered for her. Time and again he had studied at that cloudy piece of mirror Lottie had given him to keep in the barn for shaving, searching for the telltale bite marks and bruises Marissa had left during her exuberant coupling.

Of a time or two he had even grown scared she would wake up her parents in the nearby cabin, moaning so loud the way she did, mingling her passion with an uninhibited shriek every now and again. But still Lottie never said anything about her daughter's noise, and Able was likely too tired to hear.

The past few days they had labored long and hard. He and Guthrie had been finishing up splitting some shakes for the cabin's roof—working fast against the coming of autumn's harvest and another onslaught of winter. For the past two winters the Guthries had lived beneath a roof constructed of rough-sawed boards jointed with oakum to seal the seams as best the man could. Boards Able had cut into six-foot lengths and laid in overlapping rows, held in place with long, straight saplings called butting poles he pegged down by their ends to roof joists.

Folks along the frontier were always quick to learn the superstitious rites so much a part of working with native woods: a roof board rived on a waning moon would curl; a cedar post would rot before its time if set when the sign was in the feet; or timber cut when the sap was down would last far longer.

Titus listened to Marissa breathing against him for some time, then asked her, "How come you ain't got no brothers and sisters?"

She trembled slightly when he asked the question, then clutched him tightly as she answered. "I was first born. Nobody will tell me for certain, maybe they don't know for certain—but I figure me being born hurt something inside my ma. Folks always said it was just God's will that she and pa had no more children. But I know she missed out on a lot by not having a big family like she and pa had always planned on."

"That's why she's allays talking about the grandbabies you're gonna give her—"

"The grandbabies *we're* gonna give her, Titus," she corrected. "I just know ma can't wait to hold *our* babies, like they was the ones of her very own she missed out on because something got tore up inside when I was born. So you and me gonna give her the little ones she couldn't have for her own self."

Every day he found himself growing more and more comfortable with the idea of staying on there. Especially on those nights when she came to him like this and they lay together, cool flesh to cool flesh. Yet every morning after she left him to slip away in the chill, predawn air, Titus sensed his doubts of staying return, his confusion on just how to tell her resurfacing, and, oh—how to explain it to her parents?

He sensed this pull on him as if it were the tides, as if he were floundering in that swimming hole back home where he and Amy had swum as children, then made one another lovers. Floundering he was: flailing away with his arms and legs, not ever drowning, but never getting any closer to shore either. All that work and effort, only to keep his head above water . . . gasping, gasping for breath. . . .

She was talking to him now about their first night together, recalling how she had come to the bottom of the ladder and called out his name in a whisper until he had poked his head over the side of the loft and looked down at her wrapped in her sleeping gown of fine white linen cambric, one bare foot on the bottom rung. How that bare foot and those little toes had made him want her right then and there. She went on to remind him how scared he had acted when she'd asked if she could climb up the ladder, the better to sit and talk with him.

"I finally talked you into it, didn't I?" she asked. "Talked you into a lot of things. Just like I'm sure I'll talk you into falling in love with me one day real soon."

Then Marissa's chatter drifted back to that first night, how she had explained to him she wished to be kissed, to be held, just like a woman. Miserable because she believed she was getting so old, when other girls her age were spoken for, some even getting married and starting their families.

"You got lots of time," he soothed her. "Sixteen ain't old."

"Out here it's old. A girl learns to lye corn and weave nettle cloth at six or seven in this country. My pa always said if he'd had him a boy, he'd learned to hunt and trap afore that boy learned to hoe and plow—at least long before he learned how to read. Why, I know of girls marrying when they was thirteen or fourteen, Titus. Even my ma said she was late in posting her banns—she had me when she was seventeen."

Lying there, Bass winced on the seriousness of that, this custom of declaring before all that he intended to marry, as his mother had often said, to heartily cleave unto one person and only one person for the rest of his natural life. On the early frontier the parents of young couples announced their "banns": publicly posting one's intention to marry on three successive Sundays, allowing anyone who might object for whatever reason the courtesy of so doing.

Now she was running her fingertips down from his chest across his solar plexus, causing his manhood to squirm slightly as she drew nearer and nearer to it with every brush of her hot fingers.

Then she raised herself on an elbow, bit at his earlobe, and whispered to him, hot and moist, "I'll be a good mother to your children, Titus. Ain't no one gonna ever be a better woman for you than me."

"I ain't ready to have children." He fought to get the words out. They sounded low and raspy, rumbling in his throat as his own passion rose.

In moments Marissa was biting him across the shoulder, down one side of his chest, and licking across his nipples. As much as he didn't like that because it tickled, he had never once said anything to her, not daring to have her stop once she got herself worked up enough to start biting and licking his flesh. Instead, he lay there as riverbank clay in her palms, letting her shape him and move him, listening to her breathing become more and more rapid and ragged until she finally climbed over him, taking his rigid flesh in her hand and gently guiding him into her readiness as she settled her buttocks atop his hips.

As much as anything else in what they shared, he liked that part of it— when she first took hold of him and made his flesh a part of her. What fevered grappling he and Amy Whistler had shared, it had never been like this. Maybe it had been what Abigail Thresher had taught him about a woman's body, taught him about his own, showing him how to satisfy both need as well as hunger.

But maybe, just maybe—it had to do with Marissa Guthrie too.

God, how he didn't want to fall in love with her, a part of him afraid that he already had.

He looked up at her in the summer light, nothing but starshine, the crescent shadows beneath both small breasts, the rounded shadow beneath her chin as she leaned over him and let her chestnut curls tumble across his face before she met his lips with hers, opening her mouth, moist and hot and flavorful.

He was certain this was how a woman got hold of a man and would never let go. A woman's power over a man just like this. For a moment he wondered if his mother had been like this with his father—getting Thaddeus so wrought up that he couldn't leave if he had wanted to. Maybe that's why his pap stayed on the land, settled in and never again gave thought to seeing what was out there. Maybe it was this mystical power of a woman.

Titus struggled against the rising crescendo orchestrated throughout his body, coursing into his loins—vowing he would not fall in love with Marissa Guthrie because she was too much like his mother: the sort of woman who had the strength to hold a man in one place.

Slowly, slowly she rocked back, back farther still, putting her hands down near his knees as she arched her back and braced herself while she throbbed atop him, round and round in an ever-faster cadence that seemed to join itself with the rhythm of his own heart. How she did that, he didn't know. Part of the mystery that was woman.

He must not fall in love with her, for if he did, he would forever be there. Never to push on to St. Louis. Never to see what lay up the river where Levi Gamble said furs and Indians and the shaggy buffalo reigned. If he fell in love, Titus was scared down to the marrow of him that he would end up like Able Guthrie. Never to taste the caliber of the wind, never to dance on it a free man.

Like poor Able Guthrie: loving a woman who held him to her so tightly he couldn't breathe, didn't have room to roam. A good woman like Lottie, who wanted her daughter to give her the children she had been robbed of having for herself.

A good, but sad, woman.

His mother, a tired and worn woman after four children, three stillbirths, and two other babes who had died within their first year of life. A hard toll, even on a tough woman.

Now he looked at Marissa as she ground herself down onto him, as if she desired to swallow him, engulf him completely—groaning as the beast welled up within her. Did he have it in him to watch what toll childbirth took on her year after year?

He had run from the Chickasaw and fought them up so close, he could smell their sweat and their paint and even what they ate for supper. He had stood against the might of those rapids on the Ohio and held his own against the very worst the great Mississippi threw against a boatman. Titus had even dared free a slave within earshot of his masters, then shoot a slave hunter in the back when that man stood between his friends and freedom. No, let no man be so bold as to say that Titus Bass was one to shrink from fear. Instead, he had learned that fear often emboldened him—made him all the more ready to pit himself against a challenge.

But this . . . this thing of a woman and love . . . it was something that nonetheless made him shrink as never before. Afraid to his core. Frightened of Marissa? Yes, he admitted. For he had come to believe that she held the power to make him stay. For some men it might be a woman who kept them prisoner, for those like Able Guthrie. For others, like his father, it might well be the land that held Thaddeus Bass captive. The warm, steaming, fertile earth, that soil rich and black with humus. For a certain breed of man the land was no different from a heated, moist, fertile woman.

At long last he was beginning to understand his pap, and why Thaddeus stayed on and on in one place . . . almost to the point of growing enraged when his own flesh and blood did not lust after the soil every bit as much as he. Now Titus was coming to understand.

To know why he would be expected to stay here in this place with the Guthries. Not so much because of the seductive lure and hold of the land, but because of the love a man held for his woman. And all that woman needed from him.

She began thrashing her head side to side as she whimpered, raking her fingers down his chest as she reached a crescendo atop him. With great, heaving thrusts of his hips he spent himself violently within her, listening to her muted shriek in response to every last one of his explosions.

Then Marissa collapsed, murmuring in his ear to promise that she would awaken in a while and have him again before she crept off across the starshine splayed on the yard below them, slipping away to her bed in that cabin. The words were no sooner out of her mouth than he felt her breathing deepen, become rhythmic, and he knew she was sleeping.

He lay there for a long time that night, the chestnut curls spilling across his chin, her hair smelling of the musty hay where they always coupled there above the cow pens. Titus lay there knowing that if he ever did fall in love with Marissa, he vowed never to tell her.

For if he told her of his love, he would thereby be trapped in this place. He simply could not be trapped there. Not held in one place, whether held by the land or imprisoned by a woman. Never to lay eyes on the wilderness at the horizon's edge. Never to taste the bite of the wind as it roared out of those faraway places.

There and then he vowed that should he ever fall in love with Marissa Guthrie, he would have no choice but to simply convince himself that it wasn't true. Then force himself to leave.

If not for his own good, for hers.

TWENTY

A great covey of passenger pigeons beat the autumn air overhead, enough of them to blot a great shadow upon the land and he walking within it, flew right over Titus, darkening the sky so that he turned with a start and looked up, frightened. The birds passed so close above the thick and fiery orange and red canopy that he could make out the pinkish breasts until they had flapped out of sight.

He sat there on the old broken-down horse's back, watching them go, beating their way off to the south. In their wake suddenly opened in all that great expanse of blue sky sailed a lone osprey. Wide of wing it was, possessing that singular luxury of taking its time while the pigeons hurried on in flock. The osprey careened down from on high to inspect more closely this strange four-legged, two-headed creature below it, then beat its angular wings to climb back into the sparkling fall sky, circled once more over the man and horse, then disappeared beyond the horizon.

It had all taken less than a half-dozen heartbeats, his chest hammering like the devil as he watched the bird go. Wishing. Wishing . . .

He had simply stayed too long. Titus cursed himself for hanging on as long with the Guthries as he had. Was a time four years back when he had vowed to the heavens that he would never again raise blisters on his hands with farmwork. But for the sake of that warm and willing body, for the sake of that sweet ecstasy of having a woman wrapped around his manhood, for the sake of knowing he meant the world to at least one person—he had forgotten that vow.

Denied it because he had made the mistake of falling in love with Marissa Guthrie.

For sure, his young, curious, eager body may have hungered for Amy Whistler in the worst way as she'd escorted him to the brink of manhood . . . but his heart had been captured by Able Guthrie's daughter. He hadn't counted on it, no more than he had counted on running into Ebenezer Zane's flatboat and crew and floating with them on down to New Orleans. No more than he had counted on staying on all those seasons with the skinny whore who held him tightly until it was she who was ready to leave. No, he hadn't counted on a lot of things that had happened in these years since slipping away from Rabbit Hash and Boone County.

Still, he never would have dreamed things would turn out like this with Marissa. Him running again, that is.

Twice now in his young life Titus had been forced to make his choice. Both times fleeing what he feared most. First off his pap and that land Thaddeus kept clearing, more land for more crops every season. And now he'd fled the girl and the land. Running from family and children and sinking down roots—all that Marissa Guthrie represented.

Time and again he had convinced himself he wasn't really in love with her. It was only the way she felt lying next to him. That and the smell of her hair, the taste of her skin. No, it couldn't really be love that he felt for her.

Yet it was his fear that he already had fallen in love with her that drove him to leave in the first gray of a frosty dawn like some sham thief.

Five days ago he had awakened with the seeping of first light into that new barn's loft, where he lay beneath that new cedar-shake roof, awakening to the damp chill at that coldest time of day before the sun even prepared to make its rise over the earth. He had rolled over, shivering, at first attempting to go back to sleep, to secure some warmth beneath those two thick blankets he owned. Then he'd suddenly snapped awake, poking his head out to peer into the dim, ashen light. Blinking, Titus had rubbed the grit from them, then looked again—until he'd realized the fog surrounding him was his own breath. Frost borne of the chill of that early-autumn morn as the crystalline air defined the edges of all things, sharp and crisp.

Making clear what he had to do.

Already there too long. Spring had tumbled into summer. Summer had drained into fall. That ancient toll of seasons within him had once more sounded its warning knell—announcing the time for leave-taking had come. To be on the march once more, moving north to the city that had lured Levi Gamble west. The very city Able Guthrie had warned him against.

"Maybe I can take you with me to St. Louie one time of the coming winter, Titus," the settler had grunted as they had shouldered one of the roof beams across the wright pole. "Hap that you can see for yourself the devilment that lures a man away from his rightful place making the land fruitful."

Day after day that spring into summer they had harnessed Able's oxen to the long logs they'd felled and trimmed, then snaked them through the forest toward the site where they were raising Guthrie's barn. Using their hand axes, they had notched every corner before hoisting each log into position, using ropes and oak pulleys and the backs of those snorting oxen heaving the timbers ever higher.

Then the farmer had carefully shimmed and trimmed the corners as he'd needed to square them with the world. Not owning a carpenter's level, Able—like most men on the frontier—had improvised with a small bottle so filled with water that one good-sized bubble remained when it was turned on its side.

"We make every log right, Titus," Guthrie had seemed to repeat each day they'd devoted time to raising that barn. "Make every one square and level. And just like a man chooses the right tools for his job, he must choose the right wood."

Able had gone on to explain much of what Titus's grandpap had taught him years before concerning the building of a proper structure to keep out the cold and the beasts and the red man too. From generation down to generation such wisdom was passed on: that first tree cut should be hardwood, like maple, providing pegs for the job at hand; next came oak or cedar, some wood easily split for roof boards and doors, anything requiring rived planks—things made of seasoned wood carefully stacked and allowed to dry properly.

"But a man with a family to feed and protect might not always have him the time to wait on seasoned wood," Able had added. "He has to get his family behind some walls."

Each generation was taught those walls should not be of oak, for it was far too heavy when green, and even dry, tending to split with age. Beech and hickory must be avoided as well because they tended to rot beneath the onslaught of rains and snows, damps and dews. Pine too should not be used, as it decayed far too easily, fried and smelled to the eternal heavens, besides being highly flammable after seasoning.

Instead, the most solid homes on the far frontier were built of hewed cedar—when a man could have it—even the more abundant poplar, soft as it was and therefore easily worked with an adze, hewn into a rectangular instead of a square shape, which allowed a man two wall timbers from one log instead of one. Stacked on their short ends, most cabins therefore rarely required more than six timbers from doorsill to doortop.

One by one, hour by hour, a few logs a day inched the long barn walls ever higher until the final bearers of the roof timbers were in place, then wright poles notched in, secured with long iron spikes as a bed for the successive support beams. That shell of the roof was ready for the broad clapboards they eventually laid over with huge cedar shakes. Down below them in those waning days of summer Lottie and Marissa mixed water and clay, then stomped in just the right proportion of hay and daubed their recipe between every wall log to chink the barn against the coming winter.

Many were the times he had gazed down at her pigtails tied up with ribbon to pull her chestnut curls back from her mud-smeared face, finding her glancing up at him to smile before she went back to stomping more chink in that clay pit.

That dark morning of escape he had glanced below at the barn furniture they were beginning to hew out now that the roof was finished, ready to hold back the autumn rains: things like those feed boxes and water troughs, wooden latches for the stable doors, and a new shovel for mucking out manure. . . . He knew Able could finish the last details with his own hands. Alone.

From the dark timber came the howl of a wolf on the heels of an owl hoot.

Shuddering as much with anticipation as with the cold, Titus had pulled on his canvas britches and tucked in that shirt Marissa had sewn him out of mixed cloth. All that he possessed: few folks on the frontier had more than one change of clothing. After lashing his freshly tallowed moccasins around his ankles, he bent to collect what little else he owned, rolling an extra shirt, a small kettle and skillet, along with a handful of iron utensils and blacksmith tools Able Guthrie had helped him make at the hot and sooty work of the forge.

Maybe it had been all the talk over that last week or so that had rekindled the same old restlessness. What farmers there were clearing homes for their families out of that Missouri wilderness north of the old French settlement at Cape Girardeau had determined they should have themselves an autumn jubilee—to come together and celebrate the arrival of another harvest season come and gone with the bounty of the land spread across their tables, as well as an excuse to bring out a little spruce beer or cherry flip or homemade brandy. Autumn was, after all, cause for celebration.

The women had fluttered around the long line of tables strung end to end through the center of the neighbor's yard, setting every dish and pot and kettle just so while the young children needed no formal introductions and got right down to playing blindman's buff and hide-and-seek. Titus had come there with the Guthries, finding how contented it made him to watch Marissa among the womenfolk, seeing her eyes find his from time to time while he stayed with the men, old and young alike. They loaded their pipes, drank from their great clay mugs, and told their bawdy stories when there were no women about nor children playing among their legs. Stories of St. Louie. Unbelievable tales of the rouged and willing women that beckoned all passersby to come use their manhood on them, promising wild and devilish delights. Titus knew such places were not the stuff of myth and fable. He had seen Natchez-Under-the-Hill and the Swamp with his own eyes.

So he had watched Able's impassive face as the talk went on and on as the men poured down more and more of their own home brew. Then Guthrie wagged his head, knocked the black dollop from the bottom of his pipe bowl, and strode off muttering that he would be with Lottie. Titus started to move off as well at the settler's elbow.

"No, you stay with those others, son," Able said with some resignation. "Might just learn all for yourself about the sinful delights waiting to lure a man to St. Louie. Time that you listen, and pay heed."

Bass needed no further coaxing. He had seen enough down the Mississippi to whet his appetite for more. So he sipped at his spruce beer, listening wide-eyed to the farmers who had made that journey north to the mouth of the Missouri for supplies and equipment.

"Thar's Natchez, an' Norleans," a man was saying. "But the king of 'em all has to be St. Lou."

Another asked, "How come you figure it's the king?"

" 'Cause it ain't got a lick of nothing to do with the Spanish, that's why," the first answered, pounding his clay mug against his chest hard enough that he sprayed himself with cherry flip.

A third man in a scraggly beard nodded knowingly. "We all know the French can damn well show a man a better time than any else, don't we, fellers?"

The whole lot of them gushed and laughed, guffawed and poked one another in the ribs.

"Why the French better?" Titus inquired.

One of them turned and eyed the young man, then explained, "Them Spanish is mean li'l bastards, nasty and fighters."

When another agreed, "But them French, they allays been lovers."

"Never was good at fighting and such," a third piped in. "That's why the English throwed 'em out more'n fifty year ago."

"Yep, the French sure know how to show a man the time of his life."

"Why—there's so much shameful delight up that way—"

"Sh-sh! Here comes your woman, Henry," one warned, and they all went silent.

After supper, when the fiddle and squeeze-box were brought out, Titus again clung to that group regaling themselves with tales of the houses of pleasure and the great French homes built behind the tall limestone walls, stories of the stinking, brawling watering holes where a man's life might well be worth little or nothing, depending on how a man might look at another. It sounded no different from life down the Mississippi—but St. Louis was all the closer right then.

Soon she had come to Titus and asked him to dance. When he begged off, embarrassed, Marissa asked if he knew how.

"Course I know how to dance," he growled.

"Then dance with me," she begged.

"You likely dance different here in this country than I learn't back in Kentucky."

"Dancing is dancing," she pleaded. "Just come here and hold my hand, like this. Good. And put your other hand here on my hip, like that, Titus. Oh, dear—you're blushing, ain'cha?" she whispered. "Now, you've had your hand on my hip lots before."

"But these here folks never knowed it!" he rasped.

With the perfume of those hillsides matted with ivy and laurel's aro-matic green leaves and greenish-yellow flowers brought on that evening breeze, she led him away across the cropped grass in a simple pattern, slowly describing a large circle as Marissa guided him across the yard, closer and closer to meld with the other dancers. Soon enough he was whirling her in great, dizzying spins, her head flung back as she gasped and giggled, the whole world blurring around them. At times they even fell, sitting there in a heap, laughter gushing from them until they caught their breath and rose to spin again.

"I can't wait until next year," she confessed that next morning when all the celebrants had shared breakfast and families were parting for home, saying their farewells beneath the trees draped with hop vine.

"Next year?"

"Yes," Marissa replied. "Everyone's decided we need at least one good celebration a year."

"End of summer," Lottie added as she pulled her shawl over her head. "We've decided to get back together come the end of harvest next year. All that wheat and barley, corn and potatoes. Good cause to dance and laugh, don't you say?"

"I can't wait, dear," Able said, grinning, rubbing a hand across his belly.

Neither could Titus. On that long, long ride back to the Guthrie place, he thought and thought on it. One celebration a year was just not enough. To wait four whole seasons without busting loose and forgetting one's cares? Simply unreasonable. Why, it was just like the Longhunters Fair back to Boone County. Even the boatmen with their hard and dangerous life grabbed for more excitement and celebration than that! Such men reveled and made merry whenever and wherever!

Now, up to that St. Louie—that was the place, he had brooded. From the sounds of it there was a celebration going on there every night. Winter, summer, fall, or spring. The folks up there didn't wait for harvest to come around once a year. They made themselves happy just for the sprig of it!

That was the life for a young man.

But then his gaze was drawn over to Marissa, seated opposite him in the back of that big dray wagon the oxen were pulling home to the Guthrie place. And just looking at her, he doubted. Confused. Torn. Was he meant to stay? Or was he meant to go? Just to look into her eyes made him want to stay.

Oh, how he had wanted her last night after the spruce beer and the dancing and the way the aroma of her heated body rose to his nostrils as they whirled and laughed. She looked at him in that way of hers on the way home, and he knew she was coming to him that night. Titus decided he would stay.

Yet over the next eight days he changed his mind twice as many times. Lunging back and forth on the horns of his own private dilemma. Like an unbearable torture.

Until at last that morning came and he arose to the first real hard frost of the season. Knowing if he did not go then, he never would. What might hold him there was something much, much stronger than what would ever hold him to Rabbit Hash in Boone County. If he were to be free, he would have to be free of her.

Trembling even more with his fear of leaving—with his fear that he wouldn't—he had found a slip of paper. Looked to be a bill of sale as he smoothed it out across his thigh. On the back he rubbed the letters with a stub of a lead pencil, not sure of all of them as he formed the few words in making his good-bye to Marissa and her parents. Then he stood and tore a small hole in the corner of the paper, slipping it over the peg where he always hung his shirt of an evening before sinking into the blankets and the hay to await her coming to him all those hot summer nights.

That big barn smelled of oiled leather and new wood and animal sweat. His throat seized as he descended the ladder and stepped around Lottie's keeler—that shallow tub the women used for cooling milk and to catch drippings from the cheese press. From a peg he seized the hackamore he looped over the old horse Able Guthrie had given him many weeks ago: "Too old to work a plow, too weak to pull a wagon, son. It ain't much use to me nowdays, but maybe you can get the animal to ride under you."

Titus had done just that since last summer, many times taking Marissa for a ride through the cool timber, the two of them bareback atop that old, plodding plowhorse.

He led it through the low door into the cows' paddock, where he pulled out the corral rails, leading the horse through the opening, then refit the rails in their posts before he slipped into the forest just as he had that morning more than four years before. The frosty blades of dying grass crunched, the thick mat of big orange and red leaves crackled beneath his moccasins and those four old hooves.

Titus stopped back in the still-dark shadows, looking at the cabin where he had first seen her at the hearth, the fire's glow igniting the red in her chestnut curls. Bringing a blush to her cheeks, the same blush painted there when she became aroused in the hayloft with him. The merest hint of smoke rose from the chimney in a ghostly wisp above the leafy canopy turning gold and orange and sienna-brown with autumn's first cold kiss.

Maybe if he crept to the window for one last look inside . . . to see her, a last lingering look at what he was leaving behind.

Closing his eyes instead, he sought to remember that cabin where he had his first look at her. In his mind once again seeing the gleam of a hair ribbon poking from Marissa's sewing basket. The glossy spray of feathers in a turkey wing hung by the fireplace, used to stir the fire or shoo away pesky flies. The dull sheen of the black walnut highboy in a corner, atop it resting the Irish Book of Kells—that Latin manuscript of the New Testament. The white and satiny shine of a pair of slat-backed, split-bottomed chairs made from gouged buckeye where Lottie and Marissa sat as they carded and spun. Those Cumberland baskets filled with weaver's spools, warping frame, wool and cotton cards, flax and hemp hackles. The old family safe, its doors lined with hammered tin, where Mrs. Guthrie stored her flour and herbs away from the ever-present mice and spiders, its poplar wood softly yellow in the firelight from so many scrubbings.

Yes, Titus thought, forcing himself to turn quickly before he gave in. Yes, there would surely be pain in his leaving.

She loved him.

But perhaps every bit as great was the pain he felt right then at leaving without ever telling Marissa to her face that he loved her too. He hoped the few words in that note would say it for him.

He was more afraid than he had ever been. Not strong enough nor brave enough to tell Marissa to her face. To say that he loved her, but he still had to go. He wasn't man enough to do that, so he stole away before he caused her even greater pain: marrying; beginning a family; her believing they were putting down roots. Then he would up and leave her.

No. The pain he felt at that moment was nowhere near as great as her pain would be if he failed to leave right then. So he would let the note tell her, and decided to leave in silence.

Heading southwest through the timber, he kept himself deep among the trees before he circled back to the west, then pointed his feet due north. Those first moments in turning away had been so hard. All through the first hour. And that first day—the pull still so strong. Her smell clung to his shirt every time he opened his blanket coat and brought the homespun tow cloth to his nose—forced to remember what he was leaving behind, to remind himself of why he had forced himself to go.

Titus had struck the river the following day near Grand Tower Rock as the Mississippi angled lazily toward the northwest, his mind still coming back again and again to Marissa.

Now he had nothing more difficult to do but follow the river to St. Louie.

And pray that glittering old French city was enough balm to ease the sharp pain he still carried even after all these days and distance put between them.

With his heels now, he set the old horse into motion, his eyes still straining to find in all the aching autumn blue overhead that solitary osprey.

"Whereaway you bound, my son?"

With a start Titus peered up at the old man leading a fine horse up to his evening fire. Night came early, and with it the cold as he drew near the city of his dreams.

"St. Louie."

"Ah." The older man halted, staring down in study at the fire a moment, then regarded the youth and the rifle across his lap. "I am but a poor wayfarer. Do you mind if I share your fire and a bit of conversation this night?"

He tossed another limb onto the flames and shrugged. "I was just getting used to the lonesome."

Turning toward a tow sack he had tied behind his old, worn saddle, the stranger said, "I have food to offer, young man. You decide to share your fire and your talk, I'll share supper."

Looking more closely now at the dance of the firelight across the man's deeply seamed face, Titus decided he liked the gap-toothed grin. The eyes were kind, yet possessed of great, great sadness. "What you got to eat?"

"Capons. A farmyard cock—castrated to improve the flavor of his meat for the table. Fresh as can be, I suppose. Butchered this morning just before I took my leave of a farmer's place north of here—a family where I spent the night as their guest." The old man squatted, began tugging at the huge knot in the tow sack. "The truth to it, we stayed up most of the night talking on ships and kings and sealing wax."

Bass watched the bony, veiny old hands struggle over that knot, thinking how strange this stranger was—to talk in such an outlandish, confusing manner.

"I mean to say we spoke of all sorts of critical matters." The stranger tugged the tow sack open.

"Didn't know what the hell you meant."

"Aye, easy to see that on your face, young man." He pulled forth a dead bird, handing it over to Titus. "This one be yours." Then stuffed his hand into the sack again and pulled forth another, smiling with those gapped teeth. "God's rich bounty." Laying the bird aside, he next retrieved four potatoes and a half-dozen ears of corn from the sack. "I must tell you the corn might be past its prime—long gone is the sweet milk in the ear, I say. But they truly will do for a man hungry for the manna of the fields."

Titus put his hand over his mouth, catching himself about to laugh. After all these past days of loneliness and dark brooding, it brought merriment to him just listening to the way this old man talked.

So he asked of his guest, "Where are you off to?"

Raising an arm that looked more like a winter branch inside the huge, ill-fitting coat he wore, the stranger pointed off here, there, and over there. "No place special. Off to where the spirit moves me. God tells me where I am to go—as He told the wandering Israelites of Moses and Joshua of old. Yet, truth be it, I—like you—am alone. Alas, that is God's condition yoked upon the shoulders of some, is it not, son? As many as we might have around us, family and acquaintances, we are still alone in this life, and God makes the only sure friend we will ever truly have."

With a snort Titus said, "I had me lots of friends."

From beneath the bushy eyebrows that stood out like a pair of hairy caterpillars on the pronounced and bony brow, the stranger sneered, "Yes—I can see by all these companions you have brought along with you on this journey."

"They are here!" he snapped at the sudden, harsh judgment, and tapped a finger against his chest. Then added, more quietly, "Right in here."

For a long moment the stranger regarded that, then smiled warmly as he tossed Bass three ears of the corn. "Yes. I believe you might just be the sort who would hold a friend dear in your heart. But be busy now: find us something to boil our corn and potatoes in."

"I ain't got nothing near big enough—"

"Tied on the far side of my saddle," the stranger interrupted. "A wandering wayfarer like myself must always have himself an all-purpose kettle in which to boil anything and everything that God provides for the table. For a prayerful man of the Lord, nothing he finds is ill-gotten gain."

"You lost me on your track again."

"God has taken care of me for more years than you have been breathing, young man. And I trust in Him for when there are not folks to take me in and spread their board before me. At such times God will provide me the opportunity to feed myself."

Titus looked down at the capon, a castrated rooster grown plump for the table. "You . . . you didn't steal all of this, did—"

"By the heavens, no!" he roared, laughing. "The farmer I spent last night with—but I already told you, didn't I? Get that kettle of mine from the horse and see that it's filled with water from yonder creek. Once you've removed his saddle for me, you best be plucking feathers from that bird, unless you want to mud him."

Titus stopped on his knees. "M-mud him?"

"Ahh, yes," he said, regarding the fire pit. "You seem to have a good bed of coals going already. Let's mud these gamecocks tonight, my young friend. You go on about your chores and get to boiling those fruits of God's fields while you and I find a spot of dirt where we can mix in a little water to make a good, stiff mud."

"You ain't told me what the hell for."

The old man laughed easily, that gap-toothed mouth working with a throb. "Not what the hell for! For a *heavenly* repast! We're going to coat these fat little roosters with mud, a thick shell it must be. Then stuff them down in the coals to cook themselves inside that shell of temporal earth."

"They'll cook up like that?"

"And when we drag them out of the fire, prepare to dine on the outskirts of paradise, my young friend," the old man explained. "All we have to do is crack the hardened mud shell, and in pulling it off, we tear away the feathers. *Sacré bleu!* as the French in St. Louie would say. We are ready to eat!"

When it came time for everything to come off the fire and out of the coals, Titus discovered he was much hungrier than he had ever imagined. He hadn't eaten like that in days. Ever since that last of Lottie's meals . . . Lottie and Marissa's.

Something about the chill, frosty air and the crackle of the campfire gave muscle to his appetite. All of his hungers. So he tried desperately to force her into the recesses of his mind as he pushed himself back from the pile of bones and gristle and three corncobs.

"You damn near made that bird disappear," the stranger said. "Along with those potatoes, skin and all."

"I like the skin," Titus replied. "And them birds—mudded an' all."

"It was a fine feast, wasn't it?"

"A good change from pig meat."

With a visible shudder the old man wagged his head. "How I have come to hate Ned."

"Ned? Why you hate him? Who's he, anyhow?"

"Not who—what. Ned is pork. Ned is pig meat. Ned is the sustenance of the devil himself! No, I haven't partaken of Ned in so long, I cannot remember." He pointed a bony finger at Titus. "And you would do well to swear off it as well. Cloven-hooved, unclean, filthy beasts that they are."

"But if a man's hungry—"

"He's better off going hungry than biting into any Ned! God will provide for His redeemed souls . . . without any of us having to descend into the fiery depths and dine on the devil's fodder." He raised his face and arms to the sky, closed his eyes, to say, "Praise God I no longer eat such a beast." Then he quickly opened his eyes and looked directly at Titus. "Don't you hunt, son?"

"Y-yes, sir. I hunt."

"That's a fine piece of workmanship there."

Titus rubbed it, looking at what he took to be wanton envy and desire for the weapon on the stranger's face. "It was my grandpap's."

"I see." And the stranger peered into Bass's eyes again. "With such a beautiful piece, a man would never again have an excuse for eating Ned."

"No, I s'pose he wouldn't," Titus admitted, feeling backed into a corner as he watched the old man dust off the front of his clothing, so old and worn they were slickened, shiny with age.

The stranger dragged over the leather satchel he had worn over his shoulder when he'd first walked up to the fire. From it he took a pipe, then another, and finally a small pouch he pitched carelessly over his shoulder and caught in his hand behind his back dramatically.

"Would you care to share a smoke with an old man?"

"I would. Yes," Titus answered enthusiastically.

"I take it you've smoked before?" He handed over the pipe and pouch.

"Years now," Titus lied as he opened the pouch. "I been on the river. The Ohio clear down the Messessap to Norleans."

With the pouch back in the old man's possession, he asked Titus, "What brings you north to St. Lou?"

"Been wanting to go there for years now."

"Years?" And he leaned forward to snag a twig from the fire, holding it over his pipe bowl.

"For about as long as I can remember."

The stranger regarded Titus over the pipe bowl he huffed on until it glowed, watching the youth tamp the dark tobacco shreds into the pipe. "You've got it packed too tight for to draw good. Loosen it some before you try to light it."

Titus nodded, feeling the hot burn of embarrassment rise along his neck.

"It's all right, young man," the stranger confided as he leaned back against the poor saddle and blanket Titus had removed from the big, bony horse he'd brought north from the Guthries'. "Every man has to learn for himself the *feel* of filling a pipe's bowl, to sense when it is packed tightly enough. Too tight, it won't draw and you can't keep it lit. Too loose—about the same problem, and it smokes too fast or goes out on you. Rest assured, this is one of the lessons in life that all young men like yourself are bound to learn. Among many, many others."

When he had loosened the tobacco and had it going, he drew in his first long pull of smoke. It bit and burned. Coughing, he flushed with embarrassment again.

"No matter, son," the stranger said. "You go ahead and learn on your own."

"But I learn't four winters back at Louisville—"

"No need to be ashamed for a little cough or two—"

Titus interrupted, "Maybe I just be a little out of practice."

"Likely so, young man," he said with a grin. "Likely so."

At last Titus felt the heady impact of the tobacco seep across his brow, similar to the first sensations he had enjoyed from a liquid elixir, the likes of Monongahela rye or spruce beer. Titus leaned back against the stump of a tree and regarded the fire, smoking contentedly. Then he asked as maturely as he could make it sound, "What is it you're bound to the south to do?"

"Me? I always go to the south. And to the west, before I head north again to St. Lou."

"Around and around in a circle?"

He pulled the pipe from his gapped teeth. "That's what circuit-riding preachers do."

"Should've knowed you was a preacher man. From the way you . . . the way—"

"I talked?" And he chuckled. "But—I ain't one of the rappers. Trust in that."

"A r-rapper?" Titus asked.

"A queersome breed of spiritualist, to my way of thinking, young man.

One who summons communication from the dead, who make knocking sounds from the world beyond."

He felt a chill course down his spine just from the mere mention of dead spirits, that instant thinking on Ebenezer Zane. "You ain't one of them, is you?"

"Told you I wasn't," the stranger explained. "I make my circuit a month's time every trip. As far south as I can go in two weeks before turning back around to head north to the land of the wealthy and very, very Catholic French in St. Lou. What is it you'll be doing in that city you so long desired to visit?"

"I don't plan on visiting. I plan on staying awhile."

"I see," he answered, regarding his pipe bowl thoughtfully. "And pray —what can you do to provide for yourself? I take it you won't be hunting for a living?"

"Don't plan on it—but if'n I got to, I'll do it."

"Ah, yes. An enterprising young man who I am certain I will never find sitting on one of St. Louie's street corners with all the rest of the tattered beggars, hands outstretched, pleading with all who pass by to drop in their dirty hands a ha'penny, a schilling, a guinea. Any trifle so they don't have to work. Why, to think of it—there have been those who had the gall to call *me* a beggar!"

"You're a preacher, can't folks see that?"

He smiled widely, that gap between his two front teeth seeming to widen as he dusted off the front of his coat and shirt once more. "Yes. It is plain to see that while I am not a man of substance and means, I am nonetheless a man who takes care of himself and does not rely on charity. Tell me, my astute young observer of life and the manner of mankind—have you ever thought of taking up the staff of God and preaching His word?"

"Me? A preacher like you?"

"It is not easy work, let me assure you. But it is very, very satisfying."

"No, sir. I never thought on it at all. I got me my hope to make it to St. Louie. See where things sit up there. Everything on beyond is wild and open."

"Every man must find his own call. You've heard your own call, then. We'll let it rest at that," the old man said, seeming satisfied. "Yes. The beasts and the savages of the wild. Perhaps it is you are called to see them for yourself."

"Maybeso I'll get to do that one day."

"By the grace of God, you will, my son," the preacher replied. "Myself, why—I've traveled through the land of the red heathen for most of my life, and God has not once delivered me into the hands of mine enemies. Even the Shawnee, who were driven across the great Mississipp not long ago to begin a new life in the country south of Cape Girardeau. They and the Miami. On south, farther still, below the mouth of the Ohio, yes—I have gone among the Chickasaw, the Choctaw, and the Natchez of a time. All of them Eden's children: savage in every respect and by and large not ready for the teachings of God."

"So you just preach to white folks when you take your rides, make your circle?"

"It wasn't always that way, mind you," he explained, relighting his pipe with the burning twig as the night became all the deeper around them. "As a young man I first received the gift of tongues. I gave powerful sermons in the great cities of the east, dined in the finest of homes, held people in the palm of my hand by the thousands. Then one night at a camp meeting outside Philadelphia, I saw her."

"Her?"

His eyelids fell contritely. "The woman who was to be my downfall."

"Woman?"

"She sat in the second row," he replied, looking off into the distance. "Once my eyes touched her, I could not take them off her beauty. No, not that she was the most gorgeous creature I had ever seen—for there had been others prettier. But there was something so altogether striking, appealing . . . seductive about her. With the way she stirred my carnal appetites —why, I knew immediately, there and then, that she was the devil himself come to tempt me."

"The devil himself?" Titus asked in growing wonder, then swallowed, forgetting all about his pipe as he was completely drawn into the story.

"I spent the rest of the night preaching only to her. Forget the thousands who had flocked to hear my words that evening. Forget them all! I preached only to her. And in the end my faith was not enough. When the night was done and morning came through the windows of that grand hotel room, I awoke to find myself lying in bed beside that creature of temptation. I had succumbed. I had sinned. I had fallen as Adam fell—tempted by the devil made incarnate."

"You . . . you had you . . . you diddled with that woman?"

The stranger nodded, gazing now into the fire. "I suppose I could have gone on preaching in those eastern cities—but in my heart I felt the ruin. My safe, secure life of preaching to the wealthy and numerous along the Atlantic seaboard was over. I disappeared over the mountains, wandered down the Ohio, on down the Tennessee River, finding my way into the Cumberland as if guided by some unseen hand. Now I do what I have always done since leaving that rich, prosperous life behind: I ride and preach. Many a morning do I arise early to prepare myself to speak to a small congregation in some faraway place in the forest."

"How you find them?"

The old man smiled. "God takes me to them, to all those who are in need, don't you see? So I go among them, a new community nearly every day or so. Arising from my blankets before the sun and preparing my sermon. Sometimes there is a handful to listen to the word. Other times there may be fifteen or so. Faith is spread mighty thin in the wilderness, young man. Mighty thin indeed."

"But no matter," Titus commented. "You preach to 'em all, like God wants you to."

"As God *commands* me to," he answered. "Yes. Those sheep in my flock seem to suck the life energy right out of me anymore—never was it like this back east when I spoke in tongues, preaching for hours in tongues of the ancient and dead languages. But now these poor pioneering folk draw energy from me and my faith—sucking enough from this man of God that they can go from me back to their fields and their cabins to pit themselves against the harsh land for another month until I come round again."

"And so you ride on to another place?"

"Yes, I do that. I go on, at first I am weak and limp as this frostbitten grass—my power sapped by the wayward sheep. Yet, I trust in God. On I ride to my next flock, gathering my strength all the while, renewing my vigor in the Lord—for God will provide."

Titus gazed at the fire, the corn husks and chicken bones heaped beside the coals.

"Never should you doubt it, young man. The Almighty will provide."

"And He will provide for you, my son," the old preacher repeated the next morning after they had arisen, saddled, and were preparing to separate.

"I don't know that I ever asked nothing of the Lord. Never been much of a one to pray."

With that hard-boned and angular face of his, the stranger replied, "You yourself told me last night that for a long time you've been praying to get to St. Louie."

"Maybe you misunderstood me. I ain't never *prayed* to get to St. Louie—"

"But you've hoped, and dreamed, and done all that you could to get there."

"And I am getting there on my own."

A smile wrinkled the lined face. "You're getting there because God is answering your prayer."

Titus felt uneasy of a sudden, on unfamiliar ground. Frightened that he might just be in the presence of something far, far bigger than himself. "I don't know nothing about that, sir. . . . What is your name anyway?"

Removing his old felt hat from his head and dipping in a little bow, he answered, "Garrity Tremble is the name." He slapped the hat on his head and presented a hand to Titus. "Who have I had the honor of meeting and sharing so much conversation with?"

"Titus Bass."

He tugged the hat down on his brow, saying, "Well, Titus Bass. I will be looking forward to seeing you again in St. Louis in something on the order of a month. Perhaps we can talk again about prayer at that time, for I must be on my way now. There are the faithful and the faithless who beckon me into the wilderness." He swung into that old saddle atop that fine, blooded horse. "Many times have I prayed God to remove this burdensome yoke from my shoulders . . . but He will not. I certainly hope that what you pray for, Titus Bass—will not become a yoke locked about your shoulders."

In bewildered silence he watched Tremble turn the big animal away and move off into the cold, frosty stillness of the forest. Before he climbed atop the old plowhorse, Titus cautiously placed a hand upon one shoulder, as if to feel for any invisible weight there. Then touched the other shoulder in the same way. Still not satisfied, he shook his shoulders as if to rock loose anything perchance resting there. And decided it was all a little ghosty and superstitious of him to believe any preacher knew what he was talking about.

To think of it! Him, praying! Why, Titus knew he'd never prayed a prayer one in his entire life—leastways ever since he'd stopped going to church hand in hand with his mam.

Folks must just get crazy with their praying and all that talk of God and such, he decided as he urged the plodding horse into a walk. Any man who gave up everything for a woman, then gave her up and counted on God to provide everything for him from then on out had to be a fool. If not a fool, then perhaps downright touched.

A man had to provide for himself.

Just as he always had, Titus figured.

Anything else was nothing more than superstition.

He found work in St. Louis his first day.

Reporting to the crowded docks the following dawn, Titus stayed all morning long at the shoulder of the man who had hired him. There he quickly learned what was expected of him in his new position. Instead of toting the loads on and off the boats at the great riverside wharf, Bass was hired as a tallyman. To count the casks and kegs, bales and boxes, oak barrels and hemp coils coming off from boats struggling north against the current up to St. Louis, to count as well all the cargo going onto boats bound for points south.

"You can count?" the man had asked.

"Yes, sir. I can count," he had answered, a bit confused by that sort of question when he had shown up to ask for stevedore work, ready to tell of his experience in Owensboro.

"Can you write your numbers?"

"Yes, sir. It's been some time, but I figure I can—"

"Good. Come with me and see if you can catch on to what I'm doing before the dinner hour."

By noon the job was his. Struggling to control the great and unruly sheets of foolscap he had to write upon, standing at the tall but tiny desk he was instructed to place at the bottom of the cleated gangplank that stretched from the dock to a boat's gunnel. There he was given the wharfmaster's authority to make sure nothing came off, nor went on, without his first making a count of it in the proper column, in the proper box, afterward to make a final tally for his boss of what was now lashed on board for shipping, or what had just arrived for storage in one of the many stone warehouses that lined the great and bustling wharf.

By the following spring he'd had himself enough of that mind-twisting work and went off in search of something else, seeking something better to do one rainy afternoon when his labors with ink and quill at the dock were cut short as the skies opened up. By late afternoon, soaked and chilled to the marrow, Bass despaired of finding proper work for someone with such an adventuresome spirit as he. But then his keen nose caught wind of that particular scent of fiery charcoal and ironwork slaked in oil carried on the sodden air. He followed his nose, turning when necessary, until he found the livery hulking at the end of Second Street. One of the great doors was flung open, the man within standing over his hissing fire, shirtless and sweating on such a cold spring day—heaving up and down on a great bellows that shot tremendous blasts of air into that glowing bed of coals. His long graying hair he had tied back with a leather whang, worn in a queue popular at the time.

Standing there at the open doorway, drinking it all in—Bass knew why his nose had led him there. Why he was meant to work in this place.

He promised himself that he would never again despair of finding proper work for a man to do. Let others tally their counts or even carry cargo from one place to the next. But this—yes, this was proper work for a man. Fire and iron. Water and muscle. With them and his own unbounded will— Titus knew he could make anything.

There hung from nails driven into every post, and hammered along most every board that served as the livery's wall, great hanks of thick leather. Some of it crafted into bridles, bits, harnesses of all description. And laying atop most of those nails were thin black strips of iron banding. Stacked back beyond the bellows and the fire lay wide sheets of iron in all shapes and thicknesses.

He breathed deep again, taking in the fiery fragrance of this place. It so reminded him of that short time with Able Guthrie. How the settler had taught him the use of hammer and anvil and fire, to bring a piece of metal to a red heat before repairing a plowshare or making new bands to secure around a maul they had just carved out of a huge chunk of hickory.

"Something I can help you with?"

His eyes came back to the big, lantern-jawed blacksmith. "You're busy. I come back later."

"I'm always busy," the older man replied sternly, but without a hint of rancor. Then he sighed. "More work than I can do sometimes. What is it you need done?" He eyed the youngster up, then down again. "If it's that rifle of yours, that will take some time. That's close work. Not like this. And my eyes ain't all they used to—"

"My rifle? No, sir. I don't need no work done on it. Don't need nothing worked on."

The thick, heavy brows knitted. Titus watched some of the great diamonds of sweat run together in the deep crevices of that brow and become drops that tumbled into the man's eyes. They must have stung, for he blinked and yanked a great red bandanna from his waistband, swiping it down the whole of his face.

Turning away, he said, "Then I've got work to do, young'un."

With his back to Titus, his great right arm swinging up, then down with that sixteen-pound hammer clanging upon the anvil, Bass watched the man's shoulders and arms ripple as he smashed a glowing semicircle of iron band between the immutable force of that hammer and anvil. Sparks sprayed in great gusts like June fireflies with each hammer strike. Muscle swelled and bulged with every arc of the arm, sinew strained and rocked with each blow to the unmoving anvil.

Bass swallowed, forcing himself to ask. Daring to speak. To wrench the words free—words that he knew he had to say, or he would forever be sorry they went unspoken.

"You're awful busy—"

"I just said that," he snapped without anger, not taking his eyes off his work. "Now, if you don't need nothing, I'd be pleased if you were on your way. Go find another place to get warm."

"I come 'cause you . . . you 'pear to need me."

The hammer came down, this time with a dull clink, then lay still on the horseshoe he was forming for that animal tied to the nearby stall. Turning only his head, the blacksmith peered at the youngster again for a long moment. And finally turned his whole body.

"I hear you right?" he asked. "I need *you?*"

"Yes, sir. You're busier'n . . . busier'n any man deserves to be. So I figure you need my help."

The man snorted, but he didn't come right out and laugh. Not just yet. Instead, he turned back around, gripped the tongs, and stuffed the horseshoe back among the glowing cinders. Still pumping the great bellows with his left arm, the blacksmith turned back to speak.

"You ever do any of this?"

"Some. A little."

"Shoe a horse?"

"No, sir."

"Lots of horseshoeing in St. Lou, mind you."

"You can teach me."

"Maybe. If you can learn."

"I can learn. I can learn anything."

"Where you from?"

"Kentucky, sir."

"Good country, that," he said with careful appraisal of the young man once again, then regarded the muddy clay floor beneath his own boots. "Yessirree. I remember that as real good country." When he looked up at Bass again, the man resumed pumping the bellows. "Why you come here from such good country?"

"To see this country."

"Maybe even what's out there?" he asked, his head bobbing off in the general direction of the west.

"Likely, sir. But when I say I'll work for you, that means I'll work. I give my word—"

"How old are you?"

"Twenty-one, last birthday."

"And you can learn what I teach you?"

"That's how I learn't most ever'thing I know."

The older man chuckled. "If you're lucky, young'un. That's how we all learn, if we're lucky. Well, now. Come over here and let's see you make a shoe for this here ornery horse."

"M-make a shoe?"

"You said you can learn, didn't you?"

"Yes, I did—"

"Put your stuff there by the door and get over here. If you can't learn what I teach you right now, your truck will be right there by the door, so you can pick it up when I throw you out my place. But, on the other hand, if you can do like you say—learn what I can teach you—then you'll have you a job, and a place to stay, right here. So that truck and rifle of your'n can stay under this roof. Here, pull on this bellows like you was wanting to squeeze the bejesus out of it."

Bass took over the bellows handle. That first pull surprised him. It was harder than he had imagined it would be. He locked a second hand around the handle.

"No, mister." The blacksmith swung an open hand at the second wrist Titus put to work at the bellows, knocking it off the handle. "You get to use just one."

"Don't know if I'm strong 'nough—"

"Then you get your ass right on outta here and don't come back asking for nary work you can't do."

He gritted and strained, rocking the shoulder up and down, refusing to give in. He felt the pull all the way into his belly muscles. Felt the fortitude not to give in all the way to his toes.

"That's it, son! You might just have some hair in you after all," the man said. "Now, why you think I want you to do that with just one of them skinny arms of your'n?"

"D-dunno," he rasped with effort, fighting on against the bellows.

" 'Cause with the other'n you're gonna pick up those tongs and take that fired piece of horseshoe outta the coals and plop it down on the anvil."

He did as he was told, releasing the bellows when finally told to, and picked up the heavy hammer. Step by step, strike by strike, he hammered that glowing red arc of iron around the snout of the anvil, shaping, pounding, sweating even after he shucked out of his heavy, wet wool coat that steamed and stank hanging there on a nail near the fire. He didn't know who smelled worse—the older man whose great chest beaded and ran with perspiration, or him working off what little bit of tallow he had on his scrawny bones.

"There, now, you begun to get the shape," the blacksmith explained. "But the fine work's yet to come. Bring that shoe over here and let's see what we gotta do to make 'er fit this here mare."

Back and forth between the fire and anvil and the horse he sweated, refining the shape just as the blacksmith instructed. Until at last the time arrived to fasten on the fitted shoe.

From the pocket on his leather apron the man took a small iron nail. "Here. Start at the top of the shoe."

When Bass began tapping the nail through the hole he had just drilled through the softened iron, the blacksmith asked, "Say, now—you ain't a Mason, are you?"

"No, sir. I don't reckon I am," Titus answered, tapping on the nail. He put his hand out for a second nail. "But, then—I don't rightly know what a Mason is."

Placing a nail in the youth's hand, the blacksmith declared, "If you was one, you'd know. You ain't a Catholic?"

"No. If'n you mean the Catholics what . . . well, that bunch that worships God in their old way and has all them crosses with—"

"That's them. You ain't one?"

"No. Sir. I ain't."

"Good. Damned lot of 'em around here. What with the French and all. That big cathedral down the street too. I won't hire no Mason or nary no Catholic. Them's the two bunches what are the real threats to our republic. Plus slave holders and tax collectors and whiskey makers and army survey-ors—not to mention the Injuns and the damned useless postal people." He spit a stream of brown tobacco juice into a pile of manure mucked from a stall. "You ain't a Knights Templar, are you?"

"No. Dunno what—"

"Them, and all their kind, whoever they be—all can go to hell for what I care. Any bunch what meets in secret, they're a goddamned menace to this country. Slavers or bankers or even ship's captains—if they lord themselves over another, they're my enemy. Just like them Masons and Catholics—holding themselves all so high and mighty. But you said you wasn't either of 'em—right?"

"I ain't neither."

"Then shuck yourself outta that shirt of your'n and hang it on a nail, young'un."

"I . . . I got me the job?"

"We got us some teaching to do, by bloody damned. And you got yourself a passel of learning to get under your belt afore you're gonna be worth a red piss to me around here."

TWENTY-ONE

Right from that November day in 1763 when French fur traders Auguste Chouteau and Pierre Laclede Liguest pulled their dugouts out of the great Mississippi, St. Louis had flourished. Even though the Frenchmen were soon to learn that the surrounding region had recently been ceded to Spain, it made little consequence. Their trading post would prove to be the start of a very French community on Spanish soil.

It wasn't but a matter of months before the settlement had gained its broad-shouldered reputation as word spread up and down the river systems of frontier North America. Soon the muddy streets bustled with not only the French fur men and a few Spanish governing officials, but British traders, Indians in from the prairies, Creoles and Acadians, as well as black slaves, and of course American frontiersmen.

Almost from the start the waterfront was a colorful cluster of keels and flats, canoes and dugouts from the Ohio, the Missouri, the Illinois, and both ends of the great Mother of Waters. By the time Thomas Jefferson purchased Louisiana, the town could boast more than two hundred homes, most constructed of native stone. Soon thereafter Ohio flatboat merchant Moses Austin visited the city, stating that many of the homes were "large but not elegant." So while the socially elite and old-family French maintained a strict class structure in the midst of their busy provincial calendar, St. Louis was nonetheless a rowdy, rough-and-tumble, bruising city appropriately planted at the gateway to the greatest wilderness on the continent of North America.

By the autumn of 1815, when Titus began to sweat over Hysham Troost's forge, hammering iron into wagon parts, beaver traps, and locks for guns, the war with the British up at the Great Lakes and down at New Orleans had all but strangled off the western movement. American trade retreated from the upper Missouri: unrest fomented by British traders among the distant tribes in that northern country drove American trappers from those beaver-rich regions.

For the next few years the Americans pulled back, biding their time as the British took advantage of the situation—reaching out from their posts, going among the tribes with a missionary zeal, reaping rich fur harvests in that land of bounty. But over time the westward-yearning tide from America's east became undeniable. By 1820 fifty wagons a day were being ferried across the Mississippi to St. Louis. Already the most daring of settlers had pushed far beyond the city, 230 astounding miles from the mouth of the Missouri into the Boone's Lick region! Advancing settlement was taming that great river valley at the unbelievable rate of some forty miles per year. Those vanguards straining against the eastern boundary of that greatest of all American frontiers were assuredly a much hardier breed than those who at the same time were content to seep across what empty space was left throughout the Ohio and the Tennessee country. Indeed, those who left St. Louis behind to settle among the fertile bottomlands foresting the capricious valley of the Missouri more closely resembled their forefathers who had pushed down the Monongahela, hacked their way into the Cumberland, blazed trails across the canebrakes of Kentucky a hundred or more years before.

Here at the edge of all that, Titus repaired their wagons. He shod their horses. He sold them spare locks for their rifles. Then watched them go.

Farmers!

With every month and season and year he despaired that there ever would be ground left out there, in all that rumored expanse, that would not be turned by a plow, crossed by an ox, or flagged with surveyor's stakes. Some place left wild enough that farmers and settlers and merchants had no desire to go and change it in their image.

Why, he even heard talk of Indian farmers! No longer the stuff of war paint and scalp dances, but Indians who raised acres of beans and maize, working the rich, black earth in neat green rows, some even harvesting peaches and apples from pruned orchards traced with footpaths and a web of watering ditches. There were no cities of gold, the passing settlers declared as they left St. Louis behind. At least no cities like those the Spanish searched for. Instead, the land's true wealth lay in all that fertile soil among the river bottoms, ground long ago swept clear of timber by floods. Land where a man's plow could cut as easily as a hot knife through churned butter just brought up from the chill of the springhouse.

After all those years watching their kind trickle across the river to St. Louis before putting the city at their backs as they spread out in a great, wide front like a fine dusting of human spoor, Titus decided that he would never lay eyes on country yet unseen by white men. Land where he was certain his grandfather's spirit had gone to its final rest. That mythical Eden where rumor had it no man had ever, nor could he ever, reign supreme for it was ruled by the great beasts of the wilderness. If these hundreds, then thousands, of stoic settlers could push against that hardwood frontier where they intended to raise their cabins, clear the land, slash their plows into the great roll of the earth—then Bass despaired of ever finding where the buffalo had gone.

Perhaps they were mythical beasts, after all. Nothing but yarns, the stuff of nightmarish stories long ago spun for youngsters gathered at the knees of old ones first come to the Ohio and Cumberland borderlands. For certain, there must have been a few buffalo at one time—at least until the Indians and the earliest settlers had finished them off.

With the sour taste of bile in his throat Bass many times recalled his grandpap's story of how the founders of Rabbit Hash raised the alarm to put an end to the rattlesnakes in the surrounding area by once and for all raiding the dens of those serpents. All able-bodied men gathered on a succession of Sundays—the Lord's Day normally given over to the study of the Word but now spent ferreting out evil embodied in the shape of Satan's hissing serpent —the entire community marching out to climb among the stone ledges, prodding the cracks and crevices with their broadaxes and hatchets, pitchforks and hoes in hand, until the yellow and black rattlers were no more. In gleeful celebration the men tormented some of the last snakes before those too were dispatched. One of them, a yellow monster more than six feet in length, the men had teased and taunted with their hoe handles for more than an hour before the snake viciously clamped down on one of the hickory poles, therein releasing its deadly venom. Before their eyes those astonished men watched the poison rise through the grain of the wood a full twenty-two inches before the rattler's head was severed with a blow from a belt ax.

Despite what frontier folk had long claimed and Titus himself had come to believe, wanted to believe, *needed* to believe—that unlike those yellow Kentucky rattlers hunted to extinction, the buffalo had merely moved west to escape the encroachments of man—Titus finally decided he had been fooling himself.

Now he knew there simply were no buffalo left.

As his sense of loss deepened, so he came to drink more with each passing year, despairing of ever finding a new dream to replace that great and shaggy one he had carried inside him so long, the dream that had lured him away from his father's place, seduced him down the great rivers and eventually enticed him here to the gateway of the frontier.

At the first of those blurred, grog-sotted days, more than anything Titus sought a new dream to hang his fading hopes on, something to fix his future squarely on besides those long-gone buffalo.

But as the seasons rolled past, even that no longer mattered. Not dreams, not hopes, nothing that faintly rattled of the future. With a little more numbing alcohol to deaden his pain come payday each week, he found himself caring just that much less that he no longer had a reason to hope. Eventually it no longer mattered that he had ceased to dream.

How Titus came to enjoy that contented reverie he sensed with the first sip of each mug of metheglin brewed from the fermented honey found in the pods of the honey-locust tree and mixed with water; or mead, a potent brew of metheglin fermented with yeast and spices—later on fighting down the panic that swept over him when he reached the bottom of each cup and grew desperate for more. What liquid amnesia burned its way down his gullet made it easier to forget all that he had left behind to get here and seize his dream at last . . . for now he realized his dream was nothing more than that—a wisp of fantasy, hope without substance.

Drink he did these days, haunting the stinking watering holes nearly every night when he had money in his pockets. After all, Titus had little else to spend his wages on. There in his corner of Troost's livery he had enough blankets to hold winter's bite at bay, them and a chamber pot Bass would empty when he got around to it. Beyond those simple requirements all Titus needed to provide himself were his infrequent meals, taking them out and about the town whenever and wherever he chose, then returning to darken the tavern doorways that dotted the gloomy streets and narrow alleyways near the wharf, there to drink himself into another numbing stupor. More and more of those mornings-after he discovered that instead of having stumbled his way back to the livery, he more often than not woke up beside some less-than-comely wench who occasionally smelled even worse than he.

Then there were the all too frequent fights—most of them nothing more than good-natured eye-gouging romps with his fists. Nothing more than raucous brawls wherein rowdy men wore off their pent-up energies or burned off their cheap but stupefying liquor. Yet through the years Titus could recall standing in one of the wharfside grogshops or beer-sties when a fight turned poisonous, downright deadly: the combatants no longer wrestled and pummeled, no longer bit and gouged in some degree of good backwoods sportsmanship with it all. Most times it stunned him just how quickly those tests of stamina and bloodied good humor would turn murderous, knives drawn or pistols pulled—one man to stand victorious over the other who lay dying, his life oozing onto some mud-soaked, slushy floor.

Bass lost all but a handful of his fights, usually ending up as the one dragged out into the snow or the rain, there to be left unconscious for what roaming curs might happen by, drawn by the scent of blood to lick at his wounds, some to raise a leg and mark him territorially with the true measure of their disdain. No, Titus Bass wasn't really all that good with his fists, nor was he really nimble enough on his feet to dodge the hard and hammering blows, much less quick enough to make good a speedy retreat. But until that March of 1824 he could be thankful of one thing: at least he hadn't run into a man who had pulled out a gun, or a knife, or some other weapon every bit as deadly.

"Lucky you were," Hysham Troost growled at him early that cold morning. His words frosted about his head like a wreath of steam as he cradled his young apprentice's head across one arm.

Titus came to slowly, eventually blinking up at the blacksmith through one swollen eye, the other crusted shut. His puffy, bruised lips tore apart their seam of bloody crust. "L-lucky?" His tongue felt swollen to twice its size, likely bitten. And old coagulate clogged the back of his throat. "This . . . don't feel like lucky."

"From the looks of it I'd say the bastards used devil's claws on you." Troost dipped the rag back into his cherrywood piggin and wrung it out before squeezing drops into the dark and crusting tracks matted in the thick brown hair behind Titus's ear, lacerations extending on down the back of his neck, ending only at the shoulder. "You musta been turning when the feller what wore them claws smacked you. Damned lucky them cruel things didn't connect square on your face. It'd tore your eye plumb outta the skull if'n they had."

"Devil's claws," Titus groaned as the term sank into his groggy, hungover, brawl-hammered brain. He closed his eyes again to the shards of icy pain with this cleaning of those wounds. That inky blackness helped but a little. "W-what're devil's . . ."

"Just like iron knuckles, wore by them mean bastards what you'll find in them hellholes where Titus Bass goes to drink himself onto his face. In my time I've see'd just such a thing used once or twice myself." Troost pantomimed as if pulling something on his right hand, then made a fist with it, the fingers of his left hand serving as the curved claws protruding from the knuckles. "Like iron nails they are. Slip their fingers into a set of 'em. Use 'em to rake a man's face, tear up his chest, down his arms, or across his belly —opening him up like a slaughtered hog. With a swipe or two them claws can butcher you good." He wagged his head, and then with a voice grown thick with sentiment, he said quietly, "Damn, but you're lucky, Titus."

"My head . . . don't feel that way."

"The day you walked in here years ago, I had you figured for better sense. But over time you've got yourself stupid. *Real* stupid. Damn, but I just know you're gonna make me sad one of these days—me going to look for you and find you dead. Why you gotta go looking for trouble the way you do?"

"I don't . . . don't look." He squeezed his matted eye shut as Troost dribbled water across them both to loosen the crust before rubbing more of the coagulate free.

"Well, then—maybe you are just what you say you are: one unlucky son of a bitch. Trouble must come looking for you . . . because for about as long as I've knowed you—trouble's had it no problem finding Titus Bass."

"I ain't never gone to prison."

"Maybe that's a matter of time," Troost said. "Prison, or a grave."

"Prison? I never stole no man's purse, nary a horse neither. And there ain't a grave been dug what can hold me!" He lamely tried to chuckle at that, laugh at his predicament and hopelessness. But the self-deprecation did not last long for the physical hurt he caused himself.

"You know what they do to horse thieves hereabouts, don't you?" Troost asked.

Of course he knew. Over the years Bass had seen many a thief caught and brought to swift and primitive justice in old St. Louis. Down on First

Street was where they dealt with such criminals at a small, dusty patch of ground where stood three pillories and a pair of flogging posts.

"I know. They start by giving a horse thief stripes."

Behind the black and bruised lids where Troost ministered to his torn flesh swam the scenes of those he had seen lashed to the posts: their wrists bound together, pulled up high with a rope looped through a large iron ring at the top of those ten-foot posts buried firmly in the ground. Barely able to stand on their toes, the guilty were given an old-fashioned flaying with all those horrid strands of a knotted cat-o'-nine-tails.

That done, a special penalty was exacted by the town constables. First the criminal was held down while he was branded: an *H* on one cheek, *T* on the other. With his skin still sizzling, still screeching in pain, the thief was hauled out of the dirt and dragged over to one of the pillories, where a constable locked the top bar of the pillory over his neck, then nailed the thief's two ears to the wooden yoke. There the criminal remained, nailed in place and unable to move much at all for the next twenty-four hours. Only then was he freed, after the nails were cut free, ears and all, with a huge knife, just before the yoke was removed. The bleeding, branded criminal was then allowed to run, to flee, certain to carry the severity of his punishment with him the rest of his life, a marked man with a most uncertain future.

No matter what crimes of passion he had committed in his young life, Bass had never knowingly stolen anything of consequence. A few eggs, maybe a pullet here and there, but nothing that really mattered nor gave his conscience the fits at night. He'd never started out to hurt anyone, no matter how badly he ended up hurting himself.

"Damn you," Hysham Troost muttered softly as he leaned back, studying Titus side to side. "That's 'bout all I can do for you now with that horse liniment. Smells to hell, don't it? Well, you just lay there an' suffer, goddammit. I got work to do: mine and yours too now. Ain't the first time, is it? Here you lay back all bunged up again, and I gotta take up your slack—"

Titus tried to hoist himself up onto an elbow, but he hurt too much to get very far before that elbow gave out beneath him and he collapsed into the hay atop his pallet of blankets.

"Lay there, goddammit," Troost ordered gruffly. "About the worst beating I seen you get, so you'll just have to sleep this'un off. Worst I ever see'd. Damn. It just don't pay to care about you, does it?"

"Glad . . . glad you care."

"I ain't one to," Troost snapped angrily. "I don't wanna care for no man who don't care for his own self. And it sure is plain as sunshine that Titus Bass don't care for his own self. Just look at you."

"When I . . . I get better, you bring me a mirror," he croaked dry as sand, trying out half a puffy-lipped grin. "I'll look at my own self then."

Wagging his head with a weak smile, the blacksmith replied, "Damn you, Titus Bass. Here you are all cut up, your muscles knotted tighter'n new harness—and you still can make me laugh. You are a caution, son. A real, honest-to-goodness caution."

He felt the older man pat his shoulder lightly, listened as Troost rose from his side and moved out of the stall where Titus made his home in the older man's livery. Nearby sat a small iron stove radiating welcome heat as he shivered from time to time in his clothes soaked by winter's last sleety snow. Maybe it was even spring's first freezing rain that had battered St. Louis last night. No matter. Spring or winter now—they were just as cold, either one. He needed to get out of the clothes but knew he didn't have the strength and sighed.

Looking back now, Bass couldn't remember much after he had plopped himself down near the great stone fireplace at one of the grogshops and begun drinking the thick, heady stuff that burned all the way down his gullet. More and more he drank, slowly numbing his despair at ever finding what he had been seeking for so long. Just another night of punishing the whiskey and that sweet lemon-flavored rum brought upriver from New Orleans. Painkiller carried there to the mouth of the Mississippi by ship from some islands down in the great seas of the south. Another night no different from all the others gone before, he had counted on drinking his fill before stumbling out back of the saloon to one of the tiny, stinking knocking shops where women of all hues and shapes serviced the frontiersmen and riverboat crews coming and going like bees to this veritable hive at the edge of the wilderness.

For the moment there were snatches of memory, scenes that flitted behind his eyelids whether he wanted them to or not—it simply hurt to work his brain so. There in the mud and the cold rain outside the low door . . . the smoky light within . . . finding his whore and another man. Titus had shoved away. The mocking laughter. Then that stranger's friends, two—maybe three—more had come up when the argument had started.

Why he ever argued over a whore? Hadn't he learned his lesson? Whores had nearly killed him twice now. Annie Christmas's gunboat girls all the way downriver to Natchez when he was barely gone from home. And now this crooked-nosed woman he hungered for bad—a woman busy with a bull-headed, nasty sort of customer with even meaner friends.

Maybe he was lucky he had been turning, like Troost said. Whoever used those claws on him might well have killed him there by the whore's doorway. Or he might never have come to . . . if the blacksmith hadn't come hunting for him at first light. Vaguely he remembered someone rolling him over, feeling the cold bite of rain lancing against his wounds, sputtering at who took hold of him as Titus tried to get his eyes open to see, working his mushy mouth to say something to the bastard hurting him so in dragging him up and out of the icy mud and puddles of bloody water.

Just leave me be! his mind had screamed every bit as loud as his body had screamed in pain.

Then he'd been draped over someone's shoulder and hauled down the street when he'd passed out again. Had to be the blacksmith, Titus had figured just before he'd sunk again into the deep and welcome blackness of that hole he was digging for himself more and more every week, every month, every one of these last few years as he grew more and more bitter, more hopeless of ever knowing what it was his grandpap had sought, what men like Levi Gamble came west to find.

For Titus Bass there was simply nothing left to seek. Long ago when he'd begun his drinking, trying to kill himself slowly night by night an inch at a time, he had decided that his life was better short, better that than lived without hope. Better short than a life lived without that same sort of dream that had brought his grandpap to a new land.

Undeniably it was a hole he was digging for himself, a little deeper every day. For damned sure no man had yet dug the grave that could hold Titus Bass—but already he had a good start on the one he was digging for himself.

Goddamned whore.

Even the women had lost their allure for him. So why did he still seek them out? And make such an ass of himself in the process?

Titus tried to roll to the side carefully. It hurt too much, so he stayed there on his back, sensing the warmth from the tiny stove on one side, his other side still chilled and damp.

That first week he had begun work for the blacksmith years before, he and Troost had boarded up one of the stalls in a far corner of the livery. He had never made himself a door, not ever really needing one to his way of thinking. No reason to bolt things down or lock them up. He had long ago wrapped up his grandpap's rifle in an old sheet of oiled canvas and stuffed it up high in the rafters of the livery above his stall—having decided he would never have call to use the rifle again. That curly-maple stock carried so very, very many miles in that hope of reaching the place his grandpap's spirit had sought. Where the great and shaggy creatures ruled. Wherever they had disappeared, his grandpap's spirit was likely at peace there, for all time.

This was something Titus realized he would never share. That sense of peace, contentment, fulfilled of his quest.

What few possessions he owned hung above him from pegs and nails driven into the walls of his tiny cell: his grandpap's shooting pouch, odds and ends of extra clothing, a colorful bandanna, even a French-silk scarf given him by one of the dusky-skinned whores he favored in one of those knocking shops where a man degraded himself much, much more than the women he sought out in such places. Not a hell of a lot to show for his thirty years.

On the other hand, by the time his grandpap was his age, the man had brought his family into the canebrakes, fought off the French and their Indian allies, and through it all carved himself out a little place in the wilderness.

By the time Thaddeus had seen his thirtieth winter, he had cleared twice as much land as most men, raised more crops out of that rich soil than any other in Boone County, and sunk his roots down deep, deep.

Now, Titus? He had nothing to show for his years but his scars, and his miles, and the crow-foot beginnings of some wrinkles. He figured the graying would not be long in coming.

In no way was he living up to the Bass family name. He had failed in all respects, sinking lower and lower in despair and self-pity with the turn of the seasons. Failed in his attempts to accomplish anything near what the other men of his family had accomplished in their years walking the face of the earth. He had failed to make something of himself—no ground, no stock, no crops, no wife, no children. And no dream.

Nothing but his scars.

Long ago he had even considered going back home. Eventually deciding he could never return to Rabbit Hash, Boone County, Kentucky. Never to go back as Thaddeus's prodigal son. Nay, the old wounds were still too deep for him to lick, and return with his tail tucked between his legs. No home left for him back there where his brothers and sister had likely started families of their own long ago, every one of them working to clear all the more forest with Thaddeus, to push back the wilderness just that much more for the next generation to come.

"Titus," the blacksmith's voice whispered close to his ear. "If you're awake, want you to know I laid some victuals close by. Here at your left hand. It's within reach, son. I'll cover it with one of the missus's towels so the bugs don't come crawl in it right away. But you'll have to keep the mice out of it."

"Thank . . . thanks be to you, Hysham."

He patted Bass's arm gently, then rose again. "You sleep. Eat when you want. I'll get more if'n you want. Come see to you later in a while."

How lonely he felt hearing the footsteps shuffle off across the dried hay spread over the pounded clay floor of his little stall, footsteps fading down the row of stalls. In a moment he made out the distant hiss of the bellows exciting the fire, imagining the sparks sent spewing into the air like darting fireflies. Then Troost began pounding on the anvil, sure, solid, clocklike strikes with his leather-wrapped hammer.

Titus had no home.

Not Rabbit Hash. And St. Louis wasn't any more of a home to him either—even as much as Hysham Troost had taken him under his wing and shown him what a man could do with his hands when coupling fire and iron.

"Almost like a man and woman, ain't it?" Hysham had declared one day when they were fashioning rifle barrels: huge, heavy octagonal shafts of steel they would eventually cut with rifling and brown to a dull sheen. "A man and woman come together with such fire, softening their hardness in that coupling. Brought together in such a way they eventually become something new, different from 'em both by themselves. Same as what we've been doing here, Titus. It's a good life you've chose for yourself. A good life for a man, this work."

True enough. At Hysham Troost's elbow Bass had taken what rude skills he had learned from Able Guthrie and perfected them—learning to make nails, sharpen plowshares, mend wagon tires, fashion beaver traps and lock parts for rifles, as well as repair all the many mishaps befalling ironware of the day, for much of that iron was poorly made, impure in grade, and more often than not very brittle. While all farmers in the St. Louis region, like Guthrie, possessed the rudimentary skills it took to crudely fashion a horseshoe or repair a grub hoe, practically none of them had the skills and tools to accomplish anything more sophisticated in the way of repair, much less manufacture.

There in that warm corner of Troost's livery beside Hysham's forge, Titus became a part of the process—no more than a tool like the other tools he used—the huge bellows, a bench vise, a half-dozen hammers, a sledge, a shoeing hammer, a horseshoe punch, a handful of tongs, two hand vises, at least seven files and a pair of rasps, a wedge and cold chisel, along with an ax-eye punch. The whole of it could be carried by one pack animal if need be, with weight to spare . . . yet with such an outfit and an anvil—a blacksmith could forge miracles, if not repair dreams.

The frontier blacksmith was truly an important member of any community. Especially for the frontier rifle makers.

Many times over the years Hysham had given Titus a perfectly round steel rod of a certain size and a long rectangular piece of iron he was to shape, welding it inch by inch around the long rod, withdrawing the rod after each weld to cool it, reheating the iron while he did so, making weld by weld until he had his octagonal rifle barrel shaped around that rod.

A craftsman like Troost even showed Titus how to fashion his own rifling tool completely out of wood, save for the small cutting edge of fire-hardened steel. With this Titus would be given the next task of inserting the tool with its small cutting button, twisting and drawing, twisting and drawing, removing tiny curls of the barrel, making lands and grooves of a particular caliber's twist as specified by the growing rifle trade in the city.

"You need a hot fire, Titus," Troost had explained early on. "Don't know what all you've learned so far—so you pay heed what I got to teach you. Man can use seasoned hickory, or even oak bark—but I prefer to use my own charcoal. Made right out there in my own kiln."

Charcoal meant cutting and splitting wood. Across the years of sweating summer and winter, Titus came to appreciate a good, sharp, narrow—or felling—ax. With its handle or helve at two feet six inches in length, carved of shell-bark hickory and set into a head weighing no more than four and a half pounds, it was a tool no man on the frontier could do without. Many times had Titus spent a portion of a day selecting a proper piece of seasoned hickory, whittling it into rough shape for an ax handle, then smoothing it with a piece of broken glass, eventually to wedge it into the ax eye so that it would stay despite hard use.

Pity that men did not treat their axes more tenderly, Titus discovered, making sure to warm them on frosty mornings to lessen the danger of breakage to that honed edge. And woe to the boy who allowed his father's ax to bounce from wood to rocky ground, or the wife who used her husband's ax to cut the bone from a gammon of bacon.

But without just such flaws in human nature, Hysham Troost preached, "There simply wouldn't be enough work for a good blacksmith hereabouts."

Long, long after Titus heard the last ring of the old man's hammer on anvil fade from the sodden, cold air of the livery, he felt himself nudged, awakened rudely.

"Shit—you damn well don't look like you're in no shape to do no work for a man."

At the strange voice he tried to turn his face, tried easing open his puffy, crusted eyelids. Clearly this wasn't Troost kneeling nearby. A different voice. A different smell.

"Don't try to talk right now," the stranger continued. "I punched your fire up there in that leetle stove ye got yourself thar'. The warm sure does take the bite off this'r night."

Bass listened as the man shuffled about in the hay nearby like a dog making its bed, then settled back with a grunt and a sigh. The stranger was eating something, his lips smacking as he continued talking.

"Come in hyar lookin' fer a blacksmith. Ye be the blacksmith? Shit-fire. I be needin' a blacksmith in the wust way. Traps is what I got need of. Strong-assed traps, mind you. Them criks and rivers in that thar' kentry take 'em a toll of meanness on a man's beaver traps. This'r nigger cain't be takin' off fer the far lonesome 'thout a smithy like you fixin' on 'em."

This was a . . . a Negra!

But . . . the man didn't talk like no Negra Titus had ever met, sure as hell sounded nothing like the one he had known the best—Hezekiah Christmas. But, Lord and behold! The man had just called himself a nigger.

Painfully he cracked one eye open, his heart thumping with a generous mix of both fear and anticipation. In the dull glow of that squat-bellied toad of an iron stove Titus made out the dim, shadowy figure hunched in the corner of his tiny cell, chewing at what meat remained on a huge bone. Slowly he raked his sore eyes over the man, his nose suddenly pricked with the fragrance of what the man ate.

No, what Titus smelled could not be that bone the stranger tossed aside carelessly before wiping his mouth with the back of his sleeve. It had to be the clothing he wore.

In shadows that rose and fell down the man's arms and legs long fringes danced in the muted rose of the fire's dim light. Strips of dull color laced their patterns down each sleeve, over each shoulder, a round patch emblazoned at the center of the man's chest, partially covered by a long, unkempt beard he wiped his greasy hands upon, then stroked aside. From somewhere beneath the tangle of his chin whiskers he produced a small clay pipe.

Straining his eyes through the murky, smoky firelight kicked out by that small, cast-iron stove, Bass tried to make out the man's features. Sure as hell didn't look like no Negra. Not like no Negra Titus Bass had ever laid eyes on—drunk or sober. No broad nose there . . . but it was damned hard to tell for sure in this light, what with all that matted beard.

As the stranger loaded the pipe from a pouch at his side, Titus worked to tear his eyes open wider, the better to make out the man's hoary head—a mass of hair sprouting every which way in wild and greasy sprigs once he yanked off his low-crowned, wide-brimmed beaver-felt hat and carefully laid that wind-battered, rain-soaked old veteran aside. Evidently a prized possession, Bass made note.

Agonizingly Titus rolled onto an elbow about the time he cracked the second eye fully open and rocked himself up.

"Ah—thar's a leetle life left to ye, is thar now?" The stranger leaned forward, his face coming into the stove's glow as he stuffed a long piece of straw through the grate on the stove's door.

Bass nearly gasped, low and rumbling, collapsing from his elbow again. "You . . . you're a white man."

"What?" the man asked, then threw his head back and roared in great peals of laughter, rocking back into the smoky confines of the shadows skulking in that corner of Bass's little cell. "Me, a white man? Sure as sun, coon—I be a white man in sartin comp'ny, mister. But in t'other comp'ny, like these decent, God-fearin' folks hereabouts, I s'pose I be took for as Injun as Injuns come."

"I . . . thought . . . no. But you . . . said you was—"

"Spit out your piece—I said me what?"

"Call't yourself a Negra."

The stranger's brow knitted up a moment, quizzically working that over in his head; then he suddenly rocked forward, roaring in laughter again. "I'll be go to hell right hyar an' let the devil hisself chaw on my bones. If'n that don't take the circle! I call't myself a *nigger,* mister."

"That's what I said—just what you called yourself."

Leaning forward even more, the man came closer to Titus. Now Bass could see that one big upper tooth protruded outward like a hound's unruly fang. Likely from force of habit come of many years living with his affliction, the stranger constantly worked his upper lip beneath that shaggy and un-kempt mustache, sliding the lip this way, then that, doing his very best to hide that large yellowed fang that poked its way out into broad daylight despite some of the stranger's best efforts.

Around it the man rasped his explanation. "An' a feller what calls hisself a *nigger* ain't in no way calling hisself a Negra. A Negra got him black skin, black as charcoal in that forge o' your'n. An' a nigger . . . well, now." He scratched at the side of his beard, then pushed some of his long hair back over his shoulder, shrugging as if his tilt on things made all the world of sense to him. "Niggers come in all colors. No more'n that. Yest a word fellers I know come to use, s'all."

Bass licked his dry lips, then croaked, "W-where in God's earth you come from?"

"God's earth, eh? That's purty good, mister. Fer that's yest whar' I come from." He sighed. "Yessir. I yest come hyar from God's earth. Say, ye look thirsty thar'. Bet ye could do with some water?"

Titus watched him drag the red cedar piggin close and pull the dipper from it.

"Hyar. Drink up," the man commanded.

He did so, greedily too: savoring the cool, sweet taste and smooth texture of the water sliding like silk across his parched membranes.

"That ought'n limber up that talkin' hole of yer'n," the stranger declared. "My Lordee—what ye gone and done to yerself? All cut up the way ye are?"

"A fight over to a tavern last night," Bass replied, his stomach suddenly feeling very empty with the slosh of water he had just poured into it. Maybe his stomach rolled only from the smell of the stranger's food—the mere thought of eating made his belly curl up in protest.

"I see'd wust myself, mister. Blackfeet mostly. Though them Rees do a fairsome job on a nigger. When their kind get done workin' over a man—he ain't left near as purty as you. An' it ain't be all that long ago I see'd fellers wus'n yerself." He clucked, sucked his lips sideways to hide that snaggle-tooth, and wagged his head. "Leastwise, as hangdown as ye might feel, looks to be yer movin' and talkin'."

"Don't mean I ain't half near death," Titus grumbled with self-pity, his mind of a sudden feverish on something to eat after his fast of nearly twenty-four hours, despite how his stomach might protest. Then he remembered the food Troost said he'd brought in. Rocking unsteadily onto that one elbow, he craned his neck, searching for the plate in the shadows of his smoky quarters.

"Don't ye take the circle now!" the stranger exclaimed suddenly, as if it had taken more than a moment for Bass's words to sink in. "Why, if this coon ain't got him a sense of humor."

"You damn well got me wrong—I ain't much at funnin'," Titus admitted, growing impatient with his search. Troost had said he'd set that plate nearby, towel and all. "Never have been much at funnin'. Say, you see'd a plate around here? Had it a towel laid over keep the bugs out?"

"Towel, an' a plate? Like this'un hyar?" the man replied, bald-faced and innocent as could be—producing the large pewter platter, complete with a striped towel covering it all.

"Likely that's the one." Bass took it from the man, immediately sensing just how light the whole affair was. Collapsing to his side, he flung off the towel, finding the plate empty. "What . . . the hell?" he screeched two octaves too high.

"Was them yer victuals?" the stranger asked. "Pardon the bejesus out of me. When I come on in here while'st back, I nudged ye. Spoke at ye too. But nary a move. Figgered ye wasn't dead, way ye was breathin'—but had to be laid out black as night till the peep o' day. Feller in that condition surely didn't want him no victuals, so hungry as I was—I weren't about to leave 'em go to waste."

"You ate my god . . . goddamned supper?" Titus shrieked. The effort hurt, his sudden flare of hot anger shooting through every bruised scrap of tissue in his body as he rocked off his elbow, the plate clattering beside him.

"I'll go fetch ye some victuals on my own, straightaway," the stranger declared, starting to rise. "Ain't used to St. Louie City, but I'll likely find something in this'r town, even this time of night."

"What time you figure it to be?" Bass asked weakly, his brain hammering with great slashes of pain once more as he closed his eyes, laid an arm over them as he sought a soft place for the back of his head.

"Hell if I know what time to make it out to be 'cept nighttime, mister." He pointed off generally toward the rafters overhead. "From looks of the moon out there 'mongst all them clouds when I come in, had to be some past midnight."

"Jumpin' Jehoshaphat!" Titus growled nearly under his breath. "You come in here to rob a sick man of his food this time of night? Cain't you just leave a sick man to get his sleep?"

"Look who's gone an' got hisself techy," he snarled back. "Mayhaps I best find me 'nother blacksmith do my work for me tomorry an' ye can yest forget me rootin' ye out some victuals *this time of night!*"

Titus wasn't doing a damn bit of good against the steam-piston throbbing that rocked his head. As quietly as he could, he said, "Don't . . .

please don't go nowhere. Troost'd have my balls if I run off any business, mister."

"Troost?"

"My boss," Titus replied. "Man what owns this place."

"That mean . . . yer saying ye ain't the blacksmith?"

"I am. But I just work here."

"Ye any good?"

"You damn bet I am," he growled back, angry at the man. The thought of it: to be awakened by a stranger who had just eaten his food in the middle of the night, then turned around and insulted him too.

"So tell me," the man said. "Ye gonna be worth a lick to work on my traps tomorry?"

"I doubt it."

"Then I'll wait," the stranger said, smacking his lip around that fang the color of pin acorns. " 'Sides. It'll gimme time to have my spree. Come down hyar to St. Louie to have me my spree. So I got me time till ye heal yerself up."

Titus grumbled, "That's mighty kind of you."

"Ye still hungry? Said ye was hungry. I'll go fetch ye some victuals."

"Least you could do so I can consider us even," Bass replied, wagging his hammering head slightly.

The stranger slowly got to his feet and began pulling on a long blanket coat, well-greased and dirtied, blackened by the smoke of many fires. "Yer sure as sun a techy sort, ain't ye?"

"Ain't you touchy if'n some feller come in to eat your food and wake you up from a dead sleep?"

He clucked a tongue against that big front tooth, then said with a nod, "S'pose yer right, mister. I owe ye for yer hospitality. I does at that."

Titus rolled his thundering head away, easing it over onto the elbow he crooked beneath his puffy cheek. "Supper would be a damn good start at showing your thanks."

"If'n ye don't take the circle, my friend! Fer a man what's been beat as bad as ye surely be, I got to hand it to ye," the stranger said with a nod of certainty. "No matter how yer painin'—ye sure don't mind making use of that there mean mouth of yer'n, full of stupids the way it is."

"Mean?" Titus snapped, trying to rise off his blankets, straining to hold his head up and bring the stranger's face into focus. "You dance on in here the way you done, and you go off telling me *I'm* mean?"

"The way yer acting," the stranger replied, "yer gonna be yest fine, I

can see. Got lots of fight left in ye, yessirree! No matter that I find ye layin'
hyar lickin' yer wounds arter someone nigh onto kill't ye . . . but I don't
make ye out to be the sort to whimper an' moan like a bitch 'bout to pup, is
ye? Hell, no—ye still got ye sand enough in yer goddamned craw to bark at
me like a bad dog."

"Bad dog? Barking at you?"

"Yep!" And the stranger chuckled heartily. "Maybeso ye do got some
ha'r in ye after all, mister—if'n ye can bark at me while'st yer all tore up the
way ye are."

"Ain't no use in a fella feeling sorry for hisself," Titus replied, working
hard to focus on the stranger with his blood-rimmed eyes.

"Yer some, mister blacksmith. Think I yest might like gettin' to know
ye."

"Don't matter none to me if you do or if you don't," Bass snapped,
immediately sorry he had. "I . . . I don't have me many friends."

The stranger crawled over and slowly knelt near Bass, the gamy aroma
of him washing over Titus.

"Me neither, mister," the man explained quietly. "Not . . . not many
friends no more." Then he suddenly reared back and slapped both palms
down atop his thighs, rising to his feet. "Ye still hungry—I'll run off an'
fetch ye some victuals."

"I better eat," Bass admitted. "If only to give me something for my
belly to toss right back up."

"Yer meatbag paining ye, is it?" He held down his hand to Titus.
"Name's Isaac Washburn. Isaac—with two *a*'s. What's yer'n?"

"Titus Bass." He struggled some to roll off his right side, but he
eventually got the arm freed and gripped the stranger's hand. "Where was it
you said you was from, Isaac Washburn?"

"God's kentry, Titus Bass. Up the Missouri—land of the Blackfeet,
Ree, an' Assiniboin. Seen me Mandan and Pawnee kentry too. Land whar'
them red niggers take yer ha'r if'n you don't keep it locked on tight. Kentry
where the moun-tanes reach right up to scrape at the belly o' the sky, an' the
water's so cold it'll set yer back teeth on edge."

Electrified at that announcement, Bass anxiously fought to prop himself on both elbows when Washburn released his hand. The older man
clearly had a secure grip on Titus's attention.

"You . . . you been out . . . out there?" Bass asked.

Isaac grinned, knowingly. "Out thar'?" And he pointed off into the distance. "Damn right I been out thar'. Seen yest 'bout ever'thin' thar' is fer a nigger to see north on the upriver."

"Then . . . you had to seen 'em?"

"Seen what? Injuns? Yest tol't ye: I see'd more Injuns'n I ever wanna see again in my hull durn life—"

"No," Bass interrupted. "Have you see'd the buffalo?"

"Buffler?" Washburn reared back, snorting a great gust of laughter that showed Bass the underside of that great tooth all but sticking straight out of his upper gum. "Titus, I see'd buffler so thick at runoff time their rottin', stinkin' carcassees dang near clog the Missouri River her own self. From that river I see'd them critters moseying off to the north, goin' round to the south, likely to gather up in herds so big they'd cover the hull kentry far as a feller could see."

"Then you . . . you really see'd 'em!" he exclaimed under his breath, wide-eyed and aghast. Bass's heart hammered mercilessly in his chest, every bit as hard as his temples throbbed. How he hoped this was his answer. "Damn, here I am talking to a man what's see'd buffalo for real."

Washburn looped a four-inch-wide belt around his blanket coat, securing it in a huge round buckle. "My friends call me Gut."

Quickly his red eyes shot down to the stranger's belly. Nothing there that in any way remotely appeared to be a gut on the man. He was about as lean as a fella could be. Made of strap leather and latigo, most likely, Bass decided.

"Why they call you *Gut*?" Titus asked. "Ain't a man can say you got a big belly."

Isaac laughed. "No—not 'cause of my belly. Others laid that handle on me some time back—up in them Three Forks, y'ars ago it were—I s'pose fer it be my favorite food."

"You eat . . . eat gut?"

"Not gut rightly. *Bou-dans*. A parley-voo French word for sausage, s'all it is."

"Bou-dans," Titus repeated, trying out the sound of it on his tongue bitten and swollen from the beating.

"Yessirree, my friend. I'll fix 'em for us sometime while'st I'm hyar in St. Louie. Plant myself down fer a short time afore I feel the needs be pushing upriver once more." He stared off for a moment before saying, "Lord, but for once I'd love to see how a man could do getting hisself west follering the Platte."

"The Platte," Titus repeated. He had heard something of it.

Washburn pointed off with a wide jab of his arm. "Runs right out to the moun-tanes. One of them rivers what comes in off the prerra."

"All the way in from far away on the prairie?" He had seen rivers long and wide and wild. But to think of a river bringing water down from mountain snows, all the way here to St. Louis!

Washburn smacked his lips loudly, his eyes gleaming now that he had the younger man's rapt attention. "Like I said it, Titus: that water comes all the way from them moun-tanes. What moun-tanes I see'd up north in the Missouri River kentry, them moun-tanes even down south of the Powder— they was still some ways off west from the criks and rivers I was trappin' or trompin'. Word is, them moun-tanes on the headwaters of the Platte scratch the belly of the sky . . . an' go all the way south to greaser kentry."

He wagged his head in disbelief, trying to conceive of any range so high, any range that extended that great a distance. "S-same mountains?"

Washburn nodded in the dim fire's light. "Same. North, to south—far as a man can travel in a month of Sundays."

"Naw," Bass scoffed, suddenly suspicious the older man was making sport of him. Titus had seen mountains, back east. That Kentucky and Cumberland country. He damn well knew there could be nothing near as big as Isaac Washburn was claiming. "I cain't believe there's mountains what run from the Missouri where you was all the way south that far."

Squinting, the disheveled, greasy man gazed down at Bass incredulously. "Ain't ye heard, lad? Right north of St. Louie not far from hyar, a man can foller the great Missouri north to trap or trade. Goin' upriver, that man'll run onto more'n a handful of big rivers, ever' damn one of 'em coming in from the far, far moun-tanes."

"I know 'bout the beaver trade on the upper river. Been making traps for years now," Titus snapped a little impatiently. "What're they called . . . them mountains you set eyes on?"

Isaac visibly rocked back on his heels. "Called . . . the Rockies. The High Stonies. The Shining Moun-tanes."

"S-shining mountains?"

He nodded matter-of-factly. " 'Cause they allays got snow on 'em, Titus. Even in the summer."

"You seen them mountains shine for yourself?"

"Sure as hell have! I stared right up at 'em fer my first time near fifteen year ago when I was with Andy Henry on the Three Forks. Then I got me a close look again coming down the Powder this last winter with Glass's outfit; saw 'em off thar' to the west. Bigger'n yer gran'ma's titties. Why, Titus— they're even bigger'n what I ever figgered 'em to be in all my dreams growin' up back to Albermarle County."

"Where's that?"

"Virginny."

This was all coming too fast, too damned fast. He sucked in a big breath and let his answer gush forth like a limestone spring. "And the buffalo—then you're telling me them herds is real?"

For a moment Washburn stared impassively at the injured man atop his blankets in the hay. "Damn tootin' they're real, Titus. Whatever give ye the idee buffalo wasn't real?"

He wagged his head a moment, trying to find words that would describe the gut-wrenching despair suffered these long years. "I just . . . well, maybe 'cause I ain't never seen one myself—"

"I see'd enough in that north kentry along the Missouri River, up to the mouth of the Yallerstone, even round the Musselshell, and down to that Powder River kentry—I see'd 'em with my own eyes."

"Lots of 'em?"

Isaac clucked a moment on that snaggled fang, then said, "I see'd so many I thought my eyes gonna bug out . . . but then Ol' Glass—he's a friend of mine I tromped through some kentry with this'r past winter—he a way ol't hivernant from way back . . . he told me I ain't see'd all that many."

"A *hivernant?*"

"Feller what'd spent him his first winter in the far kentry. Back ago Glass was one to live with the Pawnee some. But I knowed me some hivernants afore runnin' onto Glass. Man-well Leeza had him a few hired men like that. Men so tough they growed bark right on 'em—like a tough ol' cottonwood tree. But I gotta admit, Ol' Glass had him more bark'n any man I ever knowed. Talked 'bout winterin' up quite a few with the Pawnee—"

"This Glass, he said you ain't seen very many, eh?"

Washburn jutted out his chin and slapped his chest once with a fist. " 'Many!' I bellered like a stuck calf back at Glass as we was coming 'cross from the headwaters of the Powder, making for the Platte. 'That's right,' the son of a bitch yest told me quietlike. 'If'n a man wants to see the hull consarned world covered up by buffler, he needs to take hisself on down to the prerra country come spring greenup. It's there the buff graze and breed, moseying slow as you please afore the winds of the seasons. An' they cover the hull durn earth from horizon, to horizon, to horizon.' " As he said it, Isaac pointed here, then there, then over there in emphasis. "That's what he said, the truth of it too. I believe that nigger, Glass."

"As f-far as a man can see?" Titus asked, incredulous. He had wanted to believe. Then gave up all hope. And now Isaac Washburn was telling him the whole earth was damn near black with them.

"Like a blanket coverin' ever'thing," Washburn added, kneeling slowly at Titus's side. He held his open hands up to the glow in that little stove, rubbed them. "That's the country I wanna go to see with my own eyes one day soon, Titus Bass. Clear to the moun-tanes."

"How come you been all the way out there—but you ain't never got to the mountains?"

"Hol't on there, Titus," Isaac corrected. "I been up the mighty Missouri for many a season now, trappin' beaver for that greaser he-coon named Man-well Leeza. Then of recent I been at work for my friend Andrew Henry. But that don't mean very many of us got all that close to them moun-tanes. While'st they was raised up all round us, we didn't ever go to 'em."

"Never?"

"Not once, no," Washburn answered, kneeling beside Bass once again. "An' when I was on my tromp with Ol' Glass, we sure as the devil didn't have us the time to go off lollygagging to look for no big buffler herds—man wants to keep his hair locked on, why—he keeps his head tucked into his collar out thar' in that kentry. If'n he wanders off too much, the Blackfeet or them Rees yest might take a real shine to his skelp."

"What're these here Blackfeet, and them Rees?"

Washburn shuddered. "Rees? Damn 'em. Consarn them Blackfeet too! Baddest damn two-legged beasts God ever put Him on the face of the earth. Walkin', talkin', killing things is what Blackfeet is. Some time back they struck 'em a bargain with the Englishers to keep our kind out. Over the y'ars they been doing their best to make it hard on fellers like Leeza an' Henry dealing in the Crow trade."

"Crow? The bird?"

Washburn guffawed as he rose, his knees cracking. "Crow are Injuns up in that Powder River an' Bighorn kentry. My, my—them are purty warriors—but a small tribe of 'em. They hate the Blackfeet ever' bit as bad as we do." He turned as if to shuffle away, tugging at that greasy blanket coat of his. "I'll be off to get your supper."

"Maybeso you can find us something strong to drink too."

Washburn's eyes narrowed. "Ye sure yer up to gettin' yerself bit by the same dog nearly chawed ye in half last night, Mr. Bass?"

Titus nodded, his head throbbing so—he was desperate, certain that only a little of the hair of that mongrel that had mauled him so badly would truly salve his pain.

"All right," Washburn replied. "Only ye'll swaller ye some victuals first. But I'll vow ye I'll bring us back some barleycorn. Yessir. Isaac Washburn is due him a spree! Been a few seasons since't I was last anywhere near me this hull consarn city. The up-kentry whar' I been winterin' ain't much the place fer good barleycorn whiskey and white-skinned women, no sir." He leaned forward, his face stuck down near Titus's, aglow with a red shimmer from the stove. "I'm sure a likely young feller like yerself can show Isaac Washburn whar' I can go to dip my stinger in some white gal's honey-pot . . . now, cain't ye?"

He grinned lamely. "I get myself healed up here, Isaac," Bass replied, "we're gonna both go dip our stingers in the finest honey-pots a man can find for hisself right here in St. Louie."

"Whoooeee!" Washburn exclaimed, slapping the barn wall with a flat hand as he stopped and whirled about there at the door, the bottom of his blanket coat spinning out like a wheel. "Sounds to it like ye damn well better get on the gallop and mend yer own self right quick, Mr. Titus Bass. I don't 'tend on waiting too long, now that I finally come back to St. Louie arter all these hyar winters of drinking bad-gut likker and wenching with red squaws. I owe meself a spree, young'un: white wimmens and good whiskey. An' I'm invitin' ye along fer the ride o' yer life!"

At the mere thought of swilling down a whole lot more whiskey, his head pounded unmercifully, sharp pins stabbing right behind his eyes. Titus licked his swollen, cracked lips, wanting to feel hopeful about something, desperate to feel hopeful about almost anything—especially . . . what might lie out there.

Bass asked, "You really fixing to go on out yonder this year?"

"Yonder to them moun-tanes?" He moved into the shadows at the door.

"Wait!" Titus barked with a dry-throated croak, anxious that Washburn was leaving before he got his answer. "It true you're fixing to light out there, going yonder the way you said you was—just go to the Platte and point your nose west?"

"Cutting my way right through the heart of that buffler kentry," Isaac answered, then paused.

"Damn, but I allays hoped I could . . . maybeso one day do that too."

"Maybeso, Titus Bass," Washburn eventually replied, his eyes glimmering like twelve-hour coals there in the shadows of that doorway—staring down at the younger man intently. "Maybe ye nigh well get yer chance, at that."

TWENTY-TWO

"There's some got 'em a name for that hull kentry out there," Isaac Washburn declared the next day as he chattered on and on, having found him some eager ears. "I heerd some call it the buffler palace."

Favoring the bruised ribs, Titus turned slowly to the trapper, who always lumbered close at one elbow or the other. "P-palace?"

Swaying in his drunkenness, Washburn shrugged, absently scratching at his long beard. "I s'pose at first it strikes a man as a mite queersome name—but that's what many of the boys call that prerra land out yonder. Whar' buffler's the king. Land whar' the buffler rule."

Pumping on the bellows handle with the arm that did not pain him as badly as the other, Titus let that sink in slowly over the next few moments. From what Washburn had been telling him right from last night, that country must surely be what he had dreamed it would be: the land where the buffalo had retreated toward the setting sun—seizing dominion over everything as far as a man's eye could see, a land from horizon to horizon to horizon ruled by those great, humped, mythical beasts.

"Ye mean fer true what ye said last night?" Washburn asked as he wiped some of the amber droplets from his droopy mustache.

"Said 'bout what?"

" 'Bout throwin' in with me."

"You told me a man needs him a partner to cross country like that—the Injuns an' all."

"Ye figure ye got the makin's?"

Titus turned, peering at the older man for a long time through his swollen, bloodshot eyes. "Look at me, half-beat to death . . . and you're asking me if I got the makings?"

"Damnation—ye sure as hell got enough ha'r in ye, Titus. Enough bottom to make it clear through to the moun-tanes. Yer the sort figgers something out to do, so ye put yer head down and yest go at it. That's a good thing in a man what wants to step off into the middle of the wilderness. Ain't no one else't gonna care for ye then—maybeso a partner if yer lucky enough to have one."

"You had a partner afore, Isaac?"

"Sure. Had me lots of 'em."

Bass had the fire punched now, so laid in the long piece of strap iron he was going to start forming into a spring for the first of those beaver traps he would fashion for Isaac Washburn, once more using the old square-jawed one of Hysham Troost's he kept hanging from a nearby peg as his pattern. Not that he really needed to take it down and study it, measure it, see how things fit. In the last few years Titus had hammered together the springs and jaws, pans and triggers, to make some two hundred such traps. So despite how ragged his head treated him, this morning Bass eagerly went at the sooty work over the forge with a renewed relish, well before Hysham Troost strode through the door.

Titus asked the old trapper, "Tell me how come that partner of your'n didn't come here to St. Louie to have a spree with you?"

Washburn straddled an anvil atop a huge stump that squatted on the far side of the forge and settled his rump, his eyes watching the red glow begin to bleed up long strips of iron Bass would soon begin hammering into the tempered trap springs. "Had him t'other affairs to see to."

"And miss out on a spree with his partner?"

"Like I said—other 'fairs."

"I s'pose he's got him a gal stuck away someplace, likely," Bass said, slipping on a pair of blackened leather gloves with short gauntlets.

"Ain't got a thing to do with a woman," Isaac said sourly.

"What sort of man miss out on good whiskey and white women when he finds himself this close to St. Louie?"

"Never did claim he got close to St. Louie at all."

"Did I prick you in a sore spot, Isaac?" Titus asked, shoving the iron farther down into the glowing coals, then heaving on the bellows all the more. "Sounds to me like you don't wanna talk 'bout him."

"Ain't him, rightly," Washburn finally admitted. "It's all that hurt an' p'isen he's been carrying round inside him for too long—gonna get hisself kill't from it one day soon. Shit, he yest may well gone under by now."

"Your partner?"

Isaac nodded. "I ain't been partnered up with him long, just last few months, really. But ever since't I knowed him, Glass been laughin' danger square in the face for nigh onto a y'ar now."

"Glass?"

"That's his name. Claims he's pertected by God, so he can do God's work in taking him some revenge on them what left him for dead."

"He was left for dead?"

"That's him. The one I tromped through the last winter with, gettin' to Fort Atkinson, floatin' back down the Missouri to get here with what little I got left to my outfit."

"How long you been in the mountains, in that up-country, Isaac?"

Washburn visibly relaxed as his eyes stared out the half-open livery door where a cold, spring rain drizzled in gray sheets.

"Been over fifteen winters, Titus. Damn but that do feel like a long, long time. I fust come out of Albermarle County, Virginia, in 1805. Moseyed west into the Cumberland country. Didn't come to St. Louie till the next y'ar, and by oh-seven I was hired on as engagee to Man-well Leeza. Was a big fur trader in these parts."

"I heard tell of him a lot here'bouts."

"He died not long back," Washburn continued. "Fella named Pilcher took over the company now. Howsoever, I ain't had a thing to do with it for some time."

"You went upriver to trap beaver in oh-seven?"

With a bob of his head Washburn answered, reaching beneath his long beard to take out his pipe and some tobacco. "That black-ha'red Spanyard led us north that y'ar—the winter Antoine Bisonette deserted an' Leeza sent George Drouillard to bring him back in, dead or alive."

"Did he?"

"Did he what?"

"Bring him in?"

He looked at Titus as if he were talking to a stump. "Dammit to hell—he sure did. Bisonette was wounded so bad, he weren't bound to live all that long. Leeza put him in a pirogue with two other fellers, sent 'em south back to St. Louie while'st we pushed on. Later we heerd Bisonette died. Didn't matter—wasn't many of us liked him or Drouillard neither one."

"How far you make it up the Missouri?"

"Me and others—like that friend I come to know named Henry—we went and built Leeza's post on the Yallerstone, mouth of the Bighorn. He called it Fort Raymond. Then some of us tramped on over to the Three Forks kentry."

"Three Forks?"

"Three rivers what all tangle up and make the Missouri River, see? That's Blackfeet kentry—mess of them devil's whelps."

With his tongs Titus pointed at Washburn's greasy, blackened buckskins. "That where you come onto them there? Your outfit?"

He rubbed a hand down a thigh, fingers brushing the strip of porcupine quillwork in colors dulled over time by many dunkings in high-country streams and bleached beneath a merciless sun. "Got this off'n a Mandan woman, truth of it, Titus. She kept me warm one winter, while'st I kept her an' her young'uns fed. These'r leggin's lasted me some seasons, they have. Only had to patch 'em up from time to time, down at the bottom mostly, where I soak 'em in the criks and eventual' the skin dries up an' cracks."

"Got them from that Mandan gal when you was up at the Three Forks?"

"Hell, no, I didn't, ye consarned idjit!" he roared, rocking forward off his anvil and pulling his skinning knife out of the scabbard behind his hip. "Hyar, now—lemme show ye yest how stupid a nigger yer making yerself out to be."

As Washburn went to his knees and began smoothing out some of the pounded clay floor, Titus stuffed the strip of iron back into the coals and gave the bellows another half-dozen hard heaves before he too went to his knees to hunker as close as he could while Washburn began drawing landmarks with the tip of his knife.

"These'r all along hyar—they the Rocky Moun-tanes. Hyar's whar' them three rivers tangle up to make the Missouri. All the way over hyar on the Missouri, them Mandans live in great wigwams made of earth. But back hyar is whar' the Yallerstone comes in. Sometime later on my friend Henry was to put him a post right thar'. An' on down hyar off the Yallerstone comes in the Bighorn. That's whar' Leeza had Henry build him a post to trade with them Crow."

"The Injuns you told me 'bout last night."

Washburn grinned. "Maybeso yer head weren't all so comboobled up as I thort she was!" Using his knife, he pointed back down at his crude map. "Cain't ye see how far Mandan kentry is from Blackfeet kentry?"

"Where's Blackfeet land?"

He dragged the knife tip in a great, long oval that encompassed a good portion of the land he had just described.

Bass swallowed, shifting slightly onto another knee. "All that?"

"Don't ye ever go an' doubt it, Titus. Blackfeet hold them northern moun-tanes like they was their own. An' them goddamned Rees hold the river like they owned it an' ever'thing upriver from 'em too!"

"So you been up there, in all that country, since you went up with this Manuel Lisa back to 1807?"

"No, I ain't been up there ever since, ye mule-headed idjit! Didn't take long for them Blackfeet an' Assiniboin to start whittling away at the first of us into that kentry. Some durn good men left their bones to bleach in the sun up that way. Rest of us turned tail an' come easin' back downriver in 1811. Already them British bastards was making it mighty hard for Americans to work the beaver kentry up north. They was a sneaky lot—still are, for my money. Come down from Canaydee—sellin' them blood-suckin' Injuns guns an' powder, siccin' 'em on Americans. That war we fought agin 'em didn't help, didn't help a tinker's damn up thar' in that north kentry."

Washburn spoke the truth of it. By the time the War of 1812 had worn itself out and America had negotiated a border, along with some agreements regarding exploration and control of the fur trade in the far Northwest—the Hudson's Bay Company already had consolidated everything west of the Rocky Mountains while the Northwest Company Nor'Westers had a firm hold on the entire upper Missouri country east of the continental divide. With the hostile Blackfoot confederation driving Manuel Lisa and Andrew Henry out of that prime beaver country, the whole of the upper Missouri drainage was again cleared of American interests for many years.

Nevertheless, they did leave behind one man in abandoning their Bighorn post in 1811.

"Onliest trapper we left up thar' was one of the mulatto fellers," Isaac related.

Bass turned from his anvil, beads of sweat standing out on his brow like glittering diamonds, his thick brown eyebrows soaked. "A Negra?"

"He t'weren't as dark as most Negras I see'd afore. Name o' Edward Rose—the one we left behind when we put the Bighorn post at our backs."

Bass drove the hammer down on the glowing spring metal, spacing his words between each resounding ring of hammer on steel. "Why'd he . . . stay on . . . up there . . . seeing how . . . things were . . . mighty hot . . . in that country?"

"Wanted to live on with them Crow."

The hammer came to a stop, and he stuffed the half-finished spring back into the coals, heaving down on the bellows handle to excite the fire. "Gone off to live with Injuns . . . just like a Injun?"

Washburn nodded. "Them Crow have mighty handsome wimmens, Titus." He licked his lips visibly. "Mighty, mighty handsome wimmens."

"What become of you when Manuel Lisa pulled out of that country?" Bass inquired, leaning over the red cedar piggin and bringing the ladle to his lips, drinking long and slow.

"I stayed on with Henry. He been my friend right from that first winter in that up-country. I throwed in with him whar' he was going."

With their desertion of the upper Missouri, Andrew Henry initially dropped downriver with Manuel Lisa. But while the Spaniard established a new base of operations at a new Fort Lisa raised near Council Bluffs, Andrew Henry figured he'd had himself enough of the Indian trade. He tromped on back home, while Lisa carried on a lively trade up the river as far as the Mandan villages, eastward to the Sac and Fox, from time to time bartering with bands of the westward-migrating Sioux. But due to the well-financed encroachments of the British companies coupled with the economic hardships brought the infant nation by the War of 1812, after more than a dozen years on the upper rivers, the American fur trade was no bigger when hostilities ended with the English, no stronger among the tribes in 1815 than the trade had been in 1804.

By 1819 the aggressive Lisa had nudged out many of his stodgy, conservative partners, the sort of financiers he'd believed were holding him back —replacing them with men the likes of Joshua Pilcher.

"I went with Henry when he walked away from Lisa," Washburn

explained. "Henry had him a plan, an' a good'un too. We went up to the lead mines, up north."

"Galena?"

"That's them."

"You was mining lead?"

"Same as ye buy for yer rifle, Titus. Bar lead—from St. Louis Tower. Yessir. Me an' Andrew, 'long with some others, all throwed in the muscles of their backs too. It were good, honest work—not like the Injun trade. But no matter, Henry said: thar'll always be fellers like Leeza to push open the doors to the frontier, fellers to keep them goddamned doors open."

The country Manuel Lisa wanted most to exploit was as close to virgin territory as any that then existed. The Canadians hadn't trapped it to any degree at all. What few furs had come from that country were nothing more than those the Blackfoot stole from other tribes and turned around to sell to the Canadian companies. A rich harvest, Lisa kept evangelizing among his men and financiers, an unbelievable treasure of furs lay waiting those who would take the gamble. That territory was, after all, a land where an American's scalp wasn't worth much at all, attached to a head, or hanging from some warrior's belt.

"Then Leeza died that very y'ar," Washburn explained. "Eighteennineteen. An' Joshua Pilcher takes over the comp'ny. Carried on all the ol' Spanyard's dreams too. Took him two winters to do it, but Pilcher finally got him a big outfit put together, setting off for the upper river."

Some dozen miles above the mouth of the Knife River, Joshua Pilcher rebuilt an old Lisa post and named the new fort after one of his three lieutenants, William Henry Vanderburgh. Then Pilcher pushed ahead with the two others: Robert Jones and Michael Immel. Later that year at the mouth of the Bighorn, near the spot where Lisa had raised a post in 1807, Pilcher's men built Fort Benton, christened for Missouri's newly elected senator.

By 1822 Pilcher had three hundred men trading on the upper Missouri and Yellowstone, Jones and Immel in charge of day-to-day operations. So with the Yellowstone trade secure, Pilcher next set his eye on the rich headwaters of the Missouri.

"But by that y'ar I was done with breaking my back in a galena mine."

"What become of you?" Titus asked, drawing the crimson spring from the coals.

"That once-a-time army gen'ral named Ashley come to see Andrew up to the mines—come to talk him back into the fur business. Said he needed

Henry to be his field captain for a new fur company he was puttin' together. Ashley claimed he was going back to that fur kentry—said he was headed for the land o' the beaver on the upper Missouri!"

Washburn grinned endearingly, his upper lip pulling back, taut above that snaggletooth like a hawser rope looped halfway around a wharfside post. "Spring of twenty-two it were: the two of 'em hired on some fellers what answered the notice they put in the St. Louie paper—askin' for fellers to go to the mountains an' trap beaver."

"I don't remember ever seeing that notice," Bass said quietly, slamming the hammer down onto the spring iron angrily. Watching the fireflies spew forth, the slake fly off the steel band with every blow. "Don't read much no more anyways. Ain't read much of anything in a long, long time, you know."

"My, but thar' was a bunch of 'em what did sign on for the upriver," Isaac replied, his eyes squeezed into squints as he brooded on the roll call of their names, likely recalling each face too. "That Negra Rose was back from the Crows by then, ready an' snortin' to trap again. He went, along with a greenhorn Negra named Beckwith. Then thar' was the preacher, Jedediah Smith—he carried him his Bible 'long in his possibles. Young Jim Bridger t'weren't more'n a green-broke kid, an' Davy Jackson couldn't been much older. 'Nother Span-yard, Louie Vasquez, was along too, with Tom Fitzpatrick, an' a ornery ol' hunter said he lived with the Pawnee of a time."

"That one you told me 'bout—Glass?"

"Yep." Washburn nodded. "Our bunch with Henry was the first to push off from St. Louie. The gen'ral an' his boys weren't gonna get away for the better part of a month behin't us. Whew! My ol' body gets tired yest thinking about what work it be pushin' a boat upriver. Mean work—'bout as mean as work comes: pullin' that boat of Henry's with ropes up through the brush and bramble, fightin' skeeters an' mud, warpin' them boats around trees to pull with all the gut we got—"

With a wag of his head Titus suddenly interrupted, "If I don't see another flat or keel and them big hawsers for the rest of my life—it'll be soon enough." He drew his bare, sinewy forearm across his forehead, then swiped at the large pendant of sweat hanging at the end of his nose.

Struggling upriver, the Henry brigade pushed past the town of Franklin, Missouri, and nearby Boone's Lick. Next came Fort Osage at the mouth of the Kansas River, and finally the mouth of the Platte.

"That's the place I'd leave the Missouri an' strike out for the mountanes on my own the next time."

Bass slowly laid his hammer down on the cooling steel and swallowed before asking, "The river you said what takes you into the mountains?"

"Runs smack into the heart of the Rockies."

"So you did see where it goes?"

"Not rightly—but I been on it. Ye can count plew on that."

"*Plew?*"

"Frenchie word for beaver pelt."

"You say you already was on that river—the Platte we can take to the mountains?"

"That comes later on, Titus," he replied gruffly, waving off that interruption to the flow of his story. "By an' by we pull Ashley's trade goods, 'long with our own possibles an' plunder, all the way north to them Mandan villages. It were thar' we bartered fer ponies. Ye see, the gen'ral was to rendezvous with us by then—but word reached us that his boat hit a snag and sunk clean to the bottom of the river. Not a feller to give up, Ashley turned right around to head back to St. Louie fer more trade goods. Meanin' Henry's brigade, we was on our own. Andrew looked over our bunch an' said he'd lead out the rest of us overland—makin' for the Yallerstone."

"Where you an' Rose been before."

"Yessir—we two knew some about that kentry. First night out Henry set up his run of guards—but, damn! If the Assiniboin didn't come in an' hit us a few nights later. Skedaddled off with more'n thirty of our ponies. That put Henry in a real blue funk, so bad that t'weren't long afore he decided agin tryin' to make it all the way to Three Forks that season."

"Can't see why Henry'd wanna go back there anyways," Bass said as he mopped his face there beside the glowing forge.

"Arter we was the ones went an' jabbed a stick in that Blackfoot wasps' nest more'n ten y'ar afore?" Washburn asked, then chuckled. " 'Thout all the ponies we needed so we could make a faster march of it upriver, Henry said we'd go no farther'n the mouth of the Yallerstone, wait till spring to tramp on over."

About a mile above the confluence of the two rivers, Andrew Henry's men built themselves crude log shelters chinked with riverbank mud and began laying in wood to get them through the coming season, more hints of an early and cold winter becoming apparent every day.

" 'Bout the time the leaves was really turnin'," Isaac continued, "word come upriver that Missouri Fur was coming our way. Had plans of their own to raise up a post at the Three Forks afore winter set in hard. That's when Henry changed his mind—figured to take him some men on up the Missouri. Thought it might not be a better place for us to winter in, a wee bit closer to the Forks come green-up.''

"The rest of Henry's men stayed on at the Yellowstone?"

Washburn shook his head. "Henry sent 'em off too, south by west torst the high moun-tanes we could see off a ways.''

The Missouri Fur Company didn't get as far as the Three Forks country that autumn, settling instead for erecting their post at the mouth of the Bighorn River on the Yellowstone. Henry himself didn't get all that close to the Forks either. By the time the first hard snow had squeezed down on the high plains, he and his men were scampering to get their four log shelters built, all of them enclosed by a crude stockade, there at the mouth of the Musselshell beside the Missouri River. Which placed his base about the same distance from the fabled beaver country of the Three Forks as was the Missouri Fur brigade wintering in at the mouth of the Bighorn.

"Now that his post was up an' the snow was flying," Isaac explained, "Henry was dead set on sendin' out parties to explore that kentry torst the Forks.''

"They ever get over to that Blackfeet country that winter?"

"Close to it, Titus," he answered. "An' for Henry's troubles, the men found more beaver'n any man thort possible. Ever' man's spirits was higher'n those clouds along them stony peaks above us—every last man jack of us makin' plans to get rich come spring trappin', thar' was so much prime plew to pull outta the streams in that kentry.''

Washburn nodded as if savoring that memory, swilling back some water from Titus's piggin before wiping off his chin whiskers with the back of a buckskin-covered arm. "When that winter broke, them fellers Henry sent off skedaddled back from Crow kentry. Fitzpatrick, Clyman, an' that Bible-toter, Jed Smith. Them an' the rest'd moseyed far south of Crow land, an' come back to tell of a pass they said would take a man right on over the moun-tanes.

"The wonder of it, Titus," Isaac exclaimed. "They tol't us it was so easy a man don't know he's crossed over the moun-tanes till he sees all the water flowing off to the west. A pure marvel, that pass!"

When spring came, so did the Blackfoot.

"April, it were, when they fust showed their devil faces," Washburn continued. "By May, four of Henry's twenty was kill't—running off some of them ponies we still had. I watched it all damn near take all the starch right out of Henry's backbone, it did. The man swore he was through with Blackfoot kentry, prime beaver or no. 'Missouri Fur can have it,' he vowed. 'Lock, the stock, an' the barrel too!' "

Andrew Henry retreated downriver a ways, with the intent of waiting for Ashley's main group bringing up more supplies and horses.

"Henry wasn't able to do damn much 'thout those horses," Washburn said as he stuffed his cheek full of tobacco he tore loose from a dark brown carrot of the cured leaf, then stuffed back in the pouch at his hip. "Henry said the gen'ral was headed our way with them horses, plunder, an' 'nother batch of likely young'uns wantin' to make their fortune in the moun-tanes. So he sent Jed Smith down on the best pony we had us, with word for Ashley to hurry on up. It was weeks later afore we saw Jed again—but he t'weren't leading the gen'ral our way. No, sir. The preacher come back in a lather, bellering that by the time he got to the river an' run onto Ashley, the gen'ral run hisself into a mess of trouble at them goddamned Ree villages."

"Them's the Injuns you hate just as bad as the Blackfoots," Titus observed.

"Damn right. One evenin' it seems Ashley stopped his new keelboat at them villages to trade for horses so he could carry his trade goods an' supplies overland to Henry. Most all the men with him was sleeping on the riverbank, wrapped up tight in their blankets, when them Rees started firing on 'em at the peep o' day! Must've been some fight, Titus."

Even though they were heavily outnumbered, Ashley's men held on the best they could, pinned down on that sandy beach below the bluffs where the Arikara villages stood, giving the warriors a wide field of fire. The general ordered his French keelboat crew to raise anchor and pole their way closer to shore to pick up his men—but for the longest time the boatmen refused. At last Ashley and some Americans steered the keelboat toward the men left on the bank. By the time the retreat was made, fourteen of the general's men lay dead at the edge of the Missouri. Another ten were seriously wounded. Ashley cut the anchor rope and allowed the keelboat to float downriver, far beyond the villages and fear of a second attack.

"As soon as Jed Smith told us how the gen'ral been chewed up by them Rees, Henry an' the rest of us come down on the double. A long march that was. We skirted round the village an' found Ashley's boys camped on the west bank of the river, lickin' their wounds. They buried the dead an' sat thar' waitin' fer the chance to get in some knocks. Forted up, they was, with some other traders what were headed upriver behind them. Them an' a hull mess of Colonel Leavenworth's regulars—more'n two hunnert of 'em come to punish the Rees an' get the fur traders past the villages."

But though the white soldier chief now possessed numerical superiority over the Arikara, he still did not press his advantage.

"Arter shootin' up Ashley's bunch so bad, them Rees got off scot-free!" Washburn grumped. "Goddamned army, anyways! All it done is show them Rees our backsides an' make 'em wanna thumb their noses at the white man."

"That bunch of soldiers didn't go off and attack the village?"

"Hell, no! An' that show of yaller was bound to make them red niggers harder to deal with come the next time we run into one t'other. So whar' we laid to way below the villages, on down to Fort Kioway—what some folks on the river call Fort Lookout—Henry and Ashley had themselves a real rip-snorting confab, arguing on what best be done 'bout their trapping business. All that money, all them supplies lost in that fust boat sunk to the bottom of the river, then all them trappers kill't with Henry an' down at the Ree villages too—with nothin' yet to show for it!"

"Had to be a pretty sad time of it for all of you," Bass said as he stabbed the spring into cold water with a steamy hiss.

"Well, now—it truly were some sad doin's. But the two of 'em finally decided Henry should point his nose for the Yallerstone once't again. Summer was almost gone by then. Already August—so Henry tol't us—when we pulled away from Ashley's bunch again."

"Headed back to the up-country to trap beaver?"

"That's the true of it, Titus," Isaac replied. "Johnson Gardner, Black Harris, Milt Sublette, Hugh Glass, Jim Bridger, some eight or so more of us. A small party, most every man still afoot, using what horses we had to pack the goods we took off Ashley's boat, the one the gen'ral called *The Rocky Mountain*. We pulled away from Kioway, making for the Yallerstone—three hunnert fifty miles off on the skyline, counting on doing our best to make it in ten, maybeso twelve days at most."

Henry planned to push back up along the Missouri River to that country just south of the Arikara villages, from there to strike out overland to reach the Grand.

"Damn, but we wasn't gone far when the Mandans jumped us."

"Mandans? Thought they was friends to the white man!"

"Not right then, Titus. That far upriver they'd heard tell of what the Rees got away with—how the yellow-backed army let them bastards off. So even them Mandans was willing to jump white men now that them Rees gone scot-free for what they done to Ashley's outfit. Damn, but that sours my milk!"

"Them Mandans skip off with what you had left for horses?"

"Shit! Them Mandans didn't have much the stomach to make a real fight of it—so we run them warriors off pretty quick, arter givin' 'em a good thrashin'. Ye see, Henry was bound that the word go out: don't none of them tribes dare poke a stick in his hive or they'd get stung. An' stung bad."

Bass stuffed a second length of spring steel into the fire to heat. "So you kept on heading along the Grand?"

"That's the way of it. Puttin' out hunters an' keepin' a eye on the skyline fer more red niggers wanna jump our leetle bunch. Now, that Glass feller what was along, he'd spent him some time with the Pawnee—so was no greenhorn like some of them boys. I could see that, first off."

"This the same Glass you told me of?"

"One an' the same—Hugh Glass. Me an' him struck it up—like I said: he had him some bark on him, that one. Not the sort to cow down an' do all what Henry ordered him to." Washburn spit a long brown stream into a small mound of hay mucked off to the side, wagging his head.

"Shame of it is, Titus—that Glass bein' such a ornery one likely got him in the biggest fix of his hull life, way I lays my sights to it. He had him a'purpose to be off huntin' that day—wasn't his duty that mornin'. But thar' he went, off to work the kentry way out ahead of us. Son of a bitch was nothin' if he weren't ornery, that he was, for sure an' for certain."

"What trouble he get hisself into?"

"I be comin' to that now, Titus. You yest tend to makin' your beaver traps, an' I'll tend to makin' my story." He cleared his throat dramatically before continuing. "We wasn't far up the Grand—maybe no more'n a week or so. That mornin' that ol' hunter's off by his lonesome when he gets hisself chewed up something fierce by a grizz. Shit, Titus—Glass was just healin' up from the arrer wound he took in the Ree fight. He'd come down to take a drink of water at the riverbank, an' looks up to find hisself right smack a'tween a sow grizz an' her two cubs. Nothin' makes a mama grizz madder'n that, I'll tell you."

"She kill him, kill ol' Glass, I mean?"

"She liked to—believe me! Clawin' him up, ripping chunks o' meat outta his shoulder an' his backside afore some of the other hunters heard the shouts an' come runnin'. We all put a shitload of lead in that grizz afore she fell dead: right on top of ol' Glass. Man, when we gone an' rolled that b'ar off'n him, wasn't a one of us didn't figger the ol' man for nothin' but dead.

Henry put his head down on Glass's chest—listened real keerful—then tol't us he was still alive! Can you beat that for stink? Glass was still alive arter that turrible maulin'!"

"I can't figure he lasted for long, did he?"

"No man don't last long arter wrasslin' with a grizz, Titus," Isaac explained. "But then—I was to find out that Hugh Glass wasn't yer usual feller either. The major ordered us all to make camp right there by the river, an' we all had bear steaks that night for supper. Next morning Henry was fixin' to bury Glass—they had his grave all ready for the man, cut down in the sand right aside Hugh. But that ornery cuss was still breathin'!"

"Now you're pulling my leg, you son of a bitch!" Bass roared. "He damned well couldn't still be alive!"

Washburn held a right hand up as if taking a solemn oath. "May I be struck dead with a bolt of the Lord's terrible thunder if I'm stretchin' the truth."

Bass cocked his head to the side, his eyes rolling heavenward, wary—expecting a sudden flash of lightning to come streaking through the roof over their heads.

"With the ol' man still breathin'—that give the hull bunch of us fits. Thar' we was in kentry the Rees loved to roam, an' we all knew them red niggers was still worked up and feeling like big cocks arter drivin' Americans back down the river. 'Sides, we needed to push on quick before the first snow flied. An' that was bound to be slow going if'n we hauled a dyin' man along with us."

"You didn't just leave him, did you?"

"Didn't figger on it at fust." Then with a wag of his head, Isaac replied, "We all waited 'nother day—when Henry growed tired of lollygagging. So he asked fer volunteers to stay with ol' Glass till the dyin' man breathed his last, then bury him and hurry on to catch up with the rest of us so Henry could get on fer the beaver kentry. Offered good money to them that stayed."

"Did you?"

"Naw. Wasn't one to wanna leave my ha'r in that kentry. Two did say they would stay behin't: fella named Fitzgerald, an' that young'un Jim Bridger. Next morning the rest of us pulled out, walkin' away from that camp—them two, an' Ol' Hugh Glass."

"He was still breathin'?"

"Damn if he weren't!" Then Washburn shuddered. "The way them flies smelled blood, Titus—it were a awful sight to behol't: seein' how the flies blackened ever' one of the ol' man's wounds like a swarm of crawlin' peppercorns."

Titus shuddered too. "What become of him, he up an' die on them two?"

Scratching his chin whiskers, Washburn continued. "Henry led us on to the beaver kentry, an' we made ready for the winter. Fitzgerald and that Bridger lad come in with the ol' man's plunder an' fixin's. Said they'd buried him proper whar' he was. But as that snake-eyed Fitz tol't the tale of it, I watched the boy. Bridger never looked much at any of us. Couldn't hol't a man's eye. Somethin' 'bout it yest never sat right in my craw. I s'pose I guessed the wrong of it right then an' thar'. Man cain't look you in the eye, Titus—he's got him something to hide from you. That's the sort you cain't count on watching yer backside neither. Still, something in my gut tol't me that flim-flam Fitz was the big gator in that shit-hole. I had me a feelin' he cowed the boy someway, slick-talked Bridger into doin' the wrong they done. Right then I had me no idea what they done—but I was damned certain some such smelled bad. We yest all of us went on with the fall hunt. Bridger didn't talk all that much into the fall neither. Keepin' off to hisself. Then winter finally come down on us, hard—like the slap of a man's hand right across't your cheek—"

It surprised Bass when Washburn slapped himself on the face, the sharp crack like the snap of a hickory wiping stick in that warm livery.

"One cold night not long arter the snow got serious—thar comes a poundin' at the gate," Isaac continued. "An' who you s'pose comes walkin' into our post, draggin' a bunged leg, lamed-up-like, got him a ol't buffler robe snagged round his shoulder, snow froze to his ha'r an' beard—Lordee! Lookin' ever' bit like a ghost, he was!"

"G-glass?" Bass swallowed, letting the hammer slide from his fingers onto the anvil with a resounding clunk.

"The ol' man hisself!"

Titus gulped. "H-he come back from the dead?"

"Nawwww!" Washburn growled. "I yest said it was the ol' man hisself! Not no ghost!"

Shaking his head in confusion, Bass started to mumble, but Isaac leaped right in to explain.

"He never died. Them two yest left him fer dead."

"An' he come lookin' for 'em, didn't he?" Titus roared, snapping his fingers with certainty.

"He surely did—come for them that run off with his gun, his knife, an' possibles. Leavin' him lie beside his own shaller grave. Bad part of it, only one of them two was still thar', Major Henry tol't Glass. Over to the corner huddled up young Bridger—his face gone white as the sheet on a good folks' bed. Knowin' what he done in leavin' the man fer dead—'thout nary a one of his possibles."

"Isaac—you figger he had the right to kill them two what left him in a fix like that?"

"Aye, I do, Titus. The rest of us figgered it that way too. That were mountain justice. Well, now—the place fell quiet as Ol' Glass's grave was to be, while'st outside the blizzard was howlin'. Glass pulled out his pistol, walked over to young Bridger in the corner, an' put the gun to the boy's head. He stayed it there for a long time, starin' down at Bridger's face while the boy owned up to what he done afore all of us. Bridger didn't blink— 'stead he yest kept his own eyes right there lookin' at that ol' grizz-bait, now that he was shet of what he'd done wrong. Henry an' me tol't Glass it were Fitz carried most of the blame, that he talked Bridger into it. But right is right, an' Glass had him the right to blow out the boy's candle then an' there —if he was of a mind to."

"Just put that ball through the young'un's brain?"

Washburn spit, swiped the back of his hands across his stained chin whiskers, and waited a dramatic moment as he slowly formed his hand into the shape of a pistol. Gradually he lowered his thumb. "Arter a while, Glass eased down that hammer."

"He didn't shoot Bridger?" Bass asked anxiously.

"Nope. He yest turned to the rest of us an' said, 'The boy was yest a pup. Didn't know no better. Fitzgerald's the scalp I want.' That's when Bridger started shakin', tremblin' yest like a wet pup, tears come to his eyes, him swearin' he'd never let a man down ever again."

"I'll be damned," Titus exclaimed almost under his breath, then poked more of the steel into the coals to heat.

"Glass tol't us all how he was givin' life fer life. Yest the way the Almighty Above give him his life back or somethin' such. He wasn't gonna take Bridger's life—but he was gonna run down Fitz. Claimed the Almighty Above told him vengeance would be his."

"How'd he come to get from the Grand River all the way to where you was winterin' with Henry?"

"He crawled."

"C-crawled?"

"Man gets chewed up bad as he was by a grizz . . . he's bound to have ter crawl. Tol't us all the story of it that winter night arter he'd stuffed his meatbag full of venison. Said he started out on his belly, Glass did. Some weeks later got up on his hands an' one leg, dragging the other leg what the sow chewed up so bad. Maggots wrigglin' down in his wounds—crawlin' in an' out, eatin' all the p'isen out—flies buzzin' round him something awful as he crawled on down our backtrail, foot by foot."

"Hang on there—you said he took your backtrail? Here I thought you said he come up to Henry's fort that winter."

"He did get up to that post, but—savvy as he was—first off Glass pointed his nose for Fort Kioway. Knowed it were closer. Still some three hunnert miles or so," Washburn answered, undisguised wonder a'shine in his eyes. "When ol' Hugh made it to Kioway, said he talked hisself into a new outfit an' fetched him a ride on a traders' boat going north."

"Past them troublemaking Rees?"

"Ain't you the smart one now, Titus?" Isaac exclaimed. "That's right: already Glass knowed better'n to try to poke his way on by such river niggers —so yest downriver from them villages, Glass had them traders put over and he went ashore, making overland. Kept to the brush and the timber, and what you know? It weren't long afore he heard the fight boomin' behin't him as them Rees jumped those traders. He found a hidey-hole and laid low. An' when the dust settled down, Glass turned back—found all those fellers on the boat was wiped out."

Titus dragged the steel from the fire, laying the glowing red strap over the horn on his anvil, fixing to begin hammering a bend into the spring steel. "Glass found hisself alone again?"

"Damn sure was. But that ornery hivernant run right onto some Mandans what knew better'n to jump ary a white man this time. L'arn't their lesson from us'ns with Henry. Them Mandans took Glass's ol' bones on upriver to their villages. An' from thar' he pushed on alone, walkin' up the Missouri to reach our winter digs on foot. Hate's a meal what can sure keep a man warm, no matter how cold the storm is, Titus."

Bass shuddered involuntarily as something slipped down the length of his spine—little matter how he sweated with his exertions there beside the glowing forge. He asked, "Now that he forgive Bridger, Glass was still dead set on finding this Fitzgerald?"

"Come mornin', he told us—he was leavin' off again. Wild-eyed, the ol' man was. Said he'd nursed hisself back to bein' strong, hearin' the voice of the Almighty inside his head ever' foot of the way—that voice sayin' vengeance would be his. Fitz would be delivered up to his hand. Glass knowed he had God's word on it an' it was meant to be."

"So he up an' took off the very next morning?"

"Soon as that storm broke, that ol' man disappeared. But he didn't go alone: three others told Henry they figured to go with him on that hunt for Fitz. Bound and determined to find the man truly at fault for Glass being left to die in the wilderness 'thout no possibles nor truck."

After a long silence from the old trapper, Bass looked up from his work with the hammer. Washburn was staring at him.

"Titus, I was one of them three."

"You went with Glass to hunt the man down?"

With a nod Isaac continued. "We marched west on foot—nary a one of us had a animal to ride, only one ribby horse Henry let us have for packing our blankets and plunder. We tramped up the Yallerstone to the mouth of the Powder, then turned south up the Powder. Far 'nough up toward the headwaters of the Powder we struck out south, making for the Platte. Leastways, that's what river Glass figgered it had to be when we finally run onto it. Wasn't long afore the ol' man said if we kept on trampin' east, the closer we'd come to Pawnee country."

"Same Injuns Glass'd spent him some time with, right?"

"An' run off from—so he sure didn't wanna run into those folks again," Washburn answered. "But look an' behol'! We run smack-dab into a big war party of Arikara instead! Likely they was wanderin' south, out looking for to steal some horses from the 'Rapaho or Siouxs, any band them river niggers hoped to find down there in that kentry. Wasn't s'posed to run onto them the way we was going, Glass said. But there them red niggers was."

Bass leaned close, enthralled and captivated with every new twist in the story. "What became of you and them Rees you bumped into?"

"A fight of it—that's what. They kill't two of us, right off. Shot me up a li'l"—Isaac pointed to his left arm—"an' kill't our only horse. Me an' Glass, we jumped down into a small stream slick with ice, wading on down hugging the bank and hangin' back in them bare willers real close—yest like they was a woman's soft breast. Weren't long before we found us a hole in that bank to hide in, yest big enough for our ol' bones to scrunch up in—it bein' close to low-water time and the beaver bein' moved on, leaving that hole behin't for us the way they done. Down in that stream them Rees damn well couldn't find 'em no tracks of the two white men got away. We pulled in some willer behin't us, to cover up the mouth of that hidey-hole, an' laid thar', holdin' our wind. Up an' down the crik above us Injuns hooted an' hollered fer the better part of that arternoon afore we heard 'em pull off an' leave. 'Long torst the sun goin' down we heard 'em screeching in glee off upriver. Likely they was workin' over them two other fellers started out with us from Henry's post."

"Who was they?"

"Never knowed their Christian names—damn me," Washburn admitted, wagging his head dolefully. "Likely them boys had 'em families, Glass said that night when it was gettin' dark. That was the very fust thing he said ever' since't we crawled into that hole too. An' it were the last thing he ever said about them two, from thar' on out. Arter slap-dark we finally dared stick our heads out an' started walking."

"Where the hell you head to then?" Titus asked, driving the hammer down hard, sending fireflies of sparks from the heated metal as it bent around the anvil's horn.

"Ol' Hugh claimed he felt right pert. Claimed this time he had him his gun and his fixin's. Not like the last time he'd been left to push through Injun kentry after Fitz run off with ever'thing Glass owned. It gave me the willers 'cause he kept saying, over an' over: ''Sides, us keepin' our ha'r in that fix is yest 'nother sign God's watching over me—making sure I track down Fitz, the one what left me fer dead.' ''

"Bet you fellas covered some ground that night," Bass said eagerly. "Sleep all day?"

Isaac nodded. "Found us some cover come sunup. Laid low till the night come round again. Went on like that, night arter night—making ourselves a hidey-hole ever' day. That ol' man was some walker, he was. Had him a big chest he could fill up with that cold winter air, strong legs he kept a'movin. He was one coon downright made for walking. Me? I was a man made for *riding*. I come to figger that out follerin' Hugh Glass cross't that Platte River kentry. Never been more certain of anythin' in my life: Isaac Washburn ain't cut out fer walkin'."

"So where'd you two light out for?"

"Eventual we left the Platte, struck out overland, making for Fort Kioway again. I turned to Ol' Glass. 'How far you make it from here?' asks I. 'More'n two hunnert miles,' says he. 'Closer to three hunnert likely.' I scratched my head, looked off into that night sky, darker'n the belly of your own grave, I s'pose. So I up an' asks him, 'Ain't Atkinson closer? Maybe by half?' He yest looked at me, no smile, no nothin'. 'Shore is,' Glass said. 'We'll go thar' . . . if'n you got balls big enough to walk with me through Pawnee kentry. Them niggers be wintered up all 'long the Platte this time of year. Best you recollect I runned off from the Pawnee fer a damn good reason, Isaac.' "

When Washburn paused in moving his story along, Bass grew impatient and inquired, "Which way you decide to go?"

"I tol't Hugh we'd head for Kioway."

"To stay away from them Pawnee he hated," Titus observed.

"We struck the headwaters of the Niobrara. Crossed over the divide thar' an' come on the headwaters of the White. Movin' north by east ever' night—watchin' for sign in the sky, them stars. Laying out o' sight ever' day. Comin' right through the heart of them badlands the Pawnee steer clear of. Glass said he knowed the White River take us right on to the Missouri. When we get there, we'd turn north a short piece and find ourselves at Kioway."

"He go and tell you all about that bear and him while the two of you was on your way there?"

"Times it were downright spooky bein' with Ol' Glass. Fer the longest while he'd go heap of a time 'thout talkin', then of a sudden he'd up an' growl like a dog, sayin': 'Fitz, ye g'won have yer spree while'st you can, 'cause this'r ol' child's comin' to get ye.' "

"How long did you go afore you got across that Injun country?"

"Better'n sixteen suns it took us afore I spotted that flagpole at Fort Lookout, I mean Kioway. Both of us wore down, skinnier'n hell. Been eatin' prerra dogs when we couldn't find us no game. My mocs was wored clear through—by then I was walkin' on prerra-dog skins I had tied round my feet."

"Damn," Bass said with quiet admiration, "I had me no idea, Isaac. No idea what you come through."

Washburn shrugged it off. "Could've been leaner times. As it was, all grass and gopher the hull way. Stopping only long enough ever' day to lay low an' blow arter trotting up a good pace right on through moon-time."

Bass sensed some shame rising in his gorge as he looked at the trapper there in his worn and greasy buckskins. "Isaac—I'm sorry I made such a row over you eatin' my vittles t'other night."

"Think you nothin' of it, now, Titus."

"Had I knowed you hadn't et in . . . how long it been since't you reached Fort Kiowa?"

"Not that many suns," Washburn replied. "It were there we catched us a early-spring boat headed south to Atkinson. That's a big post where the law says a man has to have him a permit to move beyond thar' into Injun kentry. Ye see: either a man is with a fur company, or he's in the army. I wasn't damn fool enough to join the army . . . and arter two trips to the upper Missouri, I'd had my fill of fur-company doin's. Fort Atkinson t'weren't the place for the likes of me."

"What come of Glass?"

"That ol' bear-bait stayed on to argue with that post commander 'bout getting his hands on Fitzgerald—since we l'arn't that snake-eyed son of a bitch had gone and join't the army. That meant if Glass kill't the bastard— the army'd turn around an' hang Glass. Last thing Hugh said to me afore we parted was, 'Of a sudden, Isaac—thar' be some big stones throwed down in the way of the Lord's own vengeance.' "

Titus asked, "After all Glass'd been through, you know if he ever got his hands on the fella left him for dead?"

Washburn screwged up his lips a bit around that snag of a fang, admitting, "I didn't wait to see what come of it, Glass's work an' the Lord's vengeance. Likely I'll never forget what that child said over an' over again to me from the time we tramped south from Henry's post: tellin' me how it was to wake up looking at buzzards flyin' overhead, roostin' on branches nigh within reach—to find his own grave scooped out aside him. Naw, Titus Bass —first chance I had I come on down hyar to St. Louie. Set on having me a real spree arter all that Injun trouble an' starvin' times I had me on up that goddamned river. Man what has him Injun trouble deserves a spree, don't he?"

"I had me some," Bass declared, "not near as bad as you had. Chicka-saw it were."

"Chickasaw?"

"They ended up killing a friend of mine. Nearly got the rest of us too. On the Messessap."

"That yer kentry down thar'?"

"It was then, I s'pose." No, he thought better of that answer. "That ain't no white man's country, Isaac. I been through there on foot—like you coming down from the Yellowstone. Walked back through that Choctaw and Chickasaw country on foot, following the Natchez Trace."

Washburn stood, stretched some kinks out of his back as if he were the one who had been pounding on trap springs that cold spring morning. "Sounds to me you put some kentry under you, Titus Bass."

His hammer came to a halt, the last ring fading in the damp air. "I have, I s'pose, at that."

Scratching his nose, Isaac spit into the pile of hay again, then looked Titus squarely in the eye to ask, "Like ye said t'other night—ye still hanker to put some more miles under ye?"

For a long moment Bass could not answer, his throat seized up with what import he sensed in those words. When he finally found his tongue, Titus asked, "Serious?"

"Isaac Washburn never been one to waste his wind, son."

His heart was pounding as he replied, "What you got in mind?"

The trapper toed the dusty floor below him with a worn and patched moccasin, saying, "Head west with me. I figger to see me them moun-tanes out thar' west on that Platte kentry. That's land I only got a wee peek of, comin' down the Powder with Glass. Maybe the two of us throw in together —if'n yer of a mind to—we can turn right at them Stonies—head up north to meet up with Major Henry, maybe some of them others, out thar' on the Yallerstone. What say ye?"

Bass realized he was gripping that heavy hammer tight enough to squeeze the hickory handle in two as he formed the words. "You . . . you saying you want me to throw in with you?"

"Yer a likely sort, Titus. Ain't a young lad no more—but I figger that runs in yer favor. Yessir, way I see it—ye got the makin's of a partner. Allays better to travel with 'nother, 'cept when that 'nother man ain't the sort can be trusted."

Lord, how his head was pounding, his eyes almost ready to swim with such tears of happiness. "Isaac, you just told me you barely lived to make it to that Kiowa post. But here you are, saying you'll head out again. Maybeso to lose your fixings and eat prairie dog again."

Washburn slapped his thigh with a snort and a grin. "Ain't it the truth? So—what d'ye say, Titus Bass? Aye? Ye got the makings to come to them moun-tanes with me?"

"I . . . I got a old horse," he stammered. "I mean—I'll get me 'nother horse. Like your'n."

"That'un?" Washburn asked, thumbing back to the animal tied outside a far stall. "He ain't no horse, Titus. No more'n a rabbit-eared, jug-headed Injun pony."

"Where you come by him?"

"Happed onto a band of Omaha north of Fort Osage—maybeso 'nother tribe," he snorted in glee. "Be fittin' if it were a Pawnee pony, don't ye figger?"

"You just took him?"

With a devilish grin and twinkle to his eye, Washburn shrugged and said, "Needed me one, Titus. So I took him. I ain't got a pot to piss in an' no window to throw it out of, so how ye figger I'm gonna buy myself a horse an' outfit now that I come to St. Louie?"

"I . . . I dunno—"

"With what, Titus? What I got to buy a horse? I lost near all my fixin's too. Takes a man money to make a new outfit."

"I got money, Isaac."

His tired old eyes lost their devilish twinkle and took on a serious light. He leaned close to the younger man. "Ye . . . said ye got money . . . money ye let me have to buy me fixings?"

"To buy *us* fixings," Bass corrected.

Straightening, Washburn appraised the younger man once again, this time more carefully than ever, and eventually shook his head. "If that hoss don't take the circle."

"Take the circle?"

"You gonna throw in with me, are ye? Puttin' up yer plews to buy our outfit?"

Bass glowed with a fire inside—few things had ever felt so right. "I got the money—you got the country. Right?"

"That's right. I got the kentry, fer damned sure," Washburn answered, tapping his forehead with one finger. "Fer the both of us, Titus Bass—I got the hull consarned Rocky Moun-tane kentry, right up here."

TWENTY-THREE

"Arr! Arr! Arrrggggg! God . . . god*damn*!"

Bass bolted awake with a start at Washburn's roar.

Isaac thrashed in his blankets, struggling to free his legs—then as suddenly the trapper awoke. Sat up. Drew his legs up against himself and wrapped his arms around them. He began to rock back and forth, staring blankly at nothing while he mumbled.

"You all right, Isaac?" Titus asked, scared at what he saw on the older man's face.

When Washburn did not reply, Bass inched closer, crawling on his hands and knees across that clay floor where he lived back in the corner of Troost's livery. Slowly, he reached out, laid his hand gently on the trapper's shoulder.

Isaac nearly jumped out of his skin at the touch, swinging an arm wildly at Bass. Titus fell back against his own blankets sprawled on the pallet of fresh hay.

"Isaac?"

"What the hell you want?"

"You . . . it's me. Titus," he tried to explain.

"I damn well know who it is," he snapped, finally turning to look directly at Bass. "What's the matter with ye—don't think I know who ye are?"

"You was screaming—sounding wild . . . wild as you would if'n that grizzly that got Hugh Glass was after you."

For a moment Washburn tried to glare Bass down, then gave in. The anger, the bravado, drained from his face, and he buried his face in his arms he had looped over his knees.

Titus asked, "You want I get you something?"

"Some of that whiskey maybe," was the mumble.

From one of the empty cherrywood pails Titus retrieved the green bottle, the glass cold against his skin. Putting the cork in his teeth, he worried it from the neck, then nudged the bottle against Washburn's hand. Isaac looked up from his arms, recognized the bottle for what it was, and took the whiskey. As Bass turned away to pry open the small stove's door, he listened as the potent liquid spilled down the old man's gullet in great, ravenous gulps.

"It were the horse, that goddamned horse again," Washburn growled low, almost under his breath.

Bass turned from punching up the fire, asking, "What horse?"

"The white one, goddammit!"

Titus tossed a last piece of firewood into the stove and latched the iron door as the tiny cell began to warm almost immediately. A little smoke leaked from that chimney—but he decided he could stuff some more chinking in it come a warm day when the whole of it cooled off enough for him to get up there and work on it.

"I don't know what white horse you're talking about, Isaac," Bass admitted as he settled before the man, watching Washburn's throat work greedily at the whiskey again. "Slow down on that a minute and tell me 'bout this here white horse of your'n."

"Same white horse. The one it's allays been," he repeated, his tone angry as he swiped amber drops off the hairs of his mustache that hung over his lips like a worn corn-bristle broom.

"Cain't be your white horse," Bass said finally, wagging his head slightly in confusion. "That pony you brung in weren't—"

He whirled his head on Titus to interrupt with a warning growl, "I damn well know that son of a bitch jug-head pony ain't white. You blamed idjit—I ain't talking about *it*, cain't you see?"

Titus eyed the green whiskey bottle, saw that it was less than half-full already. "Tell me what you want me to see, Isaac."

Then Bass glanced over at the piggin between their pallets, noticing they had only another two bottles of whiskey out of all of that they had bought last week. They had been drinking a hell of a lot of the stuff, ever since he had been on the mend and Washburn had taken to teaching him all that he knew about life in the Indian country.

"Ain't ye ever heerd tell of the white horse, Titus? Surely ye have. I tol't ye 'bout it, ain't I? Must have—many, many a time."

"I . . . can't rightly remember—"

Isaac's eyes were glazing already in stupor. "Glass said he seen the horse once't too. Tol't me hisself. See'd it fer nights in his dreams afore he bent over to take him that drink at the river."

Bass started feeling his skin go cold. "On the Grand?"

Washburn nodded. "Saw that thar' horse in his dreams, he said—many a night afore the sow grizz chawed on him."

Swallowing hard, Titus watched Washburn gulp down more of the whiskey from the bottle's dull-green glow in the orange firelight. Titus's tiny cell smelled of fresh hay and cold sweat—from the both of them. It was the smell of fear. Nothing less than pure fear of the unknown, the unseen.

"Glass saw a white horse in his dreams?"

Washburn took the bottle from his lips, licked them with the tip of his tongue as he stared at Bass with eyes that seemed as black as cinders. Deep circles of liver-colored flesh sagged beneath the man's eyes. Made them look almost like sockets in a skull. He sucked on that snaggletooth a moment, then said quietly, "I see'd that horse too, Titus."

"W-when?"

"Yest now," he whispered, belched, and stared down at the bottle in his hand. It began to tremble at first. Then the more it shook, the more frightened Washburn became until he grabbed hold of the bottle with his second hand and with both of them held it out for Bass to take.

Seizing the whiskey from Isaac, Titus welcomed a chance to swallow some for himself. When he had that satisfying burn coursing all the way down his gullet, Bass finally asked, "This ain't the first time you seen it neither, is it?"

"Said it wasn't."

"Damn," Bass muttered.

"Damn right, *damn*," Washburn echoed. "Know what that means?"

What should he say? What could he say? All he did eventually was shrug a shoulder and try to grin as he replied, "Means you and me'll just have to stay out'n the way of bears, I s'pose."

Washburn snorted, wagging his head. "It ain't yest the b'ars, Titus. That white horse . . . it's an ol', ol' legend. B'ars don't mean shit in that legend."

Titus squirmed uneasily, his eyes flicking out to the doorway's darkness. "All right—s'pose you tell me the legend."

At first the trapper eased back on his pallet, stretching out on his back, one arm crooked over his forehead, covering his eyes. "A man what sees a white horse in his dream . . . that man gonna die."

Bass let it sink in as he stared at Washburn for a long time. Then he eventually tried to cheer his friend. "We all gonna die sometime, Isaac."

Washburn rolled up on an elbow and glared at Bass angrily. "Means a man's gonna die *soon*." He plopped over onto his back once more.

"Glass didn't."

"Didn't what?"

"He didn't die," Bass retorted. "Not after he saw his white horse. Shows that's just a bunch of bunk."

For some time it appeared Washburn thought on it; then from beneath his arm he said, "He came no more'n a ha'r away from dyin', Titus. That close."

"But he didn't die, Isaac. So forget the white horse—"

"It's differ'nt: Glass didn't die 'cause the Almighty wanted him to take his revenge on them what left him!" Washburn blurted in interruption. "The Almighty's the only thing what saved Glass from dying when the white horse come to call him out."

"That what you think you seen? A white horse called you out?"

He snarled, "My time's comin', goddammit."

"You stay out'n them whiskey houses, now, Isaac," Bass suggested. "We'll keep clear of the Injuns once we head west on the Platte—"

"It don't matter, Titus."

"You can damn well make sure none of it matters 'bout that white horse, don't you see? Just be careful and watch out—"

"It don't matter—none of what I try to do. My time to go is my time," Washburn grumbled. "These here dreams mean to tell me I lived out my time an' the white horse is come to call me out."

"A man don't have to—"

"I told ye!" Washburn bellowed, then went on in a quieter voice as he turned his back on Bass, facing the wall, and yanked his blankets up to his shoulders. "It don't matter if'n I'm here in St. Louie . . . or if'n I'm out thar' on the prerra. It yest don't make a good goddamn no more now."

For the longest time Bass stared at the man's back, what he could make out of Washburn's form in the fire's dull light emitted from the grating on the stove door. He took himself a long, last drink of the whiskey, snugged the cork back in the neck, and settled it in among the other two in the piggin against that back wall of his cell.

Easing back, he rerolled his old blanket coat into a pillow for his head. Closed his eyes. Letting images swim before him. Conjuring up how that white horse must look. But the creature simply refused to take shape.

Instead, what swam behind his eyelids were images of the last few weeks with Isaac Washburn. What revelry they had shared! Haunting the grog houses, watering holes, and those stinking knocking shops where all manner of delights to the flesh were to be found—they roamed the back streets and alleyways down close to the wharf, where life lay closer to the earth—with little hope of sanctity. In those cold hours before dawn they would stagger home in the drizzle to collapse upon their blankets and sleep until Troost came in at sunrise to angrily kick Bass's foot.

"You went out an' done it again," the livery owner would grumble. "Get rid of that son of a bitch, Titus Bass—or he'll be the end of you."

"You gonna throw me out'n my job?" Bass always asked, bleary-eyed.

"I thought about it," Troost would reply. "But not yet. Get up and put in your day. And then we'll see."

So he did. Young enough that the whiskey tremors and the hard-liquor hammers in his head were not near cruel enough to keep him prisoner in that bed after a long night of chasing numbness, a long night of seeking release buried deep within the moistness of some faceless other who bit and clawed and screeched with her delight at his utter ferocity.

None of them knew. Not a one of those whores had any idea it wasn't she who made him such a beast. Whatever it was, Titus didn't know. Only that the longer he waited to be gone, the more he felt like some caged animal, trapped there in St. Louis. As if his leg were snared in one of those square-jawed traps he crafted for the two of them, caught and held as he strained to be gone, to be out there, to be reaching for the horizon.

"Not yet," Washburn always said, drunk or sober, when Bass prodded him to be about leaving. "Not yet we go."

So they drank and whored, and they fought—back to back many times. Fists up in those ear-biting, eye-gouging contests to which Titus was no stranger. A healthy letting of blood, he always figured. A good row only made them all the thirstier for the whiskey and apple beer, hungrier for a skinny one of an evening, perhaps a big and fleshy one the next night. Over the weeks Washburn had even developed his own favorites, and of them—one in particular.

"A young one," he called her, "barely old 'nough out of her school-days."

Titus knew better, for the whore had been working one brothel or another for better than ten years now. But what mattered was that Isaac was content with her, happy to consider her but a slip of a child—no matter that she weighed that much more than Washburn himself.

"I like havin' all that sweet, slick hide on a woman to grab on to when I'm ruttin'," he would explain to Bass. "When she gets to goin' under me, less'n I got some of that hide to grab on to, an' a lot of it too—that damn li'l girl's bound to heave me off!"

Isaac wasn't alone in finding a favorite. For Titus she was a recent arrival: a quadroon imported upriver from New Orleans, her skin the palest brown, almost the color of that silky mud sheen to the lower Mississippi itself.

First time Titus saw her sipping at her Lisbon wine, she wore tall and gracefully carved ivory combs in her hair dark as a moonless midnight, a velvet choker with a whalebone brooch clasped so tight at her throat that the brooch trembled with every one of her quickened pulses. Her lips full enough to more than hint at her African ancestry, it was no wonder Titus came away from her so many nights wearing the tiny blue bruises and teeth marks she left behind as she worked him over with her mouth, from shoulder on down to the flat of his belly. After swearing she was his favorite early one morning as Washburn pounded on the door and hollered that he was ready to head back to the livery, she reached up to pull a scarf down from a peg in the wall beside her narrow, short-posted muley-bed.

"You take this," she commanded as she settled her naked body back on the thin mattress beside him.

He knew not what she laid across his hands in the flickering candle-light. "What's this?"

"My scarf," she said, taking it from him to unknot. "Blue as the sea that rolls away from New Orleans to the home of my people."

"Where are your people?" he had asked her over the noise of Washburn's hammering on the doorway, his bellowing that he was about to come crashing in.

"I don't have no people no more," she said. "But I want you to be somebody special to me."

"I will be, always be," he vowed, and let her tie the scarf around his neck before they parted in the gray of that dawn.

He wore it knotted there at his neck every time he returned to see her, when he could afford her, even when he could not afford her and had to content himself with gazing at her from across the smoky room where she went about her business, talking and laughing with other customers, glancing at him once in a while, only her eyes asking why it was not he who was raising her skirts and rubbing her legs then and there in the tavern, panting to take her back to her little room.

More and more he and Isaac had other things to do with some of Titus's money.

There were blankets and trade goods, vermilion and beads, mirrors and hawks-bells, coffee and sugar and flour they were laying by as the time to go drew nigh.

"We have to leave afore June," Washburn warned. "Time we get across't the prerra, it'll be fall. An' winter don't wait long to come down on that kentry. Be ready to turn yer back on all of this come June."

So Bass worked on more traps when he could get away with it, sneaking in that time over the forge among the other jobs Troost had for him to do. What with all that he owed the blacksmith, Titus dared not fail to give full measure to Hysham Troost. Bit by bit, week by week, the livery owner gave over the coins he had been saving for Titus through all the years gone by. And with each week's payday Hysham warned that the money was disappearing far faster than Bass was earning it. Pretty soon, Hysham warned, Bass would be back to nothing but waiting on his next pay.

Far too much whiskey, and the women, for him and Washburn. Sweating the alcohol out of his pores every day over the forge while the trapper sat and talked endlessly about this piece of country, or that stream, this beaver valley, or that pass—all the landmarks Titus struggled to keep straight in his head each time Isaac drew a crude map on the clay floor there beneath the bellows, there beside the anvil where Titus sweated out the whiskey he had paid such good money for the night before.

Hour after hour Isaac told his stories of the animals and the sky. How the land went on and on for as far as a man's eye could ever hope to see—right into tomorrow, if you really tried.

They needed extra locks for their rifles, at least one spare for their pistols. Then too, a small, coarse sack of lock springs and screws, lock hammers, and several pounds of fine French amber flints. Slowly that tiny cell Titus had called home for so many winters grew even more cramped as the partners acquired everything they would need to winter up come the time they struck out for the far mountains.

"You'll need a saddle soon," Isaac said one afternoon. "An' a horse too."

Titus hadn't thought about that, but he supposed Washburn was right. "What about you? We ought'n get you something better'n that pony."

"That Injun pony do me jest fine, Titus. Ye'll see—what when we get to Injun kentry. Injun pony best, mark my word on it."

The day's work complete—counting what Troost expected him to do and what time he could squeeze in forging traps and rifle parts, harness and bits for their horses—Washburn led them upriver from the wharf a ways. There they smeared pennyroyal on their exposed flesh at ankles and wrists and necks to keep off the seed ticks, then took a belt ax to blaze a blond mark on a tree, no bigger than the width of Titus's hand, before pacing off the proper distance and toeing a line in the soft earth coming alive with the thick green springtime carpet.

Bass fired with Washburn's rifle as much as he shot that mark with his grandpap's old weapon. Slowly, every few days, week by week, Washburn moved the mark back farther and farther still. Teaching the younger man what he could about holding, breathing, letting the heavy barrel on the trapper's weapon weave across the target rather than fighting to hold the sights perfectly still before he touched off the rifle.

"Yer gettin' good thar', coon," Washburn had said one evening. "Not nowhere near good as me yet. But it's comin'. Time's come fer us go wet down our gullets an' see 'bout pokin' our stingers in a honey-pot."

Days of work, evenings at shooting, and on into the nights with the women and the whiskey, then Troost nudging him awake to start it all over again.

"When'r you going to learn me how to throw a knife?" Bass had inquired one evening they headed back toward the livery after target practice, there to pack everything away before hurrying off to one of the watering holes. "Always wanted to know how to throw a knife proper."

"I'll show you, soon enough."

"It ain't long afore June's coming."

Isaac gazed at the sky deepening in twilight. "Yep. An' afore then I'll have you throwin' a tomeehawk too."

That first evening he had hefted the weapon at the end of his arm, the memory of sights and sounds of Rabbit Hash in Boone County flooded in upon him. Struggling to soothe his mind from those haunts of youth, he drank in the smells of considerable redbud in that damp grove where the two of them made their daily pilgrimage down by the river, where the strong, acrid stench hung heavy on the air at twilight.

Nearby a half-dozen women kept a trio of huge, bubbling, steaming kettles suspended over fires they tended as they boiled down lye from wood ashes and straw kept close at hand in more than a dozen brass tubs and barrel halves.

That odor always rankled his nose, even with the merest of memory. That night and ever since he had thought on home. Thought on his mam, and how she had made her soap outside on those cool spring and autumn days, never of a hot summer's day. Always at hog-killing time. The feel of those slimy intestines slithering out of his hands as he'd spilled them into the brass kettle his mam had set to a boil until a thick grease had coated the white-oak paddle she'd used to stir the whole blamed concoction. Cooked and simmered all through the day, then cooled enough before the nastiest of the work had required them to plunge their hands into the semisoft mass, bringing out gobs of it to smear into blocks, where it would harden enough to be cut into cakes of the proper size.

From the earliest he could remember, it had been his job alone to keep the fire going beneath his mam's lye kettle. After all, Titus was the oldest of the children, the only one capable of splitting the wood, carrying armloads of it out back of the kitchen shanty built apart from their first small cabin on the ground Thaddeus was helping grandpap clear. The kitchen and that little cabin were connected by a narrow dogtrot, where Titus had got himself out of the sun on those soap-making days every spring, then again every autumn. Out of the sun and upwind from the stench of that boiling lye.

No, neither his mam nor those women down by the clearing where he and Washburn went of an evening were making a fine Windsor shaving soap, much less a fine castile. It was only the crudest sort of cleaning agent, the sort that all but made a man prefer staying dirty, caked with sweat and grime in every crevice of his fingers, a deep, brooding crescent of old labors mired back of every fingernail rather than face a hard scrubbing with lye soap.

How Thaddeus had stayed as far from bathing as he could had always made his mother livid with anger as she'd sweated over those stinking kettles, or scrubbed their children at least once a week out in that big hardwood tub they'd kept hung from a nail hammered into a side of the three-sided bathing shed attached to the kitchen.

Regular bathing bordered on pure lunacy, Thaddeus would argue. The cause of agues and croups, tick-sicks and who knew what-all fevers! A body bathed was a body defenseless against all manner of assault.

But Titus took after his mother on that account. Sitting down in a warm, sudsy tub of water every two weeks or so these days was worth the few pennies it cost him at one of the few bathhouses in the city. Letting the old women pour that water over his head as he sputtered and gasped, to be scalded and scrubbed raw, as pink as a newborn before he set off for another wildsome frolic. Outside those bathing houses a lackey kept the water boiling, the sort of slow-witted man who could find no better work—much like those who made their rounds at twilight, firing up what lamps adorned the streets of St. Louis, lamps all too often badly in need of a good scrubbing themselves: the isinglass flecked and marred with the singed and blackened bodies of so many moths and other insects that nothing more than a pale and feeble yellow light flickered down upon passersby.

Here in the dark of this early morning as he listened, the trapper began to snore. At long last Titus sensed the arms of sleep embrace him.

Contentment come.

More often than he cared to admit, Titus sorely missed the smells that had filled his senses back in that Kentucky country hard by the Ohio River: green oak stumps smoldering at the far edges of the moist, newly cleared fields; green fodder beans simmering on the fire while sweet johnnycakes toasted in the Dutch oven; his mother's white-as-snow hominy coming to a boil; his grandmam's sweet potatoes, each roasting in its own mound of warm ash heaped on the brick hearth; his pap's own corn whiskey poured steaming, fresh, potent, and with a hint of amber from the bung spout on the doubler.

In place of those memories he now savored the steamy earthiness of fresh dung from the horses he shoed or hitched to the carriages Troost hired out; the sweet lilac and gardenia perfume of the proper French ladies flouncing past in their layers of starched crinoline as they swirled by him with parasols a'twirl upon bare shoulders, devilment in their eyes; the heated closeness of the animals he brushed and curried, rank with cold sweat after the gentlemen of St. Louis returned their hire; the heavy scent of brimstone issuing from the forge; grown so accustomed to the aroma of the hardwood fire he kept glowing in that tiny stove of his cell; and the sweet elixir that was the quadroon's body calling out to his.

What a man went and got himself used to as the years passed by.

"I ain't goin' with you tonight, Isaac," Bass declared emphatically. "I ain't got no more money to buy us whiskey."

Washburn reared back, appraised the younger man, then snorted a loud guffaw. "The hell you say? You ain't bald-facin' me, are ye?"

"Bald-face?"

"Lyin' to me, Titus!"

"No," he answered quietly. "It's all . . . all gone. Ever'thing Troost saved for me across the y'ars. All drunk up—"

"—an' whored away," Isaac sighed. "Ain't that allays the way it be? Man works too damn long for what money comes his way, an' it slips right through his hands a helluva lot faster'n he can make more money."

Bass wagged his head. "We ain't even got all you said we're gonna need when we go."

"Never you mind. We'll get it," Washburn replied, looking away, his eyes squinting as if he were fitting together the pieces of a child's block puzzle in his mind. Then he suddenly looked back at Titus, a big grin on his face, the upper lip pulling back from that lone fang of a tooth in the middle of his face. "An' don't ye go frettin' yerself 'bout drinkin' money tonight neither."

"We ain't got no money to go—"

"Don't need none," he broke in. "Why, I'll bet thar's lots of fellers buy the both of us drinks in ever' place we care to walk into this fine evenin'."

"Who the hell's gonna buy us drinks?"

"Ever' man what loses his gamble with Isaac Washburn."

"Gamble?" Bass asked suspiciously. "Just what you got in mind?"

"Nothin' but a li'l game o' chance," he replied, turning to kneel at his blankets, dragging his possibles pouch over to begin rummaging through it. "There!" he exclaimed with genuine excitement, standing before Bass to slowly open his hand.

In Washburn's dirty palm lay two small pieces of what looked like quartz stone, perhaps ivory, both of them carved and painted with strange hieroglyphic symbols totally foreign to Titus.

"What's them?"

"Bones."

"You gonna gamble with them?"

He nodded matter-of-factly, his Adam's apple bobbing appropriately. "Ol' Injun game of hand. I find us a place on the floor to play, singin' out that the loser buys the drinks."

"Then what?"

"We wait till we got us someone to play."

"How you play?"

"I go an' hide one of 'em in my hand, and the unlucky son of a coon can guess till tomorry which hand's got it the bone—he ain't got a chance of winnin'. Or 'nother way the Injuns play is to bet how many of these here scratches gonna come up when I throw the both of 'em on the floor."

"But you ain't got no money to buy a fella his drink when you lose."

Washburn's face went blank with righteous indignation. "I don't ever lose at the bones, Titus. Never, ever lose."

He looked down at those two small objects, like some foreign, sacred totems they were. And his gut rumbled in warning. "I . . . I ain't goin' with you, Isaac."

"I don't never, ever lose!" he repeated. "C'mon—don't ye hear the whiskey callin' out yer name?" He slung an arm over Bass's shoulder, clacking the two bones together in his hand with the clatter of ivory dominoes on a hardwood table. "Cain't ye jest *feeeeel* that Negra gal's poon yest wrapped right around ye, squeezin' yer pecker an' makin' ye wanna go off with a roar?"

He swallowed hard. Damn, but it sounded like it could work. Washburn knew what he spoke of—on everything from Indians to the courses of the far rivers, from the valleys and passes and mountain ranges, to the ways of whiskey and the whys of women. Tempting, seductive, so damned luring was his scheme for the night—

"No, I can't go out gaming with you tonight 'thout no money," Bass answered resolutely.

"Don't be no yella-livered fool, now, Titus."

"I ain't yella!" he growled with a mighty shrug, flinging Washburn's arm off his shoulder and stepping away.

"Then c'mon with me an' have some fun."

With a shake of his head Titus said, "Better us go down to the grove where we can shoot some more. Maybeso you can show me better how to throw that belt 'hawk of your'n."

"Nope," he replied succinctly, turning to sweep up his possibles pouch, draping it over his shoulder, then pulled up the flap to drop the bones within. "Ye can find me, Titus. If'n yer of a mind to have yerself a spree with Isaac Washburn."

"You're gonna go and get yourself in 'nother fight."

He whirled on Bass. "Don't tell me ye gone and got squeamish 'bout a li'l fightin' when yer drinkin'! Why, you an' me been mixin' the fightin' an' drinkin' for better'n a hull damned moon now."

"And we gone through everything I had, 'cept what I'll make tomorry."

"What's it all track anyway, Titus? If yer money buyed us a bunch of whiskey an' a hull bunch of daubin' our stingers—then it were worth it! Yest money, an' a man allays can get him some more for the next spree he plans to have fer hisself."

Now it was Bass who turned aside, brushing past the trapper as he stepped out of his cell. "I got 'nother trap to finish."

"It'll be thar' tomorry, Titus."

"There's more lock parts I gots to file down an' polish for our guns—"

"They'll be there too," Washburn interrupted, following Bass into the livery as Titus headed for the forge. "It can all wait. It allays has."

Bass stopped, wheeled on Washburn. "Yeah, it allays has, ain't it? Long as there was enough money to give us both a hammer in our heads the next day . . . while'st you watched me pounding away at this here goddamned anvil!"

"Hell with ye, then!" Washburn roared in reply, flinging his arms in the air as he thundered past Titus. "Ye yest stay hyar, goddammit! Maybeso ye can yest stay right hyar in St. Louie when Isaac Washburn takes off fer the far places, Mr. High-an'-Mighty!"

"Isaac!"

The trapper kept on walking down the long, dusty corridor between the stalls, waving an arm in dispute of Bass's cry. "Yer a sneak an' a coward —an' not fit to eat with a dog or even drink with a nigger. Ye can yest stay behin't when I set off—"

"Isaac!"

"To hell with ye, Mr. Too-Good-to-Come-Drinkin'-with-Me!" he roared his words over his shoulder when he reached the door.

"Come back here, Isaac!"

Washburn shoved against the door with a loud scrape of wood and creak of heavy iron hinges. "I'm better on my own, ye god-blamed penny sniffer!"

And he was gone into that evening's glow as the sun sank somewhere out there to the west—far, far beyond what world Titus had ever known. For the briefest moment a golden shaft of light exploded in through that doorway flung open by Washburn, igniting the lingering particles of dust the trapper had stirred up, like flecks of crimson-fired starlight slowly settling in the shaft of light. Too quickly the sunset's fire went out, the gold swallowed by the interior darkness, the livery cold once more.

The sun gone to rest out there once more.

He turned, resolute. Looked back over his shoulder one last time, for but an instant considering that he might run to catch up the trapper—at the least to put things a'right before he returned to work, before night fell, before Washburn was off to chance a dangerous gamble to pay for his spree.

It was cold when Titus awoke to the startling, pristine silence. The fire must have all but gone out, he decided as he turned beneath the blankets, fighting the urge to lie there.

Eventually the silence alarmed fear in him.

Rolling quickly, Titus bolted upright. Washburn's blankets were empty.

Blinking, he tried to clear the webby gauze from his mind. He rubbed the grit from his eyes, then gazed through that doorway. Nothing but gloom. It must surely still be night, he assured himself. Not a thing to worry himself about.

Then he recognized the gray seep of false dawn bleeding into the livery. Enough light to realize day would not be long in arriving now.

As he sat there staring at the trapper's old, greasy blankets, what little Washburn had to truly call his own, Bass wanted to believe Isaac was at that very moment snoring beside one of his lovelies. But try as he might, Titus could not convince himself that the night remained innocent.

That he himself might not be an unwitting accomplice. Guilty for no other reason than allowing Washburn the freedom to go off with a damned fool notion playing in his head.

A drizzle began its insistent, growing patter on the shake roof overhead as he wobbled to his feet. From a tenpenny nail he took down his blanket coat, looped the wide leather belt about his waist as he reached the back door beyond the forge. Into the rain he plunged, through the soggy paddock where Troost kept his animals, over the split-rail fence and on to Market Street.

Little life stirred in lower St. Louis this time of day. Night all but done. Day yet to announce itself. Smudges of fire smoke clung low about the roofs like gray death's wreaths; at his feet tumbled the scattered clutter of fog. Wild-eyed dogs eyed him, put their noses to the air, testing for scent of the man—be he friend or danger—then slunk back into the shadows, off down an alleyway, then stopped and turned to find Titus turning into the same dark shadows of that alley before those curs loped away at a greater hurry.

Into the first of Isaac's favorite watering holes he went, stopping just inside the doorway to rake his eyes over those crumpled over the tables, collapsed in the corners, stretched out atop crude benches, their arms and legs akimbo as only the besotted can sleep. Turning to the long bar where puddles of ale and whiskey lay unattended, he nudged the tender, asleep on a curled arm.

"Whatta ye want?" the man growled without raising his head.

"Looking for a friend," Titus explained, anxious as he peered into that face swollen with fatigue and interrupted sleep. "Wears a red scarf over his head. A silver earring."

The head came up slowly. "No, nobody like that here."

"Was he? Last night."

The barman waved him away, his head sinking back to his arm pillow. "Early. Gone early. Some others throwed him out. You want a drink? If not —be off."

"No, just tell me why he was throwed—"

"Shaddup, now. You be gone an' let a man have his sleep."

"He say where he—"

"That one's lucky they didn't choose to cut his throat—that Injun game of his!"

"Where—"

"Get out before I cut your liver out me own self!"

As he turned, Titus saw several of the patrons stirring restlessly, but not a one awoke. The entire room settled back into a languorous stupor, the fire crumbling to coals in the stone fireplace.

The dogs scattered from the doorway as he hurried out, turning up the back way, feeling more desperate than ever before the dank closeness of these low-roofed shanties and whores' cribs squeezing in on that narrow, twisting passage he followed to the next of Washburn's favored haunts along the wharf.

It was much the same there, and at the next. In fact, Titus learned the trapper had visited every last one of those considered the worst of the river city's watering troughs. In most grogshops he learned how Washburn had attempted his game of chance, his sleight of hand, and for it was good-naturedly thrown out on his ear. Told to be off and take his lumbering scheme some other place.

From there Bass backtracked to the hovel where Isaac's prostitute plied her trade. Surprise crossed her face as she pulled back the heavy Russian canvas sheeting hung for a doorway.

"You got the wrong bed, don't you, lover?" she said, her voice thick with interrupted sleep. She pointed. "Your bitch is three beds down."

"I didn't come for her."

A crass smile crossed the woman's lips as she turned aside, motioning him in, then dropped the door curtain back in place behind him. Without a word the young woman stepped over to the pallet and settled to her knees, pulling up the hem of her long nightshirt until it rested at her waist, her bony, boyish hipbones straining against her pale skin, the dark triangle a stark contrast.

"I knew you'd have to have me one of these days, lover."

"No," and he wagged his head. "You don't understand."

"It don't matter," she cooed, hiking the nightshirt on up her body, over her shoulders, and flinging it into the corner, then rising up on her knees to sway provocatively as she fondled a breast. "I won't ever tell your bitch you had to come have some of the sweetest lovin' you'd get on the river."

"Please—I'm looking for Washburn."

"Isaac? Don't you worry, now—I don't think he'll be back soon," she replied, cupping her hands beneath the other small breast. "He don't have to know neither. C'mere an' taste these an' tell me they ain't ripe and juicy."

He licked his lips, trying to keep his eyes from straying below her neck. The way she moved, swayed, rocked her hips in slow, luring gyrations.

"When was he here? Early, late?"

"Middle of the night," she said, her voice deepening. "He was getting crazy awready. C'mon, lover—you know you can't leave me now."

"He tell you where he was—"

"Shut your mouth and c'mere. You got me all worked up."

"You don't know nothing more?"

"Forget about Washburn, that crazy old man," she snapped. "He stunk like nobody else I ever smelled."

Suddenly he felt very, very sorry for her. More sorry for Isaac. "That crazy ol' man thought the world of you. It'd kill him to think of you saying these things 'bout him."

Hurriedly she got to her feet, padding over to Titus, looping her arms around him and saying, "What he don't know won't never hurt 'im."

Gently pushing her bony shoulders away, he was reminded of Mincemeat. So sad was the memory that he sighed.

She tried to push his arms away and slip closer again. Rubbing her groin against his thigh. "This is all yours right now."

"Go to bed."

"That's the whole idea, sugar boy."

He shoved her backward, angry, hearing her snarl like some animal as he pushed aside the canvas flap and ducked into the low hallway that led to the door which would take him back to the narrow alley.

"I'll kill you, you ever come back again!"

How he hoped her shriek would quickly disappear behind him, swallowed by the coming gray in dawn's creeping presence. Feeling all the sadder, all the more remorse for Washburn that she was without the least shred of decency and loyalty, despite how she fed herself, kept that shabby roof over her head. There was shame, and then there was downright shameful.

Stopping outside in the rain for but a moment, he thought on his sweet quadroon, how it had been three or more nights since the last visit. Then he pried himself away, down Wharf Street and among the tortuous twists of the tree-lined pathway that led toward the docks themselves.

On and on he searched, failing to find Washburn in any of the grogshops, even the worst of the drinking dens. Yet time and again his questions aroused the smoldering anger of those who had been bested in Isaac's game of chance, before the trapper had been soundly pummeled with fists and tossed out. But where Washburn had gone after every beating, more drunk and belligerent with every new stop, no one had the least interest in helping Titus discover.

Day was coming when he finally started for the grove—hoping the trapper had gone there to sleep it off. Past the last wharves where the side-wheelers tied up to off-load, where the keelboats bobbed at their moorings to take on loads for the upriver Indian trade. Not far beyond the last of the wooden pilings the river lapped against the gentle slope of the bank. Drift-wood cluttered the sandy, muddy shore. Over and around what had at one time been dangerous sawyers or planters he trudged, his moccasins soaked.

Stopped, peered at the dark object against the muddy bank ahead. Not a snag—it bobbed half in, half out of the Mississippi . . . in the shape of a body.

Titus feared. Dared not believe. Refused to allow himself to hope as he inched closer. That faded red scarf tied round the man's head. Mud-soaked now. Washburn floated facedown in the shallow, brown water where Bass collapsed to his knees.

Dragging Isaac into his lap, he rolled the trapper over, brushing mud from the bruised and swollen face: eyes, cheeks split, lips cracked and bleed-ing, whiskers crusted with river silt. Titus sensed his own tears begin to spill as he slapped the face—hoping for life, some flicker of movement.

For the longest time Titus sat there in that cold water, cradling Wash-burn to his breast, clutched the friend beneath his chin so close he could smell the stale, sickly stench of drink about the dead man. This place, the cold unforgiving lap of the river around him, and the reek of one spree too many thick in his nostrils all brought Bass to thinking on what must have been the trapper's last minutes. Somehow limping down here after one beating too many. Coming here rather than the livery where Titus had spurned him. Perhaps Washburn stood in this very spot for some moments before he fell, staring at the water rolling out of that land far, far to the north —cursing the river that passed him by, just as so many seasons were now behind him.

Titus knew how that felt already.

Too much whiskey and too sound a thrashing—finally to crumple here into the shallow current at the edge of the muddy bank, here to drown. Never again to move. Dead drunk again.

And this time, dead.

Back and forth he rocked with the body. Then as the light ballooned in the east across the river, Titus struggled from under the weight. He nearly stumbled himself in the soft, giving mud as he got to his feet, began to drag the body out of the water.

Heaving, he brought Washburn up the bank a few yards with great exertion. Then collapsed himself beside the trapper once more. Shivering as he watched the sun continue its climb.

A new day. A little colder.

And now one friend less.

TWENTY-FOUR

The Indian pony resisted him at first, not liking the nearness of that dead body. Maybe it was true what some folks said about animals sensing death more strongly than humans ever could.

As many years as he had worked around horses and hunted the creatures of the woods, Titus had to admit he really knew damned little about the beasts whose flesh he ate, the brutes he shoed and harnessed for Hysham Troost.

With a great struggle he at last draped Washburn's body over his own shoulder, struggled to rise. Tied off to a tree, the pony sidestepped round the trunk, skittish and wide-eyed, nostrils taking the caliber of the dead man's scent as it inched away until the hackamore was wrapped around the tree and the pony's nose was snubbed right against the oak's trunk. A final heave from Bass meant the frightened pony gave one last jostle, shivering beneath the deadweight.

"There, now," he whispered to the animal, stroking its muzzle. "Last time you'll ever carry him. Easy, easy—just ease down, girl. This here's the last ride for Isaac Washburn."

Bass had returned to the livery after the sun's orange orb

had peeled itself fully off the far side of the river. Troost was already in for the day, laying out the first of the harness on his workbench, readying it for a good soaping as Titus trudged past without a word.

Perhaps it was the pain written on the young man's face and nothing more that had compelled Troost not to utter a word. Silently he had watched Bass move by on his special purpose, taking down a long braided horsehair hackamore from one of the stable posts without slowing a step. Out in the paddock behind the barn where Troost fed boscage to his oxen, he had caught up the reluctant pony, brought it among the stables, then latched the half door. Tying the animal beside the opening to his cell, Titus had reappeared with Washburn's old sleeping blankets, folding it over the pony's back.

Past Troost he had trudged, again without a word from either one of them. Near the wide double doors that fronted onto Third Street, Titus had taken down one of the mucking shovels hanging from a peg near the last stall. From the moment he had entered the livery, he had barely touched the blacksmith with his eyes. Still, through it all, he could feel Hysham's wondering, curious stare strike him dead center between his shoulder blades as Bass finally moved out of shadow and into the sunshine splashing St. Louis on that morning. He had led the pony down to the riverbank.

With the dripping, muddy corpse finally draped over the animal's back, Titus headed downriver. A mile. Another. Then two more as he sought out a place far enough from settlement, from walls of wood or stone, far enough from the walls of too many people. Eventually he stopped in a small glade and tied the pony to one of the trees that ringed the meadow. Leaves rustled in the morning breeze above him as he dragged the body from the animal's back. It reflexively backed away from Isaac Washburn, as far as the hackamore would allow it. Snorting as it sidestepped, on the far side of the tree, the pony bent its head to graze among spring's tall grass.

For some time Bass walked over every foot of that glade, then decided on a place before returning to the tree, where he took up that worn and rusted shovel he would now use to scratch at the thick carpet of green, marking out a rectangle wide enough, long enough, for the trapper. The rain-soaked earth gave easily beneath his labor, piling the moist, dark soil in a mound beside the deepening hole where he worked. Man against the ground, forcing the earth to open itself, give of itself, just wide enough for man's final pillow.

This reminded him of farming. Of Thaddeus and the others back yonder in Boone County. Slashing their shares down through the earth, forcing the soil open—demanding it give what they wanted most. Like a man prying open a reluctant woman's legs until she at last gives herself to him, where he can plant his seed—there in her moistness so that it too would grow.

But this was different, he convinced himself. This was returning something . . . someone . . . to the soil. No, he was not taking anything from the earth. This completion of the circle was something altogether different.

Down, down, down into the ground he sweated, removing first his coat, and later his shirt—those taut, lean muscles and sinews aching before he tossed out the shovel and heaved himself out of that long black hole punched out of the deep emerald green of the meadow. There in the shade, among the roots of that big elm tree. He turned, inspecting his work. Deep enough for him to stand up to his armpits.

After spreading the two blankets upon the grass and gently laying out the body, Bass carefully draped the worn and greasy wool over Washburn's face for the last time.

"It's time, Isaac," he sighed in a whisper.

Beside the hole he laid Washburn, then descended into the grave once again. Bracing himself against the side, Bass dragged the body into his arms, slowly lowering Isaac to the bottom. He quickly scrambled out once he sensed the sun inching itself ever higher, arching its way upward across the sky, warming the air. Now he sweated even more as he stabbed that mound of fresh earth, shoveling it back atop those old blankets with the solemn thump of falling sod.

"Damn you, Isaac—you wanted that spree of your'n more'n you wanted me to be your friend," Titus hurled his words down at the form wrapped in the blankets. Clod by clod, the soil spilled back into the hole.

"Went out after your whiskey, figuring it would be a better friend than I ever could make you," he growled as he hunched into his work, stung by his sweat, blinded by his tears.

"Not any different'n that ol' man Glass, was you? All's said and done —just like him you give up on folks what cared something for you. Just look at you now!" he sobbed.

Flinging the clumps of earth into that yawning pit, shovel by shovel until he was drenched with sweat, itching at the black earth smeared in great streaks across his heaving chest, tracked with tears over his cheeks, striped in beaded ribbons on his forehead. Wiping the stinging salt from his eyes, he blinked, then kept on hurling the last of that dark earth atop what remained of Isaac Washburn.

Patting the last shovelful down on that long black mound, he shuddered, resting his hands across the hickory handle. Then gazed about at the sunlit meadow he had chosen. Suddenly aware of the wildflowers. Spring's gift to the land.

Clump after clump he speared up with the old shovel, carrying them tenderly back to the grave, there to replant each bouquet with his bare hands, scratching out each hole with his fingers until that long black mound lay ablaze with color.

"These here orange ones are for the sunsets in them mountains—the ones you told me about, Isaac," he said little above a whisper, his dirty, black-caked fingers touching the soft velvet of the brilliant petals.

"And these red ones—like them hills you said the Powder River called its home. The blue'uns for the sky out yonder—the sky you told me brushes them mountains you wanted to see again so bad."

Titus swiped a grimy finger below each eye as tears began to spill across his cheeks.

"And the yellow ones, Isaac. Yellow, just as bright as that grass on the prerra you said looked like a carpet of gold—where a man can find him the buffalo ground. I put them yellow ones here special."

For the longest time Bass sat there in the shade of the tree sheltering that spot. Watching the flowers nod beneath the breeze while sunlight and shadow chased one another across the meadow . . . until at last the day grew late. Twilight's last golden kiss soon to brush the cheek of the land.

The sweat from his efforts had long ago dried by the time he pulled on his shirt, tugging it down over the black streaks of grime from that special ground. Taking up the pony's hackamore and laying the shovel over his shoulder, Titus trudged back across the belly of that glade. Miles to go before dark. Miles to go before he returned to what was, and was never to be again.

At the far line of trees rustling above him, Bass stopped. Turning, he gazed back, struck that no longer did the long black grave look so much like a dark scar in that meadow of green.

Wildflowers danced like so many bursts of color in the breeze that whispered past Isaac Washburn's final rest.

Titus had buried more than the trapper in that shady spot last spring. He had buried his hopes as well.

Then returned to town, and the livery that was all he had.

"Where's that fur man?" Hysham Troost had asked, eyeing the pony, the blankets gone from its back, when Bass had shown up late that afternoon.

"Dead."

The blacksmith stiffened. "You . . . you didn't have anything to do with it?"

Turning to look at Troost in the long shadows piercing the west doorway of that livery, Bass shook his head. "Kill't his own self."

"How?"

"Likely drunk hisself to death."

Chewing on his lower lip a minute, Troost finally volunteered, "I'm sorry, Titus."

"Not nowhere near as sorry as I am, Hysham," he replied, starting away with the pony, moving toward the paddock outside the rear door. "Damn shame Isaac Washburn died like he did. Been more fitting he died out yonder."

"You still set on going out there your own self?"

He stopped in his tracks, his back still to Troost, and wagged his head, it suddenly feeling very, very heavy upon his shoulders. "No. I ain't fixing to do nothing but go back to what I been doing all along, Hysham."

And he did.

Through that summer, on into the fall and winter's cold squeeze upon the lower Missouri, Titus threw himself back into his work. Each week Troost paid him for the last six days, Bass buried a little of it beneath a stone laid behind the small stove in his cell. The rest he used to buy himself a drink now and then, the feral pleasure of a good meal, and the company of a succession of women who each one helped Bass hold at bay the numbness slowly creeping to penetrate to his very marrow. Gone for good were the days of whiskey fever and whoring until he passed out. Gone were those days of dreaming on the buffalo.

For months there he routinely had pleasured himself one evening a week with that coffee-skinned quadroon, of times sharing a bottle of West Indian sweet rum with her before she hiked up her nettle-bark petticoat and climbed astride him. At least until the Saturday night he came to call, fresh from the bathhouse and a warm meal, ready to have that beauty work her magic on his flesh so he could swallow down what troubled him so.

The old woman who watched over the girls told Titus that his favorite was no longer there—having taken up residence in a private place farther up the hill, closer to where the rich and very French families dwelled. Bass touched the blue scarf he tied around his neck every Saturday night.

"I'll go see her there. What's the place so I'll know it?"

"You can't see her up there," she tried to explain, the wounded look in her eyes showing how she tried to understand.

"She ain't coming back?"

"Rich man bought her, took her off to the place where he's gonna keep her for himself, now on and always. Buy her all the soft clothes she'd ever wanna wear. There's a tree outside her window, she told me when she left— where she'll sit and watch the birds sing come the end of this goddamned winter."

"He married her?"

The woman had laughed at that. "Sakes, no! He's already got him a wife—likely one cold as ice. He don't ever intend to marry the girl. Just keep her in that fancy place he bought her—to be there whenever he shows up so she can pleasure only him."

"Maybeso I can see her still. Sneak up there."

The woman wagged her head sadly. "She went there on her own. That means she wasn't thinking 'bout no one else. The girl left everything behind. And that means you too. Best you forget her now."

For a moment he stared at the planks beneath their feet. Another piece of him chipped away, like a flake of plaster from one of those painted saints down at the cathedral on Rue d'Eglise. Then Titus looked into the woman's eyes, vowing he would not let it hurt. And remembered Isaac's favorite.

"What about that one with the brown hair down to the middle of her back? Think she was called Jenny."

"You're two days late, son," the woman replied morosely. "A mean bastard cut her up good. Up to the pauper's cemetery they buried Jenny in a shallow hole just this morning."

Swallowing, Bass said, "Any other'n. Any one a t'all."

"You ain't so choosy no more?"

His eyes went left down the corridor, then right. Back to the woman. "Not choosy at all."

Far from it.

From that night on Titus rutted with the fleshy ones, the pocked ones, the ones who hadn't cared to bathe in a month or more—the quality and color of whores in that city always depended upon the size of a man's purse. But it wasn't money that was determining his choice of solace for Bass. For no reason at all he simply wasn't particular where he took his pleasure, seeking only that salve to rub into all those hidden wounds he kept covered so well.

It was simply too cruel to fool himself anymore into believing in hope. Never again would he cling to any dream.

For six days a week he choked down his despair at never hoping again, daring never to dream again—pounding out his rage on that anvil, sweating on into that early spring. Of each Saturday night he found himself a new whore to stab with his anger as he rutted above her. Until he had gone through them all and by those cold days as winter waned, Titus started pleasuring his way back through what women he could afford. Frightened that each week it took just a little more of that balm to soothe his deepest wounds. Scared they never would heal.

When he found himself weakest, Titus would brood on that faraway land—mythical as it was, the stuff of children's bedtime stories. He was weakest in those moments when the whiskey could no longer stiffen his backbone, when he was drained, done with the sweating torment of driving his rage into a woman, and he lay beside her, gone limp and soft inside as well as out.

A cruel hoax his grandpap and Washburn had played on him: this stuff of longing for that place where the horizon ran black with buffalo.

Bitterness became a feast for him as he held those last days of winter's retreat at bay.

With the melting drip of that last snow slowly disappearing from the shakes on the livery roof, Titus stood gazing at the sun as it settled atop the trees from the western door of the livery. It glowed so yellow, as golden as those wildflowers he had rooted down into that black mound where he'd planted Isaac Washburn's remains. As golden as that prairie the trapper had said was the faraway kingdom of the buffalo.

Every bit as yellow as the candle faintly flickering within Titus Bass's soul.

Perhaps it was that late-winter sun. Perhaps it was the remembrance of those flowers planted for a burial shroud. Then again, maybe it was the sudden and inescapable remembrance of that distant land, admitting that some part of him still clung to hope . . . whatever it was, Bass stood there at that western door sensing for the first time that the candle of his dream was there and then being rekindled. No longer did he wish to drown its warmth in the tears of self-pity and the wrenching agony of his despair.

Before that yellow sun had settled any farther into the land beyond those trees outside Troost's livery, Titus had snatched up Washburn's old rifle and hurried with it over to Main Street, where a year before, he had his eye coveting some of the fine workmanship on display in the small shop of a local riflesmith.

"It ain't wuth very much," the old man told him.

"What you give me for it?"

The riflesmith eyed the weapon again. "Seen a lot of use."

"It was in the mountains."

The old man eyed him appraisingly now. "What you want to trade it fer?"

"To get me that'un." Titus pointed to the one hung on the big pegsnear the top of the wall.

"That's a big caliber," the riflesmith clucked.

"What's the bore?"

"Fifty-four."

Titus said, "I figure that's what it takes to bring down a buffler, don't you?"

With a grin the old man slipped the spectacles off his nose. "I wouldn't know, son. Never see'd a buffler for myself."

"I aim to," Titus promised. "And I aim to have me a gun what'll bring one down too. I'll trade you that there rifle—and bring you my pay each week till we're square."

"Had lots of fellers want that rifle—"

"But I'm the one gonna take it to the mountains," Bass said evenly, his eyes steady on the old man. "Now, you tell me what you need in the way of cash money, and we got us a deal."

For long moments the old man did not say a thing; then he eventually straightened and hobbled around the counter, over to that wall where the rifles hung on their pegs. "This'un?"

"Yes—that's the one I want."

Titus watched the man take it down off the pegs, running his old hands over the wood, the wrinkles on every finger etched with cherry-red or maple stains, browning for each weapon's iron furniture.

When he had the long flintlock down, the riflesmith asked, "You're the smithy been making them lock springs an' such Hysham Troost's sold me over the years, ain't you?"

"I am."

Step by step the old man hobbled up to Titus, handed the rifle over. "S'pose you ought'n feel how she lays agin your shoulder, son."

Once the rifle lay in his hands, went to his shoulder, rested against his cheek—their bargain was struck: Washburn's rifle, the next two weeks' pay, and a goodly order of lock parts, ramrod thimbles, front blades, and rear buckhorn sights. Enough work to keep him busy long into the night for weeks yet to come.

At long last came that Saturday afternoon he carried in the final payment in cash money and a small linen sack of polished lock springs. To the wall behind his workbench the old riflesmith turned. Reaching up, he took down a sign that hung on string from the flintlock's graceful frizzen, his own crude lettering stating:

not for
SALE

"I allays liked this gun," the man said when he passed it over the counter to Bass. "But I knowed there'd be a man come in one day that'd give me more'n just money for it. I knowed for certain there'd come a fella who'd gimme a real good reason to sell it to him. You done that, son."

How Titus caressed that .54-caliber flintlock now. Not the prettiest Pennsylvanian he had wrapped his hands around at those Longhunters Fairs in his youth back to Boone County, Kentucky, but by damned it would do for a workingman's rifle. Being a heavy Derringer, Bass knew it would shoot as true as any engraved, wire-inlaid Kentucky squirrel gun. And unlike those eastern rifles, this one would pack enough wallop to bring down the beasts where he was fixing to go.

Just as lovingly as he had touched all his women before, Titus now ran his hands over the slightly Roman-nosed stock, the big goosenecked hammer and cast-brass patchbox, its top finial filed in the shape of an eagle's head.

"What reason did I give you?" Titus asked of a sudden, remembering the certainty of the old man's declaration.

"You told me you was the one gonna take that there rifle to the mountains," the shopkeeper replied. "From what I come to know of folks in my many years—I'll wager hard money you are the man to carry this here big rifle out to that far yonder. I can see it . . . right there in your eyes."

Through the following five weeks he labored long hours to pay off Troost what he owed him in barter for what Titus had used in crafting springs and lock plates, thimbles and other furniture for the riflesmith. And without fail every one of those spring nights Bass threw the pouch over his shoulder and the saddle on that Indian pony—riding down to the grove, where he blazed a new mark on the tree where Washburn had him shoot of a bygone time. The sting of sulfur in that black homemade powder like a rich perfume in his nostrils.

So it was that the pony came to know the man's particular smell, the way he touched the animal, the way that rider felt upon its back, over the weeks, and months, and all those seasons as he brushed and curried the animal, fed it Troost's best cut grass, riding that rawboned pony every evening as he set off to practice with that big-bored full-stocked flintlock. Slowly coming to know the man all the more because Titus rode him from sunrise to sundown each Sunday—his one day off each week—not returning until the sun had milked itself from the sky, when from the pony's back he would pull the old saddle he had patched and repaired for Washburn, finally to curl up within his new wool blankets and dream on those far and Shining Mountains.

"You and me'r even," Hysham gruffly declared early of a morning as Titus strolled in from the outhouse, ready to stoke the fires in the forge for another day.

Bass stopped dead in his tracks, not sure he could believe what he had heard. "E-even?"

"Means you don't owe me 'nother day's wages, Titus," Troost explained with more than an edge of sadness, "less'n mayhaps you want to stay on and work for me 'nother eight or nine more years."

He stared, unbelieving, into the older man's glistening eyes, asking, "We . . . we're even you say?"

"Said it already," the burly blacksmith replied a little angrily, blinking at the smart of the tears. "You're free to go. And when you do, damn well be sure to take that good-for-nothing jug-head of a Injun cayuse with you. I don't want 'er around here, raising ruckus with my good studs when she comes into season again."

His heart pounding, Titus took a step closer to the blacksmith. "This . . . this means . . . I can go?"

"Gonna miss you," Troost said, volving his head slightly so Bass would not see him stab a big finger at his offending eyes. "Goddamned dust you stirred up shuffling in just now got me—"

Titus caught him in a fierce embrace before the blacksmith realized it. "You're a good man, Hysham Troost. A damned good, *good* man."

"G-g'won now, Titus Bass," he growled, trying to wiggle himself loose from the younger man's arms. "Get what all you got to take with you packed on that ol' dun mare back there."

"The . . . the mare?"

He gazed at the younger man through the haze filming his eyes. "She's as sure a packhorse as there ever was, or Hysham Troost don't know stink from horseflesh. Good of hoof, and nary a stronger back have I seen in many a year."

Bass started to turn, nearly stumbling over his own feet as part of him began to move away in giddy anticipation, yet another part of him stood rooted to the spot in fear, uncertainty, and loss he sensed beginning to well up within.

"Now, get, Titus Bass," Troost growled. "You'll find a pack frame I left for you sitting on the top rail of that last corral down aside your stall."

By then Bass was crying, bawling every bit as much as a babe. Tears spilled as he careened back close and swept up Hysham's hand, squeezing it. "You . . . I'll . . . can't never forget you for this."

"I don't 'spect you ever will, Titus," he said, his voice back to blustering. "Now, go and get yourself packed afore I find you something else to do round here."

Titus whirled frenetically about the few square feet of that tiny stall he had turned into his home for those many seasons of waiting, of moving through one day after another without hope. Quickly he lashed up within the six blankets what he had purchased with Washburn: kettles and flints, beads and mirrors, vermilion and knives, camp axes and all the rest that together he and Isaac had purchased with Titus's forge money. Then he took down that sawbuck pack saddle he had repaired just last week for Troost, realizing as he cinched it onto the back of that dun mare that the old blacksmith had planned even then to make a gift of it to Bass. New rawhide and iron rivets, brand-new sheep-hide padding. The mare turned at Titus's gentle touch and nuzzled his shoulder as the man knotted the last loop of latigo, everything he owned strapped now on the horse's back in those two pitifully small bundles of what little Titus would take west.

Sweeping up his pouch, then his rifle, Bass led the pony and the dun mare toward the street-side doors that faced Third, where Troost stood with his fists balled on his hips, the birth of that Sunday rising behind him as Titus came up and stopped.

"Light's got a head start on you already, boy. Don't 'spect you should waste any more of the day—seeing how far you got to go."

Bass couldn't say a word. Didn't, as much as he tried, his jaw working in futility the way it was. So what he did instead was grab that blacksmith again and this time plant a kiss on the gruff old man's hairy cheek.

Then he flung himself right into the old saddle as Troost stood rooted to that spot at the doorway, stunned into silence, the fingers of one huge, muscular hand brushing the cheek where Titus had left that kiss of farewell.

Blinking into the dawn's bright arrival, Hysham said, "You find that place what you're looking for, you let me know."

Shifting the fullstock rifle so that it rested across the tops of his thighs, Bass replied, "I'll be back one day. Count on that."

"Titus, I'm counting on you finding what it is calling you out there."

"I will, Hysham. I damn well will."

Troost took his hand from his cheek and held it up to the younger man. Titus gripped it in his, then let go and suddenly turned his face west as the tears began to fall, nudging his heels into that Indian pony's ribs, leading the dun mare out of the livery into that first morning of freedom.

Pointing his nose toward the Buffalo Palace.